Body of Evidence

"Cornwell has the milieu and the facts down cold . . . A complex mystery that wends a devious path through dark spaces where corpses are discovered at practically every turn."

Los Angeles Daily News

"Fascinating . . . Vivid . . . Well-plotted . . . Scarpetta is here to stay!"

Los Angeles Times Book Review

"Commanding . . . Powerful! . . . Plenty of complex, satisfying forensic sleuthing."

Publisher's Weekly

All That Remains

"Excellent . . . A series that only gets better with each book."

New York Daily News

"Strong action . . . A gripping forensic mystery . . . I just love it!"

The New York Times Book Review

"Colorful . . . Sensational . . . Dead on."

Newsweek

Patricia Cornwell

THREE COMPLETE NOVELS

Patricia Cornwell

THREE

Postmortem
Body of Evidence
All That Remains

COMPLETE NOVELS

SMITHMARK

This edition published in 1997 by
SMITHMARK Publishers
a division of U.S. Media Holdings, Inc.
115 West 18th Street
New York, NY 10011

Smithmark books are available for bulk purchase for sales promotion and premium use. For details write the manager of special sales, SMITHMARK Publishers, 115 West 18th Street, New York, NY 10011.

ISBN 0-7651-9112-1

Printed in the United States of America

99 98 97   5 4 3 2 1

Contents

Postmortem

To Joe and Dianne

1

IT WAS RAINING in Richmond on Friday, June 6.

The relentless downpour, which began at dawn, beat the lilies to naked stalks, and blacktop and sidewalks were littered with leaves. There were small rivers in the streets, and newborn ponds on playing fields and lawns. I went to sleep to the sound of water drumming the slate roof, and was dreaming a terrible dream as night dissolved into the foggy first hours of Saturday morning.

I saw a white face beyond the rain-streaked glass, a face formless and inhuman like the faces of misshapen dolls made of nylon hose. My bedroom window was dark when suddenly the face was there, an evil intelligence looking in. I woke up and stared blindly into the dark. I did not know what had awakened me until the telephone rang again. I found the receiver without fumbling.

"Dr. Scarpetta?"

"Yes." I reached for the lamp and switched it on. It was 2:33 A.M. My heart was drilling through my ribs.

"Pete Marino here. We got us one at 5602 Berkley Avenue. Think you better come."

The victim's name, he went on to explain, was Lori Petersen, a white female, thirty years old. Her husband had found her body about half an hour earlier.

Details were unnecessary. The moment I picked up the receiver and recognized Sergeant Marino's voice, I knew. Maybe I

the telephone rang. People who believe in were-
of a full moon. I'd begun to dread the hours be-
and 3:00 A.M. when Friday becomes Saturday and
conscious.

narily, the medical examiner on call is summoned to a
th scene. But this wasn't ordinary. I had made it clear after the second case that no matter the hour, if there was another murder, I was to be called. Marino wasn't keen on the idea. Ever since I was appointed chief medical examiner for the Commonwealth of Virginia less than two years ago he'd been difficult. I wasn't sure if he didn't like women, or if he just didn't like me.

"Berkley's in Berkley Downs, Southside," he said condescendingly. "You know the way?"

Confessing I didn't, I scribbled the directions on the notepad I always kept by the phone. I hung up and my feet were already on the floor as adrenaline hit my nerves like espresso. The house was quiet. I grabbed my black medical bag, scuffed and worn from years of use.

The night air was like a cool sauna, and there were no lights in the windows of my neighbors' houses. As I backed the navy station wagon out of the drive, I looked at the light burning over the porch, at the first-story window leading into the guest bedroom where my ten-year-old niece, Lucy, was asleep. This would be one more day in the child's life I would miss. I had picked her up at the airport Wednesday night. Our meals together, so far, had been few.

There was no traffic until I hit the Parkway. Minutes later I was speeding across the James River. Taillights far ahead were rubies, the downtown skyline ghostly in the rearview mirror. Fanning out on either side were plains of darkness with tiny necklaces of smudged light at the edges. Out there, somewhere, is a man, I thought. He could be anybody, walks upright, sleeps with a roof over his head, and has the usual number of fingers and toes. He is probably white and much younger than my forty years. He is ordinary by most standards, and probably doesn't drive a BMW or grace the bars in the Slip or the finer clothing stores along Main Street.

But, then again, he could. He could be anybody and he was nobody. Mr. Nobody. The kind of guy you don't remember after riding up twenty floors alone with him inside an elevator.

He had become the self-appointed dark ruler of the city,

an obsession for thousands of people he had never seen, and an obsession of mine. Mr. Nobody.

Because the homicides began two months ago, he may have been recently released from prison or a mental hospital. This was the speculation last week, but the theories were constantly changing.

Mine had remained the same from the start. I strongly suspected he hadn't been in the city long, he'd done this before somewhere else, and he'd never spent a day behind the locked doors of a prison or a forensic unit. He wasn't disorganized, wasn't an amateur, and he most assuredly wasn't "crazy."

Wilshire was two lights down on the left, Berkley the first right after that.

I could see the blue and red lights flashing two blocks away. The street in front of 5602 Berkley was lit up like a disaster site. An ambulance, its engine rumbling loudly, was alongside two un-marked police units with grille lights flashing and three white cruisers with light bars going full tilt. The Channel 12 news crew had just pulled up. Lights had blinked on up and down the street, and several people in pajamas and housecoats had wandered out to their porches.

I parked behind the news van as a cameraman trotted across the street. Head bent, the collar of my khaki raincoat turned up around my ears, I briskly followed the brick wall to the front door. I have always had a special distaste for seeing myself on the evening news. Since the stranglings in Richmond began, my office had been inundated, the same reporters calling over and over again with the same insensitive questions.

"If it's a serial killer, Dr. Scarpetta, doesn't that indicate it's quite likely to happen again?"

As if they wanted it to happen again.

"Is it true you found bite marks on the last victim, Doc?"

It wasn't true, but no matter how I answered such a question I couldn't win. "No comment," and they assume it's true. "No," and the next edition reads, "Dr. Kay Scarpetta denies that bite marks have been found on the victims' bodies . . ." The killer, who's reading the papers like everybody else, gets a new idea.

Recent news accounts were florid and frighteningly detailed. They went far beyond serving the useful purpose of warning the city's citizens. Women, particularly those who lived alone, were terrified. The sale of handguns and deadbolt locks went up fifty percent the week after the third murder, and the SPCA ran out of dogs—a phenomenon which, of course, made the front page, too. Yesterday, the infamous and prize-winning police reporter Abby Turnbull had demonstrated her usual brass by coming to my office and clubbing my staff with the Freedom of Information Act in an unsuccessful attempt at getting copies of the autopsy records.

Crime reporting was aggressive in Richmond, an old Virginia city of 220,000, which last year was listed by the FBI as having the second-highest homicide rate per capita in the United States. It wasn't uncommon for forensic pathologists from the British Commonwealth to spend a month at my office to learn more about gunshot wounds. It wasn't uncommon for career cops like Pete Marino to leave the madness of New York or Chicago only to find Richmond was worse.

What was uncommon were these sex slayings. The average citizen can't relate to drug and domestic shootouts or one wino stabbing another over a bottle of Mad Dog. But these murdered women were the colleagues you sit next to at work, the friends you invite to go shopping or to stop by for drinks, the acquaintances you chat with at parties, the people you stand in line with at the checkout counter. They were someone's neighbor, someone's sister, someone's daughter, someone's lover. They were in their own homes, sleeping in their own beds, when Mr. Nobody climbed through one of their windows.

Two uniformed men flanked the front door, which was open wide and barred by a yellow ribbon of tape, warning: CRIME SCENE—DO NOT CROSS.

"Doc." He could have been my son, this boy in blue who stepped aside at the top of the steps and lifted the tape to let me duck under.

The living room was immaculate, and attractively decorated in warm rose tones. A handsome cherry cabinet in a corner contained a small television and a compact disc player. Nearby a stand held sheet music and a violin. Beneath a curtained window overlooking the front lawn was a sectional sofa, and on the glass coffee table in front of it were half a dozen magazines neatly stacked. Among them were *Scientific American* and the *New England Journal of Medicine*. Across a Chinese dragon rug with a rose medallion against a field of cream stood a walnut bookcase. Tomes straight from a medical school's syllabi lined two shelves.

An open doorway led into a corridor running the length of the house. To my right appeared a series of rooms, to the left was the kitchen, where Marino and a young officer were talking to a man I assumed was the husband.

I was vaguely aware of clean countertops, linoleum and appliances in the off-white that manufacturers call "almond," and the pale yellow of the wallpaper and curtains. But my attention was riveted to the table. On top of it lay a red nylon knapsack, the contents of which had been gone through by the police: a stethoscope, a penlight, a Tupperware container once packed with a meal or a snack, and recent editions of the *Annals of Surgery, Lancet* and the *Journal of Trauma*. By now I was thoroughly unsettled.

Marino eyed me coolly as I paused by the table, then introduced me to Matt Petersen, the husband. Petersen was slumped in a chair, his face destroyed by shock. He was exquisitely handsome, almost beautiful, his features flawlessly chiseled, his hair jet-black, his skin smooth and hinting of a tan. He was wide-shouldered with a lean but elegantly sculpted body casually clad in a white Izod shirt and faded blue jeans. His eyes were cast down, his hands stiffly in his lap.

"These are hers?" I had to know. The medical items might belong to the husband.

Marino's "Yeah" was a confirmation.

Petersen's eyes slowly lifted. Deep blue, bloodshot, they seemed relieved as they fixed on me. The doctor had arrived, a ray of hope where there was none.

He muttered in the truncated sentences of a mind fragmented, stunned, "I talked to her on the phone. Last night. She told me she'd be home around twelve-thirty, home from VMC, the ER. I got here, found the lights out, thought she'd already gone to bed. Then I went in there." His voice rose, quivering, and he took a deep breath. "I went in there, in the bedroom." His eyes were desperate and welling, and he was pleading with me. "Please. I don't want people looking at her, seeing her like that. *Please*."

I gently told him, "She has to be examined, Mr. Petersen."

A fist suddenly banged the top of the table in a startling outburst of rage. "I know!" His eyes were wild. "But all of them, the police and everybody!" His voice was shaking. "I know how it is!

Reporters and everybody crawling all over the place. I don't want every son of a bitch and his brother staring at her!"

Marino didn't bat an eye. "Hey. I got a wife, too, Matt. I know where you're coming from, all right? You got my word she gets respect. The same respect I'd want if it was me sitting in your chair, okay?"

The sweet balm of lies.

The dead are defenseless, and the violation of this woman, like the others, had only begun. I knew it would not end until Lori Petersen was turned inside out, every inch of her photographed, and all of it on display for experts, the police, attorneys, judges and members of a jury to see. There would be thoughts, remarks about her physical attributes or lack of them. There would be sophomoric jokes and cynical asides as the victim, not the killer, went on trial, every aspect of her person and the way she lived, scrutinized, judged and, in some instances, degraded.

A violent death is a public event, and it was this facet of my profession that so rudely grated against my sensibilities. I did what I could to preserve the dignity of the victims. But there was little I could do after the person became a case number, a piece of evidence passed from hand to hand. Privacy is destroyed as completely as life.

Marino led me out of the kitchen, leaving the officer to continue questioning Petersen.

"Have you taken your pictures yet?" I asked.

"ID's in there now, dusting everything," he said, referring to the Identification section officers processing the scene. "I told 'em to give the body a wide berth."

We paused in the hallway.

On the walls were several nice watercolors and a collection of photographs depicting the husband's and the wife's respective graduating classes, and one artistic color shot of the young couple leaning against weathered piling before a backdrop of the beach, the legs of their trousers rolled up to their calves, the wind ruffling their hair, their faces ruddy from the sun. She was pretty in life, blond, with delicate features and an engaging smile. She went to Brown, then to Harvard for medical school. Her husband's undergraduate years were spent at Harvard. This was where they must have met, and apparently he was younger than she.

She. Lori Petersen. Brown. Harvard. Brilliant. Thirty years old.

About to have it all realized, her dream. After eight grueling years, at least, of medical training. A physician. All of it destroyed in a few minutes of a stranger's aberrant pleasure.

Marino touched my elbow.

I turned away from the photographs as he directed my attention to the open doorway just ahead on the left.

"Here's how he got in," he said.

It was a small room with a white tile floor and walls papered in Williamsburg blue. There was a toilet and a lavatory, and a straw clothes hamper. The window above the toilet was open wide, a square of blackness through which cool, moist air seeped and stirred the starchy white curtains. Beyond, in the dark, dense trees, cicadas were tensely sawing.

"The screen's cut." Marino's face was expressionless as he glanced at me. "It's leaning against the back of the house. Right under the window's a picnic table bench. Appears he pulled it up so he could climb in."

I was scanning the floor, the sink, the top of the toilet. I didn't see dirt or smudges or footprints, but it was hard to tell from where I was standing, and I had no intention of running the risk of contaminating anything.

"Was this window locked?" I asked.

"Don't look like it. All the other windows are locked. Already checked. Seems like she would've gone to a lot of trouble to make sure this one was. Of all the windows, it's the most vulnerable, close to the ground, in back where no one can see what's going on. Better than coming in through the bedroom window because if the guy's quiet, she's not going to hear him cutting the screen and climbing in this far down the hall."

"And the doors? Were they locked when the husband got home?"

"He says so."

"Then the killer went out the same way he came in," I decided.

"Looks that way. Tidy squirrel, don't you think?" He was holding on to the door frame, leaning forward without stepping inside. "Don't see nothing in here, like maybe he wiped up after himself to make sure he didn't leave footprints on the john or floor. It's been raining all day." His eyes were flat as they fixed on me. "His feet should've been wet, maybe muddy."

I wondered where Marino was going with this. He was hard to

read, and I'd never decided if he was a good poker player or simply slow. He was exactly the sort of detective I avoided when given a choice—a cock of the walk and absolutely unreachable. He was pushing fifty, with a face life had chewed on, and long wisps of graying hair parted low on one side and combed over his balding pate. At least six feet tall, he was bay-windowed from decades of bourbon or beer. His unfashionably wide red-and-blue-striped tie was oily around the neck from summers of sweat. Marino was the stuff of tough-guy flicks—a crude, crass gumshoe who probably had a foul-mouthed parrot for a pet and a coffee table littered with *Hustler* magazines.

I went the length of the hallway and stopped outside the master bedroom. I felt myself go hollow inside.

An ID officer was busy coating every surface with black dusting powder; a second officer was capturing everything on videotape.

Lori Petersen was on top of the bed, the blue-and-white spread hanging off the foot of the bed. The top sheet was kicked down and bunched beneath her feet, the cover sheet pulled free of the top corners, exposing the mattress, the pillows shoved to the right side of her head. The bed was the vortex of a violent storm, surrounded by the undisturbed civility of middle-class bedroom furnishings of polished oak.

She was nude. On the colorful rag rug to the right of the bed was her pale yellow cotton gown. It was slit from collar to hem, and this was consistent with the three previous cases. On the night stand nearest the door was a telephone, the cord ripped out of the wall. The two lamps on either side of the bed were out, the electrical cords severed from them. One cord bound her wrists, which were pinioned at the small of her back. The other cord was tied in a diabolically creative pattern also consistent with the first three cases. Looped once around her neck, it was threaded behind her through the cord around her wrists and tightly lashed around her ankles. As long as her knees were bent, the loop around her neck remained loose. When she straightened her legs, either in a reflex to pain or because of the assailant's weight on top of her, the ligature around her neck tightened like a noose.

Death by asphyxiation takes only several minutes. That's a very long time when every cell in your body is screaming for air.

"You can come on in, Doc," the officer with the video camera was saying. "I've got all this on film."

Watching where I walked, I approached the bed, set my bag on the floor and got out a pair of surgical gloves. Next I got out my camera and took several photographs of the body *in situ*. Her face was grotesque, swollen beyond recognition and dark bluish purple from the suffusion of blood caused by the tight ligature around her neck. Bloody fluid had leaked from her nose and mouth, staining the sheet. Her straw-blond hair was in disarray. She was moderately tall, no less than five foot seven, and considerably fleshier than the younger version captured in the photographs down the hall.

Her physical appearance was important because the absence of a pattern was becoming a pattern. The four strangling victims seemed to have had no physical characteristics in common, not even race. The third victim was black and very slender. The first victim was a redhead and plump, the second a brunette and petite. They had different professions: a schoolteacher, a free-lance writer, a receptionist, and now a physician. They lived in different areas of the city.

Fetching a long chemical thermometer from my bag, I took the temperature of the room, then of her body. The air was 71 degrees, her body 93.5. Time of death is more elusive than most people think. It can't be pinned down exactly unless the death was witnessed or the victim's Timex stopped ticking. But Lori Petersen had been dead no more than three hours. Her body had been cooling between one and two degrees per hour, and rigor had started in the small muscles.

I looked for any obvious trace evidence that might not survive the trip to the morgue. There were no loose hairs on the skin, but I found a multitude of fibers, most of which, no doubt, were from the bedcovers. With forceps I collected a sampling of them, minuscule whitish ones and several seeming to have come from a dark blue or black material. These I placed in small metal evidence buttons. The most obvious evidence was the musky smell, the patches of a residue, transparent and dried like glue, on the upper front and back of her legs.

Seminal fluid was present in all of the cases, yet it was of little serological value. The assailant was one of the twenty percent of the population who enjoyed the distinction of being a nonsecreter. This meant his blood-type antigens could not be found in his other body fluids, such as saliva or semen or sweat. Absent a blood sample, in other words, he couldn't be typed. He could have been A, B, AB or anything.

As recently as two years earlier, the killer's nonsecreter status would have been a crushing blow to the forensic investigation. But now there was DNA profiling, newly introduced and potentially significant enough to identify an assailant to the exclusion of all other human beings, provided the police caught him first and obtained biological samples and he didn't have an identical twin.

Marino was inside the bedroom right behind me.

"The bathroom window," he said, looking at the body. "Well, according to the husband in there," jerking a thumb in the direction of the kitchen, "the reason it was unlocked's because he unlocked it last weekend."

I just listened.

"He says that bathroom's hardly ever used, unless they got company. Seems he was replacing the screen last weekend, says it's possible he forgot to relock the window when he finished. The bathroom's not used all week. She"—he glanced again at the body—"has no reason to give it a thought, just assumes it's locked." A pause. "Kind of interesting the only window the killer tried, it appears, was that window. The one unlocked. The screens to the rest of 'em aren't cut."

"How many windows are in the back of the house?" I asked.

"Three. In the kitchen, the half bath and the bathroom in here."

"And all of them have slide-up sashes with a latch lock at the top?"

"You got it."

"Meaning, if you shone a flashlight on the latch lock from the outside, you probably could see whether it's fastened or not?"

"Maybe." Those flat, unfriendly eyes again. "But only if you climbed up something to look. You couldn't see the lock from the ground."

"You mentioned a picnic bench," I reminded him.

"Problem with that's the backyard's soggy as hell. The legs of the bench should've left depressions in the lawn if the guy put it up against the other windows and stood on top of it to look. I got a couple men poking around out there now. No depressions under the other two windows. Don't look like that killer went near 'em.

What it does look like is he went straight to the bathroom window down the hall."

"Is it possible it might have been open a crack, and that's why the killer went straight to it?"

Marino conceded, "Hey. Anything's possible. But if it was open a crack, maybe she would've noticed it, too, at some point during the week."

Maybe. Maybe not. It is easy to be observant retrospectively. But most people don't pay that much attention to every detail of their residences, especially to rooms scarcely used.

Beneath a curtained window overlooking the street was a desk containing other numbing reminders that Lori Petersen and I were of the same profession. Scattered over the blotter were several medical journals, the *Principles of Surgery* and Dorland's. Near the base of the brass gooseneck lamp were two computer diskettes. The labels were tersely dated "6/1" in felt-tip pen and numbered "I" and II." They were generic double-density diskettes, IBM-compatible. Possibly they contained something Lori Petersen was working on at VMC, the medical college, where there were numerous computers at the disposal of the students and physicians. There didn't appear to be a personal computer inside the house.

On a wicker chair in the corner between the chests of drawers and the window clothes were neatly laid: a pair of white cotton slacks, a red-and-white-striped short-sleeved shirt and a brassiere. The garments were slightly wrinkled, as if worn and left on the chair at the end of the day, the way I sometimes do when I'm too tired to hang up my clothes.

I briefly perused the walk-in closet and full bath. In all, the master bedroom was neat and undisturbed, except for the bed. By all indications, it was not part of the killer's *modus operandi* to ransack or commit burglary.

Marino was watching an ID officer open the dresser drawers.

"What else do you know about the husband?" I asked him.

"He's a grad student at Charlottesville, lives there during the week, comes home on Friday nights. Stays the weekend, then goes back to Charlottesville on Sunday night."

"What is his discipline?"

"Literature's what he said," Marino replied, glancing around at everything but me. "He's getting his Ph.D."

"In what?"

"Literature," he said again, slowly enunciating each syllable. "What sort of literature?"

His brown eyes finally fixed unemphatically on me. "American's what he told me. But I get the impression his main interest is plays. Seems he's in one right now. Shakespeare. *Hamlet*, I think he said. Says he's done a lot of acting, including some bit parts in movies shot around here, a couple of TV commercials, too."

The ID officers stopped what they were doing. One of them turned around, his brush poised in midair.

Marino pointed toward the computer diskettes on the desk and exclaimed loudly enough to grab everybody's attention, "Looks like we'd better take a peek at what's on these suckers. Maybe a play he's writing, huh?"

"We can take a look at them in my office. We've got a couple IBM-compatible PC's," I offered.

"PC's," he drawled. "Yo. Beats the hell out of my RC: one Royal Crapola, standard issue, black, boxy, sticky keys, the whole nine yards."

An ID officer was pulling out something from beneath a stack of sweaters in a bottom drawer, a long-bladed survival knife with a compass built into the top of the black handle and a small whetstone in a pocket on the sheath. Touching as little of it as possible, he placed it inside a plastic evidence bag.

Out of the same dresser drawer came a box of Trojans, which, I pointed out to Marino, was a little unusual, since Lori Petersen, based on what I'd seen in the master bedroom, was on oral contraceptives.

Marino and the other officers began the expected cynical speculations.

I pulled off my gloves and stuffed them in the top of my bag. "The squad can move her," I said.

The men turned in unison, as if suddenly reminded of the brutalized, dead woman in the center of the rumpled turned-down bed. Her lips were pulled back, as if in pain, from her teeth, her eyes swollen to slits and staring blindly up.

A radio message was relayed to the ambulance, and several minutes later two paramedics in blue jumpsuits came in with a stretcher, which they covered with a clean white sheet and placed flush against the bed.

Lori Petersen was lifted as I directed, the bedclothes folded over her, the gloved hands not touching her skin. She was gently placed on the stretcher, the sheet pinned at the top to ensure no trace evidence was lost or added. Velcro straps made a loud ripping sound as they were peeled apart and fastened across the white cocoon.

Marino followed me out of the bedroom and I was surprised when he announced, "I'll walk you to your car."

Matt Petersen was on his feet as we came down the hall. His face wan, his eyes glassy, he stared at me, desperately, needing something only I could give. Assurance. A word of comfort. The promise his wife died quickly and did not suffer. That she was tied up and raped after the fact. There was nothing I could say to him. Marino led me back through the living room and out the door.

The front yard was lit up with television lights floating against the background of hypnotically flashing red and blue. The staccato voices of disembodied dispatchers competed with the throbbing engines as a gentle rain began to fall through a light fog.

Reporters with notepads and tape recorders were everywhere, waiting impatiently for the moment when the body was carried down the front steps and slid into the back of the ambulance. A television crew was on the street, a woman in a snappy belted trenchcoat talking into a microphone, her face serious as a grinding camera recorded her "at the scene" for Saturday's evening news.

Bill Boltz, the Commonwealth's attorney, had just pulled up and was getting out of his car. He looked dazed and half asleep and determined to elude the press. He didn't have anything to say because he didn't know anything yet. I wondered who notified him. Maybe Marino. Cops milled around, a few of them aimlessly probing the grass with their powerful Kel lights, some of them clustered by their white cruisers and talking. Boltz zipped up his windbreaker and nodded as he briefly met my eyes, then hurried up the walk.

The chief of police and a major sat inside an unmarked beige car, the interior light on, their faces pale as they periodically nodded and made remarks to reporter Abby Turnbull. She was saying something to them through an open window. Waiting until we were on the street, she trotted after us.

Marino warded her off with the flap of a hand, a "Hey, no comment" in a "screw yourself" tone of voice.

He stepped up the pace. He was almost a comfort.

"Ain't this the pits?" Marino said with disgust as he patted himself down for his cigarettes. "A regular three-ring circus. Jesus Christ."

The rain was soft and cool on my face as Marino held the station wagon door open for me. As I turned the ignition he leaned down and said with a smirk, "Drive real careful, Doc."

2

THE WHITE CLOCK FACE floated like a full moon in the dark sky, rising high above the old domed train station, the railroad tracks and the I-95 overpass. The great clock's filigree hands stopped when the last passenger train did many years before. It was twelve-seventeen. It would always be twelve-seventeen in the city's lower end where Health and Human Services decided to erect its hospital for the dead.

Time has stopped here. Buildings are boarded up and torn down. Traffic and freight trains perpetually rumble and roar like a distant discontented sea. The earth is a poisoned shore of weed-patched raw dirt littered with debris where nothing grows and there are no lights after dark. Nothing moves here except the truckers and the travelers and the trains speeding along their tracks of concrete and steel.

The white clock face watched me as I drove through the darkness, watched me like the white face in my dream.

I nosed the station wagon through an opening in the chain-link fence and parked behind the stucco building where I'd spent virtually every day of the past two years. The only state vehicle in the lot aside from mine was the gray Plymouth belonging to Neils Vander, the fingerprints examiner. I had called him right after Marino called me. Set into effect after the second strangling was a new policy. If there was another, Vander was to meet me in the morgue immediately. By now he was inside the X-ray room and setting up the laser.

Light was spilling on the tarmac from the open bay, and two paramedics were pulling a stretcher bearing a black body pouch out of the back of an ambulance. Deliveries went on throughout the night. Anybody who died violently, unexpectedly, or suspiciously in central Virginia was sent here, no matter the hour or the day.

The young men in their blue jumpsuits looked surprised to see me as I walked through the bay and held open the door leading inside the building.

"You're out early, Doc."

"Suicide from Mecklenburg," the other attendant volunteered. "Threw himself in front of a train. Scattered him over fifty feet of tracks."

"Yo. Pieces an' parts . . ."

The stretcher bumped through the open doorway and into the white-tiled corridor. The body pouch apparently was defective or torn. Blood leaked through the bottom of the stretcher and left a trail of speckled red.

The morgue had a distinctive odor, the stale stench of death no amount of air deodorizer could mask. Had I been led here blindfolded, I would have known exactly where I was. At this hour of the morning, the smell was more noticeable, more unpleasant than usual. The stretcher clattered loudly through the hollow stillness as the attendants wheeled the suicide into the stainless steel refrigerator.

I turned right into the morgue office where Fred, the security guard, was sipping coffee from a Styrofoam cup and waiting for the ambulance attendants to sign in the body and be on their way. He was sitting on the edge of the desk, ducking out of view, just as he always did when a body was delivered. A gun to his head wouldn't have been sufficient incentive to make him escort anybody inside the refrigerator. Toe tags dangling from cold feet protruding from sheets had a peculiar effect on him.

He shot a sidelong glance at the wall clock. His ten-hour shift was almost at an end.

"We've got another strangling coming in," I bluntly told him.

"Lord, Lord! Sure am sorry." Shaking his head. "I tell you. It's hard to imagine anybody doing something like that. All them poor young ladies." Head still shaking.

"It will be here any minute and I want you to make sure the bay door is shut and remains shut after the body's brought in, Fred.

The reporters will be out in droves. I don't want *anybody* within fifty feet of this building. Is that clear?" I sounded hard and sharp, and I knew it. My nerves were singing like a power line.

"Yes, ma'am." A vigorous nod. "I'll keep an eye out, I sure will."

Lighting a cigarette, I reached for the telephone and stabbed out my home number.

Bertha picked up on the second ring and sounded drugged with sleep when she hoarsely asked, "Hello?"

"Just checking in."

"I'm here. Lucy hasn't budged, Dr. Kay. Sleeping like a log, didn't even hear me come in."

"Thank you, Bertha. I can't thank you enough. I don't know when I'll be home."

"I'll be here till I see you, then, Dr. Kay."

Bertha was on notice these days. If I got called out in the middle of the night, so did she. I'd given her a key to the front door and instructions about the operation of the burglar alarm. She probably arrived at my house just minutes after I left for the scene. It dully drifted through my mind that when Lucy got out of bed in several hours, she'd find Bertha inside the kitchen instead of her Auntie Kay.

I had promised to take Lucy to Monticello today.

On a nearby surgical cart was the blue power unit, smaller than a microwave oven, with a row of bright green lights across the front. It was suspended in the pitch darkness of the X-ray room like a satellite in empty space, a spiral cord running from it to a pencil-sized wand filled with seawater.

The laser we acquired last winter was a relatively simple device.

In ordinary light sources, atoms and molecules emit light independently and in many different wavelengths. But if an atom is excited by heat, and if light of a certain wavelength is impinged upon it, an atom can be stimulated to emit light in phase.

"Give me just another minute." Neils Vander was working various knobs and switches, his back to me. "She's slow to warm up this morning . . ." Adding in a despondent mumble, "So am I, for that matter."

I was standing on the other side of the X-ray table, watching his shadow through a pair of amber-tinted goggles. Directly below me was the dark shape of Lori Petersen's remains, the covers from her bed open but still underneath her. I stood in the darkness waiting for what seemed a very long time, my thoughts undistracted, my hands perfectly still, my senses undisturbed. Her body was warm, her life so recently ended it seemed to linger about her like an odor.

Vander announced "Ready" and flipped a switch.

Instantly spitting from the wand was a rapidly flashing syn-chronized light as brilliant as liquid chrysoberyl. It did not dispel darkness but seemed to absorb it. It did not glow but rather flowed over a small surface area. He was a flickering lab coat across the table as he began by directing the wand at her head.

We explored inches of the suffused flesh at a time. Tiny fibers lit up like hot wires and I began collecting them with forceps, my movements staccato in the strobe, creating the illusion of slow motion as I went from her body on the X-ray table to the evidence buttons and envelopes on a cart. Back and forth. Everything was disconnected. The laser's bombardment illuminated a corner of a lip, a rash of pinpoint hemorrhages on the cheekbone, or a wing of the nose, isolating each feature. My gloved fingers working the forceps seemed to belong to somebody else.

The rapidly alternating darkness and light were dizzying, and the only way I could maintain my equilibrium was to channel my concentration into one thought at a time, as if I, like the laser beam, was in phase, too—all of me in sync with what I was doing, the sum of my mental energy coalesced into a single wavelength.

"One of the guys who brought her in," Vander remarked, "told me she was a surgical resident at VMC."

I barely responded.

"Did you know her?"

The question took me by surprise. Something inside me tightened like a fist. I was on the faculty of VMC, where there were hundreds of medical students and residents. There was no reason I should have known her.

I didn't answer except to give directions such as "A little to the right," or "Hold it there for a minute." Vander was slow and deliberate and tense, as was I. A feeling of helplessness and frustration was getting to us. So far the laser had proven to be no better than a Hoover vacuum cleaner that collected miscellaneous debris.

We'd tried it on maybe twenty cases by now, only a few of

which actually merited its use. In addition to its usefulness in finding fibers and other trace evidence, it reveals various components of perspiration that fluoresce like a neon sign when stimulated by a laser. Theoretically, a fingerprint left on human skin can emit light and may be identified in cases where traditional powder and chemical methods will fail. I knew of only one case where prints on skin were found, in south Florida, where a woman was murdered inside a health spa and the assailant had tanning oil on his hands. Neither Vander nor I was expecting our luck to be any better than it had been in the past.

What we saw didn't register at first.

The wand was probing several inches of Lori Petersen's right shoulder when directly over her right clavicle three irregular smudges suddenly leapt out as if they were painted with phosphorus. We both stood still and stared. Then he whistled through his teeth as a faint chill ran up my spine.

Retrieving a jar of powder and a Magna brush, Vander delicately dusted what appeared to be three latent fingerprints left on Lori Petersen's skin.

I dared to hope. "Any good?"

"They're partials," he said abstractedly as he began taking photographs with an MP-4 Polaroid camera. "The ridge detail's damn good. Good enough to classify, I think. I'll run these babes through the computer right away."

"Looks like the same residue," I thought out loud. "The same stuff on his hands." The monster had signed his work again. It was too good to be true. The fingerprints were too good to be true.

"Looks the same, all right. But he must have had a lot more of it on his hands this time."

The killer had never left his prints in the past, but the glittery residue, which apparently caused them to fluoresce, was something we'd grown to expect. There was more of it. As Vander began probing her neck, a constellation of tiny white stars popped out like shards of glass hit by headlights on a dark street. He held the wand in place as I reached for a sterilized gauze pad.

We'd found the same glitter scattered over the bodies of the first three strangling victims, more of it in the third case than in the second, and the least amount found in the first. Samples had been sent to the labs. So far, the strange residue had not been identified beyond determining it was inorganic.

We weren't closer to knowing what it was, though by now we had quite a long list of substances it couldn't be. Over the past few weeks, Vander and I had run several series of tests, smearing everything from margarine to body lotions on our own forearms to see what reacted to the laser and what didn't. Fewer samples lit up than either of us had supposed, and nothing blazed as brightly as the unknown glittery residue.

I gently wedged a finger under the electrical cord ligature around Lori Petersen's neck, exposing an angry red furrow in the flesh. The margin wasn't clearly defined—the strangulation was slower than I'd originally thought. I could see the faint abrasions from the cord's having slipped in place several times. It was loose enough to keep her barely alive for a while. Then suddenly, it was jerked tight. There were two or three sparkles clinging to the cord, and that was all.

"Try the ligature around her ankles," I said quietly.

We moved down. The same white sparkles were there, too, but again, very few of them. There was none of this residue, what-ever it was, anywhere on her face, none in her hair or on her legs. We found several of the sparkles on her forearms, and a spangling of them over her upper arms and breasts. A constellation of the tiny white stars clung to the cords savagely binding her wrists in back, and there was a scattering of the glitter over her cut gown as well.

I moved away from the table, lit a cigarette and began reconstructing.

The assailant had some material on his hands that was deposited wherever he touched his victim. After Lori Petersen's gown was off, perhaps he gripped her right shoulder and his finger-tips left the smudges over her clavicle. One thing I felt sure of: For the concentration of this material to be so dense over her clavicle, he must have touched her there first.

This was puzzling, a piece that seemed to fit but didn't, really.

From the beginning, I'd assumed he was restraining his vic-tims immediately, subduing them, perhaps at knifepoint, and then binding them before he cut off their clothing or did anything else. The more he touched, the less of the residue was left on his hands. Why this high concentration over her clavicle? Was this area of her skin exposed when he began his assault? I wouldn't have sup-posed so. The gown was an interlocking cotton material, soft and stretchy and fashioned to look almost exactly like a long-sleeved T-shirt. There were no buttons or zippers, and the only way for her to have put it on was to pull it over her head. She would have been covered to her neck. How could the killer touch the bare skin over her clavicle if she still had her gown on? Why was there such a high concentration of the residue at all? We'd never found such a high concentration before.

I went out into the hallway where several uniformed men were leaning against the wall, chatting. I asked one of them to raise Marino on the radio and have him call me right away. I heard Marino's voice crackle back, "Ten fo'." I paced the hard tile floor inside the autopsy suite with its gleaming stainless steel tables and sinks and carts lined with surgical instruments. A faucet was dripping somewhere. Disinfectant smelled sweetly revolting, only smelled pleasant when there were worse smells lurking beneath it. The black telephone on the desk mocked me with its silence. Marino knew I was waiting by the phone. He was having a good time knowing that.

It was idle speculation to go back to the beginning and try to figure out what had gone wrong. Occasionally I thought about it anyway. What it was about me. I had been polite to Marino the first time we met, had offered him a firm and respectful handshake while his eyes went as flat as two tarnished pennies.

Twenty minutes passed before the telephone rang.

Marino was still at the Petersen house, he said, interviewing the husband, who was, in the detective's words, "as goofy as a shithouse rat."

I told him about the sparkles. I repeated what I'd explained to him in the past. It was possible they might be from some household substance consistent in all of the homicide scenes, some oddball something the killer looked for and incorporated into his ritual. Baby powder, lotions, cosmetics, cleansers.

So far, we had ruled out many things which, in a way, was the point. If the substance wasn't indigenous to the scenes, and in my heart I didn't think it was, then the killer was carrying it in with him, perhaps unaware, and this could be important and eventually lead us to where he worked or lived.

"Yeah," Marino's voice came over the line, "well, I'll poke around in the cabinets and so forth. But I got my own thought."

"Which is?"

"The husband here's in a play, right? Has practice every Friday night, which is why he gets in so late, right? Correct me if I'm wrong, but actors wear greasepaint."

"Only during dress rehearsals or performances."

"Yeah," he drawled. "Well, according to him, a dress rehearsal's exactly what he had just before he came home and supposedly found his dead wife. My little bell's ringing. My little voice is talking to me—"

I cut him off. "Have you printed him?"

"Oh, yeah."

"Place his card inside a plastic bag and when you come in bring it straight to me."

He didn't get it.

I didn't elaborate. I was in no mood to explain.

The last thing Marino told me before hanging up was "Don't know when that will be, Doc. Got a feeling I'm going to be tied up out here most of the day. No pun intended."

It was unlikely I would see him or the fingerprint card until Monday. Marino had a suspect. He was galloping down the same trail every cop gallops down. A husband could be St. Anthony and in England when his wife is murdered in Seattle, and still the cops are suspicious of him first.

Domestic shootings, poisonings, beatings, and stabbings are one thing, but a lust murder is another. Not many husbands would have the stomach for binding, raping and strangling their wives.

I blamed my disconcertedness on fatigue.

I had been up since 2:33 A.M. and it was now almost 6:00 P.M. The police officers who came to the morgue were long gone. Vander went home around lunchtime. Wingo, one of my autopsy technicians, left not long after that, and there was no one inside the building but me.

The quiet I usually craved was unnerving and I could not seem to get warm. My hands were stiff, the fingernails almost blue. Every time the telephone rang in the front office, I started.

The minimal security in my office never seemed to worry anyone but me. Budget requests for an adequate security system were repeatedly refused. The commissioner thought in terms of property loss, and no thief was going to come into the morgue even if we put out welcome mats and left the doors open wide at all hours. Dead bodies are a better deterrent than guard dogs.

The dead have never bothered me. It is the living I fear.

After a crazed gunman walked into a local doctor's office several months back and sprayed bullets into a waiting room full of patients, I went to a hardware store and bought a chain and padlock myself, which after hours and on weekends were used to reinforce the front glass double doors.

Suddenly, while I was working at my desk, someone shook those front doors so violently the chain was still swaying when I forced myself to go down the hallway to check. No one was there. Sometimes street people tried to get in to use our restrooms, but when I looked out I didn't see anyone.

I returned to my office and was so jumpy that when I heard the elevator doors opening across the hall I had a large pair of scissors in hand and was prepared to use them. It was the day-shift security guard.

"Did you try to get in through the front glass doors a little while ago?" I asked.

He glanced curiously at the scissors I was clutching and said he didn't. I'm sure it seemed an inane question. He knew the front doors were chained, and he had a set of keys to the other doors throughout the building. He had no reason to try to get in through the front.

An uneasy silence returned as I sat at my desk trying to dictate Lori Petersen's autopsy report. For some reason, I couldn't say anything, couldn't bear to hear the words out loud. It began to dawn on me that no one should hear those words, not even Rose, my secretary. No one should hear about the glittery residue, the seminal fluid, the fingerprints, the deep tissue injuries to her neck—and worst of all, the evidence of torture. The killer was degenerating, becoming more hideously cruel.

Rape and murder were no longer enough for him. It wasn't until I'd removed the ligatures from Lori Petersen's body, and was making small incisions in suspicious reddish-tinted areas of skin and palpating for broken bones that I realized what went on before she died.

The contusions were so recent they were barely visible on the surface, but the incisions revealed the broken blood vessels under the skin, and the patterns were consistent with her having been struck with a blunt object, such as a knee or a foot. Three ribs in a row on the left side were fractured, as were four of her fingers. There were fibers inside her mouth, mostly on her tongue, suggesting that at some point she was gagged to prevent her from screaming.

In my mind I saw the violin on the music stand inside the living room, and the surgical journals and books on the desk in the bedroom. Her hands. They were her most prized instruments, something with which she healed and made music. He must have deliberately broken her fingers one by one after she was bound.

The microcassette recorder spun on, recording silence. I switched it off and swiveled my judge's chair around to the computer terminal. The monitor blinked from black to the sky blue of the word-processing package, and black letters marched across the screen as I began typing the autopsy report myself.

I didn't look at the weights and notes I'd scribbled on an empty glove packet when I was performing the autopsy. I knew everything about her. I had total recall. The phrase "within normal limits" was playing nonstop inside my head. There was nothing wrong with her. Her heart, her lungs, her liver. "Within normal limits." She died in perfect health. I typed on and on and on, full pages blinking out as I was automatically given new screens until I suddenly looked up. Fred, the security guard, was standing in my doorway.

I had no idea how long I'd been working. He was due back on duty at 8:00 P.M. Everything that had transpired since I saw him last seemed like a dream, a very bad dream.

"You still here?" Then hesitantly, "Uh, there's this funeral home downstairs for a pickup but can't find the body. Come all the way from Mecklenburg. Don't know where Wingo is . . ."

"Wingo went home hours ago," I said. "What body?"

"Someone named Roberts, got hit by a train."

I thought for a moment. Including Lori Petersen, there were six cases today. I vaguely recalled the train fatality. "He's in the refrigerator."

"They say they can't find 'im in there."

I slipped off my glasses and rubbed my eyes. "Did you look?"

His face broke into a sheepish grin. Fred backed away shaking his head. "You know, Dr. Sca'petta, I don't never go inside that box! Uh-uh."

3

I PULLED INTO MY DRIVEWAY, relieved to find Bertha's boat of a Pontiac still there. The front door opened before I had a chance to select the right key.

"How's the weather?" I asked right off.

Bertha and I faced each other inside the spacious foyer. She knew exactly what I meant. We had this conversation at the end of every day when Lucy was in town.

"Been *bad*, Dr. Kay. That child been in your office all day banging on that computer of yours. I tell you! I as much as step foot in there to bring her a sandwich and ask how she be and she start hollerin' and carryin' on. But I know." Her dark eyes softened. "She just upset because you had to work."

Guilt seeped through my numbness.

"I seen the evenin' paper, Dr. Kay. Lord have mercy." She was working one arm at a time into the sleeves of her raincoat. "I know why you had to be doin' what you was doin' all day. Lord, Lord. I sure do hope the police catch that man. Meanness. Just plain meanness."

Bertha knew what I did for a living and she never questioned me. Even if one of my cases was someone from her neighborhood, she never asked.

"The evenin' paper's in there." She gestured toward the living room and collected her pocketbook from the table near the door. "I stuck it under the sofa cushion so she couldn't get hold of it.

Didn't know if you'd want her to be readin' it or not, Dr. Kay." She patted my shoulder on her way out.

I watched her make her way to her car and slowly back out of the drive. God bless her. I no longer apologized for my family. Bertha had been insulted and bullied either face-to-face or over the phone by my niece, my sister, my mother. Bertha knew. She never sympathized or criticized, and I sometimes suspected she felt sorry for me, and that only made me feel worse. Shutting the front door, I went into the kitchen.

It was my favorite room, high-ceilinged, the appliances modern but few, for I prefer to do most things, such as making pasta or kneading dough, by hand. There was a maple butcher block in the center of the cooking area, just the right height for someone not a stitch over five foot three in her stocking feet. The breakfast area faced a large picture window overlooking the wooded backyard and the bird feeder. Splashing the monochrome blonds of wooden cabinets and countertops were loose arrangements of yellow and red roses from my passionately well attended garden.

Lucy was not here. Her supper dishes were upright in the drainboard and I assumed she was in my office again.

I went to the refrigerator and poured myself a glass of Chablis. Leaning against the counter, I shut my eyes for a moment and sipped. I didn't know what I was going to do about Lucy.

Last summer was her first visit here since I had left the Dade County Medical Examiner's Office and moved away from the city where I was born and where I had returned after my divorce. Lucy is my only niece. At ten she was already doing high-school-level science and math. She was a genius, an impossible little holy terror of enigmatic Latin descent whose father died when she was small. She had no one but my only sister, Dorothy, who was too caught up in writing children's books to worry much about her flesh-and-blood daughter. Lucy adored me beyond any rational explanation, and her attachment to me demanded energy I did not have at the moment. While driving home, I debated changing her flight reservations and sending her back to Miami early. I couldn't bring myself to do it.

She would be devastated. She would not understand. It would be the final rejection in a lifelong series of rejections, another reminder she was inconvenient and unwanted. She had been looking forward to this visit all year. I'd been looking forward to it, too.

Taking another sip of wine, I waited for the absolute quiet to begin untangling my snarled nerves and smoothing away my worries.

My house was in a new subdivision in the West End of the city, where the large homes stood on wooded one-acre lots and the traffic on the streets was mostly station wagons and family cars. The neighbors were so quiet, break-ins and vandalism so rare, I couldn't recall the last time I had seen a police car cruise through. The stillness, the security, was worth any price, a necessity, a must, for me. It was soothing to my soul on early mornings to eat breakfast alone and know the only violence beyond my window would be a squirrel and a blue jay fighting over the feeder.

I took a deep breath and another sip of wine. I began to dread going to bed, dreading those moments in the dark before sleep, fearing what it would be like when I permitted my mind to be still, and therefore unguarded. I could not stop seeing images of Lori Petersen. A dam had broken and my imagination was rushing in, quickening the images into more terrible ones.

I saw him with her, inside that bedroom. I could almost see his face, but it had no features, just a glimpse of a facelike flash going by as he was with her. She would try to reason with him at first, after the paralyzing fear of waking up at the feel of cold flat steel to her throat, or at the chilling sound of his voice. She would say things, try to talk him out of it for God knows how long as he cut the cords from the lamps and began to bind her. She was a Harvard graduate, a surgeon. She would attempt to use her mind against a force that is mindless.

Then the images went wild, like a film at high speed, flapping off the reel as her attempts disintegrated into unmitigated terror. The unspeakable. I would not look. I could not bear to see any more. I had to control my thoughts.

My home office overlooked the woods in back and the blinds were typically drawn because it has always been hard for me to concentrate if I'm offered a view. I paused in the doorway, quietly letting my attention drift as Lucy vigorously tapped away on the keyboard on top of my sturdy oak desk, her back to me. I had not straightened up in here in weeks, and the sight of it was shameful. Books leaned this way and that in the bookcases, several *Law Reporters* were stacked on the floor and others were out of order. Propped against a wall were my diplomas and certificates: Cornell, Johns Hopkins, Georgetown, et al. I'd been meaning to hang them in my office downtown but had yet to get around to it. Sloppily piled on a corner of the deep blue T'ai-Ming rug were journal articles still waiting to be read and filed. Professional success meant I no longer had the time to be impeccably neat, and yet clutter bothered me as much as ever.

"How come you're spying on me?" Lucy muttered without turning around.

"I'm not spying on you." I smiled a little and kissed the top of her burnished red head.

"Yes, you are." She continued to type. "I saw you. I saw your reflection in the monitor. You've been standing in the doorway watching me."

I put my arms around her, rested my chin on the top of her head and looked at the black screen filled with chartreuse commands. It never occurred to me before this moment that the screen had a mirror effect, and I now understood why Margaret, my programming analyst, could hail by name people walking past her office though she had her back to the door. Lucy's face was a blur in the monitor. Mostly I saw a reflection of her grown-up, tortoise-rimmed glasses. She usually greeted me with a tree frog hug, but she was in a mood.

"I'm sorry we couldn't go to Monticello today, Lucy," I ventured.

A shrug.

"I'm as disappointed as you are," I said.

Another shrug. "I'd rather use the computer anyway."

She didn't mean it, but the remark stung.

"I had a shit-load of stuff to do," she went on, sharply striking the Return key. "Your data base needed cleaning up. Bet you haven't initialized it in a year." She swiveled around in my leather chair and I moved to one side, crossing my arms at my waist.

"So I fixed it up."

"You *what?*"

No, Lucy wouldn't do such a thing. Initializing was the same thing as formatting, obliterating, erasing all of the data on the hard disk. On the hard disk were—or had been—half a dozen statistical tables I was using for journal articles under deadline. The only backups were several months old.

Lucy's green eyes fixed on mine and looked owlish behind the thick lenses of her glasses. Her round, elfish face was hard as she said, "I looked in the books to see how. All you do is type IORI at the C prompt, and after it's initialized, you do the Addall and Catalog.Ora. It's easy. Any dick head could figure it out."

I didn't say anything. I didn't reprimand her for her dirty mouth.

I was feeling weak in the knees.

I was remembering Dorothy calling me, absolutely hysterical, several years ago. While she was out shopping, Lucy had gone into her office and formatted every last one of her diskettes, erasing everything on them. On two of them was a book Dorothy was writing, chapters she hadn't gotten around to printing out or backing up yet. A homicidal event.

"Lucy. You didn't."

"Ohhhh, don't worry," she said sullenly. "I exported all your data first. The book says to. And then I imported it back in and reconnected your grants. Everything's there. But it's cleaned up, space-wise, I mean."

I pulled up an ottoman and sat beside her. It was then I noticed what was beneath a layer of diskettes: the evening paper, folded the way papers are folded when they have been read. I slid it out and opened it to the front page. The banner headline was the last thing I wanted to see.

Young Surgeon Slain: Believed to be Strangler's Fourth Victim

A 30-year-old surgical resident was found brutally murdered inside her home in Berkley Downs shortly after midnight. Police say there is strong evidence that her death is related to the deaths of three other Richmond women who were strangled in their homes within the last two months.

The most recent victim has been identified as Lori Anne Petersen, a graduate of Harvard Medical School. She was last seen alive yesterday, shortly after midnight, when she left the

VMC hospital emergency room, where she was currently com-
pleting a rotation in trauma surgery. It is believed she drove
directly home from the hospital and was murdered sometime
between twelve-thirty and two this morning. The killer apparently got inside her house by cutting a screen to a bathroom
window that was unlocked . . .

It went on. There was a photograph, a grainy black-and-white
tableau of paramedics carrying her body down the front steps, and
a smaller photograph of a figure in a khaki raincoat I recognized as
me. The caption read: "Dr. Kay Scarpetta, Chief Medical Examiner,
Arriving at Murder Scene."

Lucy was staring wide-eyed at me. Bertha had been wise to
hide the paper, but Lucy was resourceful. I didn't know what to say.
What does a ten-year-old think when she reads something like this,
especially if it is accompanied by a grim photograph of her "Auntie
Kay"?

I'd never fully explained to Lucy the details of my profession.
I'd restrained myself from preaching to her about the savage world
in which we live. I didn't want her to be like me, robbed of innocence and idealism, baptized in the bloody waters of randomness
and cruelty, the fabric of trust forever torn.

"It's like the *Herald*," she quite surprised me by saying. "All
the time there's stuff in the *Herald* about people being killed.
Last week they found a man in the canal and his head was
cut off. He must have been a bad man for someone to cut his
head off."

"He may have been, Lucy. But it doesn't justify someone's doing something like that to him. And not everyone who is hurt or
murdered is bad."

"Mom says they are. She says good people don't get murdered.
Only hookers and drug dealers and burglars do." A thoughtful
pause. "Sometimes police officers, too, because they try to catch
the bad people."

Dorothy would say such a thing and, what was worse, she
would believe it. I felt a flare of the old anger.

"But the lady who got strangled," Lucy wavered, her eyes so
wide they seemed to swallow me. "She was a doctor, Auntie Kay.
How could she be bad? You're a doctor, too. She was just like you,
then."

I was suddenly aware of the time. It was getting late. I switched off the computer, took Lucy's hand, and we walked out of the office and into the kitchen. When I turned to her to suggest a snack before bed, I was dismayed to see she was biting her bottom lip, her eyes welling.

"Lucy! Why are you crying?"

She wrapped around me, sobbing. Clinging to me with fierce desperation, she cried, "I don't want you to die! I don't want you to die!"

"*Lucy* . . ." I was stunned, bewildered. Her tantrums, her arrogant and angry outbursts were one thing. But this! I could feel her tears soaking through my blouse. I could feel the hot intensity of her miserable little body as she held on to me.

"It's all right, Lucy," was all I could think to say, and I pressed her close.

"I don't want you to die, Auntie Kay!"

"I'm not going to die, Lucy."

"Daddy did."

"Nothing is going to happen to me, Lucy."

She was not to be consoled. The story in the paper affected her in a deep and pernicious way. She read it with an adult intellect yet to be weaned from a child's fearful imagination. This in addition to her insecurities and losses.

Oh, Lord. I groped for the appropriate response and couldn't come up with a thing. My mother's accusations began throbbing in some deep part of my psyche. My inadequacies. I had no children. I would have made an awful mother. "You should have been a man," my mother had said during one of our less productive encounters in recent history. "All work and ambition. It's not natural for a woman. You'll dry out like a chinch bug, Kay."

And during my emptiest moments when I felt the worst about myself, damn if I wouldn't see one of those chinch bug shells that used to litter the lawn of my childhood home. Translucent, brittle, dried out. Dead.

It wasn't something I would ordinarily do, pour a ten-year-old a glass of wine.

I took her to her room and we drank in bed. She asked me questions impossible to answer. "Why do people hurt other people?" and "Is it a game for him? I mean, does he do it for fun, sort of like MTV? They do things like that on MTV, but it's make-believe.

Nobody gets hurt. Maybe he doesn't mean to hurt them, Auntie Kay."

"There are some people who are evil," I quietly replied. "Like dogs, Lucy. Some dogs bite people for no reason. There's something wrong with them. They're bad and will always be bad."

"Because people were mean to them first. That's what makes them bad."

"In some instances, yes," I told her. "But not always. Sometimes there isn't a reason. In a way, it doesn't matter. People make choices. Some people would rather be bad, would rather be cruel. It's just an ugly, unfortunate part of life."

"Like Hitler," she muttered, taking a swallow of wine.

I began stroking her hair.

She rambled on, her voice thick with sleep, "Like Jimmy Groome, too. He lives on our street and shoots birds with his BB gun, and he likes to steal bird eggs out of nests and smash them on the road and watch the baby birds struggle. I hate him. I hate Jimmy Groome. I threw a rock at him once and hit him when he was riding by on his bike. But he doesn't know it was me because I was hiding behind the bushes."

I sipped wine and continued stroking her hair.

"God won't let anything happen to you, will He?" she asked.

"Nothing is going to happen to me, Lucy. I promise."

"If you pray to God to take care of you, He does, doesn't He?"

"He takes care of us." Though I wasn't sure I believed it.

She frowned. I'm not sure she believed it either. "Don't you ever get scared?"

I smiled. "Everybody gets scared now and then. I'm perfectly safe. Nothing's going to happen to me."

The last thing she mumbled before drifting off was "I wish I could always be here, Auntie Kay. I want to be just like you."

Two hours later, I was upstairs and still wide-awake and staring at a page in a book without really seeing the words when the telephone rang.

My response was Pavlovian, a startled reflex. I snatched up the receiver, my heart thudding. I was expecting, fearing, Marino's voice, as if last night were starting all over again.

"Hello."

Nothing.

"Hello?"

In the background I could hear the faint, spooky music I associated with early-morning foreign movies or horror films or the scratchy strains of a Victrola before the dial tone cut it off.

"Coffee?"

"Please," I said.

This sufficed for a "Good morning."

Whenever I stopped by Neils Vander's lab, his first word of greeting was "Coffee?" I always accepted. Caffeine and nicotine are two vices I've readily adopted.

I wouldn't think of buying a car that isn't as solid as a tank, and I won't start the engine without fastening my seatbelt. There are smoke alarms throughout my house, and an expensive burglar alarm system. I no longer enjoy flying and opt for Amtrak whenever possible.

But caffeine, cigarettes and cholesterol, the grim reapers of the common man—God forbid I should give them up. I go to a national meeting and sit at a banquet with three hundred other forensic pathologists, the world's foremost experts in disease and death. Seventy-five percent of us don't jog or do aerobics, don't walk when we can ride, don't stand when we can sit, and assiduously avoid stairs or hills unless they're on the decline. A third of us smoke, most of us drink, and all of us eat as if there is no tomorrow.

Stress, depression, perhaps a greater need for laughter and pleasure because of the misery we see—who can be sure of the reason? One of my more cynical friends, an assistant chief in Chicago, likes to say, "What the hell. You die. Everybody dies. So you die healthy. So what?"

Vander went to the drip coffee machine on the counter behind his desk and poured two cups. He had fixed my coffee countless times and could never remember I drink it black.

My ex-husband never remembered either. Six years I lived with Tony and he couldn't remember that I drink my coffee black or like my steaks medium-rare, not as red as Christmas, just a little pink. My dress size, forget it. I wear an eight, have a figure that will accommodate most anything, but I can't abide fluff, froth and frills. He always got me something in a six, usually lacy and gauzy and meant for bed. His mother's favorite color was spring green. She wore a size fourteen. She loved ruffles, hated pullovers, preferred zippers, was allergic to wool, didn't want to bother with anything that had to be dry-cleaned or ironed, had a visceral antagonism toward anything purple, deemed white or beige impractical, wouldn't wear horizontal stripes or paisley, wouldn't have been caught dead in Ultrasuede, believed her body wasn't compatible with pleats and was quite fond of pockets—the more the better. When it came to his mother, Tony would somehow get it right.

Vander dumped the same heaping teaspoons of whitener and sugar into my cup as he dumped into his own.

Typically, he was disheveled, his wispy gray hair wild, his voluminous lab coat smeared with black fingerprint powder, a spray of ballpoint pens and felt-tip markers protruding from his ink-stained breast pocket. He was a tall man with long, bony extremities and a disproportionately round belly. His head was shaped remarkably like a light bulb, his eyes a washed-out blue and perpetually clouded by thought.

My first winter here he stopped by my office late one afternoon to announce it was snowing. A long red scarf was wrapped around his neck, and pulled over his ears was a leather flight helmet, possibly ordered from a Banana Republic catalogue and absolutely the most ridiculous winter hat I'd ever seen. I think he would have looked perfectly at home inside a Fokker fighter plane. "The Flying Dutchman," we appropriately called him around the office. He was always in a hurry, flying up and down the halls, his lab coat flapping around his legs.

"You saw the papers?" he asked, blowing on his coffee.

"The whole blessed world saw the papers," I dismally replied.

Sunday's front page was worse than Saturday evening's. The banner headline ran across the entire width of the top of the page, the letters about an inch high. The story included a sidebar about Lori Petersen and a photograph that looked as if it came from a yearbook. Abby Turnbull was aggressive enough, if not indecent, to attempt an interview with Lori Petersen's family, who lived in Philadelphia and "were too distraught to comment."

"It sure as hell isn't helping us any," Vander stated the obvious. "I'd like to know where the information's coming from so I could string a few people up by their thumbs."

"The cops haven't learned to keep their mouths shut," I told him. "When they learn to zip their lips, they won't have leaks to bitch about anymore."

"Well, maybe it's the cops. Whatever the case, the stuff's making my wife crazy. I think if we lived in the city, she'd make us move today."

He went to his desk, which was a jumble of computer print-outs, photographs and telephone messages. There was a quart beer bottle and a floor tile with a dried bloody shoe print, both inside plastic bags and tagged as evidence. Randomly scattered about were ten small jars of formalin, each containing a charred human fingertip anatomically severed at the second joint. In cases of un-identified bodies that are badly burned or decomposed, it isn't al-ways possible to get prints by the usual method. Incongruously stationed in the midst of this macabre mess was a bottle of Vaseline Intensive Care lotion.

Rubbing a dollop of the lotion on his hands, Vander pulled on a pair of white cotton gloves. The acetone, xylene and constant hand-washing that go with his trade were brutal on his skin, and I could always tell when he'd forgotten to put on gloves while using ninhydrin, a chemical helpful for visualizing latent prints, because he'd walk around with purple fingers for a week. His morning ritual complete, he motioned me to follow him out into the fourth-floor hallway.

Several doors down was the computer room, clean, almost sterile, and filled with light-silver modular hardware of various boxy shapes and sizes, bringing to mind a space-age Laundromat. The sleek, upright unit most closely resembling a set of washers and dryers was the fingerprint matching processor, its function to match unknown prints against the multimillion fingerprint data base stored on magnetic disks. The FMP, as it was known, with its advanced pipeline and parallel processing was capable of eight hundred matches per second. Vander didn't like to sit around and wait for the results. It was his habit to let the thing cook overnight so he had something to look forward to when he came to work the next morning.

The most time-consuming part of the process was what Vander did Saturday, feeding the prints into the computer. This required his taking photographs of the latent prints in question, enlarging them five times, placing a sheet of tracing paper over each photo-graph and with a felt-tip pen tracing the most significant char-acteristics. Next he reduced the drawing to a one-to-one sized photograph, precisely correlating to the actual size of the print. He glued the photograph to a latent-print layout sheet, which he fed into the computer. Now it simply was a matter of printing out the results of the search.

Vander seated himself with the deliberation of a concert pianist about to perform. I almost expected him to flip up his lab coat in back and stretch his fingers. His Steinway was the remote input station, consisting of a keyboard, a monitor, an image scanner and a fingerprint image processor, among other things. The image scanner was capable of reading both ten-print cards and latent prints. The fingerprint image processor (or FIP, as Vander referred to it) automatically detected fingerprint characteristics.

I watched him type in several commands. Then he punched the print button, and lists of potential suspects were rapidly hammered across the green-striped paper.

I pulled up a chair as Vander tore off the printout and ripped the paper into ten sections, separating his cases.

We were interested in 88-01651, the identification number for the latents found on Lori Petersen's body. Computerized print comparison is analogous to a political election. Possible matches are called candidates, and ranked according to score. The higher the score, the more points of comparison a candidate has in common with the unknown latents entered into the computer. In the case of 88-01651 there was one candidate leading by a wide margin of more than one thousand points. This could mean only one thing.

A hit.

Or as Vander glibly put it, "A hot one."

The winning candidate was impersonally listed as NIC112.

I really hadn't expected this.

"So whoever left the prints on her has prints on file with the data base?" I asked.

"That's right."

"Meaning it's possible he has a criminal record?"

"Possible, but not necessarily." Vander got up and moved to the verification terminal. He lightly rested his fingers on the keyboard and stared into the CRT display.

He added, "Could be he was printed for some other reason. If he's in law enforcement, or maybe applied for a taxi license once."

He began calling up fingerprint cards from the depths of image retrieval. Instantly, the search-print image, an enlarged aggregation of loops and whorls in turquoise blue, was juxtaposed to the candidate-print image. To the right was a column listing the sex, race, date of birth and other information revealing the candidate's identification. Producing a hard copy of the prints, he handed it over.

I studied it, read and reread the identity of NIC112.

Marino would be thrilled.

According to the computer, and there could be no mistake about it, the latents the laser picked up on Lori Petersen's shoulder were left by Matt Petersen, her husband.

4

I WAS NOT UNDULY SURPRISED that Matt Petersen touched her body. Often it is a reflex to touch someone who appears dead, to feel for a pulse or to grip a shoulder lightly the way one does to wake up the person. What dismayed me were two things. First, the latents were picked up because the individual who left them had a residue of the perplexing sparkles on his fingers—evidence also found in the previous strangling cases. Second, Matt Petersen's ten-print card had not been turned in to the lab yet. The only reason the computer got a hit was he *already* had prints on file with the data base.

I was telling Vander we needed to find out why and when Petersen was printed in the past, if he had a criminal record, when Marino walked in.

"Your secretary said you was up here," he announced by way of a greeting.

He was eating a doughnut I recognized as having come from the box by the coffee machine downstairs. Rose always brought in doughnuts on Monday mornings. Glancing around at the hardware, he casually shoved a manila envelope my way. "Sorry, Neils," he mumbled. "But the Doc here says she's got first dibs."

Vander looked curiously at me as I opened the envelope. Inside was a plastic evidence bag containing Petersen's ten-print card. Marino had put me on the spot, and I didn't appreciate it. The card, under ordinary circumstances, should have been receipted directly to the fingerprints lab—not to me. It is this very sort of maneuver that creates animosity on the part of one's colleagues. They assume you're violating their turf, assume you're preempting them when, in truth, you may be doing nothing of the sort.

I explained to Vander, "I didn't want this left on your desk, out in the open where it might be handled. Matt Petersen supposedly was using greasepaint before he came home. If there was a residue on his hands, it may also be on his card."

Vander's eyes widened. The thought appealed to him. "Sure. We'll run it under the laser."

Marino was staring sullenly at me.

I asked him, "What about the survival knife?"

He produced another envelope from the stack wedged between his elbow and waist. "Was on my way to take it to Frank."

Vander suggested, "We'll take a look at it with the laser first."

Then he printed out another hard copy of NIC112, the latents that Matt Petersen had left on his wife's body, and presented it to Marino.

He studied it briefly, muttering, "Ho-ly shit," and he looked up straight at me.

His eyes smiled in triumph. I was familiar with the look, which I had expected. It said, "So there, *Ms. Chief*. So maybe you got book-learning, but me, I know the street."

I could feel the investigative screws tightening on the husband of a woman who I still believed was slain by a man not known to any of us.

Fifteen minutes later, Vander, Marino and I were inside what was the equivalent of a darkroom adjoining the fingerprint lab. On a countertop near a large sink were the ten-print card and the survival knife. The room was pitchblack. Marino's big belly was unpleasantly brushing my left elbow as the dazzling pulses ignited a scattering of sparkles on the inky smudges of the card. In addition, there were sparkles on the handle of the knife, which was hard rubber and too coarse for prints.

On the knife's wide shiny blade was a smattering of virtually microscopic debris and several distinct partial prints that Vander dusted and lifted. He leaned closer to the ten-print card. A quick visual comparison with his eagle, expert eye was enough for him to tentatively say, "Based on an initial ridge comparison, they're his, the prints on the blade are Petersen's."

The laser went off, throwing us into complete blackness, and presently we were squinting in the rude glare of overhead lights that had suddenly returned us to the world of dreary cinder block and white Formica.

Pushing back my goggles, I began the litany of objective reminders as Vander fooled around with the laser and Marino lit a cigarette.

"The prints on the knife may not mean anything. If the knife belonged to Petersen, you'd expect to find his prints. As for the sparkling residue—yes, it's obvious he had something on his hands when he touched his wife's body and when he was fingerprinted. But we can't be sure the substance is the same as the glitter found elsewhere, particularly in the first three strangling cases. We'll give scanning electron microscopy a shot at it, hopefully determine if the elemental compositions or infrared spectrums are the same as those in the residues found on other areas of her body and in the previous cases."

"What?" Marino asked, incredulously. "You thinking Matt had one thing on his hands and the killer had something else, and they ain't the same but both look the same under the laser?"

"Almost everything that reacts strongly to the laser looks the same," I told him in slow, measured words. "It glows like white neon light."

"Yeah, but most people don't have white neon crap on their hands, to my knowledge."

I had to agree. "Most people don't."

"Sort of a weird little coincidence Matt just happens to have the stuff on his hands, whatever it is."

"You mentioned he'd just come home from a dress rehearsal," I reminded him.

"That's his story."

"It might not be a bad idea to collect the makeup he was using Friday night and bring it in for testing."

Marino stared disdainfully at me.

In my office was one of the few personal computers on the second floor. It was connected to the main computer down the hall, but it wasn't a dumb terminal. Even if the main computer was down, I could use my PC for word processing if nothing else.

Marino handed over the two diskettes found on the desk inside the Petersen bedroom. I slipped them into the drives and executed a directory command for each one.

An index of files, or chapters, of what clearly was Matt Petersen's dissertation appeared on the screen. The subject was Tennessee Williams, "whose most successful plays reveal a frustrating world in which sex and violence lie beneath the surface of romantic gentility," read the opening paragraph of the Introduction.

Marino was peering over my shoulder shaking his head.

"Jeez," he muttered, "this is only getting better. No wonder the squirrel freaked out when I told him we was taking these disks in. Look at this stuff."

I rolled down the screen.

Flashing past were Williams's controversial treatments of homosexuality and cannibalism. There were references to the brutish Stanley Kowalski and to the castrated gigolo in *Sweet Bird of Youth*. I didn't need clairvoyant powers to read Marino's mind, which was as banal as the front page of a tabloid. To him, this was the stuff of garden-variety porn, the fuel of the psychopathic minds that feed on fantasies of sexual aberrancies and violence. Marino wouldn't know the difference between the street and the stage if he were pistol-whipped with a Drama 101 course.

The people like Williams, and even Matt Petersen, who create such scenarios rarely are the individuals who go around living them.

I looked levelly at Marino. "What would you think if Petersen were an Old Testament scholar?"

He shrugged, his eyes shifting away from me, glancing back at the screen. "Hey. This ain't exactly Sunday school material."

"Neither are rapes, stonings, beheadings and whores. And in real life, Truman Capote wasn't a mass murderer, Sergeant."

He backed away from the computer and went to a chair. I swiveled around, facing him across the wide expanse of my desk. Ordinarily, when he stopped by my office he preferred to stand, to remain on his feet towering over me. But he was sitting, and we were eye to eye. I decided he was planning to stay awhile.

"How about seeing if you can print out this thing? You mind? Looks like good bedtime reading." He smiled snidely. "Who knows? Like, maybe this American lit freak quotes the Marquis-Sade-what's-his-face in there, too."

"The Marquis de Sade was French."

"Whatever."

I restrained my irritation. I was wondering what would happen if one of my medical examiners' wives were murdered. Would Marino look in the library and think he'd struck pay dirt when he found volume after volume on forensics and perverse crimes in history?

His eyes narrowed as he lit another cigarette and took a big drag. He waited until he'd blown out a thin stream of smoke before saying, "You've apparently got a high opinion of Petersen. What's it based on? The fact he's an artist or just that he's a hotshot college kid?"

"I have no opinion of him," I replied. "I know nothing about him except he doesn't profile right to be the person strangling these women."

He got thoughtful. "Well, I do know about him, Doc. You see, I talked to him for several hours." He reached inside a pocket of his plaid sports jacket and tossed two microcassette tapes on the blotter, within easy reach of me. I got out my cigarettes and lit one, too.

"Let me tell you how it went down. Me and Becker are in the kitchen with him, okay? The squad's just left with the body when bingo! Petersen's personality completely changes. He sits up straighter in the chair, his mind clears, and his hands start gesturing like he's on stage or something. It was friggin' unbelievable. His eyes tear up now and then, his voice cracks, he flushes and gets pale. I'm thinking to myself, this ain't an interview. It's a damn performance."

Settling back in the chair, he loosened his tie. "I'm thinking where I've seen this before, you know. Mainly back in New York with the likes of Johnny Andretti with his silk suits and imported cigarettes, charm oozing out his ears. He's so smooth you start falling all over yourself to accommodate 'im and begin suppressing the minor detail that he's whacked more than twenty people during his career. Then there's Phil the Pimp. He beats his girls with coat hangers, two of them to death, and tears up inside his restaurant, which is just a front for his escort service. Phil's all broken up about his dead hookers and he's leaning across the table, saying to me, 'Please find who did this to them, Pete. He has to be an animal. Here, try a little of this Chianti, Pete. It's nice.'

"Point is, Doc, I've been around the block more than once.

And Petersen's setting off the same alarm toads like Andretti and Phil did. He's giving me this performance, I'm sitting there and asking myself, 'What's this Harvard highbrow think? I'm a bimbo or what?' "

I inserted a tape inside my microcassette player without saying anything.

Marino nodded for me to press the Play button. "Act one," he drolly announced. "The setting, the Petersen kitchen. The main character, Matt. The role, tragic. He's pale and wounded about the eyes, okay? He's staring off at the wall. Me? I'm seeing a movie in my head. Never been to Boston and wouldn't know Harvard from a hole in the ground, but I'm seeing old brick and ivy."

He fell silent as the tape abruptly began with Petersen mid-sentence. He was talking about Harvard, answering questions about when he and Lori had met. I'd heard my share of police in-terviews over the years, and this one was perplexing me. Why did it matter? What did Petersen's courting of Lori back in their college days have to do with her murder? At the same time I think a part of me knew.

Marino was probing, drawing Petersen out. Marino was looking for anything—*anything*—that might show Petersen to be obsessive and warped and possibly capable of overt psychopathy.

I got up to shut the door so we wouldn't be interrupted, as the recorded voice quietly went on.

". . . I'd seen her before. On campus, this blonde carrying an armload of books and oblivious, as if she was in a hurry and had a lot on her mind."

Marino: "What was it about her that made you notice her, Matt?"

"It's hard to say. But she intrigued me from a distance. I'm not sure why. But part of it may have been that she was usually alone, in a hurry, on her way somewhere. She was, uh, confident and seemed to have purpose. She made me curious."

Marino: "Does that happen very often? You know, where you see some attractive woman and she makes you curious, from a distance, I'm saying?"

"Uh, I don't think so. I mean, I notice people just like every-body else does. But with her, with Lori, it was different."

Marino: "Go on. So you met her, finally. Where?"

"It was at a party. In the spring, early May. The party was in an off-campus apartment belonging to a buddy of my roommate, a guy who turned out to be Lori's lab partner, which was why she'd come. She walked in around nine, just about the time I was getting ready to leave. Her lab partner, Tim, I think was his name, popped open a beer for her and they started talking. I'd never heard her voice before. Contralto, soothing, very pleasant to listen to. The sort of voice that makes you turn around to find the source of it. She was telling anecdotes about some professor and the people around her were laughing. Lori had a way of getting everybody's attention without even trying."

Marino: "In other words, you didn't leave the party after all. You saw her and decided to stick around."

"Yes."

"What did she look like back then?"

"Her hair was longer, and she was wearing it up, the way ballet dancers do. She was slender, very attractive . . ."

"You like slender blondes, then. You find those qualities attractive in a woman."

"I just thought she was attractive, that's all. And there was more to it. It was her intelligence. That's what made her stand out."

Marino: "What else?"

"I don't understand. What do you mean?"

Marino: "I'm just wondering what attracted you to her." A pause. "I find it interesting."

"I can't really answer that. It's mysterious, that element. How you can meet a person and be so aware. It's as if something inside you wakes up. I don't know why . . . God . . . I don't know."

Another pause, this one longer.

Marino: "She was the kind of lady people notice."

"Absolutely. All the time. Whenever we went places together, or if my friends were around. She'd upstage me, really. I didn't mind. In fact, I liked it. I enjoyed sitting back and watching it happen. I'd analyze it, try to figure out what it was that drew people to her. Charisma is something you have or you don't have. You can't manufacture it. You can't. She didn't try. It just was."

Marino: "You said when you used to see her on campus, she seemed to keep to herself. What about at other times? What I'm wondering is if it was her habit to be friendly with strangers. You know, like if she was in a store or at a gas station, did she talk to people she didn't know? Or if someone came by the house, a delivery-eryman, for example, was she the type to invite the person in, be friendly?"

"No. She rarely talked to strangers, and I know she didn't invite strangers into the house. Never. Especially when I wasn't here. She'd lived in Boston, was acclimated to the dangers of the city. And she worked in the ER, was familiar with violence, the bad things that happen to people. She wouldn't have invited a stranger in or been what I consider particularly vulnerable to that sort of thing. In fact, when the murders started happening around here, it frightened her. When I'd come home on the weekends, she hated it when I'd leave . . . hated it more than ever. Because she didn't like being alone at night. It bothered her more than it used to."

Marino: "Seems like she would have been careful about keeping all the windows locked if she was nervous because of the murders around here."

"I told you. She probably thought it was locked."

"But you accidentally left it, the bathroom window, unlocked last weekend when you was replacing the screen."

"I'm not sure. But that's the only thing I can figure . . ."

Becker's voice: "Did she mention anybody coming by the house, or an encounter somewhere, with someone who made her nervous? Anything at all? Maybe a strange car she noticed in your neighborhood, or the suspicion at some point that maybe she was being followed or observed? Maybe she meets some guy and he puts the move on her."

"Nothing like that."

Becker: "Would she have been likely to tell you if something like that had happened?"

"Definitely. She told me everything. A week, maybe two weeks ago, she thought she heard something in the backyard. She called the police. A patrol car came by. It was just a cat messing with the garbage cans. The point is, she told me everything."

Marino: "What other activities was she involved in besides work?"

"She had a few friends, a couple of other women doctors at the hospital. Sometimes she went out to dinner with them or shopping, maybe a movie. That was about it. She was so busy. In the main, she worked her shift and came home. She'd study, sometimes practice the violin. During the week, she generally worked, came home and slept. The weekends she kept open for me. That was our time. We were together on the weekends."

Marino: "Last weekend was the last time you saw her?"

"Sunday afternoon, around three. Right before I drove back to Charlottesville. We didn't go out that day. It was raining, raw. We stayed in, drank coffee, talked . . ."

Marino: "How often did you talk to her during the week?"

"Several times. Whenever we could."

Marino: "The last time was last night, Thursday night?"

"I called to tell her I'd be in after play practice, that I might be a few minutes later than usual because of dress rehearsal. She was supposed to be off this weekend. If it was nice, we were thinking of driving to the beach."

Silence.

Petersen was struggling. I could hear him taking a deep breath, trying to steady himself.

Marino: "When you talked to her last night, did she have anything to report, any problems, any mention of anybody coming by the house? Anyone bothering her at work, maybe weird phone calls, anything?"

Silence.

"Nothing. Nothing at all like that. She was in good spirits, laughing . . . looking forward, uh, looking forward to the weekend."

Marino: "Tell us a little more about her, Matt. Every little thing you can think of might help. Her background, her personality, what was important to her."

Mechanically, "She's from Philadelphia, her dad's an insurance salesman, and she has two brothers, both younger. Medicine was the most important thing to her. It was her calling."

Marino: "What kind of doctor was she studying to be?"

"A plastic surgeon."

Becker: "Interesting. Why did she decide on that?"

"When she was ten, eleven, her mother got breast cancer, underwent two radical mastectomies. She survived but her self-esteem was destroyed. I think she felt deformed, worthless, untouchable. Lori talked about it sometimes. I think she wanted to help people. Help people who have been through things like that."

Marino: "And she played the violin."

"Yes."

Marino: "Did she ever give concerts, play in the symphony, anything public like that?"

"She could have, I think. But she didn't have time."

Marino: "What else? For example, you're big on acting, in a play right now. Was she interested in that kind of thing?"

"Very much so. That's one of the things that fascinated me about her when we first met. We left the party, the party where we met, and walked the campus for hours. When I started telling her about some of the courses I was taking, I realized she knew a lot about the theater, and we started talking about plays and such. I was into Ibsen then. We got into that, got into reality and illusion, what's genuine and what's ugly in people and society. One of his strongest themes is the feeling of alienation from home. Uh, of separation. We talked about that.

"And she surprised me. I'll never forget it. She laughed and said, 'You artists think you're the only ones who can relate to these things. Many of us have the same feelings, the same emptiness, the same loneliness. But we don't have the tools to verbalize them. So we carry on, we struggle. Feelings are feelings. I think people's feelings are pretty much the same all over the world.'

"We got into an argument, a friendly debate. I disagreed. Some people feel things more deeply than others, and some people feel things the rest of us don't. This is what causes isolation, the sense of being apart, different . . ."

Marino: "This is something you relate to?"

"It is something I understand. I may not feel everything other people feel, but I understand the feelings. Nothing surprises me. If you study literature, drama, you get in touch with a vast spectrum of human emotions, needs and impulses, good and bad. It's my nature to step into other characters, to feel what they feel, to act as they do, but it doesn't mean these manifestations are genuinely my own. I think if anything makes me feel different from others, it's my need to experience these things, my need to analyze and understand the vast spectrum of human emotions I just mentioned."

Marino: "Can you understand the emotions of the person who did this to your wife?"

Silence.

Almost inaudibly, "Good God, no."

Marino: "You sure about that?"

"No. I mean, yes, I'm sure! I don't want to understand it!"

Marino: "I know it's a hard thing for you to think about, Matt. But you could help us a lot if you had any ideas. For example, if you was designing the role for a killer like this, what would he be like—"

"I don't know! The filthy son of a bitch!" His voice was breaking, exploding with rage. "I don't know why you're asking me! You're the fucking cops! You're supposed to be the ones figuring it out!"

He abruptly fell silent, as if a needle had been lifted off a record.

The tape played a long stretch in which nothing was heard except Marino clearing his throat and a chair scraping back.

Then Marino asked Becker, "You wouldn't by chance have an extra tape in your car?"

It was Petersen who mumbled, and I think he was crying, "I've got a couple of them back in the bedroom."

"Well, now," Marino's voice coolly drawled, "that's mighty nice of you, Matt."

Twenty minutes later, Matt Petersen got to the subject of finding his wife's body.

It was awful to hear and not see. There were no distractions. I drifted on the current of his images and recollections. His words were taking me into dark areas where I did not want to go.

The tape played on.

". . . Uh, I'm sure of it. I didn't call first. I never did, just left. Didn't hang around or anything. As I was saying, uh, I left Charlottesville as soon as rehearsal was over and the props and costumes were put away. I guess this was close to twelve-thirty. I was in a hurry to get home. I hadn't seen Lori all week.

"It was close to two when I parked in front of the house, and my first reaction was to notice the lights out and realize she'd already gone to bed. Her schedule was very demanding. On twelve hours and off twenty-four, the shift out of sync with human biological clocks and never the same. She worked Friday until midnight, was to be off Saturday, uh, today. And tomorrow she would be on from midnight to noon Monday. Off Tuesday, and on Wednesday from noon to midnight again. That's how it went.

"I unlocked the front door and flipped on the living room light. Everything looked normal. Retrospectively, I can say that even though I had no reason to be looking for anything out of the ordinary. I do remember the hall light was off. I noticed because usually she left it on for me. It was my routine to go straight to the bedroom. If she wasn't too exhausted, and she almost never was, we would sit up in bed and drink wine and talk. Uh, stay up, and then sleep very late.

"I was confused. Uh. Something was confusing me. The bedroom. I couldn't see anything much at first because the lights . . . the lights, of course, were out. But something felt wrong immediately. It's almost as if I sensed it before I saw it. Like an animal senses things. And I thought I was smelling something but I wasn't sure and it only added to my confusion."

Marino: "What sort of smell?"

Silence.

"I'm trying to remember. I was only vaguely aware of it. But aware enough to be puzzled. It was an unpleasant smell. Sort of sweet but putrid. Weird."

Marino: "You mean a body-odor-type smell?"

"Similar, but not exactly. It was sweetish. Unpleasant. Rather pungent and sweaty."

Becker: "Something you've smelled before?"

A pause. "No, it wasn't quite like anything I've ever smelled before, I don't think. It was faint, but maybe I was more aware of it because I couldn't see anything, couldn't hear anything the instant I walked into the bedroom. It was so quiet inside. The first thing that struck my senses was this peculiar odor. And it flickered in my mind, oddly, it flickered in my mind—maybe Lori had been eating something in bed. I don't know. It was, uh, it was like waffles, maybe syrupy. Pancakes. I thought maybe she was sick, had been eating junk and gotten sick. Uh, sometimes she went on binges. Uh, ate fattening things when she was stressed or anxious. She gained a lot of weight after I started commuting to Charlottesville . . ."

His voice was trembling very badly now.

"Uh, the smell was sick, unhealthy, as if maybe she was sick and had been in bed all day. Explaining why all the lights were out, why she hadn't waited up for me."

Silence.

Marino: "Then what happened, Matt?"

"Then my eyes began to adjust and I didn't understand what I was seeing. The bed materialized in the dimness. I didn't understand the covers, the way they were hanging off. And her. Lying on top in this strange position and not having anything on. God. My heart was coming out of my chest before it even registered. And when I flipped on the light, and saw her . . . I was screaming, but I couldn't hear my own voice. Like I was screaming inside my head. Like my brain was floating out of my skull. I saw the stain on the sheet, the red, the blood coming out of her nose and mouth. Her face. I didn't think it was her. It wasn't her. It didn't even look like her. It was somebody else. A prank, a terrible trick. It wasn't her."

Marino: "What did you do next, Matt? Did you touch her or disturb anything inside the bedroom?"

A long pause and the sound of Petersen's shallow, rapid breathing: "No. I mean, yes. I touched her. I didn't think. I just touched her. Her shoulder, her arm, I don't remember. She was warm. But when I started to feel for a pulse, I couldn't find her wrists. Because she was on top of them, they were behind her back, tied. And I started to touch her neck and saw the cord embedded in her skin. I think I tried to feel her heart beating or hear it but I don't remember. I knew it. I knew she was dead. The way she looked. She had to be dead. I ran into the kitchen. I don't remember what I said or even remember dialing the phone. But I know I called the police and then I paced. Just paced. I paced in and out of the bedroom. I leaned against the wall and cried and talked to her. I talked to her. I talked to her until the police got here. I told her not to let it be real. I kept going over to her and backing off and begging her not to let it be real. I kept listening for someone to get here. It seemed to take forever . . ."

Marino: "The electrical cords, the way she was tied. Did you disturb anything, touch the cords or do anything else? Can you remember?"

"No. I mean, I don't remember if I did. Uh, but I don't think I did. Something stopped me. I wanted to cover her. But something stopped me. Something told me not to touch anything."

Marino: "Do you own a knife?"

Silence.

Marino: "A knife, Matt. We found a knife, a survival knife with a whetstone in the sheath and a compass in the handle."

Confused: "Oh. Uh-huh. I got it several years ago. One of those mail-order knives you could get for five-ninety-five or something. Uh, I used to take it with me when I went hiking. It's got fishing line, matches inside the handle."

Marino: "Where did you see it last?"

"On the desk. It's been on the desk. I think Lori was using it as a letter opener. I don't know. It's just been sitting there for months. Maybe it made her feel better to have it out. Being alone at night and all. I told her we could get a dog. But she's allergic."

Marino: "If I hear what you're saying, Matt, you're telling me the knife was on the desk last time you saw it. That would have been when? Last Saturday, Sunday, when you was home, the weekend when you replaced the screen in the bathroom window?"

No response.

Marino: "You know any reason your wife might've had to move the knife, like maybe tuck it in a drawer or something? She ever done that in the past?"

"I don't think so. It's been on the desk, near the lamp for months."

Marino: "Can you explain why we found this knife in the bottom dresser drawer, underneath some sweaters and beside a box of condoms? Your dresser drawer, I'm guessing?"

Silence.

"No. I can't explain it. That's where you found it?"

Marino: "Yes."

"The condoms. They've been in there a long time." A hollow laugh that was almost a gasp. "From before Lori went on the pill."

Marino: "You sure about that? About the condoms?"

"Of course I'm sure. She went on the pill about three months after we got married. We got married just before we moved here. Less than two years ago."

Marino: "Now, Matt, I've got to ask you several questions of a personal nature, and I want you to understand I'm not picking on you or trying to embarrass you. But I have reasons. There's things we got to know, for you own good, too. Okay?"

Silence.

I could hear Marino lighting a cigarette. "All right then. The condoms. Did you have any relations outside your marriage, with anybody else, I'm saying?"

"Absolutely not."

Marino: "You was living out of town during the week. Now me, I would have been tempted—"

"Well, I'm not you. Lori was everything to me. I have nothing with anybody else."

Marino: "No one in the play with you, maybe?"

"No."

Marino: "See, the point is, we do these little things. I mean, they're human nature, okay? A good-looking guy like you—hey, the women probably throw themselves at you. Who could blame you? But if you was seeing someone, we need to know. There could possibly be a connection."

Almost inaudibly. "No. I've told you, no. There could be no connection unless you're accusing me of something."

Becker: "No one's accusing you of anything, Matt."

There was the sound of something sliding across the table. The ashtray, perhaps.

And Marino was asking, "When was the last time you had sex with your wife?"

Silence.

Petersen's voice was shaking. "Jesus Christ."

Marino: "I know it's your business, personal. But you need to tell us. We got our reasons."

"Sunday morning. Last Sunday."

Marino: "You know there will be tests run, Matt. Scientists will be examining everything so we can get blood types, make other comparisons. We need samples from you just like we needed your prints. So we can sort things out and know what's yours, and what's hers, and what maybe's from—"

The tape abruptly ended. I blinked and my eyes focused for what seemed the first time in hours.

Marino reached for the recorder, turned it off and retrieved his tapes.

He concluded, "After that we took him down to Richmond General and got the suspect kit. Betty's examining his blood even as we speak to see how it compares."

I nodded, glancing at the wall clock. It was noon. I felt sick.

"Something, huh?" Marino stifled a yawn. "You see it, don't you? I'm telling you, the guy's off. I mean there's something off about any guy who can sit there after finding his wife like that and talk the way he does. Most of 'em, they don't talk much. He would have rattled on till Christmas if I'd let 'im. A lot of pretty words and poetry, you ask me. He's slick. You want my opinion, that's it. He's so slick it gives me the willies."

I slipped off my glasses and kneaded my temples. My brain was heated up, the muscles in my neck on fire. The silk blouse beneath my lab coat was damp. My circuits were so overloaded that what I wanted to do was place my head on my arms and sleep.

"His world is words, Marino," I heard myself say. "An artist would have painted the picture for you. Matt painted it with words. This is how he exists, how he expresses himself, through words and more words. To think a thought is to express it verbally for people like him." I put my glasses back on and looked at Marino. He was perplexed, his meaty, shopworn face flushed.

"Well, take that bit about the knife, Doc. It's got his prints on it, even though he says his wife's the one who's been using it for months. It's got that sparkle crap on the handle, just like he had on his hands. And the knife was in his dresser drawer, like maybe someone was hiding it. Now that gives you a pause, don't you think?"

"I think it is possible the knife was on top of Lori's desk just as it had been, that she rarely used it and had no reason to touch the blade when she did if she simply opened letters with it, occasionally." I was seeing this in my head, so vividly I almost believed the images were memories of an event that had actually occurred. "I think it's possible the killer saw the knife too. Perhaps he took it out of the sheath to look at it. Perhaps he used it—"

"Why?"

"Why not?" I asked.

A shrug.

"To jerk everyone around, perhaps," I suggested. "Perversity, if nothing else. We have no idea what went on, for God's sake. He may have asked her about the knife, tormented her with her own—or her husband's own—weapon. And if she talked with him as I suspect she did, then he may have learned the knife belongs to her husband. He thinks, 'I'll use it. I'll put it in a drawer where the cops are sure to find it.' Or maybe he doesn't think much about it at all. Maybe his reason was utilitarian. In other words, maybe it was a bigger knife than the one he'd brought in with him, it caught his eye, appealed to him, he used it, didn't want to take it out with him, stuck it in a drawer hoping we wouldn't know he used it—and it was that simple."

"Or maybe Matt did it all," Marino flatly said.

"Matt? Think about it. Could a husband rape and bind his wife? Could he fracture her ribs and break her fingers? Could he slowly strangle her to death? This is someone he loves or once loved. Someone he sleeps with, eats with, talks to, lives with. A person, Sergeant. Not a stranger or depersonalized object of lust and violence. How are you going to connect a husband murdering his wife with the first three stranglings?"

Clearly, he'd already thought about this. "They occurred after midnight, on early Saturday mornings. Right about the time Matt was getting home from Charlottesville. Maybe his wife got suspicious about him for some reason and he decides he's got to whack her. Maybe he does her like the others to make us think the serial killer did her. Or maybe the wife's who he was after all along, and he does the other three first to make it look like his wife was done by this anonymous and same killer."

"A wonderful plot for Agatha Christie." I was pushing back my chair and getting up. "But as you know in real life murder is usually depressingly simple. I think these murders are simple. They are exactly what they appear to be, impersonal random murders committed by someone who stalks his victims long enough to figure out when to strike."

Marino got up, too. "Yeah, well in real life, Doc-tor Scarpetta, bodies don't have freaky little sparkles all over 'em that match the same freaky sparkles found on the hands of the husband who discovers the body and leaves his prints all over the damn place. And the victims don't have pretty-boy actors for husbands, squirrels writing dissertations on sex and violence and cannibals and faggots."

I calmly asked him, "The odor Petersen mentioned. Did you smell anything like that when you arrived on the scene?"

"Naw. Didn't smell a damn thing. So maybe he was smelling seminal fluid, if he's telling the truth."

"I should think he would know what that smells like."

"But he wouldn't be expecting to smell it. No reason it should come to mind at first. Now me, when I went in the bedroom, I didn't smell nothing like he was describing."

"Do you recall smelling anything peculiar at the other strangling scenes?"

"No, ma'am. Which just further corroborates my suspicion that either Matt imagined it or is making it up, to throw us off track."

Then it came to me. "In the three previous cases, the women weren't found until the next day, after they'd been dead at least twelve hours."

Marino paused in the doorway, his face incredulous. "You suggesting Matt got home just after the killer left, that the killer's got some weird case of B.O.?"

"I'm suggesting it's possible."

His face tightened with anger, and as he stalked down the hall I heard him mutter, "Goddam women . . ."

5

THE SIXTH STREET MARKETPLACE is a Bayside without the water, one of these open, sunny malls built of steel and glass, on the north edge of the banking district in the heart of downtown. It wasn't often I went out for lunch, and I certainly didn't have time for the luxury this afternoon. I had an appointment in less than an hour, and there were two sudden deaths and one suicide in transport, but I needed to unwind.

Marino bothered me. His attitude toward me reminded me of medical school.

I was one of four women in my class at Hopkins. I was too naïve in the beginning to realize what was happening. The sudden creaking of chairs and loud shuffling of papers when a professor would call on me were not coincidence. It was not chance when old tests made the rounds but were never available to me. The excuses—"You wouldn't be able to read my writing" or "Someone else is borrowing them right now"—were too universal when I went from student to student on the few occasions I missed a lecture and needed to copy someone else's notes. I was a small insect faced with a formidable male network web in which I might be ensnared but never a part.

Isolation is the cruelest of punishments, and it had never occurred to me that I was something less than human because I wasn't a man. One of my female classmates eventually quit, another suffered a complete nervous breakdown. Survival was my only hope, success my only revenge.

I'd thought those days were behind me, but Marino brought all of it back. I was more vulnerable now because these murders were affecting me in a way others had not. I did not want to be alone in this; but Marino seemed to have his mind made up, not only about Matt Petersen, but also about me.

The midday stroll was soothing, the sun bright and winking on windshields of the passing traffic. The double glass doors leading inside the Marketplace were open to let the spring breeze in, and the food court was as crowded as I knew it would be. Waiting my turn at the carry-out salad counter, I watched people go by, young couples laughing and talking and lounging at small tables. I was aware of women who seemed alone, preoccupied professional women wearing expensive suits and sipping diet colas or nibbling on pita bread sandwiches.

It could have been in a place like this he first spotted his victims, some large public place where the only thing the four women had in common was that he took their orders at one of the counters.

But the overwhelming and seemingly enigmatic problem was that the murdered women did not work or live in the same areas of the city. It was unlikely they shopped or dined out or did their banking or anything else in the same places. Richmond has a large land area with thriving malls and business areas in the four major quandrants. People who live Northside are catered to by the Northside merchants, the people south of the river patronize the Southside businesses, and the same is true in the eastern part of the city. I mainly restricted myself to the malls and restaurants in the West End, for example, except when I was at work.

The woman at the counter who took my order for a Greek salad paused for a moment, her eyes lingering on my face as if I looked familiar to her. I uncomfortably wondered if she'd seen my picture in the Saturday evening paper. Or she could have seen me in the television footage and court sketches the local television stations were constantly pulling out of their files whenever murder was big news in central Virginia.

It has always been my wish to be unnoticed, to blend. But I was at a disadvantage for several reasons. There were few women chief medical examiners in the country, and this prompted reporters to be unduly tenacious when it came to pointing cameras in my direction or excavating for quotes. I was easily recognized because I am "distinctive" in appearance, "blond" and "handsome" and Lord knows what else I've been called in print. My ancestors are from northern Italy where there is a segment of blue-eyed, fair natives who share blood with the people of Savoy, Switzerland and Austria.

The Scarpettas are a traditionally ethnocentric group, Italians who have married other Italians in this country to keep the bloodline pure. My mother's greatest failure, so she has told me numerous times, is that she bore no son and her two daughters have turned out to be genetic dead ends. Dorothy sullied the lineage with Lucy, who is half Latin, and at my age and marital status it wasn't likely I would be sullying anything.

My mother is prone to weeping as she bemoans the fact that her immediate family is at the end of its line. "All that good blood," she would sob, especially during the holidays, when she should have been surrounded by a bevy of adorable and adoring grandchildren. "Such a shame. All that good blood! Our ancestors! Architects, painters! Kay, Kay, to let that go to waste, like fine grapes on the vine."

We are traced back to Verona, the province of Romeo of Montague and Juliet Capulet, of Dante, Pisano, Titian, Bellini and Paolo Cagliari, according to my mother. She persists in believing we are somehow related to these luminaries, despite my reminders that Bellini, Pisano and Titian, at any rate, influenced the Veronese School but were really native to Venice, and the poet Dante was Florentine, exiled after the Black Guelf triumph and relegated to wandering from city to city, his stay in Verona but a pit stop along the way to Ravenna. Our direct ancestors, in truth, were with the railways or were farmers, a humble people who immigrated to this country two generations ago.

A white bag in hand, I eagerly embraced the warm afternoon again. Sidewalks were crowded with people wandering to and from lunch, and as I waited on a corner for the light to change, I instinctively turned toward the two figures emerging from the Chinese restaurant across the street. The familiar blond hair had caught my eye. Bill Boltz, the Commonwealth's attorney for Richmond City, was slipping on a pair of sunglasses and seemed in the midst of an intense discussion with Norman Tanner, the director of public safety. For a moment, Boltz was staring straight at me, but he didn't return my wave. Maybe he really didn't see me. I didn't wave again. Then the two men were gone, swept up in the congested flow of anonymous faces and scuffling feet.

When the light turned green after an interminably long time, I crossed the street, and Lucy came to mind as I approached a computer software store. Ducking in, I found something she was sure to like, not a video game but a history tutorial complete with art, music and quizzes. Yesterday we had rented a paddle-boat in the park and drifted around the small lake. She ran us into the fountain to give me a tepid shower, and I found myself childishly paying her back. We fed bread to the geese and sucked on grape snow cones until our tongues turned blue. Thursday morning she would fly home to Miami, and I would not see her again until Christmas, if I saw her again at all this year.

It was quarter of one when I walked into the lobby of the Office of the Chief Medical Examiner, or OCME, as it was called. Benton Wesley was fifteen minutes early and sitting on the couch reading the *Wall Street Journal*.

"Hope you got something to drink in that bag," he said drolly, folding the newspaper and reaching for his briefcase.

"Wine vinegar. You'll love it."

"Hell. Ripple—I don't care. Some days I'm so desperate I fantasize the water cooler outside my door's full of gin."

"Sounds like a waste of imagination to me."

"Nawwww. Just the only fantasy I'm going to talk about in front of a lady."

Wesley was a suspect profiler for the FBI and located in Richmond's field office, where he actually spent very little time. When he wasn't on the road, he was usually at the National Academy in Quantico teaching death-investigation classes and doing what he could to coax VICAP through its rocky adolescence. VICAP is an acronym for Violent Criminal Apprehension Program. One of VICAP's most innovative concepts was regional teams, which yoke a Bureau profiler with an experienced homicide detective. Richmond P.D. called in VICAP after the second strangling. Marino, in addition to being a detective sergeant for the city, was Wesley's regional team partner.

"I'm early," Wesley apologized, following me into the hallway. "Came straight here from a dental appointment. Won't bother me if you eat while we talk."

"Well, it *will* bother me," I said.

His blank look was followed by a sheepish grin as it suddenly occurred to him. "I forgot. You're not Doc Cagney. You know, he used to keep cheese crackers on the desk in the morgue. In the middle of a post he'd take a break for a snack. It was unbelievable."

We turned off into a room so small it was really an alcove, where there was a refrigerator, a Coke machine and a coffeemaker. "He's lucky he didn't get hepatitis or AIDS," I said.

"AIDS." Wesley laughed. "That would have been poetic justice."

Like a lot of good ole boys I've known, Dr. Cagney was reputed to be acutely homophobic. "Just some goddam queer," he was known to say when persons of a certain persuasion were sent in for examination.

"AIDS . . ." Wesley was still enjoying the thought as I tucked my salad inside the refrigerator. "Wouldn't I love to hear him explain his way out of that one."

I'd gradually warmed up to Wesley. The first time I met him I had my reservations. At a glance, he made one a believer in stereotypes. He was FBI right down to his Florsheim shoes, a sharp-featured man with prematurely silver hair suggesting a mellow disposition that wasn't there. He was lean and hard and looked like a trial lawyer in his precisely tailored khaki suit and blue silk paisley-printed tie. I couldn't recall ever seeing him in a shirt that wasn't white and lightly starched.

He had a master's degree in psychology and had been a high school principal in Dallas before enlisting in the Bureau, where he worked first as a field agent, then undercover in fingering members of the Mafia, before ending up where he'd started, in a sense. Profilers are academicians, thinkers, analysts. Sometimes I think they are magicians.

Carrying our coffees out, we turned left and stepped inside the conference room. Marino was sitting at the long table and going through a fat case file. I was mildly surprised. For some reason, I just assumed he would be late.

Before I had a chance to so much as pull out a chair, he launched in with the laconic announcement, "I stopped by serology a minute ago. Thought you might be interested in knowing Matt Petersen's A positive and a nonsecreter."

Wesley looked keenly at him. "This the husband you were telling me about?"

"Yo. A *nonsecreter*. Same as the guy snuffing these women."

"Twenty percent of the population is nonsecreter," I matter-of-factly stated.

"Yeah," Marino said. "Two out of ten."

"Or approximately forty-four thousand people in a city the size of Richmond. Twenty-two thousand if half of that number is male," I added.

Lighting a cigarette, Marino squinted up at me over the Bic flame. "You know what, Doc?" The cigarette wagged with each syllable. "You're beginning to sound like a damn defense attorney."

A half hour later I was at the head of the table, the two men on either side. Spread out before us were photographs of the four murdered women.

This was the most difficult and time-consuming part of the investigation—profiling the killer, profiling the victims, and then profiling the killer again.

Wesley was describing him. This was what he did best, and quite often was uncannily accurate when he read the emotion of a crime scene, which in these cases was cold, calculating rage.

"I'm betting he's white," he was saying. "But I won't stake my reputation on it. Cecile Tyler was black, and an interracial mix in victim selection is unusual unless the killer is rapidly decompensating." He picked up a photograph of Cecile Tyler, dark-skinned, lovely in life, and a receptionist at a Northside investment firm. Like Lori Petersen, she was bound, strangled, her nude body on top of the bed.

"But we're getting more of them these days. That's the trend, an increase of sexual slaying in which the assailant is black, the woman white, but rarely the opposite—white men raping and murdering black women, in other words. Hookers are an exception." He glanced blandly at the array of photographs. "These women certainly weren't hookers. I suppose if they had been," he muttered, "our job would be a little easier."

"Yeah, but theirs wouldn'ta been," Marino butted in.

Wesley didn't smile. "At least there would be a connection that maybe makes sense, Pete. The selection." He shook his head. "It's peculiar."

"So what does Fortosis have to say these days?" Marino asked, referring to the forensic psychiatrist who had been reviewing the cases.

"Not a whole hell of a lot," Wesley replied. "Talked to him briefly this morning. He's being noncommittal. I think the murder of this doctor's causing him to rethink a few things. But he's still damn sure the killer's white."

The face from my dream violated my mind, the white face without features.

"He's probably between twenty-five and thirty-five." Wesley continued staring into his crystal ball. "Because the murders aren't related to any particular locality, he's got some way of getting around, a car versus a motorcycle or a truck or a van. My guess is he's stashing his wheels in some inconspicuous spot, going the rest of the way on foot. His car's an older model, probably American, dark or plain in color, such as beige or gray. It wouldn't be the least bit uncommon for him to drive, in other words, the very sort of car plainclothes law-enforcement officers drive."

He wasn't being funny. This type of killer is frequently fascinated by police work and may even emulate cops. The classic postoffense behavior for a psychopath is to become involved in the investigation. He wants to help the police, to offer insights and suggestions, and assist rescue teams in their search for a body he dumped in the woods somewhere. He's the kind of guy who wouldn't think twice about hanging out at the Fraternal Order of Police lounge clacking beer mugs with the off-duty cops.

It has been conjectured that at least one percent of the population is psychopathic. Genetically, these individuals are fearless; they are people users and supreme manipulators. On the right side, they are terrific spies, war heroes, five-star generals, corporate billionaires and James Bonds. On the wrong side, they are strikingly evil: the Neros, the Hitlers, the Richard Specks, the Ted Bundys, antisocial but clinically sane people who commit atrocities for which they feel no remorse and assume no blame.

"He's a loner," Wesley went on, "and has a difficult time

with close relationships, though he may be considered pleasant or even charming to acquaintances. He wouldn't be close to any one person. He's the type to pick up a woman in a bar, have sex with her and find it frustrating and highly unsatisfactory."

"Don't I know the feeling," Marino said, yawning.

Wesley elaborated, "He would gain far more satisfaction from violent pornography, detective magazines, S&M, and probably entertained violent sexual fantasies long before he began to make the fantasies reality. The reality may have begun with his peeping into the windows of houses or apartments where women live alone. It gets more real. Next he rapes. The rapes get more violent, culminating in murder. This escalation will continue as he continues to become more violent and abusive with each victim. Rape is no longer the motive. Murder is. Murder is no longer enough. It has to be more sadistic."

His arm extended, exposing a perfect margin of stiff white cuff, he reached for Lori Petersen's photographs. Slowly he looked through them, one at a time, his face impassive. Lightly pushing the stack away from him, he turned to me. "It seems clear to me that in her case, in Dr. Petersen's case, the killer introduced elements of torture. An accurate assessment?"

"Accurate," I replied.

"What? Busting her fingers?" Marino posed the question as if looking for an argument. "The Mob does shit like that. Sex murderers usually don't. She played the violin, right? Busting her fingers seems kinda personal. Like the guy who did it knew her."

As calmly as possible I said, "The surgical reference books on her desk, the violin—the killer didn't have to be a genius to pick up a few clues about her."

Wesley considered, "Another possibility is her broken fingers and fractured ribs are defense injuries."

"They aren't." I was sure of this. "I didn't find anything to send me the message she struggled with him."

Marino turned his flat, unfriendly eyes my way. "Really? I'm curious. What do you mean by defense injuries? According to your report, she had plenty of bruises."

"Good examples of defense injuries"—I met his gaze and held it—"are broken fingernails, scratches or injuries found in the areas of the hands and arms that would have been exposed had the victim attempted to ward off blows. Her injuries are inconsistent with this."

Wesley summarized, "Then we're all in agreement. He was more violent this time."

"Brutal's the word," Marino quickly said as if this were his favorite point to make. "That's what I'm talking about. Lori Petersen's different from the other three."

I suppressed my fury. The first three victims were tied up, raped and strangled. Wasn't that *brutal?* Did they need to have their bones broken, too?

Wesley grimly predicted, "If there's another one, there will be more pronounced signs of violence, of torture. He kills because it's a compulsion, an attempt to fill some need. The more he does it the stronger this need becomes and the more frustrated he gets, therefore the stronger the urge will become. He's becoming increasingly desensitized and it's taking more with each killing to satiate him. The satiation is temporary. Over the subsequent days or weeks, the tension builds until he finds his next target, stalks her and does it again. The intervals between each killing may get shorter. He may escalate, finally, into a spree murderer, as Bundy did."

I was thinking of the time frame. The first woman had been murdered on April 19, the second on May 10, the third on May 31. Lori Petersen was murdered a week later, on the seventh of June.

The rest of what Wesley said was fairly predictable. The killer was from a "dysfunctional home" and might have been abused, either physically or emotionally, by his mother. When he was with a victim, he was acting out his rage, which was inextricably connected to his lust.

He was above average in intelligence, an obsessive-compulsive, and very organized and meticulous. He might be prone to obsessive behavior patterns, phobias or rituals, such as neatness, cleanliness, his diet—anything that maintained his sense of controlling his environment.

He had a job, which is probably menial—a mechanic, a repairman, a construction worker or some other labor-related occupation . . .

I noticed Marino's face getting redder by the moment. He was looking restlessly around the conference room.

"For him," Wesley was saying, "the best part of what he does is the antecedent phase, the fantasy plan, the environmental cue that activates his fantasy. Where was the victim when he became aware of her?"

We did not know. She may not have known were she alive to tell. The interface may have been as tenuous and obscure as a shadow crossing her path. He caught a glimpse of her somewhere. It may have been at a shopping mall or perhaps while she was inside her car and stopped at a red light.

"What triggered him?" Wesley went on. "Why this particular woman?"

Again, we did not know. We knew only one thing. Each of the women was vulnerable because she lived alone. Or was thought to live alone as in Lori Petersen's case.

"Sounds like your all-American Joe." Marino's acid remark stopped us cold.

Flicking an ash, he leaned aggressively forward. "Hey. This is all very good and nice. But me, I don't intend to be no Dorothy going down no Yellow Brick Road. They don't all lead to Emerald City, okay? We say he's a plumber or something, right? Well, Ted Bundy was a law student, and a couple years back there's this serial rapist in D.C. who turns out to be a dentist. Hell, the Green Valley strangler out there in the land of fruits and nuts could be a Boy Scout for all anybody knows."

Marino was getting around to what was on his mind. I'd been waiting for him to start in.

"I mean, who's to say he ain't a student? Maybe even an actor, a creative type whose imagination's gone apeshit. One lust murder don't look much different from another no matter who's committed it unless the squirrel's into drinking blood or barbecuing people on spits—and this squirrel we're dealing with ain't a Lucas. The reason these brands of sex murders all profile pretty much the same, you want my opinion, is because, with few exceptions, people are people. Doctor, lawyer or Indian chief. People think and do pretty much the same damn things, going back to the days when cavemen dragged women off by their hair."

Wesley was staring off. He slowly looked over at Marino and quietly asked, "What's your point, Pete?"

"I'll tell you what the hell my point is!" His chin was jutted out, the veins in his neck standing out like cords. "This goddamn crap about who profiles right and who don't. It frosts me. What I got here is a guy writing his friggin' dissertation on sex and violence, cannibals, queers. He's got glitter crap on his hands that looks like the same stuff found on all the bodies. His prints are on his dead wife's skin and on the knife stashed in one of his drawers—a knife that also has this glitter crap on the handle. He gets home every weekend right about the time the women get whacked. But no. Hell, no. He can't be the guy, right? And why? 'Cause he ain't blue collar. He ain't trashy enough."

Wesley was staring off again. My eyes fell to the photographs spread out before us, full-blown color shots of women who never in their worst nightmares would have believed anything like this could happen to them.

"Well, let me just lay this one on you." The tirade wasn't about to end. "Pretty-boy Matt, here—it just so happens he ain't exactly pure as the driven snow. While I was upstairs checking with serology, I buzzed by Vander's office again to see if he'd turned up anything else. Petersen's prints are on file, right? You know why?" He stared hard at me. "I'll tell you why. Vander looked into it, did his thing with his gizmos. Pretty-boy Matt got arrested six years ago in New Orleans. This was the summer before he went off to college, long before he met his surgeon lady. She probably never even knew about it."

"Knew about what?" Wesley asked.

"Knew her lover-boy actor was charged with rape, that's what."

No one said anything for a very long time.

Wesley was slowly turning his Mont Blanc pen end over end on the table top, his jaw firmly set. Marino wasn't playing by the rules. He wasn't sharing information. He was ambushing us with it as if this were court and Wesley and I were opposing counsel.

I finally proposed, "If Petersen was, in fact, charged with rape, then he was acquitted. Or else the charges were dropped."

Those eyes of his fixed on me like two gun barrels. "You know that, do you? I ain't run a record check on him yet."

"A university like Harvard, Sergeant Marino, doesn't make it a practice to accept convicted felons."

"If they know."

"True," I agreed. "If they know. It's hard to believe they wouldn't know, if the charge stuck."

"We'd better run it down" was all Wesley had to say about the matter.

With that, Marino abruptly excused himself.

I assumed he was going to the men's room.

Wesley acted as if there was nothing out of the ordinary about Marino's outburst or anything else. He casually asked, "What's the word from New York, Kay? Anything back from the lab yet?"

"DNA testing takes a while," I abstractedly replied. "We didn't send them anything until the second case. I should be getting those results soon. As for the second two, Cecile Tyler and Lori Petersen, we're talking next month at the earliest."

He persisted in his "nothing's wrong" mode. "In all four cases the guy's a nonsecreter. That much we know."

"Yes. We know that much."

"There's really no doubt in my mind it's the same killer."

"Nor in mine," I concurred.

Nothing more was said for a while.

We sat tensely, waiting for Marino's return, his angry words still ringing in our ears. I was perspiring and could feel my heart beating.

I think Wesley must have been able to read the look on my face that I wanted nothing more to do with Marino, that I had relegated him to the oblivion I reserve for people who are impossible and unpleasant and professionally dangerous.

He said, "You have to understand him, Kay."

"Well, I don't."

"He's a good detective, a very fine one."

I didn't comment.

We sat silently.

My anger began to rise. I knew better, but there was no stopping the words from boiling out. "Damn it, Benton! These women deserve our best effort. We screw it up and someone else may die. I don't want him screwing it up because he's got some problem!"

"He won't."

"He already is." I lowered my voice. "He's got a noose around Matt Petersen's neck. It means he's not looking at anybody else."

Marino, thank God, was taking his sweet time coming back.

Wesley's jaw muscles were flexing and he wouldn't meet my eyes. "I haven't dismissed Petersen yet either. I can't. I know killing his wife doesn't fit with the other three. But he's an unusual case. Take Gacy. We've got no idea how many people he murdered. Thirty-three kids. Possibly it was hundreds. Strangers, all of them strangers to him. Then he does his mother and stuffs pieces of her down the garbage disposal . . ."

I couldn't believe it. He was giving me one of his "young agents" lectures, rattling on like a sweaty-palmed sixteen-year-old on his first date.

"Chapman's toting around *Catcher in the Rye* when he wastes John Lennon. Reagan, Brady get shot by some jerk who's obsessed with an actress. Patterns. We try to predict. But we can't always. It isn't always predictable."

Next he began reciting statistics. Twelve years ago the clearance rate for homicides averaged at ninety-five, ninety-six percent. Now it was more like seventy-four percent, and dropping. There were more stranger killings as opposed to crimes of passion, and so on. I was barely hearing a word of it.

". . . Matt Petersen worries me, to tell you the truth, Kay." He paused.

He had my attention.

"He's an artist. Psychopaths are the Rembrandts of murderers. He's an actor. We don't know what roles he's played out in his fantasies. We don't know that he isn't making them reality now. We don't know that he isn't diabolically clever. His wife's murder might have been utilitarian."

"*Utilitarian?*" I stared at him with wide, disbelieving eyes, stared at the photographs taken of Lori Petersen at the scene. Her face a suffused mask of agony, her legs bent, the electrical cord as taut as a bowstring in back and wrenching her arms up and cutting into her neck. I was seeing everything the monster did to her. Utilitarian? I wasn't hearing this.

Wesley explained, "Utilitarian in the sense he may have had a need to get rid of her, Kay. If, for example, something happened to make her suspect he'd killed the first three women, he may have panicked, decided he had to kill her. How can he do that and get away with it? He can make her death look like the other ones."

"I've heard shades of this before," I said evenly. "From your partner."

His words were slow and steady like the beat of a metronome, "All possible scenarios, Kay. We have to consider them."

"Of course we do. And that's fine as long as Marino considers *all* possible scenarios and doesn't wear blinders because he's getting obsessed or has a problem."

Wesley glanced toward the open door. Almost inaudibly, he said, "Pete's got his prejudices. I won't deny that."

"I think you'd better tell me exactly what they are."

"Let it suffice to say that when the Bureau decided he was a good candidate for a VICAP team, we did some checking into his background. I know where he grew up, how he grew up. Some things you never get over. They set you off. It happens."

He wasn't telling me anything I hadn't already figured out. Marino grew up poor on the wrong side of the tracks. He was uncomfortable around the sort of people who had always made him uncomfortable. The cheerleaders and homecoming queens never gave him a second glance because he was a social misfit, because his father had dirt under his nails, because he was "common."

I'd heard these cop sob stories a thousand times before. The guy's only advantage in life is he's big and white, so he makes himself bigger and whiter by carrying a gun and a badge.

"We don't get to excuse ourselves, Benton," I said shortly. "We don't get to excuse criminals because they had screwed-up childhoods. We don't get to use the powers entrusted to us to punish people who remind us of our own screwed-up childhoods."

I wasn't lacking in compassion. I understood exactly where Marino was coming from. I was no stranger to his anger. I'd felt it many times when facing a defendant in court. No matter how convincing the evidence, if the guy's nice-looking, clean-cut and dressed in a two-hundred-dollar suit, twelve working men and women don't, in their hearts, believe he's guilty.

I could believe just about anything of anybody these days. But only if the evidence was there. Was Marino looking at the evidence? Was he even looking at all?

Wesley pushed back his chair and stood up to stretch. "Pete has his spells. You get used to it. I've known him for years."

He stepped into the open doorway and looked up and down the hall. "Where the hell is he, anyway? He fall in the john?"

Wesley concluded his depressing business with my office and disappeared into the sunny afternoon of the living where other felonious activities demanded his attention and his time.

We'd given up on Marino. I had no idea where he'd gone, but his trip to the men's room apparently took him out of the building. Nor did I have a chance to wonder about it for very long, because Rose came through the doorway linking my office with hers just as I was locking the case files back inside my desk.

I knew instantly by her weighty pause and the grim set of her mouth that she had something on her mind I didn't want to hear.

"Dr. Scarpetta, Margaret's been looking for you and asked me to tell you the minute you came out of your meeting."

My impatience showed before I could check it. There were autopsies to look in on downstairs and innumerable phone calls to return. I had enough to do to keep half a dozen people busy and I wanted nothing else added to the list.

Handing me a stack of letters to be signed, she looked like a formidable headmistress as she peered at me over her reading glasses and added, "She's in her office, and I don't think the matter can wait."

Rose wasn't going to tell me, and though I really couldn't fault her, I was annoyed. I think she knew everything that went on throughout the entire statewide system, but it was her style to direct me to the source instead of filling me in directly. In a word, she assiduously avoided being the bearer of bad news. I supposed she'd learned the hard way after working for my predecessor Cagney most of her life.

Margaret's office was midway down the hall, a small Spartan room of cinder-block walls painted the same insipid crème-de-menthe color as the rest of the building. The dark green tile floor always looked dusty no matter how often it was swept, and spilling over her desktop and every other surface were reams of computer printouts. The bookcase was crammed with instruction manuals and printer cables, extra ribbons and boxes of diskettes. There were no personal touches, no photographs, posters or knickknacks. I don't know how Margaret lived with the sterile mess, but I'd never seen a computer analyst's office that wasn't.

She had her back to the door and was staring at the monitor, a programmer manual opened in her lap. Swiveling around, she rolled the chair to one side when I came in. Her face was tense, her short black hair ruffled as if she'd been raking her fingers through it, her dark eyes distracted.

"I was at a meeting most of the morning," she launched in. "When I got here after lunch I found this on the screen."

She handed me a printout. On it were several SQL commands that allowed one to query the data base. At first my mind was blank as I stared at the printout. A Describe had been executed on the case table, and the upper half of the page was filled with column names. Below this were several simple Select statements. The first one asked for the case number where the last name was "Petersen," the first name "Lori." Under it was the response, "No Records Found." A second command asked for the case numbers and first names of every decedent whose record was in our data base and whose last name was "Petersen."

Lori Peterson's name was not included in the list because her case file was inside my desk. I had not handed it over to the clerks up front for filing yet.

"What are you saying, Margaret? You didn't type in these commands?"

"I most certainly didn't," she replied with feeling. "Nobody did it up front either. It wouldn't have been possible."

She had my complete attention.

"When I left Friday afternoon," she went on to explain, "I did the same thing I always do at the end of the day. I left the computer in answer mode so you could dial in from home if you wanted to. There's no way anyone used my computer, because you can't use it when it's in answer mode unless you're at another PC and dialing in by modem."

That much made sense. The office terminals were networked to the one Margaret worked on, which we referred to as the "server." We were not linked to the Health and Human Services Department's mainframe across the street, despite the commissioner's on-going pressure for us to do so. I had refused and would continue to do so because our data was highly sensitive, many of the cases under active criminal investigation. To have everything dumped in a central computer shared by dozens of other HHSD agencies was an invitation to a colossal security problem.

"I didn't dial in from home," I told her.

"I never assumed you did," she said. "I couldn't imagine why you would type in these commands. You of all people would know Lori Petersen's case isn't in yet. Someone else is responsible, some-one other than the clerks up front or the other doctors. Except for your PC and the one in the morgue, everything else is a dumb terminal."

A dumb terminal, she went on to remind me, is rather much what it sounds like—a brainless unit consisting of a monitor and a keyboard. The dumb terminals in our office were linked to the server in Margaret's office. When the server was down or frozen, as was true when it was in answer mode, the dumb terminals were down or frozen, too. In other words, they'd been out of commission since late Friday—*before* Lori Petersen's murder.

The data base violation had to have occurred over the weekend or at some point earlier today.

Someone, an outsider, got in.

This person had to be familiar with the relational data base we used. A popular one, I reminded myself, and not impossible to learn. The dial-up number was Margaret's extension, which was listed in the HHSD's in-house directory. If you had a computer loaded with a communications software package, if you had a compatible modem, and if you knew Margaret was the computer analyst and tried her number, you could dial in. But that's as far as you would get. You couldn't access any office applications or data. You couldn't even get into the electronic mailboxes without knowing the user names and passwords.

Margaret was staring at the screen through her tinted glasses. Her brow was slightly furrowed and she was nipping at a thumbnail.

I pulled up a chair and sat down. "How? The user name and password. How did anyone have access to these?"

"That's what I'm puzzling over. Only a few of us know them, Dr. Scarpetta. You, me, the other doctors, and the people who enter the data. And our user names and passwords are different from the ones I assigned to the districts."

Though each of my other districts was computerized with a network exactly like ours, they kept their own data and did not have on-line access to the Central Office data. It wasn't likely—in fact, I did not think it was possible—that one of my deputy chiefs from one of the other offices was responsible.

I made a lame suggestion.

"Maybe someone guessed and got lucky."

She shook her head. "Next to impossible. I know. I've tried before when I've changed someone's electronic mail password and can't remember what it is. After about three tries, the computer isn't forgiving, the phone line's disconnected. In addition, this version of the data base doesn't like illegal log-ons. If you type in enough of them when you're trying to get into SQL or into a table, you get a context error, whack the pointers out of alignment and crash the data base."

"There's no other place the passwords might be?" I asked. "No other place in the computer, for example, where someone might be able to find out what they are? What if the person were another programmer . . .?"

"Wouldn't work." She was sure. "I've been careful about it. There *is* a system table where the user names and passwords are listed, but you could get into that only if you know what you're doing. And it doesn't matter anyway because I dropped that table a long time ago to prevent this very sort of problem."

I didn't say anything.

She was tentatively searching my face, looking for a sign of displeasure, for a glint in my eyes telling her I was angry or blaming her.

"It's awful," she blurted out. "Really. I don't have a clue, don't know what all the person did. The DBA isn't working, for example."

"Isn't working?" The DBA, or data base administrator, was a grant giving select persons, such as Margaret or me, authority to access all tables and do anything we wished with them. For the DBA not to be working was the equivalent of being told the key to my front door no longer fit. "What do you mean *it isn't working?*" It was getting very difficult to sound calm.

"Exactly that. I couldn't get into any of the tables with it. The password was invalid for some reason. I had to reconnect the grant."

"How could *that* have happened?"

"I don't know." She was getting more upset. "Maybe I should change all of the grants, for security reasons, and assign new passwords?"

"Not now," I automatically replied. "We'll simply keep Lori Petersen's case out of the computer. Whoever the person is, at least he didn't find what he was looking for." I got out of the chair.

"This time he didn't."

I froze, staring down at her.

Two spots of color were forming on her cheeks. "I don't know. If it's happened before, I have no way of knowing, because the

echo was off. These commands here"—she pointed to the printout—"are the echo of the commands typed on the computer that
dialed up this one. I always leave the echo off so if you're dialing
in from home, whatever you're doing isn't echoed on this screen.
Friday I was in a hurry. Maybe I inadvertently left the echo on or
set it on. I don't remember, but it was on." Ruefully she added, "I
guess it's a good thing—"

We both turned around at the same time.

Rose was standing in the doorway.

That look on her face—*Oh, no, not again.*

She waited for me to come out into the hallway, then said, "The
ME in Colonial Heights is on line one. A detective from Ashland's
on line two. And the commissioner's secretary just called—"

"What?" I interrupted. Her last remark was the only one I
really heard. "Amburgey's secretary?"

She handed me several pink telephone slips as she replied,
"The commissioner wants to see you."

"About what, for God's sake?" If she told me one more time I'd
have to hear the details for myself, I was going to lose my temper.

"I don't know," Rose replied. "His secretary didn't say."

6

I COULDN'T BEAR to sit at my desk. I had to move about and distract myself before I lost my composure.

Someone had broken into my office computer, and Amburgey wanted to see me in an hour and forty-five minutes. It wasn't likely that he was merely inviting me to tea.

So I was making evidence rounds. Usually this entailed my receipting evidence to the various labs upstairs. Other times I simply stopped by to see what was going on with my cases—the good doctor checking in on her patients. At the moment, my routine was a veiled and desperate peregrination.

The Forensic Science Bureau was a beehive, a honeycomb of cubicles filled with laboratory equipment and people wearing white lab coats and plastic safety glasses.

A few of the scientists nodded and smiled as I passed their open doorways. Most of them didn't look up, too preoccupied with whatever they were doing to pay a passerby any mind. I was thinking about Abby Turnbull, about other reporters I didn't like.

Did some ambitious journalist pay a computer hack to break into our data?

How long had the violations been going on?

I didn't even realize I'd turned in to the serology lab until my eyes were suddenly focusing on black countertops cluttered with beakers, test tubes, and Bunsen burners. Jammed on glass-enclosed shelves were bags of evidence and jars of chemicals, and in the center of the room was a long table covered with the spread and sheets removed from Lori Petersen's bed.

"You're just in time," Betty greeted me. "If you want acid indigestion, that is."

"No, thanks."

"Well, I'm getting it already," she added. "Why should you be immune?"

Close to retirement, Betty had steel-gray hair, strong features and hazel eyes that could be unreadable or shyly sensitive depending on whether you took the trouble to get to know her. I liked her the first time I met her. The chief serologist was meticulous, her acumen as sharp as a scalpel. In private she was an ardent bird-watcher and an accomplished pianist who had never been married or sorry about the fact. I think she reminded me of Sister Martha, my favorite nun at St. Gertrude's parochial school.

The sleeves of her long lab coat were rolled up to her elbows, her hands gloved. Arranged over her work area were test tubes containing cotton-tipped swabs, and a physical evidence recovery kit—or PERK—comprising the cardboard folder of slides and the envelopes of hair samples from Lori Petersen's case. The file of slides, the envelopes and the test tubes were identified by computer-generated labels initialed by me, the fruits of yet one more of Margaret's programs.

I vaguely recalled the gossip at a recent academy meeting. In the weeks following the mayor of Chicago's sudden death, there were some ninety attempts at breaking into the medical examiner's computer. The culprits were thought to be reporters after the autopsy and toxicology results.

Who? Who broke into my computer?

And why?

"He's coming along well," Betty was saying.

"I'm sorry . . ." I smiled apologetically.

She repeated, "I talked with Dr. Glassman this morning. He's coming along well with the samples from the first two cases and should have results for us in a couple of days."

"You sent up the samples from the last two yet?"

"They just went out." She was unscrewing the top of a small brown bottle. "Bo Friend will be hand-delivering them—"

"*Bo Friend?*" I interrupted.

"Or Officer Friendly, as he's known by the troops. That's his name. Bo Friend. Scout's honor. Let's see, New York's about a six-hour drive. He should get them to the lab sometime this evening. I think they drew straws."

I looked blankly at her. "Straws?"

What could Amburgey want? Maybe he was interested in how the DNA testing was going. It was on everyone's mind these days.

"The cops," Betty was saying. "Going to New York and all. Some of them have never been."

"Once will be enough for most of them," I commented abstractedly. "Wait until they try changing lanes or finding a parking place."

But he could have just sent a memo through the electronic mail if he'd had a question about DNA tests or anything else. That's what Amburgey usually did. In fact, that's what he'd always done in the past.

"Huh. That's the least of it. Our man Bo was born and bred in Tennessee and never goes anywhere without his piece."

"He went to New York without his piece, I hope." My mouth was talking to her. The rest of me was elsewhere.

"Huh," she said again. "His captain told him to, told him about the gun laws up there in Yankeeville. Bo was smiling when he came up to get the samples, smiling and patting what I presume was a shoulder holster under his jacket. He's got one of these John Wayne revolvers with a six-inch barrel. These guys and their guns. It's so Freudian it's boring . . ."

The back of my brain was recalling news accounts of virtual children who had broken into the computers of major corporations and banks.

Beneath the telephone on my desk at home was a modem enabling me to dial up the computer here. It was off-limits, strictly verboten. Lucy understood the seriousness of her ever attempting to access the OCME data. Everything else she was welcome to do, despite my inward resistance, the strong sense of territory that comes from living alone.

I recalled the evening paper Lucy found hidden under the sofa cushion. I recalled the expression on her face as she questioned me about the murder of Lori Petersen, and then the list of my staff's office and home telephone numbers—including Margaret's extension—tacked to the cork bulletin board above my home desk.

I realized Betty hadn't said anything for quite a long time. She was staring strangely at me.

"Are you all right, Kay?"

"I'm sorry," I said again, this time with a sigh.

Silent for a moment, she spoke sympathetically. "No suspects yet. It's eating at me, too."

"I suppose it's hard to think of anything else." Even though I'd hardly given the subject a thought in the last hour or so, and I should be giving it my full attention, I silently chastised myself.

"Well, I hate to tell you, but DNA's not worth a tinker's damn unless they catch *somebody*."

"Not until we reach the enlightened age where genetic prints are stored in a central data base like fingerprint records," I muttered.

"Will never happen as long as the ACLU has a thing to say about it."

Didn't anybody have anything positive to offer today? A headache was beginning to work its way up from the base of my skull.

"It's weird." She was dripping naphthyl acid phosphate on small circles of white filter paper. "You would think somebody *somewhere* has seen this guy. He's not invisible. He doesn't just beam into the women's houses, and he's got to have seen them at some point in the past to have picked them and followed them home. If he's hanging out in parks or malls or the likes, someone should have noticed him, seems to me."

"If anybody's seen anything, we don't know about it. It isn't that people aren't calling," I added. "Apparently the Crime Watch hot lines are ringing off the hook morning, noon and night. But so far, based on what I've been told, nothing is panning out."

"A lot of wild goose chases."

"That's right. A lot of them."

Betty continued to work. This stage of testing was relatively simple. She took the swabs from the test tubes I'd sent up to her, moistened them with water and smeared filter paper with them. Working in clusters, she first dripped naphthyl acid phosphate, and then added drops of fast-blue B salt, which caused the smear to pop up purple in a matter of seconds if seminal fluid was present.

I looked at the array of paper circles. Almost all of them were coming up purple.

"The bastard," I said.

"A lousy shot at that." She began describing what I was seeing.

"These are the swabs from the back of her thighs," she said, pointing. "They came up immediately. The reaction wasn't quite as quick with the anal and vaginal swabs. But I'm not surprised. Her own body fluids would interfere with the tests. In addition, the oral swabs are positive."

"The bastard," I repeated quietly.

"But the ones you took of the esophagus are negative. Obviously, the most substantial residues of seminal fluid were left outside the body. Misfires, again. The pattern's almost identical to what I found with Brenda, Patty, and Cecile."

Brenda was the first strangling, Patty the second, Cecile the third. I was startled by the note of familiarity in Betty's voice as she referred to the slain women. They had, in an odd way, become part of our family. We'd never met them in life and yet now we knew them well.

As Betty screwed the medicine dropper back inside its small brown bottle, I went to the microscope on a nearby counter, stared through the eyepiece and began moving the wetmount around on the stage. In the field of polarized light were several multicolored fibers, flat and ribbon-shaped with twists at irregular intervals. The fibers were neither animal hair nor man-made.

"These what I collected from the knife?" I almost didn't want to ask.

"Yes. They're cotton. Don't be thrown off by the pinks and greens and white you're seeing. Dyed fabrics are often made up of a combination of colors you can't detect with the naked eye."

The gown cut from Lori Petersen was cotton, a pale yellow cotton.

I adjusted the focus. "I don't suppose there's any chance they could be from a cotton rag paper, something like that. Lori apparently was using the knife as a letter opener."

"Not a chance, Kay. I've already looked at a sample of fibers from her gown. They're consistent with the fibers you collected from the knife blade."

That was expert-witness talk. Consistent-this and reasonable-that. Lori's gown was cut from her body with her husband's knife. Wait until Marino gets this lab report, I thought. Damn.

Betty was going on, "I can also tell you right off the fibers you're looking at aren't the same as some of the ones found on her body and on the frame of the window the police think the killer came through. Those are dark—black and navy blue with some red, a polyester-and-cotton blend."

The night I'd seen Matt Petersen he was wearing a white Izod shirt that I suspected was cotton and most certainly would not have contained black, red or navy blue fibers. He was also wearing jeans, and most denim jeans are cotton.

It was highly unlikely he left the fibers Betty just mentioned, unless he changed his clothes before the police arrived.

"Yeah, well, Petersen ain't stupid," I could hear Marino say. "Ever since Wayne Williams half the world knows fibers can be used to nail your ass."

I went out and followed the hallway to the end, turning left into the tool marks and firearms lab, with its countertops and tables cluttered with handguns, rifles, machetes, shotguns and Uzis, all tagged as evidence and waiting their day in court. Handgun and shotgun cartridges were scattered over desktops, and in a back corner was a galvanized steel tank filled with water and used for test fires. Floating placidly on the water's surface was a rubber duck.

Frank, a wiry white-haired man retired from the army's CID, was hunched over the comparison microscope. He relit his pipe when I came in and didn't tell me anything I wanted to hear.

There was nothing to be learned from the cut screen removed from Lori Petersen's window. The mesh was a synthetic, and therefore useless as far as tool marks or even the direction of the cut was concerned. We couldn't know if it had been cut from the inside or the outside of the house because plastic, unlike metal, doesn't bend.

The distinction would have been an important one, something I very much would have liked to know. If the screen was cut from the *inside* of the house, then all bets were off. It would mean the killer didn't break in but out of the Petersen house. It would mean, quite likely, Marino's suspicions of the husband were correct.

"All I can tell you," Frank said, puffing out swirls of aromatic smoke, "is it's a clean cut, made with something sharp like a razor or a knife."

"Possibly the same instrument used to cut her gown?"

He absently slipped off his glasses and began cleaning them with a handkerchief. "Something sharp was used to cut her gown but I can't tell you if it was the same thing used to cut the screen. I can't even give you a classification, Kay. Could be a stiletto. Could be a saber or a pair of scissors."

The severed electrical cords and survival knife told another story.

Based on a microscopic comparison, Frank had good reason to believe the cords had been cut with Matt Petersen's knife. The tool marks on the blade were consistent with those left on the severed ends of the cords. Marino, I dismally thought again. This bit of circumstantial evidence wouldn't amount to much had the survival knife been found out in the open and near the bed instead of hidden inside Matt Petersen's dresser drawer.

I was still envisioning my own scenario. The killer saw the knife on top of Lori's desk and decided to use it. But why did he hide it afterward? Also, if the knife was used to cut Lori's gown, and if it was also used to cut the electrical cords, then this changed the sequence of events as I had imagined them.

I'd assumed when the killer entered Lori's bedroom he had his own cutting instrument in hand, the knife or sharp instrument he used to cut the window screen. If so, then why didn't he cut her gown and the electrical cords with it? How is it he ended up with the survival knife? Did he instantly spot it on the desk when he entered her bedroom?

He couldn't have. The desk was nowhere near the bed, and when he first came in, the bedroom was dark. He couldn't have seen the knife.

He couldn't have seen it until the lights were on, and by then Lori should have been subdued, the killer's knife at her throat. Why should the survival knife on the desk have mattered to him? It didn't make any sense.

Unless something interrupted him.

Unless something happened to disrupt and alter his ritual, unless an unexpected event occurred that caused him to change course.

Frank and I batted this around.

"This is assuming the killer's not her husband," Frank said.

"Yes. This is assuming the killer is a stranger to Lori. He has his pattern, his MO. But when he's with Lori, something catches him off guard."

"Something she does . . ."

"Or says," I replied, then proposed, "She may have said something that momentarily stalled him."

"Maybe." He looked skeptical. "She may have stalled him long enough for him to see the knife on the desk, long enough for him to get the idea. But it's more likely, in my opinion, he found the knife on the desk earlier in the evening because he was already inside her house when she got home."

"No. I really don't think so."

"Why not?"

"Because she was home for a while before she was assaulted." I'd gone through it many times.

Lori drove home from the hospital, unlocked her front door and relocked it from the inside. She went into the kitchen and placed her knapsack on the table. Then she had a snack. Her gastric contents indicated she'd eaten several cheese crackers very close to the time she was assaulted. The food had scarcely begun to digest. Her terror when she was attacked would have caused her digestion to completely shut down. It's one of the body's defense mechanisms. Digestion shuts down to keep blood flowing to the extremities instead of to the stomach, preparing the animal for fight or flight.

Only it hadn't been possible for her to fight. It hadn't been possible for her to flee anywhere.

After her snack, she went from the kitchen to the bedroom. The police had found out it was her habit to take her oral contraceptive at night, right before bed. Friday's tablet was missing from the foil pack inside the master bathroom. She took her tablet, perhaps brushed her teeth and washed her face, then changed into her gown and placed her clothing neatly on the chair. I believed she was in bed when he attacked her not long afterward. He may have been watching her house from the darkness of the trees or the shrubbery. He may have waited until the lights were out, until he assumed she was asleep. Or he may have observed her in the past and known exactly what time she came home from work and went to bed.

I remembered the bedcovers. They were turned down as if

she'd been under them, and there was no evidence of a struggle anywhere else in the house.

There was something else coming to me.

The smell Matt Petersen mentioned, the sweaty, sweet smell.

If the killer had a peculiar and pronounced body odor, it was going to be wherever he was. It would have lingered inside her bedroom had he been hiding there when Lori got home.

She was a physician.

Odors are often indications of diseases and poisons. Physicians are trained to be very sensitive to smells, so sensitive I can often tell by the odor of blood at a scene that the victim was drinking shortly before he was shot or stabbed. Blood or gastric contents reminiscent of musky macaroons, of almonds, may indicate the presence of cyanide. A patient's breath smelling of wet leaves may indicate tuberculosis—

Lori Petersen was a physician, like me.

Had she noticed a peculiar odor the moment she walked into her bedroom, she would not have undressed or done anything else until she determined the source of it.

Cagney did not have my worries, and there were times when I felt haunted by the spirit of the predecessor I had never met, a reminder of a power and invulnerability I would never have. In an unchivalrous world he was an unchivalrous knight who wore his position like a panache, and I think a part of me envied him.

His death was sudden. He literally dropped dead as he was crossing the living room rug to switch on the Super Bowl. In the predawn silence of an overcast Monday morning he became the subject of his own instruction, a towel draped over his face, the autopsy suite sealed off from everyone but the pathologist whose lot it was to examine him. For three months, no one touched his office. It was exactly as he'd left it, except, I suppose, that Rose had emptied the cigar butts out of the ashtray.

The first thing I did when I moved to Richmond was to strip his inner sanctum to a shell and banish the last remnant of its former occupant—including the hard-boiled portrait of him dressed in his academic gown, which was beneath a museum light behind his formidable desk. That was relegated to the Pathology Department at VMC, as was an entire bookcase filled with macabre mementos forensic pathologists are expected to collect, even if most of us don't.

His office—my office, now—was well-lighted and carpeted in royal blue, the walls arranged with prints of English landscapes and other civilized scenes. I had few mementos, and the only hint of morbidity was the clay facial reconstruction of a murdered boy whose identity remained a mystery. I'd arranged a sweater around the base of his neck and perched him on top of a filing cabinet where he watched the open doorway with plastic eyes and waited in sad silence to be called by name.

Where I worked was low-profile, comfortable but business-like, my impedimenta deliberately unrevealing and bland. Though I somewhat smugly assured myself it was better to be viewed as a professional than as a legend, I secretly had my doubts.

I still felt Cagney's presence in this place.

People were constantly reminding me of him through stories that became more apocryphal the longer they lived on. He rarely wore gloves while doing a post. He was known to arrive at scenes eating his lunch. He went hunting with the cops, he went to bar-becues with the judges, and the previous commissioner was obse-quiously accommodating because he was absolutely intimidated by Cagney.

I paled by comparison and I knew comparisons were con-stantly being made. The only hunts and barbecues I was invited to were courtrooms and conferences in which targets were drawn on me and fires lit beneath my feet. If Dr. Alvin Amburgey's first year in the commissioner's office was any indication, his next three prom-ised to be the pits. My turf was his to invade. He monitored what I did. Not a week went by that I didn't get an arrogant electronic memo from him requesting statistical information or demanding an answer as to why the homicide rate continued to rise while other crimes were slightly on the decline—as if somehow it was my fault people killed each other in Virginia.

What he had never done to me before was to schedule an impromptu meeting.

In the past, when he had something to discuss, if he didn't send a memo he sent one of his aides. There was no doubt in my mind his agenda was not to pat me on the back and tell me what a fine job I was doing.

I was abstractedly looking over the piles on my desk and trying to find something to arm myself with—files, a notepad, a clipboard. For some reason, the thought of going in there empty-handed made me feel undressed. Emptying my lab-coat pockets of the miscellaneous debris I had a habit of collecting during the day, I settled for tucking in a pack of cigarettes, or "cancer sticks," as Amburgey was known to call them, and I went out into the late afternoon.

He reigned across the street on the twenty-fourth floor of the Monroe Building. No one was above him except an occasional pigeon roosting on the roof. Most of his minions were located below on floor after floor of HHSD agencies. I'd never seen his office. I'd never been invited.

The elevator slid open onto a large lobby where his receptionist was ensconced within a U-shaped desk rising from a great field of wheat-colored carpet. She was a bosomy redhead barely out of her teens, and when she looked up from her computer and greeted me with a practiced, perky smile, I almost expected her to ask if I had reservations and needed a bellhop to manage my bags.

I told her who I was, which didn't seem to fan the smallest spark of recognition.

"I have a four o'clock appointment with the commissioner," I added.

She checked his electronic calendar and cheerily said, "Please make yourself comfortable, Mrs. Scarpetta. Dr. Amburgey will be with you shortly."

As I settled myself on a beige leather couch, I searched the sparkling glass coffee and end tables bearing magazines and arrangements of silk flowers. There wasn't an ashtray, not a single one, and at two different locations were "Thank You for Not Smoking" signs.

The minutes crept by.

The redheaded receptionist was sipping Perrier through a straw and preoccupied with her typing. At one point she thought to offer me something to drink. I smiled a "no, thank you," and her fingers flew again, keys rapidly clicked, and the computer complained with a loud beep. She sighed as if she'd just gotten grave news from her accountant.

My cigarettes were a hard lump in my pocket and I was tempted to find a ladies' room and light up.

At four-thirty her telephone buzzed. Hanging up—that

cheery, vacant smile again—she announced, "You may go in, Mrs. Scarpetta."

Defrocked and decidedly out of sorts, "Mrs." Scarpetta took her at her word.

The commissioner's door opened with a soft click of its rotating brass knob and instantly on their feet were three men—only one of whom I was expecting to see. With Amburgey were Norman Tanner and Bill Boltz, and when it came Boltz's turn to offer his hand, I looked him straight in the eye until he glanced away uncomfortably.

I was hurt and a little angry. Why hadn't he told me he was going to be here? Why hadn't I heard a word from him since our paths had crossed briefly at Lori Petersen's home?

Amburgey granted me a nod that seemed more a dismissal, and added "Appreciate your coming" with the enthusiasm of a bored traffic court judge.

He was a shifty-eyed little man whose last post had been in Sacramento, where he picked up enough West Coast ways to disguise his North Carolina origins; he was the son of a farmer, and not proud of the fact. He had a penchant for string ties with silver slides, which he wore almost religiously with a pin-striped suit, and on his right ring finger was a hunk of silver set with turquoise. His eyes were hazy gray, like ice, the bones of his skull sharply pronounced through his thin skin. He was almost bald.

An ivory wing chair had been pulled out from the wall and seemed to be there for me. Leather creaked, and Amburgey stationed himself behind his desk, which I had heard of but never seen. It was a huge, ornately carved masterpiece of rosewood, very old and very Chinese.

Behind his head was an expansive window affording him a vista of the city, the James River a glinting ribbon in the distance and Southside a patchwork. With a loud snap he opened a black ostrich-skin briefcase before him and produced a yellow legal pad filled with his tight, snarled scrawl. He had outlined what he was going to say. He never did anything without his cue cards.

"I'm sure you're aware of the public distress over these recent stranglings," he said to me.

"I'm very aware of it."

"Bill, Norm and I had an emergency summit meeting, so to speak, yesterday afternoon. This was apropos of several things, not the least of which was what was in the Saturday evening and Sunday morning papers, Dr. Scarpetta. As you may know, because of this fourth tragic death, the murder of the young surgeon, the news has gone out over the wire."

I didn't know. But I wasn't surprised.

"No doubt you've been getting inquiries," Amburgey blandly went on. "We've got to nip this in the bud or we're going to have sheer pandemonium on our hands. That's one of the things the three of us have been discussing."

"If you can nip the murders in the bud," I said just as blandly, "you'll deserve a Nobel Prize."

"Naturally, that's our top priority," said Boltz, who had unbuttoned his dark suit jacket and was leaning back in his chair. "We've got the cops working overtime on them, Kay. But we're all in agreement there's one thing we must control for the time being—these leaks to the press. The news stories are scaring the hell out of the public and letting the killer know everything we're up to."

"I couldn't agree more." My defenses were going up like a drawbridge, and I instantly regretted what I said next: "You can rest assured I have issued no statements from my office other than the obligatory information of cause and manner."

I'd answered a charge not yet made, and my legal instincts were bridling at my foolishness. If I were here to be accused of indiscretion, I should have forced them—forced Amburgey, anyway—to introduce such an outrageous subject. Instead, I'd sent up the flare I was on the run and it gave them justification to pursue.

"Well, now," Amburgey commented, his pale, unfriendly eyes resting briefly on me, "you've just laid something on the table I think we need to examine closely."

"I haven't laid anything on the table," I unemphatically replied. "I'm just stating a fact, for the record."

With a light knock, the redheaded receptionist came in with coffee, and the room abruptly froze into a mute tableau. The heavy silence seemed completely lost on her as she went to considerable lengths to make sure we had everything we needed, her attention hovering about Boltz like a mist. He may not have been the best

Commonwealth's attorney the city had ever known, but he was by far the best looking—one of those rare blond men to whom the passing years were generous. He was losing neither his hair nor his physique, and the fine lines at the corners of his eyes were the only indication he was creeping close to forty.

When she was gone, Boltz said to no one in particular, "We all know the cops occasionally have a problem with kiss and tell. Norm and I have had a few words with the brass. No one seems to know exactly where the leaks are coming from."

I restrained myself. What did they expect? One of the majors is in tight with Abby Turnbull or whoever and this guy's going to confess, "Yeah, sorry about that. I squawked"?

Amburgey flipped a page in his legal pad. "So far a leak cited as 'a medical source' has been quoted seventeen times in the papers since the first murder, Dr. Scarpetta. This makes me a little uneasy. Clearly, the most sensational details, such as the ligatures, the evidence of sexual assault, how the killer got in, where the bodies were found, and the fact DNA testing is in the works have been attributed to this medical source." He glanced up at me. "Am I to assume the details are accurate?"

"Not entirely. There were a few minor discrepancies."

"Such as?"

I didn't want to tell him. I didn't want to talk about these cases at all with him. But he had the right to the furniture inside my office if he wanted it. I reported to him. He reported to no one but the governor.

"For example," I replied, "in the first case, the news reported there was a tan cloth belt tied around Brenda Steppe's neck. The ligature was actually a pair of pantyhose."

Amburgey was writing this down. "What else?"

"In Cecile Tyler's case, it was reported her face was bleeding, that the bedspread was covered with blood. An exaggeration, at best. She had no lacerations, no injuries of this nature. There was a little bloody fluid coming out of her nose and mouth. A postmortem artifact."

"These details," Amburgey asked as he continued to write, "were they mentioned in the CME-1 reports?"

I had to take a moment to compose myself. It was becoming clear what was going through his mind. The CME-1's were the medical examiner's initial report of investigation. The responding

ME simply wrote down what he saw at the scene and learned from the police. The details were not always completely accurate because the ME on call was surrounded by confusion, and the autopsy hadn't been performed yet.

In addition, ME's were not forensic pathologists. They were physicians in private practice, virtual volunteers who got paid fifty dollars a case to be jerked out of bed in the middle of the night or have their weekends wrecked by car crashes, suicides and homicides. These men and women provided a public service; they were the troops. Their primary job was to determine whether the case merited an autopsy, to write everything down and take a lot of photographs. Even if one of my ME's had confused a pair of pantyhose with a tan belt, it wasn't relevant. My ME's didn't talk to the press.

Amburgey persisted, "The bit about the tan cloth belt, the bloody bedspread. I'm wondering if these were mentioned in the CME-1's."

"In the manner the press made reference to the details," I firmly replied, "no."

Tanner drolly remarked, "We all know what the press does. Takes a mustard seed and turns it into a mountain."

"Listen," I said, looking around at the three men, "if your point is that one of my medical examiners is leaking details about these cases, I can tell you with certainty you're way off base. It isn't happening. I know both of the ME's who responded to the first two scenes. They've been ME's in Richmond for years and have always been unimpeachable. I myself responded to the third and fourth scenes. The information is not coming from my office. The details, all of them, could have been divulged by anyone who was there. Members of the rescue squads who responded, for example."

Leather quietly creaked as Amburgey shifted in his chair. "I've looked into that. Three different squads responded. No one paramedic was present at all four scenes."

I said levelly, "Anonymous sources are often a blend of numerous sources. A medical source could have been a combination of what a squad member said, what a police officer said, and what the reporter overheard or saw while waiting around outside the residence where the body was found."

"True." Amburgey nodded. "And I don't believe any of us really think the leaks are coming from the Medical Examiner's Office—at least not intentionally—"

"*Intentionally?*" I broke out. "Are you implying the leaks may be coming from my office *unintentionally?*" Just as I was about to retort self-righteously what a lot of nonsense this was, I was suddenly struck silent.

A flush began creeping up my neck as it came back to me with swift simplicity. My office data base. It had been violated by an outsider. Was this what Amburgey was alluding to: How could he possibly know about it?

Amburgey went on as if he hadn't heard me, "People talk, employees talk. They tell their family, their friends, and they don't intend any harm in most instances. But you never know where the buck stops—maybe on a reporter's desk. These things happen. We're objectively looking into the matter, turning over every stone. We have to. As you must realize, some of what's been leaked has the potential of doing serious damage to the investigation."

Tanner laconically added, "The city manager, the mayor, they aren't pleased with this type of exposure. The homicide rate's already given Richmond a black eye. Sensational national news accounts of a serial murderer are the last thing the city needs. All these new hotels going up are dependent on big conferences, visitors. People don't want to come to a city where they fear for their lives."

"No, they don't," I coldly agreed. "Nor would people want to think the city's major concern over these murders is they're an inconvenience, an embarrassment, a potential obstruction to the tourist trade."

"Kay," Boltz quietly reasoned, "nobody's implying anything outrageous like that."

"Of course not," Amburgey was quick to add. "But we have to face certain hard realities, and the fact is there's a lot simmering beneath the surface. If we don't handle the matter with extreme care, I'm afraid we're in for a major eruption."

"Eruption? Over what?" I warily asked, and automatically looked at Boltz.

His face was tight, his eyes hard with restrained emotion. Reluctantly he said, "This last murder's a powder keg. There are certain things about Lori Petersen's case no one's talking about. Things that, thank God, the reporters don't know yet. But it's just a matter of time. Someone's going to find out, and if we haven't handled the problem first, sensibly and behind the scenes, the situation's going to blow sky-high."

Tanner took over, his long, lantern-shaped face very grim, "The city is at risk for, well, litigation." He glanced at Amburgey, who signaled him with a nod to proceed.

"A very unfortunate thing happened, you see. Apparently Lori Petersen called the police shortly after she got home from the hospital early Saturday morning. We learned this from one of the dispatchers on duty at the time. At eleven minutes before one A.M., a 911 operator got a call. The Petersen residence came up on the computer screen but the line was immediately disconnected."

Boltz said to me, "As you may recall from the scene, there was a telephone on the bedside table, the cord ripped out of the wall. Our conjecture is Dr. Petersen woke up when the killer was inside her house. She reached for the phone and got as far as dialing 911 before he stopped her. Her address came up on the computer screen. That was it. No one said anything. Nine-one-one calls of this nature are dispatched to the patrolmen. Nine times out of ten they're cranks, kids playing with the phone. But we can't ever be sure of that. Can't be sure the person isn't suffering a heart attack, a seizure. In mortal danger. Therefore, the operator's supposed to give the call a high priority. Then the dispatcher broadcasts it to the units on the street without delay, prompting an officer to drive past the residence and at least check to make sure everything's all right. This wasn't done. A certain 911 operator, who even as we speak is suspended from duty, gave the call a priority four."

Tanner interjected, "There was a lot of action on the street that night. A lot of radio traffic. The more calls there are, the easier it is to rank something lower in importance than you maybe otherwise would. Problem is, once something's been given a number, there's no going back. The dispatcher's looking at the numbers on his screen. He's not privy to the nature of the calls until he gets to them. He's not going to get to a four anytime soon when he's got a backlog of ones and twos and threes to send out to the men on the street."

"No question the operator dropped the ball," Amburgey mildly said. "But I think one can see how such a thing could have happened."

I was sitting so rigidly I was barely breathing.

Boltz resumed in the same dull tone, "It was some forty-five minutes later when a patrol car finally cruised past the Petersen residence. The officer says he shone his spotlight over the front of the house. The lights were out, everything looked, quote, 'secure.' He gets a call of a domestic fight in progress, speeds off. It wasn't long after this Mr. Petersen apparently came home and found his wife's body."

The men continued to talk, to explain. References were made to Howard Beach, to a stabbing in Brooklyn, in which the police were negligent in responding and people died.

"Courts in D.C., New York, have ruled a government can't be held liable for failing to protect people from crime."

"Makes no difference what the police do or don't do."

"Doesn't matter. We win the suit, if there is one, we still lose because of the publicity."

I was scarcely hearing a word of it. Horrible images were playing crazily inside my mind. The 911 call, the fact it was aborted, made me see it.

I knew what happened.

Lori Petersen was exhausted after her ER shift, and her husband had told her he would be in later than usual that night. So she went to bed, perhaps planning to sleep just awhile, until he got home—as I used to do when I was a resident and waiting for Tony to come home from the law library at Georgetown. She woke up at the sound of someone inside the house, perhaps the quiet sound of this person's footsteps coming down the hallway toward the bedroom. Confused, she called out the name of her husband.

No one answered.

In that instant of dark silence that must have seemed an eternity, she realized there was someone inside the house and it wasn't Matt.

Panicking, she flicked on the bedside lamp so she could see to dial the phone.

By the time she'd stabbed out 911, the killer had gotten to her. He jerked the phone line from the wall before she had a chance to cry out for help.

Maybe he grabbed the receiver out of her hand. Maybe he yelled at her or she began to plead with him. He'd been interrupted, momentarily knocked off guard.

He was enraged. He may have struck her. This may be when

he fractured her ribs, and as she cowered in stunned pain he wildly looked around. The lamp was on. He could see everything inside the bedroom. He could see the survival knife on her desk.

Her murder was preventable. It could have been stopped!

Had the call been given a priority one, had it immediately been dispatched over the air, an officer would have responded within minutes. He would have noticed the bedroom light was on—the killer couldn't see to cut cords and tie up his victim in the dark. The officer might have gotten out of his car and heard something. If nothing else, had he taken the time to shine his light over the back of her house, the removed window screen, the picnic bench, the open window would have been noticed. The killer's ritual took time. The police might have been able to get inside before he killed her!

My mouth was so dry I had to take several sips of coffee before I could ask, "How many people know this?"

Boltz replied, "No one's talking about it, Kay. Not even Sergeant Marino knows. Or at least it's doubtful he does. He wasn't on duty when the call was broadcast. He was contacted at home after a uniform man had already arrived at the scene. The word's out in the department. Those cops aware of what happened are not to discuss the matter with anyone."

I knew what that meant. Loose lips would send the guy back to traffic or stick him behind a desk in the uniform room.

"The only reason we're apprising you of this unfortunate situation"—Amburgey carefully chose his words—"is because you need the background in order to understand the steps we feel compelled to take."

I sat tensely, looking hard at him. The point of all this was about to be made.

"I had a conversation with Dr. Spiro Fortosis last night, the forensic psychiatrist who has been good enough to share his insights with us. I've discussed the cases with the FBI. It's the opinion of the people who are experts in profiling this type of killer that publicity exacerbates the problem. This type of killer gets off on it. He gets excited, hyper, when he reads about what he's done. It pushes him into overdrive."

"We can't curtail the freedom of the press," I bluntly reminded him. "We have no control over what reporters print."

"We do." Amburgey was gazing out the window. "They can't

print much if we don't give them much. Unfortunately, we've given them a lot." A pause. "Or at least someone has."

I wasn't sure where Amburgey was going but the road signs definitely pointed in my direction.

He continued, "The sensational details—the leaks—we've already discussed have resulted in graphic, grisly stories, banner headlines. It's the expert opinion of Dr. Fortosis this may be what prompted the killer to strike again so soon. The publicity excites him, puts him under incredible stress. The urge peaks again and he has to find release in selecting another victim. As you know, there was only a week between the slayings of Cecile Tyler and Lori Petersen—"

"Have you talked to Benton Wesley about this?" I interrupted.

"Didn't have to. Talked to Susling, one of his colleagues at the Behavioral Science Unit in Quantico. He's well known in the field, has published quite a lot on the subject."

Thank God. I couldn't endure knowing Wesley had just been sitting in my conference room several hours before and had made no mention of what I was now being told. He would be just as incensed as I was, I thought. The commissioner was wedging his foot in the investigation. He was going around me, around Wesley, around Marino, and taking matters into his own hands.

"The probability that sensational publicity, which has been ignited by loose talk, by leaks," Amburgey went on, "the fact the city may be liable because of the 911 mishap, means we have to take serious measures, Dr. Scarpetta. All information dispensed to the public, from this point forward, will be channeled through Norm or Bill, as far as the police end of it goes. And nothing will be coming from your office unless it is released by me. Are we clear?"

There had never been a problem with my office before, and he knew it. We had never solicited publicity, and I'd always been circumspect when releasing information to the press.

What would the reporters—what would anybody—think when they were told they were being referred to the commissioner for information that historically had come from my agency? In the forty-two-year history of the Virginia medical examiner system, this had never happened. By gagging me it would appear I'd been relieved of my authority because I couldn't be trusted.

I looked around. No one would meet my eyes. Boltz's jaw was

firmly set as he absently studied his coffee cup. He refused to grant me so much as a reassuring smile.

Amburgey began perusing his notes again. "The worst offender is Abby Turnbull, which isn't anything new. She doesn't win prizes for being passive." This to me: "Are you two acquainted?"

"She rarely gets past my secretary."

"I see." He casually flipped another page.

"She's dangerous," Tanner volunteered. "The *Times* is part of one of the biggest chains in the country. They have their own wire service."

"Well, there's no question that Miss Turnbull is the one doing the damage. All the other reporters are simply reprinting her scoops and kicking the stuff around on the air," Boltz slowly commented. "What we've got to find out is where the hell she's getting the goods." This to me: "We'd be wise to consider all channels. Who else, for example, has access to your records, Kay?"

"Copies are sent to the CA and to the police," I replied evenly—he and Tanner *were* the CA and the police.

"What about the families of the victims?"

"So far I've gotten no requests from the women's families, and in cases such as these I most likely would refer the relative to your office."

"What about insurance companies?"

"If requested. But after the second homicide I instructed my clerks to refrain from sending out any reports, except to your office and to the police. The reports are provisional. I've been stalling for as long as possible to keep them out of circulation."

Tanner asked, "Anybody else? What about Vital Statistics? Didn't they used to keep your data on their mainframe, requiring you to send them copies of all your CME-1's and autopsy reports?"

Startled, I didn't respond right away. Tanner certainly had done his homework. There was no reason he should have been privy to such a mundane housekeeping concern.

"We stopped sending VS any paper reports after we became computerized," I told him. "They'll get data from us eventually. When they begin working on their annual report—"

Tanner interrupted with a suggestion that had the impact of a pointed gun.

"Well, that leaves your computer." He began idly swirling the coffee in his Styrofoam cup. "I assume you have very restricted access to the data base."

"That was my next question," Amburgey muttered.

The timing was terrible.

I almost wished Margaret hadn't told me about the computer violation.

I was desperately trying to think what to say as I was seized by panic. Was it possible the killer might have been caught earlier and this gifted young surgeon might still be alive had these leaks not occurred? Was it possible the anonymous "medical source" wasn't a person after all, but my office computer?

I think it was one of the worst moments in my life when I had no choice but to admit, "Despite all precautions, it appears someone has gotten into our data. Today we discovered evidence that someone tried to pull up Lori Petersen's case. It was a fruitless attempt because she hasn't been entered into the computer yet."

No one spoke for a few moments.

I lit a cigarette. Amburgey stared angrily at it, then said, "But the first three cases are in there."

"Yes."

"You're sure it wasn't a member of your staff, or perhaps one of your deputy chiefs from one of the districts?"

"I'm reasonably sure."

Silence again. Then he asked, "Could it be whoever this infiltrator is, he may have gotten in before?"

"I can't be sure it hasn't happened before. We routinely leave the computer in answer mode so either Margaret or I can dial in after hours. We have no idea how an outsider gained access to the password."

"How did you discover the violation?" Tanner looked confused. "You discovered it today. Seems like you would have discovered it in the past if it's happened before."

"My computer analyst discovered it because the echo was inadvertently left on. The commands were on the screen. Otherwise we would never have known."

Something flickered in Amburgey's eyes and his face was turning an angry red. Idly picking up a cloisonné letter opener, he ran his thumb along the blunt edge for what seemed a long moment. "Well," he decided, "I suppose we'd better take a look at your screens. See what sort of data this individual might have looked at. It may not have anything to do with what's been in the papers. I'm sure this's what we'll discover. I also want to review the four strangling cases, Dr. Scarpetta. I'm getting asked a lot of questions. I need to know exactly what we're dealing with."

I sat helplessly. There was nothing I could do. Amburgey was usurping me, opening the private, sensitive business carried on in my office to bureaucratic scrutiny. The thought of him going through these cases, of him staring at the photographs of these brutalized, murdered women made me tremble with rage.

"You may review the cases across the street. They are not to be photocopied, nor are they to leave my office." I added coldly, "For security reasons, of course."

"We'll take a look at them now." Glancing around. "Bill, Norm?"

The three men got up. As we filed out, Amburgey told his receptionist he would not be back today. Her gaze longingly followed Boltz out the door.

7

WE WAITED IN THE BRIGHT SUN for a break in rush-hour traffic and hurried across the street. No one talked, and I walked several paces ahead of them, leading them around to the back of the building. The front doors would be chained by now.

Leaving them inside the conference room, I went to collect the files from a locked drawer in my desk. I could hear Rose shuffling paper next door. It was after five and she was still here. This comforted me a little. She was lingering because she sensed something bad was going on for me to have been summoned to Amburgey's office.

When I returned to the conference room, the three men had pulled their chairs close together. I sat across from them, quietly smoking and silently daring Amburgey to ask me to leave. He didn't. So I sat.

Another hour went by.

There was the sound of pages turning, of reports being riffled through, of comments and observations made in low voices. Photographs were fanned out on the table like playing cards. Amburgey was busily taking notes in his niggling, fussy scrawl. At one point several case files slid off Boltz's lap and splashed on the carpet.

"I'll pick it up." Tanner unenthusiastically scooted his chair to one side.

"I've got it." Boltz seemed disgusted as he began to collect the paperwork scattered under and around the table. He and Tanner were considerate enough to sort everything by the proper case numbers while I numbly looked on. Amburgey, meanwhile, continued to write as if nothing had happened.

The minutes took hours to go by, and I sat.

Sometimes I was asked a question. Mostly, the men just looked and talked among themselves as if I were not there.

At half past six we moved into Margaret's office. Seating myself before the computer, I deactivated answer mode, and momentarily the case screen was before us, a pleasing orange and blue construction of Margaret's design. Amburgey glanced at his notes and read me the case number of Brenda Steppe, the first victim.

Entering it, I hit the query key. Almost instantly, her case was up.

The case screen actually comprised more than half a dozen tables which were joined. The men began scanning the data filling the orange fields, glancing at me each time they were ready for me to page-down.

Two pages later, we all saw it at the same time.

In the field called "Clothing, Personal Effects, etc." was a description of what came in with Brenda Steppe's body, including the ligatures. Written in black letters as big as life was "tan fabric belt around neck."

Amburgey leaned over me and silently ran his finger across the screen.

I opened Brenda Steppe's case file and pointed out that this was not what I had dictated in the autopsy protocol, that typed in my paper record was "a pair of nude pantyhose around her neck."

"Yes," Amburgey jogged my memory, "but take a look at the rescue squad's report. A tan cloth belt is listed, is it not?"

I quickly found the squad sheet and scanned it. He was right. The paramedic, in describing what he had seen, mentioned the victim was bound with electrical cords around the wrists and ankles, and a "tannish cloth beltlike article" was around her neck.

Boltz suggested, as if trying to be helpful, "Perhaps one of your clerks was going through this record as she typed it, and she saw the squad sheet and mistakenly typed in the bit about the belt—in other words, she didn't notice this was inconsistent with what you dictated in the autopsy report."

"It's not likely," I objected. "My clerks know to get the data only from the autopsy and lab reports and the death certificate."

"But it's possible," Amburgey said, "because this belt is mentioned. It's in the record."

"Of course it's possible."

"Then it's also possible," Tanner decided, "the source of this tan belt, which was cited in the paper, came from your computer. That maybe a reporter has been getting into your data base, or has been getting someone else to get into it for him. He printed inaccurate information because he read an inaccuracy in your office's data."

"Or he got the information from the paramedic who listed the belt in his squad report," I countered.

Amburgey backed away from the computer. He said coldly, "I'll trust you to do something to ensure the confidentiality of your office records. Get the girl who looks after your computer to change the password. Whatever it takes, Dr. Scarpetta. And I'll expect a written statement from you pertaining to the matter."

He moved to the doorway, hesitating long enough to toss back at me, "Copies will be given to the appropriate parties, and then it remains to be seen if any further measures will have to be taken."

With that he was gone, Tanner at his heels.

⸻

When all else fails, I cook.

Some people go out after a god-awful day and slam a tennis ball around or jog their joints to pieces on a fitness course. I had a friend in Coral Gables who would escape to the beach with her folding chair and burn off her stress with sun and a slightly pornographic romance she wouldn't have been caught dead reading in her professional world—she was a district court judge. Many of the cops I know wash away their miseries with beer at the FOP lounge.

I've never been particularly athletic, and there wasn't a decent beach within reasonable driving distance. Getting drunk never solved anything. Cooking was an indulgence I didn't have time for most days, and though Italian cuisine isn't my only love, it has always been what I do best.

"Use the finest side of the grater," I was saying to Lucy over the noise of water running in the sink.

"But it's so hard," she complained, blowing in frustration.

"Aged parmigiano-reggiano is hard. And watch your knuckles, okay?"

I finished rinsing green peppers, mushrooms and onions, patted them dry and placed them on the cutting board. Simmering on the stove was sauce made last summer from fresh Hanover tomatoes, basil, oregano and several cloves of crushed garlic. I always kept a good supply in the freezer for times like these. Luganega sausage was draining on paper towels near other towels of browned lean beef. High-gluten dough was on the counter rising beneath a damp dish towel, and crumbled in a bowl was whole-milk mozzarella imported from New York and still packed in its brine when I'd bought it at my favorite deli on West Avenue. At room temperature the cheese is soft like butter, when melted is wonderfully stringy.

"Mom always gets the boxed kind and adds a bunch of junk to it," Lucy said breathlessly. "Or she buys the kind already made in the grocery store."

"That's deplorable," I retorted, and I meant it. "How can she eat such a thing?" I began to chop. "Your grandmother would have let us starve first."

My sister has never liked cooking. I've never understood why. Some of the happiest times when we were growing up were spent around the dinner table. When our father was well, he would sit at the head of the table and ceremoniously serve our plates with great mounds of steaming spaghetti or fettuccine or—on Fridays—frittata. No matter how poor we were, there was always plenty of food and wine, and it was always a joy when I came home from school and was greeted by delicious smells and promising sounds coming from the kitchen.

It was sad and a violation of tradition that Lucy knew nothing of these things. I assumed when she came home from school most days she walked into a quiet, indifferent house where dinner was a drudgery to be put off until the last minute. My sister should never have been a mother. My sister should never have been Italian.

Greasing my hands with olive oil, I began to knead the dough, working it hard until the small muscles in my arms hurt.

"Can you twirl it like they do on TV?" Lucy stopped what she was doing, staring wide-eyed at me.

I gave her a demonstration.

"Wow!"

"It's not so hard." I smiled as the dough slowly spread out over my fists. "The trick is to keep your fingers tucked in so you don't poke holes in it."

"Let me do it."

"You haven't finished grating the cheese," I said with mock severity.

"*Please . . .*"

She got down from her footstool and came over to me. Taking her hands in mine, I bathed them with olive oil and folded them into fists. It surprised me that her hands were almost the size of mine. When she was a baby her fists were no bigger than walnuts. I remembered the way she would reach out to me when I was visiting back then, the way she would grab my index finger and smile while a strange and wonderful warmth spread through my breast. Draping the dough over Lucy's fists, I helped her flop it around awkwardly.

"It gets bigger and bigger," she exclaimed. "This is neat!"

"The dough spreads out because of centrifugal force—similar to the way people used to make glass. You know, you've seen the old glass windows with ripples in them?"

Nodding.

"The glass was spun into a large, flat disk—"

We both looked up as gravel crunched beneath tires in the drive. A white Audi was pulling in and Lucy's mood immediately began to sink.

"Oh," she said unhappily. "*He's* here."

Bill Boltz was getting out of the car and collecting two bottles of wine from the passenger's seat.

"You'll like him very much." I was deftly laying the dough in the deep pan. "He very much wants to meet you, Lucy."

"He's your boyfriend."

I washed my hands. "We just do things together, and we work together . . ."

"He's not married?" She was watching him follow the walkway to the front door.

"His wife died last year."

"Oh." A pause. "How?"

I kissed the top of her head and went out of the kitchen to answer the door. Now was not the time for me to answer such a question. I wasn't sure how Lucy would take it.

"You recovering?" Bill smiled and lightly kissed me.

I shut the door. "Barely."

"Wait till you've had a few glasses of this magic stuff," he said, holding up the bottles as if they were prize catches from a hunt. "From my private stock—you'll love it."

I touched his arm and he followed me to the kitchen.

Lucy was grating cheese again, up on her footstool, her back to us. She didn't even glance around when we walked in.

"Lucy?"

Still grating.

"Lucy?" I led Bill over to her. "This is Mr. Boltz, and Bill, this is my niece."

Reluctantly, she stopped what she was doing and looked straight at me. "I scraped my knuckle, Auntie Kay. See?" She held up her left hand. A knuckle was bleeding a little.

"Oh, dear. Here, I'll get a Band-Aid . . ."

"Some of it got in the cheese," she went on, as if suddenly on the verge of tears.

"Sounds to me like we need an ambulance," Bill announced, and he quite surprised Lucy by plucking her off the stool and locking his arms under her thighs. She was in a ridiculously funny sitting position. "Rerrrrrr—RERRRRRRRRRR . . ." He was wailing like a siren and carrying her over to the sink. "Three-one-six, bringing in an emergency—cute little girl with a bleeding knuckle." He was talking to a dispatcher now. "Please have Dr. Scarpetta ready with a Band-Aid . . ."

Lucy was shrieking with laughter. Momentarily her knuckle was forgotten and she was staring with open adoration at Bill as he uncorked a bottle of wine.

"You have to let it breathe," he was gently explaining to her. "See, it's sharper now than it will be in an hour or so. Like everything else in life, it gets mellower with time."

"Can I have some?"

"Well, now," he replied with exaggerated gravity, "all right by me if your Auntie Kay says so. But we wouldn't want you getting silly on us."

I was quietly putting the pizza together, spreading the dough with sauce and overlaying this with the meats, vegetables and parmesan cheese. Topping it with the crumbled mozzarella, I slid it into the oven. Soon the rich garlicky aroma was filling the kitchen and I was busying myself with the salad and setting the table while Lucy and Bill chatted and laughed.

We didn't eat until late, and Lucy's glass of wine turned out to be a good thing. By the time I was clearing the table, her eyes were half shut and she was definitely ready for bed, despite her unwillingness to say good-night to Bill, who had completely won her heart.

"That was rather amazing," I said to him after I'd tucked her in and we were sitting at the kitchen table. "I don't know how you managed it. I was worried about her reaction . . ."

"You thought she'd view me as competition." He smiled a little.

"Let's just put it this way. Her mother's in and out of relation-ships with just about anything on two legs."

"Meaning she doesn't have much time for her daughter." He refilled our glasses.

"To put it mildly."

"That's too damn bad. She's something, smart as hell. Must have inherited your brains." He slowly sipped his wine, adding, "What does she do all day long while you're working?"

"Bertha's here. Mostly Lucy stays in my office hours on end banging on the computer."

"Playing games on it?"

"Hardly. I think she knows more about the damn thing than I do. Last time I checked, she was programming in Basic and reorganizing my data base."

He began studying his wineglass. Then he asked, "Can you use your computer to dial up the one downtown?"

"Don't even suggest it!"

"Well." He looked at me. "You'd be better off. Maybe I was hoping."

"Lucy wouldn't do such a thing," I said with feeling. "And I'm not sure how I would be better off were it true."

"Better your ten-year-old niece than a reporter. It would get Amburgey off your back."

"Nothing would get him off my back," I snapped.

"That's right," he said dryly. "His reason for getting up in the morning is to jerk you around."

"I'm frankly beginning to wonder that."

Amburgey was appointed in the midst of the city's black community publicly protesting that the police were indifferent to homicides unless the victims were white. Then a black city councilman was shot in his car, and Amburgey and the mayor considered it good public relations, I supposed, to appear unannounced at the morgue the next morning.

Maybe it wouldn't have turned out so badly had Amburgey thought to ask questions while he watched me perform the autopsy, had he kept his mouth shut afterward. But the physician combined with the politician, compelling him to confidently inform the press waiting outside my building that the "spread of pellet wounds" over the dead councilman's upper chest "indicates a shotgun blast at close range." As diplomatically as possible, I explained when the reporters questioned me later that the "spread" of holes over the chest was actually marks of therapy made when ER attendants inserted large-gauge needles into the subclavian arteries to transfuse blood. The councilman's lethal injury was a small-caliber gunshot wound to the back of the head.

The reporters had a field day with Amburgey's blunder.

"The problem is he's a physician by training," I was saying to Bill. "He knows just enough to think he's an expert in forensic medicine, to think he can run my office better than I can, and a lot of his opinions are flat-out full of shit."

"Which you make the mistake of pointing out to him."

"What am I supposed to do? Agree and look as incompetent as he is?"

"So it's a simple case of professional jealousy," he said with a shrug. "It happens."

"I don't know *what* it is. How the hell do you explain these things? Half of what people do and feel doesn't make a damn bit of sense. For all I know, I could remind him of his mother."

My anger was mounting with fresh intensity, and I realized by the expression on his face that I was glaring at him.

"Hey," he objected, raising his hand, "don't be pissed at me. I didn't do anything."

"You were there this afternoon, weren't you?"

"What do you expect? I'm supposed to tell Amburgey and Tanner I can't be in on the meeting because you and I have been seeing each other?"

"Of course you couldn't tell them that," I said in a miserable way. "But maybe I wanted you to. Maybe I wanted you to punch Amburgey's lights out or something."

"Not a bad idea. But I don't think it would help me much come reelection time. Besides, you'd probably let my ass rot in jail. Wouldn't even post my bond."

"Depends on how much it was."

"Shit."

"Why didn't you tell me?"

"Tell you what?"

"About the meeting. You must have known about it since yesterday." Maybe you'd known about it longer, I started to say, and that's why you didn't so much as call me over the weekend! Restraining myself, I stared tensely at him.

He was studying his wineglass again. After a pause, he replied, "I didn't see any point in telling you. All it would have done was worry you, and it was my impression the meeting was *pro forma*—"

"*Pro forma?*" I looked incredulously at him. "Amburgey's gagged me and spent half the afternoon tearing apart my office and that's *pro forma?*"

"I feel sure some of what he did was sparked by your disclosure of the computer violation, Kay. And I didn't know about that yesterday. Hell, you didn't even know about that yesterday."

"I see," I said coldly. "No one knew about it until I told them."
Silence.

"What are you implying?"

"It just seemed an incredible coincidence we discovered the violation just hours before he called me to his office. I had the peculiar thought that maybe he knew . . ."

"Maybe he did."

"That certainly reassures me."

"It's moot anyway," he easily went on. "So what if Amburgey knew about the violation by the time you came to his office this afternoon? Maybe somebody talked—your computer analyst, for example. And the rumor drifted up to the twenty-fourth floor." He shrugged. "It just gave him one more worry, right? You didn't trip yourself up, if that's the case, because you were smart enough to tell the truth."

"I always tell the truth."

"Not always," he remarked slyly. "You routinely lie about us—by omission—"

"So maybe he knew," I cut him off. "I just want to hear you didn't."

"I didn't." He looked intensely at me. "I swear. If I'd heard anything about it, I would have forewarned you, Kay. I would have run to the nearest phone booth—"

"And charged out as Superman."

"Hell," he muttered, "now you're making fun of me."

He was in his boyish wounded manifestation. Bill had a lot of roles and he played all of them extraordinarily well. Sometimes it was hard for me to believe he was so smitten with me. Was that a role as well?

I think he had a starring role in the fantasies of half the city's women, and his campaign manager was shrewd enough to take advantage of it. Photographs of Bill had been plastered over restaurant and storefronts, and nailed to telephone poles on virtually every city block. Who could resist that face? He was stunningly handsome, his hair streaked straw-blond, his complexion perpetually sunburned from the many hours he spent each week at his tennis club. It was hard not to stare openly at him.

"I'm not making fun of you," I said wearily. "Really, Bill. And let's not fight."

"Fine by me."

"I'm just sick. I don't have any idea what to do."

Apparently he'd already thought about this, and he said, "It would be helpful if you could figure out who's been getting into your data." A pause. "Or better, if you could prove it."

"Prove it?" I looked warily at him. "Are you suggesting you have a suspect?"

"Not based on any fact."

"Who?" I lit a cigarette.

His attention drifted across the kitchen. "Abby Turnbull is top on my list."

"I thought you were going to tell me something I couldn't have figured out on my own."

"I'm dead serious, Kay."

"So she's an ambitious reporter," I said irritably. "Frankly, I'm getting a little tired of hearing about her. She's not as powerful as everyone makes her out to be."

Bill set his wineglass on the table with a sharp click. "The hell she isn't," he retorted, staring at me. "The woman's a goddam snake. I know she's an ambitious reporter and all that shit. But she's worse than anybody imagines. She's vicious and manipulative and extremely dangerous. The bitch would stoop to anything."

His vehemence startled me into silence. It was uncharacteristic of him to use such vitriolic terms in describing anyone. Especially someone I assumed he scarcely knew.

"Remember that story she did on me a month or so back?"

Not long ago the *Times* finally got around to the obligatory profile of the city's new Commonwealth's attorney. The story was a rather lengthy spread that ran in the Sunday paper, and I didn't remember in detail what Abby Turnbull had written except that the piece struck me as unusually colorless considering its author.

I said as much to him, "As best I recall, the story was toothless. It did no harm; neither did it do any good."

"There's a reason for that," he fired back at me. "I suspect it wasn't something she wanted to write, particularly."

He wasn't hinting that the assignment had been a boring one. Something else was coming and my nerves were coiling tightly again.

"My session with her was pretty damn terrible. She spent an entire day with me, riding around in my car, going from meeting to meeting, hell, even to my dry cleaner's. You know how these reporters are. They'll follow you into the men's room if you let them. Well, let's just say that as the evening progressed, things took a rather unfortunate and definitely unexpected turn."

He hesitated to see if I got his implication.

I got it all too well.

Glancing at me, his face hard, he said, "It completely broadsided me. We got out of the last meeting around eight. She insisted we go to dinner. You know, it was on the paper and she had a few questions to finish up. We'd no sooner pulled out of the restaurant's parking lot when she said she wasn't feeling well. Too much wine or something. She wanted me to drop her off at her house instead of taking her back to the paper, where her car was parked. So I did. Took her home. And when I pulled in front of her house, she was all over me. It was awful."

"And?" I asked as if I didn't care.

"And I didn't handle it worth a damn. I think I humiliated her without intending to. She's been out to jerk the hell out of me ever since."

"What? She's calling you, sending you threatening letters?" I wasn't exactly serious. Nor was I prepared for what he said next.

"This shit she's been writing. The fact maybe it's coming from your computer. As crazy as it may sound, I think her motivation is mostly personal—"

"The *leaks*? Are you suggesting she's breaking into my computer and writing lurid details about these cases to jerk you around?"

"If these cases are compromised in court, who the hell gets hurt?"

I didn't respond. I was staring in disbelief at him.

"*I* do. I'll be the one prosecuting the cases. Cases as sensational and heinous as these get screwed up because of all this shit in the papers, and no one's going to be sending me flowers or thank-you notes. She sure as hell knows that, Kay. She's sticking it to me, that's what she's doing."

"Bill," I said, lowering my voice, "it's her job to be an aggressive reporter, to print everything she can get her hands on. More important, the cases would get screwed up in court only if the sole evidence was a confession. Then the defense gets to make him change his mind. He takes it all back. The party line is the guy's psychotic and knows the details of the murders because he read about them in the paper. He imagined he committed the crimes. That sort of rubbish. The monster who's killing these women isn't about to turn himself in or confess to anything."

He drained his glass and refilled it. "Maybe the cops develop him as a suspect and get him to talk. Maybe that's the way it happens. And it might be the only thing linking him to the crimes. There isn't a shred of physical evidence that's amounted to anything—"

"No shred of physical evidence?" I interrupted. Surely I hadn't heard him right. Was the wine dulling his senses? "He's leaving a load of seminal fluid. He gets caught and DNA will nail him to—"

"Oh, yeah. *Sure* it will. DNA printing's only gone to trial a couple of times in Virginia. There are very few precedents, very few convictions nationwide—every damn one of them still being appealed. Try explaining to a Richmond jury the guy's guilty because of DNA. I'll be lucky if I can find a juror who can *spell* DNA. Anybody's got an IQ over forty and the defense will find a reason to exclude him, that's what I put up with week after week . . ."

"Bill . . ."

"Hell." He began to pace the kitchen floor. "It's hard enough to get a conviction if fifty people swear they saw the guy pull the trigger. The defense will drag in a herd of expert witnesses to muddy the waters and hopelessly confuse everything. You of all people know how complicated this DNA testing is."

"Bill, I've explained just as difficult things to juries in the past."

He started to say something but caught himself. Staring across the kitchen again, he took another swallow of wine.

The silence was drawn out and heavy. If the outcome of the trial depended solely on the DNA results, this placed me in the position of being a key witness for the prosecution. I'd been in such a position many times in the past and I couldn't recall it ever unduly worrying Bill.

Something was different this time.

"What is it?" I forced myself to ask. "Are you unsettled because of our relationship? You're thinking someone's going to figure it out and accuse us of being professionally in bed together—accuse me of rigging the results to suit the prosecution?"

He glanced at me, his face flushed. "I'm not thinking that at all. It's a fact we've been together, but big deal? So we've gone out to dinner and taken in a few plays . . ."

He didn't have to complete the sentence. Nobody knew about us. Usually he came to my house or we went to some distant place, such as Williamsburg or D.C., where it wasn't likely we would run into anybody who would recognize us. I'd always been more worried about the public seeing us together than he seemed to be.

Or was he alluding to something else, something far more biting?

We were not lovers, not completely, and this remained a subtle but uncomfortable tension between us.

I think we'd both been aware of the strong attraction, but we'd completely avoided doing anything about it until several weeks ago. After a trial that didn't end until early evening, he casually offered to buy me a drink. We walked to a restaurant near the courthouse and two Scotches later we were heading to my house. It was that sudden. It was adolescent in its intensity, our lust as tangible as heat. The forbiddenness of it made it all the more frantic, and then quite suddenly while we were in the dark on my living room couch, I panicked.

His hunger was too much. It exploded from him, invaded instead of caressed as he pushed me down hard into the couch. It was at that moment I had a vivid image of his wife slumped against pale blue satin pillows in bed like some lovely life-size doll, the front of her white negligee stained dark red, the nine-millimeter automatic just inches from her limp right hand.

I'd gone to the suicide scene knowing only that the wife of the man running for Commonwealth's attorney apparently had committed suicide. I did not know Bill then. I examined his wife. I literally held her heart in my hands. Those images, all of them, flashed graphically behind my eyes in my dark living room so many months later.

Physically, I withdrew from him. I'd never told him the real reason why, although in the days that followed he continued to pursue me even more vigorously. Our mutual attraction remained but a wall had gone up. I could not seem to tear it down or climb over it much as I wanted to.

I was scarcely hearing a word he was saying.

". . . and I don't see how you could rig DNA results unless you're involved in a conspiracy that includes the private lab conducting the tests and half the forensic bureau, too—"

"What?" I asked, startled. "Rig DNA results?"

"You haven't been listening," he blurted out impatiently.

"Well, I missed something, that's certain."

"I'm saying no one could accuse you of rigging anything—that's my point. So our relationship has nothing to do with what I'm thinking."

"Okay."

"It's just . . ." He faltered.

"Just *what*?" I asked. Then, as he drained his glass again, I added, "Bill, you have to drive . . ."

He waved it off.

"Then what is it?" I demanded again. "What?"

He pressed his lips together and wouldn't look at me. Slowly, he drew it out. "It's just I'm not sure where you'll be in the eyes of the jurors by then."

I couldn't have been more stunned had he struck me with his open palm.

"My God . . . You do know something. What? What! What is that son of a bitch plotting? He'd going to fire me because of this goddam computer violation, is this what he's said to you?"

"Amburgey? He's not plotting anything. Hell, he doesn't have to. If your office gets blamed for the leaks, and if the public eventually believes the inflammatory news stories are why the killer's striking with increased frequency, then your head will be on the block. People need someone to blame. I can't afford my star witness to have a credibility or popularity problem."

"Is this what you and Tanner were discussing so intensely after lunch?" I was just a blink away from tears. "I saw you on the sidewalk, coming out of The Peking . . ."

A long silence. He had seen me, too, then but had pretended otherwise. Why? Because he and Tanner probably were talking about me!

"We were discussing the cases," he replied evasively. "Discussing a lot of things."

I was so enraged, so stung, I didn't trust myself to say a word.

"Listen," he said wearily as he loosened his tie and unfastened the top button of his shirt. "This didn't go right. I didn't mean for it to come out like this. I swear to God. Now you're all upset, and I'm all upset. I'm sorry."

My silence was stony.

He took a deep breath. "It's just we have real things to worry about and we should be working on them together. I'm painting worst-case scenarios so we can be prepared, okay?"

"What exactly do you expect me to do?" I measured each word to keep my voice steady.

"Think five times about everything. Like tennis. When you're down or psyched you've got to play it careful. Concentrate on every shot, don't take your eye off the ball for a second."

His tennis analogies got on my nerves sometimes. Right now was a good example. "I always think about what I'm doing," I said testily. "You don't need to tell me how to do my job. I'm not known for missing shots."

"It's especially important now. Abby Turnbull's poison. I think she's setting us up. Both of us. Behind the scenes. Using you or your office computer to get to me. Not giving a damn if she maims justice in the process. The cases get blown out of the water and you and I are both blown out of office. It's that simple."

Maybe he was right, but I was having a hard time accepting that Abby Turnbull could be so evil. Surely if she had even a drop of human blood in her veins she would want the killer punished. She wouldn't use four brutally murdered young women as pawns in her vindictive machinations if she were guilty of vindictive machinations, and I wasn't convinced she was.

I was about to tell him he was exaggerating, his bad encounter with her had momentarily distorted his reason. But something stopped me.

I didn't want to talk about this anymore.

I was afraid to.

It was nagging at me. He'd waited until now to say anything. Why? His encounter with her was weeks ago. If she were setting us up, if she were so dangerous to both of us, then why hadn't he told me this before now?

"I think what you need is a good night's sleep," I said quietly. "I think we'd be wise to strike this conversation, at least certain portions of it, go on as if it never happened."

He pushed back from the table. "You're right. I've had it. So have you. Christ, I didn't mean for it to go like this," he said again. "I came over here to cheer you up. I feel terrible . . ."

His apologies continued as we went down the hall. Before I could open the door, he was kissing me and I could taste the wine on his breath and feel his heat. My physical response was always immediate, a frisson of spine-tingling desire and fear running through me like a current. I involuntarily pulled away from him and muttered, "Good night."

He was a shadow in the darkness heading to his car, his profile briefly illuminated by the interior light as he opened the door and climbed in. I was still standing numbly on the porch long after red taillights had burned along the vacant street and disappeared behind trees.

8

THE INSIDE of Marino's silver Plymouth Reliant was as cluttered and slovenly as I would have expected it to be—had I ever given the matter a moment's thought.

On the floor in back were a chicken-dinner box, crumpled napkins and Burger King bags, and several coffee-stained Styrofoam cups. The ashtray was overflowing, and dangling from the rearview mirror was an evergreen-scented air freshener shaped like a pine tree and about as effective as a shot of Glade aimed inside a Dumpster. Dust and lint and crumbs were everywhere, and the windshield was practically opaque with smoker's soot.

"You ever give this thing a bath?" I was fastening my seatbelt.

"Not anymore I don't. Sure, it's assigned to me, but it ain't mine. They don't let me take it home at night or over the weekend or nothing. So I wax it to a spit shine and use up half a bottle of Armor All on the inside and what happens? Some drone's going to be in it while I'm off duty. I get it back looking just like this. Never fails. After a while, I started saving everybody the trouble. Started trashing it myself."

Police traffic quietly crackled as the scanner light blinked from channel to channel. He pulled out of the parking lot behind my building. I hadn't heard a word from him since he abruptly left the conference room on Monday. It was late Wednesday afternoon now, and he had mystified me moments ago by suddenly appearing in my doorway with the announcement that he wanted to take me on a "little tour."

The "tour," it turned out, entailed a retrospective visit to the crime scenes. The purpose, as best I could ascertain, was for me to fix a map of them in my head. I couldn't argue. The idea was a good one. But it was the last thing I was expecting from him. Since when did he include me in anything unless he absolutely had no choice?

"Got a few things you need to know," he said, as he adjusted the side mirror.

"I see. I suppose the implication is had I not agreed to your 'little tour' then you might never have gotten around to telling me these few things I need to know?"

"Whatever."

I waited patiently as he returned the lighter to its socket. He took his time settling more comfortably behind the wheel.

"Might interest you to know," he began, "we gave Petersen a polygraph yesterday and the sucker passed it. Pretty telling, but it don't completely let him off the hook. It's possible to pass it if you're one of these psychopaths who can lie as easy as other people breathe. He's an actor. He probably could say he's Christ crucified and his hands wouldn't sweat, his pulse would be steadier than yours and mine when we're in church."

"That would be highly unusual," I said. "It's pretty hard, close to impossible, to beat a polygraph. I don't care who you are."

"It's happened before. That's one reason it's not admissible in court."

"No, I won't go so far as to say it's infallible."

"Point is," he went on, "we don't have probable cause to pop him or even tell him not to skip town. So I've got him under surveillance. What we're really looking for is his activities after hours. Like, what he does at night. Like, maybe does he get in his car and drive through various neighborhoods, cruising, getting the lay of the land."

"He hasn't gone back to Charlottesville?"

Marino flicked an ash out the window. "He's hanging around for a while, says he's too upset to go back. He's moved, staying in an apartment on Freemont Avenue, says he can't set foot in the house after what happened. I think he's gonna sell the joint. Not that he'll need the money." He glanced over at me and I was briefly faced with a distorted image of myself in his mirrored shades. "Turns out the wife had a hefty life insurance policy. Petersen's going to be about two hundred grand richer. Guess he'll be able to write his plays and not have to worry about making a living."

I didn't say anything.

"And I guess we just let it slide he was brought up on rape charges the summer after he graduated from high school."

"You've looked into that?" I knew he had or he wouldn't have mentioned it.

"Turns out he was doing summer theater in New Orleans and made the mistake of taking some groupie too seriously. I've talked with the cop who investigated the case. According to him, Petersen's the lead actor in some play, and this babe in the audience gets the hots for him, comes to see him night after night, leaves him notes, the whole nine yards. Then she turns up backstage and they end up bar-hopping in the French Quarter. Next thing you know, she's calling the cops at four in the morning, all hysterical, claiming she's been raped. He's in hot water because her PERK's positive and the fluids pop up nonsecreter, which is what he is."

"Did the case go to court?"

"Damn grand jury threw it out. Petersen admitted having sex with her inside her apartment. Said it was consensual, she came on to him. The girl was pretty bruised up, even had a few marks on her neck. But no one could prove how fresh the bruises were and if Petersen caused 'em by working her over. See, the grand jury takes one look at a guy like him. They take into account he's in a play and this girl initiated the encounter. He still had her notes inside the dressing room, which clearly showed the girl had a thing for him. And he was real convincing when he testified she had bruises when he was with her, that she supposedly told him she'd been in a fight several days earlier with some guy she was in the process of breaking up with. Nobody's going to throw the book at Petersen. The girl had the morals of a guppy and was either a Froot Loop or else she made a stupid mistake, laid herself wide open, so to speak, for getting a number done on her."

"Those kinds of cases," I quietly commented, "are almost impossible to prove."

"Well, you just never know. It's also sort of coincidental," he added as a by-the-way for which I was completely unprepared, "that Benton called me up the other night to tell me the big mother computer in Quantico got a hit on the MO of whoever's whacking these women here in Richmond."

"Where?"

"Waltham, Massachusetts, as a matter of fact," he replied, glancing over at me. "Two years ago, right at the time Petersen was a senior at Harvard, which is about twenty miles east of Waltham. During the months of April and May, two women was raped and strangled inside their apartments. Both lived alone in first-floor apartments, was tied up with belts, electrical cords. The killer apparently got in through unsecured windows. Both times it occurred on the weekend. The crimes are a carbon copy of what's been happening here."

"Did the murders stop after Petersen graduated and moved here?"

"Not exactly," he replied. "There was one more later that summer which Petersen couldn't have committed because he was living here, his wife just starting at VMC. But there were a few differences in the third case. The victim was a teenager and lived about fifteen miles from where the other two homicides occurred. She didn't live alone, was shacked up with a guy who was out of town at the time. The cops speculated her murder was a copycat—some squirrel read about the first two in the papers and got the idea. She wasn't found for about a week, was so decomposed there wasn't a hope in hell of finding seminal fluid. Typing the killer wasn't possible."

"What about typing the first two cases?"

"Nonsecreter," he slowly said, staring straight ahead.

Silence. I reminded myself there are millions of men in the country who are nonsecreters and sex slayings happen every year in almost every major city. But the parallels were jolting.

We had turned onto a narrow, tree-lined street in a recently developed subdivision where all of the ranch-style houses looked alike and hinted of cramped space and low-budget building materials. There were realtor signs scattered about, and some of the homes were still under construction. Most of the lawns were newly seeded and landscaped with small dogwoods and fruit trees.

Two blocks down on the left was the small gray house where Brenda Steppe had been slain not quite two months ago. The house had not been rented or sold. Most people in the market for a new home aren't keen on the idea of moving into a place where someone has been brutally murdered. Planted in the yards of the houses on either side were "For Sale" signs.

We parked in front and sat quietly, the windows rolled down.

There were few streetlights, I noted. At night it would be very dark, and if the killer was careful and wearing dark clothing, he wasn't going to be seen.

Marino said, "He got in the kitchen window around back. It appears she got home at nine, nine-thirty that night. We found a shopping bag in the living room. The last item she bought had the computer-printed time on it of eight-fifty P.M. She goes home and cooks a late dinner. That weekend it was warm, and I'm assuming she left the window open to air out the kitchen. Especially since it appears she'd been frying ground beef and onions."

I nodded, recalling Brenda Steppe's gastric contents.

"Cooking hamburger and onions usually smokes or smells up the kitchen. Least it does in my damn house. And there was a ground-beef wrapper, an empty spaghetti sauce jar, onion skins, in the trash under the sink, plus a greasy frying pan soaking." He paused, adding thoughtfully, "Kind of weird to think her choice of what to cook for dinner maybe resulted in her ending up murdered. You know, maybe if she'd had a tuna casserole, a sandwich or something, she wouldn't have left the window open."

This was a favorite rumination of death investigators: What if? What if the person had not decided to buy a pack of cigarettes at a convenience store where two armed robbers were holding the clerk hostage in the back? What if someone hadn't decided to step outside and empty the cat-litter box at the very moment a prison escapee was nearing the house? What if someone hadn't had a fight with his lover, resulting in his driving off in a huff at the exact moment a drunk driver was rounding a curve on the wrong side of the road?

Marino asked, "You notice the turnpike's less than a mile from here?"

"Yes. There's a Safeway on the corner, just before you turn off in this neighborhood," I recalled. "A possible place for him to have left his car, assuming he came the rest of the way on foot."

He cryptically observed, "Yeah, the Safeway. It closes at midnight."

I lit another cigarette and played on the adage that in order for a detective to be good, he has to be able to think like the people he's out to get.

"What would you have done," I asked, "if it were you?"

"If what were me?"

"If you were this killer."

"Depending on whether I'm some squirrely artist like Matt Petersen or just your run-of-the-mill maniac who gets off on stalking women and strangling them?"

"The latter," I evenly said. "Let's assume the latter."

He was baiting me, and he laughed rather rudely. "See, you missed it, Doc. You should've asked how it would be different. Because it wouldn't be. What I'm telling you is if I was either type, I'd pretty much do it the same way—don't matter who or what I am during my regular hours when I'm working and acting like everybody else. When I get into it, I'm just every other drone who's ever done it or ever will. Doctor, lawyer or Indian chief."

"Go on."

He did.

"It starts with me seeing her, having some sort of contact with her somewhere. Maybe I'm coming to her house, selling something or delivering flowers, and when she comes to the door, that little voice in my head says, 'This is the one.' Maybe I'm doing construction in the neighborhood and see her coming and going alone. I fix on her. I might follow her for as long as a week, learning as much about her, about her habits, as possible. Like what lights left on means she's up, what lights off means she's asleep, what her car looks like."

"Why her?" I asked. "Of all the women in the world, why this one?"

He briefly considered this. "She sets something off in me."

"Because of the way she looks?"

He was still thinking. "Maybe. But maybe it's her attitude. She's a working woman. Got a pretty nice crib, meaning she's smart enough to earn a decent living. Sometimes career women are snooty. Maybe I didn't like the way she treated me. Maybe she assaulted my masculinity, like I'm not good enough for her or something."

"All of the victims are career women," I said, adding, "but then, most women who live alone work."

"That's right. And I'm going to know she lives alone, going to make sure of it, going to think I'm sure of it, anyway. I'm going to fix her, show her who's got the power. The weekend comes and I'm feeling like doing it. So I get in the car late, after midnight. I've already cased the area, have the whole scenario planned. Yeah. I might leave my car in the Safeway parking lot, but the problem is it's after hours. The lot's going to be empty, meaning my ride's going to stick out like a sore thumb. Now, it just so happens there's an Exxon station on the same corner as the grocery store. Me, I'd probably leave my car there. Why? Because the service station closes at ten and you expect to see cars waiting for repairs left in service station lots after hours. No one's going to think twice about it, not even the cops, and that's who I'm most worried about. Some cop on patrol seeing my car in an empty parking lot and maybe checking it out or calling in a ten-twenty-eight to find out who owns it."

He described in chilling detail every move. Dressed in dark clothing, he stayed in the shadows as he walked through the neighborhood. When he got to this address his adrenaline began to pump as he realized the woman, whose name he probably did not know, was home. Her car was in the drive. All the lights, except the porch light, were out. She was asleep.

Taking his time, he stayed out of sight as he assessed the situation. He looked around, making sure no one spotted him, then went around to the back of the house where he began to feel a surge of confidence. He was invisible from the street, and the houses one row over are an acre away, the lights out, not a sign of anybody stirring. It was pitch dark in back.

Quietly, he approached the windows and immediately noted the one open. It was simply a matter of running a knife through the screen and releasing the latches inside. Within seconds, the screen was off and on the grass. He slid the window open, pulled himself up and found himself staring at the shadowy shapes of kitchen appliances.

"Once inside," Marino was saying, "I stand still for a minute, listening. Once satisfied I don't hear nothing, I find the hallway and start looking for the room where she's at. A crib small as this," a shrug, "and there aren't too many possibilities. I find the bedroom right off and can hear her sleeping inside. By now I got something over my head, a ski mask, for example . . ."

"Why bother?" I asked. "She isn't going to live to identify you."

"Hairs. Hey, I ain't stupid. I probably pick forensic science books for bedtime reading, probably have memorized all the cop's ten codes. No chance anybody's going to be finding my hairs on her or anywhere else."

"If you're so smart"—now I was the one baiting him—"why aren't you worried about DNA? Don't you read the newspapers?"

"Well, I'm not going to wear no damn rubber. And you aren't ever going to develop me as a suspect because I'm too damn slick. No suspect, no comparison, and your DNA hocus-pocus isn't worth a dime. Hairs are a little more personal. You know, maybe I don't want you to know if I'm black or white, a blond or a redhead."

"What about fingerprints?"

He smiled. "Gloves, babe. The same as you wear when you're examining my victims."

"Matt Petersen wasn't wearing gloves. If he had been, he wouldn't have left his prints on his wife's body."

Marino said easily, "If Matt's the killer, he wouldn't worry about leaving prints in his own house. His prints are gonna be all over the place anyway." A pause. "*If.* Fact is, we're looking for a squirrel. Fact is, Matt's a squirrel. Fact is, he ain't the only squirrel in the world—there's one behind every bush. Fact is, I really don't know who the hell whacked his wife."

I saw the face from my dreams, the white face with no features. The sun breaking through the windshield was hot but I couldn't seem to get warm.

He continued, "The rest's pretty much what you'd imagine. I'm not going to startle her. Going to ease my way to the edge of the bed and wake her up by putting one hand over her mouth, the knife to her throat. I'm probably not going to carry a gun because if she struggles and it goes off maybe I get shot, maybe she does before I've had a chance to do my thing. That's real important to me. It's got to go down the way I planned or I'm real upset. Also, I can't take the chance of anyone hearing gunfire and calling the cops."

"Do you say anything to her?" I asked, clearing my throat.

"I'm going to talk low, tell her if she screams I'll kill her. I'll tell her that over and over again."

"What else? What else will you say to her?"

"Probably nothing."

He shoved the car in gear and turned around. I took one last look at the house where what he just described happened, or at least I almost believed it happened exactly as he said. I was seeing it as he was saying it. It did not seem speculation but an eyewitness revelation. An unemotional, unremorseful confession.

I was formulating a different opinion of Marino. He wasn't slow. He wasn't stupid. I think I liked him less than ever.

We headed east. The sun was caught in the leaves of the trees and rush hour was at its peak. For a while we were trapped in a sluggish flow of congestion, cars occupied by anonymous men and women on their way home from work. As I looked at the passing faces I felt out of synch, detached, as if I did not belong in the same world other people lived in. They were thinking about supper, perhaps the steaks they would cook on the grill, their children, the lover they would soon be seeing, or some event that had taken place during the day.

Marino was going down the list.

"Two weeks before her murder UPS delivered a package. Already checked out the delivery guy. Zip," he said. "Not long before that some guy came by to work on the plumbing. He squares okay, too, best we can tell. So far, we've come up with nothing to suggest any service person, delivery guy, what have you, is the same in the four cases. Not a single common denominator. No overlapping or similarities where the victims' jobs are concerned either."

Brenda Steppe was a fifth-grade teacher who taught at Quinton Elementary, not far from where she lived. She moved to Richmond five years ago, and had recently broken off her engagement to a soccer coach. She was a full-figured redhead, bright and good-humored. According to her friends and her former fiancé, she jogged several miles every day and neither smoked nor drank.

I probably knew more about her life than her family in Georgia did. She was a dutiful Baptist who attended church every Sunday and the suppers every Wednesday night. A musician, she played the guitar and led the singing at the youth group retreats. Her college major was English, which was also what she taught. Her favorite form of relaxation, in addition to jogging, was reading, and she was reading Doris Betts, it appeared, before switching off her bedside light that Friday night.

"The thing that sort of blew my mind," Marino told me, "is something I recently found out, one possible connection between her and Lori Petersen. Brenda Steppe was treated in the VMC ER about six weeks ago."

"For what?" I asked, surprised.

"A minor traffic accident. She got hit when she was backing out of her driveway one night. No big deal. She called the cops herself, said she'd bumped her head, was a little dizzy. An ambulance was dispatched. She was held a few hours in the ER for observation, X-rays. It was nothing."

"Was she treated during a shift when Lori Petersen was working?"

"That's the best part, maybe the only hit we've gotten so far. I checked with the supervisor. Lori Petersen was on that night. I'm running down everybody else who might've been around, orderlies, other doctors, you name it. Nothing so far except the freaky thought the two women may have met, having no idea that this very minute their murders would be in the process of being discussed by you and yours truly."

The thought went through me like a low-voltage shock. "What about Matt Petersen? Any chance he might have been at the hospital that night, perhaps to see his wife?"

Marino replied, "Says he was in Charlottesville. This was a Wednesday, around nine-thirty, ten P.M."

The hospital certainly could be a connection, I thought. Anyone who works there and has access to the records could have been familiar with Lori Petersen and might also have seen Brenda Steppe, whose address would be listed on her ER chart.

I suggested to Marino that everyone who may have been working at VMC the night she was treated should be turned inside out.

"We're only talking five thousand people," he replied. "And for all we know, the squirrel who took her out might've been treated in the ER that night, too. So I'm juggling that ball, too, and it don't look real promising at the moment. Half the people treated that shift was women. The other half was either old geezers suffering heart attacks or a couple of Young Turks who was tanked when they got in their cars. They didn't make it, or else are hanging around in comas even as we speak. A lot of people was in and out, and just between you and me, the record-keeping in that joint stinks. I may never know who was there. I'm never going to know who might've wandered in off the street. Could be the guy's some vulture who drifts in and out of hospitals, looking for victims — nurses, doctors, young women with minor problems."

He shrugged. "Could be he delivers flowers and is in and out of hospitals."

"You've mentioned this twice," I commented. "The bit about flower deliveries."

Another shrug. "Hey. Before I became a cop, I delivered flowers for a while, okay? Most flowers is sent to women. If I was going around wanting to meet women to whack, me, I'd deliver flowers."

I was sorry I'd asked.

"That's how I met my wife, as a matter of fact. Delivered a Sweetheart Special to her, nice arrangement of red and white carnations and a couple of sweetheart roses. From some drone she was dating. She ends up more impressed with me than with the flowers, and her boyfriend's gesture puts him out of business. This was in Jersey, a couple years before I moved to New York and signed on with the P.D."

I was seriously considering never accepting delivered flowers again.

"It's just something that jumps into my mind. Whoever he is, he's got some gig going. It puts him in touch with women. That's it, plain and simple."

We crept past Eastland Mall and took a right.

Soon we were out of traffic and gliding through Brookfield Heights, or the Heights, as it's usually called. The neighborhood is situated on a rise that almost passes for a hill. It's one of the older parts of town the young professionals have begun to take over during the last ten years. The streets are lined with row houses, some of them dilapidated and boarded up, most of them beautifully restored, with intricate wrought-iron balconies and stained-glass windows. Just a few blocks north the Heights deteriorates into a skid row; a few blocks beyond are federal housing projects.

"Some of these cribs are going to a hundred g's and up," Marino said as he slowed the car to a crawl. "I wouldn't take one if you gave it to me. I've been inside a few of 'em. Incredible. But no way you'd catch me living in this neighborhood. A fair number of single women here, too. Crazy. Just crazy."

I'd been eyeing the odometer. Patty Lewis's row house was exactly 6.7 miles from where Brenda Steppe lived. The neighborhoods were so different, so far from each other, I couldn't imagine anything about the locations that might link the crimes. There was construction going on here just as there was in Brenda's neighborhood, but it wasn't likely the companies or the crews were the same.

Patty Lewis's house was squeezed between two others, a lovely brownstone with a stained-glass window over the red front door. The roof was slate, the front porch girdled in freshly painted wrought iron. In back was a walled-in yard dense with big magnolias.

I'd seen the police photographs. It was hard to look at the graceful elegance of this turn-of-the-century home and believe anything so horrible happened inside it. She came from old money in the Shenandoah Valley, which was why, I assumed, she was able to afford living here. A free-lance writer, she struggled over a typewriter for many years and was just reaching the tier where rejection letters were war stories from the past. Last spring a story was published by *Harper's*. A novel was due out this fall. It would be a posthumous work.

Marino reminded me the killer, once again, got in through a window, this one leading into her bedroom, which faced the backyard.

"It's the one there on the end, on the second story," he was saying.

"Your theory is he climbed that magnolia closest to the house, got up on the porch roof and then through the window?"

"It's more than a theory," he retorted. "I'm sure of it. No other way he could've done it unless he had a ladder. It's more than possible to climb the tree, get on the porch roof and reach over to slide up the window. I know. I tried it myself to see if it could be done. Did it without a hitch. All the guy needs is sufficient upper-body strength to grab the edge of the roof from that thick lower tree branch," he pointed, "and pull himself up."

The brownstone had ceiling fans but no air-conditioning. According to an out-of-town friend who used to come to visit several times a year, Patty often slept with the bedroom window open. Simply put, it was a choice between being comfortable or being secure. She chose the former.

Marino made a lazy U-turn in the street and we headed northeast.

Cecile Tyler lived in Ginter Park, the oldest residential neighborhood in Richmond. There are monstrous three-story Victorian houses with wraparound porches wide enough to roller-skate on, and turrets, and dentil work along the eaves. Yards are thick with magnolias, oaks and rhododendrons. Grape vines climb over porch posts and arbors in back. I was envisioning dim living rooms beyond the blank windows, faded Oriental rugs, ornate furniture and cornices, and knickknacks jammed in every nook and cranny. I wouldn't have wanted to live here. It was giving me the same claustrophobic case of the creeps that ficus trees and Spanish moss do.

Hers was a two-story brick house, modest by her neighbors' standards. It was exactly 5.8 miles from where Patty Lewis lived. In the waning sun the slate roof glinted like lead. Shutters and doors were naked, stripped to the wood and still waiting for the fresh paint Cecile would have applied had she lived long enough.

The killer got in through a basement window behind a boxwood hedge on the north wing of the house. The lock was broken and, like everything else, waiting to be repaired.

She was a lovely black woman, recently divorced from a dentist now living in Tidewater. A receptionist at an employment agency, she was attending college classes at night to complete a degree in business. The last time she'd been seen alive was at approximately 10:00 P.M., a week ago Friday, about three hours before her death, I had estimated. She had dinner that night with a woman friend at a neighborhood Mexican restaurant, then went straight home.

Her body was found the next afternoon, Saturday. She was supposed to go shopping with her friend. Cecile's car was in the drive, and when she didn't answer the phone or the door, her friend got worried and peered through the slightly parted curtains of the bedroom window. The sight of Cecile's nude, bound body on top of the disarrayed bed wasn't something the friend was likely ever to forget.

"Bobbi," Marino said. "She's white, you know."

"Cecile's friend?" I'd forgotten her name.

"Yo. Bobbi. The rich bitch who found Cecile's body. The two of 'em was always together. Bobbi's got this red Porsche, a dynamite-looking blonde, works as a model. She's at Cecile's crib all the time, sometimes don't leave until early morning. Think the two of 'em were sweet on each other, you want my opinion. Blows my mind. I mean, it's hard to figure. Both of 'em good-looking enough to pop your eyes out. You'd think men would be hitting on 'em all the time . . ."

"Maybe that's your answer," I said in annoyance. "If your suspicions about the women are founded."

Marino smiled slyly. He was baiting me again.

"Well, my point is," he went on, "maybe the killer's cruising the neighborhood and sees Bobbi climbing into her red Porsche late one night. Maybe he thinks she lives here. Or maybe he follows her one night when she's on her way to Cecile's house."

"And he murders Cecile by mistake? Because he thought Bobbi lived here?"

"I'm just running it up the pole. Like I said, Bobbi's white. The other victims are white."

We sat in silence for a moment, staring at the house.

The racial mix continued to bother me, too. Three white women and one black woman. Why?

"One more thing I'll run up the pole," Marino said. "I've been wondering if the killer's got several candidates for each of these murders, like he chooses from the menu, ends up getting what he can afford. Sort of strange each time he sets out to kill one of 'em, she just happens to have a window unlocked or open or broke. It's either, in my opinion, a random situation, where he cruises and looks for anyone who seems to be alone and whose house is insecure, or else he's got access to a number of women and their addresses, and maybe makes the rounds, maybe cases a lotta residences in one night before finding the one that'll work for him."

I didn't like it.

"I think he stalked each of these women," I said, "that they were specific targets. I think he may have cased their homes before and either not found them in or found the windows locked. It may be the killer habitually visits the place where his next victim lives and then strikes when the opportunity presents itself."

He shrugged, playing with the idea. "Patty Lewis was murdered several weeks after Brenda Steppe. And Patty also was out of town visiting a friend the week prior to her murder. So it's possible he tried the weekend before and didn't find her home. Sure. Maybe it happened like that. Who's to say? Then he hits Cecile Tyler three weeks later. But he got to Lori Petersen exactly one week after that—who knows? Maybe he scored right off. A window was unlocked because the husband forgot to lock it. The killer could have had some sort of contact with Lori Petersen as recently as several days before he murdered her, and if her window hadn't been unlocked last weekend he'd be back this weekend, trying again."

"The weekend," I said. "That seems to be important to him, important to strike on a late Friday night or in the first hour or so of Saturday morning."

Marino nodded. "Oh, yeah. It's calculated. Me, I think it's because he works Monday through Friday, has the weekend off to chill out after he's done it. Probably he likes the pattern for another reason, too. It's a way of jerking us around. Friday comes and he knows the city, people like you and me, are nervous as a cat in the middle of a freeway."

I hesitated, then broached the subject. "Do you think his pattern is escalating? That the murders are more closely spaced because he's getting more stressed, perhaps by all the publicity?"

He didn't comment right away. Then he spoke very seriously, "He's a friggin' addict, Doc. Once he starts, he can't stop."

"You're saying the publicity has nothing to do with his pattern?"

"No," he replied, "I'm not saying that. His pattern's to lay low and keep his mouth shut, and maybe he wouldn't be so cool if the reporters wasn't making it so damn easy for him. The sensational stories are a gift. He don't have to do any work. The reporters are rewarding him, giving it to him free. Now if nobody was writing up nothing, he'd get frustrated, more reckless maybe. After a while, maybe he'd start sending notes, making phone calls, doing something to get the reporters going. He might screw up."

We were quiet awhile.

Then Marino caught me off guard.

"Sounds like you been talking to Fortosis."

"Why?"

"The stuff about it escalating and the news stories stressing him, making his urge peak quicker."

"Is this what he's told you?"

He casually slipped off his sunglasses and set them on the dash. When he looked at me his eyes were faintly glinting with anger. "Nope. But he's told a couple people near and dear to my heart. Boltz, for one. Tanner, for another."

"How do you know that?"

"Because I got as many snitches inside the department as I got on the street. I know exactly what's going down and where it's going to end—maybe."

We sat in silence. The sun had dipped below rooftops and long shadows were creeping over the lawns and street. In a way, Marino had just cracked the door that would take us into each other's confidence. He knew. He was telling me he knew. I wondered if I dared push the door open wider.

"Boltz, Tanner, the powers-that-be are very upset by the leaks to the press," I said cautiously.

"May as well have a nervous breakdown over the rain. It happens. 'Specially when you got 'Dear Abby' living in the same city."

I smiled ruefully. How appropriate. Spill your secrets to "Dear Abby" Turnbull and she prints every one of them in the paper.

"She's a big problem," he went on. "Has the inside track, a line hooked straight into the heart of the department. I don't think the chief takes a whiz without her knowing it."

"Who's telling her?"

"Let's just say I got my suspicions but I haven't got the goods yet to go nowhere with them, okay?"

"You know someone's been getting into my office computer," I said as if it were common knowledge.

He glanced sharply at me. "Since when?"

"I don't know. Several days ago someone got in and tried to pull up Lori Petersen's case. It was luck we discovered it—a onetime oversight made by my computer analyst resulted in the perpetrator's commands appearing on the screen."

"You're saying someone could've been getting in for months and you wouldn't know?"

"That's what I'm saying."

He got quiet, his face hard.

I pressed him. "Changes your suspicions?"

"Huh," he said shortly.

"That's it?" I asked in exasperation. "You don't have anything to say?"

"Nope. Except your ass must be getting close to the fire these days. Amburgey know?"

"He knows."

"Tanner, too, I guess."

"Yes."

"Huh," he said again. "Guess that explains a couple things."

"Like what?" My paranoia was smoldering and I knew Marino could see I was squirming. "What things?"

He didn't reply.

"*What things?*" I demanded.

He slowly looked over at me. "You really want to know?"

"I think I'd better." My steady voice belied my fear, which was quickly mounting into panic.

"Well, I'll put it to you like this. If Tanner knew you and me was riding around together this afternoon, he'd probably jerk my badge."

I stared at him in open bewilderment. "What are you saying?"

"See, I ran into him at HQ this morning. He called me aside for a little chat, said he and some of the brass are clamping down on the leaks. Tanner told me to be real tight-lipped about the investigation. As if I needed to be told that. Hell. But he said something else that didn't make a whole lot of sense at the time. Point is, I'm not supposed to be telling anyone at your office—meaning you—shit about what's going on anymore."

"What—"

He went on, "How the investigation's going and what we're thinking, I'm saying. You're not supposed to be told squat. Tanner's orders are for us to get the medical info from you but not give you so much as the time of day. He said too much has been floating around and the only way to put a stop to it is not say a word to anyone except those of us who got to know in order to work the cases . . ."

"That's right," I snapped. "And that includes me. These cases are within my jurisdiction—or has everyone suddenly forgotten that?"

"Hey," he said quietly, staring at me. "We're sitting here, right?"

"Yes," I replied more calmly. "We are."

"Me, I don't give a shit what Tanner says. So maybe he's just antsy because of your computer mess. Doesn't want the cops blamed for giving out sensitive information to Dial-a-Leak at the ME's office."

"Please . . ."

"Maybe there's another reason," he muttered to himself.

Whatever it was, he had no intention of telling me.

He roughly shoved the car in gear and we were off toward the river, south to Berkley Downs.

For the next ten, fifteen, twenty minutes—I wasn't really aware of the time—we didn't say a word to each other. I was left sitting in a miserable silence, watching the roadside flash by my window. It was like being the butt of a cruel joke or a plot to which everyone was privy but me. My sense of isolation was becoming unbearable, my fears so acute I no longer was sure of my judgment, my acumen, my reason. I don't think I was sure of anything.

All I could do was picture the debris of what just days ago was a desirable professional future. My office was being blamed for the leaks. My attempts at modernization had undermined my own rigid standards of confidentiality.

Even Bill was no longer sure of my credibility. Now the cops were no longer supposed to talk to me. It wouldn't end until I had been turned into the scapegoat for all the atrocities caused by these murders. Amburgey probably would have no choice but to ease me out of office if he didn't outright fire me.

Marino was glancing over at me.

I'd scarcely been aware of his pulling off the road and parking.

"How far is it?" I asked.

"From what?"

"From where we just were, from where Cecile lived?"

"Exactly seven-point-four miles," he replied laconically, without a glance at the odometer.

In the light of day, I almost didn't recognize Lori Petersen's house.

It looked empty and unlived in, wearing the patina of neglect. The white clapboard siding was dingy in the shadows, the Wedgwood shutters seeming a dusky blue. The lilies beneath the front windows had been trampled, probably by investigators combing every inch of the property for evidence. A tatter of yellow crime-scene tape remained tacked to the door frame, and in the overgrown grass was a beer can that some thoughtless passerby had tossed out of his car.

Her house was the modest tidy house of middle-class America, the sort of place found in every small town and every small neighborhood. It was the place where people got started in life and migrated back to during their later years: young professionals, young couples and, finally, older people retired and with children grown and gone.

It was almost exactly like the Johnsons' white clapboard house where I rented a room during my medical school years in Baltimore. Like Lori Petersen, I had existed in a grueling oblivion, out the door at dawn and often not returning until the following evening. Survival was limited to books, labs, examinations, rotations, and sustaining the physical and emotional energy to get through it all. It would never have occurred to me, just as it never occurred to Lori, that someone I did not know might decide to take my life.

"Hey . . ."

I suddenly realized Marino was talking to me.

His eyes were curious. "You all right, Doc?"

"I'm sorry. I didn't catch what you were saying."

"I asked what you thought. You know, you got a map in your head. What do you think?"

I abstractedly replied, "I think their deaths have nothing to do with where they lived."

He didn't agree or disagree. Snatching up his hand mike, he told the dispatcher he was EOT. He was marking off for the day. The tour was over.

"Ten-four, seven-ten," the cocky voice crackled back. "Eighteen-forty-five hours, watch the sun in your eyes, same time tomorrow they'll be playing our song . . ."

Which was sirens and gunfire and people crashing into each other, I assumed.

Marino snorted. "When I was coming along, you so much as gave a 'Yo' instead of a ten-four the inspector'd write up your ass."

I briefly shut my eyes and kneaded my temples.

"Sure ain't what it used to be," he said. "Hell, nothing is."

9

THE MOON WAS a milk-glass globe through gaps in the trees as I drove through the quiet neighborhood where I lived.

Lush branches were moving black shapes along the roadside, and the mica-flecked pavement glittered in the sweep of my headlights. The air was clear and pleasantly warm, perfect for convertibles or windows rolled down. I was driving with my doors locked, my windows shut, and the fan on low.

The very sort of evening I would have found enchanting in the past was now unsettling.

The images from the day were before me, as the moon was before me. They haunted me and wouldn't let me go. I saw each of those unassuming houses in unrelated parts of the city. How had he chosen them? And why? It wasn't chance. I strongly believed that. There had to be some element consistent with each case, and I was continually drawn back to the sparkling residue we'd been finding on the bodies. With absolutely no evidence to go on, I was profoundly sure this glitter was the missing link connecting him to each of his victims.

That was as far as my intuition would take me. When I attempted to envision more, my mind went blank. Was the glitter a clue that could lead us to where he lived? Was it related to some profession or recreation that gave him his initial contact with the women he would murder? Or stranger yet, did the residue originate with the women themselves?

Maybe it *was* something each victim had in her house—or even on her person or in her workplace. Maybe it was something each woman purchased from him. God only knew. We couldn't test every item found in a person's house or office or some other place frequently visited, especially if we had no idea what we were looking for.

I turned into my drive.

Before I'd parked my car, Bertha was opening the front door. She stood in the glare of the porch light, her hands on her hips, her purse looped over a wrist. I knew what this meant—she was in one big hurry to leave. I hated to think what Lucy had been like today.

"Well?" I asked when I got to the door.

Bertha started shaking her head. "Terrible, Dr. Kay. That child. Uh-uh! Don't know what in the world's got in her. She been bad, bad, bad."

I'd reached the ragged edge of this worn-out day. Lucy was in a decline. In the main, it was my fault. I hadn't handled her well. Or perhaps I'd *handled* her, period, and that was a better way to state the problem.

Not accustomed to confronting children with the same forthrightness and bluntness that I used with relative impunity on adults, I hadn't questioned her about the computer violation, nor had I so much as alluded to it. Instead, after Bill left my house Monday night, I had disconnected the telephone modem in my office and carried it upstairs to my closet.

My rationale was Lucy would assume I took it downtown, in for repairs, or something along these lines, if she noticed its absence at all. Last night she made no mention of the missing modem, but was subdued, her eyes fleeting and hinting of hurt when I caught her watching me instead of the movie I'd inserted in the VCR.

What I did was purely logical. If there were even the slightest chance it was Lucy who broke into the computer downtown, then the removal of the modem obviated her doing it again without my accusing her or instigating a painful scene that would tarnish our memories of her visit. If the violation did recur, it would prove Lucy couldn't be the perpetrator, should there ever be a question.

All this when I know human relationships are not founded on reason any more than my roses are fertilized with debate. I know seeking asylum behind the wall of intellect and rationality is a selfish retreating into self-protectiveness at the expense of another's well-being.

What I did was so intelligent it was as stupid as hell.

I remembered my own childhood, how much I hated the games my mother used to play when she would sit on the edge of my bed and answer questions about my father. He had a "bug" at first, something that "gets in the blood" and causes relapses every so often. Or he was fighting off "something some colored person" or "Cuban" carried into his grocery store. Or "he works too hard and gets himself run down, Kay." Lies.

My father had chronic lymphatic leukemia. It was diagnosed before I entered the first grade. It wasn't until I was twelve and he deteriorated from stage-zero lymphocytosis to stage-three anemia that I was told he was dying.

We lie to children even though we didn't believe the lies we were told when we were their age. I don't know why we do that. I didn't know why I'd been doing it with Lucy, who was as quick as any adult.

By eight-thirty she and I were sitting at the kitchen table. She was fiddling with a milk shake and I was drinking a much-needed tumbler of Scotch. Her change in demeanor was unsettling and I was fast losing my nerve.

All the fight in her had vanished; all of the petulance and resentment over my absences had retreated. I couldn't seem to warm her or cheer her up, not even when I said Bill would be dropping by just in time to say good-night to her. There was scarcely a glimmer of interest. She didn't move or respond, and she wouldn't meet my eyes.

"You look sick," she finally muttered.

"How would you know? You haven't looked at me once since I've been home."

"So. You still look sick."

"Well, I'm not sick," I told her. "I'm just very tired."

"When Mom gets tired she doesn't look sick," she said, halfway accusing me. "She only looks sick when she fights with Ralph. I hate Ralph. He's a dick head. When he comes over, I make him do 'Jumble' in the paper just because I know he can't. He's a stupid-ass dick head."

I didn't admonish her for her dirty mouth. I didn't say a word.

"So," she persisted, "you have a fight with Ralph?"

"I don't know any Ralphs."

"Oh." A frown. "Mr. Boltz is mad at you, I bet."

"I don't think so."

"I bet he is too. He's mad because I'm here—"

"Lucy! That's ridiculous. Bill likes you very much."

"Ha! He's mad 'cause he can't *do it* when I'm here!"

"Lucy . . ." I warned.

"That's it. Ha! He's mad 'cause he's gotta keep his pants on."

"Lucy," I spoke severely. "Stop it this minute!"

She finally gave me her eyes and I was startled by their anger. "See. I knew it!" She laughed in a mean way. "And you wish I wasn't here so I couldn't get in the way. Then he wouldn't have to go home at night. Well, I don't care. So there. Mom sleeps with her boyfriends all the time and I don't care!"

"I'm not your Mom!"

Her lower lip quivered as if I'd slapped her. "I never said you were! I wouldn't want you to be anyway! I hate you!"

Both of us sat very still.

I was momentarily stunned. I couldn't remember anyone's ever saying he hated me, even if it was true.

"Lucy," I faltered. My stomach was knotted like a fist. I felt sick. "I didn't mean it like that. What I meant was I'm not like your mother. Okay? We're very different. Always have been very different. But this doesn't mean I don't care very much for you."

She didn't respond.

"I know you don't really hate me."

She remained stonily silent.

I dully got up to refresh my drink. Of course she didn't really hate me. Children say that all the time and don't mean it. I tried to remember. I never told my mother I hated her. I think I secretly did, at least when I was a child, because of the lies, and because when I lost my father I lost her, too. She was as consumed by his dying as he was consumed by his disease. There was nothing warm-blooded left for Dorothy and me.

I had lied to Lucy. I was consumed, too, not by the dying but by the dead. Every day I did battle for justice. But what justice was there for a living little girl who didn't feel loved? Dear Lord. Lucy didn't hate me but maybe I couldn't blame her if she did. Returning to the table, I approached the forbidden subject as delicately as possible.

"I guess I look worried because I am, Lucy. You see, someone got into the computer downtown."

She was quiet, waiting.

I sipped my drink. "I'm not sure this person saw anything that matters, but if I could explain how it happened or who did it, it would be a big load off my mind."

Still, she said nothing.

I forced it.

"If I don't get to the bottom of it, Lucy, I might be in trouble."

This seemed to alarm her.

"Why would you be in trouble?"

"Because," I calmly explained, "my office data is very sensitive, and important people in city and state government are concerned over the information that is somehow ending up in the newspapers. Some people are worried the information might be coming from my office computer."

"Oh."

"If a reporter somehow got in, for example . . ."

"Information about what?" she asked.

"These recent cases."

"The lady doctor who got killed."

I nodded.

Silence.

Then she said sullenly, "That's why the modem's gone, isn't it, Auntie Kay? You took it because you think I did something bad."

"I don't think you did anything bad, Lucy. If you dialed into my office computer, I know you didn't do it to be bad. I wouldn't blame you for being curious."

She looked up at me, her eyes welling. "You took away the modem 'cause you don't trust me anymore."

I didn't know how to respond to this. I couldn't lie to her, and the truth would be an admission that I didn't really trust her.

Lucy had lost all interest in her milk shake and was sitting very still, chewing her bottom lip as she stared down at the table.

"I did remove the modem because I wondered if it was you," I confessed. "That wasn't the right thing for me to do. I should have just asked you. But maybe I was hurt. It hurt me to think you might have broken our trust."

She looked at me for a long time. She seemed strangely pleased, almost happy when she asked, "You mean my doing something bad hurt your feelings?"—as if this gave her some sort of power or validation she desperately wanted.

"Yes. Because I love you very much, Lucy," I said, and I think it was the first time I'd ever told her that so clearly. "I didn't intend to hurt your feelings any more than you intended to hurt mine. I'm sorry."

"It's okay."

The spoon clacked the side of the glass as she stirred her milk shake and cheerfully exclaimed, "Besides, I knew you hid it. You can't hide things from me, Auntie Kay. I saw it in your closet. I looked while Bertha was making lunch. I found it on the shelf right next to your .38."

"How did you know it's a .38?" I blurted without thinking.

" 'Cause Andy has a .38. He was before Ralph. Andy has a .38 on his belt, right here," pointing to the small of her back. "He owns a pawnshop and that's why he always wears a .38. He used to show it to me and how it works. He'd take all the bullets out and let me shoot it at the TV. Bang! Bang! It's really neat! Bang! Bang!" Shooting her finger at the refrigerator. "I like him better than Ralph but Mom got tired of him, I guess."

This was what I was sending her home to tomorrow? I started lecturing her on handguns, reciting all the lines about how they aren't toys and can hurt people, when the telephone rang.

"Oh, yeah," Lucy remembered as I got out of the chair. "Grans called before you got home. Twice."

She was the last person I wanted to talk to right now. No matter how well I disguised my moods she always managed to sense them and wouldn't let them alone.

"You sound depressed," my mother said two sentences into the conversation.

"I'm just tired." That shopworn line again.

I could see her as if she were before me. No doubt she was sitting up in bed, several pillows behind her back, the television softly playing. I have my father's coloring. My mother is dark, her black hair white now and softly framing her round, full face, her brown eyes large behind her thick glasses.

"Of course you're tired," she started in. "All you do is work. And those horrible cases in Richmond. There was a story about them in the *Herald* yesterday, Kay. I've never been so surprised in my life. I didn't even see it until this afternoon when Mrs. Martinez dropped by with it. I stopped getting the Sunday paper. All those inserts and coupons and ads. It's so fat I can't be bothered. Mrs. Martinez came by with it because your picture's in it."

I groaned.

"Can't say I would have recognized you. It's not very good, taken at night, but your name's under it, sure enough. And wearing no hat, Kay. Looked like it was raining or wet and nasty out and here you are not wearing a hat. All those hats I've crocheted for you and you can't even bother to wear one of your mother's hats so you don't catch pneumonia . . ."

"Mother . . ."

She went on.

"Mother!"

I couldn't stand it, not tonight. I could be Maggie Thatcher and my mother would persist in treating me like a five-year-old who doesn't have sense enough to come out of the rain.

Next came the run of questions about my diet and whether I was getting enough sleep.

I abruptly derailed her. "How's Dorothy?"

She hesitated. "Well, that's why I'm calling."

I scooted over to a chair and sat down as my mother's voice went up an octave and she proceeded to tell me Dorothy had flown to Nevada—to get married.

"Why Nevada?" I stupidly asked.

"You tell me! You tell me why your only sister meets with some book person she's only talked to over the phone in the past, and suddenly calls her mother from the airport to say she's on her way to Nevada to get married. You tell me how my daughter could do something like that. You think she had macaroni for brains . . .

"What sort of book person?" I glanced at Lucy. She was watching me, her face stricken.

"I don't know. Some illustrator she called him, I guess he draws the pictures for her books, was in Miami a few days ago for some convention and got with Dorothy to discuss her current project or something. Don't ask me. His name's Jacob Blank. Jewish, I just know it. Though Dorothy certainly couldn't tell me. Why should she tell her mother she's marrying a Jew I've never met who's twice her age and draws kiddy pictures, for crummy sake?"

I didn't even ask.

To send Lucy home in the midst of yet another family crisis was unthinkable. Her absences from her mother had been prolonged before, whenever Dorothy had to dash out of town for an editorial meeting or a research trip or one of her numerous "book talks" that always seemed to detain her longer than anyone had supposed. Lucy would remain with her grandmother until the wandering writer eventually made it back home. Maybe we had learned to accept these lapses into blatant irresponsibility. Maybe even Lucy had. But eloping? Good God.

"She didn't say when she'd be back?" I turned away from Lucy and lowered my voice.

"What?" my mother said loudly. "Tell *me* such a thing? Why should she tell her mother that? Oh! How could she do this again, Kay! He's *twice* her age! Armando was twice her age and look what happened to him! He drops dead by the pool before Lucy's even old enough to ride a bicycle . . ."

It took me a while to ease her out of hysteria. After I hung up, I was left with the fallout.

I couldn't think of a way to cushion the news. "Your mother's gone out of town for a little while, Lucy. She's gotten married to Mr. Blank, who illustrates her books for her . . ."

She was as still as a statue. I reached out my arms to pull her into an embrace.

"They're in Nevada at the moment—"

The chair jerked back and fell against the wall as she wrenched away from me and fled to her room.

How could my sister do this to Lucy? I was sure I would never forgive her, not this time. It was bad enough when she married Armando. She was barely eighteen. We warned her. We did everything to talk her out of it. He hardly spoke English, was old enough to be her father, and we were uneasily suspicious of his wealth, of his Mercedes, his gold Rolex and his posh waterfront apartment. Like a lot of people who appear mysteriously in Miami, he enjoyed a high-rolling life-style that couldn't be explained logically.

Damn Dorothy. She knew about my work, knew how demanding and relentless it was. She knew I'd been hesitant about Lucy's coming at all right now because of these cases! But it was planned, and Dorothy cajoled and convinced with her charms.

"If it gets too inconvenient, Kay, you can just send her back and we'll reschedule," she had said sweetly. "*Really*. She's so desperately looking forward to it. It's all she talks about these days. She simply *adores* you. A genuine case of hero worship if I ever saw it."

Lucy was sitting stiffly on the edge of her bed, staring at the floor.

"I hope they get killed in a plane crash" was the only thing she said to me as I helped her into her pajamas.

"You don't mean that, Lucy." I smoothed the daisy-spangled spread beneath her chin. "You can stay with me for a while. That will be nice, won't it?"

She squeezed her eyes shut and turned her face to the wall.

My tongue felt thick and slow. There were no words that would ease her pain, so I sat looking helplessly at her for a while. Hesitantly, I moved closer to her and began to rub her back. Gradually her misery seemed to fade, and eventually she began breathing the deep, regular breaths of sleep. I kissed the top of her head and softly shut her door.

Halfway back to the kitchen, I heard Bill pull in.

I got to the door before he had a chance to ring the bell.

"Lucy's asleep," I whispered.

"Oh," he playfully whispered back. "Too bad—so I wasn't worth waiting up for—"

He suddenly turned, following my startled eyes out to the street. Headlights cut around the bend and were instantly extinguished at the same time a car I could not make out came to an abrupt stop. Now it was accelerating in reverse, the engine loudly straining.

Pebbles and grit popped as it turned around beyond the trees and sped away.

"Expecting company?" Bill muttered, staring out into the darkness.

I slowly shook my head.

He stole a glance at his watch and lightly nudged me into the foyer.

Whenever Marino came to the OCME, he never failed to needle Wingo, who was probably the best autopsy technician I'd ever worked with and by far the most fragile.

". . . Yo. It's what's known as a close encounter of the *Ford* kind . . ." Marino was loudly going on.

A bay-windowed state trooper who arrived at the same time Marino did guffawed again.

Wingo's face was bright red as he stabbed the plug of the Stryker saw into the yellow cord reel dangling over the steel table.

Up to my wrists in blood, I mumbled under my breath, "Ignore it, Wingo."

Marino cut his eyes at the trooper, and I waited for the limp wrist act to follow.

Wingo was much too sensitive for his own good and I sometimes worried about him. He so keenly identified with the victims it wasn't uncommon for him to cry over unusually heinous cases.

The morning had presented one of life's cruel ironies. A young woman had gone to a bar in a rural area of a neighboring county last night, and as she started walking home around 2:00 A.M. she was struck by a car that kept on going. The state trooper, examining her personal effects, had just discovered inside her billfold a slip of paper from a fortune cookie which predicted, "You will soon have an encounter that will change the course of your life."

"Or maybe she was looking for Mr. HOODbar . . ."

I was just on the verge of blowing up at Marino when his voice was drowned out by the Stryker saw, which sounded like a loud dentist's drill as Wingo began cutting through the dead woman's skull. A bony dust unpleasantly drifted on the air and Marino and the trooper retreated to the other end of the suite where the autopsy of Richmond's latest shooting homicide was being performed on the last table.

When the saw was silenced and the skull cap removed, I stopped what I was doing to make a quick inspection of the brain. No subdural or subarachnoid hemorrhages . . .

"It isn't funny," Wingo began his indignant litany, "not the least bit funny. How can anybody laugh at something like that . . ."

The woman's scalp was lacerated but that was it. What killed her were multiple pelvic fractures, the blow to her buttocks so violent the pattern of the vehicle's grille was clearly visible on her skin. She wasn't struck by something low to the ground, such as a sports car. Might have been a truck.

"She saved it because it meant something to her. Like it was something she wanted to believe. Maybe that's why she went to the bar last night. She was looking for someone she'd been waiting for all her life. Her *encounter*. And it turns out to be some drunk driver who knocks her fifty feet into a ditch."

"Wingo," I said wearily as I began taking photographs, "it's better if you don't imagine some things."

"I can't help it . . ."

"You have to learn to help it."

He cast wounded eyes in the direction of Marino, who was never satisfied unless he got a rise out of him. Poor Wingo. Most members of the rough-and-tumble world of law enforcement were more than a little put off by him. He didn't laugh at their jokes or particularly relish their war stories, and more to the point, he was, well, different.

Tall and lithely built, he had black hair cropped close on the sides with a cockatoo spray on top and a rat tail curling at the nape of his neck. Delicately handsome, he looked like a model in the loose-fitting designer clothes and soft leather European shoes he wore. Even his indigo-blue scrubs, which he bought and laundered himself, were stylish. He didn't flirt. He didn't resent having a woman tell him what to do. He never seemed remotely interested in what I looked like beneath my lab coat or all-business Britches of Georgetown suits. I'd grown so comfortable around him that on the few occasions when he accidentally walked into the locker room while I was changing into my scrubs, I was scarcely aware of him.

I suppose if I'd wondered about his proclivities when he interviewed for the job several months ago I might have been less enthusiastic about hiring him. It was something I didn't like to admit.

But it was all too easy to stereotype because I saw the worst example of every sort in this place. There were the transvestites with their falsies and padded hips, and the gays who flew into jealous rages and murdered their lovers, and the chicken hawks who cruised parks and video arcades and got carved up by homophobic rednecks. There were the prisoners with their obscene tattoos and histories of sodomizing anything on two legs inside the cell blocks, and there were the profligate purveyors in bathhouses and bars who didn't care who else got AIDS.

Wingo didn't fit. Wingo was just Wingo.

"You can handle it from here?" He was angrily rinsing off his gloved and bloody hands.

"I'll finish up," I replied abstractedly as I resumed measuring a large tear of the mesentery.

Walking off to a cabinet, he began to collect spray bottles of disinfectants, rags and the other odds and ends he used for cleaning. Slipping a small set of headphones over his ears, he switched on the tape player attached to the waistband of his scrubs, momentarily shutting out the world.

Fifteen minutes later he was cleaning out the small refrigerator where evidence was stored inside the autopsy suite over the weekend. I vaguely noticed him pulling something out and looking at it for a long moment.

When he came over to my table, he was wearing his headphones around his neck like a collar, and he had a puzzled, uneasy expression on his face. In his hand was a small cardboard slide folder from a PERK.

"Uh, Dr. Scarpetta," he said, clearing his throat, "this was inside the fridge."

He didn't explain.

He didn't need to.

I set down the scalpel as my stomach tightened. Printed on the slide folder label was the case number, name and date of the autopsy of Lori Petersen—whose evidence, all of it, had been turned in four days earlier.

"You found this in the refrigerator?"

There had to be some mistake.

"In the back, on the bottom shelf." Hesitantly, he added, "Uh, it's not initialed. I mean, you didn't initial it."

There had to be an explanation.

"Of course I didn't initial it," I said sharply. "I collected only one PERK in her case, Wingo."

Even as I said the words, doubt wavered deep inside me like a windblown flame. I tried to remember.

I stored Lori Petersen's samples in the refrigerator over the weekend, along with the samples from all of Saturday's cases. I distinctly remembered receipting her samples in person to the labs Monday morning, including a cardboard folder of slides smeared with anal, oral and vaginal swabs. I was sure I used only one cardboard folder of slides. I never sent up a slide folder bare—it was always enclosed inside a plastic bag containing the swabs, envelopes of hair, test tubes and everything else.

"I have no idea where this came from," I told him too adamantly.

He uncomfortably shifted his weight to his other foot and averted his eyes. I knew what he was thinking. I'd screwed up and he hated to be the one who had to point it out to me.

The threat had always been there. Wingo and I had gone over it numerous times in the past, ever since Margaret loaded the PC in the autopsy suite with the label programs.

Before one of the pathologists started a case he went to that PC and typed in information about the decedent whose autopsy he was about to perform. A run of labels was generated for every sample one might possibly collect, such as blood, bile, urine, stomach contents and a PERK. It saved a lot of time and was perfectly acceptable provided the pathologist was careful to stick the right label on the right tube and remembered to initial it.

There was one feature of this bit of automated enlightenment that had always made me nervous. Inevitably there were leftover labels because one didn't, as a rule, collect every possible sample, especially when labs were overworked and understaffed. I wasn't going to send fingernail clippings to trace evidence, for example, if the decedent was an eighty-year-old man who died of a myocardial infarct while cutting his grass.

What to do with leftover labels? You certainly didn't want to leave them lying around where they might find their way onto the wrong test tubes. Most of the pathologists tore them up. It was my habit to file them with the person's case folder. It was a quick way to know what was tested for, what wasn't, and how many tubes of this or that I'd actually sent upstairs.

Wingo had trotted across the suite and was running a finger down the pages of the morgue log. I could feel Marino staring across the suite at me as he waited to collect the bullets from his homicide case. He wandered my way just as Wingo got back.

"We had six cases that day," Wingo reminded me as if Marino were not there. "Saturday. I remember. There were a lot of labels on the counter over there. Maybe one of them—"

"No," I said loudly. "I don't see how. I didn't leave any leftover labels from her case lying around. They were with my paperwork, clipped to my clipboard—"

"Shit," Marino said in surprise. He was looking over my shoulder. "That what I think it is?"

Frantically pulling off my gloves, I took the folder from Wingo and slit the tape with a thumbnail. Inside were four slides, three of which were definitely smeared with something, but they were not hand-marked with the standard "O," "A," or "V," designating which samples they were. They weren't marked at all, except by the computer label on the outside of the folder.

"So, maybe you labeled this thinking you were going to use it, changed your mind or something?" Wingo suggested.

I didn't reply right away. I couldn't remember!

"When was the last time you went inside the refrigerator?" I asked him.

A shrug. "Last week, maybe a week ago Monday when I got out the stuff so the doctors could take it up. I wasn't in this past Monday. This is the first time I've looked in the fridge this week."

I slowly recalled that Wingo had taken comp time on Monday. I myself had gotten Lori Petersen's evidence out of the refrigerator before making evidence rounds. Was it possible I overlooked this cardboard folder? Was it possible I was so fatigued, so distracted, I got her evidence mixed up with evidence from one of the five other cases we had that day? If so, which cardboard folder of slides was really from her case—the one I receipted upstairs, or this one? I couldn't believe this was happening. I was always so careful!

I rarely wore my scrubs out of the morgue. Almost never. Not even when there was a fire drill. Several minutes later, lab workers glanced curiously at me as I walked briskly down the third-floor hall in my blood-spattered greens. Betty was inside her cramped office taking a coffee break. She took one look at me and her eyes froze.

"We've got a problem," I said right off.

She stared at the cardboard folder, at the label on it.

"Wingo was cleaning out the evidence refrigerator. He found it a few minutes ago."

"Oh, God," was all she said.

As I followed her into the serology lab, I was explaining I had no recollection of labeling two folders from PERKs in Lori's case. I was clueless.

Working her hands into a pair of gloves, she reached for bottles inside a cabinet as she attempted to reassure me. "I think the ones you sent me, Kay, have to be right. The slides were consistent with the swabs, with everything else you receipted. Everything came up as nonsecreter, was consistent. This must be an extra you don't remember taking."

Another tremor of doubt. I had taken only one folder of slides, or had I? Could I swear to it? Last Saturday seemed a blur. I couldn't retrace my every step with certainty.

"No swabs with this, I take it?" she asked.

"None," I replied. "Just this folder of slides. That's all Wingo found."

"Hmm." She was thinking. "Let's see what we have here." She placed each slide under the phase microscope, and after a long silence, said, "We've got big squamous cells, meaning these could be oral or vaginal, but not anal. And"—she looked up—"I'm not seeing any sperm."

"Lord," I groaned.

"We'll try again," she answered.

Tearing open a packet of sterilized swabs, she moistened them with water and began gently rolling one at a time over a portion of each smear on each slide—three in all. Next she smeared the swabs over small circles of white filter paper.

Getting out the medicine droppers, she began deftly dripping naphthyl acid phosphate over the filter paper. Then came the fast-blue B salt. We stared, waiting for the first hint of purple.

The smears didn't react. They sat there in tiny wet stains tormenting me. I continued to stare beyond the brief period of time the smears needed to react as if I could somehow will them into testing positive for seminal fluid. I wanted to believe this was an extra file of slides. I wanted to believe I *had* taken two PERKs in Lori's case and just didn't remember. I wanted to believe anything except what was becoming patently clear.

The slides Wingo had found were not from Lori's case. They couldn't be.

Betty's impassive face told me she was worried, too, and doing her best not to let it show.

I shook my head.

She was forced to conclude, "Then it doesn't seem likely these are from Lori's case." A pause. "I'll do what I can to group them, of course. See if there are any Barr bodies present, that sort of thing."

"Please." I took a deep breath.

She went on, trying to make me feel better. "The fluids I separated out from the killer's fluids are consistent with Lori's blood samples. I don't think you have a worry. There's no doubt in my mind about the first file sent in . . ."

"The question has been raised," I said, miserable.

Lawyers would love it. Good God, would they love it. They'd have a jury doubting any of the samples were Lori's, including the tubes of blood. They'd have a jury wondering if the samples sent to New York for DNA testing were the right ones. Who was to say that they weren't from some other dead body?

My voice was on the verge of trembling when I told her, "We had six cases that day, Betty. Three of them merited PERKs, were potential sexual assaults."

"All female?"

"Yes," I muttered. "All of them women."

What Bill said Wednesday night when he was stressed, his tongue lubricated by liquor, was branded in my mind. What would happen to these cases should my credibility be compromised? Not only would Lori's case come into question, all of them would. I was cornered, absolutely and with no way out. I couldn't pretend this file didn't exist. It did exist and what it meant was I couldn't honestly swear in the court the chain of evidence was intact.

There was no second chance. I couldn't collect the samples again, start from scratch. Lori's samples had already been hand-delivered to the New York lab. Her embalmed body had been buried Tuesday. An exhumation, forget it. It wouldn't be profitable. It would be, however, a sensational event sparking enormous public curiosity. Everyone would want to know why.

Betty and I both glanced toward the door at the same time as Marino casually walked in.

"I just had a freaky little thought, Doc." He paused, his face hard as his eyes wandered to the slides and filter paper on the countertop.

I stared numbly at him.

"Me, I'd take this PERK here over to Vander. Maybe you left it in the fridge. Then again, maybe you didn't."

A sense of alarm fluttered through my blood before the jolt of comprehension.

"What?" I asked, as if he were crazy. "Someone else put it there?"

He shrugged. "I'm just suggesting you consider every possibility."

"Who?"

"Got no idea."

"How? How could that be possible? Someone would have to have gotten inside the autopsy suite, had access to the refrigerator. And the file is labeled . . ."

The labels: it was coming to me. The computer-generated labels left over from Lori's autopsy. They were inside her case file. No one had been inside her file except me—and Amburgey, Tanner and Bill.

When the three men left my office early Monday evening, the front doors were chained. All of them went out through the morgue. Amburgey and Tanner had left first, and Bill a little later.

The autopsy suite was locked, but the walk-in refrigerator was not. We had to leave the refrigerator unlocked so funeral homes and rescue squads could deliver bodies after hours. The walk-in refrigerator had two doors, one opening onto the hallway, another leading into the autopsy suite. Had one of the men gone though the refrigerator and into the suite? On a shelf near the first table were stacks of evidence kits, including dozens of PERKs. Wingo always kept the shelves fully stocked.

I reached for the phone and instructed Rose to unlock my desk drawer and open Lori Petersen's case file.

"There should be some evidence labels inside," I told her.

While she checked, I tried to remember. There were six, maybe seven labels left over, not because I didn't collect a lot of samples but because I collected so many of them—almost twice as many as usual, resulting in my generating not one, but two runs of computerized labels. Left over should be labels for heart, lung, kidney and other organs, and an extra one for a PERK.

"Dr. Scarpetta?" Rose was back. "The labels are here."

"How many?"

"Let me see. Five."

"For what?"

She replied, "Heart, lung, spleen, bile and liver."

"And that's all?"

"Yes."

"You're sure there isn't one for a PERK?"

A pause. "I'm sure. Just these five."

Marino said, "You slapped the label on this PERK, and your prints should be on it, seems to me."

"Not if she was wearing gloves," said Betty, who was watching all this with dismay.

"I generally don't wear gloves when I'm labeling things," I muttered. "They're bloody. The gloves would be bloody."

Marino blandly went on, "Okay. So you wasn't wearing gloves and Dingo was—"

"Wingo," I irritably said. "His name's Wingo!"

"Whatever." Marino turned to leave. "Point is, you touched the PERK with bare hands, meaning your prints should be on it." He added from the hall, "But maybe nobody else's should be."

10

NOBODY ELSE'S WERE. The only identifiable prints on the card-board file were mine.

There were a few smudges—and something else so completely unexpected that I had, for the moment, completely forgotten the unhappy reason for coming to see Vander at all.

He was bombarding the file with the laser and the cardboard was lit up like a night sky of pinpoint stars.

"This is just crazy," he marveled for the third time.

"The damn stuff must have come from my hands," I said incredulously. "Wingo was wearing gloves. So was Betty . . ."

Vander flipped on the overhead light and shook his head from side to side. "If you were male, I'd suggest the cops take you in for questioning."

"And I wouldn't blame you."

His face was intense: "Rethink what you've been doing this morning, Kay. We've got to make sure this residue's from you. If it is, we might have to reconsider our assumptions about the strangling cases, about the glitter we've been finding—"

"No," I interrupted. "It isn't possible I've been leaving the resi-due on the bodies, Neils. I wore gloves the entire time I worked with them. I took my gloves *off* when Wingo found the PERK. I was touching the file with my bare hands."

He persisted, "What about hair sprays, cosmetics? Anything you routinely use?"

"Not possible," I repeated. "This residue hasn't shown up when we've examined other bodies. It's shown up only in the strangling cases."

"Good point."

We thought for a minute.

"Betty and Wingo were wearing gloves when they handled this file?" He wanted to make sure.

"Yes, they were, which is why they left no prints."

"So it isn't likely the residue came from their hands?"

"Had to have come from mine. Unless someone else touched the file."

"Some other person who may have planted it in the refrigerator, you're still thinking." Vander looked skeptical. "Yours were the only prints, Kay."

"But the smudges, Neils. Those could be from anyone."

Of course they could be. But I knew he didn't believe it.

He asked, "What exactly were you doing just before you came upstairs?"

"I was posting a hit-and-run."

"Then what?"

"Then Wingo came over with the slide folder and I took it straight to Betty."

He glanced unemphatically at my bloodstained scrubs and observed, "You were wearing gloves while doing the post."

"Of course, and I took them off when Wingo brought me the file, as I've already explained—"

"The gloves were lined with talc."

"I don't think that could be it."

"Probably not, but it's a place to start."

I went back down to the autopsy suite to fetch an identical pair of latex gloves. Several minutes later, Vander was tearing open the packet, turning the gloves inside out, and shooting them with the laser.

Not even a glimmer. The talc didn't react, not that we really thought it would. In the past we'd tested various body powders from the murdered women's scenes in hopes of identifying the glittery substance. The powders, which had a talc base, hadn't reacted either.

The lights went on again. I smoked and thought. I was trying to envision my every move from the time Wingo showed me the slide file to when I ended up in Vander's office. I was engrossed in coronary arteries when Wingo walked up with the PERK. I set down the scalpel, peeled off my gloves and opened the file to look at the slides. I walked over to the sink, hastily washed my hands and patted them dry with a paper towel. Next I went upstairs to see Betty. Did I touch anything inside her lab? I didn't recall if I had.

It was the only thing I could think of. "The soap I used downstairs when I washed up. Could that be it?"

"Unlikely," Vander said without pause. "Especially if you rinsed off. If your everyday soap reacted even after rinsing we'd be finding the glittery stuff all the time on bodies and clothes. I'm pretty certain this residue is coming from something granular, a powdery substance of some sort. The soap you used downstairs is a disinfectant, a liquid, isn't it?"

It was, but that wasn't what I'd used. I was in too big of a rush to go back to the locker room and wash with the pink disinfectant kept in bottles by the sinks. Instead, I went to the sink nearest me, the one in the autopsy suite where there was a metal dispenser filled with the same grainy, gray soap powder used throughout the rest of the building. It was cheap. It was what the state purchased by the truckload. I had no idea what was in it. It was almost odorless and didn't dissolve or lather. It was like washing up with wet sand.

There was a ladies' room down the hall. I left for a moment and returned with a handful of the grayish powder. Lights out and Vander switched on the laser again.

The soap went crazy, blazing neon white.

"I'll be damned . . ."

Vander was thrilled. I wasn't exactly feeling the same way. I desperately wanted to know the origin of the residue we'd been finding on the bodies. But I'd never, not in my wildest fantasies, hoped it would turn out to be something found in every bathroom inside my building.

I still wasn't convinced. Did the residue on this file come from my hands? What if it didn't?

We experimented.

Firearms examiners routinely conduct a series of test fires to determine distance and trajectory. Vander and I were conducting a series of test washings to determine how thoroughly one had to rinse his hands in order for none of the residue to show up in the laser.

He vigorously scrubbed with the powder, rinsed well, and carefully dried his hands with paper towels. The laser picked up one or two sparkles, and that was it. I tried to reenact my handwashing, doing it exactly as I did it when I was downstairs. The result was a multitude of sparkles that were easily transferred to the countertop, the sleeve of Vander's lab coat, anything I touched. The more I touched, obviously, the fewer sparkles there were left on my hands.

I returned to the ladies' room and presently was back with a coffee cup full of the soap. We washed and washed, over and over again. Lights went on and off, the laser spitting, until the entire area of the sink looked like Richmond from the air after dark.

One interesting phenomenon became apparent. The more we washed and dried, the more the sparkles accumulated. They got under our nails, clung to our wrists and the cuffs of our sleeves. They ended up on our clothing, found their way to our hair, our faces, our necks—everywhere we touched. After about forty-five minutes of dozens of experimental washings, Vander and I looked perfectly normal in normal light. In the laser, we looked as if we'd been decorated with Christmas glitter.

"Shit," he exclaimed in the dark. It was an expletive I'd never heard him use. "Would you look at this stuff? The bastard must be a clean freak. To leave as much of the stuff as he does, he must be washing his hands twenty times a day."

"*If* this soap powder's the answer," I reminded him.

"Of course, of course."

I prayed the scientists upstairs could make their magic work. But what couldn't be determined by them or anyone else, I thought, was the origin of the residue on the slide file—and how the file had gotten inside the refrigerator to begin with.

My anxious inner voice was nagging at me again.

You just can't accept you made a mistake, I admonished myself. You just can't handle the truth. You mislabeled this PERK, and the residue on it came from your own hands.

But what if? What if the scenario were a more pernicious one? I silently argued. What if someone maliciously planted the file inside the refrigerator, and what if the glittery residue was from this person's hands instead of mine? The thought was strange, the poison of an imagination gone berserk.

So far a similar residue had been found on the bodies of four murdered women.

I knew Wingo, Betty, Vander and I had touched the file. The only other people who might have touched it were Tanner, Amburgey or Bill.

His face drifted through my mind. Something unpleasant and chilling shifted inside me as Monday afternoon slowly replayed in my memory. Bill was so distant during the meeting with Amburgey and Tanner. He was unable to look at me then, or later when the three men were going though the cases inside my conference room.

I saw case files slipping off Bill's lap and falling to the floor in a commingled, god-awful mess. Tanner quickly offered to pick them up. His helpfulness was so automatic. But it was Bill who picked up the paperwork, paperwork that would have included leftover labels. Then he and Tanner sorted through everything. How easy it would have been to tear off a label and slip it into a pocket . . .

Later, Amburgey and Tanner left together, but Bill remained with me. We talked in Margaret's office for ten or fifteen minutes. He was affectionate and full of promises that a couple of drinks and an evening together would soothe my nerves.

He left long before I did, and when he went out of the building he was alone and unwatched . . .

I blanked the images out of my mind, refused to see them anymore. This was outrageous. I was losing control. Bill would never do such a thing. In the first place, there would be no point. I couldn't imagine how such an act of sabotage could possibly profit him. Mislabeled slides could only damage the very case he eventually would be prosecuting in court. Not only would he be shooting himself in the foot, he'd be shooting himself in the head.

You want someone to blame because you can't face the fact that you probably screwed up!

These strangling cases were the most difficult of my career, and I was gripped by the fear I was becoming too caught up in them. Maybe I was losing my rational, methodical way of doing things. Maybe I was making mistakes.

Vander was saying, "We've got to figure out the composition of this stuff."

Like thoughtful shoppers, we needed to find a box of the soap and read the ingredients.

"I'll hit the ladies' rooms," I volunteered.

"I'll hit the men's."

What a scavenger hunt this turned out to be.

After wandering in and out of the ladies' rooms throughout the building I got smart and found Wingo. One of his jobs was to fill all the soap dispensers in the morgue. He directed me to the janitor's closet on the first floor, several doors down from my office. There, on a top shelf, right next to a pile of dusting rags, was an industrial-sized gray box of Borawash hand soap.

The main ingredient was borax.

A quick check in one of my chemical reference books hinted at why the soap powder lit up like the Fourth of July. Borax is a boron compound, a crystalline substance that conducts electricity like a metal at high temperatures. Industrial uses of it range from the making of ceramics, special glass, washing powders and disinfectants, to the manufacturing of abrasives and rocket fuels.

Ironically, a large percentage of the world's supply of borax is mined in Death Valley.

Friday night came and went, and Marino did not call.

By seven o'clock the following morning I had parked behind my building and uneasily began checking the log inside the morgue office.

I shouldn't have needed convincing. I knew better. I would have been one of the first to be alerted. There were no bodies signed in I wasn't expecting, but the quiet seemed ominous.

I couldn't shake the sensation another woman was waiting for me to tend to her, that it was happening again. I kept expecting Marino to call.

Vander rang me up from his home at seven-thirty.

"Anything?" he asked.

"I'll call you immediately if there is."

"I'll be near the phone."

The laser was upstairs in his lab, loaded on a cart and ready to be brought down to the X-ray room should we need it. I'd reserved the first autopsy table, and late yesterday afternoon Wingo had scrubbed it mirror-bright and set up two carts with every conceivable surgical tool and evidence-collection container and device. The table and carts remained unused.

My only cases were a cocaine overdose from Fredericksburg and an accidental drowning from James City County.

Just before noon Wingo and I were alone, methodically finishing up the morning's work.

His running shoes squeaked across the damp tile floor as he leaned a mop against the wall and remarked to me, "Word is they had a hundred cops working overtime last night."

I continued filling out a death certificate. "Let's hope it makes a difference."

"Would if I was the guy." He began hosing down a bloody table. "The guy'd be crazy to show his face. One cop told me they're stopping everybody out on the street. They see you walking around late they're going to check you out. Taking plate numbers, too, if they see your car parked somewhere late."

"What cop?" I looked up at him. We had no cases from Richmond this morning, no cops in from Richmond either. "What cop told you this?"

"One of the cops who came in with the drowning."

"From James City County? How did he know what was going on in Richmond last night?"

Wingo glanced curiously at me. "His brother's a cop here in the city."

I turned away so he couldn't see my irritation. Too many people were talking. A cop whose brother was a cop in Richmond just glibly told Wingo, a stranger, this? What else was being said? There was too much talk. Too much. I was reading the most innocent remark differently, becoming suspicious of everything and everybody.

Wingo was saying, "My opinion's the guy's gone under. He's cooling his heels for a while, until everything quiets down." He paused, water drumming down on the table. "Either that or he hit last night and no one's found the body yet."

I said nothing, my irritation becoming acute.

"Don't know, though." His voice was muffled by splashing water. "Kind of hard to believe he'd try it. Too risky, you ask me. But I know some of the theories. They say some guys like this get really bold after a while. Like they're jerking everybody around, when the truth is they want to be caught. Could be he can't help himself and is begging for someone to stop him . . ."

"Wingo . . ." I warned.

He didn't seem to hear me and went on, "Has to be some kind of sickness. He knows he's sick. I'm pretty sure of it. Maybe he's begging someone to save him from himself . . ."

"Wingo!" I raised my voice and spun around in my chair. He'd turned off the water but it was too late. My words were out and startlingly loud in the still, empty suite—

"He doesn't want to be caught!"

His lips parted in surprise, his face stricken by my sharpness. "Gee. I didn't mean to upset you, Dr. Scarpetta. I . . ."

"I'm not upset," I snapped. "But people like this bastard don't want to be caught, okay? He isn't *sick*, okay? He's antisocial, he's evil and he does it because he *wants* to, okay?"

Shoes quietly squeaking, he slowly got a sponge out of a sink and began wiping down the sides of the table. He wouldn't look at me.

I stared after him in a defeated way.

He didn't look up from his cleaning.

I felt bad. "Wingo?" I pushed back from the desk. "Wingo?" He reluctantly came over to me, and I lightly touched his arm. "I apologize. I have no reason to be short with you."

"No problem," he said, and the uneasiness in his eyes unnerved me. "I know what you're going through. With what's been happening and all. Makes me crazy, you know. Like I'm sitting around all the time trying to figure out something to do. All this stuff you're getting hit with these days and I can't figure out anything. I just, well, I just wish I could do something . . ."

So that was it! I hadn't hurt his feelings as much as I had reinforced his worries. Wingo was worried about *me*. He knew I wasn't myself these days, that I was strung tight to the point of breaking. Maybe it was becoming apparent to everyone else, too. The leaks, the computer violation, the mislabeled slides. Maybe no one would be surprised if I were eventually accused of incompetence—

"We saw it coming," people would say. "She was getting unhinged."

For one thing, I wasn't sleeping well. Even when I tried to relax, my mind was a machine with no Off switch. It ran on and on until my brain was overheated and my nerves were humming like power lines.

Last night I had tried to cheer up Lucy by taking her out to dinner and a movie. The entire time we were inside the restaurant and the theater I was waiting for my pager to go off, and every so often I tested it to make sure the batteries were still charged. I didn't trust the silence.

By 3:00 P.M. I'd dictated two autopsy reports and demolished a stack of micro dictations. When I heard my phone ring as I was getting on the elevator, I dashed back to my office and snatched up the receiver.

It was Bill.

"We still on?"

I couldn't say no. "Looking forward to it," I replied with enthusiasm I didn't feel. "But I'm not sure my company is worth writing home about these days."

"I won't write home about it, then."

I left the office.

It was another sunny day, but hotter. The grass border around my building was beginning to look parched, and I heard on the radio as I was driving home that the Hanover tomato crop was going to be damaged if we didn't get more rain. It had been a peculiar and volatile spring. We had long stretches of sunny, windy weather, and then quite out of nowhere, a fierce black army of clouds would march across the sky. Lightning would knock out electricity all over the city, and the rain would billow down in sheets. It was like dashing a bucket of water in the face of a thirsty man—it happened too fast for him to drink a drop.

Sometimes I was struck by certain parallels in life. My relationship with Bill had been little different from the weather. He marched in with an almost ferocious beauty, and I discovered all I wanted was a gentle rain, something quiet to quench the longing of my heart. I was looking forward to seeing him tonight, and yet I wasn't.

He was punctual, as always, and drove up at five exactly.

"It's good and it's bad," he remarked when we were on my back patio lighting the grill.

"Bad?" I asked. "I don't think you mean it quite like that, Bill."

The sun was at a sharp angle and still very hot, but clouds were streaming across the face of it, throwing us into intervals of shade and white light. The wind had whipped up and the air was pregnant with change.

He wiped his forehead on his shirtsleeve and squinted at me. A gust of wind bent the trees and sent a paper towel fluttering across the patio. "Bad, Kay, because his getting quiet may mean he's left the area."

We backed away from the smoldering coals and sipped from bottles of beer. I couldn't endure the thought that the killer might have moved on. I wanted him here. At least we were familiar with what he was doing. My nagging fear was he might begin striking in other cities where the cases would be worked by detectives and medical examiners who did not know what we knew. Nothing could foul up an investigation like a multijurisdictional effort. Cops were jealous of their turf. Each investigator wanted to make the arrest, and he thought he could work the case better than anyone else. It got to the point one thought a case belonged to him.

I supposed I was not above feeling possessive either. The victims had become my wards, and their only hope for justice was for their killer to be caught and prosecuted here. A person can be charged with only so many capital murders, and a conviction somewhere else might preclude a trial here. It was an outrageous thought. It would be as if the deaths of the women in Richmond were practice, a warm-up, and utterly in vain. Maybe it would turn out that everything happening to me was in vain, too.

Bill was squirting more lighter fluid on the charcoal. He backed away from the grill and looked at me, his face flushed from the heat. "How about your computer?" he asked. "Anything new?"

I hesitated. There was no point in my being evasive. Bill knew very well that I'd ignored Amburgey's orders and hadn't changed the password or done anything else to, quote, "secure" my data. Bill was standing right over me last Monday night when I activated answer mode and set the echo on again as if I were inviting the perpetrator to try again. Which was exactly what I was doing.

"It doesn't appear anyone else has gotten in, if that's what you mean."

"Interesting," he mused, taking another swallow of beer. "It doesn't make much sense. You'd think the person would try to get into Lori Petersen's case."

"She isn't in the computer," I reminded him. "Nothing new is going into the computer until these cases are no longer under active investigation."

"So the case isn't in the computer. But how's the person getting in going to know that unless she looks?"

"*She?*"

"She, he—whoever."

"Well, she—he—whoever looked the first time and couldn't pull up Lori's case."

"Still doesn't make a lot of sense, Kay," he insisted. "Come to think of it, it doesn't make a lot of sense someone would have tried in the first place. Anybody who knows much about computer entry would have realized a case autopsied on Saturday isn't likely to be in the office data base by Monday."

"Nothing ventured, nothing gained," I muttered.

I was edgy around Bill. I couldn't seem to relax or give myself up to what should have been a lovely evening.

Inch-thick ribeyes were marinating in the kitchen. A bottle of red wine was breathing on the counter. Lucy was making the salad, and she was in fine spirits considering we hadn't heard a word from her mother, who was off somewhere with her illustrator. Lucy seemed perfectly content. In her fantasies she was beginning to believe she would never leave, and it troubled me that she'd begun hinting at how nice it would be "when Mr. Boltz" and I "got married."

Sooner or later I would have to dash her dreams against the hard rock of reality. She would be going home just as soon as her mother returned to Miami, and Bill and I were not going to get married.

I'd begun scrutinizing him as though for the first time. He was staring pensively at the flaming charcoal, his beer absently cradled in both hands, the hair on his arms and legs gold like pollen in the sun. I saw him through a veil of rising heat and smoke, and it seemed a symbol of the distance growing between us.

Why did his wife kill herself with his gun? Was it simply utilitarian, that his gun was the most convenient means of instantly snuffing herself out? Or was it her way of punishing him for sins I knew nothing of?

His wife shot herself in the chest while she was sitting up in bed—in their bed. She pulled the trigger that Monday morning just hours, maybe even minutes, after they made love. Her PERK was positive for sperm. The faint scent of perfume still lingered on her body when I examined her at the scene. What was the last thing Bill said to her before he left for work?

"Earth to Kay . . ."

My eyes focused. Bill was staring at me. "Off somewhere?" he asked, slipping an arm around my waist, his breath close to my cheek. "Can I come?"

"I was just thinking."

"About what? And don't tell me it's about the office . . ."

I came out with it. "Bill, there's some paperwork missing from one of the case files you, Amburgey and Tanner were looking through the other day . . ."

His hand kneading the small of my back went still. I could feel the anger in the pressure of his fingers. "What paperwork?"

"I'm not real sure," I nervously replied. I didn't dare get specific, didn't dare mention the PERK label missing from Lori Petersen's file. "I was just wondering if you may have noticed anyone accidentally picking up anything—"

He abruptly removed his arm and blurted out, "Shit. Can't you push these goddam cases out of your mind for one goddam evening?"

"Bill . . ."

"Enough, all right?" He plunged his hands into the pockets of his shorts and wouldn't look at me. "Jesus, Kay. You're going to make me crazy. They're dead. The women are fucking dead. Dead. Dead! You and I are alive. Life goes on. Or at least it's supposed to. It's going to do you in—it's going to do *us* in—if you don't stop obsessing over these cases."

But for the rest of the evening, while Bill and Lucy were chatting about inconsequential matters at the dinner table, my ear was turned toward the phone. I kept expecting it to ring. I was waiting for Marino's call.

When it rang early in the morning the rain was lashing my house and I was sleeping restlessly, my dreams fragmented, worrisome.

I fumbled for the receiver.

No one was there.

"Hello?" I said again as I flicked on the lamp.

In the background a television was faintly playing. I could hear the murmur of distant voices reciting lines I could not make out, and as my heart thudded against my ribs I slammed down the receiver in disgust.

———

It was Monday now, early afternoon. I was going over the preliminary lab reports of the tests the forensic scientists were conducting upstairs.

They had given the strangling cases a top priority. Everything else—blood alcohol levels, street drugs and barbiturates—was temporarily on hold. I had four very fine scientific minds focused on trace amounts of a glittery residue that might be a cheap soap powder found in public restrooms all over the city.

The preliminary reports weren't exactly thrilling. So far, we couldn't even say very much about the known sample, the Borawash soap we used in the building. It was approximately twenty-five percent "inert ingredient, an abrasive," and seventy-five percent sodium borate. We knew this because the manufacturer's chemists had told us so. Scanning electron microscopy wasn't so sure. Sodium borate, sodium carbonate and sodium nitrate, for example, all came up as flat-out sodium in SEM. The trace amounts of the glittery residue came up the same way—as sodium. It's about as specific as saying something contains trace elements of lead, which is everywhere, in the air, in the soil, in the rain. We never tested for lead in gunshot residues because a positive result wouldn't mean a thing.

In other words, all that glitters isn't borax.

The trace evidence we'd found on the slain women's bodies could be something else, such as a sodium nitrate with uses ranging from fertilizer to a component of dynamite. Or it could be a crystal carbonate used as a constituent in photography developers. Theoretically, the killer could spend his working hours in a darkroom or in a greenhouse or on a farm. How many substances out there contain sodium? God only knows.

Vander was testing a variety of other sodium compounds in the laser to see if they sparkled. It was a quick way to mark items off our list.

Meanwhile, I had my own ideas. I wanted to know who else in the greater Richmond metropolitan area ordered Borawash, who in addition to the Health and Human Services Department. So I

called the distributor in New Jersey. I got some secretary who referred me to sales who referred me to accounting who referred me
to data processing who referred me to public relations who referred
me back to accounting.

Next, I got an argument.

"Our list of clients is confidential. I'm not allowed to release
that. You're what kind of examiner?"

"Medical examiner," I measured out each word. "This is Dr.
Scarpetta, chief medical examiner in Virginia."

"Oh. You grant licenses to physicians, then—"

"No. We investigate deaths."

A pause. "You mean a coroner?"

There was no point in explaining that, no, I was not a coroner.
Coroners are elected officials. They usually aren't forensic pathologists. You can be a gas station attendant and get elected coroner in
some states. I let him think he was in the right ballpark and this
only made matters worse.

"I don't understand. Are you suggesting someone is saying
Borawash is fatal? That just isn't possible. To my knowledge, it
isn't toxic, absolutely not. We've never had any problems of that
nature. Did someone eat it? I'm going to have to refer you to my
supervisor . . ."

I explained a substance that may be Borawash had been found
at several related crime scenes but the cleanser had nothing to do
with the deaths, the potential toxicity of the soap wasn't my concern. I told him I could get a court order, which would only waste
more of his time and mine. I heard keys clicking as he went into a
computer.

"I think you're going to want me to send this to you, ma'am.
There are seventy-three names here, clients in Richmond."

"Yes, I would very much appreciate it if you would send me a
printout as quickly as possible. But if you would, read me the list
over the phone, please."

Decidedly lacking in enthusiasm, he did, and a lot of good it
did. I didn't recognize most of the businesses except for the Department of Motor Vehicles, Central Supply for the city, and of
course, HHSD. Collectively speaking, they included probably ten
thousand employees, everyone from judges to public defenders to
prosecutors to the entire police force to mechanics at the state and

city garages. Somewhere within this great pool of people was a Mr. Nobody with a fetish for cleanliness.

I was returning to my desk a little after 3:00 P.M. with another cup of coffee when Rose buzzed me and transferred a call.

"She's been dead awhile," Marino was saying.

I grabbed my bag and was out the door.

11

ACCORDING TO MARINO, the police had yet to find any neighbors who had seen the victim over the weekend. A friend she worked with tried to call Saturday and Sunday and didn't get an answer. When the woman didn't show up to teach her one o'clock class the friend called the police. An officer arrived at the scene and went around to the back of the house. A window on the third floor was wide open. The victim had a roommate who apparently was out of town.

The address was less than a mile from downtown and on the fringes of Virginia Commonwealth University, a sprawling physical plant with more than twenty thousand students. Many of the schools that made up the university were located in restored Victorian homes and brownstones along West Main. Summer classes were in session, and students were walking and riding bicycles along the street. They lingered at small tables on restaurant terraces, sipping coffee, their books stacked by their elbows as they talked with friends and luxuriated in the sunny warmth of a lovely June afternoon.

Henna Yarborough was thirty-one and taught journalism at the university's School of Broadcasting, Marino had told me. She had moved to the city from North Carolina last fall. We knew nothing more about her except that she was dead and had been dead for several days.

Cops, reporters were all over the place.

Traffic was slow rolling past the dark red brick, three-story house, with a blue-and-green handmade flag fluttering over the entrance. There were windowboxes bright with pink and white geraniums, and a blue-steel roof with an Art Nouveau flower design in pale yellow.

The street was so congested I was forced to park almost half a block away, and it didn't escape my notice that the reporters were more subdued than usual. They scarcely stirred as I passed. They didn't jam cameras and microphones in my face. There was something almost militaristic in their bearing—stiff, quiet, definitely not at ease—as if they sensed this was another one. Number five. Five women like themselves or their wives and lovers who had been brutalized and murdered.

A uniformed man lifted the yellow tape barring the front doorway at the top of the worn granite steps. I went into a dim foyer and up three flights of wooden stairs. On the top landing I found the chief of police, several high-ranking officers, detectives and uniformed men. Bill was there, too, closest to an open doorway and looking in. His eyes briefly met mine, his face ashen.

I was hardly aware of him as I paused in the doorway and looked inside the small bedroom filled with the pungent stench of decomposing human flesh that is unlike any other odor on earth. Marino's back was to me. He was squatting on his heels and opening dresser drawers, his hands deftly shuffling through layers of neatly folded clothing.

The top of the dresser was sparsely arranged with bottles of perfume and moisturizers, a hairbrush and a set of electric curlers. Against the wall to the left of it was a desk, and the electric typewriter on top of it was an island in the midst of a sea of paper and books. More books were on a shelf overhead and stacked on the hardwood floor. The closet door was open a crack, the light off inside. There were no rugs or knickknacks, no photographs or paintings on the walls—as if the bedroom had not been lived in very long or else her stay was temporary.

Far to my right was a twin bed. From a distance I saw disarrayed bedcovers and a splay of dark, tangled hair. Watching where I stepped, I went to her.

Her face was turned toward me, and it was so suffused, so bloated by decomposition, I could not tell what she had looked like in life except she was white, with shoulder-length dark brown hair.

She was nude and resting on her left side, her legs drawn up, her hands behind her and tightly bound. It appeared the killer used the cords from venetian blinds, and the knots, the pattern, were joltingly familiar. A dark blue bedspread was thrown over her hips in a manner still ringing of careless cold contempt. On the floor at the foot of the bed was a pair of shorty pajamas. The top was buttoned, and it was slit from the collar to the hem. The bottoms appeared to be slit along the sides.

Marino slowly crossed the bedroom and stood next to me. "He climbed up the ladder," he said.

"What ladder?" I asked.

There were two windows. The one he was staring at was open and nearer the bed. "Against the brick outside," he explained, "there's an old iron fire escape ladder. That's how he got in. The rungs are rusty. Some of it flaked off and is on the sill, probably from his shoes."

"And he went out that way, too," I assumed aloud.

"Can't say for sure, but it would appear so. The door downstairs was locked. We had to bust it open. But outside," he added, looking toward the window again, "there's tall grass under the ladder. No footprints. It rained cats and dogs Saturday night so that don't help our cause worth a damn either."

"This place air-conditioned?" My skin was crawling, the airless room hot and damp and bristling with decay.

"Nope. No fans either. Not a single one." He wiped his flushed face with his hand. His hair was clinging like gray string to his wet forehead, his eyes bloodshot and darkly ringed. Marino looked as if he hadn't been to bed or changed his clothes in a week.

"Was the window locked?" I asked.

"Neither of them was—" He got a surprised look on his face as we turned in unison toward the doorway. "What the hell . . .?"

A woman had started screaming in the foyer two floors below. Feet were scuffing, male voices were arguing.

"Get out of my house! Oh, God . . . Get out of my house, you goddam son of a bitch!" screamed the woman.

Marino abruptly brushed past me, and his steps thudded loudly on the wooden stairs. I could hear him saying something to someone, and almost immediately the screaming stopped. The loud voices faded to a murmur.

I began the external examination of the body.

She was the same temperature as the room, and rigor already had come and gone. She got cool and stiff right after death, and then as the temperature outside rose so did the temperature of her body. Finally, her stiffness passed, as if the initial shock of death vanished with time.

I did not have to pull back the bedspread much to see what was beneath it. For an instant, I wasn't breathing and my heart seemed to stop. I gently laid the spread back in place and began peeling off my gloves. There was nothing more I could do with her here. Nothing.

When I heard Marino coming back up the stairs, I turned to tell him to be sure the body came to the morgue wrapped in the bedcovers. But the words stuck in my throat. I stared in speechless astonishment.

In the doorway next to him was Abby Turnbull. What in God's name did Marino think he was doing? Had he lost his mind? Abby Turnbull, the ace reporter, the shark that made Jaws seem like a goldfish.

Then I noticed she was wearing sandals, a pair of blue jeans and a white cotton blouse that wasn't tucked in. Her hair was tied back. She wasn't wearing makeup. She carried no tape recorder or notepad, just a canvas tote bag. Her wide eyes were riveted to the bed, her face twisted by terror.

"*God, no!*" As she placed her hand over her open mouth.

"It's her, then," Marino said in a low voice.

She moved closer, staring. "My God. Henna. Oh, my God . . ."

"This was her room?"

"Yes. Yes. Oh, please, God . . ."

Marino jerked his head, motioning a uniformed man I couldn't see to come upstairs and escort Abby Turnbull out. I heard their feet on the stairs, heard her moaning.

I quietly asked Marino, "You know what you're doing?"

"Hey. I always know what I'm doing."

"That was her screaming," I numbly went on. "Screaming at the police?"

"Nope. Boltz had just come down. She was yelling at him."

"Boltz?" I couldn't think.

"Can't say I blame her," he replied unemphatically. "It's her house. Can't blame her for not wanting us crawling all over the damn place, telling her she can't come in . . ."

"Boltz?" I asked idiotically. "Boltz told her she couldn't come in?"

"And a couple of the guys." Shrugging. "She's going to be something to talk to. Totally off the wall." His attention drifted to the body on the bed, and something flickered in his eyes. "This lady here's her sister."

━━━━━

The living room was filled with sunlight and potted plants. It was on the second floor. And had been recently and expensively refurbished. The polished hardwood floor was almost completely covered with a dhurrie rug of pale blue and green geometrical designs against a field of white, and the furniture was white and angular with small pillows in pastels. On the whitewashed walls was an enviable collection of abstract monotype prints by Richmond artist Gregg Carbo. It was an impractical room, one Abby designed with no one in mind but herself, I suspected. An impressive frosty lair, it bespoke success and a lack of sentiment and seemed very much in character with what I'd always thought of its creator.

Curled up in a corner of the white leather couch, she was nervously smoking a long thin cigarette. I'd never seen Abby up close, and she was so peculiar looking she was striking. Her eyes were irregular, one slightly greener than the other, and her full lips did not seem to belong on the same face as the prominent, narrow nose. She had brown hair, which was graying and just brushing her shoulders, and her cheekbones were high, her complexion finely lined at the corners of her eyes and mouth. Long-legged and slender, she was my age, perhaps a few years younger.

She stared at us with the unblinking glassy eyes of a frightened deer. A uniformed man left and Marino quietly shut the door.

"I'm real sorry. I know how hard this is . . ." Marino started in with the usual windup. He calmly explained the importance that she answer all questions, remember everything about her sister—her habits, her friends, her routines—in as much detail as she could. Abby sat woodenly and said nothing. I sat opposite her.

"I understand you've been out of town," he was saying.

"Yes." Her voice trembled and she shivered as if she were cold. "I left Friday afternoon for a meeting in New York."

"What sort of meeting?"

"A book. I'm in the process of negotiating a book contract. Had a meeting with my agent. Stayed over with a friend."

The microcassette recorder on top of the glass coffee table silently turned. Abby stared blindly at it.

"So, you have any contact with your sister while you was in New York?"

"I tried to call her last night to tell her what time my train was coming in." She took a deep breath. "When I didn't get an answer, I was puzzled, I guess. Then I just assumed she'd gone out somewhere. I didn't try after I pulled into the station. The train station. I knew she had classes this afternoon. I got a cab. I had no idea. It wasn't until I got here and saw all the cars, the police . . ."

"How long's your sister been living with you?"

"Last year she and her husband separated. She wanted a change, time to think. I told her to come here. Told her she could live with me until she got settled or went back to him. That was fall. Late August. She moved in with me last August and started her job at the university."

"When was the last time you saw her?"

"Friday afternoon." Her voice rose and caught. "She drove me to the train station." Her eyes were welling.

Marino pulled a rumpled handkerchief out of a back pocket and handed it to her. "You have any idea what her plans for the weekend were?"

"Work. She told me she was going to stay in, work on class preparations. As far as I know, she didn't have any plans. Henna wasn't very outgoing, had one or two good friends, other professors. She had a lot of class preparation, told me she would do the grocery shopping on Saturday. That's all."

"And where was that? What store?"

"I have no idea. It doesn't matter. I know she didn't go. The other policeman in here a minute ago had me check the kitchen. She didn't go to the grocery store. The refrigerator's as bare as it was when I left. It must have happened Friday night. Like the other ones. All weekend I've been in New York and she's been here. Been here like this."

No one said anything for a moment. Marino was looking around the living room, his face unreadable. Abby shakily lit a cigarette and turned to me.

I knew what she was going to ask before the words were out.

"Is it like the other ones? I know you looked at her." She hesitated, trying to compose herself. She was like a violent storm about to break when she quietly asked, "What did he do to her?"

I found myself giving her the "I won't be able to tell you anything until I've examined her in a good light" response.

"For God's sake, she's my sister!" she cried. "I want to know what the animal did to her! Oh, God! Did she suffer? Please tell me she didn't suffer . . ."

We let her cry, deep, heaving moans of naked anguish. Her pain carried her far beyond the realm where any mortal could reach her. We sat. Marino watched her with unwavering, unreadable eyes.

I hated myself at times like this, cold, clinical, the consummate professional unmoved by another person's pain. What was I supposed to say? Of course she suffered! When she found him inside her room, when she began to realize what was going to happen, her terror, which would have been that much worse because of what she'd read in the papers about the other murdered women, chilling accounts written by her own sister. And her pain, her physical pain.

"Fine. Of course you're not going to tell me," Abby began in rapid jerky sentences. "I know how it is. You're not going to tell me. She's my sister. And you're not going to tell me. You keep all your cards close to your vest. I know how it goes. And for what? How many does the bastard have to murder? Six? Ten? Fifty? Then maybe the cops figure it out?"

Marino continued to stare blandly at her. He said, "Don't blame the police, Miss Turnbull. We're on your side, trying to help—"

"Right!" She cut him off. "You and your help! Like a lot of help you were last week! Where the shit were you then?"

"Last week? What are you referring to, exactly?"

"I'm referring to the redneck who tailed me all the way home from the newspaper," she exclaimed. "He was right on top of me, turning everywhere I did. I even stopped at a store to get rid of him. Then I come out twenty minutes later and there he is again. The same goddam car! Following me! I get home and immediately call the cops. And what do they do? *Nothing.* Some officer stops by *two hours later* to make sure everything's all right. I give him a description, even the plate number. Did he ever follow up? Hell no, I never heard a word. For all I know, the pig in the car's the one who did it! My sister's dead. Murdered. Because some cop couldn't be bothered!"

Marino was studying her, his eyes interested. "When exactly was this?"

She faltered. "Tuesday, I think. A week ago Tuesday. Late, maybe ten, ten-thirty at night. I worked late in the newsroom, finishing up a story . . ."

He looked confused. "Uh, correct me if I'm wrong, but I thought you was on the graveyard beat, six to two A.M., or something."

"That Tuesday one of the other reporters was working my beat. I had to come in early, during the day, to finish up something the editors wanted for the next edition."

"Yeah," Marino said. "Okay, so this car. When did it start following you?"

"It's hard to know. I didn't really notice it until several minutes after I'd pulled out of the parking deck. He could have been waiting for me. Maybe he saw me at some point. I don't know. But he was right on my rear bumper, his high beams on. I slowed down, hoping he'd go around me. He slowed down, too. I speeded up. Same thing. I couldn't shake him. I decided to go to Farm Fresh. I didn't want him following me home. He did anyway. He must have gone by and come back, waited for me in the parking lot or on a nearby street. Waited until I came back out and drove off."

"You positive it was the same car?"

"A new Cougar, black. I'm absolutely sure. I got a contact at DMV to run the plate number since the cops couldn't be bothered. It's a rental car. I've got the address of the dealership, the car's plate number written down if you're interested."

"Yeah, I'm interested," Marino told her.

She dug inside her tote bag and found a folded piece of notepaper. Her hand trembled as she gave it to him.

He glanced at it and tucked it inside a pocket. "So what then? The car followed you. It followed you all the way home?"

"I had no choice. I couldn't drive around all night. Couldn't do a damn thing. He saw where I live. I came in and went straight to the phone. I guess he drove past, went on. When I looked out the window, I didn't see him anywhere."

"You ever seen the car before?"

"I don't know. I've seen black Cougars before. But I can't say that I've ever seen that exact car before."

"You get a look at the driver?"

"It was too dark and he was behind me. But there was definitely just one person inside the car. Him, the driver."

"Him? You're sure about that?"

"All I saw was a big shape, someone with short hair, okay? Of course it was a *him*. It was awful. He was sitting rigidly, staring straight at the back of my head. Just this shape, staring. Right on my bumper. I told Henna. I told her about it. I told her to be careful, to keep an eye out for a black Cougar and if she saw a car like that near the house to call 911. She knew what was going on in the city. The murders. We talked about it. Dear God! I can't believe it! She knew! I told her not to leave her windows unlocked! To be careful!"

"So it was normal for her to have a window or two unlocked, maybe open."

Abby nodded and wiped her eyes. "She's always slept with windows open. It's hot in here sometimes. I was going to get air-conditioning, have it installed by July. I just moved in right before she came. In August. There was so much else to do and fall, winter, wasn't that far off. Oh, God. I told her a thousand times. She was always off in her own world. Just oblivious. I couldn't get it to sink in. Just like I never could get her to fasten her seatbelt. She's my baby sister. She's never liked me telling her what to do. Things slid right over her, it's like she didn't even hear them. I'd tell her. I'd tell her the things that go on, the crimes. Not just the murders, but the rapes, the robberies, all of it. And she'd get impatient. She didn't want to hear it. She'd say, 'Oh, Abby, you see only the horrible things. Can't we talk about something else?' I have a handgun. I told her to keep it by her bed when I wasn't here. But she wouldn't touch it. No way. I offered to teach her how to shoot it, to get her one of her own. But no way. No way! And now this! She's gone! Oh, God! And all these things I'm supposed to tell you about her, about her habits and everything, it doesn't matter!"

"It does matter. Everything matters . . ."

"None of it matters because I know it wasn't her he was after! He didn't even know about her! He was after me!"

Silence.

"What makes you think that?" Marino calmly asked.

"If it was him in the black car, then I know he was after me.

No matter who he is, I'm the one who's been writing about him. He's seen my byline. He knows who I am."

"Maybe."

"Me! He was after me!"

"You may have been his target," Marino matter-of-factly told her. "But we can't know that for sure, Miss Turnbull. Me, I've got to consider all possibilities, like maybe he seen your sister somewhere, maybe on the campus or in a restaurant, a shop. Maybe he didn't know she lived with somebody, especially if he followed her while you was at work—if he followed her at night and saw her come in when you wasn't home, I'm saying. He may not have had any idea you're her sister. It could be a coincidence. Was there any place she frequented, a restaurant, a bar, any place?"

Wiping her eyes again, she tried to remember. "There's a deli on Ferguson within walking distance of the school. The School of Broadcasting. She ate lunch there once or twice a week, I think. She didn't go to bars. Now and then we ate out at Angela's on Southside but we were always together on those occasions—she wasn't alone. She may have gone other places, shops, I mean. I don't know. I don't know every single thing she did every minute of the day."

"You say she moved in last August. She ever leave, maybe for the weekend, take any trips, that sort of thing?"

"Why?" She was bewildered. "You thinking someone followed her, someone from out of town?"

"I'm just trying to ascertain when she was here and when she wasn't."

She said shakily, "Last Thursday she went back to Chapel Hill to see her husband and spend some time with a friend. She was gone most of the week, got back on Wednesday. Today classes started, the first day of classes for the summer session."

"He ever come here, the husband?"

"No," she warily replied.

"He have any history of being rough with her, of violence—"

"No!" she blurted out. "Jeff didn't do this to her! They both wanted a trial separation! There wasn't any animosity between them! The pig who did this is the same pig who's been doing it!"

Marino stared at the tape recorder on the table. A tiny red light was flashing. He checked the pockets of his jacket and looked irritated. "I'm gonna have to go out to the car for a minute."

He left Abby and me alone in the bright white living room.

There was a long, uncomfortable silence before she looked at me.

Her eyes were bloodshot, her face puffy. Bitterly, miserably, she said to me, "All those times I've wanted to talk to you. And now, here it is. This. You're probably secretly glad. I know what your opinion of me is. You probably think I deserve it. I get a dose of what the people I write about must feel. Poetic justice."

The remark cut me to the bone. I said with feeling, "Abby, you don't deserve this. I would never wish this on you or anyone."

Staring down at her tightly clenched hands, she painfully went on, "Please take care of her. Please. My sister. Oh, God. Please take care of Henna . . ."

"I promise I'll take care of her . . ."

"You can't let him get away with this! You can't!"

I didn't know what to say.

She looked up at me and I was startled by the terror in her eyes. "I don't understand anything anymore. I don't understand what's going on. All these things I've been hearing. And this happens. I tried. I tried to find out, tried to find out from you. Now this. I don't know who's us or them anymore!"

Quietly, I said, "I don't think I understand, Abby. *What* did you try to find out from me?"

She talked very fast. "That night. Earlier in the week. I tried to talk to you about it. But he was there . . ."

It was coming to me. I dully asked, "What night?"

She looked confused, as if she couldn't remember. "Wednesday," she said. "Wednesday night."

"You drove to my house late that night and then quickly drove off? Why?"

She stammered, "You . . . you had company."

Bill. I remembered we stood in the glare of the front porch light. We were in plain view and his car was parked in my drive. It was her. Abby was the one who drove up that night, and she saw me with Bill, but this didn't explain her reaction. Why did she panic? It seemed a frightened visceral reflex when she extinguished her headlights and slammed the car into reverse.

She was saying, "These investigations. I've heard things. Rumors. Cops can't talk to you. Nobody's supposed to talk to you. Something's screwed up and that's why all calls are being referred to Amburgey. I had to ask you! And now they're saying you screwed up the serology in the surgeon . . . Lori Petersen's case. That the entire investigation's screwed up because of your office and if it wasn't for that the cops might have caught the killer by now . . ." She was angry and uncertain, staring wildly at me. "I have to know if it's true. I have to know! I have to know what's going to happen to my sister!"

How did she know about the mislabeled PERK? Surely Betty wouldn't tell her. But Betty had concluded her serology tests on the slides, and copies—*all* copies of *all* reports—were being sent straight to Amburgey. Did he tell Abby? Did someone in his office tell her? Did he tell Tanner? Did he tell Bill?

"Where did you hear this?"

"I hear a lot of things." Her voice trembled.

I looked at her miserable face, at her body drawn in by grief, by horror. "Abby," I said very calmly, "I'm quite sure you hear a lot of things. I'm also quite sure a lot of them aren't true. Or even if there is a grain of truth, the interpretation is misleading, and perhaps you might ask yourself why someone would tell you these things, what this person's real motive is."

She wavered. "I just want to know if it's true, what I've heard. If your office is at fault."

I couldn't think how to respond.

"I'm going to find out anyway, I'll tell you that right now. Don't underestimate me, Dr. Scarpetta. The cops have screwed up big time. Don't think I don't know. They screwed up with me when that damn redneck followed me home. And they screwed up with Lori Petersen when she dialed 911 and no one responded until almost an hour later. When she was already dead!"

My surprise was visible.

"When this breaks," she went on, her eyes bright with tears, with rage, "the city's going to rue the day I was ever born! People are going to pay! I'll make sure certain people pay, and you want to know why?"

I was staring dumbly at her.

"Because nobody who counts gives a damn when women are raped and murdered! The same bastards who work the cases go out on the town and watch movies about women being raped, strangled, slashed. To them it's sexy. They like to look at it in magazines. They fantasize. They probably get their rocks off by looking at the scene photographs. The cops. They make *jokes* about it. I hear it. I hear them laughing at scenes, hear them laughing inside the ER!"

"They don't really mean it like that." My mouth was dry. "It's one of the ways they cope."

Footsteps were coming up the stairs.

Glancing furtively toward the door, she went into her tote bag and clumsily got out a business card and scribbled a number on it. "Please. If there's anything you can tell me after it's—it's done . . ." She took a deep breath. "Will you call me?" She handed me the card. "It's got my pager number. I don't know where I'll be. Not in this house. Not for a while. Maybe never."

Marino was back.

Abby's eyes fixed angrily on him. "I know what you're going to ask," she said as he shut the door. "And the answer's no. There weren't any men in Henna's life, nobody here in Richmond. She wasn't seeing anyone, she wasn't sleeping with anyone."

Wordlessly, he clicked in a new tape and depressed the Record button.

He slowly looked up at her. "What about you, Miss Turnbull?"

Her breath caught in her throat. Stammering, "I have a close relationship, am close to someone in New York. Nobody here. Just a lot of business associations."

"I see. And just what exactly's your definition of a business association?"

"What do you mean?" Her eyes got wide with fear.

He looked thoughtful for a moment, then casually said, "What I'm wondering is if you're aware that this 'redneck' who followed you home the other night, has, in fact, been keeping an eye on you for several weeks now. The guy in the black Cougar. Well, he's a cop. Plainclothes, works out of Vice."

She stared at him in disbelief.

"See," Marino laconically went on, "that's why nobody got real upset when you called in the complaint, Miss Turnbull. Well, strike that. It would've upset me, if I'd known about it at the time—because the guy's supposed to be better than that. If he's following you, you're not supposed to know it, is what I'm saying."

He was getting chillier by the second, his words beginning to bite.

"But this particular cop don't like you none too well. Fact is, when I went out to the car a minute ago, I raised him on the radio, got the straight skinny from him. He admits he was hassling you deliberately, lost his cool a little bit when he was tailing you that night."

"What is this?" she cried in a spasm of panic. "He was harassing me because I'm a *reporter?*"

"Well, it's a little more personal than that, Miss Turnbull." Marino casually lit a cigarette. "You remember a couple years back you did that big exposé on the Vice cop who was dipping into the contraband and got himself hooked on coke? Sure, you remember that. He ended up eating his service revolver, blew his damn brains out. You gotta remember that clear as a bell. That particular Vice cop was the partner of the guy following you. Thought his interest in you would motivate him to do a good job. Looks like he went a little overboard . . ."

"*You!*" she cried incredulously. "You asked him to follow me? Why?"

"I'll tell you. Since it appears my friend overplayed his hand, the gig's up. You would have found out eventually he's a cop. May as well put all of it out on the table, right here in front of the doc, since, in a way, it concerns her, too."

Abby glanced frantically at me. Marino took his time tapping an ash.

He took another drag and said, "Just so happens the ME's office is taking a lot of heat right now because of these alleged leaks to the press, which translates directly into leaks to you, Miss Turnbull. Someone's been breaking into the doc's computer. Amburgey's twisting the blade in the doc, here, causing a lot of problems and making a lot of accusations. Me, I'm of a different opinion. I think the leaks got nothing to do with the computer. I think someone's breaking into the computer to make it look like that's where the information's coming from in order to disguise the fact that the only data base being violated is the one between Bill Boltz's ears."

"That's insane!"

Marino smoked, his eyes fixed on her. He was enjoying watching her squirm.

"I absolutely had nothing to do with any computer violations!" she exploded. "Even if I knew how to do such a thing, I would never, never, do it! I can't believe this! My sister's dead . . . Jesus Christ . . ." Her eyes were wild and swimming in tears. "Oh, God! What does any of this have to do with Henna?"

Marino coldly said, "I'm to the point of not having any idea who or what's got to do with anything. I do know some of the stuff you've been printing ain't common knowledge. Someone in the know's singing, singing to you. Someone's screwing up the investigation behind the scenes. I'm curious why anybody would be doing that unless he's got something to hide or something to gain."

"I don't know what you're getting—"

"See," he interrupted, "I just think it's a little strange that about five weeks ago, right after the second strangling, you did a big spread on Boltz, a day-in-the-life-of story. A big profile of the city's favorite golden boy. The two of you spend a day together, right? It just so happens I was out that night, saw the two of you driving away from Franco's around ten o'clock. Cops is nosy, especially if we've got nothing better to do, you know, if it's slow on the street. And it just so happens I tagged along after you . . ."

"Stop it," she whispered, shaking her head side to side. "Stop it!"

He ignored her. "Boltz don't drop you off at the newspaper. See, he takes you to your house and when I breeze by several hours later—bingo! The fancy white Audi's still there, all the lights in the house off. What do you know? Right after that, all these juicy details start showing up in your stories. I guess that's your definition of a *professional association*."

Abby was trembling all over, her face in her hands. I couldn't look at her. I couldn't look at Marino. I was knocked so off balance it was barely penetrating—the unwarranted cruelty of his hitting her with this now, after all that had happened.

"I didn't sleep with him." Her voice shook so badly she could barely talk. "I didn't. I didn't want to. He . . . he took advantage of me."

"Right." Marino snorted.

She looked up and briefly shut her eyes. "I was with him all day. The last meeting we went to wasn't over until seven that night. I offered dinner, said the newspaper would buy him dinner. We went to Franco's. I had one glass of wine, that was all. One glass. I start getting woozy, just incredibly woozy. I hardly remember leaving the restaurant. The last thing I remember is getting into his car. Him reaching for my hand, saying something about how he'd never made it with a police reporter before. What happened that night, I don't remember any of it. I woke up early the next morning. He was there . . ."

"Which reminds me." Marino stabbed out the cigarette. "Where was your sister during all this?"

"Here. She was in her room, I guess. I don't remember. It doesn't matter. We were downstairs. In the living room. On the couch, on the floor, I don't remember—I'm not sure she even knew!"

He looked disgusted.

She hysterically went on, "I couldn't believe it. I was terrified, sick like I'd been poisoned. All I can figure is when I got up to go to the ladies' room at one point during dinner he slipped something in my drink. He knew he had me. He knew I wouldn't go to the cops. Who would believe me if I called and said the Commonwealth's attorney. . . he did such a thing? No one! No one would believe me!"

"You got that straight," Marino butted in. "Hey, he's a good-looking guy. He don't need to slip a lady a mickey to get her to give up the goods."

Abby screamed, "He's scum! He's probably done it a thousand times and gotten away with it! He threatened me, told me if I mentioned a word he'd make me out to be a slut, he'd ruin me!"

"Then what?" Marino demanded. "Then he feels guilty and starts leaking information to you?"

"No! I've had nothing to do with the bastard! If I got within ten feet of him I'd be afraid I'd blow his goddam head off! None of my information has come from him!"

It couldn't be true.

What Abby was saying. It couldn't be true. I was trying to ward off the statements. They were terrible, but they were adding up despite my desperate inward denials.

She must have recognized Bill's white Audi on the spot. That was why she panicked when she saw it parked in my drive. Earlier she found Bill inside her house and shrieked at him to leave because she hated the very sight of him.

Bill warned me she would stoop to anything, that she was vengeful, opportunistic and dangerous. Why did he tell me that? Why really? Was he laying the groundwork for his own defense should Abby ever accuse him?

He had lied to me. He didn't spurn her so-called advances when he drove her to her house after the interview. His car was still parked there early the next morning—

Images were flashing through my mind of the few occasions

early on when Bill and I were alone on my living room couch. I became sickened by the memory of his sudden aggression, the raw brute force that I attributed to whisky. Was this the dark side of him? Was the truth that he found pleasure only in overpowering? In taking?

He was here, inside this house, at the scene, when I arrived. No wonder he was so quick to respond. His interest was more than professional. He wasn't merely doing his job. He would have recognized Abby's address. He probably knew whose house it was before anybody else did. He wanted to see, to make sure.

Maybe he was even hoping the victim was Abby. Then he would never have to worry this moment would happen, that she would tell.

Sitting very still, I willed my face to turn to stone. I couldn't let it show. The wrenching disbelief. The devastation. Oh, God, don't let it show.

A telephone started ringing in some other room. It rang and rang and nobody answered it.

Footsteps were coming up the stairs, metal making muffled clangs against wood and radios blaring unintelligible static. Paramedics were carrying a stretcher up to the third floor.

Abby was fumbling with a cigarette and she suddenly threw it and the burning match into the ashtray.

"If it's true you've been having me followed"—she lowered her voice, the room filled with her scorn—"and if your reason was to see if I was meeting him, sleeping with him to get information, then you ought to know what I'm saying is true. After what happened that night I haven't been anywhere near the son of a bitch."

Marino didn't say a word.

His silence was his answer.

Abby had not been with Bill since.

Later, as paramedics were carrying the stretcher down, Abby leaned against the door frame, clutching it with white-knuckled emotion. She watched the white shape of her sister's body go past, stared after the retreating men, her face a pallid mask of abject grief.

I gripped her arm with unspoken feeling and went out in the wake of her incomprehensible loss. The odor lingered on the stairs, and when I stepped into the dazzling sunshine on the street, for a moment I was blind.

12

HENNA YARBOROUGH'S FLESH, wet from repeated rinsings, glistened like white marble in the overhead light. I was alone inside the morgue with her, suturing the last few inches of the Y incision, which ran in a wide seam from her pubis to her sternum and forked over her chest.

Wingo took care of her head before he left for the night. The skullcap was exactly in place, the incision around the back of her scalp neatly closed and completely covered by her hair, but the ligature mark around her neck was like a rope burn. Her face was bloated and purple, and neither my efforts nor those of the funeral home were ever going to change that.

The buzzer sounded rudely from the bay. I glanced up at the clock. It was shortly after 9:00 P.M.

Cutting the twine with a scalpel, I covered her with a sheet and peeled off my gloves. I could hear Fred, the security guard, saying something to someone down the hall as I pulled the body onto a gurney and began to wheel it into the refrigerator.

When I reemerged and shut the great steel door, Marino was leaning against the morgue desk and smoking a cigarette.

He watched me in silence as I collected evidence and tubes of blood and began to initial them.

"Find anything I need to know?"

"Her cause of death is asphyxiation due to strangulation due to the ligature around her neck," I said mechanically.

"What about trace?" He tapped an ash on the floor.

"A few fibers—"

"Well," he interrupted, "I gotta couple of things."

"Well," I said in the same tone, "I want to get the hell out of here."

"Yo, Doc. Exactly what I had in mind. Me, I'm thinking of taking a ride."

I stopped what I was doing and stared at him. His hair was clinging damply to his pate, his tie was loose, his short-sleeved white shirt was badly wrinkled in back as if he'd been sitting for a long time in his car. Strapped under his left arm was his tan shoulder holster with its long-barreled revolver. In the harsh glare of the overhead light he looked almost menacing, his eyes deeply set in shadows, his jaw muscles flexing.

"Think you need to come along," he added unemphatically. "So, I'll just wait while you get out of your scrubs there and call home."

Call home? How did he know there was anyone at home I needed to call? I'd never mentioned my niece to him. I'd never mentioned Bertha. As far as I was concerned, it was none of Marino's goddam business I even had a home.

I was about to tell him I had no intention of riding anywhere with him when the hard look in his eyes stopped me cold.

"All right," I muttered. "All right."

He was still leaning against the desk smoking as I walked across the suite and went into the locker room. Washing my face in the sink, I got out of my gown and back into skirt and blouse. I was so distracted, I opened my locker and reached for my lab coat before I realized what I was doing. I didn't need my lab coat. My pocketbook, briefcase and suit jacket were upstairs in my office.

Somehow I collected all of these things and followed Marino to his car. I opened the passenger door and the interior light didn't go on. Slipping inside, I groped for the shoulder harness and brushed crumbs and a wadded paper napkin off the seat.

He backed out of the lot without saying a word to me. The scanner light blinked from channel to channel as dispatchers transmitted calls Marino didn't seem interested in and which often I didn't understand. Cops mumbled into the microphone. Some of them seemed to eat it.

"Three-forty-five, ten-five, one-sixty-nine on chan'l three."

"One-sixty-nine, switchin' ov'."

"You free?"

"Ten-ten. Ten-seventeen the breath room. With subj't."

"Raise me whenyurten-twen-fo'."

"Ten-fo'."

"Four-fifty-one."

"Four-fifty-one X."

"Ten-twenty-eight on Adam Ida Lincoln one-seven-zero . . ."

Calls went out and alert tones blared like a bass key on an electric organ. Marino drove in silence, passing through downtown where storefronts were barred with the iron curtains drawn at the end of the day. Red and green neon signs in windows garishly advertised pawnshops and shoe repairs and greasy-spoon specials. The Sheraton and Marriott were lit up like ships, but there were very few cars or pedestrians out, just shadowy clusters of peripatetics from the projects lingering on corners. The whites of their eyes followed us as we passed.

It wasn't until several minutes later that I realized where we were going. On Winchester Place we slowed to a crawl in front of 498, Abby Turnbull's address. The brownstone was a black hulk, the flag a shadow limply stirring over the entrance. There were no cars in front. Abby wasn't home. I wondered where she was staying now.

Marino slowly pulled off the street and turned into the narrow alleyway between the brownstone and the house next door. The car rocked over ruts, the headlights jumping and illuminating the dark brick sides of the buildings, sweeping over garbage cans chained to posts and broken bottles and other debris. About twenty feet inside this claustrophobic passageway he stopped and cut the engine and the lights. Directly left of us was the backyard of Abby's house, a narrow shelf of grass girdled by a chainlink fence with a sign warning the world to "Beware" of a "Dog" I knew didn't exist.

Marino had the car searchlight out and the beam was licking over the rusting fire escape against the back of the house. All of the windows were closed, the glass glinting darkly. The seat creaked as he moved the light around the empty yard.

"Go on," he said. "I'm waiting to hear if you're thinking what I am."

I stated the obvious. "The sign. The sign on the fence. If the killer thought she had a dog, it should have given him pause. None of his victims had dogs. If they had, the women would probably still be alive."

"Bingo."

"And," I went on, "my suspicion is you're concluding the killer must have known the sign didn't mean anything, that Abby—or Henna—didn't have a dog. And how could he know that?"

"Yo. How could he know that," Marino echoed slowly, "unless he had a reason to know it?"

I said nothing.

He jammed in the cigarette lighter. "Like if maybe he'd been inside the house before."

"I don't think so . . ."

"Cut the playing-dumb act, Doc," he said quietly.

I got out my cigarettes, too, and my hands were trembling.

"I'm picturing it. I think you're picturing it. Some guy who's been inside Abby Turnbull's house. He don't know her sister's here, but he does know there ain't no damn dog. And Miss Turnbull here's someone he don't like none too well because she knows something he don't want anybody in the whole goddamn world to know."

He paused. I could feel him glancing over at me, but I refused to look at him or say a word.

"See, he's already had his piece of her, right? And maybe he couldn't help himself when he did his number because he's got some kind of compulsion, some screw loose, so to speak. He's worried. He's worried she's going to tell. Shit. She's a goddam reporter. She *gets paid* to tell people's dirty secrets. It's going to come out, what he did."

Another glance my way, and I remained stonily silent.

"So what's he do? He decides to whack her and make her look like the other ones. Only little problem is he don't know about Henna. Don't know where Abby's bedroom is either, see, because when he's been inside the house in the past, he never got any farther than the living room. So he goes in the wrong bedroom—Henna's bedroom—when he breaks in last Friday night. Why? Because that's the one with the lights on, because Abby's out of town. Well, it's too late. He's committed himself. He's got to go through with it. He murders her . . ."

"He couldn't have done it." I was trying to keep my voice from shaking. "Boltz would never do such a thing. He's not a murderer, for God's sake."

Silence.

Then Marino slowly looked over at me and flicked an ash. "Interesting. I didn't mention no names. But since you did, maybe we ought to pursue the subject, go a little deeper."

I was quiet again. It was catching up to me and I could feel my throat swelling. I refused to cry. Dammit! I wasn't going to let Marino see me cry!

"Listen, Doc," he said, and his voice was considerably calmer, "I'm not trying to jerk you around, all right? I mean, what you do in private's none of my damn business, all right? You're both consenting adults, unattached. But I know about it. I've seen his car at your place . . ."

"My house?" I asked, bewildered. "What—"

"Hey. I'm all over this goddam city. You live in the city, right? I know your state car. I know your damn address, and I know his white Audi. I know when I seen it at your house on several occasions over the past few months he wasn't there taking a deposition . . ."

"That's right. Maybe he wasn't. And it's none of your business, either."

"Well, it is." He flicked the cigarette butt out the window and lit another one. "It is my business now because of what he done to Miss Turnbull. That makes me wonder what else he's been doing."

"Henna's case is virtually the same as the other ones," I coldly told him. "There's no doubt in my mind she was murdered by the same man."

"What about her swabs?"

"Betty will work on them first thing in the morning. I don't know . . ."

"Well, I'll save you the trouble, Doc. Boltz is a nonsecreter. I think you know that, too, have known it for months."

"There are thousands of men in the city who are nonsecreters. You could be one, for all I know."

"Yeah," he said shortly. "Maybe I could be, for all you know. But fact is, you don't know. Fact is, you do know about Boltz. When you posted his wife last year, you PERKed her and found sperm, her husband's sperm. It's right there on the damn lab report that the guy she had sex with right before she took herself out is a nonsecreter. Hell, even I remember that. I was at the scene, remember?"

I didn't respond.

"I wasn't going to rule out nothing when I first walked into that bedroom and found her sitting up in her pretty little nightie, a big hole in her chest. Me, I always think murder first. Suicide's last on my list because if you don't think murder first, it's a little late after the fact. The only friggin' mistake I made back then was not taking a suspect's kit from Boltz. Suicide seemed so obvious after you did the post I marked the case exceptionally cleared. Maybe I shouldn't have. Back then I had a good reason to get his blood, to make sure the sperm inside her was his. He said it was, said they had sex early that morning. I let it go. I didn't get squat from him. Now I can't even ask. I don't got probable cause."

"You have to get more than blood," I said idiotically. "If he's A negative, B negative in the Lewis blood group system, you can't tell if he's a nonsecreter—you have to get saliva . . ."

"Yo. I know how to take a suspect kit, all right? It don't matter. We know what he is, right?"

I said nothing.

"We know the guy whacking these women is a nonsecreter. And we know Boltz would know the details of the crimes, know 'em so well he could take out Henna and make it look like the other ones."

"Well, get your kit and we'll get his DNA," I said angrily. "Just go ahead. That will tell you definitely."

"Hey. Maybe I will. Maybe I'll run him under the damn laser, too, and see if he sparkles."

The glittery residue on the mislabeled PERK flashed in my mind. Did the residue really come from my hands? Did Bill routinely wash his hands with Borawash soap?

"You found the sparkles on Henna's body?" Marino was asking.

"On her pajamas. The bedcovers, too."

Neither of us spoke for a while.

Then I said, "It's the same man. I know what my findings are. It's the same man."

"Yeah. Maybe it is. But that don't make me feel any better."

"You're sure what Abby said is true?"

"I buzzed by his office late this afternoon."

"You went to see him, to see Boltz?" I stammered.

"Oh, yeah."

"And did you get your confirmation?" My voice was rising.

"Yeah." He glanced over at me. "I got it more or less."

I didn't say anything. I was afraid to say anything.

" 'Course, he denied everything and got right hot about it. Threatened to sue her for slander, the whole nine yards. He won't, though. No way he'll make a peep about it because he's lying and I know it and he knows I know it."

I saw his hand go toward his left outer thigh and I suddenly panicked. His microcassette recorder!

"If you're doing what I think you're doing . . ." I blurted out.

"What?" he asked, surprised.

"If you've got a goddam tape recorder going . . ."

"Hey!" he protested. "I was scratching, all right? Hell, pat me down. Do a strip search if it'll make you feel better."

"You couldn't pay me enough."

He laughed. He was honestly amused.

He went on, "Want to know the truth? It makes me wonder what really happened to his wife."

I swallowed hard and said, "There was nothing suspicious about the physical findings. She had powder residues on her right hand—"

He cut me off. "Oh, sure. She pulled the trigger. I don't doubt that, but maybe we know why now, huh? Maybe he's been doing this for years. Maybe she found out."

Cranking the engine, he turned on his lights. Momentarily, we were rocking between houses and emerging on the street.

"Look." He wasn't going to give it a rest. "I don't mean to pry. Better put, it ain't my idea of a good time, okay? But you know him, Doc. You been seeing him, right?"

A transvestite was sashaying along a sidewalk, his yellow skirt swishing around his shapely legs, his false breasts firm and high, the false nipples erect beneath a tight white shell. Glassy eyes glanced our way.

"You been seeing him, right?" he asked again.

"Yes." My voice was almost inaudible.

"What about last Friday night?"

I couldn't remember at first. I couldn't think. The transvestite languidly turned around and went the other way.

"I took my niece to dinner and a movie."

"He with you?"

"No."

"You know where he was last Friday night?"

I shook my head.

"He didn't call or nothing?"

"No."

Silence.

"Shit," he muttered in frustration. "If only I'd known about it then, known what I know about him now, I would've driven past his crib. You know, checked to see where the hell he was. Shit."

Silence.

He tossed the cigarette butt out the window and lit up again. He was smoking one right after another. "So, how long you been seeing him?"

"Several months. Since April."

"He seeing any other ladies, or just you?"

"I don't think he's been seeing anybody else. I don't know. Obviously there's a lot about him I don't know."

He went on with the relentlessness of a threshing machine, "You ever pick up on anything? Anything *off* about him, I'm saying?"

"I don't know what you mean." My tongue was getting thick. I was almost slurring my words as if I were falling asleep.

"*Off*," he repeated. "Sex-wise."

I said nothing.

"He ever rough with you? Force anything?" A pause. "What's he like? He the animal Abby Turnbull described? Can you see him doing something like that, like what he done to her?"

I was hearing him and not hearing him. My thoughts were ebbing and flowing as if I were slipping in and out of consciousness.

". . . like aggression, I'm saying. Was he aggressive? You notice anything strange . . . ?"

The images. Bill. His hands crushing me, tearing at my clothes, pushing me down hard on the couch.

". . . guys like that, they have a pattern. It ain't sex they're really after. They have to *take* it. You know, a conquest . . ."

He was so rough. He was hurting me. He thrust his tongue

into my mouth. I couldn't breathe. It wasn't he. It was as if he'd become somebody else.

"Don't matter a damn he's good-looking, could have it when he wants it. You see that? People like that, they're *off. OFF . . .*"

Like Tony used to do when he was drunk and angry with me.

". . . I mean, he's a *friggin' rapist*, Doc. I know you don't want to hear it. But, goddam it, it's true. Seems like you might have picked up on something . . ."

He drank too much. Bill did. He was worse when he had too much to drink.

". . . happens all the time. You wouldn't believe the reports I get, these young ladies calling me to their cribs two months after the fact. They finally get around to telling someone. Maybe a friend convinces them to come forward with the info. Bankers, businessmen, politicians. They meet some babe in a bar, buy her a drink and slip in a little chloral hydrate. Boom. Next thing, she's waking up with this animal in her bed, feels like a friggin' truck's been run through her . . ."

He would never have tried such a thing with me. He cared about me. I wasn't an object, a stranger . . . Or maybe he'd simply been cautious. I know too much. He would never have gotten away with it.

". . . the toads get away with it for years. Some of 'em get away with it their whole lives. Go to their graves with as many notches on their belts as Jack the Giant Killer . . ."

We were stopped at a red light. I had no idea how long we'd been sitting here, not moving.

"That's the right al-lusion, ain't it? The drone who killed flies, put a notch on his belt for each one . . ."

The light was a bright red eye.

"He ever do it to you, Doc? Boltz ever rape you?"

"What?" I slowly turned toward him. He was staring straight ahead, his face pale in the red glow of the traffic light.

"What?" I asked again. My heart was pounding.

The light blinked from red to green, and we were moving again.

"Did he ever rape you?" Marino demanded, as if I were someone he didn't know, as if I were one of the "babes" whose "cribs" he was called to in the past.

I could feel the blood creeping up my neck.

"He ever hurt you, try to choke you, anything like . . ."

Rage exploded from me. I was seeing flecks of light. As if something were shorting out. Blinded as blood pounded inside my head. *"No! I've told you every goddam thing I know about him! Every goddam thing I'm going to tell you! PERIOD!"*

Marino was stunned into silence.

I didn't know where we were at first.

The great white clock face floated directly ahead as shadows and shapes materialized into the small trailer park of mobile unit laboratories beyond the back parking lot. There was no one else around as we crept to a halt beside my state car.

I unfastened my seatbelt. I was trembling all over.

Tuesday it rained. Water poured from gray skies and my wipers couldn't clear the windshield fast enough. I was part of the barely moving string of traffic creeping along the interstate.

The weather mirrored my mood. The encounter with Marino left me feeling physically sick, hung over. How long had he known? How often had he seen the white Audi parked in my drive? Was it more than idle curiosity when he cruised past my house? He wanted to see how the uppity lady chief lived. He probably knew what the Commonwealth paid me and what my mortgage was each month.

Spitting flares forced me to merge into the left lane, and as I crept past an ambulance, and police directing traffic around a badly mangled van, my dark thoughts were interrupted by the radio.

"... Henna Yarborough was sexually assaulted and strangled, and it is believed she was murdered by the same man who has killed four other Richmond women in the past two months ..."

I turned up the volume and listened to what I'd already heard several times since leaving my house. Murder seemed to be the only news in Richmond these days.

"... the latest development. According to a source close to the investigation, Dr. Lori Petersen may have attempted to dial 911 just before she was murdered ..."

This juicy revelation had been on the front page of the morning newspaper.

"... Director of Public Safety Norman Tanner was reached at his home ..."

Tanner read an obviously prepared statement. "The police bureau has been apprised of the situation. Due to the sensitivity of these cases, I can't make any comment . . ."

"Do you have any idea who the source of this information is, Mr. Tanner?" the reporter asked.

"Not at liberty to make any comments about that . . ."

He couldn't comment because he didn't know.

But I did.

The so-called source close to the investigation had to be Abby herself. Her byline was nowhere to be found. Obviously, her editors would have taken her off the stories. She was no longer reporting the news, now she was making it, and I remembered her threat: "Someone will pay . . ." She wanted Bill to pay, the police to pay, the city to pay, God Himself to pay. I was waiting for news of the computer violation and the mislabeled PERK. The person who would pay was going to be me.

I didn't get to the office until almost eight-thirty, and by then the phones were already ringing up and down the hall.

"Reporters," Rose complained as she came in and deposited a wad of pink telephone message slips on my blotter. "Wire services, magazines and a minute ago some guy from New Jersey who says he's writing a book."

I lit a cigarette.

"The bit about Lori Petersen calling the police," she added, her face lined with anxiety. "How awful, if it's true . . ."

"Just keep sending everybody across the street," I interrupted. "Anybody who calls about these cases gets directed to Amburgey."

He had already sent me several electronic memos demanding I have a copy of Henna Yarborough's autopsy report on his desk "immediately." In the most recent memo, "immediately" was under-lined and included was the insulting remark "Expect explanation about *Times* release."

Was he implying I was somehow responsible for this latest "leak" to the press? Was he accusing me of telling a reporter about the aborted 911 call?

Amburgey would get no explanation from me. He wasn't go-ing to get a damn thing from me today, not even if he sent twenty memos and appeared in person.

"Sergeant Marino's here," Rose quite unnerved me by adding. "Do you want to see him?"

I knew what he wanted. In fact, I'd already made a copy of my report for him. I supposed I was hoping he'd stop by later in the day, when I was gone.

I was initialing a stack of toxicology reports when I heard his heavy footsteps down the hall. When he came in, he was wearing a dripping-wet navy blue rain slicker. His sparse hair was plastered to his head, his face haggard.

"About last night . . ." he ventured as he approached my desk. The look in my eyes shut him up.

Ill at ease, he glanced around as he unsnapped his slicker and dug inside a pocket for his cigarettes. "Raining cats and dogs out there," he muttered. "Whatever the hell that means. Don't make any sense, when you think of it." A pause. " 'Sposed to burn off by noon."

Wordlessly, I handed him a photocopy of Henna Yarborough's autopsy report, which included Betty's preliminary serological findings. He didn't take the chair on the other side of my desk but stood where he was, dripping on my rug, as he began to read.

When he got to the gross description, I could see his eyes riveted about halfway down the page. His face was hard when he looked at me and asked, "Who all knows about this?"

"Hardly anybody."

"The commissioner seen it?"

"No."

"Tanner?"

"He called a while ago. I told him only her cause of death. I made no mention of her injuries."

He perused the report a little while longer. "Anybody else?" he asked without looking up.

"No one else has seen it."

Silence.

"Nothing in the papers," he said. "Not on the radio or the tube either. In other words, our leak out there don't know these details."

I stared stonily at him.

"Shit." He folded the report and tucked it inside a pocket. "The guy's a damn Jack the Ripper." Glancing at me, he added, "I take it you ain't heard a peep from Boltz. If you do, dodge him, make yourself scarce."

"And what's that supposed to mean?" The mere mention of Bill's name physically bit into me.

"Don't take his call, don't see him. Whatever's your style. I don't want him having a copy of anything right now. Don't want him seeing this report or knowing anything more than he already knows."

"You're still considering him a suspect?" I asked as calmly as possible.

"Hell, I'm not sure what I'm considering anymore," he retorted. "Fact is, he's the CA and has a right to whatever he wants, okay? Fact also is I don't give a rat's ass if he's the damn governor. I don't want him getting squat. So I'm just asking you to do what you can to avoid him, to give him the slip."

Bill wouldn't be by. I knew I wouldn't hear from him. He knew what Abby had said about him, and he knew I was present when she said it.

"And the other thing," he went on, snapping up his slicker and turning the collar up around his ears, "if you're gonna be pissed at me, then be pissed. But last night I was just doing my job and if you're thinking I enjoyed it, you're flat-out wrong."

He turned around at the sound of a throat clearing. Wingo hesitated in my doorway, his hands in the pockets of his stylish white linen trousers.

A look of disgust passed over Marino's face, and he rudely brushed past Wingo and left.

Nervously jingling change, Wingo came to the edge of my desk and said, "Uh, Dr. Scarpetta, there's another camera crew in the lobby . . ."

"Where's Rose?" I asked, slipping off my glasses. My eyelids felt as if they were lined with sandpaper.

"In the ladies' room or something. Uh, you want me to tell the guys to leave or what?"

"Send them across the street," I said, adding irritably, "just like we did to the last crew and the crew before that."

"Sure," he muttered, and he made no move to go anywhere. He was nervously jingling change again.

"Anything else?" I asked with forced patience.

"Well," he said, "there's something I'm curious about. It's about him, uh, about Amburgey. Uh, isn't he an antismoker and makes a lot of noise about it, or have I got him mixed up with somebody else?"

My eyes lingered on his grave face. I couldn't imagine why

it mattered as I replied, "He's strongly opposed to smoking and frequently takes public stands on the issue."

"Thought so. Seems like I've read stuff about it on the editorial page, heard him on TV, too. As I understand it, he plans to ban smoking from all HHSD buildings by next year."

"That's right," I replied, my irritation flaring. "By this time next year, your chief will be standing outside in the rain and cold to smoke—like some guilt-ridden teenager." Then I looked quizzically at him and asked, "Why?"

A shrug. "Just curious." Another shrug. "I take it he used to smoke and got converted or something."

"To my knowledge, he has never smoked," I told him.

My telephone rang again, and when I glanced up from my call sheet, Wingo was gone.

If nothing else, Marino was right about the weather. That afternoon I drove to Charlottesville beneath a dazzling blue sky, the only evidence of this morning's storm the mist rising from the rolling pastureland on the roadsides.

Amburgey's accusations continued to gnaw at me, so I intended to hear for myself what he had actually discussed with Dr. Spiro Fortosis. At least this was my rationale when I had made an appointment with the forensic psychiatrist. Actually, it wasn't my only reason. We'd known each other from the beginning of my career, and I'd never forgotten he had befriended me during those chilly days when I attended national forensic meetings and scarcely knew a soul. Talking to him was the closest I could comfortably get to unburdening myself without going to a shrink.

He was in the hallway of the dimly lit fourth floor of the brick building where his department was located. His face broke into a smile, and he gave me a fatherly hug, planting a light peck on the top of my head.

Professor of medicine and psychiatry at UVA, he was older by fifteen years, his hair white wings over his ears, his eyes kindly behind rimless glasses. Typically, he was dressed in a dark suit, a white shirt and a narrow striped tie that had been out of fashion long enough to come into vogue again. I'd always thought he could be a Norman Rockwell painting of the "town doctor."

"My office is being repainted," he explained, opening a dark wooden door halfway down the hall. "So if it won't bother you being treated like a patient, we'll go in here."

"Right now I feel like one of your patients," I said as he shut the door behind us.

The spacious room had all the comforts of a living room, albeit a somewhat neutral, emotionally defused one.

I settled into a tan leather couch. Scattered about were pale abstract watercolors and several nonflowering potted plants. Absent were magazines, books and a telephone. The lamps on end tables were switched off, the white designer blinds drawn just enough to allow sunlight to seep peacefully into the room.

"How's your mother, Kay?" Fortosis said as he pulled up a beige wing chair.

"Surviving. I think she'll outlive all of us."

He smiled. "We always think that of our mothers, and unfortunately it's rarely true."

"Your wife and daughters?"

"Doing quite well." His eyes were steady on me. "You look very tired."

"I suppose I am."

He was quiet for a moment.

"You're on the faculty of VMC," he began, in his mild unthreatening way. "I've been wondering if you might have known Lori Petersen in life."

With no further prompting, I found myself telling him what I had not admitted to anyone else. My need to verbalize it was overwhelming.

"I met her once," I said. "Or at least I'm fairly sure of it."

I had probed my memory exhaustively, especially during those quiet, introspective times when I was driving to or from work, or when I was out in my yard, tending to my roses. I would see Lori Petersen's face and try to superimpose it on the vague image of one of the countless VMC students gathered around me at labs, or in the audiences at lectures. By now, I'd convinced myself that when I studied the photographs of her inside her house, something clicked. She looked familiar.

Last month I had given a Grand Rounds lecture, "Women in Medicine." I remembered standing behind the podium and looking out over a sea of young faces lining the tiers rising up to the back of the medical college auditorium. The students had brought their lunches and were sitting comfortably in the red-cushioned seats as they ate and sipped their soft drinks. The occasion was like all others before it, nothing extraordinary or particularly memorable about it, except retrospectively.

I did not know for a fact but believed Lori was one of the women who came forward afterward to ask questions. I saw the hazy image of an attractive blonde in a lab coat. The only feature I remembered clearly was her eyes, dark green and tentative, as she asked me if I really thought it was possible for a woman to manage a family and a career as demanding as medicine. This stood out because I momentarily faltered. I managed one but certainly not the other.

Obsessively I'd replayed that scene, going over and over it in my mind, as if the face would come into focus if I conjured it up enough. Was it she or wasn't it? I would never be able to walk the halls of VMC again without looking for that blond physician. I did not think I would find her. I think she was Lori briefly appearing before me like a ghost from a future horror that would relegate her to nothing but a past.

"Interesting," Fortosis remarked in his thoughtful way. "Why do you suppose it's important that you met her then or at any other time?"

I stared at the smoke drifting up from my cigarette. "I'm not sure, except that it makes her death more real."

"If you could go back to that day, would you?"

"Yes."

"What would you do?"

"I would somehow warn her," I said. "I would somehow undo what he did."

"What her killer did?"

"Yes."

"Do you think about him?"

"I don't want to think about him. I just want to do everything I can to make sure he is caught."

"And punished?"

"There's no punishment equal to the crime. No punishment would be enough."

"If he's put to death, won't that be punishment enough, Kay?"

"He can die only once."

"You want him to suffer, then." His eyes wouldn't let me go.

"Yes," I said.

"How? Pain?"

"Fear," I said. "I want him to feel the fear they felt when they knew they were going to die."

I wasn't aware of how long I'd talked but the inside of the room was darker when I finally stopped.

"I suppose it's getting beneath my skin in a way other cases haven't," I admitted.

"It's like dreams." He leaned back in the chair and lightly tapped his fingertips together. "People often say they don't dream, when it's more accurate to say that they *don't remember* their dreams. It gets under our skin, Kay. All of it does. We just manage to cage in most of the emotions so they don't devour us."

"Obviously, I'm not managing that too well these days, Spiro."

"Why?"

I suspected he knew very well but he wanted me to say it. "Maybe because Lori Petersen was a physician. I relate to her. Maybe I'm projecting. I was her age once."

"In a sense, you *were* her once."

"In a sense."

"And what happened to her—it could have been you?"

"I don't know if I've pushed it that far."

"I think you have." He smiled a little. "I think you've been pushing a lot of things pretty far. What else?"

Amburgey. What did Fortosis actually say to him?

"There are a lot of peripheral pressures."

"Such as?"

"Politics." I brought it up.

"Oh, yes." He was still tapping his fingertips together. "There's always that."

"The leaks to the press. Amburgey's concerned they might be coming from my office." I hesitated, looking for any sign that he was already privy to this.

His impassive face told me nothing.

"According to him, it's your theory the news stories are making the killer's homicidal urge peak more quickly, and therefore the leaks could be indirectly responsible for Lori's death. And now Henna Yarborough's death, too. I'll be hearing that next, I'm sure."

"Is it possible the leaks are coming from your office?"

"Someone—an outsider—broke into our computer data base. That makes it possible. Better put, it places me in a somewhat indefensible position."

"Unless you find out who's responsible," he matter-of-factly stated.

"I don't see a way in the world to do that." I pressed him, "You talked to Amburgey."

He met my eyes. "I did. But I think he's overemphasized what I said, Kay. I would never go so far as to claim information allegedly leaked from your office is responsible for the last two homicides. The two women would be alive, in other words, were it not for the news accounts. I can't say that. I didn't say that."

I was sure my relief was visible.

"However, if Amburgey or anyone else intends to make a big deal of the so-called leaks that may have come from your office computer, I'm afraid there isn't much I can do about it. In truth, I feel strongly there's a significant link between publicity and the killer's activity. If sensitive information is resulting in more inflammatory stories and bigger headlines, then yes, Amburgey—or anybody else for that matter—may take what I objectively say and use it against your office." He looked at me for a long moment. "Do you understand what I'm saying?"

"You're saying you can't defuse the bomb," I replied, my spirits falling.

Leaning forward, he flatly told me, "I'm saying I can't defuse a bomb I can't even see. What bomb? Are you suggesting someone's setting you up?"

"I don't know," I replied carefully. "All I can tell you is the city stands to have a lot of egg on its face because of the 911 call Lori Petersen made to the police right before she was murdered. You read about that?"

He nodded, his eyes interested.

"Amburgey called me in to discuss the matter long before this morning's story. Tanner was there. So was Boltz. They said there might be a scandal, a lawsuit. At this point, Amburgey mandated that all further information to the press would have to be routed through him. No comments whatsoever are to come from me. He said you think the leaks to the press, the subsequent stories are escalating the killer's activities. I was questioned at length about the leaks, about the potentiality of their source being my office. I had no choice but to admit someone's gotten into our data base."

"I see."

"As all this progressed," I continued, "I began to get the unsettling impression if any scandal erupts, it's going to be over what's supposedly been happening inside my office. The implication: I've hurt the investigation, perhaps indirectly caused more women to die . . ." I paused. My voice was starting to rise. "In other words, I have visions of everyone ignoring the city's screwup with the 911 call because everyone's so busy being enraged with the OCME, with me."

He made no comment.

I lamely added, "Maybe I'm getting bent over nothing."

"Maybe not."

It wasn't what I wanted to hear.

"Theoretically," he explained, "it could happen exactly as you've just outlined it. If certain parties wanted it to happen that way, because they're trying to save their own skins. The medical examiner is an easy scapegoat. The public, in the main, doesn't understand what the ME does, has rather ghastly, objectionable impressions and assumptions. People tend to resist the idea of someone cutting up a loved one's body. They see it as mutilation, the final indignity—"

"Please," I broke out.

He mildly went on, "You get my point."

"All too well."

"It's a damn shame about the computer break-in."

"Lord. It makes me wish we were still using typewriters."

He stared through the window. "To get lawyerly with you, Kay." His eyes drifted toward me, his face grim. "I propose you be very careful. But I strongly advise you not to get so caught up in this that you let it distract you from the investigation. Dirty politics, or the fear of them, can be unsettling to the point you can make mistakes sparing your antagonists the trouble of manufacturing them."

The mislabeled slides flashed in my mind. My stomach knotted.

He added, "It's like people on a sinking ship. They can become savage. Every man for himself. You don't want to be in the way. You don't want to put yourself in a vulnerable position when people are panicking. And people in Richmond are panicking."

"Certain people are," I agreed.

"Understandably. Lori Petersen's death was preventable. The police made an unforgivable error when they didn't give her 911 call a high priority. The killer hasn't been caught. Women are continuing to die. The public is blaming the city officials, who in turn have to find someone else to blame. It's the nature of the beast. If the police, the politicians, can pass the buck on down the line, they will."

"On down the line and right to my doorstep," I said bitterly, and I automatically thought of Cagney.

Would this have happened to him?

I knew what the answer was, and I voiced it out loud. "I can't help but think I'm an easy mark because I'm a woman."

"You're a woman in a man's world," Fortosis replied. "You'll always be considered an easy mark until the ole boys discover you have teeth. And you do have teeth." He smiled. "Make sure they know it."

"How?"

He asked. "Is there anyone in your office you trust implicitly?"

"My staff is very loyal . . ."

He waved off the remark. "*Trust*, Kay. I mean trust with your life. Your computer analyst, for example?"

"Margaret's always been faithful," I replied hesitantly. "But trust with my life? I don't think so. I scarcely know her, not personally."

"My point is, your security—your best defense, if you want to think of it as such—would be to somehow determine who's been breaking into your computer. It may not be possible. But if there's a chance, then I suspect it would take someone who's sufficiently trained in computers to figure it out. A technological detective, someone you trust. I think it would be unwise to involve someone you scarcely know, someone who might talk."

"No one comes to mind," I told him. "And even if I found out, the news might be bad. If it *is* a reporter getting in, I don't see how finding that out will solve my problem."

"Maybe it wouldn't. But if it were I, I'd take the chance."

I wondered where he was pushing me. I was getting the feeling he had his own suspicions.

"I'll keep all this in mind," he promised, "if and when I get calls about these cases, Kay. If someone pressures me, for example, about the news accounts escalating the killer's peak, that sort of thing." A pause. "I have no intention of being used. But I can't lie, either. The fact is, this killer's reaction to publicity, his MO, in other words, is a little unusual."

I just listened.

"Not all serial killers love to read about themselves, in truth. The public tends to believe the vast majority of people who commit sensational crimes want recognition, want to feel important. Like Hinckley. You shoot the President and you're an instant hero. An inadequate, poorly integrated person who can't keep a job and maintain a normal relationship with anyone is suddenly internationally known. These types are the exception, in my opinion. They are one extreme.

"The other extreme is your Lucases and Tooles. They do what they do and often don't even stick around in the city long enough to read about themselves. They don't want anybody to know. They hide the bodies and cover their tracks. They spend much of their time on the road, drifting from place to place, looking for their next targets along the way. It's my impression, based on a close examination of the Richmond killer's MO, that he's a blend of both extremes: He does it because it's a compulsion, and he absolutely doesn't want to be caught. But he also thrives on the attention, he wants everyone to know what he's done."

"This is what you told Amburgey?" I asked.

"I don't think it was quite this clear in my mind when I talked to him or anyone else last week. It took Henna Yarborough's murder to convince me."

"Because of Abby Turnbull."

"Yes."

"If she was the intended victim," I went on, "what better way to shock the city and make national news than to kill the prize-winning reporter who's been covering the stories."

"If Abby Turnbull was the intended victim, her selection strikes me as rather personal. The first four, it appears, were impersonal, stranger killings. The women were unknown to the assailant, he stalked them. They were targets of opportunity."

"The DNA test results will confirm whether it's the same man," I said, anticipating where I assumed his thoughts were going. "But

I'm sure of it. I don't for a minute believe Henna was murdered by somebody else, a different person who might have been after her sister."

Fortosis said, "Abby Turnbull is a celebrity. On the one hand, I asked myself, if she was the intended victim, does it fit that the killer would make a mistake and murder her sister instead? On the other, if the intended victim was Henna Yarborough, isn't the coincidence she's Abby's sister somewhat overwhelming?"

"Stranger things have happened."

"Of course. Nothing is certain. We can conjecture all our lives and never pin it down. Why this or why that? Motive, for example. Was he abused by his mother, was he molested, et cetera, et cetera? Is he paying back society, showing his contempt for the world? The longer I'm in this profession the more I believe the very thing most psychiatrists don't want to hear, which is that many of these people kill because they enjoy it."

"I reached that conclusion a long time ago," I angrily told him.

"I think the killer in Richmond is enjoying himself," he calmly continued. "He's very cunning, very deliberate. He rarely makes mistakes. We're not dealing with some mental misfit who has damage to his right frontal lobe. Nor is he psychotic, absolutely not. He is a psychopathic sexual sadist who is above average in intelligence and able to function well enough in society to maintain an acceptable public persona. I think he's gainfully employed in Richmond. Wouldn't surprise me in the least if he's involved in an occupation, a hobby, that brings him in contact with distraught or injured people, or people he can easily control."

"What sort of occupation, exactly?" I asked uneasily.

"Could be just about anything. I'm willing to bet he's shrewd enough, competent enough, to do just about anything he likes."

"Doctor, lawyer, Indian chief," I heard Marino say.

I reminded Fortosis, "You've changed your mind. Originally you assumed he might have a criminal record or history of mental illness, maybe both. Someone who was just let out of a mental institution or prison—"

He interrupted, "In light of these last two homicides, particularly if Abby Turnbull figures in, I don't think that at all. Psychotic offenders rarely, if ever, have the wherewithal to repeatedly elude the police. I'm of the opinion that the killer in Richmond is experienced, has probably been murdering for years in other places, and has escaped apprehension as successfully in the past as he's escaping it now."

"You're thinking he moves to a new place and kills for several months, then moves on?"

"Not necessarily," he replied. "He may be disciplined enough to move to a new place and get himself settled in his job. It's possible he can go for quite a while until he starts. When he starts, he can't stop. And with each new territory it's taking more to satisfy him. He's becoming increasingly daring, more out of control. He's taunting the police and enjoying making himself the major preoccupation of the city, that is, through the press—and possibly through his victim selection."

"Abby," I muttered. "If he really was after her."

He nodded. "That was new, the most daring, reckless, thing he's done—if he set out to murder a highly visible police reporter. It would have been his greatest performance. There could be other components, ideas of reference, projection. Abby writes about him and he thinks he has something personal with her. He develops a relationship with her. His rage, his fantasies, focus on her."

"But he screwed up," I angrily retorted. "His so-called greatest performance and he completely screws it up."

"Exactly. He may not have been familiar enough with Abby to know what she looks like, know that her sister moved in with her last fall." His eyes were steady as he added, "It's entirely possible he didn't know until he watched the news or read the papers that the woman he murdered wasn't Abby."

I was startled by the thought. It hadn't occurred to me.

"And this worries me considerably." He leaned back in the chair.

"What? He might come after her again?" I seriously doubted it.

"It worries me." He seemed to be thinking out loud now. "It didn't happen the way he planned. In his own mind, he made a fool of himself. This may only serve to make him more vicious."

"How violent does he have to be to qualify as 'more vicious'?" I blurted out loudly. "You know what he did to Lori. And now Henna . . ."

The look on his face stopped me.

"I rang up Marino shortly before you got here, Kay."

Fortosis knew.

He knew Henna Yarborough's vaginal swabs were negative.

The killer probably misfired. Most of the seminal fluid I collected was on the bedcovers and her legs. Or else the only instrument he successfully inserted was his knife. The sheets beneath her were stiff and dark with dried blood. Had he not strangled her, she probably would have bled to death.

We sat in oppressive silence with the terrible image of a person who could take pleasure in causing such horrendous pain to another human being.

When I looked at Fortosis his eyes were dull, his face drained. I think it was the first time I'd ever realized he was old beyond his years. He could hear, he could see what happened to Henna. He knew these things even more vividly than I. The room closed in on us.

We both got up at the same time.

I took the long way back to my car, veering across the campus instead of following the direct route of the narrow road leading to the parking deck. The Blue Ridge Mountains were a hazy frozen ocean in the distance, the dome of the rotunda bright white, and long fingers of shadow were spreading across the lawn. I could smell the scent of trees and grass still warm in the sun.

Knots of students drifted past, laughing and chatting and paying me no attention. As I walked beneath the spreading arms of a giant oak, my heart jumped into my throat at the sudden sound of running feet behind me. I abruptly spun around, and a young jogger met my startled gaze, his lips parting in surprise. He was a flash of red shorts and long brown legs as he cut across a sidewalk and was gone.

13

THE NEXT MORNING I was at the office by six. No one else was in, the phones up front still coded to roll over to the state switchboard.

While coffee was dripping, I stepped into Margaret's office. The computer in answer mode was still daring the perpetrator to try again. He hadn't.

It didn't make sense. Did he know we had discovered the break-in after he tried to pull up Lori Petersen's case last week? Did he get spooked? Did he suspect nothing new was being entered?

Or was there some other reason? I stared at the dark screen. Who are you? I wondered. What do you want from me?

The ringing started again down the hall. Three rings and abrupt silence as the state operator intervened.

"He's very cunning, very deliberate . . ."

Fortosis didn't need to tell me that.

"We're not dealing with some mental misfit . . ."

I wasn't expecting him to be anything like us. But he could be. Maybe he was.

". . . able to function well enough in society to maintain an acceptable public persona . . ."

He might be competent enough to work in any profession. He might use a computer on his job or he might have one at home.

He would want to get inside my mind. He would want to get inside my mind as much as I wanted to get inside his. I was the only real link between him and his victims. I was the only living witness. When I examined the contusions, the fractured bones, and the deep tissue cuts, I alone realized the force, the savageness required to inflict the injuries. Ribs are flexible in young, healthy people. He broke Lori's ribs by smashing his knees down on top of her rib cage with all of his weight. She was on her back then. He did this after her jerked the telephone cord out of the wall.

The fractures to her fingers were twist fractures, the bones violently wrenched out of joint. He gagged and tied her, then broke her fingers one by one. He had no reason except to cause her excruciating pain and give her a taste of what was to come.

All the while, she was panicking for air. Panicking as the constricted blood flow ruptured vessels like small balloons and made her head feel as if it were going to explode. Then he forced himself inside her, into virtually every orifice.

The more she struggled, the more the electrical cord tightened around her neck until she blacked out for the last time and died.

I had reconstructed all of it. I had reconstructed what he did to all of them.

He was wondering what I knew. He was arrogant. He was paranoid.

Everything was in the computer, everything he did to Patty, to Brenda, to Cecile . . . The description of every injury, every shred of evidence we'd found, every laboratory test I'd instigated.

Was he reading the words I dictated? Was he reading my mind?

My low-heeled shoes clicked sharply along the empty hallway as I ran back to my office. In a burst of frantic energy, I emptied the contents of my billfold until I found the business card, off-white with the *Times* masthead in raised black Gothic print across the center. On the back was the ballpoint scribbling of an unsteady hand.

I dialed Abby Turnbull's pager number.

———

I scheduled the meeting for the afternoon because when I spoke to Abby her sister's body had not yet been released. I didn't want Abby inside the building until Henna was gone and in the care of the funeral home.

Abby was on time. Rose quietly showed her to my office and I just as quietly shut both doors.

She looked terrible. Her face was more deeply lined, her color almost gray. Her hair was loose and bushy over her shoulders, and she was dressed in a wrinkled white cotton blouse and khaki skirt. When she lit a cigarette, I noticed she was shaking. Somewhere deep within the emptiness of her eyes was a glint of grief, of rage.

I began by telling her what I told the loved ones of any of the victims whose cases I worked.

"The cause of your sister's death, Abby, was strangulation due to the ligature around her neck."

"How long?" She blew out a tremulous stream of smoke. "How long did she live after . . . after he got to her?"

"I can't tell you exactly. But the physical findings lead me to suspect her death was quick."

Not quick enough, I did not say. I found fibers inside Henna's mouth. She had been gagged. The monster wanted her alive for a while and he wanted her quiet. Based on the amount of blood loss, I'd classified her cutting injuries as perimortem, meaning I could say with certainty only that they were afflicted around the time of death. She bled very little into surrounding tissues after the assault with the knife. She may already have been dead. She may have been unconscious.

More likely it was worse than that. I suspected the cord from the venetian blinds was jerked tight around her neck when she straightened her legs in a violent reflex to pain.

"She had petechial hemorrhages in the conjunctivae, and facial and neck skin," I said to Abby. "In other words, rupture of the small, superficial vessels of the eyes and face. This is caused by pressure, by cervical occlusion of the jugular veins due to the ligature around her neck."

"How long did she live?" she dully asked again.

"Minutes," I repeated.

That's as far as I intended to go. Abby seemed slightly relieved. She was seeking solace in the hope her sister's suffering was minimal. Someday, when the case was closed and Abby was stronger, she would know. God help her, she would know about the knife.

"That's all?" she asked shakily.

"That's all I can say now," I told her. "I'm sorry. I'm so terribly sorry about Henna."

She smoked for a while, taking nervous jerky drags as if she didn't know what to do with her hands. She was biting her lower lip, trying to keep it from trembling.

When she finally met my eyes, her own were uneasy, suspicious.

She knew I hadn't asked her here for this. She sensed there was something else.

"It's really not why you called, is it?"

"Not entirely," I replied frankly.

Silence.

I could see the resentment, the anger building.

"What?" she demanded. "What is it you want from me?"

"I want to know what you're going to do."

Her eyes flashed. "Oh, I get it. You're worried about your goddam self. Jesus Christ. You're just like the rest of them!"

"I'm not worried about myself," I said very calmly. "I'm beyond that, Abby. You have enough to cause me trouble. If you want to run my office and me into the ground, then do it. That's your decision."

She looked uncertain, her eyes shifting away.

"I understand your rage."

"You couldn't possibly understand it."

"I understand it better than you might imagine." Bill flashed in my mind. I could understand Abby's rage very well.

"You couldn't. Nobody could!" she exclaimed. "He stole my sister from me. He stole a part of my life. I'm so damn tired of people taking things from me! What kind of world is this," she choked, "where someone can do something like that? Oh, Jesus! I *don't know* what I'm going to do . . ."

I said firmly, "I know you intend to investigate your sister's death on your own, Abby. Don't do it."

"Somebody's got to!" she cried out. "What? I'm supposed to leave it up to the Keystone Kops?"

"Some matters you must leave to the police. But you can help. You can if you really want to."

"Don't patronize me!"

"I'm not."

"I'll do it my own way . . ."

"No. You won't do it your own way, Abby. Do it for your sister."

She stared blankly at me with red-rimmed eyes.

"I asked you here because I'm taking a gamble. I need your help."

"Right! You need me to help by leaving town and keeping the hell out of it . . ."

I was slowly shaking my head.

She looked surprised.

"Do you know Benton Wesley?"

"The profiler," she replied hesitantly. "I know who he is."

I glanced up at the wall clock. "He'll be here in ten minutes."

She stared at me for a long time. "What? What is it, exactly, you want me to do?"

"Use your journalistic connections to help us find him."

"*Him?*" Her eyes widened.

I got up to see if there was any coffee left.

Wesley was reluctant when I had explained my plan over the telephone, but now that the three of us were in my office it seemed clear to me he'd accepted it.

"Your complete cooperation is nonnegotiable," he said to Abby emphatically. "I've got to have your assurance you'll do exactly what we agree upon. Any improvisation or creative thinking on your part could blow the investigation right out of the water. Your discretion is imperative."

She nodded, then pointed out, "If it's the killer breaking into the computer, why's he done it only once?"

"Once we're aware of," I reminded her.

"Still, it hasn't happened again since you discovered it."

Wesley suggested, "He's been running like hell. He's murdered two women in two weeks and there's probably been sufficient information in the press to satisfy his curiosity. He could be sitting pretty, feeling smug, because by all news accounts we don't have anything on him."

"We've got to inflame him," I added. "We've got to do something to make him so paranoid he gets reckless. One way to do this is to make him think my office has found evidence that could be the break we've been waiting for."

"If he's the one getting into the computer," Wesley summarized, "this could be sufficient incentive for him to try again to discover what we supposedly know." He looked at me.

The fact was we had no break in the case. I'd indefinitely

banished Margaret from her office and the computer was to be left in answer mode. Wesley had set up a tracer to track all calls made to her extension. We were going to use the computer to lure the murderer by having Abby's paper print a story claiming the forensic investigation had come up with a "significant link."

"He's going to be paranoid, upset enough to believe it," I predicted. "If he's ever been treated in a hospital around here, for example, he's going to worry now that we might track him through old charts. If he gets any special medications from a pharmacy, he's got that to worry about, too."

All of this hinged on the peculiar odor Matt Petersen mentioned to the police. There was no other "evidence" to which we could safely allude.

The one piece of evidence the killer would have trouble with was DNA.

I could bluff him from hell to breakfast with it, and it might not even be a bluff.

Several days ago, I had gotten copies of the reports from the first two cases. I studied the vertical array of bands of varying shades and widths, patterns that looked remarkably like the bar codes stamped on supermarket packaged foods. There were three radioactive probes in each case, and the position of the bands in each probe for Patty Lewis's case was indistinguishable from the position of the bands in the three probes in Brenda Steppe's.

"Of course this doesn't give us his identity," I explained to Abby and Wesley. "All we can say is if he's black, then only one out of 135 million men theoretically can fit the same pattern. If he's Caucasian, only one out of 500 million men."

DNA is the microcosm of the total person, his life code. Genetic engineers in a private laboratory in New York had isolated the DNA from the samples of seminal fluid I collected. They snipped the samples at specific sites, and the fragments migrated to discrete regions of an electrically charged surface covered with a thick gel. A positively charged pole was at one end of the surface, a negatively charged pole at the other.

"DNA carries a negative charge," I went on. "Opposites attract."

The shorter fragments traveled farther and faster in the positive direction than the longer ones did, and the fragments spread out across the gel, forming the band pattern. This was transferred to a nylon membrane and exposed to a probe.

"I don't get it," Abby interrupted. "What *probe?*"

I explained. "The killer's double-stranded DNA fragments were broken, or denatured, into single strands. In more simplistic terms, they were unzipped like a zipper. The probe is a solution of single-stranded DNA of a specific base sequence that's labeled with a radioactive marker. When the solution, or probe, was washed over the nylon membrane, the probe sought out and bonded with complementary single strands—with the killer's complementary single strands."

"So the zipper is zipped back up?" she asked. "But it's radioactive now?"

"The point is that his pattern can now be visualized on X-ray film," I said.

"Yeah, his *bar code.* Too bad we can't run it over a scanner and come up with his name," Wesley dryly added.

"Everything about him is there," I continued. "The problem is the technology isn't sophisticated enough yet to read the specifics, such as genetic defects, eye and hair color, that sort of thing. There are so many bands present covering so many points in the person's genetic makeup it's simply too complex to definitively make anything more out of it than a match or a nonmatch."

"But the killer doesn't know that." Wesley looked speculatively at me.

"That's right."

"Not unless he's a scientist or something," Abby interjected.

"We'll assume he isn't," I told them. "I suspect he never gave DNA profiling a thought until he started reading about it in the papers. I doubt he understands the concept very well."

"I'll explain the procedure in my story," Abby thought out loud. "I'll make him understand it just enough to freak him."

"Just enough to make him think we know about his defect," Wesley agreed. "If he has a defect . . . That's what worries me, Kay." He looked levelly at me. "What if he doesn't?"

I patiently went over it again. "What continues to stand out to me is Matt Petersen's reference to 'pancakes,' to the smell inside the bedroom reminding him of pancakes, of something sweet but sweaty."

"Maple syrup," Wesley recalled.

"Yes. If the killer has a body odor reminiscent of maple syrup, he may have some sort of anomaly, some type of metabolic disorder. Specifically, 'maple syrup urine disease.' "

"And it's genetic?" Wesley had asked this twice.

"That's the beauty of it, Benton. If he has it, it's in his DNA somewhere."

"I've never heard of it," Abby said. "This disease."

"Well, it's not exactly your common cold."

"Then *exactly* what is it?"

I got up from my desk and went to a bookcase. Sliding out the fat *Textbook of Medicine*, I opened it to the right page and set it before them.

"It's an enzyme defect," I explained as I sat back down. "The defect results in amino acids accumulating in the body like a poison. In the classic or acute form, the person suffers severe mental retardation and/or death at infancy, which is why it's rare to find healthy adults of sound mind who suffer from the disease. But it's possible. In its mild form, which would have to be what the killer suffers from if this is his affliction, postnatal development is normal, symptoms are intermittent, and the disease can be treated through a low-protein diet, and possibly through dietary supplements—specifically, thiamine, or vitamin B_1, at ten times the normal daily intake."

"In other words," Wesley said, leaning forward and frowning as he scanned the book, "he could suffer from the mild form, lead a fairly normal life, be smart as hell—but stink?"

I nodded. "The most common indication of maple syrup urine disease is a characteristic odor, a distinctive maple-syrupy odor of the urine and perspiration. The symptoms are going to be more acute when he's under stress, the odor more pronounced when he's doing what stresses him most, which is committing these murders. The odor's going to get into his clothing. He's going to have a long history of being self-conscious about his problem."

"You wouldn't smell it in his seminal fluid?" Wesley asked.

"Not necessarily."

"Well," Abby said, "if he's got this body odor, then he must take a lot of showers. If he works around people. They'd notice it, the smell."

I didn't respond.

She didn't know about the glittery residue, and I wasn't going to tell her. If the killer has this chronic odor, it wouldn't be the least bit unusual for him to be compulsive about washing his armpits, his face and hands, frequently throughout the day while he's exposed to people who might notice his problem. He might be washing himself while at work, where there might be a dispenser of borax soap in the men's room.

"It's a gamble." Wesley leaned back in his chair. "Jeez." Shaking his head. "If the smell Petersen mentioned was something he imagined or something he confused with another odor—maybe a cologne the killer was wearing—we're going to look like fools. The squirrel's going to be all the more certain we don't know what the hell we're doing."

"I don't think Petersen imagined the smell," I said with conviction. "As shocked as he was when he found his wife's body, the smell had to be unusual and potent for Petersen to notice and remember it. I can't think of a single cologne that would smell like sweaty maple syrup. I'm speculating the killer was sweating profusely, that he'd left the bedroom maybe minutes before Petersen walked in."

"The disease causes retardation . . ." Abby was flipping through the book.

"If it's not treated immediately after birth," I repeated.

"Well, this bastard isn't retarded." She looked up at me, her eyes hard.

"Of course he isn't," Wesley agreed. "Psychopaths are anything but stupid. What we want to do is make the guy *think* we think he's stupid. Hit him where it hurts—his goddam pride, which is hooked up with his grandiose notions of his off-the-charts IQ."

"This disease," I told them, "could do that. If he has it, he's going to know it. Possibly it runs in his family. He's going to be hypersensitive, not only about his body odor, but also about the mental deficiencies the defect is known to cause."

Abby was making notes to herself. Wesley was staring off at the wall, his face tense. He didn't look happy.

Blowing in frustration, he said, "I just don't know, Kay. If the guy doesn't have this maple syrup whatever . . ." He shook his head. "He'll be on to us in a flash. It could set the investigation back."

"You can't set back something that is already backed into a corner," I said evenly. "I have no intention of naming the disease in the article." I turned to Abby. "We'll refer to it as a metabolic disorder. This could be a number of things. He's going to worry. Maybe it's something he doesn't know he has. He thinks he's in perfect health? How can he be sure? He's never had a team of genetic engineers studying his body fluids before. Even if the guy's a physician, he can't rule out the possibility he has an abnormality that's been latent most of his life, sitting there like a bomb waiting to go off. We'll plant the anxiety in his head. Let him stew over it. Hell, let him think he's got something fatal. Maybe it will send him to the nearest clinic for a physical. Maybe it will send him to the nearest medical library. The police can make a check, see who seeks out a local doctor or frantically begins riffling through medical reference books at one of the libraries. If he's the one who's been breaking into the computer here, he'll probably do it again. Whatever happens, my gut tells me *something* will happen. It's going to rattle his cage."

The three of us spent the next hour drafting the language in Abby's article.

"We can't have attribution," she insisted. "No way. If these quotes are attributed to the chief medical examiner, it will sound fishy because you've refused to talk in the past. And you've been ordered not to talk now. It's got to look like the information was leaked."

"Well," I commented dryly, "I suppose you can pull your famous 'medical source' out of your hat."

Abby read the draft aloud. It didn't set well with me. It was too vague. "Alleged" this and "possible" that.

If only we had his blood. The enzyme defect, if it existed, could be assayed in his leukocytes, his white blood cells. If only we had *something*.

As if on cue my telephone buzzed. It was Rose. "Dr. Scarpetta, Sergeant Marino's here. He says it's urgent."

I met him in the lobby. He was carrying a bag, the familiar gray plastic bag used to hold clothing connected to criminal cases.

"You ain't gonna believe this." He was grinning, his face flushed. "You know Magpie?"

I was staring at the bulging bag, my confusion apparent.

"You know, *Magpie*. All over the city with all his earthly belongings in a grocery cart he swiped somewhere. Spends his hours rummaging through garbage cans and Dumpsters."

"A street person?" What was Marino talking about?

"Yo. The Grand Dragon of street persons. Well, over the week-end he's fishing around in this Dumpster less than a block from where Henna Yarborough was whacked and guess what? He finds himself a nice navy blue jumpsuit, Doc. Flips him right out because the damn thing's stained with blood. He's a snitch of mine, see. Has the brains to stuff the thing in a trash bag, and's been wheeling the damn thing around for days, looking for me. So he waves me down on the street a little while ago, charges me the usual ten-spot, and Merry Christmas."

He was untwisting the tie around the top of the bag.

"Take a whiff."

It almost knocked me over, not just the stench of the days-old bloody garment but a powerful maple-sweetish, sweaty odor. A chill ran down my spine.

"Hey," Marino went on, "I bopped by Petersen's apartment before I come over here. Had him take a whiff."

"Is it the odor he remembers?"

He shot his finger at me and winked. "Bingo."

⸻

For two hours Vander and I worked on the blue jumpsuit. It would take a while for Betty to analyze the bloodstains, but there was little doubt in our minds the jumpsuit was worn by the killer. It sparkled under the laser like mica-flecked blacktop.

We suspected when he assaulted Henna with the knife he got very bloody and wiped his hands on his thighs. The cuffs of the sleeves were also stiff with dried blood. Quite likely it was his habit to wear something like a jumpsuit over his clothes when he struck. Maybe it was routine for him to toss the garment into a Dumpster after the crime. But I doubted it. He tossed this one because he made this victim bleed.

I was willing to bet he was smart enough to know bloodstains are permanent. If he were ever picked up, he had no intention of having anything hanging in his closet that might be stained with old blood. He had no intention of anyone's tracing the jumpsuit either. The label had been removed.

The fabric looked like a cotton and synthetic blend, dark blue, the size a large or perhaps an extra-large. I was reminded of the dark fibers found on Lori Petersen's window sill and on her body. There were a few dark fibers on Henna's body as well.

The three of us had said nothing to Marino about what we were doing. He was out on the street somewhere, maybe at home drinking beer in front of the TV. He didn't have a clue. When the news broke, he was going to think it was legitimate, that the information was leaked and related to the jumpsuit he turned in and to the DNA reports recently sent to me. We wanted *everybody* to think the news was legitimate.

In fact, it probably was. I could think of no other reason for the killer's having such a distinctive body odor, unless Petersen was imagining things and the jumpsuit just happened to be tossed on top of a Mrs. Butterworth's maple syrup bottle inside the Dumpster.

"It's perfect," Wesley was saying. "He never thought we'd find it. The toad had it all figured out, maybe even knew where the Dumpster was before he went out that night. He never thought we'd find it."

I stole a glance at Abby. She was holding up amazingly well.

"It's enough to run with," Wesley added.

I could see the headline:

DNA, NEW EVIDENCE: SERIAL KILLER MAY HAVE METABOLIC DISORDER

If he truly did have maple syrup urine disease, the front-page story ought to knock him off his feet.

"If your purpose is to entice him with the OCME computer," Abby said, "we have to make him think the computer figures in. You know, the data are related."

I thought for a minute. "Okay. We can do that if we say the computer got a hit on a recent data entry, information relating to a peculiar smell noted at one of the scenes and associated with a recently discovered piece of evidence. A search hit on an unusual enzyme defect that could cause a similar odor, but sources close to the investigation would not say exactly what this defect or disease might be, or if the defect has been verified by the results of recently completed DNA tests."

Wesley liked it. "Great. Let him sweat."

He didn't catch the pun.

"Let him wonder if we found the jumpsuit," he went on. "We don't want to give details. Maybe you can just say the police refused to disclose the exact nature of the evidence."

Abby continued to write.

I said, "Going back to your 'medical source,' it might be a good idea to have some pointed quotes coming from this person's mouth."

She looked up at me. "Such as?"

I eyed Wesley and replied, "Let this medical source refuse to reveal the specific metabolic disorder, as we've agreed. But have this source say the disorder can result in mental impairment, and in acute stages, retardation. Then add, uh . . ." I composed out loud, "An expert in human genetics stated that certain types of metabolic disorders can cause severe mental retardation. Though police believe the serial killer cannot possibly be severely mentally impaired, there is evidence to suggest he might suffer a degree of deficiency that manifests itself in disorganization and intermittent confusion."

Wesley muttered, "He'll be off the wall. It will absolutely enrage him."

"It's important we don't question his sanity," I continued. "It will come back to haunt us in court."

Abby suggested, "We'll simply have the source say so. We'll have the source distinguish between slowness and mental illness."

By now, she had filled half a dozen pages in her reporter's notepad.

She asked as she wrote, "This maple syrup business. Do we want to be that specific about the smell?"

"Yes," I said without pause. "This guy may work around the public. He's going to have colleagues, if nothing else. Someone may come forward."

Wesley considered. "One thing's damn certain, it will further unhinge him. Should make him paranoid as hell."

"Unless he really doesn't have a weird case of B.O.," Abby said.

"How is he going to know he doesn't?" I asked.

Both of them looked surprised.

"Ever heard the expression, 'A fox never smells its own'?" I added.

"You mean he could stink and not know it?" she asked.

"Let *him* wonder that," I replied.

She nodded, bending over her notepad again.

Wesley settled back in his chair. "What else do you know about this defect, Kay? Should we be checking out the local pharmacies, see if someone buys a lot of oddball vitamins or prescription drugs?"

"You could check to see if someone regularly comes in to buy large doses of B_1," I said. "There's also MSUD powder, a dietary supplement available. I think it's over-the-counter, a protein supplement. He may be controlling the disease through diet, through a limiting of normal high-protein foods. But I think he's too careful to be leaving those kinds of tracks, and in truth, I don't think his disease has been acute enough for him to be on a very restricted diet. I suspect in order for him to function as well as he does he leads a fairly normal life. His only problem is he has a strange-smelling body odor that gets more noticeable when he's under stress."

"Emotional stress?"

"Physical stress," I replied. "MSUD tends to flare up under physical stress, such as when the person is suffering from a respiratory infection, the flu. It's physiological. He's probably not getting enough sleep. It takes a lot of physical energy to stalk victims, break into houses, do what he does. Emotional stress and physical stress are connected—one adds to the other. The more emotionally stressed he becomes, the more physically stressed he becomes and vice versa."

"Then what?"

I looked impassively at him.

"Then what happens," he repeated, "if the disease flares up?"

"Depends on whether it becomes acute."

"Let's say it does."

"He's got a real problem."

"Meaning?"

"Meaning, the amino acids build up in his system. He's going to get lethargic, irritable, ataxic. Symptoms similar to severe hyperglycemia. It may be necessary for him to be hospitalized."

"English," Wesley said. "What the hell's *ataxic* mean?"

"Unsteady. He's going to walk around like he's drunk. He's not going to have the wherewithal to scale fences and climb through windows. If it gets acute, if his stress level continues to climb, and if he goes untreated, it could get out of control."

"Out of control?" he persisted. "We stress him—that's our purpose, right? His disease gets out of control?"

"Possibly."

"Okay." He hesitated. "What next?"

"Severe hyperglycemia, and his anxiety increases. If it isn't controlled, he's going to get confused, overwrought. His judgment may be impaired. He'll suffer mood changes."

I stopped right there.

But Wesley wasn't going to let me. He was leaning forward in his chair, staring at me.

"You didn't just think of this maple syrup urine disease business, did you?" he pushed.

"It's been in my differential."

"And you didn't say anything."

"I wasn't at all sure," I replied. "I saw no reason to suggest it until now."

"Right. Okay. You say you want to rattle his cage, stress him right out of his mind. Let's do it. What's the last stage? I mean, *what if his disease gets really bad?*"

"He may become unconscious, have convulsions. If this is prolonged, it may lead to a severe organic deficit."

He stared incredulously at me as his eyes filled with comprehension. "Jesus. You're trying to kill the son of a bitch."

Abby's pen stopped. Startled, she looked up at me.

I replied, "This is all theoretical. If he's got the disease, it's mild. He's lived with it all his life. It's highly unlikely MSUD's going to kill him."

Wesley continued to stare. He didn't believe me.

14

I COULDN'T SLEEP all night. My mind wouldn't shut down and I tossed miserably between unsettling realities and savage dreams. I shot somebody and Bill was the medical examiner called to the scene. When he arrived with his black bag, he was accompanied by a beautiful woman I did not know . . .

My eyes flew open in the dark, my heart squeezed as if by a cold hand. I got out of bed long before my alarm went off and drove to work in a fog of depression.

I don't know when in my life I'd ever felt so lonely and withdrawn. I scarcely spoke to anyone at the office, and my staff began to cast nervous, strange glances my way.

Several times I came close to calling Bill, my resolve trembling like a tree about to fall. It finally fell shortly before noon. His secretary brightly told me "Mr. Boltz" was on vacation and wouldn't be back until the first of July.

I left no message. The vacation wasn't planned, I knew. I also knew why he didn't say a word about it to me. In the past he would have told me. The past was past. There would be no resolution or lame apologies or outright lies. He'd cut me off forever because he couldn't face his own sins.

After lunch I went upstairs to serology and was surprised to find Betty and Wingo with their backs to the door, their heads together as they looked at something white inside a small plastic bag.

I said, "Hello," and came inside.

Wingo nervously tucked the bag in a pocket of Betty's lab coat, as if slipping her money.

"You finished downstairs?" I pretended I was too preoccupied to have noticed this peculiar transaction.

"Uh, yeah. Sure am, Dr. Scarpetta," he quickly replied, on his way out. "McFee, the guy shot last night—released him a little while ago. And the burn victims coming in from Albemarle won't be in till four or so."

"Fine. We'll hold them until the morning."

"You got it," I heard him say from the hallway.

Spread out on the wide table in the center of the room was the reason for my visit. The blue jumpsuit. It looked flat and mundane, neatly smoothed out and zipped up to the collar. It could have belonged to anybody. There were numerous pockets, and I think I must have checked each one half a dozen times hoping to find anything that might hint at who he was, but they were empty. There were large holes cut in the legs and sleeves where Betty had removed swatches of bloodstained fabric.

"Any luck grouping the blood?" I asked, trying not to stare at the plastic bag peeking out of the top of her pocket.

"I've got some of it worked out." She motioned me to follow her to her office.

On her desk was a legal pad scribbled with notes and numbers that would look like hieroglyphics to the uninitiated.

"Henna Yarborough's blood type is B," she began. "We're lucky on that count because it's not all that common. In Virginia, about twelve percent of the population's type B. Her PGM's one-plus, one-minus. Her PEP is A-one, EAP is CB, ADA-one and AK-one. The subsystems, unfortunately, are very common, up there in the eighty-nine percent and above of Virginia's population."

"How common is the actual configuration?" The plastic peeking out of the top of her pocket was beginning to unsettle me.

She started stabbing out digits on a calculator, multiplying the percentages and dividing by the number of subsystems she had. "About seventeen percent. Seventeen out of a hundred people could have that configuration."

"Not exactly rare," I muttered.

"Not unless sparrows are rare."

"What about the bloodstains on the jumpsuit?"

"We were lucky. The jumpsuit must have already air-dried by the time the street person found it. It's in amazingly good shape. I got all the subsystems except an EAP. It's consistent with Henna Yarborough's blood. DNA should be able to tell us with certainty, but we're talking about a month to six weeks."

I commented abstractedly, "We ought to buy stock in the lab."

Her eyes lingered on me and grew soft. "You look absolutely ragged, Kay."

"That obvious, is it?"

"Obvious to me."

I didn't say anything.

"Don't let all this get to you. After thirty years of this misery, I've learned the hard way . . ."

"What's Wingo up to?" I foolishly blurted out.

Surprised, she faltered. "Wingo? Well . . ."

I was staring at her pocket.

She laughed uneasily, patted it. "Oh, this. Just a little private work he's asked me to do."

That was as much as she intended to say. Maybe Wingo had other real worries in his life. Maybe he was having an HIV test done on the sly. Good God, don't let him have AIDS.

Gathering my fragmented thoughts, I asked, "What about the fibers? Anything?"

Betty had compared fibers from the jumpsuit to fibers left at Lori Petersen's scene and to a few fibers found on Henna Yarborough's body.

"The fibers found on the Petersen windowsill could have come from the jumpsuit," she told me, "or they could have come from any number of dark blue cotton-polyester blend twills."

In court, I dismally thought, the comparison's not going to mean a thing because the twill is about as generic as dime-store typing paper—you start looking for it and you're going to find it all over the place. It could have come from someone's work pants. It could, for that matter, have come from a paramedic's or cop's uniform.

There was another disappointment. Betty was sure the fibers I found on Henna Yarborough's body were not from the jump-suit.

"They're cotton," she was saying. "They may have come from something she was wearing at some point earlier in the day, or even a bath towel. Who knows? People carry all sorts of fibers on their person. But I'm not surprised the jumpsuit didn't leave fibers."

"Why?"

"Because twill fabrics, such as the fabric of the jumpsuit, are very smooth. They rarely leave fibers unless the fabric comes in contact with something abrasive."

"Such as a brick window ledge or a rough wooden sill, as in Lori's case."

"Possibly, and the dark fibers we found in her case may have come from a jumpsuit. Maybe even this one. But I don't think we're ever going to know."

I went back downstairs to my office and sat at my desk for a while, thinking. Unlocking the drawer, I pulled out the five murdered women's cases.

I began looking for anything I might have missed. Once again, I was groping for a connection.

What did these five women have in common? Why did the killer pick them? How did he come in contact with them?

There had to be a link. In my soul, I didn't believe it was a random selection, that he just cruised around looking for a likely candidate. I believed he selected them for a reason. He had some sort of contact with them first, and perhaps followed them home.

Geographics, jobs, physical appearances. There was no common denominator. I tried the reverse, the least common denominator, and I continued to go back to Cecile Tyler's record.

She was black. The four other victims were white. I was bothered by this in the beginning, and I was still bothered by it now. Did the killer make a mistake? Perhaps he didn't realize she was black. Was he really after somebody else? Her friend Bobbi, for example?

I flipped pages, scanning the autopsy report I'd dictated. I perused evidence receipts, call sheets and an old hospital chart from St. Luke's, where she'd been treated five years earlier for an ectopic pregnancy. When I got to the police report, I looked at the name of the only relative listed, a sister in Madras, Oregon. From her Marino got information about Cecile's background, about her failed marriage to the dentist now living in Tidewater.

X rays sounded like saw blades bending as I pulled them out of manila envelopes and held them up, one by one, to the light of my desk lamp. Cecile had no skeletal injuries other than a healed impaction fracture of her left elbow. The age of the injury was impossible to tell but I knew it wasn't fresh. It could go back too many years to matter.

Again, I contemplated the VMC connection. Both Lori Petersen and Brenda Steppe had recently been in the hospital's ER. Lori was there because her rotation was trauma surgery. Brenda was treated there after her automobile accident. Perhaps it was too farfetched to think Cecile might have been treated there as well for the fractured elbow. At this point, I was willing to explore anything.

I dialed Cecile's sister's number listed on Marino's report.

After five rings the receiver was picked up.

"Hello?"

It was a poor connection and clearly I'd made a mistake.

"I'm sorry, I must have the wrong number," I quickly said.

"Pardon?"

I repeated myself, louder.

"What number were you dialing?" The voice was cultured and Virginian and seemed that of a female in her twenties.

I recited the number.

"That's this number. With whom did you wish to speak?"

"Fran O'Connor," I read from the report.

The young, cultured voice replied, "Speaking."

I told her who I was and heard a faint gasp. "As I understand it, you are Cecile Tyler's sister."

"Yes. Dear Lord. I don't want to talk about it. Please."

"Mrs. O'Connor, I'm terribly sorry about Cecile. I'm the medical examiner working her case, and I'm calling to find out if you know how your sister fractured her left elbow. She has a healed fracture of her left elbow. I'm looking at the X rays now."

Hesitation. I could hear her thinking.

"It was a jogging accident. She was jogging on a sidewalk and tripped, landing on her hands. One of her elbows was fractured from the impact. I remember because she wore a cast for three months during one of the hottest summers on record. She was miserable."

"That summer? Was this in Oregon?"

"No, Cecile never lived in Oregon. This was in Fredericksburg, where we grew up."

"How long ago was the jogging accident?"

Another pause. "Nine, maybe ten years ago."

"Where was she treated?"

"I don't know. A hospital in Fredericksburg. I can't remember the name."

Cecile's impaction fracture wasn't treated at VMC, and the injury had occurred much too long ago to matter. But I no longer cared.

I never met Cecile Tyler in life.

I never talked to her.

I just assumed she would sound "black."

"Mrs. O'Connor, are you black?"

"Of course I'm black." She sounded upset.

"Did your sister talk like you?"

"Talk like me?" she asked, her voice rising.

"I know it seems an odd question . . ."

"You mean did she talk *white* like me?" she went on, outraged. "Yes! She did! Isn't that what education's all about? So *black* people can talk *white?*"

"Please," I said with feeling. "I certainly didn't intend to offend you. But it's important . . ."

I was apologizing to a dial tone.

Lucy knew about the fifth strangling. She knew about all of the slain young women. She also knew I kept a .38 in my bedroom and had asked me about it twice since dinner.

"Lucy," I said as I rinsed plates and loaded them in the dishwasher, "I don't want you thinking about guns. I wouldn't own one if I didn't live alone."

I'd been strongly tempted to hide it where she would never think to look. But after the episode with the modem, which I had guiltily reconnected to my home computer days ago, I vowed to be up front with her. The .38 remained high on my closet shelf, inside its shoebox, while Lucy was in town. The gun wasn't loaded. These days, I unloaded it in the morning and reloaded it before bed. As for the Silvertip cartridges—those I hid where she would never think to look.

When I faced her, her eyes were huge. "You know why I have a gun, Lucy. I think you understand how dangerous they are . . ."

"They kill people."

"Yes," I replied as we went into the living room. "They most certainly can."

"You have it so you can kill somebody."

"I don't like to think about that," I told her seriously.

"Well, it's true," she persisted. "That's why you keep it. Because of bad people. That's why."

I picked up the remote control and switched on the television.

Lucy pushed up the sleeves of her pink sweatshirt and complained, "It's hot in here, Auntie Kay. Why's it always so hot in here?"

"Would you like me to turn up the air-conditioning?" I abstractedly flipped through the television schedule.

"No. I hate air-conditioning."

I lit a cigarette and she complained about that, too.

"Your office is hot and always stinks like cigarettes. I open the window and still it stinks. Mom says you shouldn't smoke. You're a doctor and you smoke. Mom says you should know better."

Dorothy had called late the night before. She was somewhere in California, I couldn't remember where, with her illustrator husband. It was all I could do to be civil to her. I wanted to remind her, "You have a daughter, flesh of your flesh, bone of your bone. Remember Lucy? Remember her?" Instead, I was reserved, almost gracious, mostly out of consideration for Lucy, who was sitting at the table, her lips pressed together.

Lucy talked to her mother for maybe ten minutes, and had nothing to say afterward. Ever since, she'd been all over me, critical, snappish and bossy. She'd been the same way during the day, according to Bertha, who this evening had referred to her as a "fusspot." Bertha told me Lucy scarcely set foot outside my office. She sat in front of the computer from the moment I left the house until the moment I returned. Bertha gave up calling her into the kitchen for meals. Lucy ate at my desk.

The sitcom on the set seemed all the more absurd because Lucy and I were having our own sitcom in the living room.

"Andy says it's more dangerous to own a gun and not know how to use it than if you don't own one," she loudly announced.

"Andy?" I said absentmindedly.

"The one before Ralph. He used to go to the junkyard and shoot bottles. He could hit them from a long ways away. I bet you couldn't." She looked accusingly at me.

"You're right. I probably couldn't shoot as well as Andy."

"See!"

I didn't tell her I actually knew quite a lot about firearms. Before I bought my stainless-steel Ruger .38, I went down to the indoor range in the basement of my building and experimented with an assortment of handguns from the firearms lab, all this under the professional supervision of one of the examiners. I practiced from time to time, and I wasn't a bad shot. I didn't think I would hesitate if the need ever arose. I also didn't intend to discuss the matter further with my niece.

Very quietly I asked, "Lucy, why are you picking on me?"

"Because you're a stupid ass!" Her eyes filled with tears. "You're just an old stupid ass and if you tried to, you'd hurt yourself or he'd get it away from you! And then you'd be gone, too! If you tried to, he'd shoot you with it just like it happens on TV!"

"If I tried to?" I puzzled. "If I tried to *what*, Lucy?"

"If you tried to get somebody first."

She angrily wiped away tears, her narrow chest heaving. I stared blindly at the family circus on TV and didn't know what to say. My impulse was to retreat to my office and shut the door, to lose myself in my work for a while, but hesitantly I moved over and pulled her close. We sat like this for the longest time, saying nothing.

I wondered who she talked to at home. I couldn't imagine her having any conversations of substance with my sister. Dorothy and her children's books had been lauded by various critics as "extraordinarily insightful" and "deep" and "full of feeling." What a dismal irony. Dorothy gave the best she had to juvenile characters who didn't exist. She nurtured them. She spent long hours contemplating their every detail, from the way their hair was combed to the clothes they wore, to their trials and rites of passage. All the while Lucy was starved for attention.

I thought of the times Lucy and I spent together when I lived in Miami, of the holidays with her, my mother and Dorothy. I thought of Lucy's last visit here. I couldn't recall her ever mentioning the names of friends. I don't think she had any. She would talk about her teachers, her mother's ragtag assortment of "boyfriends," Mrs. Spooner across the street, Jake the yardman and the endless parade of maids. Lucy was a tiny, bespectacled know-it-all whom older children resented and children her age didn't understand.

She was out of sync. I think I was exactly like her when I was her age.

A peaceful warmth had settled over both of us. I said into her hair, "Someone asked me a question the other day."

"About what?"

"About trust. Someone asked me who I trusted more than anybody else in the world. And you know what?"

She leaned her head back, looking up at me.

"I think that person is you."

"Do you really?" she asked, incredulously. "More than *anybody?*"

I nodded and quietly went on, "That being the case, I'm going to ask you to help me with something."

She sat up and stared at me, her eyes alert and utterly thrilled. "Oh, sure! Just ask me! I'll help you, Auntie Kay!"

"I need to figure out how someone managed to break into the computer downtown . . ."

"I didn't do it," she instantly blurted out, a stricken look on her face. "I already told you I didn't."

"I believe you. But someone did it, Lucy. Maybe you can help me figure it out?"

I didn't think she could but had felt an impulse to give her a chance.

Energized and excited again, she said confidently, "Anybody could do it because it's easy."

"Easy?" I had to smile.

"Because of System/Manager."

I stared at her in open astonishment. "How do you know about System/Manager?"

"It's in the book. He's God."

At times like these I was reminded, if not unnerved. Lucy's IQ. The first time she was given an IQ test she scored so high the counselor insisted on testing her again because there had to be "some mistake." There was. The second time Lucy scored ten points higher.

"That's how you get into SQL to begin with," she was rattling on. "See, you can't create any grants unless you got one to start with. That's why you've got System/Manager. God. You get into SQL with Him, and then you can create anything you want."

Anything you want, it dawned on me. Such as all of the user

names and passwords assigned to my offices. This was a terrible revelation, so simplistic it had never occurred to me. I supposed it never occurred to Margaret either.

"All someone's got to do is get in," Lucy matter-of-factly went on. "And if he knows about God, he can create any grant he wants, make it the DBA, and then he can get into your data base."

In my office, the data base administrator, or DBA, was "DEEP/THROAT." Margaret did have a sense of humor now and then.

"So you get into SQL by connecting System/Manager, then you type in: GRANT CONNECT, RESOURCE, DBA TO AUNTIE IDENTIFIED BY KAY."

"Maybe that's what happened," I thought out loud. "And with the DBA, someone not only could view but actually alter the data."

"Sure! He could do anything because God's told him he can. The DBA is Jesus."

Her theological allusions were so outrageous I laughed in spite of myself.

"That's how I got into SQL to begin with," she confessed. "Since you didn't tell me any passwords or anything. I wanted to get into SQL so I could try out some of the commands in the book. I just gave your DBA user name a password I made up so I could get in."

"Wait a minute," I slowed her down. "Wait a minute! What do you mean you assigned a password you made up to my DBA user name? How did you know what my user name is? I didn't tell you."

She explained, "It's in your grants file. I found it in the Home directory where you have all the INP's for the tables you created. You have a file called 'Grants.SQL' where you created all the public synonyms for your tables."

Actually, I hadn't created those tables. Margaret did last year and I loaded my home computer with the boxes of backup diskettes she gave me. Was it possible there was a similar "Grants" file in the OCME computer?

I took hold of Lucy's hand and we got up from the couch. Eagerly, she followed me into my office. I sat her down in front of the computer and pulled up the ottoman.

We got into the communications software package and typed in the number for Margaret's office downtown. We watched the countdown at the bottom of the screen as the computer dialed. Almost immediately it announced we were connected, and several commands later the screen was dark and flashing with a green C prompt. My computer suddenly was a looking glass. On the other side were the secrets of my office ten miles from here.

It made me slightly uneasy to know that even as we worked the call was being traced. I'd have to remember to tell Wesley so he didn't waste his time figuring out that the perpetrator, in this instance, was me.

"Do a find file," I said, "for anything that might be called 'Grants.' "

Lucy did. The C prompt came back with the message "No files found." We tried again. We tried looking for a file called "Synonyms" and still had no luck. Then she got the idea of trying to find any file with the extension "SQL" because ordinarily that was the extension for any file containing SQL commands, commands such as the ones used to create public synonyms on the office data tables. Scores of file names rolled up the screen. One caught our attention. It was called "Public.SQL."

Lucy opened the file and we watched it roll past. My excitement was equaled by my dismay. It contained the commands Margaret wrote and executed long ago when she created public synonyms for all of the tables she created in the office data base—commands like CREATE PUBLIC SYNONYM CASE FOR DEEP.CASE. I was not a computer programmer. I'd heard of public synonyms but was not entirely sure what they were.

Lucy was flipping through a manual. She got to the section on public synonyms and confidently volunteered, "See, it's neat. When you create a table, you have to create it under a user name and password." She looked up at me, her eyes bright behind her thick glasses.

"Okay," I said. "That makes sense."

"So if your user name is 'Auntie' and your password is 'Kay,' then when you create a table called 'Games' or something, the name the computer gives it is really 'Auntie.Games.' It attaches the table name to the user name it was created under. If you don't want to bother typing in 'Auntie.Games' every time you want to get into the table, you create a public synonym. You type the command CREATE PUBLIC SYNONYM GAMES FOR AUNTIE.GAMES. It sort of renames the table so it's just called 'Games.' "

I stared at the long list of commands on the screen, a list revealing every table in the OCME computer, a list revealing the DBA user name each table was created under.

I puzzled, "But even if someone saw this file, Lucy, he wouldn't know the password. Only the DBA user name is listed, and you can't get into a table, such as our case table, without knowing the password."

"Wanna bet?" Her fingers were poised over the keys. "If you know the DBA user name, you can change the password, make it anything you want and then you can get in. The computer doesn't care. It lets you change passwords anytime you want without messing up your programs or anything. People like to change their passwords for security reasons."

"So you could take the user name 'Deep' and assign it a new password and get into our data?"

She nodded.

"Show me."

She looked at me with uncertainty. "But you told me not to ever go into your office data base."

"I'm making an exception this one time."

"And if I give 'Deep' a new password, Auntie Kay, it will get rid of the old one. The old one won't be there anymore. It won't work."

I was jolted by the memory of what Margaret mentioned when we first discovered someone tried to pull up Lori Petersen's case: something about the DBA password not working, causing her to have to connect the DBA grant again.

"The old password won't work anymore because it's been re-placed by the new one I made up. So you can't log on with the old one." Lucy glanced furtively at me. "But I was going to fix it."

"Fix it?" I was barely listening.

"Your computer here. Your old password won't work anymore because I changed it to get into SQL. But I was going to fix it, you know, I promise."

"Later," I quickly said. "You can fix it later. I want you to show me exactly how someone could get in."

I was trying to make sense of it. It seemed likely, I decided, that the person who got into the OCME data base knew enough about it to realize he could create a new password for the user name found in the Public.SQL file. But he didn't realize that in doing so he would invalidate the old password, preventing us from getting in the next time we tried. Of course we would notice that. Of course we would wonder about it, and the idea the echo might be on and echoing his commands on the screen apparently didn't occur to him either. The break-in had to have been a onetime event!

If the person had broken in before, even if the echo was off, we would have known because Margaret would have discovered the password "Throat" no longer worked. Why?

Why did this person break in and try to pull up Lori Petersen's case?

Lucy's fingers were clicking away on the keyboard.

"See," she was saying, "pretend I'm the bad guy trying to break in. Here's how I do it."

She got into SQL by typing in System/Manager, and executed a connect/resource/DBA command on the user name "Deep" and a password she made up—"jumble." The grant was connected. It was the new DBA. With it she could get into any of the office tables. It was powerful enough for her to do anything she wished.

It was powerful enough for her to alter data.

It was powerful enough, for example, for someone to have altered Brenda Steppe's case record so that the item "tan cloth belt" was listed in the "Clothing, Personal Effects" field.

Did *he* do this? He knew the details of the murders he'd committed. He was reading the papers. He was obsessing over every word written about him. He would recognize an inaccuracy in the news accounts before anybody else would. He was arrogant. He wanted to flaunt his intelligence. Did he change my office data to jerk me around, to taunt me?

The break-in had occurred almost two months *after* the detail was printed in Abby's account of Brenda Steppe's death.

Yet the data base was violated only once, and only recently.

The detail in Abby's story could not have come from the OCME computer. Was it possible the detail in the computer came from the newspaper account? Perhaps he carefully went through the strangling cases in the computer, looking for something inconsistent with what Abby was writing. Perhaps when he got to Brenda Steppe's case he found his inaccuracy. He altered the data by typing "tan cloth belt" over "a pair of nude pantyhose." Perhaps the last thing he did before logging off was to try to pull up Lori Petersen's case, out of curiosity, if for no other reason. This would explain why those commands were what Margaret found on the screen.

Was my paranoia running off with my reason?

Could there be a connection between this and the mislabeled PERK as well? The cardboard file was spangled with a glittery residue. What if it hadn't come from my hands?

"Lucy," I asked, "would there be any way to know if someone has altered data in my office computer?"

She said without pause, "You back up the data, don't you? Someone does an export, doesn't he?"

"Yes."

"Then you could get an export that's old, import it into a computer and see if the old data's different."

"The problem," I considered, "is even if I discovered an alteration, I can't say for sure it wasn't the result of an update to the record one of my clerks made. The cases are in a state of constant flux because reports trickle in for weeks, months, after the case has been initially entered."

"I guess you got to ask them, Auntie Kay. Ask them if they changed it. If they say no, and if you find an old export that's different from the stuff in the computer now, wouldn't that help?"

I admitted, "It might."

She changed the password back to what it was supposed to be. We logged off and cleared the screen so no one would see the commands on the OCME computer in the morning.

It was almost eleven o'clock. I called Margaret at home and she sounded groggy as I questioned her about the export disks and asked if she might have anything dating back prior to the time the computer was broken into.

She offered me the expected disappointment. "No, Dr. Scarpetta. The office wouldn't have anything that old. We do a new export at the end of every day, and the previous export is formatted, then updated."

"Damn. Somehow I've got to get hold of a version of the data base that hasn't been updated for the past several weeks."

Silence.

"Wait a minute," she muttered. "I might have a flat file . . ."

"Of what?"

"I don't know . . ." She hesitated. "I guess the last six months of data or so. Vital Statistics wants our data, and a couple of weeks ago I was experimenting, importing the districts' data into one partition and spooling all the case data off into a file to see how it looks. Eventually, I'm supposed to ship it to them over the phone, straight into their mainframe—"

"How many weeks ago?" I interrupted. "How many weeks ago did you spool it off?"

"The first of the month . . . let's see, I think I did it around the first of June."

My nerves were buzzing. I had to know. At the very least, my office couldn't be blamed for leaks if I could prove data were altered in the computer *after* the stories appeared in the papers.

"I need a printout of that flat file immediately," I told her.

There was a long silence. She seemed uncertain when she replied, "I had some problems with the procedure." Another pause. "But I can give you what I've got, first thing in the morning."

Glancing at my watch, I next dialed Abby's pager number.

Five minutes later, I had her on the line.

"Abby, I know your sources are sacred, but there's something I must know."

She didn't respond.

"In your account of Brenda Steppe's murder, you wrote she was strangled with a tan cloth belt. Where did you get this detail?"

"I can't—"

"Please. It's very important. I simply must know the source."

After a long pause, she said, "No names. A squad member. It was a squad member, okay? One of the guys at the scene. I know a lot of squad members . . ."

"The information in no shape or form came from my office?"

"Absolutely not," she said emphatically. "You're worrying about the computer break-in Sergeant Marino mentioned . . . I swear, nothing I've printed came from that, came from your office."

It was out before I thought twice. "Whoever got in, Abby, may have typed this tan cloth belt detail into the case table to make it appear you got it from my office, that my office is the leak. The detail is inaccurate. I don't believe it was ever in our computer. I think whoever broke in got the detail from your story."

"Good God" was all she said.

15

MARINO DROPPED THE MORNING NEWSPAPER on top of the conference table with a loud slap that sent pages fluttering and inserts sliding out.

"What the hell is this?" His face was an angry red and he needed a shave. "Je-sus Christ!"

Wesley's reply was to calmly kick out a chair, inviting him to sit.

Thursday's story was front-page, above the fold, with the banner headline:

DNA, NEW EVIDENCE RAISE POSSIBILITY STRANGLER HAS GENETIC DEFECT

Abby's byline was nowhere to be found. The account was written by a reporter who usually covered the court beat.

There was a sidebar about DNA profiling, including an artist's sketch of the DNA "fingerprinting" process. I wondered about the killer, imagined him reading and rereading the paper in a rage. My guess was wherever he worked, he called in sick today.

"What I want to know is how come I wasn't told any of this?" Marino glared at me. "I turn in the jumpsuit. Do my job. Next thing, I'm reading this crap! What *defect*? Some DNA reports just come in some asshole's already leaked, or what?"

I didn't say anything.

Wesley replied levelly, "It doesn't matter, Pete. The newspaper story isn't our concern. Consider it a blessing. We know the killer's got a strange body odor, or at least it seems likely he does. He thinks Kay's office is on to something, maybe he makes a stupid move." He looked at me. "Anything?"

I shook my head. So far there'd been no attempts at breaking into the OCME computer. Had either man come into the conference room twenty minutes earlier, he would have found me ankle-deep in paper.

It was no wonder Margaret had been hesitant last night when I asked her to print out the flat file. It included about three thousand statewide cases through the month of May, or a run of green-striped paper that stretched practically the length of the building.

What was worse, the data were compressed in a format not meant to be readable. It was like fishing for complete sentences in a bowl of alphabet soup.

It took me well over an hour to find Brenda Steppe's case number. I don't know if I felt thrilled or horrified—maybe it was both—when I discovered the listing under "Clothing, Personal Effects": "Pair of nude pantyhose around neck." There was no mention of a tan cloth belt anywhere. None of my clerks remembered changing the entry or updating the case after it was entered. The data had been altered. It was altered by someone other than my staff.

"What about this mental impairment stuff?" Marino rudely shoved the newspaper my way. "You find out something in this DNA hocus-pocus to make you think he ain't operating on all cylinders?"

"No," I honestly replied. "I think the point of the story is some metabolic disorders can cause problems like that. But I have come up with no evidence to suggest such a thing."

"Well, it sure as hell ain't my opinion the guy's got brain rot. Me, I'm hearing the same garbage again. The squirrel's stupid, nothing more than a lowlife. Probably works in a car wash, cleans out the city sewers or something . . ."

Wesley was beginning to register impatience. "Give it a rest, Pete."

"I'm supposed to be in charge of this investigation and I gotta read the damn newspaper to know what the hell's going on . . ."

"We've got a bigger problem, all right?" Wesley snapped.

"Well, what?" Marino asked.

So we told him.

We told him about my telephone conversation with Cecile Tyler's sister.

He listened, the anger in his eyes retreating. He looked baffled.

We told him all five women definitely had one thing in common. Their voices.

I reminded him of Matt Petersen's interview. "As I recall, he said something about the first time he met Lori. At a party, I believe. He talked about her voice. He said she had the sort of voice that caught people's attention, a very pleasant contralto voice. What we're considering is the link connecting these five murders is voice. Perhaps the killer didn't see them. He *heard* them."

"It never occurred to us," Wesley added. "When we think of stalkers, we think of psychopaths who *see* the victim at some point. In a shopping mall, out jogging, or through a window in the apartment or house. As a rule, the telephone, if it figures in at all, comes after the initial contact. He sees her. Maybe he calls her later, just dials her number to hear her voice so he can fantasize. What we're considering now is far more frightening, Pete. This killer may have some occupation that involves his calling women he doesn't know. He has access to their numbers and addresses. He calls. If her voice sets him off, he selects her."

"Like this really narrows it down," Marino complained. "Now we got to find out if all these women was listed in the city directory. Next we got to consider occupation possibilities. I mean, not a week goes by the missus don't get a call. Some drone selling brooms, light bulbs, condos. Then there's the pollsters. The let-me-ask-you-fifty-questions type. They want to know if you're married, single, how much money you earn. Whether you put your pants on one leg at a time and floss after brushing."

"You're getting the picture," Wesley muttered.

Marino went on without pause, "So you got some guy who's into rape and murder. He could get paid eight bucks an hour to sit on his ass at home and run through the phone book or city directory. Some woman tells him she's single, earns twenty g's a year. A week later," this to me, "she's coming through your joint. So I ask you. How the hell we going to find him?"

We didn't know.

The possible voice connection didn't narrow it down. Marino was right. In fact, it made our job more difficult instead of easier. We might be able to determine who a victim saw on any given day. But it was unlikely we could find every person she talked to on the phone. The victim might not even know, were she alive to tell. Telephone solicitors, pollsters and people who dial wrong numbers rarely identify themselves. All of us get multiple calls day and night we neither process nor remember.

I said, "The pattern of when he hits makes me wonder if he has a job outside of the home, if he goes to work somewhere Monday through Friday. Throughout the week his stress builds. Late Friday night or after midnight, he hits. If he's using a borax soap twenty times a day, then it isn't likely this is something he has in his household bathroom. Hand soaps you buy at your local grocery store don't contain borax, to my knowledge. If he's washing up with borax soap, I suspect he's doing so at work."

"We're sure it's borax?" Wesley asked.

"The labs determined it through ion chromatography. The glittery residue we've been finding on the bodies contains borax. Definitely."

Wesley considered this for a moment. "If he's using borax soap on the job and gets home at five, it's not likely he'd have such a buildup of this glittery residue at one o'clock in the morning. He may work an evening shift. There's borax soap in the men's room. He gets off sometime before midnight, one A.M., and goes straight to the victim's residence."

The scenario was more than plausible, I explained. If the killer worked at night, this gave him ample opportunity during the day while the rest of the world was at work to cruise through the neighborhood of his next victim and look over the area. He could drive by again late, maybe after midnight, to take another look. The victims were either out or asleep, as were most of their neighbors. He wasn't going to be seen.

What night jobs involve the telephone?

We batted that around for a while.

"Most telephone solicitors call right in the middle of the dinner hour," Wesley said. "It seems to me it's unusual for them to call much later than nine."

We agreed.

"Pizza deliverers," Marino proposed. "They're out all hours. Could be it's the drone who takes the call. You dial up and the first thing the operator asks is your phone number. If you've ever called before, your address pops up on the computer screen. Thirty minutes later some squirrel's at your door with a pepperoni-hold-the-onions. It could be the delivery guy who figures out in a hurry he's got some woman who lives alone. Maybe it's the operator. He likes her voice, knows her address."

"Check it," Wesley said. "Get a couple of guys to go around to the various pizza delivery places pronto."

Tomorrow was Friday!

"See if there's any one pizza place all five women called from time to time. It should be in the computer, easy to track."

Marino left for a moment, returning with the Yellow Pages. He found the pizza section and started scribbling down names and addresses.

We kept coming up with more and more possible occupations. Switchboard operators for hospitals and telephone companies were up all hours answering calls. Fund-raisers didn't hesitate to interrupt your favorite television program as late as ten P.M. Then there was always the possibility of someone playing roulette with the city directory or telephone book—a security guard with nothing better to do while he's sitting inside the lobby of the Federal Reserve, or a gas station attendant bored late at night during the slow hours.

I was getting more confused. I couldn't sort through it all.

Yet there was something bothering me.

You're making it too complicated, my inner voice was telling me. You're getting farther and farther removed from what you actually know.

I looked at Marino's damp, meaty face, at his eyes shifting here and there. He was tired, stressed. He was still nursing a deep-seated anger. Why was he so touchy? What was it he said about the way the killer would think, something about him not liking professional women because they're snooty?

Every time I tried to get hold of him, he was "on the street." He'd been to every strangling scene.

At Lori Petersen's scene he was wide-awake. Had he even been to bed that night? Wasn't it a little odd he was so rabid in trying to pin the murders on Matt Petersen?

Marino's age doesn't profile right, I told myself.

He spends most of his time in his car and doesn't answer the phone for a living, so I can't see the connection between him and the women.

Most important, he doesn't have a peculiar body odor, and if the jumpsuit found in the Dumpster was his, why would he bring it in to the lab?

Unless, I thought, he's turning the system inside out, playing it against itself because he knows so much. He is, after all, an expert, in charge of the investigation and experienced enough to be a savior or a satan.

I suppose all along I'd been harboring the fear that the killer might be a cop.

Marino didn't fit. But the killer might be someone he'd worked around for months, someone who bought navy blue jumpsuits at the various uniform stores around the city, someone who washed his hands with the Borawash soap dispensed in the department's men's rooms, someone who knew enough about forensics and criminal investigation to be able to outsmart his brothers and me. A cop gone bad. Or someone drawn to law enforcement because this is often a very attractive profession to psychopaths.

We'd tracked down the squads that responded to the homicide scenes. What we'd never thought to do was to track down the uniformed men who responded when the bodies were discovered.

Maybe some cop was thumbing through the telephone or city directory during his shift or after hours. Maybe his first contact with the victims was voice. Their voices set him off. He murdered them and made sure he was on the street or near a scanner when each body was found.

"Our best bet is Matt Petersen," Wesley was saying to Marino. "He still in town?"

"Yeah. Last I heard."

"I think you'd better go see him, find out if his wife ever mentioned anything about telephone soliciting, about someone calling up to say she'd won a contest, someone taking a poll. Anything involving the phone."

Marino pushed back his chair.

I hedged. I didn't come right out and say what I was thinking.

Instead, I asked, "How tough would it be to get printouts or tape recordings of the calls made to the police when the bodies were found? I want to see the exact times the homicides were called in, what time the police arrived, especially in Lori Petersen's case. Time of death may be very important in helping us determine what time the killer gets off work, assuming he works at night."

"No problem," Marino replied abstractedly. "You can come along with me. After we hit Petersen, we'll swing by the radio room."

We didn't find Matt Petersen at home. Marino left his card under the brass knocker of his apartment.

"I don't expect him to return my call," he mumbled as he crept back out into traffic.

"Why not?"

"When I dropped by the other day he didn't invite me in. Just stood in the doorway like a damn barricade. Was big enough to sniff the jumpsuit before basically telling me to buzz off, practically slammed the door in my face, said in the future to talk to his lawyer. Petersen said the polygraph cleared him, said I was harassing him."

"You probably were," I commented dryly.

He glanced at me and almost smiled.

We left the West End and headed back downtown.

"You said some ion test came up with borax." He changed the subject. "This mean you didn't get squat on the greasepaint?"

"No borax," I replied. "Something called 'Sun Blush' reacted to the laser. But it doesn't contain borax, and it seems quite likely the prints Petersen left on his wife's body were the result of his touching her while he had some of this 'Sun Blush' on his hands."

"What about the glittery stuff on the knife?"

"The trace amounts were too small to test. But I don't think the residue is 'Sun Blush.' "

"Why not?"

"It isn't a granular powder. It's a cream base—you remember the big white jar of dark pink cream you brought into the lab?"

He nodded.

"That was 'Sun Blush.' Whatever the ingredient is that makes it sparkle in the laser, it's not going to accumulate all over the place the way borax soap does. The creamy base of the cosmetic is more likely to result in high concentrations of sparkles left in discrete smudges, wherever the person's fingertips come in firm contact with some surface."

"Like over Lori's collarbone," he supposed.

"Yes. And over Petersen's ten-print card, the areas of the paper his fingertips actually were pressed against. There were no random sparkles anywhere else on the card, only over the inky ridges. The sparkles on the handle of the survivor knife were not clustered in a pattern like this. They were random, scattered, in very much the same way the sparkles were scattered over the women's bodies."

"You're saying if Petersen had this 'Sun Blush' on his hands and took hold of the knife, there'd be glittery smudges versus individual little sparkles here and there."

"That's what I'm saying."

"Well, what about the glitter you found on the bodies, on the ligatures and so on?"

"There were high-enough concentrations in the areas of Lori's wrists for testing. It came up as borax."

He turned his mirrored eyes toward me. "Two different types of glittery stuff, after all, then."

"That's right."

"Hmm."

Like most city and state buildings in Richmond, Police Headquarters is built of stucco that is almost indistinguishable from the concrete in the sidewalks. Pale and pasty, its ugly blandness is broken only by the vibrant colors of the state and American flags fluttering against the blue sky over the roof. Pulling around in back, Marino swung into a line of unmarked police cars.

We went into the lobby and walked past the glass-enclosed information desk. Officers in dark blue grinned at Marino and said, "Hi, Doc," to me. I glanced down at my suit jacket, relieved I'd remembered to take off my lab coat. I was so used to wearing it, sometimes I forgot. When I accidentally wore it outside of my building, I felt as if I were in my pajamas.

We passed bulletin boards plastered with composite sketches of child molesters, flimflam artists, basic garden-variety thugs.

There were mug shots of Richmond's Ten Most Wanted robbers, rapists and murderers. Some of them were actually smiling into the camera. They'd made the city's hall of fame.

I followed Marino down a dim stairwell, the sound of our feet a hollow echo against metal. We stopped before a door where he peered through a small glass window and gave somebody the high sign.

The door unlocked electronically.

It was the radio room, a subterranean cubicle filled with desks and computer terminals hooked up to telephone consoles. Through a wall of glass was another room of dispatchers for whom the entire city was a video game; 911 operators glanced curiously at us. Some of them were busy with calls, others were idly chatting or smoking, their headphones down around their necks.

Marino took me around to a corner where there were shelves jammed with boxes of large reel-to-reel tapes. Each box was labeled by a date. He walked his fingers down the rows and slipped out one after another, five in all, each one spanning the period of one week.

Loading them in my arms, he drawled, "Merry Christmas."

"What?" I looked at him as if he'd lost his mind.

"Hey." He got out his cigarettes. "Me, I got pizza joints to hit. There's a tape machine over there." He jerked his thumb toward the dispatcher's room beyond the glass. "Either listen up in there, or take 'em back to your office. Now if it was me, I'd take them the hell outa this animal house, but I didn't tell you that, all right? They ain't supposed to leave the premises. Just hand 'em back over when you're through, to me personally."

I was getting a headache.

Next he took me into a small room where a laser printer was sweeping out miles of green-striped paper. The stack of paper on the floor was already two feet high.

"I buzzed the boys down here before we left your office," he laconically explained. "Had 'em print out everything from the computer for the last two months."

Oh, God.

"So the addresses and everything are there." His flat brown eyes glanced at me. "You'll have to look at the hard copies to see what came up on the screen when the calls was made. Without the addresses, you won't know which call's what."

"Can't we just pull up exactly what we want to know on the computer?" I broke out in exasperation.

"You know anything about mainframes?"

Of course I didn't.

He looked around. "Nobody in this joint knows squat about the mainframe. We got one computer person upstairs. Just so happens he's at the beach right now. Only way to get in an expert is if there's a crash. Then they call DP and the department gets knocked up for seventy bucks an hour. Even if the department's willing to co-operate with you, those DP dipsticks are as slow coming around as payday. The guy's going to get around to it late tomorrow, Monday, sometime next week, and that's if Lady Luck's on your side, Doc. Fact is, you was lucky I could find somebody smart enough to hit a Print button."

We stood in the room for thirty minutes. Finally, the printer stopped and Marino ripped off the paper. The stack was close to three feet high. He put it inside an empty printer-paper box he found somewhere and hoisted it up with a grunt.

As I followed him back out of the radio room, he tossed over his shoulder to a young, nice-looking black communications officer, "If you see Cork, I gotta message for him."

"Shoot," the officer said with a yawn.

"Tell him he ain't driving no eighteen-wheeler rig no more and this ain't *Smokey and the Bandit*."

The officer laughed. He sounded exactly like Eddie Murphy.

For the next day and a half I didn't even get dressed but was sequestered inside my home wearing a nylon warmup suit and headphones.

Bertha was an angel and took Lucy on an all-day outing.

I was avoiding my downtown office, where I was sure to be interrupted every five minutes. I was racing against time, praying I came up with something before Friday dissolved into the first few hours of Saturday morning. I was convinced he would be out there again.

I'd already checked in with Rose twice. She said Amburgey's office had tried to get me four times since I drove off with Marino. The commissioner was demanding I come see him immediately, demanding I provide him with an explanation of yesterday morning's front-page story, of "this latest and most outrageous leak," in his words. He wanted the DNA report. He wanted the report on this "latest evidence" turned in. He was so furious he actually got on the phone himself threatening Rose, who had plenty of thorns.

"What did you say to him?" I asked her in amazement.

"I told him I'd leave the message on your desk. When he threatened to have me fired if I didn't hook him up with you immediately, I told him that was fine. I've never sued anybody before . . ."

"You *didn't*."

"I most certainly did. If the little jerk had another brain it would rattle."

My answering machine was on. If Amburgey tried to call me at home he was only going to get my mechanical ear.

It was the stuff of nightmares. Each tape covered seven twenty-four-hour days. Of course, the tapes weren't that many hours long because often there were only three or four two-minute calls per hour. It simply depended on how busy the 911 room was on any given shift. My problem was finding the exact time period when I thought one of the homicides was called in. If I got impatient, I might whiz right on by and have to back up. Then I lost my place. It was awful.

Also, it was as depressing as hell. Emergency calls ranged from the mentally disenfranchised whose bodies were being invaded by aliens, to people roaring drunk, to poor men and women whose spouses had just keeled over from a heart attack or a stroke. There were a lot of automobile accidents, suicide threats, prowlers, barking dogs, steroes up too loud and firecrackers and car backfires that came in as shootings.

I was skipping around. So far I had managed to find three of the calls I was looking for. Brenda's, Henna's and, just now, Lori's. I backed up the tape until I found the aborted 911 call Lori apparently made to the police right before she was murdered. The call came in at exactly 12:49 A.M., Saturday, June 7, and all that was on the tape was the operator picking up the line and crisply saying, "911."

I folded back sheet after sheet of continuous paper until I found the corresponding printout. Lori's address appeared on the

911 screen, her residence listed in the name of L. A. Petersen. Giving the call a priority four, the operator shipped it out to the dispatcher behind the wall of glass. Thirty-nine minutes later patrol unit 211 finally got the call. Six minutes after this he cruised past her house, then sped off on a domestic call.

The Petersen address came up again exactly sixty-eight minutes after the aborted 911 call, at 1:57 A.M., when Matt Petersen found his wife's body. If only he hadn't had dress rehearsal that night, I thought. If only he'd gotten home an hour, an hour and a half earlier . . .

The tape clicked.

"911."

Heavy breathing. "My wife!" In panic. "Somebody killed my wife! Please hurry!" Screaming. "Oh, God! *Somebody killed her!* Please hurry!"

I was paralyzed by the hysterical voice. Petersen couldn't speak in coherent sentences or remember his address when the operator asked if the address on his screen was correct.

I stopped the tape and did some quick calculations. Petersen arrived home twenty-nine minutes after the first responding officer shone his light over the front of the house and reported everything looked "secure." The aborted 911 call came in at 12:49 A.M. The officer finally arrived at 1:34 A.M.

Forty-five minutes had elapsed. The killer was with Lori no longer than that.

By 1:34 A.M., the killer was gone. The bedroom light was out. Had he still been inside the bedroom, the light would have been on. I was sure of it. I couldn't believe he could see well enough to find electrical cords and tie elaborate knots in the dark.

He was a sadist. He would want the victim to see his face, especially if it were masked. He would want his victim to see everything he did. He would want her to anticipate in unthinkable terror every horrendous thing he planned to do . . . as he looked around, as he cut the cords, as he began to bind her . . .

When it was over, he calmly flicked off the bedroom light and climbed back out the bathroom window, probably minutes before the patrol car cruised by and less than half an hour before Petersen walked in. The peculiar body odor lingered like the stench of garbage.

So far I'd found no common patrol unit that had responded to

Brenda, Lori and Henna's scenes. My disappointment was robbing me of the energy to go on.

I took a break when I heard the front door open. Bertha and Lucy were back. They gave me a full account and I did my best to smile and listen. Lucy was exhausted.

"My stomach hurts," she complained.

"It's no wonder," Bertha started in. "I told you not to eat all that trash. Cotton candy, corn dogs . . ." Shaking her head.

I fixed Lucy chicken broth and put her to bed.

Returning to my office, I reluctantly slipped the headphones on again.

I lost track of the time as though I were in suspended animation.

"911." "911."

Over and over again it played in my head.

Shortly after ten I was so weary I could barely think. I dully rewound a tape trying to find the call made when Patty Lewis's body was discovered. As I listened, my eyes drifted over pages of the computer printout unfolded in my lap.

What I saw didn't make sense.

Cecile Tyler's address was printed halfway down the page and dated May 12, at 21:23 hours, or 9:23 P.M.

That couldn't be right.

She wasn't murdered until May 31.

Her address shouldn't have been listed on this portion of the printout. It shouldn't be on this tape!

I fast-forwarded, stopping every few seconds. It took me twenty minutes to find it. I played the segment three times trying to figure out what it meant.

At exactly 9:23 a male voice answered, "911."

A soft, cultured female voice said in surprise, after a pause, "Oh, dear. I'm sorry."

"Is there a problem, ma'am?"

An embarrassed laugh. "I meant to dial Information. I'm sorry." Another laugh. "I guess I hit a nine instead of a four."

"Hey, no problem, that's good, always glad when there's no problem." Adding jauntily, "You have a nice evening."

Silence. A click, and the tape went on.

On the printout the slain black woman's address was listed, simply, under her name: Cecile Tyler.

Suddenly I knew. "Jesus. Dear Jesus," I muttered, momentarily sick to my stomach.

Brenda Steppe had called the police when she had her automobile accident. Lori Petersen had called the police, according to her husband, when she thought she heard a prowler that turned out to be a cat getting into the garbage cans. Abby Turnbull had called the police when the man in the black Cougar followed her. Cecile Tyler had called the police by mistake—it was a wrong number.

She dialed 911 instead of 411.

A wrong number!

Four of the five women. All of the calls were made from their homes. Each address immediately flashed on the 911 computer screen. If the residences were in the women's names, the operator knew they probably lived alone.

I ran into the kitchen. I don't know why. There was a telephone in my office.

I frantically stabbed out the number for the detective division.

Marino wasn't in.

"I need his home number."

"I'm sorry, ma'am, we're not allowed to give those out."

"Goddam it! This is Dr. Scarpetta, the chief medical examiner! Give me his goddam home phone number!"

A startled pause. The officer, whoever he was, began apologizing profusely. He gave me the number.

I dialed again.

"Thank God," I gushed when Marino answered.

"No shit?" he said after my breathless explanation. "Sure, I'll look into it, Doc."

"Don't you think you'd better get down to the radio room to see if the bastard's there?" I practically screamed.

"So, what'd the guy say? You recognize the voice?"

"Of course I didn't recognize the voice."

"Like what exactly did he say to this Tyler lady?"

"I'll let you hear it." I ran back into the office and picked up that extension. Rewinding the tape, I unplugged the headphones and turned the volume up high.

"You recognize it?" I was back on the line.

Marino didn't reply.

"Are you there?" I exclaimed.

"Hey. Chill out for a while, Doc. It's been a rough day, right? Just leave it to yours truly here. I promise I'll look into it."

He hung up.

I sat staring at the receiver in my hand. I sat without moving until the loud dial tone went dead and a mechanical voice began to complain, "If you'd like to make a call, please hang up and try again . . ."

I checked the front door, made sure the burglar alarm was set and went upstairs. My bedroom was at the end of the hall and overlooked the woods in back. Fireflies winked in the inky blackness beyond the glass, and I nervously yanked the blinds shut.

Bertha had this irrational idea sunlight ought to stream into rooms whether anyone was inside them or not. "Kills germs, Dr. Kay," she would say.

"Fades the rugs and the upholstery," I would counter.

But she was set in her ways. I hated it when I came upstairs after dark and found the blinds open. I'd shut them before turning on the light to make sure nobody could see me, if there was anybody out there. But I'd forgotten tonight. I didn't bother to take off my warm-up suit. It would do for pajamas.

Stepping up on a footstool I kept inside the closet, I slid out the Rockport shoe box and opened the lid. I tucked the .38 under my pillow.

I was sick with the worry the telephone would ring and I'd be summoned out into the black morning and have to say to Marino, "I told you so, you stupid bastard! I told you so!"

What was the big lug doing right now, anyway? I flicked off the lamp and pulled the covers up to my ears. He was probably drinking beer and watching television.

I sat up and flicked the lamp back on. The telephone on the bedside table taunted me. There was no one else I could call. If I called Wesley, he would call Marino. If I called the detective division, whoever listened to what I had to say—provided he took me seriously—would call Marino.

Marino. He was in charge of this damn investigation. All roads led to Rome.

Switching off the lamp again, I stared up into the darkness.

"911."

"911."

I kept hearing the voice as I tossed on my bed.

It was past midnight when I crept back down the stairs and found the bottle of cognac in the bar. Lucy hadn't stirred since I had tucked her in hours ago. She was out cold. I wished I could say the same for me. Downing two shots like cough medicine, I miserably returned to my bedroom and switched off the lamp again. I could hear the minutes go by on the digital clock.

Click.

Click.

Seeping in and out of consciousness, I fitfully tossed.

". . . So what exactly did he say to this Tyler woman?"

Click. The tape went on.

"I'm sorry." An embarrassed laugh. "I guess I hit a nine instead of a four . . ."

"Hey, no problem, . . . You have a nice evening."

Click.

". . . I hit a nine instead of a four . . ."

"911."

"Hey . . . He's a good-looking guy. He don't need to slip a lady a mickey to get her to give up the goods . . ."

"He's scum!"

". . . Because he's out of town right now, Lucy. Mr. Boltz went on vacation."

"Oh." Eyes filled with infinite sadness. "When's he coming back?"

"Not until July."

"Oh. Why couldn't we go with him, Auntie Kay? Did he go to the beach?"

". . . You routinely lie by omission about us." His face shimmered behind the veil of rising heat and smoke, his hair gold in the sun.

"911."

I was inside my mother's house and she was saying something to me.

A bird was circling lazily overhead as I rode in a van with someone I neither knew nor could see. Palm trees flowed by. Longnecked white egrets were sticking up like porcelain periscopes in the Everglades. The white heads turned as we passed. Watching us. Watching me.

Turning over, I tried to get more comfortable by resting on my back.

My father sat up in bed and watched me as I told him about my day at school. His face was ashen. His eyes didn't blink and I couldn't hear what I was saying to him. He didn't respond but continued to stare. Fear was constricting my heart. His white face stared. The empty eyes stared.

He was dead.

"*Daddddyyyyy!*"

My nostrils were filled with a sick, stale sweatiness as I buried my face in his neck . . .

The inside of my brain went black.

I surfaced into consciousness like a bubble floating up from the deep. I was aware. I could feel my heart beating.

The smell.

Was it real or was I dreaming?

The putrid smell! *Was I dreaming?*

An alarm was going off inside my head and slamming my heart against my ribs.

As the foul air stirred and something brushed against the bed.

16

THE DISTANCE BETWEEN MY RIGHT HAND and the .38 beneath my pillow was twelve inches, no more.

It was the longest distance I'd ever known. It was forever. It was impossible. I wasn't thinking, just feeling that distance, as my heart went crazy, flailing against my ribs like a bird against the bars of its cage. Blood was roaring in my ears. My body was rigid, every muscle and tendon straining, stiff and quivering with fear. It was pitch-black inside my bedroom.

Slowly I nodded my head, the metallic words ringing, the hand crushing my lips against my teeth. I nodded. I nodded to tell him I wouldn't scream.

The knife against my throat was so big it felt like a machete. The bed tilted to the right and with a click I went blind. When my eyes adjusted to the lamplight, I looked at him and stifled a gasp.

I couldn't breathe or move. I felt the razor-thin blade biting coldly against my skin.

His face was white, his features flattened beneath a white nylon stocking. Slits were cut in it for eyes. Cold hatred poured from them without seeing. The stocking sucked in and out as he breathed. The face was hideous and inhuman, just inches from mine.

"One sound, I'll cut your head off."

Thoughts were sparks flying so fast and in so many directions. Lucy. My mouth was getting numb and I tasted the salty blood.

Lucy, don't wake up. Tension ran through his arm, through his hand, like power through a high-voltage line. I'm going to die.

Don't. You don't want to do this. You don't have to do this.

I'm a person, like your mother, like your sister. You don't want to do this. I'm a human being like you. There are things I can tell you. About the cases. What the police know. You want to know what I know.

Don't. I'm a person. A person! I can talk to you! You have to let me talk to you!

Fragmented speeches. Unspoken. Useless. I was imprisoned by silence. Please don't touch me. Oh, God, don't touch me.

I had to get him to take away his hand, to talk to me.

I tried to will my body to go limp, to relax. It worked a little. I loosened up a little, and he sensed it.

He eased the grip of his hand over my mouth, and I swallowed very slowly.

He was wearing a dark blue jumpsuit. Sweat stained the collar, and there were wide crescent moons under his arms. The hand holding the knife to my throat was sheathed in the translucent skin of a surgical glove. I could smell the rubber. I could smell him.

I saw the jumpsuit in Betty's lab, smelled the syrupy putrid smell of it as Marino was untying the plastic bag . . .

"Is it the smell he remembers?" played in my mind like the rerun of an old movie. Marino's finger pointing at me as he winked, *"Bingo . . ."*

The jumpsuit flattened on the table inside the lab, a large or an extra large with bloody swatches cut out of it . . .

He was breathing hard.

"Please," I barely said without moving.

"Shut up!"

"I can tell you . . ."

"Shut up!" The hand tightened savagely. My jaw was going to shatter like an eggshell.

His eyes were darting, looking around, looking at everything inside my bedroom. They stopped at the draperies, at the cords hanging down. I could see him looking at them. I knew what he was thinking. I knew what he was going to do with them. Then the eyes darted frantically to the cord leading out of my bedside lamp. Something white flashed out of his pocket and he stuffed it into my mouth and moved the knife away.

My neck was so stiff it was on fire. My face was numb. I tried to work the dry cloth forward in my mouth, pushing it around with my tongue without him noticing. Saliva was trickling down the back of my throat.

The house was absolutely silent. My ears were filled with the pounding of my blood. Lucy. Please, God.

The other women did what he said. I saw their suffused faces, their dead faces . . .

As I tried to remember what I knew about him, tried to make sense of what I knew about him. The knife was just inches from me, glinting in the lamplight. Lunge for the lamp and smash it to the floor.

My arms and legs were under the covers. I couldn't kick or grab or move. If the lamp crashed to the floor, the room would go black.

I wouldn't be able to see. He had the knife.

I could talk him out of it. If only I could talk, I could reason with him.

Their suffused faces, the cords cutting into their necks.

Twelve inches, no more. It was the longest distance I'd ever known.

He didn't know about the gun.

He was nervous, jerky, and seemed confused. His neck was flushed and dripping with sweat, his breathing labored and fast.

He wasn't looking at my pillow. He was looking around at everything, but he wasn't looking at my pillow.

"You move . . ." He lightly touched the needle point of the knife to my throat.

My eyes were widely fixed on him.

"You're going to enjoy this, bitch." It was a low, cold voice straight out of hell. "I've been saving the best for last." The stocking sucking in and out. "You want to know how I've been doing it. Going to show you real slow."

The voice. It was familiar.

My right hand. Where was the gun? Was it farther to the right or to the left? Was it directly centered under my pillow? I couldn't remember. I couldn't think! He had to get to the cords. He couldn't cut the cord to the lamp. The lamp was the only light on. The switch to the overhead light was near the door. He was looking at it, at the vacant dark rectangle.

I eased my right hand up an inch.

The eyes darted toward me, then toward the draperies again.

My right hand was on my chest, almost to my right shoulder under the sheet.

I felt the edge of the mattress lift as he got up from the bed. The stains under his arms were bigger. He was soaking wet with sweat.

Looking at the light switch near the blank doorway, looking across the bedroom at the draperies again, he seemed indecisive.

It happened so fast. The hard cold shape knocked against my hand and my fingers seized it and I was rolling off the bed, pulling the covers with me, thudding to the floor. The hammer clicked back and locked and I was sitting straight up, the sheet twisted around my hips, all of it happening at once.

I don't remember doing it. I don't remember doing any of it. It was instinct, someone else. My finger was against the trigger, hands trembling so badly the revolver was jumping up and down.

I don't remember taking the gag out.

I could only hear my voice.

I was screaming at him.

"You son of a bitch! You goddam son of a bitch!"

The gun was bobbing up and down as I screamed, my terror, my rage exploding in profanities that seemed to be coming from someone else. Screaming, I was screaming at him to take off his mask.

He was frozen on the other side of the bed. It was an odd detached awareness. The knife in his gloved hand, I noticed, was just a folding knife.

His eyes were riveted to the revolver.

"TAKE IT OFF!"

His arm moved slowly and the white sheath fluttered to the floor . . .

As he spun around . . .

I was screaming and explosions were going off, spitting fire and splintering glass, so fast I didn't know what was happening.

It was madness. Things were flying and disconnected, the knife flashing out of his hand as he slammed against the bedside table, pulling the lamp to the floor as he fell, and a voice said something. The room went black.

A frantic scraping sound was coming from the wall near the door . . .

"Where're the friggin' lights in this joint . . . ?"

<hr>

I would have done it.

I know I would have done it.

I never wanted to do anything so badly in my life as I wanted to squeeze that trigger.

I wanted to blow a hole in his heart the size of the moon.

We'd been over it at least five times. Marino wanted to argue. He didn't think it happened the way it did.

"Hey, the minute I saw him going through the window, Doc, I was following him. He couldn'ta been in your bedroom no more than thirty seconds before I got there. And you didn't have no damn gun out. You went for it and rolled off the bed when I busted in and blew him out of his size-eleven jogging shoes."

We were sitting in my downtown office Monday morning. I could hardly remember the past two days. I felt as if I'd been under water or on another planet.

No matter what he said, I believed I had my gun on the killer when Marino suddenly appeared in my doorway at the same time his .357 pumped four bullets into the killer's upper body. I didn't check for a pulse. I made no effort to stop the bleeding. I just sat in the twisted sheet on the floor, my revolver in my lap, tears streaming down my cheeks as it dawned on me.

The .38 wasn't loaded.

I was so upset, so distracted when I went upstairs to bed, I'd forgotten to load my gun. The cartridges were still in their box tucked under a stack of sweaters inside one of my dresser drawers where Lucy would never think to look.

He was dead.

He was dead when he hit my rug.

"He didn't have his mask off either," Marino was going on. "Memory plays weird tricks, you know? I pulled the damn stocking off his face soon as Snead and Riggy got there. By then he was already dead as dog food."

He was just a boy.

He was just a pasty-faced boy with kinky dirty-blond hair. His mustache was nothing more than a dirty fuzz.

I would never forget those eyes. They were windows through which I saw no soul. They were empty windows opening onto a darkness, like the ones he climbed through when he murdered women whose voices he'd heard over the phone.

"I thought he said something," I muttered to Marino. "I thought I heard him say something as he was falling. But I can't remember." Hesitantly, I asked, "Did he?"

"Oh, yeah. He said one thing."

"What?" I shakily retrieved my cigarette from the ashtray.

Marino smiled snidely. "Same last words recorded on them little black boxes of crashed planes. Same last words for a lot of poor bastards. He said, 'Oh, shit.' "

One bullet severed his aorta. Another took out his left ventricle. One more went through a lung and lodged in his spine. The fourth one cut through soft tissue, missing every vital organ, and shattered my window.

I didn't do his autopsy. One of my deputy chiefs from northern Virginia left the report on my desk. I don't remember calling him in to do it but I must have.

I hadn't read the papers. I couldn't stomach it. Yesterday's headline in the evening edition was enough. I caught a glimpse of it as I hastily stuffed the paper in the garbage seconds after it landed on my front stoop:

**STRANGLER SLAIN
BY DETECTIVE
INSIDE CHIEF MEDICAL EXAMINER'S
BEDROOM**

Beautiful. I asked myself, Who does the public think was inside my bedroom at two o'clock in the morning, the killer or Marino?

Beautiful.

The gunned-down psychopath was a communications officer hired by the city about a year ago. Communications officers in Richmond are civilians, they aren't really cops. He worked the six-to-midnight shift. His name was Roy McCorkle. Sometimes he worked 911. Sometimes he worked as a dispatcher, which was why Marino recognized the CB voice on the 911 tape I played for him over the phone. Marino didn't tell me he recognized the voice. But he did.

McCorkle wasn't on duty Friday night. He called in sick. He

hadn't been to work since Abby's Thursday morning front-page story. His colleagues didn't have much of an opinion of him one way or another except they found his CB phone manner and jokes amusing. They used to kid him about his frequent trips to the men's room, as many as a dozen during a shift. He was washing his hands, his face, his neck. A dispatcher walked in on him once and found McCorkle practically taking a sponge bath.

In the communications men's room was a dispenser of Borawash soap.

He was an "all-right guy." No one who worked with him really knew him well. They assumed he had a woman he was seeing after hours, "a good-looking blonde" named "Christie." There was no Christie. The only women he saw after hours were the ones he butchered. No one who worked with him could believe he was the one, the strangler.

McCorkle, we were considering, may have murdered the three women in the Boston area years ago. He was driving a rig back then. One of his stops was Boston, where he delivered chickens to a packing plant. But we couldn't be sure. We may never know just how many women he murdered all over the United States. It could be dozens. He probably started out as a peeper, then progressed to a rapist. He had no police record. The most he'd ever gotten was a speeding ticket.

He was only twenty-seven.

According to his résumé on file with the police department, he'd worked a number of jobs: trucker, dispatcher for a cement company in Cleveland, mail deliveryman and as a deliveryman for a florist in Philadelphia.

Marino wasn't able to find him Friday night but he didn't look very hard. From eleven-thirty Marino was on my property, out of sight behind shrubbery, watching. He was wearing a dark blue police jumpsuit so he would blend with the night. When he switched on the overhead light inside my bedroom, and I saw him standing there in the jumpsuit, the gun in hand, for a paralyzing second I didn't know who was the killer and who was the cop.

"See," he was saying, "I'd been thinking about the Abby Turnbull connection, about the possibility the guy was after her and ended up with the sister by mistake. That worried me. I asked myself, what other lady in the city's he getting hooked into?" He looked at me, his face thoughtful.

When Abby was followed from the newspaper late one night and dialed 911, it was McCorkle who answered the call. That was how he knew where she lived. Maybe he'd already thought of killing her, or maybe it didn't occur to him until he heard her voice and realized who she was. We would never know.

We did know all five women had dialed 911 in the past. Patty Lewis did less than two weeks before she was murdered. She called at 8:23 on a Thursday night, right after a bad rainstorm, to report a traffic light out a mile from her house. She was being a good citizen. She was trying to prevent an accident. She didn't want anybody to get hurt.

Cecile Tyler hit a nine instead of a four. A wrong number.

I never dialed 911.

I didn't need to..

My number and address were in the phone directory because medical examiners had to be able to reach me after business hours. Also I talked with several dispatchers on several occasions over the past few weeks when I was trying to find Marino. One of them might have been McCorkle. I'd never know. I don't think I wanted to know.

"Your picture's been in the paper and on TV," Marino went on. "You've been working all his cases, he's been wondering what you know. He's been thinking about you. Me, I was worried. Then all that shit about his metabolic disorder and your office having something on him." He paced as he talked. "Now he's going to be hot. Now it's gotten personal. The snooty lady doctor here's maybe insulting his intelligence, his masculinity."

The phone calls I was getting at late hours—

"This pushes his button. He don't like no broad treating him like he's a stupid ass. He's thinking, 'The bitch thinks she's smart, better'n me. I'll show her. I'll fix her.' "

I was wearing a sweater under my lab coat. Both were buttoned up to the collar. I couldn't get warm. For the last two nights I'd slept in Lucy's room. I was going to redecorate my bedroom. I was thinking of selling my house.

"So I guess that big newspaper spread on him the other day rattled his cage all right. Benton said it was a blessing. That maybe he'd get reckless or something. I was pissed. You remember that?"

I barely nodded.

"You want to know the big reason I was so damned pissed?"

I just looked at him. He was like a kid. He was proud of himself. I was supposed to praise him, be thrilled, because he shot a man at ten paces, mowed him down inside my bedroom. The guy had a buck knife. That was it. What was he going to do, throw it?

"Well, I'll tell you. For one thing, I got a little tip sometime back."

"A tip?" My eyes focused. "What tip?"

"Golden Boy Boltz," he replied matter-of-factly as he flicked an ash. "Just so happens he was big enough to pass along something right before he blew out of town. Told me he was worried about you . . ."

"About me?" I blurted.

"Said he dropped by your house late one night and there was this strange car. It cruised up, cut its lights and sped off. He was antsy you was being watched, maybe it was the killer . . ."

"That was Abby!" I crazily broke out. "She came to see me, to ask me questions, saw Bill's car and panicked . . ."

Marino looked surprised, just for an instant. Then shrugged. "Whatever. Just as well it caught our attention, huh?"

I didn't say anything. I was on the verge of tears.

"It was enough to give me the jitters. Fact is, I've been watching your house for a while. Been watching it a lot of late nights. Then comes the damn story about the DNA link. I'm thinking this squirrel's maybe already casing the doc. Now he's really going to be off the wall. The story ain't going to lure him to the computer. It's going to lure him straight to her."

"You were right," I said, clearing my throat.

"You're damn right I was right."

Marino didn't have to kill him. No one would ever know except the two of us. I'd never tell. I wasn't sorry. I would have done it myself. Maybe I was sick inside because if I tried I would have failed. The .38 wasn't loaded. Click. That's as far as I would have gotten. I think I was sick inside because I couldn't save myself and I didn't want to thank Marino for my life.

He was going on and on. My anger started to simmer. It began creeping up my throat like bile.

When suddenly Wingo walked in.

"Uh." Hands in his pockets, he looked uncertain as Marino eyed him in annoyance.

"Uh, Dr. Scarpetta. I know this isn't a good time and all. I mean, I know you're still upset . . ."

"I'm not upset!"

His eyes widened. He blanched.

Lowering my voice, I said, "I'm sorry, Wingo. Yes. I'm upset. I'm ragged. I'm not myself. What's on your mind?"

He reached in a pocket of his powder-blue silk trousers and pulled out a plastic bag. Inside was a cigarette butt, Benson & Hedges 100's.

He placed it lightly on my blotter.

I looked blankly at him, waiting.

"Uh, well, you remember me asking about the commissioner, about whether he's an antismoker and all that?"

I nodded.

Marino was getting restless. He was looking around as if he were bored.

"You see, my friend Patrick. He works in accounting across the street, in the same building where Amburgey works. Well." He was blushing. "Patrick and I, we meet sometimes at his car and go off for lunch. His assigned parking place is about two rows down from where Amburgey's is. We've seen him before."

"Seen him before?" I asked, baffled. "Seen Amburgey before? Doing what?"

Wingo leaned over and confided, "Seen him smoking, Dr. Scarpetta." He straightened up. "I swear. Late morning and right after lunchtime, Patrick and me, we're sitting in the car, in Patrick's car, just talking, listening to tunes. We've seen Amburgey get into his black New Yorker and light up. He doesn't even use the ashtray because he doesn't want anybody to know. He's looking around the whole time. Then he flicks the butt out the window, looks around some more and strolls back toward the building squirting freshener in his mouth . . ."

He stared at me, bewildered.

I was laughing so hard I was crying. It must have been hysteria. I couldn't stop. I was pounding the top of my desk and wiping my eyes. I'm sure people could hear me up and down the hall.

Wingo started laughing, uneasily, then he couldn't stop either.

Marino scowled at both of us as if we were imbeciles. Then he was fighting a smile. In a minute he was choking on his cigarette and guffawing.

Wingo finally went on, "The thing is . . ." He took a deep breath. "The thing is, Dr. Scarpetta, I waited until he did it and right after he left his car I ran over and collected the butt. I took it straight up to serology, to Betty, had her test it."

I gasped. "You did what? You took the butt to Betty? That's what you took up to her the other day? To what? Have his saliva tested? What for?"

"His blood type. It's AB, Dr. Scarpetta."

"My God."

The connection was that fast. The blood type that came up on the mislabeled PERK Wingo found inside the evidence refrigerator was AB.

AB is extremely rare. Only four percent of the population has type AB.

"I was wondering about him," Wingo explained. "I know how much he, uh, hates you. It's always hurt me he treats you so bad. So I asked Fred . . ."

"The security guard?"

"Yeah. I asked Fred about seeing anybody. You know, if he'd seen anybody going inside our morgue who wasn't supposed to be there. He said he saw this one dude on an early Monday evening. Fred was starting his rounds and stopped off to use the john down there. He's coming out just as this white dude's coming in, into the john, I'm saying. Fred told me the white dude had something in his hands, some paper packets of some sort. Fred just went on out, went about his business."

"Amburgey? It was Amburgey?"

"Fred didn't know. He said most white folks look alike to him. But he remembered this dude because he had on a real nice silver ring with a real big blue stone in it. An older guy, scrawny, and about bald."

It was Marino who proposed, "So maybe Amburgey went into the john and swabbed himself—"

"They're oral," I recalled. "The cells that showed up on the slides. And no Barr bodies. Y chromosome, in other words—male."

"I love it when you talk dirty." Marino grinned at me, and went on, "So he swabs the inside of his cheeks—the ones above his friggin' neck, I hope. Smears some slides from a PERK, slaps a label on it—"

"A label he got from Lori Petersen's file," I interrupted him again, this time incredulously.

"Then he tucks it inside the fridge to make you think you screwed up. Hell, maybe he's the one breaking into the computer, too. Unbelievable." Marino was laughing again. "Don't you love it? We'll nail his ass!"

The computer had been broken into over the weekend, sometime after hours on Friday, we believed. Wesley noticed the commands on the screen Saturday morning when he came in for McCorkle's autopsy. Someone had tried to pull up Henna Yarborough's case. The call, of course, could be traced. We were waiting for Wesley to get the goods from the telephone company.

I'd been assuming it was McCorkle who might have gotten in at some point Friday evening before he came after me.

"If the commissioner's the one breaking into the computer," I reminded them, "he's not in trouble. He has the right, ex officio, to my office data and anything else he cares to peruse. We'll never be able to prove he altered a record."

All eyes fell to the cigarette butt inside the plastic bag.

Evidence tampering, fraud, not even the governor could take such liberties. A felony is a felony. I doubted it could be proved.

I got up and hung my lab coat on the back of the door. Slipping on my suit jacket, I collected a fat folder off a chair. I was due in court in twenty minutes to testify in yet one more homicide case.

Wingo and Marino walked me out to the elevator. I left them and stepped inside.

Through the closing doors I blew them each a kiss.

Three days later, Lucy and I sat in the back of a Ford Tempo heading to the airport. She was returning to Miami, and I was going with her for two very good reasons.

I intended to see about the situation with her mother and the illustrator she had married, and I desperately needed a vacation.

I planned to take Lucy to the beach, to the Keys, to the Everglades, to the Monkey Jungle and the Seaquarium. We'd watch the Seminoles wrestle alligators. We'd watch the sun set over Biscayne Bay and go see the pink flamingos in Hialeah. We'd rent the movie

Mutiny on the Bounty, and then tour the famous ship at Bayside and imagine Marlon Brando on deck. We'd go shopping along Coconut Grove, and eat grouper and red snapper and Key lime pie until we were sick. We'd do everything I wished I could have done when I was her age.

We'd also talk about the shock of what she'd been through. Miraculously, she had slept through everything until Marino opened fire. But Lucy knew her aunt was almost murdered.

She knew the killer got in through my office window, which was closed but unlocked, because Lucy forgot to lock it after opening it several days earlier.

McCorkle cut the wires to the burglar alarm system outside the house. He came in through the first-floor window, walked within feet of Lucy's room and quietly went up the stairs. How did he know my bedroom was on the second floor?

I don't think he could have unless he'd watched my house in the past.

Lucy and I had a lot of talking to do. I needed to talk to her as much as she needed for me to talk to her. I planned to hook her up with a good child psychologist. Maybe both of us should go.

Our chauffeur was Abby. She was kind enough to insist on driving us to the airport.

She pulled in front of the airline gate, turned around and smiled wistfully.

"I wish I were going with you."

"You're welcome to," I responded with feeling. "Really. We'd love it, Abby. I'll be down there for three weeks. You have my mother's phone number. If you can get away, hop a plane and we'll all go to the beach together."

An alert tone sounded on her scanner. She absently reached around to turn up the volume and adjust the squelch.

I knew I wouldn't hear from her. Not tomorrow or the next day or the day after that.

By the time our plane took off, she would be chasing ambulances and police cars again. It was her life. She needed reporting like other people need air.

I owed her a lot.

Because of what she set up behind the scenes we discovered it was Amburgey breaking into the OCME computer. The call was traced back to his home telephone. He was a computer hack and had a PC at home with a modem.

I think he broke in the first time simply because he was monitoring my work, as usual. I think he was rolling through the strangling cases when he noticed a detail in Brenda Steppe's record different from what Abby reported in the paper. He realized the leak couldn't be my office. But he so desperately wanted it to be, he altered the record to make it appear that way.

Then he deliberately keyed on the echo and tried to pull up Lori Petersen's case. He wanted us to find those commands on the screen the following Monday, just hours before he called me to his office in front of Tanner and Bill.

One sin led to another. His hatred blinded his reason, and when he saw the computer labels in Lori's case file he wasn't able to restrain himself. I'd thought a long time about the meeting in my conference room, when the men were going through the files. I'd assumed the PERK label was stolen when several cases slipped off Bill's lap and scattered over the floor. But as I went over it I recalled Bill and Tanner sorting out the paperwork by the proper case numbers. Lori's case was not among them because Amburgey was perusing it at the time. He took advantage of the confusion and quickly tore off the PERK label. Later, he left the computer room with Tanner but stayed behind alone in the morgue to use the men's room. He planted the slides.

That was his first mistake. His second mistake was underestimating Abby. She was livid when she realized someone was using her reporting to jeopardize my career. It didn't matter whose career, I suspected. Abby simply didn't cotton to being used. She was a crusader: truth, justice and the American way. She was all dressed up with rage with no place to go.

After her story hit the racks, she went to see Amburgey. She was already suspicious of him, she'd confessed to me, because he was the one who slyly gave her access to the information about the mislabeled PERK. He had the serology report on his desk, and notes to himself about the "fouled-up chain of evidence," and the "inconsistency of these results with those from earlier tests." While Abby was seated on one side of his famous Chinese desk, he stepped out, leaving her alone for a minute—long enough for her to see what was on his blotter.

It was obvious, what he was doing. His feelings for me were no secret. Abby wasn't stupid. She became the aggressor. Last Friday morning she had gone back to see him and confronted him about the computer violation.

He was cagey, feigning horror that she might print such a thing, but he was salivating. He could taste my disgrace.

She set him up by admitting she didn't have enough to go on. "The computer violation's only happened once," she told him. "If it happens again, Dr. Amburgey, I'll have no choice but to print it and other allegations I've heard, because the public will have to know there's a problem at the OCME."

It had happened again.

The second computer violation had nothing to do with the planted news story, because it wasn't the killer who needed to be lured back to the OCME computer. It was the commissioner.

"By the way," Abby told me as we got the bags out of the trunk, "I don't think Amburgey's going to be a problem anymore."

"A leopard can't change its spots," I remarked, glancing at my watch.

She smiled at some secret she wasn't going to divulge. "Just don't be surprised when you come back to find he's no longer in Richmond."

I didn't ask.

She had plenty on Amburgey. Someone had to pay. She couldn't touch Bill.

He had called me yesterday to say he was glad I was all right, that he had heard about what had happened. He had made no references to his own crimes, and I had not so much as alluded to them when he calmly said he didn't think it was a good idea for us to see each other anymore.

"I've given it a lot of thought, and I just don't think it's going to work, Kay."

"You're right," I agreed, surprised by my own sense of relief. "It just isn't going to work, Bill."

I gave Abby a big hug.

Lucy frowned as she struggled with a very large pink suitcase.

"Shoot," she complained. "Mom's computer's got nothing but word processing on it. Shoot. No data base or nothing."

"We're going to the beach." I shouldered two bags and followed her through the opening glass doors. "We're going to have a good time, Lucy. You can just lay off the computer for a while. It's not good for your eyes."

"There's a software store about a mile from my house . . ."

"The beach, Lucy. You need a vacation. Both of us need a vacation. Fresh air, sunshine, it will be good for you. You've been cooped up inside my office for two weeks."

We continued bickering at the ticket counter.

I shoved the bags on the scale, straightened Lucy's collar in back and asked her why she hadn't carried her jacket. "The air-conditioning in planes is always too high."

"Auntie Kay . . ."

"You're going to be cold."

"Auntie Kay!"

"We've got time for a sandwich."

"I'm not hungry!"

"You need to eat. From here we're stuck in Dulles for an hour and there's no lunch on the plane from there. You need something in your stomach."

"You sound just like Grans!"

Body of Evidence

For Ed,
Special Agent and Special Friend

Prologue

August 13
KEY WEST

Dear M,

Thirty days have passed in measured shades of sunlit color and changes in the wind. I think too much and do not dream.

Most afternoons I'm at Louie's writing on the porch and looking out at the sea. The water is mottled emerald green over the mosaic of sandbars, and aqua as it deepens. The sky goes on forever, clouds white puffs always moving like smoke. A constant breeze washes out the sounds of people swimming and sailboats anchoring just beyond the reef. The porch is covered and when a sudden storm whips up, as it often does late afternoon, I stay at my table smelling the rain and watching it turn the water nappy like fur rubbed the wrong way. Sometimes it pours and the sun shines at the same time.

Nobody bothers me. By now I am part of the restaurant's family, like Zulu, the black Lab who splashes after Frisbees, and the stray cats who silently wander up to politely wait for scraps. Louie's four-legged wards eat better than any human. It is a comfort to watch the world treat its creatures kindly. I cannot complain about my days.

It is the nights I dread.

When my thoughts creep back into dark crevices and spin their fearful webs I pitch myself into crowded Old Town streets, drawn to noisy bars like a moth to light. Walt and PJ have refined my nocturnal habits to an art. Walt returns to the rooming house first, at twilight because his silver jewelry business in Mallory Square grinds to a halt after dark. We open bottles of beer and wait for PJ. Then out we go, bar to bar, usually ending up at Sloppy Joe's. We are becoming inseparable. I hope the two of them will always be inseparable. Their love no longer seems out of the ordinary to me. Nothing does, except the death I see.

Men emaciated and wan, their eyes windows through which I see tormented souls. AIDS is a holocaust consuming the offerings of this small island. Odd I should feel at home with the exiled and the dying. I may be survived by all of them. When I lie awake at night listening to the whirring of the window fan I'm seized by images of how it will happen.

Every time I hear a telephone ring, I remember. Every time I hear someone walking behind me, I turn around. At night I look in my closet, behind the curtain and under my bed, then prop a chair in front of the door.

Dear God, I don't want to go home.

                                                                    Beryl

September 30
KEY WEST

Dear M,

Yesterday at Louie's, Brent came out to the porch and said the phone was for me. My heart raced as I went inside and was answered by long distance static and the line going dead.

The way that made me feel! I've been telling myself I'm too paranoid. He would have said something, and delighted in my fear. It's impossible he knows where I am, impossible he could have tracked me here. One of the waiters is named Stu. He recently broke off with a friend up north, then moved here. Maybe his friend called and the connection was bad. It sounded like he asked for "Straw" instead of "Stu," and then when I answered he hung up.

I wish I had never told anyone my nickname. I am Beryl. I am Straw. I am frightened.

The book isn't finished. But I'm almost out of money, and the weather has turned. This morning it's dark and there's a fierce wind. I've stayed in my room because if I tried to work at Louie's the pages would blow out to sea. Streetlights have blinked on. Palm trees are struggling against the wind, fronds like inside-out umbrellas. The world moans outside my window like something wounded, and when the rain hits the glass it sounds as if a dark army has marched in and Key West is under siege.

I must leave soon. I will miss the island. I will miss PJ and Walt. They have made me feel cared for and safe. I don't know what I'll do when I get back to Richmond. Perhaps I should move right away, but I don't know where I will go.

Beryl

1

RETURNING THE KEY WEST LETTERS to their manila folder, I got out a packet of surgical gloves, tucked it inside my black medical bag, and took the elevator down one floor to the morgue.

The tile hallway was damp from being mopped, the autopsy suite locked and closed for business. Diagonally across from the elevator was the stainless-steel refrigerator, and opening its massive door, I was greeted by the familiar blast of cold, foul air. I located the gurney inside without bothering to check toe tags, recognizing the slender foot protruding from a white sheet. I knew every inch of Beryl Madison.

Smoky-blue eyes stared dully from slitted lids, her face slack and marred with pale open cuts, most of them on the left side. Her neck was laid wide open to her spine, the strap muscles severed. Closely spaced over her left chest and breast were nine stab wounds spread open like large red buttonholes and almost perfectly vertical. They had been inflicted in rapid succession, one right after the other, the force so violent there were hilt marks in her skin. Cuts to her forearms and hands ranged from a quarter of an inch to four and a half inches in length. Counting two on her back, and excluding her stab wounds and cut throat, there were twenty-seven cutting injuries, all of them inflicted while she was attempting to ward off the slashing of a wide, sharp blade.

I would not need photographs or body diagrams. When I closed my eyes I could see Beryl Madison's face. I could see in sickening detail the violence inflicted upon her body. Her left lung was punctured four times. Her carotid arteries were almost transected. Her aortic arch, pulmonary artery, heart, and pericardial sac were penetrated. She was, for all practical purposes, dead by the time the madman almost decapitated her.

I was trying to make sense of it. Someone had threatened to murder her. She fled to Key West. She was terrified beyond reason. She did not want to die. The night she returned to Richmond it happened.

Why did you let him into your house? Why in God's name did you?

Rearranging the sheet, I returned the gurney to the others bearing bodies against the refrigerator's back wall. By this time tomorrow her body would be cremated, her ashes en route to California. Beryl Madison would have turned thirty-four next month. She had no living relatives, no one in this world, it seemed, except a half sister in Fresno. The heavy door sucked shut.

The tarmac of the parking lot behind the Office of the Chief Medical Examiner was warm and reassuring beneath my feet, and I could smell the creosote of nearby railroad trestles baking in the unseasonably warm sun. It was Halloween.

The bay door was open wide, one of my morgue assistants hosing off the concrete. He playfully arched water, slapping it close enough for me to feel mist around my ankles.

"Hey, Dr. Scarpetta, you keeping banker's hours now?" he called out.

It was a little past four-thirty. I rarely left the office before six.

"Need a lift somewhere?" he added.

"I've got a ride. Thanks," I answered.

I was born in Miami. I was no stranger to the part of the world where Beryl had hidden during the summer. When I closed my eyes I saw the colors of Key West. I saw bright greens and blues and sunsets so gaudy only God can get away with them. Beryl Madison should never have come home.

A brand-new LTD Crown Victoria, shining like black glass, slowly pulled into the lot. Expecting the familiar beat-up Plymouth, I was startled when the new Ford's window hummed open. "You waiting for the bus or what?" Mirrored shades reflected my surprised face. Lieutenant Pete Marino was trying to look blasé as electronic locks opened with a firm click.

"I'm impressed," I said, settling into the plush interior.

"Went with my promotion." He revved the engine. "Not bad, huh?"

After years of broken-down dray horses, Marino had finally gotten himself a stallion.

I noticed the hole in the dash as I got out my cigarettes. "You been plugging in your bubble light or just your electric razor?"

"Oh, hell," he complained. "Some drone swiped my lighter. At the car wash. I mean, I'd only had the car a day, you believe it? I take her in, right? Was too busy bitching after the fact, the brushes broke off the antenna, was giving the drones holy hell about that . . ."

Sometimes Marino reminded me of my mother.

". . . wasn't until later I noticed the damn lighter gone." He paused, digging in his pocket as I rummaged through my purse for matches.

"Yo, Chief, thought you was gonna quit smoking," he said rather sarcastically, dropping a Bic lighter in my lap.

"I am," I muttered. "Tomorrow."

The night Beryl Madison was murdered I was out enduring an overblown opera followed by drinks in an overrated English pub with a retired judge who became something less than honorable as the evening progressed. I wasn't wearing my pager. Unable to reach me, the police had summoned Fielding, my deputy chief, to the scene. This would be the first time I had been inside the slain author's house.

Windsor Farms was not the sort of neighborhood where one would expect anything so hideous to happen. Homes were large and set back from the street on impeccably landscaped lots. Most had burglar alarm systems, and all featured central air, eliminating the need for open windows. Money can't buy eternity, but it can buy a certain degree of security. I had never had a homicide case from the Farms.

"Obviously she had money from somewhere," I observed as Marino halted at a stop sign.

A snowy-haired woman walking her snowy Maltese squinted at us as the dog sniffed a tuft of grass, which was followed by the inevitable.

"What a worthless fuzz ball," he said, staring disdainfully at the woman and the dog moving on. "Hate mutts like that. Yap their damn heads off and piss all over the place. Gonna have a dog, ought to be something with teeth."

"Some people simply want company," I said.

"Yeah." He paused, then picked up on my earlier statement. "Beryl Madison had money, most of it tied up in her crib. Apparently whatever savings she had, she blew the dough down there in Queer West. We're still sorting through her paperwork."

"Had any of it been gone through?"

"Don't look like it," he replied. "Found out she didn't do half bad as a writer—bucks-wise. Appears she used several pen names. Adair Wilds, Emily Stratton, Edith Montague." The mirrored shades turned my way again.

None of the names were familiar except Stratton. I said, "Her middle name is Stratton."

"Maybe accounting for her nickname, Straw."

"That and her blond hair," I remarked.

Beryl's hair was honey blond streaked gold by the sun. She was petite, with even, refined features. She may have been striking in life. It was hard to say. The only photograph from life I had seen was the one on her driver's license.

"When I talked to her half sister," Marino was explaining, "I found out Beryl was called Straw by the people she was close to. Whoever she was writing down there in the Keys, this person was aware of her nickname. That's the impression I get." He adjusted the visor. "Can't figure why she Xeroxed those letters. Been chewing on that. I mean, how many people do you know who make photocopies of personal letters they write?"

"You've indicated she was an inveterate record keeper," I reminded him.

"Right. That's bugging me, too. Supposedly the squirrel's been threatening her for months. What'd he do? What'd he say? Don't know, because she didn't tape his calls or write nothing down. The lady makes photocopies of personal letters but don't keep a record when someone's threatening to whack her. Tell me if that makes sense."

"Not everybody thinks the way we do."

"Well, some people don't *think* because they're in the middle of something they don't want nobody to know about," he argued.

Pulling into a drive, he parked in front of the garage door. The grass was badly overgrown and spangled with tall dandelions swaying in the breeze, and there was a FOR SALE sign planted near the mailbox. Still tacked across the gray front door was a ribbon of yellow crime-scene tape.

"Her ride's inside the garage," Marino said as we got out. "A nice black Honda Accord EX. Some details about it you might find interesting."

We stood on the drive and looked around. The slanted rays of the sun were warm on the back of my shoulders and neck. The air was cool, the pervasive hum of autumn insects the only sound. I took a slow, deep breath. I was suddenly very tired.

Her house was International style, modern and starkly simplistic with a horizonal frontage of large windows supported by ground-floor piers, bringing to mind a ship with an open lower deck. Built of fieldstone and gray-stained wood, it was the sort of house a wealthy young couple might build—big rooms, high ceilings, a lot of expensive and wasted space. Windham Drive dead-ended at her lot, which explained why no one had heard or seen anything until it was too late. The house was cloistered by oaks and pines on two sides, drawing a curtain of foliage between Beryl and her nearest neighbors. In back, the yard sharply dropped off into a ravine of underbrush and boulders, leveling out into an expanse of virgin timber stretching as far as I could see.

"Damn. Bet she had deer," Marino said as we wandered around back. "Something, huh? You look out your windows, think you got the world to yourself. Bet the view's something when it snows. Me, I'd love a crib like this. Build a nice fire in the winter, pour yourself a little bourbon, and just look out at the woods. Must be nice to be rich."

"Especially if you're alive to enjoy it."

"Ain't that the truth," he said.

Fall leaves crackled beneath our shoes as we rounded the west wing. The front door was level with the patio, and I noted the peephole. It stared at me like a tiny empty eye. Marino flicked a cigarette butt, sent it sailing into the grass, then dug in a pocket of his powder-blue trousers. His jacket was off, his big belly hanging over his belt, his short-sleeved white shirt open at the neck and wrinkled around his shoulder holster.

He produced a key attached to a yellow evidence tag, and as I watched him open the dead-bolt lock I was startled anew by the size of his hands. Tan and tough, they reminded me of baseball mitts.

He would never have made a musician or a dentist. Somewhere in his early fifties, with thinning gray hair and a face as shopworn as his suits, he was still formidable enough to give most people pause. Big cops like him rarely get in fights. The street punks take one look and sit on their bravado.

We stood in a rectangle of sunlight inside the foyer and worked on pairs of gloves. The house smelled stale and dusty, the way houses smell when they have been shut up for a while. Though the Richmond police department's Identification Unit, or ID, had thoroughly processed the scene, nothing had been moved. Marino had assured me the house would look exactly as it had when Beryl's body was found two nights earlier. He shut the door and flipped on a light.

"As you can see," his voice echoed, "she had to have let the guy in. No sign of forcible entry, and the joint's got a triple A burglar alarm." He directed my attention to the panel of buttons by the door, adding, "Deactivated at the moment. But it was in working order when we got here, screaming bloody murder, which is why we found her so fast to begin with."

He went on to remind me the homicide was originally called in as an audible alarm. At shortly after eleven P.M., one of Beryl's neighbors dialed 911 after the alarm had been going for nearly thirty minutes. A patrol unit responded and the officer found the front door ajar. Minutes later he was on his radio requesting backups.

The living room was in shambles, the glass coffee table on its side. Magazines, a crystal ashtray, several art deco bowls and a flower vase were strewn over the dhurrie rug. A pale blue leather wingchair was overturned, a cushion from the matching sectional sofa nearby. On the whitewashed wall left of a door leading into a hallway were dark spatters of dried blood.

"Does her alarm have a time delay?" I asked.

"Oh, yeah. You open the door and the alarm hums about fifteen seconds, long enough for you to punch in your code before it goes off."

"Then she must have opened the door, deactivated the alarm, let the person in, and then reset the alarm while he was still here. Otherwise, it would never have gone off later, when he left. Interesting."

"Yeah," Marino replied, "interesting as shit."

We were inside the living room, standing near the overturned coffee table. It was sooty with dusting powder. The magazines on the floor were news and literary publications, all of them several months old.

"Did you find any recent newspapers or magazines?" I asked. "If she bought a paper locally, it could be important. Anywhere she went after getting off the plane is worth checking."

I saw his jaw muscles flex. Marino hated it when he assumed I was telling him how to do his job.

He said, "There were a couple of things upstairs in her bedroom where her briefcase and bags was. A Miami *Herald* and something called the *Keynoter*, has mostly real estate listings for the Keys. Maybe she was thinking of moving down there? Both papers came out Monday. She must've bought them, maybe picked them up in the airport on her way back to Richmond."

"I'd be interested in what her realtor has to say . . ."

"Nothing, that's what he has to say," he interrupted. "Has no idea where Beryl was and only showed her house once while she was gone. Some young couple. Decided the price was too high. Beryl was asking three hundred Gs for the joint." He looked around, his face impervious. "Guess someone could get a deal now."

"Beryl took a taxi home from the airport the night she got in." I doggedly pursued the details.

He got out a cigarette and pointed with it. "Found the receipt in the foyer there, on that little table by the door. Already checked out the driver, a guy named Woodrow Hunnel. Dumb as a bag of hammers. Said he was waiting in the line of cabs at the airport. She flagged him down. This was close to eight, it was raining cats and dogs. He let her out here at the house maybe forty minutes later, said he carried her two suitcases to the door, then split. The fare was twenty-six bucks, including the tip. He was back at the airport about half an hour later picking up another fare."

"You're sure, or is this what he told you?"

"Sure as I'm damn standing here." He tapped the cigarette on his knuckle and began fingering the filtered tip with his thumb. "We checked out the story. Hunnel was shooting straight with us. He didn't touch the lady. There wasn't time."

I followed his eyes to the dark spatters near the doorway. The killer's clothing would have been bloody. It wasn't likely a cabdriver with bloody clothes was going to be picking up fares.

"She hadn't been home long," I said. "Got in around nine and a neighbor calls in her alarm at eleven. It had been going for a half hour, meaning the killer was gone by around ten-thirty."

"Yeah," he answered. "That's the hardest part to figure. Based on those letters, she was scared shitless. So she sneaks back to the city, locks herself inside her house, even has her three-eighty on the kitchen counter—show you that when we get there. Then, boom! The doorbell rings or what? Next thing you know, she's let the squirrel in and reset the burglar alarm behind him. Had to be somebody she knew."

"I wouldn't rule out a stranger," I said. "If the person is very smooth, she may have trusted him, let him in for some other reason."

"At that hour?" His eyes flicked me as they went around the room. "What? He's selling magazine subscriptions, Good Humor bars at ten o'clock at night?"

I didn't reply. I didn't know.

We stopped at the open doorway leading into a hallway. "This is the first blood," Marino said, looking at the dried spatters on the wall. "She got cut right here, the first cut. I figure she's running like hell and he's slashing."

I envisioned the cuts on Beryl's face, arms, and hands.

"My guess," he went on, "is he cut her left arm or back or face at this point. The blood on the wall here's cast off from blood slinging off the blade. He'd already cut her at least once, the blade was bloody, and when he swung again drops flew off and hit the wall."

The stains were elliptical, about six millimeters in diameter, and became increasingly elongated the farther they arched left of the doorframe. The spread of drops spanned at least ten feet. The assailant had been swinging with the vigor of a hard-hitting squash player. I felt the emotion of the crime. It wasn't anger. It was worse than that. *Why did she let him in?*

"Based on the location of this spatter, I'm thinking the drone was right about here," Marino said, positioning himself several yards back from the doorway and slightly to the left of it. "He swings, cuts her again, and as the blade follows through, blood flies off and hits the wall. The pattern, as you can see, starts here." He gestured toward the highest drops, which were almost level with the top of his head. "Then sweeps down, stopping several inches from the floor." He paused, his eyes challenging me. "You examined her. What do you think? He's right-handed or left-handed?"

The cops always wanted to know that. No matter how often I told them it was anybody's guess, they still asked.

"It's not possible to tell from this blood spatter," I said, the inside of my mouth dry and tasting like dust. "It depends entirely on where he was standing in relation to her. As for the stab injuries to her chest, they're slightly angled from left to right. That might make him left-handed. But again, it depends on where he was in relation to her."

"I just think it's interesting almost all her defense injuries are located on the left side of her body. You know, she's running. He's coming at her from the left instead of the right. Makes me suspicious he's left-handed."

"It all depends on the victim and assailant's positions in relation to each other," I repeated impatiently.

"Yo," he muttered shortly. "Everything depends on something."

Through the doorway was a hardwood floor. A runway had been chalked off to enclose drips of blood leading to a stairway some ten feet to our left. Beryl had fled this way and up the stairs. Her shock and terror were greater than her pain. On the left wall at almost every step was a bloody smear made by her cut fingers reaching out for balance and dragging across the paneling.

The black spots were on the floor, on the walls, on the ceiling. Beryl had run to the end of the upstairs hall, where she was momentarily cornered. In this area there was a great deal of blood. The chase resumed after she apparently fled from the end of the hall into her bedroom, where she may have eluded him by climbing over the queen-size bed as he came around it. At this point, either she threw her briefcase at him or, more likely, it was on top of the bed and was knocked off. The police found it on the rug, open and upside down like a tent, papers scattered nearby, including the photocopies of the letters she had written from Key West.

"What other papers did you find in here?" I asked.

"Receipts, a couple tourist guides, including a brochure with a street map," Marino answered. "I'll make copies for you if you want."

"Please," I said.

"Also found a stack of typed pages on her dresser there." He pointed. "Probably what she was writing in the Keys. A lot of notes scribbled in the margins in pencil. No prints worth nothing, a few smudges and a few partials that are hers."

Her bed was stripped to the bare mattress, its blood-stained quilted spread and sheets having been sent to the lab. She had been slowing down, losing motor control, getting weak. She had stumbled back out into the hall, where she'd fallen over an Oriental prayer rug I remembered from the scene photographs. There were bloody drag marks and handprints on the floor. Beryl had crawled into the guest bedroom beyond the bath, and it was here, finally, that she died.

"Me," Marino was saying, "I think it wasn't any fun unless he chased her. He could've grabbed her, killed her down there in the living room, but that would've ruined the sport. He was probably smiling the whole time, her bleeding and screaming and begging. When she finally makes it in here, she collapses. The gig's up. No fun anymore. He ends it."

The room was wintry, decorated in yellow as pale as January sunshine. The hardwood floor was black near the twin bed, and there were black streaks and splashes on the whitewashed wall. In the scene photographs Beryl was on her back, her legs spread, her arms up around her head, her face turned toward the curtained window. She was nude. When I had first studied the photographs I could not tell what she looked like or even the color of her hair. All I saw was red. The police had found a pair of bloody khaki slacks near her body. Her blouse and undergarments were missing.

"The cabdriver you mentioned—Hunnel or whatever his name was—did he remember what Beryl was wearing when he picked her up at the airport?" I asked.

"It was dark," Marino replied. "He wasn't sure but thought she was wearing pants and a jacket. We know she was wearing pants when she was attacked, the khaki ones we found in here. There was a matching jacket on a chair inside her bedroom. I don't think she changed clothes when she got home, just tossed her jacket on the chair. Whatever else she was wearing—a blouse, her underclothes—the killer took them."

"A souvenir," I thought aloud.

Marino was staring at the dark-stained floor where her body had been found.

He said, "The way I'm seeing it, he has her down in here, takes her clothes off, rapes her or tries to. Then he stabs her and nearly cuts her head off. A damn shame about her PERK," he added, referring to her Physical Evidence Recovery Kit, swabs from which were negative for sperm. "Guess we can kiss DNA good-bye."

"Unless some of the blood we're analyzing is his," I replied. "Otherwise, yes. Forget DNA."

"And no hairs," he said.

"None except a few consistent with hers."

The house was so quiet our voices were unnervingly loud. Everywhere I looked I saw the ugly stains. I saw the images in my mind: the stab wounds, the hilt marks, the savage wound in her neck gaping like a yawning red mouth. I went out into the hall. The dust was irritating my lungs. It was hard to breathe.

I said, "Show me where you found her gun."

When the police had arrived at the scene that night, they'd found Beryl's .380 automatic on the kitchen counter near the microwave oven. The gun was loaded, the safety on. The only partial prints the lab could identify were her own.

"She kept the box of cartridges inside a table by her bed," Marino said. "Probably kept the gun there, too. I figure she carried her bags upstairs, unpacked and dumped most of her clothes in the bathroom hamper, and put her suitcases back in the bedroom closet. At some point during all this, she got out her piece. A sure sign she was antsy as hell. What you wanta bet she checked out every room with it before she started winding down?"

"I know I would have," I commented.

He looked around the kitchen. "So maybe she came in here for a snack."

"She may have thought about a snack, but she didn't eat one," I answered. "Her gastric contents were about fifty milliliters, or less than two ounces, of dark brown fluid. Whatever she ate last was fully digested by the time she died—or better put, by the time she was attacked. Digestion shuts down during acute stress or fear. If she'd just eaten a snack when the killer got to her, the food wouldn't have cleared her stomach."

"Not much to munch on anyway," he said as if this were an important point to make as he opened the refrigerator door.

Inside we found a shriveled lemon, two sticks of butter, a block of moldy Havarti cheese, condiments, and a bottle of tonic water. The freezer was a little more promising, but not much. There were a few packages of chicken breasts, Le Menus, and lean ground beef. Cooking, it appeared, was not a pleasure for Beryl but a utilitarian exercise. I knew what my own kitchen was like. This one was depressingly sterile. Motes of dust were suspended in the pale light seeping through slits of the gray designer blinds in the window over the sink. The drainboard and sink were empty and dry. The appliances were modern and looked unused.

"The other thought is she came in here for a drink," Marino speculated.

"Her STAT alcohol was negative," I said.

"Don't mean she didn't think about it."

He opened a cabinet above the sink. There wasn't an inch to spare on three shelves: Jack Daniel's, Chivas Regal, Tanqueray, liqueurs, and something else that caught my attention. In front of the Cognac on the top shelf was a bottle of Haitian Barbancourt Rhum, aged fifteen years and as expensive as unblended Scotch.

Lifting it out with a gloved hand, I set it on the counter. There was no strip stamp, and the seal around the gold cap was unbroken.

"I don't think she got this around here," I told Marino. "My guess is she got it in Miami, Key West."

"So you're saying she brought it back from Florida?"

"It's possible. Clearly, she was a connoisseur of good booze. Barbancourt's wonderful."

"Guess I should start calling you Doc-tor Connoisseur," he said.

The bottle of Barbancourt wasn't dusty, even though many of the bottles near it were.

"It might explain why she was in the kitchen," I went on. "Perhaps she came downstairs to put away the rum. She may have been contemplating a nightcap when someone arrived at her door."

"Yeah, but what it don't explain is why she left her piece in here on the counter when she answered the door. She was supposed to be spooked, right? Still makes me think she was expecting company, knew the squirrel. Hey, she's got all this fancy booze, right? She drinks the stuff alone? Don't make sense. Makes more sense to think she did a little entertaining from time to time, had some guy in. Hell, maybe it's this 'M' she was writing down there in the Keys. Maybe that's who she was expecting the night she was whacked."

"You're entertaining the possibility 'M' is the killer," I said.

"Wouldn't you be?"

He was getting combative, and his toying with the unlit cigarette was beginning to grate on my nerves.

"I would entertain every possibility," I replied. "For example, I would also entertain the possibility she *wasn't* expecting company. She was in the kitchen putting away her rum and possibly thinking of pouring herself a drink. She was nervous, had her automatic nearby on the counter. She was startled when the doorbell rang or someone started knocking—"

"Right," he cut me off. "She's startled, jumpy. So why does she leave her piece here in the kitchen when she goes to the damn door?"

"Did she practice?"

"Practice?" he said as our eyes met. "Practice *what*?"

"Shooting."

"Hell . . . I donno . . ."

"If she didn't, it wasn't a natural reflex for her to arm herself but a conscious deliberation. Women carry Mace in their pocketbooks. They're assaulted and the Mace never enters their minds until after the fact because defending themselves isn't a reflex."

"I don't know . . ."

I *did* know. I had a Ruger .38 revolver loaded with Silvertips, one of the most destructive cartridges money could buy. The only reason it would occur to me to arm myself with the handgun was I practiced, took it down to the range inside my building several times a month. When I was home alone, I was more comfortable with the handgun than without it.

There was something else. I thought of the living room, of the fireplace tools upright in their brass stand on the hearth. Beryl had struggled with her assailant in that room and it never occurred to her to arm herself with the poker or the shovel. Defending herself was not a reflex. Her only reflex was to run, whether it was up the stairs or to Key West.

I explained, "She may have been a stranger to the gun, Marino. The doorbell rings. She's unnerved, confused. She goes into the living room and looks through the peephole. Whoever it is, she trusts the person enough to open the door. The gun is forgotten."

"Or else she was expecting her visitor," he said again.

"That is entirely possible. Providing somebody knew she was back in town."

"So maybe *he* knew," he said.

"And maybe he's 'M.' " I told him what he wanted to hear as I replaced the bottle of rum on the shelf.

"Bingo. Making more sense now, isn't it?"

I shut the cabinet door. "She was threatened, terrorized for months, Marino. I find it hard to believe it was a close friend and Beryl wasn't the least bit suspicious."

He looked annoyed as he glanced at his watch and dug another key out of a pocket. It made no sense at all that Beryl would have opened the door to a stranger. But it made even less sense that someone she trusted could have done this to her. *Why did she let him in?* The question wouldn't stop nagging at me.

A covered breezeway joined the house to the garage. The sun had dipped below the trees.

"I'll tell you right off," Marino said, the lock clicking open, "I only went in here right before I called you. Could've busted down the door the night of her murder but didn't see no point." He shrugged, lifting those massive shoulders of his as if to make sure I understood he really could tackle a door or a tree or a Dumpster if he were so inclined. "She hadn't been in here since she left for Florida. Took us a while to find the friggin' key."

It was the only paneled garage I had ever seen, the floor a gorgeous dragon skin of expensive red Italian tile.

"Was this *really* designed to be a garage?" I asked.

"It's got a garage door, don't it?" He was pulling several more keys out of a pocket. "Some place to keep your ride out of the rain, huh?"

The garage was airless and smelled dusty, but it was spotless. Other than a rake and a broom leaning against a corner, there was no sign of the usual tools, lawnmowers, and other impedimenta one would expect to find. The garage looked more like a car dealership showroom, the black Honda parked in the center of the tile floor. The car was so clean and shiny it could have passed for new and never driven.

Marino unlocked the driver's door and opened it.

"Here. Be my guest," he said.

Momentarily, I was settled back in the soft ivory leather seat, staring through the windshield at the paneled wall.

Stepping back from the car, he added, "Just sit there, okay? Get the feel of it, look around the interior, tell me what comes to mind."

"You want me to start it?"

He handed me the key.

"Then please open the garage door so we don't asphyxiate ourselves," I added.

Frowning as he glanced around, he found the right button and cracked the door.

The car turned over the first time, the engine dropping several octaves and purring throatily. The radio and air conditioning were on. The gas tank was a quarter full, the odometer registering less than seven thousand miles, the sunroof partially open. On the dash was a dry cleaning slip dated July eleventh, a Thursday, when Beryl took in a skirt and a suit jacket, garments she obviously never picked up. On the passenger's seat was a grocery receipt dated July twelfth at ten-forty in the morning, when she bought one head of lettuce, tomatoes, cucumbers, ground beef, cheese, orange juice, and a roll of mints, the total nine dollars and thirteen cents out of a ten she gave the check-out clerk.

Next to the receipt was a slender white bank envelope that was empty. Beside it a pebbly tan Ray Ban sunglasses case—also empty.

In the backseat was a Wimbledon tennis racket, and a rumpled white towel I reached over the seat to get. Stamped in small blue letters on a terrycloth border was WESTWOOD RACQUET CLUB, the same name printed on a red vinyl tote bag I had noted upstairs in Beryl's closet.

Marino had saved his theatrics for last. I knew he had looked over all of these items and wanted me to see them *in situ*. They weren't evidence. The killer had never gone inside the garage. Marino was baiting me. He had been baiting me since we had first stepped inside the house. It was a habit of his that irritated the hell out of me.

Turning off the engine, I got out of the car, the door shutting with a muffled solid thud.

He looked speculatively at me.

"A couple of questions," I said.

"Shoot."

"Westwood is an exclusive club. Was she a member?"

A nod.

"You checked out when she last reserved a court?"

"Friday, July twelfth, at nine in the morning. She had a lesson with the pro. Took a lesson once a week, that was about the extent of her playing."

"As I recall, she flew out of Richmond early Saturday morning, July thirteenth, arriving in Miami shortly after noon."

Another nod.

"So she took her lesson, then went straight to the grocery store. After that, she may have gone to the bank. Whatever the case, at some point after she did her shopping, she suddenly decided to leave town. If she'd known she was leaving town the next day, she wouldn't have bothered going to the grocery store. She didn't have time to eat everything she bought, and she didn't leave the food in the refrigerator. Apparently she threw away everything except the ground beef, the cheese and possibly the mints."

"Sounds reasonable," he said unemphatically.

"She left her glasses case and other items on the seat," I continued. "Plus, the radio and air conditioning were left on, the sunroof partially open. Looks like she drove into the garage, cut the engine, and hurried into the house with her sunglasses on. Makes me wonder if something happened while she was out in the car driving home from tennis and her errands . . ."

"Oh yeah. I'm pretty damn sure it did. Walk around, take a look at the other side—specifically at the passenger's door."

I did.

What I saw scattered my thoughts like marbles. Gouged into the glossy black paint right below the door handle was the name BERYL enclosed in a heart.

"Kind of gives you the creeps, don't it?" he said.

"If he did this while her car was parked at the club or the grocery store," I reasoned, "it seems someone would have seen him."

"Yo. So maybe he did it earlier." He paused, casually perusing the graffiti. "When's the last time you looked at *your* passenger's door?"

It could have been days. It could have been a week.

"She went grocery shopping." He finally lit the damn cigarette. "Didn't buy much." He took a deep, hungry drag. "And it probably all fit inside one bag, right? When my wife's got just one or two bags, she always sticks them up front, on the floor mat, maybe on the seat. So maybe Beryl went around to the passenger's side to put the groceries in the car. That's when she noticed what was scratched into the paint. Maybe she knew it had to have been done that day. Maybe she didn't. Don't matter. Freaked her right out, pushed her over the edge. She makes tracks home or maybe to the bank for cash. Books the next flight out of Richmond and runs to Florida."

I followed him out of the garage and back to his car. Night was falling fast, a chill in the air. He cranked the engine while I stared mutely out the side window at Beryl's house. Its sharp angles were deteriorating in the shadows, the windows dark. Suddenly the porch and living room lights blinked on.

"Geez," Marino muttered. "Trick or treat."

"A timer," I said.

"No kidding."

2

THERE WAS A FULL MOON over Richmond as I followed the long road home. Only the most tenacious trick-or-treaters were still making the rounds, their ghastly masks and menacing child-size silhouettes lit up by my headlights. I wondered how many times my doorbell had gone unanswered. My house was a favorite because I was excessively generous with candy, not having children of my own to indulge. I would have four unopened bags of chocolate bars to dole out to my staff in the morning.

The phone started ringing as I was climbing the stairs. Just before my answering machine intervened, I snatched up the receiver. The voice was unfamiliar at first, then recognition grasped my heart.

"Kay? It's Mark. Thank God you're home . . ."

Mark James sounded as if he were talking from the bottom of an oil drum, and I could hear cars passing in the background.

"Where are you?" I managed to ask, and I knew I sounded unnerved.

"On Ninety-five, about fifty miles north of Richmond."

I sat down on the edge of the bed.

"At a phone booth," he went on to explain. "I need directions to your house." After another gust of traffic, he added, "I want to see you, Kay. I've been in D.C. all week, been trying to get you since late afternoon, finally took a chance and rented a car. Is it all right?"

I didn't know what to say.

"Thought we could have a drink, catch up," said this man who had once broken my heart. "I've got reservations at the Radisson downtown. Tomorrow morning, early, there's a flight out of Richmond back to Chicago. I just thought . . . Actually, there's something I want to discuss with you."

I couldn't imagine what Mark and I could have to discuss.

"Is it all right?" he asked again.

No, it wasn't all right! What I said was "Of course, Mark. It will be wonderful to see you."

After giving him directions, I went into the bathroom to freshen up, pausing long enough to take inventory. More than fifteen years had come and gone since our days together in law school. My hair was more ash than blond, and it had been long when Mark and I had last seen each other. My eyes were hazier, not as blue as they used to be. The unbiased mirror went on to remind me rather coldly that I would never see thirty-nine again and there was such a thing as face-lifts. In my memory Mark had remained barely twenty-four, when he became an object of passion and dependency that ultimately led to abject despair. After it was over, I did nothing but work.

He still drove fast and liked fine automobiles. Less than forty-five minutes later, I opened the front door and watched him get out of his rental Sterling. He was still the Mark I remembered, the same trim body and long-legged confident walk. Briskly mounting the steps, he smiled a little. After a quick hug, we stood awkwardly in the foyer for a moment and couldn't think of a significant thing to say.

"Still drinking Scotch?" I finally asked.

"That hasn't changed," he said, following me to the kitchen.

Retrieving the Glenfiddich from the bar, I automatically fixed his drink exactly as I had so long ago: two jiggers, ice, and a splash of seltzer water. His eyes followed me as I moved about the kitchen and set our drinks on the table. Taking a sip, he stared into his glass and began slowly swirling ice the way he used to when he was tense. I took a good, long look at him, at his refined features, high cheekbones, and clear gray eyes. His dark hair had begun to turn a little at the temples.

I shifted my attention to the ice slowly spinning inside his glass. "You're with a firm in Chicago, I assume?"

Leaning back in his chair, he looked up and said, "Doing

strictly appeals, trial work only now and then. I run into Diesner occasionally. That's how I found out you're here in Richmond."

Diesner was the chief medical examiner in Chicago. I saw him at meetings and we were on several committees together. He had never mentioned he was acquainted with Mark James, and how he even knew I was once acquainted with Mark was a mystery.

"I made the mistake of telling him I'd known you in law school, think he brings you up from time to time to needle me," Mark explained, reading my thoughts.

That I could believe. Diesner was as gruff as a billy goat, and he was none too fond of defense attorneys. Some of his battles and theatrics in court had become the stuff of legends.

Mark was saying, "Like most forensic pathologists, he's pro prosecution. I represent a convicted murderer and I'm the bad guy. Diesner will make a point of looking for me and as a by-the-way telling me about the latest journal article you published or some gruesome case you worked. Dr. Scarpetta. The famous Chief Scarpetta." He laughed, but his eyes didn't.

"I don't think it's fair to say we're pro prosecution," I answered. "It seems that way because if the evidence is pro defendant, the case never sees a courtroom."

"Kay, I know how it works," he said in that give-it-a-rest tone of voice I remembered so well. "I know what you see. And if I were you, I'd want all the bastards to fry, too."

"Yes. You know what I see, Mark," I started to say. It was the same old argument. I couldn't believe it. He had been here less than fifteen minutes and we were picking up right where we had left off. Some of our worst fights used to be over this very subject. I was already an M.D. and enrolled in law school at Georgetown when Mark and I met. I had seen the darker side, the cruelty, the random tragedies. I had placed my gloved hands on the bloody spoils of suffering and death. Mark was the splendid Ivy Leaguer whose idea of a felony was for someone to nick the paint on his Jaguar. He was going to be a lawyer because his father and grandfather were lawyers. I was Catholic, Mark was Protestant. I was Italian, he was as Anglo as Prince Charles. I was brought up poor, he was brought up in one of the wealthiest residential districts of Boston. I had once thought ours would be a marriage made in heaven.

"You haven't changed, Kay," he said. "Except maybe you radiate a certain resolve, a hardness. I bet you're a force to be reckoned with in court."

"I wouldn't like to think I'm hard."

"I don't mean it as a criticism. I'm saying you look terrific." He glanced around the kitchen. "And successful. You happy?"

"I like Virginia," I answered, looking away from him. "My only complaint is the winters, but I suppose you have a bigger complaint in that department. How do you stand Chicago six months out of the year?"

"Never gotten used to it, you want to know the truth. You'd hate it. A Miami hothouse flower like you wouldn't last a month." He sipped his drink. "You're not married."

"I was."

"Hmmmm." He frowned as he thought. "Tony somebody. . . I recall you started seeing Tony . . . Benedetti, right? The end of our third year."

Actually, I was surprised Mark would have noticed, much less remembered. "We're divorced, have been for a long time," I said.

"I'm sorry," he said softly.

I reached for my drink.

"Seeing anybody nice?" he asked.

"No one at the moment, nice or otherwise."

Mark didn't laugh as much as he used to. He volunteered matter-of-factly, "I almost got married a couple of years ago but it didn't work out. Or maybe I should be honest enough to say that at the last minute I panicked."

It was hard for me to believe he had never been married. He must have read my mind again.

"This was after Janet died." He hesitated. "I *was* married."

"Janet?"

He was swirling the ice in his glass again. "Met her in Pittsburgh, after Georgetown. She was a tax lawyer in the firm."

I was watching him closely, perplexed by what I saw. Mark had changed. The intensity that had once drawn me to him was different. I couldn't put my finger on it, but it was darker.

"A car accident," he was explaining. "A Saturday night. She went out for popcorn. We were going to stay up, watch a late movie. A drunk driver crossed over into her lane. Didn't even have his headlights on."

"God, Mark. I'm sorry," I said. "How awful."

"That was eight years ago."

"No children?" I asked quietly.

He shook his head.

We fell silent.

"My firm's opening an office in D.C.," he said as our eyes met.

I did not respond.

"It's possible I may be relocated, move to D.C. We've been expanding like crazy, got a hundred-some lawyers and offices in New York, Atlanta, Houston."

"When would you be moving?" I asked very calmly.

"It could be by the first of the year, actually."

"You're definitely going to do it?"

"I'm sick to death of Chicago, Kay, need a change. I wanted to let you know—that's why I'm here, at least the major reason. I didn't want to move to D.C. and have us run into each other at some point. I'll be living in northern Virginia. You have an office in northern Virginia. Odds are we would run into each other in a restaurant, at the theater one of these days. I didn't want that."

I imagined sitting inside the Kennedy Center and spotting Mark three rows ahead whispering into the ear of his beautiful young date. I was reminded of the old pain, a pain once so intense it was physical. He'd had no competition. He had been my entire emotional focus. At first a part of me had sensed it wasn't mutual. Later, I was sure of it.

"This was my *major* reason," he repeated, now the lawyer making his opening statement. "But there's something else that really has nothing to do with us personally."

I remained silent.

"A woman was murdered here in Richmond a couple of nights ago. Beryl Madison . . ."

The look of astonishment on my face briefly stopped him.

"Berger, the managing partner, told me about it when he called me at my hotel in D.C. I want to talk to you about it—"

"How does it concern you?" I asked. "Did you *know* her?"

"Remotely. I met her once, in New York last winter. Our office there dabbles in entertainment law. Beryl was having publishing problems, a contract dispute, and she retained Orndorff & Berger to set things straight. I happened to be in New York on the same day she was conferring with Sparacino, the lawyer who took her case. Sparacino ended up inviting me to join the two of them for lunch at the Algonquin."

"If there's any possibility this *dispute* you mentioned could be connected with her murder, you need to be talking to the police, not to me," I said, getting angry.

"Kay," he replied. "My firm doesn't even know I'm talking to you, okay? When Berger called yesterday, it was about something else, all right? He happened to mention Beryl Madison's murder in the course of the conversation, said for me to check the area papers, see what I could find out."

"Right. Translated into see what you could find out from your ex—" I felt a flush creeping up my neck. Ex-*what*?

"It isn't like that." He glanced away. "I was thinking about you, thinking of calling you up before Berger called, before I even knew about Beryl. For two damn nights I actually had my hand on the phone, had already gotten your number from Information. But I couldn't bring myself to do it. And maybe I never would have had Berger not told me what happened. Maybe Beryl gave me the excuse. I'll concede that much. But it's not the way you think . . ."

I didn't listen. It dismayed me that I wanted to believe him so much. "If your firm has an interest in her murder, tell me what it is, exactly."

He thought for a moment. "I'm not sure if we have an interest in her murder legitimately. Maybe it's personal, a sense of horror. A shock for those of us who had any exposure to her while she was alive. I will also tell you that she was in the midst of a rather bitter dispute, was getting royally screwed because of a contract she signed eight years ago. It's very complicated. Has to do with Cary Harper."

"The novelist?" I said, baffled. "*That* Cary Harper?"

"As you probably know," Mark said, "he doesn't live far from here, in some eighteenth-century plantation called Cutler Grove. It's on the James River, in Williamsburg."

I was trying to remember what I had read about Harper, who produced one novel some twenty years ago that won a Pulitzer Prize. A legendary recluse, he lived with a sister. Or was it an aunt? There had been much speculation about Harper's private life. The more he refused interviews and eluded reporters, the more the speculation grew.

I lit a cigarette.

"I was hoping you'd quit," he said.

"It would take the removal of my frontal lobe."

"Here's what little I know. Beryl had some sort of relationship with Harper when she was in her teens, early twenties. For a time, she actually lived in the house with him and his sister. Beryl was the aspiring writer, the talented daughter Harper never had. His protégée. It was through his connections she got her first novel published when she was only twenty-two, some sort of quasiliterary romance she published under the name Stratton. Harper even conceded to giving a comment for the book jacket, some quote about this exciting new writer he'd discovered. It raised a lot of eyebrows. Her novel was more a commercial book than literature, and no one had heard a word from Harper in years."

"What does this have to do with her contract dispute?"

Mark answered wryly, "Harper may be a sucker for a hero-worshiping young lady, but he's a cagey bastard. Before he got her published, he forced her to sign a contract prohibiting her from ever writing a word about him or anything relating to him as long as he and his sister are alive. Harper's only in his mid-fifties, his sister a few years older. Basically, the contract trussed Beryl for life, preventing her from writing her memoirs because how could she do that and leave out Harper?"

"Maybe she could," I replied, "but minus Harper, the book wouldn't sell."

"Exactly."

"Why did she resort to pen names? Was this part of her agreement with Harper?"

"I think so. My guess is he wanted Beryl to remain his secret. He granted her literary success but wanted her locked away from the world. The name Beryl Madison's not exactly well known, even though her novels have been financially successful."

"Am I to assume she was on the verge of violating this contract, and that's why she sought out Orndorff & Berger?"

He sipped his drink. "Let me remind you that she wasn't my client. So I don't know all of the details. But my impression is that she was burned out, wanted to write something of significance. And this is the part that you probably already know about. Apparently she was having problems, somebody was threatening her, harassing her . . ."

"When?"

"Last winter, about the time I met her at lunch. I guess it was late February."

"Go on," I said, intrigued.

"She had no idea who was threatening her. Whether this began before she decided to write what she was currently working on or afterward, I can't say with certainty."

"How was she going to get away with violating her contract?"

"I'm not sure she would have, not entirely," Mark replied. "But the direction Sparacino was going was to inform Harper he had a choice. He could cooperate, and the finished product would be fairly harmless—in other words, Harper would have limited powers of censorship. Or else he could be a son of a bitch and Sparacino would give the newspapers, 'Sixty Minutes,' a crack at it. Harper was in a bind. Sure, he could sue Beryl, but she didn't have that much cash, a drop in the bucket compared to what he's worth. A suit would only make everybody run out to buy Beryl's book. Harper really couldn't win."

"Couldn't he have gotten an injunction to stop the publication?" I asked.

"More publicity. And to halt the presses would have run him into the millions."

"Now she's dead." I watched my cigarette smoldering in the ashtray. "The book isn't finished, I presume. Harper doesn't have any worries. Is this what you're getting at, Mark? That Harper may be involved in her murder?"

"I'm just giving you the background," he said.

Those clear eyes were looking into mine. Sometimes they could be so incredibly unreachable, I remembered uncomfortably.

"What do you think?" he was asking.

I did not say what I really thought, which was that it struck me as very strange that Mark was telling me all this. It did not matter that Beryl was not his client. He was familiar with the canons of legal ethics, which make it quite clear that the knowledge of one member of a firm is imputed to all its members. He was just a shade away from impropriety, and this was as out of character for the scrupulous Mark James I remembered as if he had shown up at my house sporting a tattoo.

"I think you'd better have a talk with Marino, the head of the investigation," I replied. "Or else I'd better tell him what you just told me. In either event, he'll be looking up your firm, asking questions."

"Fine. I don't have a problem with that."

We fell silent for a moment.

"What was she like?" I asked, clearing my throat.

"As I said, I met her only once. But she was memorable. Dynamic, witty, attractive, dressed in white. A fabulous winter-white suit. I'd also describe her as rather distant. She kept a lot of secrets. There was a depth to her no one was ever going to reach. And she drank a lot, at least she did that day at lunch—had three cocktails, which struck me as rather excessive considering it was the middle of the day. It may not have been in character, though. She was nervous, upset, tense. Her reason for coming to Orndorff & Berger wasn't a happy one. I'm sure all this business about Harper had to be upsetting her."

"What did she drink?"

"Pardon?"

"The three cocktails. What were they?" I asked.

He frowned, staring off across the kitchen. "Hell, I don't know, Kay. What difference does it make?"

"I'm not sure it makes a difference," I said, recalling her liquor cabinet. "Did she talk about the threats she'd been getting? In your presence, I mean?"

"Yes. And Sparacino's mentioned them. All I know is she started receiving phone calls that were very specific in nature. Always the same voice, wasn't somebody she knew, or at least this is what she said. There were other strange events. I can't remember the details—it was a long time ago."

"Was she keeping a record of these events?" I asked.

"I don't know."

"And she had no idea who was doing this or why?"

"That's the impression she gave." He scooted back his chair. It was getting close to midnight.

As I led him to the front door, something suddenly occurred to me. "Sparacino," I said. "What's his first name?"

"Robert," he replied.

"He doesn't go by the initial M, does he?"

"No," he said, looking curiously at me.

There was a tense pause.

"Drive carefully."

"Good night, Kay," he said, hesitating.

Maybe it was my imagination, but for an instant I thought he was going to kiss me. Then he walked briskly down the steps, and I was back inside my house when I heard him drive off.

The following morning was typically frantic. Fielding informed us in staff meeting that we had five autopsies, including a "floater," or decomposed body from the river, a prospect that never failed to make everybody groan. Richmond had sent in its two latest shootings, one of which I managed to post before dashing off to the John Marshall Court House to testify in another homicidal shooting, and afterwards to the Medical College to have lunch with one of my student advisees. All the while, I was working hard at pushing Mark's visit completely from my mind. The more I tried not to think about him, the more I thought about him. He was cautious. He was stubborn. It was out of character for him to contact me after more than a decade of silence.

It wasn't until early afternoon that I gave in and called Marino.

"Was just about to ring you up," he launched in before I had barely said two words. "On my way out. Can you meet at Benton's office in an hour, hour and a half?"

"What's this about?" I hadn't even told him why I was calling.

"Got my hands on Beryl's reports. Thought you'd wanna be there."

He hung up as he always did, without saying good-bye.

At the appointed time, I drove along East Grace Street and parked in the first metered space I could find within a reasonable walk of my destination. The modern ten-story office building was a lighthouse watching over a depressing shore of junk shops parading as antique stores and small ethnic restaurants whose "specials" weren't. Street people drifted along cracked sidewalks.

Identifying myself at the guard station inside the lobby, I took the elevator to the fifth floor. At the end of the hall was an un-marked wooden door. The location of Richmond's FBI field office was one of the city's best-kept secrets, its presence as unannounced and unobtrusive as its plainclothes agents. A young man sitting be-hind a counter that stretched halfway across the back wall glanced at me as he talked on the phone. Placing his hand over the mouth-piece, he raised his eyebrows in a "May I help you?" expression. I explained my reason for being here, and he invited me to take a seat.

The lobby was small and decidedly male, with furniture upholstered in sturdy dark-blue leather, the coffee table stacked with various sports magazines. On paneled walls were a rogue's gal-lery of past directors of the FBI, service awards, and a brass plaque engraved with the names of agents who had died in action. The outer door opened occasionally, and tall, fit men in somber suits and sunglasses passed through without a glance in my direction.

Benton Wesley could be as Prussian as the rest of them, but over the years he had won my respect. Beneath his Bureau boiler-plate was a human being worth knowing. He was brisk and ener-getic, even when he was sitting, and he was typically dapper in his dark suit trousers and starched white shirt. His necktie was fash-ionably narrow and perfectly knotted, the black holster on his belt lonely for its ten-millimeter, which he almost never wore indoors. I hadn't seen Wesley in a while and he hadn't changed. He was fit and handsome in a hard way, with premature silver-gray hair that never failed to surprise me.

"Sorry to keep you waiting, Kay," he said, smiling.

His handshake was reassuringly firm and absent of any hint of macho. The grip of some cops and lawyers I know are a thirty-pound squeeze on a three-pound trigger that damn near breaks my fingers.

"Marino's here," Wesley added. "I needed to go over a few more things with him before we brought you in."

He held the door and I followed him down an empty hallway. Steering me inside his small office, he left to get coffee.

"The computer finally came up last night," Marino said. He was leaning back comfortably in his chair and examining a .357 revolver that looked brand new.

"Computer? What computer?" Had I forgotten my cigarettes? No. On the bottom of my purse again.

"At HQ. Goes down all the friggin' time. Anyway, I finally got hard copies of those offense reports. Interesting. Least I think so."

"Beryl's?" I asked.

"You got it." He set the handgun on Wesley's desk, adding, "Nice piece. The lucky bastard won it as a door prize at the police chiefs' convention in Tampa last week. Me, I can't even win two bucks in the lottery."

My attention drifted. Wesley's desk was cluttered with telephone messages, reports, videotapes, and thick manila envelopes containing details and photographs, I assumed, of various crimes police jurisdictions had brought to his attention. Behind panes of glass in the bookcase against one wall were macabre weapons—a sword, brass knuckles, a zip gun, an African spear—trophies from the hunt, gifts from grateful protégés. An outdated photograph showed William Webster shaking hands with Wesley before a backdrop of a Marine Corps helicopter at Quantico. There wasn't the faintest hint Wesley had a wife and three kids. FBI agents, like most cops, jealously guard their personal lives from the world, especially if they have gotten close enough to evil to feel its horror. Wesley was a suspect profiler. He knew what it was to review photographs of unthinkable slaughter and then visit penitentiaries and stare the Charles Mansons, the Ted Bundys, straight in the eye.

Wesley was back with two Styrofoam cups of coffee, one for Marino, one for me. Wesley always remembered I drink my coffee black and need an ashtray within easy reach.

Marino collected a thin stack of photocopied police reports from his lap and began to go through them.

"For starters," he said, "there's only three of 'em. Three reports we got a record of. The first one's dated March eleventh, nine-thirty on a Monday morning. Beryl Madison dialed 911 the night before and requested that an officer come to her house to take a complaint. The call, unsurprisingly, was given a low priority because the street was hopping. A uniform man didn't swing by until the next morning, uh, Jim Reed, been with the department about five years." He glanced up at me.

I shook my head. I didn't know Reed.

Marino began skimming the report. "Reed reported the complainant, Beryl Madison, was very agitated and stating she'd received a phone call of a threatening nature at eight-fifteen the night before—Sunday night. During this phone call, a voice she identified as male, and possibly white, said the following: 'Bet you've been missing me, Beryl. But I'm always watching over you even though you can't see me. I see you. You can run but you can't hide.' The complainant went on to report that this caller stated he'd observed Miss Madison buying a newspaper in front of a Seven-Eleven earlier that morning. The subject described what she'd been wearing, 'a red warm-up suit and no bra.' She confirmed she did drive to the Seven-Eleven on Rosemount Avenue at approximately ten o'clock Sunday morning, and that she was dressed in the described fashion. She parked in front of the Seven-Eleven and bought a *Washington Post* from a vending machine and didn't go inside the store or notice anybody in the area. She was upset the caller knew these details and stated he must be following her. When asked if she was aware of anybody following her at any time, she stated she was not."

Marino turned to the second page, the confidential section of the report, and resumed: "Reed reports here Miss Madison was reluctant to divulge specific details pertaining to the actual threat communicated by the caller. When questioned at length, she finally stated the caller became 'obscene' and said when he imagined what she looked like with her clothes off it made him want to 'kill' her. At this point, Miss Madison hung up the phone, she said."

Marino placed the photocopy on the edge of Wesley's desk.

"What advice did Officer Reed give her?" I asked.

"The usual," Marino said. "Advised her to start keeping a log. When she got a call, to write down the date, time and what occurred. He also advised her to keep her doors locked, her windows shut and locked, maybe to think about getting an alarm system installed. And if she noted any strange vehicles, to write down the plate numbers, call the police."

I remembered what Mark had told me about his lunch with Beryl last February. "Did she say that this threat, the one she reported on March eleventh, was the first one she'd gotten?"

It was Wesley who replied as he reached for the report, "Apparently not." He flipped a page. "Reed mentions she claimed to have been receiving harassing calls since the first of the year, but didn't notify the police until this occasion. It seems the previous calls were infrequent and not as specific as the one she received Sunday night, the night of March tenth."

"She was certain the previous calls were made by the same man?" I asked Marino.

"She told Reed the voice sounded the same," he replied. "A white male she described as soft-spoken and articulate. It wasn't the voice of anyone she knew—or at least this was what she claimed."

Marino resumed, the second report in hand: "Beryl called Officer Reed's pager number on a Tuesday evening at seven-eighteen. She said she needed to see him, and he arrived at her house less than an hour later, at shortly after eight. Again, according to his report, she was very upset, stating she'd got another threatening call right before she'd dialed Reed's pager number. It was the same voice, the same subject who'd called in the past, she said. In this instance his message was similar to the March tenth call."

Marino began reading the report word for word. " 'I know you've been missing me, Beryl. I'll be coming for you soon. I know where you live, know everything about you. You can run but you can't hide.' He went on to state he knew she drove a new car, a black Honda, and he'd broken off the antenna the night before while it was parked in her driveway. The complainant confirmed that her car had been parked in her driveway the night before, and when she went out this same Tuesday morning she did notice the antenna was broken. It was still attached to the car, but bent back at an extreme angle and too damaged to be operative. This officer did go out to look at the vehicle and found the antenna to be in the condition the complainant described."

"What action did Officer Reed take?" I asked.

Marino flipped to the second page and said, "Advised her to begin parking her car inside the garage. She stated she never used the garage, was planning to turn it into an office. He then suggested she ask her neighbors to begin watching out for strange vehicles in the area or anybody on her property at any time. He notes in this report she inquired as to whether she should get a handgun."

"That's all?" I asked. "What about the log Reed told her to keep. Any mention of that?"

"No. He also made the following note in the confidential part of the report: 'Complainant's response to the damaged antenna seemed excessive. She became extremely upset and at one point was abusive to this officer.' " Marino looked up. "Translated, Reed's implying he didn't believe her. Maybe she broke the antenna herself, was making up the shit about the threatening calls."

"Oh, Lord," I muttered in disgust.

"Hey. You got any idea how many frootloops call in this kind of crap on a regular basis? Ladies call all the time, got cuts on 'em, scratches, screaming rape. Some of 'em make it up. They got some screw loose that makes 'em need the attention. . . ."

I knew all about fictitious illnesses and injuries, about Munchausens and maladjustments and manias that will cause people to wish and even induce terrible sickness and violence upon themselves. I didn't need a lecture from Marino.

"Go on," I said. "What happened next?"

He placed the second report on Wesley's desk and began reading the third one. "Beryl called Reed again, this time on July sixth, a Saturday morning at eleven-fifteen. He responded to her house that afternoon at four o'clock and found the complainant hostile and upset . . ."

"I guess so," I said shortly. "She'd been waiting five damn hours for him."

"On this occasion"—Marino ignored me and read word for word—"Miss Madison stated the same subject called her at eleven A.M. and communicated the following message: 'Still missing me? Soon, Beryl, soon. I came by last night for you. You weren't home. Do you bleach your hair? I hope not.' At this point, Miss Madison, who is blond, said she tried to talk to him. She pleaded with him to leave her alone, asked him who he was and why he was doing this to her. She said he didn't respond and hung up. She did confirm she was out the night before when the caller claimed to have come by. When this officer asked her where she was, she became evasive and would state only that she was out of town."

"And what did Officer Reed do this time to help the lady in distress?" I asked.

Marino looked blandly at me. "He advised her to get a dog, and she stated she was allergic to dogs."

Wesley opened a file folder. "Kay, you're looking at this in retrospect, in light of a terrible crime already committed. But Reed was coming at it from the other end. Look at it through his eyes. Here's this young woman who lives alone. She's getting hysterical. Reed does the best he can for her—even gives her his pager number. He responds quickly, at least at first. But she's evasive when asked pointed questions. She's got no evidence. Any officer would have been skeptical."

"If it had been me," Marino concurred, "I know what I would have thought. I would have been suspicious the lady was lonely, wanted the attention, wanted to feel like someone gave a rat's ass about her. Or maybe she'd been burned by some guy and was setting the stage to pay him back."

"Right," I said before I could stop myself. "And if it had been her husband or boyfriend threatening to kill her, you'd think the same thing. And Beryl would still turn up dead."

"Maybe," Marino said testily. "But if it was her husband—saying she had one—at least I would have a damn suspect and could get a damn warrant and the judge could slap the drone with a restraining order."

"Restraining orders aren't worth the paper they're written on," I retorted, my anger nudging me closer to the limits of self-control. Not a year went by that I didn't autopsy half a dozen brutalized women whose husbands or boyfriends had been slapped with restraining orders.

After a long silence, I asked Wesley, "Didn't Reed at any point suggest placing a trap on her line?"

"Wouldn't have done any good," he answered. "Pin taps or traps aren't easy to get. The phone company needs a long list of calls, hard evidence the harassment is occurring."

"She didn't have hard evidence?"

Wesley slowly shook his head. "It would take more calls than she was getting, Kay. A lot of them. A pattern of when they were occurring. A solid record of them. Without all that, you can forget a trap."

"By all appearances," Marino added, "Beryl was getting only one or two calls a month. And she wasn't keeping the damn log Reed told her to keep. Or if she was, we haven't found it. Apparently she didn't tape any of the calls either."

"Good God," I muttered. "Someone threatens your life and it takes a damn act of Congress to get anyone to take it seriously."

Wesley didn't reply.

Marino snorted. "It's like in your place, Doc. No such thing as preventive medicine. We're nothing but a damn cleanup crew. Can't do a damn thing until after the fact, when there's hard evidence. Like a dead body."

"Beryl's behavior ought to have been evidence enough," I answered. "Look over these reports. Everything Officer Reed suggested, she did. He told her to get an alarm system and she did. He told her to start parking her car in the garage and she did, even though she was planning to turn the garage into an office. She asked him about a handgun, then went out and bought one. And whenever she called Reed it was *directly after* the killer had called and threatened her. In other words, she didn't wait and call the police hours, days later."

Wesley began spreading out the photocopies of Beryl's letters from Key West, the scene sketches and report, and a series of Polaroid photographs of her yard, the inside of her house, and finally of her body in the bedroom upstairs. He perused the items in silence, his face hard. He was sending the clear signal it was time to move on, we had argued and complained enough. What the police did or didn't do wasn't important. Finding the killer was.

"What's bothering me," Wesley began, "is there's an inconsistency in the MO. The history of threats she was receiving are in keeping with a psychopathic mentality. Someone who stalked and threatened Beryl for months, someone who seemed to know her only from a distance. Unquestionably, he derived most of his pleasure from fantasy, the antecedent phase. He drew it out. He may have finally struck when he did because she'd frustrated him by leaving town. Maybe he feared she was going to move altogether, and he murdered her the moment she got back."

"She finally pissed him off big time," Marino interjected.

Wesley continued looking at the photographs. "I'm seeing a lot of rage, and this is where the inconsistency comes in. His rage seems personally directed at her. The mutilation of her face, specifically." He tapped a photograph with an index finger. "The face is the person. In the typical homicide committed by a sexual sadist, the victim's face isn't touched. She's depersonalized, a symbol. In a sense, she has no face to the killer because she's a nobody to him. Areas of the body he mutilates, if he's into mutilation, are the breasts, the genitalia . . ." He paused, his eyes perplexed. "There are personal elements in Beryl's murder. The cutting of her face, the overkill, fit with the killer's being someone she knew, perhaps even well. Someone who had a private, intense obsession with her. But watching her from a distance, stalking her, don't fit with that at all. These are acts more in keeping with a stranger killer."

Marino was toying with Wesley's .357 door prize again. Idly spinning the cylinder, he said, "Want my opinion? I think the squirrel's got a God complex. You know, as long as you play by his rules he don't whack you. Beryl broke the rules by leaving town and sticking a FOR SALE sign in her yard. No fun anymore. You break the rules, you get punished."

"How are you profiling him?" I asked Wesley.

"White, mid-twenties to mid-thirties. Bright, from a broken home in which he was deprived of a father figure. He may also have been abused as a child, physically, psychologically, or both. He's a loner. This doesn't mean he lives alone, however. He could be married because he's skilled at maintaining a public persona. He leads a double life. There is the one man the world sees, then this darker side. He's obsessive-compulsive, and he's a voyeur."

"Yo," Marino muttered sardonically. "Sounds like half the drones I work with."

Wesley shrugged. "Maybe I'm shooting blanks, Pete. I haven't sorted through it yet. He could be some loser still living at home with his mother, could have priors, been in and out of institutions, prisons. Hell, he could work downtown in a big securities firm and have no criminal or psychiatric history at all. It seems he usually called Beryl at night. The one call we know about that he made during the day was on a Saturday. She worked out of her home, was there most of the time. He called when it was convenient for him versus when he was likely to find her in. I'm leaning toward thinking he has a regular nine to five job and is off on the weekends."

"Unless he was calling her while he was at work," Marino said.

"There's always that possibility," Wesley conceded.

"What about his age?" I asked. "You don't think it's possible he might be older than you just proposed?"

"It would be unusual," Wesley said. "But anything's possible."

Sipping my coffee, which was cool by now, I got around to telling them what Mark had told me about Beryl's contract conflicts and her enigmatic relationship with Cary Harper. When I was finished, Wesley and Marino were staring curiously at me. For one thing, this Chicago lawyer's impromptu visit late at night did sound a little odd. For another, I had thrown them a curve. The thought probably had not occurred to Marino or Wesley and, before last night, certainly not to me, that there actually might be a motive in Beryl's slaying. The most common motive in sexual homicides is no motive at all. The perpetrators do it because they enjoy it and because the opportunity is there.

"A buddy of mine's a cop in Williamsburg," Marino commented. "Tells me Harper's a real squirrel, a hermit. Drives around in an old Rolls-Royce and never talks to nobody. Lives in this big mansion on the river, never has nobody in, nothing. And the guy's *old*, Doc."

"Not so old," I disagreed. "In his mid-fifties. But yes, he's reclusive. I think he lives with his sister."

"It's a long shot," Wesley said, and he looked very tense. "But see how far you can run with it, Pete. If nothing else, maybe Harper would have a few guesses about this 'M' Beryl was writing. Obviously, it was someone she knew well, a friend, a lover. Someone out there has got to know who it is. We find that out, we're getting somewhere."

Marino didn't like it. "I know what I've heard," he said. "Harper ain't going to talk with me and I don't got probable cause to force him into it. I also don't think he's the guy who whacked Beryl even if he did have motive, maybe. Seems to me he would have done it and been done with it. Why draw it out for nine, ten months? And she'd recognize his voice if it was him calling."

"Harper could have hired somebody," Wesley said.

"Right. And we would have found her a week later with a nice clean gunshot wound in the back of her head," Marino answered. "Most hit men don't stalk their victims, call 'em up, use a blade, rape 'em."

"Most of them don't," Wesley agreed. "But we can't be sure rape occurred, either. There was no seminal fluid." He glanced at me, and I nodded a confirmation. "The guy may be dysfunctional. Then again, the crime could be staged, her body positioned to looked like a sexual assault when it really wasn't. It all depends on who was hired, if this is the case, and what the plan was. For example, if Beryl turned up shot while she was in the middle of a dispute with Harper, the cops put him first on the list. But if her murder looks like the work of a sexual sadist, a psychopath, Harper doesn't enter anybody's mind."

Marino was staring off at the bookcase, his meaty face flushed. Slowly turning uneasy eyes on me, he said, "What else you know about this book she was writing?"

"Only what I've said, that it was autobiographical and possibly threatening to Harper's reputation," I replied.

"That's what she was working on down there in Key West?"

"I would assume so. I can't be certain," I said.

He hesitated. "Well, I hate to tell you, but we didn't find nothing like that inside her house."

Even Wesley looked surprised. "The manuscript in her bedroom?"

"Oh, yeah." Marino reached for his cigarettes. "I've glanced at it. Another novel with all this Civil War/romance shit in it. Sure don't sound like this other thing the doc's describing."

"Does it have a title or a date on it?" I asked.

"Nope. Don't even look like it's all there, for that matter. About this thick." Marino measured off about an inch with his fingers. "Got a lot of notes written in the margins, about ten more pages written in longhand."

"We'd better take a second look through all of her papers, her computer disks, make sure this autobiographical manuscript isn't there," Wesley said. "We also need to find out who her literary agent or editor is. Maybe she mailed the manuscript to someone before she left Key West. What we'd better make sure of is that she didn't return to Richmond with the thing. If she did and now it's gone, that's significant, to say the least."

Glancing at his watch, Wesley pushed back his chair as he announced apologetically, "I've got another appointment in five minutes." He escorted us out to the lobby.

I couldn't get rid of Marino. He insisted on walking me to my car.

"You got to keep your eyes open." He was at it again, giving me one of the "street smart" lectures he had given me numerous times in the past. "A lot of women, they never think about that. I see 'em all the time walking along and not having the foggiest idea who's looking at 'em, maybe following 'em. And when you get to your car, have your damn keys out and look *under* it, okay? Be surprised how many women don't think about that either. If you're driving along and realize someone's following you, what do you do?"

I ignored him.

"You head to the nearest fire station, okay? Why? Because there's always somebody there. Even at two in the morning on Christmas. That's the first place you head."

Waiting for a break in traffic, I began digging for my keys. Glancing across the street, I noticed an ominous white rectangle under the wiper blade of my state car. Hadn't I put in enough change? Damn.

"They're all over the place," Marino went on. "Just start looking for 'em on your way home or when you're running around doing your shopping."

I shot him one of my looks, then hurried across the street.

"Hey," he said when we got to my car, "don't get hot at me, all right? Maybe you should feel lucky I hover over you like a guardian angel."

The meter had run out fifteen minutes ago. Snatching the ticket off the windshield, I folded it and stuffed it in his shirt pocket.

"When you *hover* back to headquarters," I said, "take care of this, please."

He was scowling at me as I drove off.

3

TEN BLOCKS AWAY I pulled into another metered space and dropped in my last two quarters. I kept a red MEDICAL EXAMINER plate in plain view on the dash of my state car. Traffic cops never seemed to look. Several months ago, one of them had the nerve to write me up while I was downtown working a homicide scene the police had called me to in the middle of the day.

Hurrying up cement steps, I pushed through a glass door and went inside the main branch of the public library, where people moved about noiselessly and wooden tables were stacked with books. The hushed ambiance inspired the same reverence in me as it had when I was a child. Locating a row of microfiche machines halfway across the room, I began pulling up an index of books written under Beryl Madison's various pen names and jotting down the titles. The most recent work, a historical novel set during the Civil War and published under the pen name Edith Montague, had come out a year and a half ago. Probably irrelevant, and Mark was right, I thought. Over the past ten years, Beryl had published six novels. I had never heard of a single one of them.

Next I began a search of periodicals. Nothing. Beryl wrote books. Apparently she had not published anything, nor had there been any interviews of her, in magazines. Newspaper clips should be more promising. There were a few book reviews published in the Richmond *Times* over the past few years. But they were useless because they referred to the author by pen name. Beryl's killer knew her by her real name.

Screen after screen of hazy white type went by. "Maberly," "Macon," and finally "Madison." There was one very short piece about Beryl published in the *Times* last November:

AUTHOR TO LECTURE

Novelist Beryl Stratton Madison will lecture to the Daughters of the American Revolution this Wednesday at the Jefferson Hotel at Main and Adams streets. Ms. Madison, protégée of Pulitzer Prize-winner Cary Harper, is most known for historical fiction set during the American Revolution and the Civil War. She will speak on "The Viability of Legend as a Vehicle for Fact."

Jotting down the pertinent information, I lingered long enough to locate several of Beryl's books and check them out. Back at the office, I busied myself with paperwork, my attention continually tugged toward the phone. *It's none of your business.* I was well aware of the boundary separating my jurisdiction from that of the police.

The elevator across the hall opened and custodians began talking in loud voices as they went to the janitorial closet several doors down. They always arrived at around six-thirty. Mrs. J. R. McTigue, listed in the paper as being in charge of reservations, wasn't going to answer anyway. The number I had copied was probably the DAR's business office, which would have closed at five.

The phone was picked up on the second ring.

After a pause, I asked, "Is this Mrs. J. R. McTigue?"

"Why, yes. I'm Mrs. McTigue."

It was too late. There was no point in being anything other than direct. "Mrs. McTigue, this is Dr. Scarpetta . . ."

"Dr. *who*?"

"Scarpetta," I repeated. "I'm the medical examiner investigating the death of Beryl Madison . . ."

"Oh, my! Yes, I read about that. Oh, my, oh, my. She was such a lovely young woman. I just couldn't believe it when I heard—"

"I understand she spoke at the November DAR meeting," I said.

"We were so thrilled when she agreed to come. You know, she didn't do much of that sort of thing."

Mrs. McTigue sounded quite elderly, and already I had the

sinking feeling this had been the wrong move. Then she surprised me.

"You see, Beryl did it as a favor. That's the only reason it happened. My late husband was a friend of Cary Harper, the writer. I'm sure you've heard of him. Joe set it up, really. He knew it would mean so much to me. I've always loved Beryl's books."

"Where do you live, Mrs. McTigue?"

"The Gardens."

Chamberlayne Gardens was a retirement home not far from downtown. It was just one more grim landmark in my professional life. Over the past few years, I'd had several cases from the Gardens and virtually every other retirement community or nursing home in the city.

"I'm wondering if I could stop by for a few minutes on my way home," I said. "Would that be possible?"

"I think so. Why, yes. I suppose that would be fine. You're Dr. *who*?"

I repeated my name slowly.

"I'm in apartment three-seventy-eight. When you come into the lobby, take the elevator up to the third floor."

I already knew a lot about Mrs. McTigue because of where she lived. Chamberlayne Gardens catered to the elderly who did not have to rely on Social Security to survive. Deposits for its apartments were substantial, the monthly fee steeper than most people's mortgages. But the Gardens, like others of its kind, was a gilded cage. No matter how lovely it was, no one really wanted to be there.

On the western fringes of downtown, it was a modern brick high rise that looked like a depressing blend of a hotel and a hospital. Parking in a visitor slot, I headed toward a lighted portico that promised to be the main entrance. The lobby gleamed with Williamsburg reproductions, many of the pieces bearing arrangements of silk flowers in heavy cut-crystal vases. On top of the wall-to-wall red carpet were machine-made Oriental rugs, and overhead was a brass chandelier. An old man was perched on a couch, cane in hand, eyes vacant beneath the brim of a tweedy English cap. A decrepit woman was trekking across the rug with a walker.

A young man looked bored behind a potted plant on the front

desk and paid me no mind as I headed to the elevator. The doors
eventually opened and took forever to close, as is common in places
where people need plenty of time to ambulate. Riding up three
floors alone, I stared abstractedly at the bulletins taped to the paneled interior, reminders of field trips to area museums and plan-
tations, of bridge clubs, arts and crafts, and a deadline for knitted
items needed by the Jewish Community Center. Many of the an-
nouncements were outdated. Retirement homes, with their cemetery names like Sunnyland or Sheltering Pines or Chamberlayne
Gardens, always made me feel slightly queasy. I didn't know what
I would do when my mother could no longer live alone. Last time
I called her she was talking about getting a hip replacement.

Mrs. McTigue's apartment was halfway down on the left,
and my knock was promptly answered by a wizened woman with
scanty hair tightly curled and yellowed like old paper. Her face was
dabbed with rouge, and she was bundled in an oversize white car-
digan sweater. I smelled floral-scented toilet water and the aroma
of baking cheese.

"I'm Kay Scarpetta," I said.

"Oh, it's so nice of you to come," she said, lightly patting my
offered hand. "Will you have tea or something a little stronger?
Whatever you like, I have it. I'm drinking port."

All this as she led me into the small living room and showed
me to a wing chair. Switching off the television, she turned on
another lamp. The living room was as overwhelming as the set of
the opera *Aïda*. On every available space of the faded Persian
rug were heavy pieces of mahogany furniture: chairs, drum tables,
a curio table, crowded bookcases, corner cupboards jammed with
bone china and stemware. Closely spaced on the walls were dark
paintings, bell pulls, and several brass rubbings.

She returned with a small silver tray bearing a Waterford de-
canter of port, two matching pieces of stemware, and a small plate
arranged with homemade cheese biscuits. Filling our glasses, she
offered me the plate and lacy linen napkins that looked old and
freshly ironed. It was a ritual that took quite a long time. Then
she seated herself on a worn end of a sofa where I suspected she
sat most hours of the day while she was reading or watching television. She was pleased to have company even if the reason for it
was somewhat less than sociable. I wondered who, if anyone, ever
came to see her.

"As I mentioned earlier, I'm the medical examiner working Beryl Madison's case," I said. "At this point there is very little those of us investigating her death know about her or the people who might have known her."

Mrs. McTigue sipped her port, her face blank. I was so accustomed to going straight to the point with the police and attorneys I sometimes forgot the rest of the world needs lubrication. The biscuit was buttery and really very good. I told her so.

"Why, thank you." She smiled. "Please help yourself. There's plenty more."

"Mrs. McTigue," I tried again, "were you acquainted with Beryl Madison before you invited her to speak to your group last fall?"

"Oh, yes," she replied. "At least I was indirectly, because I've been quite a fan of hers for years. Her books, you see. Historical novels are my favorite."

"How did you know she wrote them?" I asked. "Her books were written under pen names. There is no mention of her real name on the jacket or in an author's note." I had glanced through several of Beryl's books on my way out of the library.

"Very true. I suppose I'm one of the few people who knew her identity—because of Joe."

"Your husband?"

"He and Mr. Harper were friends," she answered. "Well, as much as anyone is really Mr. Harper's friend. They were connected through Joe's business. That's how it started."

"What was your husband's business?" I asked, deciding that my hostess was much less confused than I had previously assumed.

"Construction. When Mr. Harper bought Cutler Grove, the house was badly in need of restoration. Joe spent the better part of two years out there overseeing the work."

I should have made the connection right away. McTigue Contractors and McTigue Lumber Company were the biggest construction companies in Richmond, with offices throughout the commonwealth.

"This was well over fifteen years ago," Mrs. McTigue went on. "And it was during the time Joe was working at the Grove that he first met Beryl. She came to the site several times with Mr. Harper, and soon moved into the house. She was very young." She paused. "I remember Joe telling me back then that Mr. Harper had adopted a beautiful young girl who was a very talented writer. I think she was an orphan. Something sad like that. This was all kept very quiet, of course." She carefully set down her glass and slowly made her way across the room to the secretary. Sliding open a drawer, she pulled out a legal-size creamy envelope.

"Here," she said. Her hands trembled as she presented it to me. "It's the only picture of them I have."

Inside the envelope was a blank sheet of heavy rag stationery, an old, slightly overexposed black-and-white photograph protected within its folds. On either side of a delicately pretty blond teen-age girl were two men, imposing and tan and dressed for outdoors. The three figures stood close to each other, squinting in the glare of a brilliant sun.

"That's Joe," Mrs. McTigue said, pointing to the man standing to the left of a girl I was certain was the young Beryl Madison. The sleeves of his khaki shirt were rolled up to the elbows of his muscular arms, his eyes shielded by the brim of an International Harvester cap. To Beryl's right was a big white-haired man who Mrs. McTigue went on to explain was Cary Harper.

"It was taken by the river," she said. "Back then when Joe was working on the house. Mr. Harper had white hair even then. I 'spect you've heard the stories. Supposedly his hair turned white while he was writing *The Jagged Corner*, when he was barely in his thirties."

"This was taken at Cutler Grove?"

"Yes, at Cutler Grove," she answered.

I was haunted by Beryl's face. It was a face too wise and knowing for one so young, a wistful face of longing and sadness that I associate with children who have been mistreated and abandoned.

"Beryl was just a child then," Mrs. McTigue said.

"I suppose she would have been sixteen, maybe seventeen?"

"Well, yes. That sounds about right," she replied, watching me fold the sheet of paper around the photograph and tuck both back inside the envelope. "I didn't find this until after Joe passed on. I 'spect one of the members of his crew must have taken it."

She returned the envelope to its drawer, and when she had reseated herself, she added, "I think one of the reasons Joe got on so well with Mr. Harper is Joe was a one-way street when it came to other people's business. There was quite a lot I'm sure he never even told me." Smiling wanly, she stared off at the wall.

"Apparently, Mr. Harper told your husband about Beryl's books when they began to get published," I commented.

She shifted her attention back to me and looked surprised. "You know, I'm not sure Joe ever told me how he knew that, Dr. Scarpetta—such a lovely name. Spanish?"

"Italian."

"Oh! I'll bet you're quite a cook, then."

"It's something I enjoy," I said, sipping my port. "So apparently Mr. Harper told your husband about Beryl's books."

"Oh, my." She frowned. "How curious you should bring that up. It's something I never considered. But Mr. Harper must have told him at some point. Why, yes, I can't think of how else Joe would have known. But he did. When *Flag of Honor* first came out, he gave me a copy of it for Christmas."

She got up again. Searching several bookshelves, she pulled out a thick volume and carried it over to me. "It's autographed," she added proudly.

I opened it and looked at the generous signature of "Emily Stratton," which had been penned in December ten years before.

"Her first book," I said.

"Possibly one of the few she ever signed." Mrs. McTigue beamed. "I believe Joe got it through Mr. Harper. Of course, there's no other way he could have gotten it."

"Do you have any other signed editions?"

"Not of hers. Now, I have all of her books, have read every one of them, most of them two or three times." She hesitated, her eyes widening. "Did it happen the way the papers depicted?"

"Yes." I wasn't telling the whole truth. Beryl's death was much more brutal than anything reported by the news.

She reached for another cheese biscuit, and for an instant seemed on the verge of tears.

"Tell me about last November," I said. "It was almost a year ago when she came to speak to your group, Mrs. McTigue. This was for the Daughters of the American Revolution?"

"It was our annual author's luncheon. The highlight of the year, when we have in a special speaker, an author—usually someone quite well known. It was my turn to head the committee, to work out the arrangements, find the speaker. I knew from the start I wanted Beryl, but immediately ran into obstacles. I had no idea how to locate her. She didn't have a listed telephone number and

I had no idea where she lived, had no earthly idea she lived right here in Richmond! Finally, I asked Joe to help me out." She hesitated, laughing uncomfortably. "You know, I 'spect I wanted to see if I could take care of the matter on my own. And Joe was so busy. Well, he called Mr. Harper one night, and the very next morning my telephone rang. I'll never forget my surprise. Why, I was almost speechless when she identified herself."

Her telephone. It hadn't occurred to me that Beryl's number was unlisted. There was no mention of this detail in the reports Officer Reed had taken. Did Marino know?

"She accepted the invitation, much to my delight, then asked the usual questions," Mrs. McTigue said. "What size group we expected. I told her between two and three hundred. The time, how long she should talk, that sort of thing. She was most gracious, charming. Not chatty, though. And it was unusual. She didn't care to bring books. Authors always want to bring books, don't you know. They sell them afterward, autograph them. Beryl said that wasn't her practice, and she refused the honorarium as well. It was quite out of the ordinary. She was very sweet and modest, I thought."

"Was your group all women?" I asked.

She tried to remember. "I think a few members did bring their husbands, but most of those who attended were women. Almost always are."

I expected as much. It was improbable Beryl's killer had been among her admirers that November day.

"Did she accept invitations like yours very often?" I asked.

"Oh, no," Mrs. McTigue was quick to say. "I know she didn't, at least not around here. I would have heard about something like that and been the first to sign up. She struck me as a very private young woman, someone who wrote for the joy of it and didn't really care for the attention. Explaining why she used pen names. Writers who mask their identities the way she did rarely venture out in public. And I'm sure she wouldn't have made the exception in my case had it not been for Joe's connections with Mr. Harper."

"Sounds like he would do most anything for Mr. Harper," I commented.

"Why, yes. I 'spect that's so."

"Have you ever met him?"

"Yes."

"What was your impression of him?"

"I 'spect he may have been shy," she said. "But I sometimes thought he was an unhappy man and perhaps considered himself a bit better than everybody else. I will say he cut an impressive figure." She was staring off again, and the light had gone out of her eyes. "Certainly my husband was devoted to him."

"When was the last time you saw Mr. Harper?" I asked.

"Joe passed away last spring."

"You haven't seen Mr. Harper since your husband died?"

She shook her head and left me for a private bitter place I knew nothing of. I wondered what had really transpired between Cary Harper and Mr. McTigue. Bad business deals? An influence on Mr. McTigue that eventually made him less than the man his wife had loved? Perhaps it was simply that Harper was egotistical and rude.

"He has a sister, I understand. Cary Harper lives with his sister?" I said.

Mrs. McTigue baffled me by pressing her lips together, her eyes tearing up.

Setting my glass on an end table, I reached for my pocketbook. She followed me to the door.

I persisted, carefully. "Did Beryl ever write to you or perhaps to your husband?"

She shook her head.

"Are you aware of any other friends she had? Did your husband ever mention anyone?"

Again, she shook her head.

"What about anyone she may have referred to as 'M,' the initial M?"

Mrs. McTigue stared sadly into the empty hallway, her hand on the door. When she looked at me, her eyes were weepy and unfocused. "There's a 'P' and an 'A' in two of her novels. Union spies, I believe. Oh, my. I don't think I turned the oven off." She blinked several times as if staring into sunlight. "You'll come see me again, I hope?"

"That would be very nice." Kindly touching her arm, I thanked her and left.

I called my mother as soon as I got home and for once was relieved to receive the usual lectures and reminders, to hear that strong voice loving me in its no-nonsense way.

"It's been in the eighties all week and I saw on the news

it's been dropping as low as forty in Richmond," she said. "That's almost freezing. It hasn't snowed yet?"

"No, Mother. It hasn't snowed. How's your hip?"

"As well as can be expected. I'm crocheting a lap robe, thought you could cover your legs with it while you work in your office. Lucy's been asking about you."

I hadn't talked to my niece in weeks.

"She's working on some science project at school right now," my mother went on. "A talking robot, of all things. Brought it over the other night and scared poor Sinbad under the bed. . . ."

Sinbad was a sinful, bad, mean, nasty cat, a gray- and black-striped stray who had tenaciously begun following Mother while she was shopping in Miami Beach one morning. Whenever I came to visit, Sinbad's hospitality extended to his perching on top of the refrigerator like a vulture and giving me the fish-eye.

"You'll never guess who I saw the other day," I began a little too breezily. The need to tell someone was overwhelming. My mother knew my past, or at least most of it. "Do you remember Mark James?"

Silence.

"He was in Washington and stopped by."

"Of course I remember him."

"He stopped by to discuss a case. You remember, he's a lawyer. Uh, in Chicago." I was rapidly retreating. "He was on business in D.C." The more I said, the more her disapproving silence closed in on me.

"*Huh*. What I remember is he nearly killed you, Katie."

When she called me "Katie" I was ten years old again.

4

AN OBVIOUS ADVANTAGE of having the forensic science labs inside my building was I didn't have to wait for paper reports. Like me, the scientists often knew a lot before they began writing anything down. I had submitted Beryl Madison's trace evidence exactly one week ago. It would probably be several more weeks before the report was on my desk, but Joni Hamm would already have her opinions and private interpretations. Having finished the morning's cases and in a mood to speculate, I keyed myself up to the fourth floor, a cup of coffee in hand.

Joni's "office" was little more than an alcove sandwiched between the trace and drug analysis labs at the end of the hall. When I walked in she was sitting at a black countertop peering into the ocular lens of a stereoscopic microscope, a spiral notebook at her elbow filled with neatly written notes.

"A bad time?" I inquired.

"No worse than any other time," she said, glancing around distractedly.

I pulled up a chair.

Joni was a petite young woman with short black hair and wide, dark eyes. A Ph.D. candidate taking classes at night and the mother of two young children, she always looked tired and a bit harried. But then, most of the lab workers did, and in fact the same was often said of me.

"Checking in on Beryl Madison," I said. "What have you found?"

"More than you bargained for, I have a feeling." She turned

back through pages in the notebook. "Beryl Madison's trace is a nightmare."

I wasn't surprised. I had turned in a multitude of envelopes and evidence buttons. Beryl's body was so bloody it had picked up debris like flypaper. Fibers, in particular, were difficult to examine because they had to be cleaned before Joni could put them under the scope. This required placing each individual fiber inside a container of soapy solution, which in turn was placed inside an ultrasound bath. After blood and dirt were gently agitated free, the solution was strained through sterile filter paper and each fiber was mounted on a glass slide.

Joni was scanning her notes. "If I didn't know better," she went on, "I'd suspect Beryl Madison was murdered somewhere other than her house."

"Not possible," I answered. "She was murdered upstairs, and she hadn't been dead long when the police got there."

"I understand that. We'll start with fibers indigenous to her house. There were three collected from the bloody areas of her knees and palms. They're wool. Two of them dark red, one gold."

"Consistent with the Oriental prayer rug in the upstairs hallway?" I recalled from the scene photographs.

"Yes," she said. "A very good match with the exemplars brought in by the police. If Beryl Madison were on her hands and knees and on the rug, it would explain the fibers you collected and their location. That's the easy part."

Joni reached for a stack of stiff cardboard slide folders, sorting through them until she found what she was looking for. Opening the flaps, she perused rows of glass slides as she talked. "In addition to those fibers, there were a number of white cotton fibers. They're useless, could have come from anywhere and possibly were transferred from the white sheet covering her body. I also looked at ten other fibers collected from her hair, the bloody areas of her neck and chest, and her fingernail scrapings. Synthetics." She glanced up at me. "And they aren't consistent with any of the exemplars the police sent in."

"They don't match up with her clothing or bed covers?" I asked.

Joni shook her head and said, "Not at all. They appear foreign to the scene, and because they were adhering to blood or were under her nails, the likelihood is strong they're the result of a passive transfer from the assailant to her."

This was an unexpected reward. When Deputy Chief Fielding finally got hold of me the night of Beryl's murder, I had instructed him to wait for me at the morgue. I got there shortly before one A.M. and we spent the next several hours examining Beryl's body under the laser and collecting every particle and fiber that lit up. I had just assumed most of what we found would prove worthless debris from Beryl's own clothing or house. The idea of finding ten fibers deposited by the assailant was astonishing. In most cases I was lucky to find one unknown fiber and considered myself blessed to find two or three. I frequently had cases where I didn't find any. Fibers are hard to see, even with a lens, and the slightest disturb-ance of the body or the faintest stirring of air can dislodge them long before the medical examiner arrives at the scene or the body is transported to the morgue.

"What sort of synthetics?" I asked.

"Olefin, acrylic, nylon, polyethylene, and Dynel, with the ma-jority of them being nylon," Joni replied. "The colors vary: red, blue, green, gold, orange. Microscopically they're inconsistent with each other as well."

She began placing one slide after another on the stereoscope's stage and peering through the lens.

She explained, "Logitudinally, some are striated, some aren't. Most of them contain titanium dioxide in a variety of densities, meaning some are a semidull luster, others dull, a few bright. The diameters are all rather coarse, suggestive of carpet-type fibers, but on cross section the shapes vary."

"*Ten* different origins?" I asked.

"That's the way it looks at this point," she said. "Definitely atypical. If these fibers were transferred by the assailant, he was carrying an unusual variety of fibers on his person. Obviously, the coarser ones aren't from his clothing because they're carpet-type fibers. And they're not from any of the carpets inside her house. For him to have such a variety is peculiar for another reason. You pick up fibers all day long, but they don't stay with you. You sit somewhere and pick up fibers, and a little later they're brushed off when you sit somewhere else. Or the air dislodges them."

It got more perplexing. Joni turned another page in her note-book and said, "I've also put the vacuumings under the scope, Dr. Scarpetta. The debris Marino vacuumed off the prayer rug, in particular, is a real hodgepodge." She skimmed a list. "Tobacco ash, pinkish paper particles consistent with the stamp on cigarette packs, glass beads, a couple bits of broken glass consistent with beer bottle and headlight glass. As usual, there are pieces and parts of bugs, vegetable debris, also one spherical metal ball. And a lot of salt."

"As in table salt?"

"That's right," she said.

"All this was on her prayer rug?" I asked.

"Also from the area of the floor where her body was found," she replied. "And a lot of the same debris was on her body, in her nail scrapings, and in her hair."

Beryl didn't smoke. There was no reason for tobacco ash or particles from a cigarette pack stamp to be found inside her house. Salt is associated with food, and it didn't make sense for salt to be upstairs or on her body.

"Marino brought in six different vacuumings, all of them from carpets and areas of the floor where blood was found," Joni said. "In addition, I've looked at the control sample vacuumings taken from areas of her house or carpets where there was no blood or evidence of a struggle—areas where the police think the killer didn't go. The vacuumings are significantly different. The debris I just listed was found only in those areas where the killer was thought to have been, suggesting that most of this material was transferred from him to the scene and her body. It may have been clinging to his shoes, his clothing, his hair. Everywhere he went, everything he brushed up against collected some of this debris."

"He must be a veritable Pig Pen," I said.

"This stuff is almost invisible to the naked eye," the ever-serious Joni reminded me. "He probably wouldn't have a clue he was carrying so much trace on his person."

I studied her handwritten lists. There were only two types of cases from my past experience that might account for such an abundance of debris. One was when a body was dumped in a landfill or some other dirty place such as a road shoulder or gravel parking lot, the other when it was transported from one scene to another in the dirty trunk or on the dirty floor of a car. Neither scenario applied to Beryl.

"Break it down for me by color," I said. "Which of these are likely to be carpet versus garment fibers?"

"The six nylon fibers are red, dark red, blue, green, greenish yellow, and dark green. The greens may actually be black," she added. "Black doesn't look black under the scope. All of these are coarse, consistent with carpet-type fibers, and I'm suspicious some of them may be from vehicle versus household carpeting."

"Why?"

"Because of the debris I found. For example, the glass beads are often associated with reflectorized paint, such as is used in street signs. The metal spheres I find quite often in car vacuumings. They're solder balls from the assembling of the vehicle's under-carriage. You don't see them, but they're there. Bits of broken glass—broken glass is all over the place, especially along road shoulders and in parking lots. You pick it up on the bottom of your shoes and track it into your car. Same goes for the cigarette debris. Finally, we're left with salt, and that makes me most suspicious the origin of Beryl's trace is vehicular. People go to McDonald's. They eat french fries inside their cars. Probably every car in this city has salt in it."

"Let's say you're right," I said. "Let's say these fibers are from car carpeting. That still doesn't explain why there would be pos-sibly six different nylon carpet fibers. It's not likely this guy has six different types of carpet inside his vehicle."

"No, that's not likely," Joni said. "But the fibers could have been transferred to the inside of his car. Maybe he works in a profession that exposes him to carpets. Maybe he has an occu-pation that puts him in and out of different cars throughout the day."

"A car wash?" I asked, envisioning Beryl's car. It was spotless inside and out.

Joni thought about this, her young face intense. "Could very well be something like that. If he works in one of these car washes where attendants clean the interiors, the trunks, he'd be exposed to a variety of carpet fibers all day long. It's inevitable he's going to pick up some of them. Another possibility is he works as a car mechanic."

I reached for my coffee. "Okay. Let's get to the other four fibers. What can you tell me about them?"

She glanced over her paperwork. "One is acrylic, one olefin, one polyethylene, the other Dynel. Again, the first three are consis-tent with carpet-type fibers. The Dynel fiber is interesting because I don't see Dynel very often. It's generally associated with fake fur coats, furlike rugs, wigs. But this Dynel fiber is rather fine, more consistent with garment material."

"The only clothing fiber you found?"

"I'm inclined that way," she answered.

"Beryl was thought to have been wearing a tannish pants suit . . ."

"It's not Dynel," she said. "At least her slacks and jacket aren't. They're a cotton and polyester blend. It's possible her blouse was Dynel, no way to know since it hasn't turned up." She retrieved another slide from the file folder and mounted it on the stage. "As for the orange fiber I mentioned, the only acrylic one I found, it has a shape at cross section I've never seen before."

She drew a diagram to demonstrate, three circles joined in the center, bringing to mind a three-leaf clover without a stem. Fibers are manufactured by forcing a melted or dissolved polymer through the very fine holes of a spinneret. Cross-sectionally, the resulting filaments, or fibers, will be the same shape as the spinneret holes, just as a line of toothpaste will be the same cross-sectional shape as the opening in the tube it was squeezed through. I had never seen the clover-leaf shape before, either. Most acrylics are a peanut, dog bone, dumbbell, round, or mushroom shape at cross section.

"Here." Joni moved to one side, making room for me.

I peered through the ocular lens. The fiber looked like a blotchy twisted ribbon, its varying shades of bright orange lightly peppered with black particles of titanium dioxide.

"As you can see," she explained, "the color is also a little awkward. The orange. Uneven, and moderately dense with delustering particles to dull the fiber's shine. All the same, the orange is garish, a real Halloween orange, which I find peculiar for clothing or carpet fibers. The diameter is moderately coarse."

"Which would make it consistent with carpeting," I ventured. "Despite the peculiar color."

"Possibly."

I began thinking about what materials I had come across that were bright orange. "What about traffic vests?" I asked. "They're bright orange, and a fiber from that would fit with the vehicle-type debris you've identified."

"Unlikely," she replied. "Most traffic vests I've seen are nylon versus acrylic, usually a very coarse mesh that isn't likely to shed. In addition, windbreakers and jackets you might associate with road crews or traffic cops are smooth, also unlikely to shed, and they're usually nylon." She paused, adding thoughtfully, "It also seems to me you aren't likely to find much, if any, delustering particles — you wouldn't want a traffic vest to appear dull."

I backed away from the stereoscope. "Whatever the case, this fiber is so distinctive I suspect it's patented. Someone out there should recognize it even if we don't have a known material for comparison."

"Good luck."

"I know. Proprietary blackouts," I said. "The textile industry is as secretive about their patents as people are about their assignations."

Joni stretched her arms and massaged the back of her neck. "It's always struck me as miraculous the Feds were able to get so much cooperation in the Wayne Williams case," she said, referring to the grisly twenty-two-month spree in Atlanta, in which it is believed that as many as thirty black children were murdered by the same serial killer. Fibrous debris recovered from twelve of the victims' bodies was linked to the residence and automobiles used by Williams.

"Maybe we should get Hanowell to take a look at these fibers, especially this orange one," I said.

Roy Hanowell was an FBI special agent in the Microscopic Analysis Unit in Quantico. He examined the fibers in the Williams case, and ever since had been inundated with other investigative agencies worldwide wanting him to look at everything from cashmere to cobwebs.

"Good luck," Joni said again, just as drolly.

"You'll call him?" I asked.

"I doubt he'll be inclined to look at something that's already been examined," she said, adding, "You know how the Feds are."

"We'll both call him," I decided.

When I returned to my office there were half a dozen pink telephone messages. One jumped out at me. Written on it was a number with a New York City exchange and the note: "Mark. Please return call ASAP." There was only one reason I could think of for his being in New York. He was seeing Sparacino, Beryl's attorney. Why was Orndorff & Berger so intensely interested in Beryl Madison's murder?

The telephone number apparently was Mark's direct line because he picked up on the first ring.

"When's the last time you were in New York?" he asked casually.

"I beg your pardon?"

"There's a flight leaving Richmond in exactly four hours. It's nonstop. Can you can be on it?"

"What is this about?" I asked quietly, my pulse quickening.

"I don't think it wise to discuss the details over the phone, Kay," he said.

"I don't think it wise for me to come to New York, Mark," I responded.

"Please. It's important. You know I wouldn't ask if it wasn't."

"It's not possible . . ."

"I just spent the morning with Sparacino," he interrupted as long-suppressed emotions wrestled with my resolve. "There's a couple of new developments having to do with Beryl Madison and your office."

"My office?" I no longer sounded unmoved. "What could you possibly be discussing that has to do with my office?"

"Please," he said again. "Please come."

I hesitated.

"I'll meet you at La Guardia." Mark's urgency cut off my attempts at retreat. "We'll find someplace quiet to talk. The reservation's already made. All you need to do is pick up your ticket at the check-in counter. I've booked a room for you, taken care of everything."

Oh God, I thought as I hung up, and then I was inside Rose's office.

"I have to go to New York this afternoon," I explained in a tone that invited no questions. "It has to do with Beryl Madison's case, and I'll be out of the office at least through tomorrow." I evaded her eyes. Though my secretary knew nothing about Mark, I feared that my motivation was as obvious as a billboard.

"Is there a number where you can be reached?" Rose asked.

"No."

Opening the calendar, she immediately began scanning for the appointments she would need to cancel as she informed me, "The

Times called earlier, something about doing a features article, a profile of you."

"Forget it," I answered irritably. "They just want to corner me about Beryl Madison's case. It never fails. Whenever there's a particularly brutal case I refuse to discuss, suddenly every reporter in town wants to know where I went to college, if I have a dog or ambivalence about capital punishment, and what my favorite color, food, movie, and mode of death are."

"I'll decline," she muttered, reaching for the phone.

I left the office in time to make it home, throw a few things into a suit bag, and beat the rush-hour traffic. As Mark promised, my ticket was waiting for me at the airport. He had booked me in first class, and within the hour I was settled in a row all to myself. For the next hour I sipped Chivas on the rocks and tried to read as my thoughts shifted like the clouds in the darkening sky beyond my oval window.

I wanted to see Mark. I realized it wasn't professional necessity, but a weakness that I had believed I had completely overcome. I was alternately thrilled and disgusted with myself. I did not trust him, but I wanted to desperately. *He's not the Mark you once knew, and even if he was, remember what he did to you.* And no matter what my mind said, my emotions would not listen.

I went through twenty pages of a novel written by Beryl Madison as Adair Wilds and had no earthly idea what I had read. Historical romances are not my favorite, and this one, in truth, wouldn't win any prizes. Beryl wrote well, her prose sometimes breaking into song, but the story limped along on wooden feet. It was the sort of pulp that was written almost to formula, and I wondered if she might have succeeded at the literature she aspired to write had she lived.

The pilot's voice suddenly announced we would be landing in ten minutes. Below, the city was a dazzling circuit board with tiny lights moving along highways and tower lights winking red from the tops of skyscrapers.

Minutes later, I pulled my suit bag out of the storage compartment and passed through the boarding bridge into the madness of La Guardia. I turned, rather startled, at the pressure of a hand on my elbow. Mark was behind me, smiling.

"Thank God," I said with relief.

"What? You thought I was a purse snatcher?" he asked dryly.

"If you had been, you wouldn't be standing," I said.

"I don't doubt that." He began steering me through the terminal. "Your only bag?"

"Yes."

"Good."

Out front, we got a cab piloted by a bearded Sikh in a maroon turban whose name was Munjar, according to the ID clamped to his visor. He and Mark shouted at each other until Munjar appeared to understand our destination.

"You haven't eaten, I hope," Mark said to me.

"Nothing but smoked almonds . . ." I fell against his shoulder as we screeched from lane to lane.

"There's a good steak house not far from the hotel," Mark said loudly. "Figured we'd just eat there since I don't know a damn thing about getting around in this city."

Just getting to the hotel would do, I thought, as Munjar began an unsolicited monologue about how he had come to this country to get married, and had a December wedding planned even though he had no prospects for a wife at the moment. He went on to inform us that he had been driving a cab for only three weeks, and had learned how to drive in the Punjab, where he had started driving a tractor at the age of seven.

The traffic was bumper to bumper, with yellow cabs whirling dervishes in the dark. When we arrived in midtown we passed a steady flow of people in evening dress adding to the long line outside Carnegie Hall. The bright lights and people in furs and black ties stirred old memories. Mark and I used to love the theater, the symphony, the opera.

The cab stopped at the Omni Park Central, an impressive tower of lights near the theater district at the corner of Fifty-fifth and Seventh. Mark snatched up my bag and I followed him inside the elegant lobby, where he checked me in and had my bag sent up to my room. Minutes later we were walking through the sharp night air. I was grateful I had brought my overcoat. It felt cold enough to snow. In three blocks we were at Gallagher's, the nightmare of every cow and coronary artery and the fantasy of every red meat lover. The front window was a meat locker behind glass, an enormous display of every cut of meat imaginable. Inside was a shrine to celebrities, autographed photographs covering the walls.

The din was loud and the bartender mixed our drinks very

strong. I lit a cigarette and took a quick survey. Tables were arranged close together, typical for New York restaurants. Two businessmen were engrossed in conversation to our left, the table to our right empty, the one beyond that occupied by a strikingly handsome young man working on the *New York Times* and a beer. I took a long look at Mark, trying to read his face. He was tight around the eyes and playing with his Scotch.

"Why am I really here, Mark?" I asked.

"Maybe I just wanted to take you out to dinner," he said.

"Seriously."

"I'm serious. You aren't enjoying yourself?"

"How can I enjoy myself when I'm waiting for a bomb to drop?" I said.

He unbuttoned his suit jacket. "We'll order first, then we'll talk."

He used to do this to me all the time. He would get me going only to make me wait. Maybe it was the lawyer in him. It used to drive me crazy. It still did.

"The prime rib comes highly recommended," he said as we looked over the menus. "That's what I'm going to have, and a spinach salad. Nothing fancy. But the steaks are supposed to be the best in town."

"You've never been here?" I asked.

"No. Sparacino has," he answered.

"He recommended this place? And the hotel, too, I presume?" I asked, my paranoia kicking in.

"Sure," he replied, interested in the wine list now. "It's SOP. Clients fly to town and stay in the Omni because it's convenient to the firm."

"And your clients eat here, too?"

"Sparacino's been here before, usually after the theater. That's how he knows about it," Mark said.

"What else does Sparacino know about?" I asked. "Did you tell him you were meeting me?"

He met my eyes and said, "No."

"How is that possible if your firm is putting me up and if Sparacino recommended the hotel and the restaurant?"

"He recommended the hotel to *me*, Kay. I have to stay somewhere. I have to eat. Sparacino invited me to go out with a couple of other lawyers tonight. I declined, said I needed to look over some paperwork and would probably just find a steak somewhere. What did he recommend? And so on."

It was beginning to dawn on me and I wasn't sure if I felt embarrassed or unnerved. Probably it was both. Orndorff & Berger wasn't paying for this trip. Mark was. His firm knew nothing about it.

The waiter was back and Mark placed the order. I was fast losing my appetite.

"I flew in last night," he resumed. "Sparacino got hold of me in Chicago yesterday morning, said he needed to see me right away. As you may have guessed, it's about Beryl Madison." He looked uncomfortable.

"And?" I prodded him, my uneasiness increasing.

He took a deep breath and said, "Sparacino knows about my connection, uh, about you and me. Our past . . ."

My stare stopped him.

"Kay . . ."

"You bastard." I pushed back my chair and dropped my napkin on the table.

"Kay!"

Mark grabbed my arm, pulling me back into the seat. I angrily shook him off and sat rigidly in my chair, glaring at him. It was in a Georgetown restaurant many years ago that I had snatched off the heavy gold bracelet he had given me and dropped it into his clam chowder. It was a childish thing to do. It was one of the rare moments in my life when I had completely lost my composure and made a scene.

"Look," he said, lowering his voice, "I don't blame you for what you're thinking. But it isn't like that. I'm not taking advantage of our past. Just listen for a minute, please. It's very involved, has to do with things you know nothing about. I have your best interests in mind, I swear. I'm not supposed to be talking to you. If Sparacino, if Berger knew, my ass would be nailed to the nearest tree."

I didn't say anything. I was so upset I couldn't think.

He leaned forward. "Start with this thought. Berger's after Sparacino and, right now, Sparacino's after you."

"After *me*?" I blurted out. "I've never met the man. How could he be after me?"

"Again, it's all got to do with Beryl," he repeated. "The truth is, he's been her lawyer since the beginning of her career. He didn't join our firm until we opened the office here in New York. Before that, he was on his own. We needed an attorney who specialized in entertainment law. Sparacino's been in New York for thirty-some years. He had all the connections. He brought over his clients, brought us a lot of business up front. You remember my mentioning when I first met Beryl, the lunch at the Algonquin?"

I nodded, the fight in me fading.

"That was a setup, Kay. I wasn't there by accident. Berger sent me."

"Why?"

Glancing around the restaurant, he replied, "Because Berger's worried. The firm's just getting started in New York, and you've got to be aware how hard it is to break into this city, to build up a solid clientele, a good reputation. Last thing we need is an asshole like Sparacino driving the firm's name into the gutter."

He fell silent as the waiter appeared with the salads and ceremoniously uncorked a bottle of cabernet sauvignon. Mark took the obligatory first sip and glasses were filled.

"Berger knew when he hired Sparacino the guy's flamboyant, likes to play fast and loose," Mark resumed. "You think, well, it's just his style. Some lawyers are conservative, others like to make a lot of noise. Problem is, it wasn't until some months back that Berger and a few of us began to see just how far Sparacino was willing to go. You remember Christie Riggs?"

It took a moment for the name to click. "The actress who married the quarterback?"

Nodding, he said, "Sparacino masterminded that one from soup to nuts. Christie's a struggling model doing a few TV commercials here in the city. This was about two years ago, at the same time Leon Jones was making the covers of all the magazines. The two of them meet at a party and some photographer snaps a picture of them leaving together and getting inside Jones's Maserati. Next thing, Christie Riggs is sitting in the lobby of Orndorff & Berger. She's got an appointment with Sparacino."

"Are you telling me Sparacino was behind what happened?" I asked in disbelief.

Christie Riggs and Leon Jones had been married last year and divorced about six months later. Their tempestuous relationship and dirty divorce had entertained the world night after night on the news.

"Yes." Mark sipped his wine.

"Explain."

"Sparacino fixes on Christie," he said. "She's gorgeous, smart, ambitious. But the real thing she's got going for her at the moment is she's dating Jones. Sparacino gives her the game plan. She wants to be a household name. She wants to be rich. All she's got to do is draw Jones into her web and later start crying in front of cameras about their lives behind shut doors. She accuses him of slapping her around, says he's a drunk, a psychopath, fooling around with cocaine, smashing up the furniture. Next thing you know, she and Jones are splitting and she's signed a million-dollar book contract."

"Makes me have a little more sympathy for Jones," I muttered.

"The worse part is I think he really loved her and didn't have the smarts to know what he was up against. He started playing lousy ball, ended up in the Betty Ford Clinic. He's since dropped out of sight. One of America's greatest quarterbacks is washed up, ruined, and indirectly you can thank Sparacino for it. This kind of muckraking and slandering isn't our style. Orndorff & Berger is an old, distinguished firm, Kay. When Berger began to get a scent of what his entertainment lawyer was doing, Berger wasn't exactly happy."

"Why doesn't your firm just get rid of him?" I asked, picking at my salad.

"Because we can't prove anything, not at this point. Sparacino knows how to slide through without a snag. He's powerful, especially in New York. It's like grabbing hold of a snake. How the hell do you let go without getting bit? And the list goes on." Mark's eyes were angry. "When you start looking back through Sparacino's professional history and examine some of the cases he handled when he was a one-man show, it really makes you wonder."

"What cases, for example?" I almost hated to ask.

"A lot of suits. Some hatchet writer decides to do an unauthorized biography of Elvis, John Lennon, Sinatra, and when it comes pub time, the celebrity, his relatives sue the biographer and it makes the network talk shows, *People* magazine. The book comes out anyway, with the benefit of incredible free publicity. Everybody's fighting over it because it's got to be juicy to have caused such a stink. We're suspicious Sparacino's method is to represent the writer, then go behind the scenes and offer the 'victim' or 'victims' money under the table to raise hell. It's all staged, works like a charm."

"Makes you wonder what to believe." In fact, I wondered that most of the time.

The prime rib arrived. When the waiter was gone I asked, "How in the world did Beryl Madison ever get hooked up with him?"

"Through Cary Harper," Mark said. "That's the irony. Sparacino represented Harper for a number of years. When Beryl was coming along, Harper sent her to him. Sparacino has been shepherding her since the beginning, a combination agent, lawyer and godfather. I think Beryl was very vulnerable to older powerful men, and her career was pretty bland until she decided to do this autobiographical work. My guess is Sparacino originally suggested it. Whatever the case, Harper hasn't published anything since his Great American Novel. He's history, only valuable to someone like Sparacino if there's a possibility for exploitation."

I considered. "Is it possible Sparacino was playing his game with them? In other words, Beryl decides to break her silence—and break her contract with Harper—and Sparacino plays both sides. Goes behind the scenes and goads Harper into causing a problem."

He refilled our glasses and answered, "Yes, I think he was staging a dogfight and neither Beryl nor Harper was aware of it. As I've said, it's Sparacino's style."

We ate in silence for a moment. Gallagher's was living up to its reputation. You could cut the prime rib with a fork.

Mark finally said, "What's so awful, at least for me, Kay"—he looked up at me, his face hard—"that day we had lunch at the Algonquin, when Beryl mentioned she was being threatened, that someone was threatening to kill her . . ." He hesitated. "To tell you the truth, knowing what I did about Sparacino . . ."

"You didn't believe her." I finished the sentence for him.

"No," he confessed. "I didn't. Frankly, it struck me as another publicity stunt. I was suspicious Sparacino put her up to it, had her stage the whole thing to help sell her book. Not only does she have this battle with Harper, but now someone's threatening to kill her. I didn't give what she said much credence." He paused. "And I was wrong."

"Sparacino wouldn't go that far," I dared to suggest. "You're not implying . . ."

"I really think it's more likely he might have agitated Harper to the point he freaked, got so enraged maybe he came to see her and lost it. Or Harper hired someone else to do it."

"If that's the case," I said quietly, "he must have a lot to hide about what went on when Beryl lived with him."

"He might," Mark said, returning his attention to his meal. "Even if he doesn't, he knows Sparacino, knows how he operates. Truth or fiction, it doesn't matter. When Sparacino wants to raise a stink, he does, and nobody remembers the outcome, only the accusations."

"And now he's after me?" I asked dubiously. "I don't understand. How do I fit in?"

"Simple. Sparacino wants Beryl's manuscript, Kay. Now more than ever the book's a hot property because of what happened to the author." He looked up at me. "He believes the manuscript was turned in to your office as evidence. Now it's missing."

I reached for the sour cream and was very calm when I asked, "What makes you think it's missing?"

"Sparacino somehow managed to get his hands on the police report," Mark said. "You've seen it, I assume?"

"It was fairly routine," I answered.

He jogged my memory. "On the back sheet's an itemized list of evidence collected—including papers found on her bedroom floor and a manuscript from her dresser."

Oh, God, I thought. Marino *had* found a manuscript. It was simply that he had found the wrong one.

"He talked to the investigator this morning," Mark said. "A lieutenant named Marino. He told Sparacino the cops don't have it, said all evidence was turned into the labs in your building. He suggested Sparacino call the medical examiner—you, in other words."

"It's *pro forma*," I said. "The cops send everyone to me and I send everyone back to them."

"Try telling Sparacino that. He's claiming it was turned in to you, that it came in with Beryl's body. And now it's missing. He's holding your office responsible."

"That's ridiculous!"

"Is it?" Mark looked speculatively at me. I felt as if I were being cross-examined when he said, "Isn't it true some evidence comes in with the body and you personally receipt it to the labs or store it in your evidence room?"

Of course it was true.

"Are you part of the chain of evidence in Beryl's case?" he asked.

"Not in terms of what was found at the scene, such as in the instance of any personal papers," I said tensely. "Those were receipted to the labs by the cops, not by me. In fact, most of the items collected from her house would be in the P.D.'s property room."

Again he said, "Try telling Sparacino that."

"I never saw the manuscript," I said flatly. "My office doesn't have it, never had it. And as far as I know, it hasn't turned up, period."

"It hasn't turned up? You mean it wasn't in her house? The cops didn't find it?"

"No. The manuscript they found isn't the one you're talking about. It's an old one, possibly from a book published years ago, and it's incomplete, just a couple hundred pages at most. It was in her bedroom on the dresser. Marino took it in, had Fingerprints check in the event the killer might have touched it."

He leaned back in his chair.

"If you didn't find it," he asked quietly, "then where is it?"

"I have no idea," I answered. "I suppose it could be anywhere. Perhaps she mailed it to someone."

"She have a computer?"

"Yes."

"You check out her hard disk?"

"Her computer doesn't have a hard disk, just two floppy drives," I said. "Marino's checking the floppies. I don't know what's on them."

"Doesn't make sense," he went on. "Even if she did mail the manuscript to someone, it doesn't make sense she wouldn't have made a copy first, that there wasn't a copy somewhere inside her house."

"It doesn't make sense her godfather Sparacino wouldn't have a copy," I said pointedly. "I can't believe he hasn't seen the book. In fact, I can't believe he doesn't have a draft somewhere, maybe even the latest version."

"He says he doesn't, and I'm inclined to believe him for one good reason. From what I've gathered about Beryl, she was very private when it came to her writing, didn't let anybody—including Sparacino—see what she was doing until it was finished. She'd kept him posted on her progress through telephone conversations, letters. According to him, the last time he heard from her was about a month ago. She supposedly told him she was busy revising and should have the book ready to submit for publication by the first of the year."

"A month ago?" I asked warily. "She wrote to him?"

"Called him."

"From where?"

"Hell, I don't know. Richmond, I guess."

"Is that what he told you?"

Mark thought for a moment. "No, he didn't mention *where* she was calling from." He paused. "Why?"

"She'd been out of town for a while," I replied as if it didn't matter. "I'm just wondering if Sparacino knew where she was."

"The cops don't know where she was?"

"There's a lot the cops don't know," I said.

"That's not an answer."

"A better answer is we really shouldn't be discussing her case, Mark. I've already said too much, and I'm not sure why you're so interested."

"And you're not sure my motives are pure," he said. "You're not sure that I'm not trying to wine you and dine you because I want information."

"Yes, to be honest," I answered as our eyes met.

"I'm worried, Kay." I could tell by the tension in his face—a face that still had power over me—that he was. I could scarcely take my eyes off him.

"Sparacino's up to something," he said. "I don't want you squeezed." He drained the last of the wine into our glasses.

"What's he going to do, Mark?" I asked. "Call me and demand a manuscript I don't have? So what?"

"I have a feeling he knows you don't have it," he said. "Problem is, it doesn't matter. Yes, he wants it. And he'll get it eventually, has to unless it's lost. He's the executor of her estate."

"That's cozy," I said.

"I just know he's up to something." He seemed to be talking to himself.

"Another one of his publicity schemes?" I offered a bit too breezily.

He sipped his wine.

"I can't imagine what," I went on. "Not anything involving me."

"I can imagine it," he said seriously.

"Then please spell it out," I said.

He did. "Headline: 'Chief Medical Examiner Refuses to Release Controversial Manuscript.' "

I laughed. "That's ridiculous!"

He didn't smile. "Think about it. A controversial autobiography written by a reclusive woman who ends up brutally murdered. Then the manuscript disappears and the medical examiner is accused of stealing it. The damn thing's disappeared from the *morgue*. Christ. When the book finally comes out, it will be a runaway bestseller and Hollywood will be fighting over the movie rights."

"I'm not worried," I said unconvincingly. "It's all so farfetched, I can't imagine it."

"Sparacino's a whiz at making something out of nothing, Kay," he warned. "I just don't want you ending up like Leon Jones." He looked around for the waiter, his eyes freezing in the direction of the front door. Quickly looking down at his half-eaten prime rib, he mumbled, "Oh, shit."

It took every bit of my self-restraint not to turn around. I didn't look up or act the least bit aware until the big man was at our table.

"Well, hello, Mark. Thought I might find you here."

He was a soft-spoken man in his late fifties or early sixties, with a fleshy face made hard by small eyes as blue as they were lacking in warmth. Flushed, he was breathing hard, as if the exertion of merely carrying his formidable weight strained every cell in his body.

"On a whim, I decided to wander by and offer you a drink, old boy." Unbuttoning his cashmere coat, he turned to me, offering his hand and a smile. "I don't believe we've met. Robert Sparacino."

"Kay Scarpetta," I said with surprising poise.

5

SOMEHOW WE HAD MANAGED to drink liqueur with Sparacino for an hour. It was awful. He acted as if I were a stranger. But he knew who I was, and I was sure the encounter hadn't been accidental. In a city the size of New York, how could it have been accidental?

"You sure there's no way he knew I was coming?" I asked.

"I don't see how," Mark said.

I could feel the urgency in his fingertips as he steered me right on to Fifty-fifth Street. Carnegie Hall was empty, a few people strolling past on the sidewalk. It was getting close to one A.M., and my thoughts were floating in alcohol, nerves taut.

Sparacino had gotten more animated and obsequious with each Grand Marnier until he was finally slurring his words.

"He doesn't miss a trick. You think he's soused and won't remember a thing in the morning. Hell, he's on red alert even when he's sound asleep."

"You're not making me feel any better," I said.

We headed straight for the elevator, where we rode up in self-conscious silence, watching the floor light blink from number to number. Our feet were quiet on the carpeted hallway. Hoping my bag was there, I was relieved to see it on the bed when I stepped inside my room.

"Are you nearby?" I asked.

"A couple doors down." His eyes were darting around. "You going to offer me a nightcap?"

"I didn't bring anything . . ."

"There's a bar fully stocked. Take my word for it," he said.

We needed another drink like a hole in the head.

"What's Sparacino going to do?" I asked.

The "bar" was a small refrigerator filled with beer, wine, and jigger-sized bottles.

"He sees us together," I added. "What's going to happen?"

"Depends on what I tell him," Mark said.

I handed him a plastic cup of Scotch. "Let me ask it this way. What are you planning to tell him, Mark?"

"A lie."

I sat down on the edge of the bed.

He pulled a chair close and began slowly swirling the amber liquor. Our knees were almost touching.

"I'll tell him I was trying to find out what I could from you," he said, "trying to help him out."

"That you were using me," I said, my thoughts breaking apart like a bad radio transmission. "That you were able to do that. Because of our past."

"Yes."

"And that's a lie?" I demanded.

He laughed, and I had forgotten how much I loved the sound of his laugh.

"I fail to see the humor," I protested. It was hot inside the room. I felt flushed from the Scotch. "If that's a lie, Mark, then what's the truth?"

"Kay," he said, still smiling, and his eyes wouldn't let me go. "I've already told you the truth." He was silent for a moment. Then he leaned over and touched my cheek, and I was frightened by how much I wanted him to kiss me.

He leaned back in his chair. "Why don't you stay, at least until tomorrow afternoon? Maybe we should both go talk to Sparacino in the morning."

"No," I said. "That's exactly what he'd like me to do."

"Whatever you say."

Hours later, after Mark left, I lay awake staring up into the darkness, aware of the cool emptiness of the other side of the bed. In the old days Mark never stayed the night, and the next morning I would go around the apartment collecting various articles of clothing, dirty glasses, dishes, and wine bottles, and emptying the ashtrays. Both of us smoked then. We would sit up until one, two, three A.M., talking, laughing, touching, drinking, smoking. We also argued. I hated the debates, which all too often turned into vicious exchanges, blow for blow, tit for tat, Code section this for philosophical that. I was always waiting to hear him say he was in love with me. He never did. In the morning I had the same empty feeling I'd had as a child when Christmas was over and I helped my mother gather up the discarded gift paper strewn under the tree.

I didn't know what I wanted. Maybe I never had. The emotional distance was never worth the togetherness, and yet I didn't learn. Nothing had changed. Had he reached for me, I would have forgotten to behave sensibly. Desire has no reason, and the need for intimacy had never stopped. I had not conjured up the images in years, his lips on mine, his hands, the urgency of our hunger. Now I was tormented by the memories.

I had forgotten to request a wake-up call and didn't bother with the clock by the bed. Setting my mental alarm for six, I woke up exactly on time. I sat straight up and felt as bad as I looked. A hot shower and careful grooming did not hide the dark puffy circles under my eyes or my wan complexion. The bathroom lighting was brutally honest. I called United Airlines and was tapping on Mark's door at seven.

"Hi," he said, looking disgustingly fresh and chipper. "You change your mind?"

"Yes," I said. The familiar scent of his cologne rearranged my thoughts like bright shards of glass inside a kaleidoscope.

"I knew you would," he said.

"And how did you know that?" I asked.

"Never knew you to duck a fight," he said, watching me in the dresser mirror as he resumed knotting his tie.

———

Mark and I had agreed to meet at the Orndorff & Berger offices in the early afternoon. The firm's lobby was a heartless, deep space. Rising from black carpet was a massive black console beneath polished-brass track lighting, with a solid block of brass serving as a table between two black acrylic chairs nearby. Remarkably, there was no other furniture, no plants or paintings, nothing else but a few pieces of twisted sculpture desposited like shrapnel to break the vast emptiness of the room.

"May I help you?" The receptionist gave me a practiced smile from the depths of her station.

Before I could respond, a door indistinguishable from the dark walls silently opened and Mark was taking my suit bag and ushering me inside a long, wide hallway. We passed doorway after doorway opening onto spacious offices with plate-glass windows offering a gray vista of Manhattan. I didn't see a soul. I supposed everybody was at lunch.

"Who in God's name designed your lobby?" I whispered.

"The person we're going to see," Mark said.

Sparacino's office was twice the size of the others I had passed, his desk a beautiful block of ebony scattered with polished gemstone paperweights and surrounded by walls of books. No less intimidating than he had seemed last night, this lawyer to luminaries and the literati was dressed in what looked like an expensive John Gotti suit, the handkerchief in his breast pocket offering a contrasting touch of bloodred. He did not budge from his casual repose when we walked in and helped ourselves to chairs. For a chilly moment he did not even look at us.

"Understand you're on your way to lunch," he finally said as cool blue eyes lifted up and thick fingers shut a file folder. "I promise not to hold you up long, Dr. Scarpetta. Mark and I have been reviewing a few details pertaining to the case of my client, Beryl Madison. As her attorney and the executor of her estate, I have some fairly clear needs, and I'm confident you can assist me in complying with her wishes."

I said nothing, my search for an ashtray fruitless.

"Robert needs her papers," Mark said unemphatically. "Specifically the manuscript of the book she was writing, Kay. I was explaining to him before you got here that the medical examiner's office is not the custodian of these personal effects, at least not in this instance."

We had rehearsed this meeting over breakfast. Mark was supposed to "handle" Sparacino before I arrived. Already I was getting the feeling that I was the one being handled.

I looked straight at Sparacino and said, "The items receipted to my office are of an evidentiary nature and do not include any papers you might need."

"You're telling me you don't have the manuscript," he said.

"That's correct."

"You don't know where it is, either," he said.

"I have no idea."

"Well, now, I've got a few problems with what you're saying."

His face was expressionless as he opened the file folder and produced a photocopy I recognized as Beryl's police report.

"According to the police, a manuscript was recovered at the scene," he said. "Now I'm being told there isn't a manuscript. Can you help me make sense of that?"

"Pages of a manuscript were recovered," I answered. "But I don't think they're what you're interested in, Mr. Sparacino. They do not appear to be part of a current work and, more to the point, they were never receipted to me."

"How many pages?" he asked.

"I've not actually seen them," I said.

"Who has?"

"Lieutenant Marino. He's the one you really need to talk to," I said.

"I already have, and he tells me he hand delivered this manuscript to you."

I did not believe Marino had actually said such a thing. "A miscommunication," I replied. "I think Marino must have been referring to his receipting a partial manuscript to the forensic labs, pages of which may be an earlier work. The Bureau of Forensic Science is a separate division. It happens to be located in my building."

I glanced at Mark. His face was hard and he was perspiring.

Leather creaked as Sparacino shifted in the chair.

"I'm going to shoot straight with you, Dr. Scarpetta," he said. "I don't believe you."

"I have no control over what you believe or don't believe," I replied very calmly.

"I've been giving the matter a lot of thought," he said, just as calmly. "The fact is, the manuscript's a lot of worthless paper unless you realize its value to certain parties. I know of at least two people, not including publishers, who would pay a high price for the book she was working on when she died."

"All of this is of no concern to me," I answered. "My office does not have the manuscript you've mentioned. Furthermore, we never had it."

"Someone has it." He stared out the window. "I knew Beryl

better than anyone did, knew her habits, Dr. Scarpetta. She'd been out of town for quite a while, had been home only a few hours before she was murdered. I find it impossible to think she didn't have her manuscript close by. In her office, in her briefcase, in a suitcase." The small blue eyes fixed back on me. "She doesn't have a lock box in a bank, no other place she might have kept it—not that she would have, anyway. She had it with her while she was out of town, was working on it. Obviously, when she came back to Richmond she would have had the manuscript with her."

"She'd been out of town for quite a while," I repeated. "You're sure of that?"

Mark wouldn't look at me.

Sparacino leaned back in his chair and laced his fingers over his big belly.

He said to me, "I knew Beryl wasn't home. I had been trying to call her for weeks. Then she called me about a month ago. She wouldn't tell me where she was but said she was, quote, safe, and proceeded to give me a progress report on her book, said she was hard at work on it. To make a long story short, I didn't pry. Beryl was running scared because of this psycho threatening her. It didn't really matter to me where she was, just that she was well and working hard at meeting her deadline. Might sound insensitive, but I had to be pragmatic."

"We don't know where Beryl was," Mark informed me. "Apparently, Marino wouldn't say."

His choice of pronouns bit into me. "We" as in he and Sparacino.

"If you're asking me to answer that question—"

"That's exactly what I'm asking," Sparacino cut in. "It's going to come out eventually that for the past few months she was staying in North Carolina, Washington, Texas—hell, wherever it was. I need to know *now*. You're telling me your office doesn't have the manuscript. The police are telling me they don't have it. One sure way for me to get to the bottom of this is to find out where she was last, begin tracking the manuscript that way. Maybe someone drove her to the airport. Maybe she made friends wherever she was. Maybe someone has an inkling as to what happened to her book. For example, did she have it in hand when she boarded the plane?"

"You'll have to get that information from Lieutenant Marino,"

I replied. "I'm not at liberty to discuss the details of her case with you."

"I didn't expect you to be," Sparacino said. "Probably because you know she had it with her when she got on that plane to come home to Richmond. Probably because it came into your office with her body and now it's gone." He paused, his eyes cold on mine. "How much did Cary Harper or his sister or both pay you to turn it over to them?"

Mark was tuned out, his face without expression.

"How much? Ten, twenty, fifty thousand?"

"I believe this terminates our conversation, Mr. Sparacino," I said, reaching for my pocketbook.

"No. I don't believe it does, Dr. Scarpetta," Sparacino answered.

He casually shuffled through the file folder. Just as casually, he tossed several sheets of paper across the desk in my direction.

I felt the blood drain from my face as I picked up what I recognized as photocopies of articles the Richmond newspapers had published more than a year ago. The story on top was depressingly familiar:

MEDICAL EXAMINER ACCUSED OF STEALING FROM BODY

When Timothy Smathers was shot to death last month in front of his residence, he was wearing a gold wristwatch, a gold ring, and had $83 cash in his pants pockets, according to his wife, who was witness to the homicide allegedly committed by a disgruntled former employee. Police and members of the rescue squad responding to Smathers' residence after the shooting claim that these valuables accompanied Smathers' body when it was sent in to the Medical Examiner's Office for an autopsy. . . .

There was more, and I didn't have to read on to know what the other clippings said. The Smathers case had precipitated some of the worst publicity my office had ever received.

I passed the photocopies to Mark's outstretched hand. Sparacino had me on a hook and I was determined not to squirm.

"As you'll note if you've read the stories," I said, "there was a full investigation of that situation, and my office was cleared of any wrongdoing."

"Yes, indeed," Sparacino said. "You personally receipted the valuables in question to the funeral home. It was after this that the items disappeared. The problem was proving it. Mrs. Smathers is still of the opinion the OCME stole her husband's jewelry and money. I've talked to her."

"Her office was cleared, Robert," Mark offered in a monotone as he looked over the articles. "Even so, it says here that Mrs. Smathers was issued a check for an amount commensurate with what the items were worth."

"That's correct," I said coldly.

"There's no price tag on sentimental value," Sparacino remarked. "You could have issued her a check for *ten times* the amount, and she's going to be unhappy."

That was definitely a joke. Mrs. Smathers, whom the police still suspected was behind her husband's murder, married a wealthy widower before the grass had even started growing on her husband's grave.

"And as the news stories point out," Sparacino was saying, "your office was unable to produce the evidence receipt that would verify you did indeed turn over Mr. Smathers's personal effects to the funeral home. Now, I know the details. The receipt was supposedly misplaced by your administrator, who has since gone to work elsewhere. It boiled down to your word against the funeral home's, and though the matter was never resolved, at least not to my satisfaction, by now nobody remembers or cares."

"What's your point?" Mark asked in the same flat tone.

Sparacino glanced at Mark, then returned his attention to me. "The Smathers situation, unfortunately, isn't the end of this sort of accusation. Last July your office received the body of an elderly man named Henry Jackson, who died of natural causes. His body came into your office with fifty-two dollars cash in a pocket. Again, it seems, the money disappeared and you were forced to issue a check to the dead man's son. The son complained to a local television news station. I've got a videotape of what went out over the air if you'd like to see it."

"Jackson came in with fifty-two dollars cash in his pockets," I responded, about to lose my temper. "He was badly decomposed, the money so putrid not even the most desperate thief would have touched it. I don't know what happened to it, but it seems likely the money inadvertently got incinerated along with Jackson's equally putrid and maggot-infested clothing."

"Jesus," Mark muttered under his breath.

"Your office has got a problem, Dr. Scarpetta." Sparacino smiled.

"Every office has its problems," I snapped, getting up. "You want Beryl Madison's property, deal with the police."

"I'm sorry," Mark said when we were riding down on the elevator. "I had no idea the bastard was going to hit you with this shit. You could have told me, Kay . . ."

"Told you?" I stared incredulously at him. "Told you *what*?"

"About the items missing, the bad publicity. It's just the sort of stink Sparacino thrives on. I didn't know and I walked both of us into an ambush. Damn!"

"I didn't tell you," I said, my voice rising, "because it isn't relevant to Beryl's case. The situations he mentioned were tempests in a teapot, the sort of housekeeping snafus that inevitably occur when bodies land on the doorstep in every possible condition and where funeral homes and cops are in and out all day long to pick up personal effects—"

"Please don't get angry with me."

"I'm not angry with you!"

"Look, I've warned you about Sparacino. I'm trying to protect you from him."

"Maybe I'm not sure what you're trying to do, Mark."

We continued to talk in heated voices as he cast about for a cab. The street was almost at a standstill. Horns were blaring, engines rumbling, and my nerves were to the point of snapping. A cab finally appeared and Mark opened the back door, placing my suit bag on the floor. When he handed the driver a couple of bills after I got in, I realized what was happening. Mark wasn't joining me. He was sending me back to the airport alone and without lunch. Before I could roll down the window to talk to him, the cab jerked back out into traffic.

I rode in silence to La Guardia and still had three hours to spare before my flight departed. I was angry, hurt, and bewildered. I couldn't stand parting like this. Finding an empty chair inside a bar, I ordered a drink and lit a cigarette. I watched blue smoke curl up and dissipate in the hazy air. Minutes later I was feeding a quarter into a pay phone.

"Orndorff & Berger," the businesslike female voice announced.

I envisioned the black console as I said, "Mark James, please."

After a pause, the woman replied, "I'm sorry, you must have the wrong number."

"He's with your Chicago office. He's visiting. In fact, I met him at your office earlier today," I said.

"Can you hold?"

I was treated to a Muzak rendition of Jerry Rafferty's "Baker Street" for what must have been two minutes.

"I'm sorry," the receptionist informed me when she returned, "there's no one here by that name, ma'am."

"He and I met in your lobby less than two hours ago," I exclaimed impatiently.

"I checked, ma'am. I'm sorry, but perhaps you have us confused with another firm."

Cursing under my breath, I slammed down the receiver. Dialing directory assistance, I got the number for Orndorff & Berger's Chicago office and stabbed in my credit card number. I would leave a message for Mark telling him to call me as soon as possible.

My blood ran cold when the Chicago receptionist announced, "I'm sorry, ma'am. There is no Mark James at this firm."

6

MARK WASN'T LISTED in the Chicago directory. There were five Mark Jameses and three M Jameses, and after I got home I tried each number and either got a woman or some unfamiliar man on the line. I was so bewildered I couldn't sleep.

It didn't occur to me until the next morning to call Diesner, the chief medical examiner in Chicago whom Mark had claimed to run into.

Deciding being direct was my best recourse, I said to Diesner after the usual pleasantries, "I'm trying to track down Mark James, a Chicago lawyer I believe you might know."

"James . . ." Diesner repeated thoughtfully. "Afraid the name's not familiar, Kay. You say he's a lawyer here in Chicago?"

"Yes." My heart sank. "With Orndorff & Berger."

"Now, I know Orndorff & Berger. A very well respected firm. But I can't recall, uh, a Mark James . . ." I heard a drawer opening and pages flipping. After a long moment, Diesner was saying, "Nope. Don't see him listed in the Yellow Pages either."

After I hung up, I poured myself another cup of black coffee and stared out the kitchen window at the empty bird feeder. The gray morning threatened rain. I had a desk downtown requiring a bulldozer. It was Saturday. Monday was a state holiday. The office would be deserted, my staff already enjoying the three-day weekend. I should go in and take advantage of the peace and quiet. But I didn't care. I couldn't think of anything but Mark. It was as if he didn't exist, as if the man was imaginary, a dream. The more

I tried to sort through it, the more tangled my thoughts became. What the hell was going on?

To the point of desperation, I tried to get Robert Sparacino's home number from Directory Assistance and was secretly relieved to find it was unlisted. It would be suicidal for me to call him. Mark had lied to me. he told me he worked for Orndorff & Berger, told me he lived in Chicago and knew Diesner. None of it was true! I kept hoping the phone would ring, hoping Mark would call. I put on a pot of tomato sauce, made meatballs, and went through the mail.

The phone didn't ring until five P.M.

"Yo, Doc? Marino here," the familiar voice greeted me. "Don't mean to be bothering you on the weekend, but been trying to find you for two damn days. Wanted to make sure you was all right."

Marino was playing guardian angel again.

"Got a videotape I want you to see," he said. "Thought if you was going to be in, I'd just drop it by your house. You got a VCR?"

He knew I did. He had "dropped by" videotapes before. "What sort of videotape?" I asked.

"This drone I spent the entire morning with. Interviewing him about Beryl Madison." He paused. I could tell he was pleased with himself.

The longer I knew Marino, the more he had begun subjecting me to show-and-tell. In part I attributed this phenomenon to his saving my life, a horrific event that had served to bond us into an unlikely pair.

"You on duty?" I asked.

"Hell, I'm always on duty," he grumbled.

"Seriously."

"Not officially, okay? Knocked off at four, but the wife's off in Jersey visiting her mother and I got more loose ends to tie up than a damn rug maker."

His wife was gone. His kids were grown. It was a gray, raw Saturday. Marino didn't want to go home to an empty house. I wasn't exactly feeling contented and cheery inside my empty house, either. I stared at the pot of sauce simmering on the stove.

"I'm not going anywhere," I said. "Drop by with your videotape and we'll watch it together. You like spaghetti?"

He hesitated. "Well . . ."

"With meatballs. And I'm getting ready to make the pasta now. You'll eat with me?"

"Yeah," he said. "I guess I can do that."

───────────

When Beryl Madison wanted a clean car, it was her habit to visit Masterwash on Southside.

Marino had found this out by hitting every high-class car wash in the city. There weren't that many, a dozen at most that offered to roll your driverless car automatically through an assembly line of "hula skirts" gyrating over sudsy paint as spray jets fired needle streams of water. Following a quick hot-air drying, the car was manned by a human being and driven to a bay where attendants vacuumed, waxed, buffed, dressed the bumpers, and all the rest of it. A Masterwash "Super Deluxe," Marino informed me, was fifteen dollars.

"I was lucky as hell," Marino said as he guided spaghetti onto his fork with a soup spoon. "How do you track down something like that, huh? The drones wipe off, what, seventy, a hundred rides a day? And you think they're gonna notice a black Honda? Hell, no."

He was the happy hunter. He had bagged the big one. I knew when I had given him the preliminary fiber report last week he would start hitting every car wash and body shop in the city. One thing about Marino, if there was one bush in the desert, he had to look behind it.

"Hit pay dirt yesterday," he went on. "Buzzed by Masterwash. Was close to last on my list because of its location. Me, I figured Beryl would take her Honda to some West Endy joint. But she didn't, took it Southside, and the only reason I can figure for that is the place has a body and detail shop. Turns out she took her car in shortly after she bought it last December and had one of those hundred-buck jobs done to seal the undercoating and paint. Next thing, she's opened an account there, made herself a member so she could get two bucks knocked off each wash and the perk of the week thrown in free."

"That's how you found out about it?" I asked. "Because of this membership deal?"

"Oh, yeah," he said. "They don't have a computer. Had to look through all their damn receipts. But I found a copy of when she paid for her membership, and based on the condition of her car when we found it in her garage, I was guessing she had it washed not long before she ran off to Key West. Been rooting through her paperwork, too, looking at her charge-card bills. Only one listing for Masterwash, and that's the hundred-buck job I told you about. Apparently she paid cash when she had her ride cleaned after that."

"The car wash attendants," I said. "What do they wear?"

"Nothing orange that might fit with that oddball fiber you found. Most of 'em wear jeans, running shoes—all of 'em have on these blue shirts with 'Masterwash' embroidered in white on the pocket. I looked over everything while I was there. Nothing hit me. Only other fabric-type shit I saw was the barrels of white towels they use to wipe down the cars."

"Doesn't sound very promising," I remarked, pushing away my plate. At least Marino had an appetite. My stomach was still knotted from New York, and I was debating whether to tell him what had happened.

"Maybe not," he said. "But one guy I talked to made my antenna go up."

I waited.

"Name's Al Hunt, twenty-eight, white. Zeroed in on him right away. Saw him standing out there supervising the busy beavers. Something clicked. He looked out of place. Clean-cut, smart, like he ought have been wearing a three-piece suit and carrying a briefcase. I start asking myself, 'What's a guy like him doing in a dead end like this?' " He paused to sop his plate with garlic bread. "So I wander his way and start shooting the breeze. I ask him about Beryl, show him her picture from her driver's license. Ask if maybe he remembers seeing her there, and boom! He starts getting antsy."

I couldn't help but think I would start getting antsy, too, if Marino "wandered" my way. He probably ran over the poor man like a Mack truck.

"Then what?" I asked.

"Then we go inside, get coffee, and get down to serious business," Marino replied. "This Al Hunt's a first-class squirrel. To start with, the guy's been to graduate school. Gets a master's degree in psychology, then goes to work as a *male nurse* at Metropolitan for a couple years, if you can friggin' believe that. And when I ask him why he left the hospital for Masterwash, I find out his old man owns the damn place. Old man Hunt's got his fingers in pies all over the city. Masterwash is just one of his investments. He also owns a number of parking lots and is a slumlord for half of Northside. I'm supposed to automatically assume young Al's being groomed to move into his daddy's shoes, right?"

I was getting interested.

"Thing is, though, Al ain't wearing a suit even if he looks like he should be, right? Translated, Al's a loser. The old man don't trust him in pinstripes and sitting behind a desk. I mean, the guy's standing out there in the lot telling drones how to wax cars and dress the bumpers. Tells me right away something's off up here." He pointed a greasy finger at his head.

"Maybe you should ask his father that," I said.

"Right. He's going to tell me his great white hope's a dumb ass."

"How do you plan to follow up?"

"Already did," he answered. "Witness the videotape I brought, Doc. Spent the entire morning with Al Hunt down at HQ. This guy will talk the wood off a door, and he's overly curious about what happened to Beryl, said he read about it in the papers—"

"How did he know who Beryl was?" I interrupted. "The papers and television stations didn't have any photographs of her. Did he recognize her name?"

"Said he didn't, had no idea it was the blond lady he'd seen at the car wash until I showed him the picture on her driver's license. Then he put on the big act of being shocked, real tore up about it. He was hanging on my every word, wanted to talk about her, was real intense for someone who supposedly didn't know her from Adam's house cat." He placed his rumpled napkin on the table. "Best thing's for you to hear it yourself."

I put on a pot of coffee, gathered the dirty dishes, and we went into the living room and started the tape. The setting was familiar. I had seen it numerous times before. The police department's interrogation room was a small, paneled cubicle with nothing but a bare table in the middle of the carpeted floor. Near the door was a light switch, and only an expert or the initiated would notice the top screw was missing. On the other side of the tiny black hole was a video room equipped with a special wide-angle camera.

At a glance, Al Hunt didn't look frightening. He was fair, with receding light blond hair and a pasty complexion. He wouldn't have been unattractive were it not for a weak chin that caused his face to disappear into his neck. He was wearing a maroon leather jacket and jeans, his tapered fingers nervously fidgeting with a can of 7-Up as he watched Marino, who was sitting directly across from him.

"What was it about Beryl Madison, exactly?" Marino asked. "What made you notice her? You get a lot of cars in your car wash every day. Do you remember all your clients?"

"I remember more of them than you might think," Hunt replied. "Regular customers in particular. Maybe I don't remember their names, but I remember their faces because most people generally stand out in the lot while the attendants are wiping down their cars. Many of the customers supervise, if you know what I mean. They keep an eye on their cars, make sure nothing is forgotten. Some of them will pick up one of the cloths and help out, especially if they're in a hurry—if they're the kind of people who can't stand still, have to be doing something."

"Was Beryl that kind of person? Did she supervise?"

"No, sir. We have a couple of benches out there. It was her habit to sit outside on a bench. Sometimes she read the paper, a book. She really didn't pay any attention to the attendants and wasn't what I would call friendly. Maybe that's why I noticed her."

"What do you mean?" Marino asked.

"I mean she sent out these signals. I picked up on them."

"Signals?"

"People send out all kinds of signals," Hunt explained. "I'm attuned to them, pick them up. I can tell a lot about a person by the signals he or she sends out."

"Am I sending out signals, Al?"

"Yes, sir. Everybody sends them."

"What signals am I sending?"

Hunt's face was very serious as he answered, "Pale red."

"Huh?" Marino looked baffled.

"I pick up signals as colors. Maybe you think that's strange, but it's not unique. There are some of us who sense colors radiating from others. These are the signals I'm referring to. The signals I pick up from you are a pale red. Somewhat warm but also somewhat angry. Like a warning signal. It draws you in but suggests a danger of some sort—"

Marino stopped the tape and smiled snidely at me.

"Is the guy a squirrel or what?" he asked.

"Actually, I think he's rather astute," I said. "You *are* sort of warm, angry, and dangerous."

"Shit, Doc. The guy's goofy. To hear him talk, the whole friggin' population's a walking rainbow."

"There's some psychological validity to what he's saying," I replied matter-of-factly. "Various emotions are associated with colors. It's a legitimate basis for color schemes chosen for public places, hotel rooms, institutions. Blue, for example, is associated with depression. You won't find many psychiatric hospital rooms decorated in blue. Red is angry, violent, passionate. Black is morbid, ominous, and so on. As I recall, you told me Hunt has a master's degree in psychology."

Marino looked annoyed and restarted the tape.

"—I assume this may have to do with the role you're playing. You're a detective," Hunt was saying. "You need my cooperation at the moment, but you also don't trust me and could be dangerous to me if I have something to hide. That's the warning part of the pale red I sense. The warm part is your outgoing personality. You want people to feel close to you. Maybe you want to be close to people. You act tough, but you want people to like you . . ."

"All right," Marino interrupted. "What about Beryl Madison? You pick up colors from her, too?"

"Oh, yes. That struck me right away about her. She was different, really different."

"How so?" Marino's chair creaked loudly as he leaned back and crossed his arms.

"Very aloof," Hunt replied. "I picked up arctic colors from her. Cool blue, pale yellow like weak sunlight, and white so cold it was hot like dry ice, as if she would burn you if you ever touched her. It's the white part that was different. I pick up the pastel shades from a lot of women. Feminine shades that fit with the colors they wear. Pink, yellow, light blues and greens. The ladies passive, cool, fragile. Sometimes I'll see a woman who sends out dark, strong colors like navy or burgundy or red. She's a stronger type. Usually aggressive, may be a lawyer or doctor or business-woman, and often wears suits in the colors I just described. They're the type who stand out by their cars, their hands on their hips as they supervise everything the attendants are doing. And they don't hesitate to point out streaks on the windshield or any spots of dirt."

"Do you like that type of woman?" Marino asked.

He hesitated. "No, sir. To be honest."

Marino laughed, leaned forward and said to him, "Hey. Me, I don't like those types either. Like the pastel babes better."

I gave the real Marino one of my looks.

He ignored me as on-screen he said to Hunt, "Tell me some more about Beryl, about what you picked up."

Hunt frowned, thinking hard. "The pastel shades she sent out weren't all that unusual except I didn't interpret them as fragile, exactly. Not passive, either. The shades were cooler, arctic, as I've said, versus flower shades. As if she were telling the world to keep away from her, to give her a lot of space."

"Like maybe she was frigid?"

Hunt fidgeted with his 7-Up can again. "No, sir, I don't think I can say that. In fact, I don't think I was picking up that. Distance is what came to mind. A vast distance one would have to travel to get to her. But if you did, if she ever let you get close, she would burn you with her intensity. That's where the white-hot signals came in, the thing that made her stand out to me. She was intense, very intense. I had the feeling she was very intelligent, very complicated. Even when she was off sitting alone on her bench and not paying anybody any attention, her mind was working. She was picking up on everything around her. She was distant and white-hot like a star."

"Did you notice she was single?"

"She wasn't wearing a wedding ring," Hunt replied without pause. "I assumed she was single. I didn't notice anything about her car to tell me otherwise."

"I don't get it." Marino looked confused. "How could you tell from her car?"

"I think it was the second time she brought it in. I was watching one of the guys clean out the interior and there wasn't anything masculine inside. Her umbrella, for example—it was on the floor in back and was one of these slender blue umbrellas women usually carry, versus the black ones with big wooden handles men carry. Her dry cleaning was also in the back and it looked like women's clothing in the bags, no men's garments. Most married ladies pick up their husband's clothing when they pick up their own. Also, the trunk. No tools, jumper cables. Nothing masculine. It's interesting, but when you see cars all day long, you start to notice these details and make assumptions about the drivers without really thinking about it."

"Sounds like you did think about it in her case," Marino said. "Did it ever cross your mind to ask her out, Al? You sure you didn't know her name, didn't notice it on her dry cleaning slip, maybe on a piece of mail she left inside her car?"

Hunt shook his head. "I didn't know her name. Maybe I didn't want to know it."

"Why not?"

"I don't know . . ." He became uneasy, confused.

"Come on, Al. You can tell me. Hey, maybe I would have wanted to ask her out, you know? She's a good-looking lady, interesting. Hey, I would have thought about it, probably would have gotten her name on the sly, maybe even tried to ring her up."

"Well, I didn't." Hunt stared down at his hands. "I didn't try any of that."

"Why not?"

Silence.

Marino said, "Maybe because you had a woman like her once and she burned you?"

Silence.

"Hey, it happens to all of us, Al."

"In college," Hunt replied almost inaudibly. "I went out with a girl. For two years. She ended up with some guy in med school. Women like that . . . they look for certain types. You know, when they start thinking about settling down."

"They look for the big shots." Marino's voice was getting sharp around the edges. "The lawyers, doctors, bankers. They don't look for guys working in car washes."

Hunt's head jerked up. "I wasn't working in a car wash then."

"Don't matter, Al. The blue-chip babes like Beryl Madison ain't likely to give you the time of day, right? Bet Beryl didn't even know you were alive, right? Bet she wouldn't have recognized you if you'd run into her damn car on a street some-where . . ."

"Don't say things like that—"

"True or false?"

Hunt stared at his clenched fists.

"So maybe you had a thing for Beryl, huh?" Marino continued relentlessly. "Maybe you was thinking about this white-hot lady all the time, fantasizing, wondering what it would be like to get with her, date her, have sex with her. Maybe you just didn't have the guts to talk to her directly because you figured she'd consider you a lowlife, beneath her—"

"Stop it! You're picking on me! Stop it! Stop it!" Hunt cried shrilly. "Leave me alone!"

Marino stared unemotionally across the table at him.

"Sound just like your old man, don't I, Al?" Marino lit up a cigarette and waved it as he talked. "Old Man Hunt who thinks his only kid's a fuckin' fairy because you're not a mean-ass-son-of-a-bitch slumlord who don't give a shit about anybody's welfare or feelings." He exhaled a stream of smoke, then spoke gently. "I know about the Almighty Old Man Hunt. Also know he told all his buddies you was a pansy, was ashamed to have his blood in your veins when you went to work as a male nurse. Fact is, you came over to his damn car wash because he said if you didn't, you'd be disinherited."

"You know that? How did you know that?" Hunt stammered.

"I know a lot of things. Also know, as a matter of fact, the people at Metropolitan said you was topflight, had a real gentle way with patients. They was sorry as hell to see you leave. Think the word they used to describe you was 'sensitive,' maybe too sensitive for your own good, huh, Al? Explaining why you don't date, don't have no ladies. You're scared. Beryl scared the shit out of you, didn't she?"

Hunt took a deep breath.

"That why you didn't want to know her name? Then you wouldn't be tempted to call her, try anything?"

"I just noticed her," Hunt responded nervously. "Really, there wasn't anything more to it than that. I didn't think about her in the manner you've suggested. I was just, uh, just very aware of her. But I didn't cultivate it. I never even talked to her until the last time she came in—"

Marino hit the Stop button again. He said, "This is the important part . . ." He paused and looked closely at me. "Hey, you all right?"

"Was it really necessary to be so brutal?" I answered emotionally.

"You ain't been around me much if you think that was brutal," Marino said.

"Sorry. I forgot I was sitting in my living room with Attila the Hun."

"It's all acting," he said, hurt.

"Remind me to nominate you for an Academy Award."

"Come off it, Doc."

"You absolutely demoralized him," I said.

"It's a tool, okay? You know, a way to shake things loose, make people say things maybe they wouldn't have thought of otherwise." He turned back toward the set and added, as he hit the Play button, "The entire interview was worth what he tells me next."

"When was this?" Marino asked Hunt. "The last time she came in was when?"

"I'm not sure of the exact date," Hunt answered. "A couple months ago, but I do remember it was a Friday, uh, late morning. The reason I remember is I was supposed to have lunch with my father that day. I always have lunch with him on Friday so we can discuss the business." He reached for his 7-Up. "I always dress a little better on Friday. I was wearing a tie that day."

"So Beryl comes in late morning on this Friday to have her car washed," Marino prompted him. "And on this occasion you talked to her?"

"She actually talked to me first," Hunt replied as if this was important. "Her car was coming out of the bay when she walked up to me, told me she spilled something on the carpet inside the trunk and wanted to know if we could get it out. She took me to her car, opened the trunk, and I saw the carpet was soaked. Apparently, she had groceries in the trunk and a half-gallon bottle of orange juice broke. I guess that's why she decided to drive her car in to be washed right away."

"Was the groceries still in the trunk when she brought her car in?"

"No," Hunt replied.

"Do you remember what she was wearing that day?"

Hunt hesitated. "Tennis clothes, sunglasses. Uh, it looked like she'd just played. I remember because I'd never seen her come in like that. In the past she was always in street clothes. I also remember her tennis racket and a few other things were in the trunk because she took these things out when we started shampooing. I remember she wiped them off and placed them in the backseat."

Marino pulled a datebook out of his breast pocket. Opening

it and flipping back several pages, he said, "Is it possible this was the second week of July? Friday the twelfth?"

"It could have been."

"Do you remember anything else? Did she say anything else?"

"She was almost friendly," Hunt answered. "I remember that well. I assume it was because I was helping her out, making sure we took care of her trunk when I really didn't have to. I could have told her she'd have to take her car to the detail shop and pay thirty dollars for a shampoo. But I wanted to help her. And I was hanging around while the guys worked when I happened to notice the passenger's side of her car. The door was messed up. It was weird. It looked as if someone had taken his key and gouged a heart and some letters on the door right below the handle. When I asked her how it happened, she went around to the door and inspected the damage. She just stood there staring. I swear, she turned white as a sheet. Apparently she hadn't noticed the damage until I pointed it out. I tried to calm her down, told her I didn't blame her for being upset. The Honda's brand new, not a scratch on it, about a twenty-thousand-dollar car. Then some jerk does something like that. Probably some kid with nothing better to do."

"What else did she say, Al?" Marino asked. "Did she have any explanation for the damage?"

"No, sir. She didn't say much of anything. It's like she got scared, was looking around, really upset. Then she asked me where the nearest phone was and I told her there was a pay phone inside. By the time she came back out, the car was finished and she left—"

Marino stopped the tape and popped it out of the VCR. Remembering coffee, I went into the kitchen and fixed two cups.

"Looks like that answers one of our questions," I said when I returned.

"Oh, yeah," Marino said, reaching for the cream and sugar. "The way I'm picturing it, Beryl probably used the pay phone to call her bank or maybe the airlines to make a reservation. Finding that little Valentine scratched in her door was the last straw. She freaked. From the car wash she heads straight to her bank. I've checked out where she had her account. On July twelfth at twelve-fifty P.M., she withdrew almost ten thousand dollars cash, cleaning out her account. Was a top-drawer customer. Didn't get an argument."

"Did she get traveler's checks?"

"No, if you can believe it," he said. "Tells me she was more scared of someone finding her than she was of being robbed. She pays cash for everything down there in the Keys. No one has to know her name if she's not using credit cards or traveler's checks."

"She must have been terrified," I said quietly. "I can't imagine carrying that much cash. I'd have to be crazy or frightened to the point of utter desperation."

He lit a cigarette. I did the same.

Shaking out the match, I asked, "Do you think it's possible the heart was scratched on her car while it was being washed?"

"I asked Hunt the same question to see how he reacted," Marino replied. "He swore it couldn't have been done at the car wash, said someone would have seen it, seen the person doing it. I'm not so sure. Hell, you leave fifty cents in your change box at those joints and it's gone when you get your ride back. People steal like bandits. Change, umbrellas, checkbooks, you name it, and no one saw a thing when you ask. Hunt could have done it, for all I know."

"He is a little unusual," I conceded. "I find it peculiar he was so vividly aware of Beryl. She was one of a very large number of people through that place every day. She was coming in what? Once a month, maybe less?"

He nodded. "But she stood out like a neon sign to him. Could be perfectly innocent. Then again, maybe not."

I recalled what Mark had said about Beryl's being "memorable."

Marino and I sipped our coffees in silence, darkness settling over my thoughts again. Mark. There had to be some mistake, some logical explanation for why he wasn't listed with Orndorff & Berger. Perhaps his name had been left out of the directory or the firm had recently become computerized and he was improperly coded, and his name didn't come up when the receptionist keyed it into her computer. Maybe both receptionists were new and didn't know many of the lawyers. But why wasn't he listed in Chicago at all?

"You look like something's eating you," Marino finally said. "Been looking like that ever since I got here."

"I'm just tired," I answered.

"Bullshit." He sipped his coffee.

I almost choked on mine when he said, "Rose told me you

skipped town. You have a productive little chat with Sparacino in New York?"

"When did Rose tell you that?"

"Don't matter. And don't go getting hot at your secretary," he said. "She just said you had to go out of town. Didn't say where, who, or what for. The rest of it I found out on my own."

"How?"

"You just told me, that's how," he said. "Didn't deny it, did you? So what did you and Sparacino talk about?"

"He said he talked to you. Maybe you should tell me about that conversation first," I answered.

"Nothing to it." Marino retrieved his cigarette from the ashtray. "He calls me the other night at home. Don't ask me how the hell he got my name and number. He wants Beryl's papers and I'm not about to hand them over. Maybe I would have been more inclined to be more cooperative, but the guy's an asshole. Started giving orders, acting like King Tut. Said he's the executor of her estate, started threatening."

"And you did the honorable thing by sending the shark to my office," I said.

Marino looked blankly at me. "No. I didn't even mention you."

"You're sure?"

"Sure I'm sure. The conversation lasted maybe three minutes. That was it. Your name didn't come up."

"What about the manuscript you listed in the police report? Did Sparacino ask about it?"

"He did," Marino said. "I didn't give him any details, told him all her papers was being processed as evidence, gave him the usual about not being at liberty to discuss her case."

"You didn't tell him the manuscript you found was receipted to my office?" I asked.

"Hell, no." He looked strangely at me. "Why would I tell him that? It isn't true. I had Vander check the thing for prints, stood there while he did it. Then I took it back out of the building with me. It's in the property room with all her other shit even as we speak." He paused. "Why? What did Sparacino tell you?"

I got up to refill our coffee cups. When I returned, I told Marino everything. When I was finished, he was staring at me in disbelief, and there was something else in his eyes that thoroughly unnerved me. I think it was the first time I had ever seen Marino scared.

"What are you going to do if he calls?" he asked.

"If Mark does?"

"No. If the Seven Dwarfs does," Marino said sarcastically.

"Ask him to explain. Ask him how he can work for Orndorff & Berger, ask him how he can live in Chicago when there's no record of it." My frustration was mounting. "I don't know, but I'll try to find out what the hell is really going on."

Marino looked away, his jaw muscles flexing.

"You're wondering if Mark's involved . . . tied in with Sparacino, involved in illegal activities, crime," I said, barely able to put into words this chilling suspicion.

He angrily lit another cigarette. "What else am I supposed to think? You haven't seen your ex-Romeo for more than fifteen years, haven't even talked to him, heard a word about his whereabouts. It's like he fell off the edge of the earth. Then he's suddenly on your doorstep. How do you know what he's really been doing all this time? You don't. You only know what he tells you—"

We both started at the clangor of the telephone. I instinctively glanced at my watch as I went to the kitchen. It was not quite ten, and my heart was tight with fear as I picked up the receiver.

"Kay?"

"Mark?" I swallowed hard. "Where are you?"

"Home. Flew back to Chicago, just got in . . ."

"I tried to get you in New York and Chicago, at the office . . ." I stammered. "Called while I was at the airport."

There was a pregnant pause.

"Listen, I don't have much time. I just wanted to call to tell you I'm sorry about how it went and to make sure you're all right. I'll be in touch."

"Where are you?" I asked again. "Mark? Mark!"

I was answered by a dial tone.

7

THE NEXT DAY, Sunday, I slept through the alarm. I slept through Mass. I slept through lunch and felt sluggish and unsettled when I finally climbed out of bed. I could not remember my dreams, but I knew they had been unpleasant.

My telephone rang at a little past seven P.M. as I was chopping onions and peppers for an omelet I wasn't destined to eat. Minutes later I was speeding along a dark stretch of 64 East, a slip of paper on the dash scribbled with directions to Cutler Grove. My mind was like a computer program caught in a loop, thoughts going round and round, processing the same information. Cary Harper had been murdered. An hour ago he drove home from a Williamsburg tavern and was attacked as he got out of his car. It happened very fast. The crime was very brutal. Like Beryl Madison, he'd had his throat cut.

It was dark out, pockets of fog reflecting the low beams of my headlights back into my eyes. Visibility was reduced to almost zero, and the highway I had traveled countless times in the past suddenly seemed strange. I wasn't sure where I was. I was tensely lighting a cigarette when I realized headlights were gaining on me. A dark car I could not make out rushed alarmingly close, then gradually dropped back. The car maintained the same distance from me mile after mile whether I sped up or slowed down. When I finally found the exit I was looking for, I turned off, as did the car behind me.

The unpaved road I turned onto next wasn't marked. The headlights remained fixed to my bumper. My .38 was at home. I had nothing but a small canister of chemical Mace in my medical bag. I was so relieved I said, "Thank you, Lord," out loud when the great house appeared around a bend, its semicircular drive pulsing with emergency lights and lined with cars. I parked, and the car still tailing me rocked to a halt at my rear. I stared in amazement as Marino climbed out and flipped his coat collar up around his ears.

"*Good God*," I exclaimed irritably. "I can't believe it."

"Ditto," he grumbled, his long strides bringing him to my side. "I can't believe it, either." He scowled into the bright circle of lights set up around an old white Rolls-Royce parked near the mansion's back entrance. "Shit. That's all I got to say. Shit!"

Cops were all over the place. Their faces seemed unnaturally pale in the flood of artificial light. Engines rumbled loudly and the static of fragmented sentences from radios drifted on the damp frigid air. Crime-scene tape tied to the back-step railings sealed off the area in an ominous yellow rectangle.

A plainclothes officer wearing an old brown leather jacket headed our way. "Dr. Scarpetta?" he said. "I'm Detective Poteat."

I was opening my medical bag to get out a packet of surgical gloves and a flashlight.

"No one's disturbed the body," Poteat informed me. "I done exactly what Doc Watts said to do."

Dr. Watts was a general practitioner, one of my five hundred appointed MEs statewide, and one of my top ten pains in the ass. After the police called him earlier this evening, he immediately called me. It was SOP to notify the chief medical examiner whenever there was a suspicious or unexpected death of a well-known personage. It was also SOP for Watts to avoid any case he could, to pass it along or pass it by because he couldn't be bothered with the inconvenience or the paperwork. He was notoriously bad about not responding to scenes, and I saw neither hide nor hair of him at this one.

"Got here about the same time the squad did," Poteat was explaining. "Made sure the guys didn't do nothing more'n necessary. Didn't turn him over or remove his clothes or nothing. He was DOA."

"Thank you," I said abstractedly.

"Looks like he was beaten about the head, cut. Maybe shot. Bird shot all over the place. You'll see in a minute. We ain't found a weapon. Appears he pulled in around quarter of seven, parked where his car is now. Best we can figure, he was attacked as he got out."

He looked over at the white Rolls-Royce. The area around it was thick with shadows cast by boxwoods older and taller than he was.

"Was the driver's door open when you got here?" I asked.

"No, ma'am," Poteat answered. "The car keys is on the ground, like he had 'em in his hand when he went down. Like I said, we ain't touched nothing, was waiting till you got here or till the weather forced us to proceed. Gonna rain." He squinted up at the layer of dense clouds. "Could be snow. No sign of any disturbance inside the car, no sign of a struggle at all. We're figuring the assailant was waiting for him, hiding in the bushes prob'ly. All I can tell you is it happened mighty fast, Doc. His sister in there didn't hear a gun go off, nothing, she says."

I left him to talk to Marino as I ducked under the tape and approached the Rolls-Royce, my eyes instinctively probing everywhere I stepped. The car was parallel parked less than ten feet from the back steps, the driver's door toward the house. Rounding the hood with its distinctive ornament, I stopped and got out my camera.

Cary Harper was on his back, his head just inches from the car's front tire. The white fender was speckled and streaked with blood, his beige fisherman's knit sweater almost solid red. Not far from his hips was a ring of keys. In the glare of floodlights all I saw was glistening sticky red. His white hair was matted with blood, his face and scalp laid open by lacerations caused when he was struck with severe force by a blunt instrument that had split the skin. His throat was cut from ear to ear, almost severing his head from his neck, and everywhere I directed the flashlight bird shot glinted like tiny beads of pewter. There were hundreds of them on his body and around it, even a few scattered over the hood of the car. The bird shot had not been fired from any sort of gun.

I moved around taking photographs, then squatted and got out the long chemical thermometer, which I slid carefully under his sweater and wedged in the fold of his left arm. The temperature of the body was 92.4 degrees, the temperature of the air 31. The body was cooling at the rapid rate of approximately three degrees per hour because it was below freezing out and Harper wasn't heavyset or heavily dressed. Rigor had already started in the small muscles. I estimated he had been dead less than two hours.

Next I began looking for any trace evidence that might not survive the trip to the morgue. Fibers, hairs or any other debris adhering to blood could wait. I was worried about anything loose, slowly scanning his body and the area directly around it, when the narrow beam licked over something not far from his neck. I leaned closer without touching, puzzling over a small green-ish lump of what looked remarkably like Play-Doh. Embedded in it were several more pellets. I was carefully sealing this in-side a plastic envelope when the back door opened and I found myself staring directly up into the terrified eyes of a woman standing inside the foyer beside a police officer holding a metal clipboard.

Approaching footsteps belonged to Marino and Poteat. They ducked under the tape and were joined by the officer with the clipboard. The back door quietly shut.

"Will there be someone to stay with her?" I asked.

"Oh, yeah," the officer with the clipboard responded, his breath smoking out. "Miss Harper's got a friend coming, says she'll be okay. We'll have a couple units staked out nearby to make sure the guy doesn't come back for an encore."

"What we looking for?" Poteat asked me.

He slipped his hands in the pockets of his jacket and hunched his shoulders against the cold. Snowflakes as big as quarters were beginning to spiral down.

"More than one weapon," I replied. "The injuries to his head and face are blunt-force trauma." I pointed a bloody gloved fin-ger. "Obviously, the injury to his neck was inflicted by a sharp in-strument. As for the bird shot, the pellets aren't deformed, and it doesn't appear that any of them penetrated his body."

Marino looked positively baffled as he stared at the pellets scattered everywhere.

"That was my impression," Poteat said, nodding. "Don't ap-pear the shot was fired, but I couldn't be sure. Then we're prob'ly not looking for a shotgun. A knife and maybe something like a tire tool?"

"Possibly but not necessarily," I answered. "All I can tell you with certainty right now is his neck was cut with something sharp, and he was beaten with something blunt and linear."

"That could be a lot of things, Doc," Poteat remarked, frowning.

"Yes, it could be a lot of things," I agreed.

Though I had my suspicions about the bird shot, I refrained from speculating, having learned the hard way from past experiences. Generalities often got interpreted literally, and at one crime scene the cops walked right past a bloody upholstery needle in the victim's living room because I had said that the weapon was "consistent with" an ice pick.

"The squad can move him," I announced, peeling off my gloves.

Harper was wrapped in a clean white sheet and zipped inside a body pouch. I stood next to Marino and watched the ambulance slowly head back down the dark, deserted drive. There were no lights or sirens—no need to rush when transporting the dead. The snow was coming down harder and it was sticking.

"You leaving?" Marino asked me.

"What are you going to do, follow me again?" I wasn't smiling.

He stared off at the old Rolls-Royce in the circle of milky light at the edge of the drive. Snowflakes melted as they hit the area of gravel stained with Harper's blood.

"I wasn't following you," Marino said seriously. "Got the radio message when I was almost back to Richmond—"

"Almost back to Richmond?" I interrupted. "Almost back from *where?*"

"From here," he said, fishing in a pocket for his keys. "Found out Harper was a regular at Culpeper's Tavern. I decide to button-hole him. Was with him maybe a half hour before he basically tells me to screw myself. Then he splits. So I head out, am maybe fifteen miles from Richmond when Poteat gets a dispatcher to raise me and tell me what's gone down. I'm hauling ass back in this direction when I recognize your ride, stay with you to make sure you don't get lost."

"You're telling me you actually talked to Harper at the tavern tonight?" I asked in amazement.

"Oh, yeah," he said. "Then he leaves me and gets whacked about five minutes later." Agitated and restless, he started moving toward his car. "Gonna meet with Poteat, see what all I can find out. And I'll be by in the morning to look in on the post if you've got no objections."

I watched him walk off, shaking snow out of his hair. He

was gone by the time I turned the key in the Plymouth's ignition. The wipers pushed back a thin layer of snow, then stopped cold in the middle of the windshield. The engine of my state car made one last sick attempt before it became the second DOA of the night.

The Harper library was a warm, vibrant room of red Persian rugs and antiques crafted from the finest woods. I was fairly certain the sofa was a Chippendale, and I had never touched, much less sat on, a genuine Chippendale anything before. The high ceiling was ornamented in rococo molding, the walls lined with books, most of them leatherbound. Directly across from me was a marble fireplace recently stoked with split logs.

Leaning forward, I stretched my hands toward the flames and resumed studying the oil portrait over the mantel. The subject was a lovely young girl in white seated on a small bench, her hair long and very blond, her hands loosely curled around a silver hairbrush in her lap. She shimmered darkly in the rising heat, her eyes heavy lidded, her moist lips parted, the deeply scooped neckline of her dress exposing a porcelain-white, undeveloped bosom. I was wondering why this peculiar portrait was so prominently displayed when Cary Harper's sister came in and shut the door as quietly as she had opened it.

"I thought this might warm you," she said, handing me a glass of wine.

Setting the tray on the coffee table, she seated herself on the red velvet cushion of a baroque side chair, tucking her feet to one side the way proper ladies are taught to sit by their proper female elders.

"Thank you," I said, and again I apologized.

The battery in my state car was no longer in this world, and jumper cables were not going to bring it back. The police had radioed for a wrecker, and had promised to give me a lift back to Richmond as soon as they finished processing the scene. There was no choice. I wasn't going to stand outside in the snow or sit for an hour inside a squad car. So I had knocked on Miss Harper's back door.

She sipped her wine and stared vacantly into the fire. Like the expensive objects surrounding her, she was beautifully crafted, one of the most elegant women I thought I had ever seen. Silver-white hair softly framed her patrician face. Her cheekbones were high, her features refined, her figure lithe but shapely in a beige cowl-necked sweater and corduroy skirt. When I looked at Sterling Harper, the word "spinster" definitely did not enter my mind.

She was silent. Snow coldly kissed the windows and the wind moaned around the eaves. I could not imagine living alone in this house.

"Do you have any other family?" I asked.

"None living," she said.

"I'm sorry, Miss Harper . . ."

"Really. You must stop saying that, Dr. Scarpetta."

A large cut-emerald ring flashed in the firelight as she lifted her glass again. Her eyes focused on me. I remembered the terror in those eyes when she opened the door while I was examining her brother. She was remarkably steady now.

"Cary knew better," she suddenly commented. "I suppose what surprises me most is the *way* it happened. I wouldn't have expected someone to be so bold as to wait for him at the house."

"And you didn't hear anything?" I asked.

"I heard him drive up. I heard nothing after that. When he didn't come inside the house, I opened the door to check. I immediately called 911."

"Did he frequent any other places besides Culpeper's?" I asked.

"No. No other place. He went to Culpeper's every night," she said, her eyes drifting away from me. "I warned him about going to that place, about the dangers in this day and age. He always carried cash, you see, and Cary was quite skilled at offending people. He never stayed at the tavern long. An hour, at the most two hours. He used to tell me it was for inspiration, to mingle with the common man. Cary had nothing else to say after *The Jagged Corner*."

I had read the novel at Cornell and remembered only impressions: a gothic South of violence, incest, and racism as seen through the eyes of a young writer growing up on a Virginia farm. I remembered it had depressed me.

"My brother was one of these unfortunate talents who had but one book in him," Miss Harper added.

"There have been other very fine writers like that," I said.

"He lived only what he was forced to live when he was young," she went on in the same unnerving monotone. "After that he became the hollow man, the life of quiet desperation. His writing was a series of false starts that he would eventually toss into the fire, scowling as he watched the pages burn. Then he would roam about the house like a angry bull until he was ready to try again. That is the way it has been for more years than I care to recall."

"You seem awfully hard on your brother," I remarked quietly.

"I'm awfully hard on myself, Dr. Scarpetta," she said as our eyes met. "Cary and I are cut from the same cloth. The difference between the two of us is I don't feel compelled to be analytical about what can't be altered. He was constantly excavating his nature, his past, the forces that shaped him. It won him a Pulitzer Prize. As for me, I have chosen not to fight what has always been so clear."

"Which is?"

"The Harper family is at the end of its line, overbred and barren. There will be no one after us," she said.

The wine was an inexpensive domestic burgundy, dry with a faint metallic bite. How much longer until the police finished? I thought I'd heard the rumble of a truck a while ago, the wrecker coming to tow away my car.

"I accepted it as my lot in life to take care of my brother, to ease the family into extinction," Miss Harper said. "I will miss Cary only because he was my brother. I'm not going to sit here and lie about how wonderful he was." She sipped her wine again. "I'm sure I must sound cold to you."

Cold wasn't the word for it. "I appreciate your honesty," I said.

"Cary had imagination and volatile emotions. I have little of either, and were this not the case I couldn't have managed. Certainly, I wouldn't have lived here."

"Living in this house would be isolating." I supposed this was what Miss Harper meant.

"It isn't the isolation I mind," she said.

"What is it you mind, then, Miss Harper?" I queried, reaching for my cigarettes.

"Would you like another glass of wine?" she asked, one side of her face obscured by the shadow of the fire.

"No, thank you."

"I wish we'd never moved here. Nothing good happens in this house," she said.

"What will you do, Miss Harper?" The emptiness of her eyes chilled me. "Will you stay here?"

"I have no place else to go, Dr. Scarpetta."

"I would think selling Cutler Grove wouldn't be hard," I answered, my attention wandering back to the portrait over the mantel. The young girl in white smiled eerily in the firelight at secrets she would never tell.

"It is hard to leave your iron lung, Dr. Scarpetta."

"I beg your pardon?"

"I'm too old for change," she explained. "I'm too old to pursue good health and new relationships. The past breathes for me. It is my life. You are young, Dr. Scarpetta. Someday you will see what it is like to look back. You will find it inescapable. You will find your personal history drawing you back into familiar rooms where, ironically, events occurred that set into motion your eventual estrangement from life. You will find the hard furniture of heartbreak more comfortable and the people who failed you friendlier with time. You will find yourself running back into the arms of the pain you once ran away from. It is easier. That's all I can say. It is easier."

"Do you have any idea who did this to your brother?" I asked her directly, desperate to change the subject.

She said nothing as she stared wide-eyed into the fire.

"What about Beryl?" I persisted.

"I know she was being harassed months before it happened."

"Months before her death?" I asked.

"Beryl and I were very close."

"You knew she was being harassed?"

"Yes. The threats she was getting," she said.

"She *told you* she was being threatened, Miss Harper?"

"Of course," she said.

Marino had been through Beryl's phone bills. He hadn't found any long-distance calls made to Williamsburg. Nor had he turned up any letters written to her by Miss Harper or her brother.

"Then you maintained close contact with her over the years?" I said.

"Very close contact," she replied. "At least, as much as that was possible. Because of this book she was writing and the clear violation of her agreement with my brother. Well, it all got very ugly. Cary was enraged."

"How did he know what she was doing? Did she tell him what she was writing?"

"Her lawyer did," she said.

"Sparacino?"

"I don't know the details of what he told Cary," she said, her face hard. "But my brother was informed of Beryl's book. He knew enough to be extremely out of sorts. The lawyer agitated the matter behind the scenes. Going from Beryl to Cary, back and forth, acting as if he were an ally with one or the other, depending on whom he was talking to."

"Do you know the status of her book now?" I asked carefully. "Does Sparacino have it? Is it in the process of being published?"

"Several days ago he called Cary. I overheard snatches of their conversation, enough to ascertain the manuscript has disappeared. Your office was mentioned. I heard Cary say something about the medical examiner. You, I suppose. And at this point he was getting angry. I concluded Mr. Sparacino was trying to determine whether it was possible my brother might have the manuscript."

"Is that possible?" I wanted to know.

"Beryl would never have turned it over to Cary," she answered with emotion. "It would make no sense for her to have relinquished her work to him. He was adamantly opposed to what she was doing."

We were silent for a moment.

Then I asked, "Miss Harper, what was your brother so afraid of?"

"Life."

I waited, watching her closely. She was staring into the fire again.

"The more he feared it, the more he retreated from it," she said in a strange voice. "Reclusiveness does peculiar things to one's mind. Turns it inside out, puts a spin on thoughts and ideas until they begin to bounce off center and at crazy angles. I think Beryl was the only person my brother ever loved. He clung to her. He had an overwhelming need to possess her, to keep her wedded to him. When he thought she was betraying him, that he no longer had power over her, his madness became more extreme. I'm sure he began to imagine all sorts of nonsense she might divulge about him. About our situation here."

When she reached for her wine again, her hand trembled. She was talking about her brother as if he had been dead for years. There was an edge to her voice when she spoke of him, the well of love for her brother lined with hard bricks of rage and pain.

"Cary and I had no one left when Beryl came along," she continued. "Our parents were dead. We had no one but each other. Cary was difficult. A devil who wrote like an angel. He needed taking care of. I was willing to facilitate his desire to leave his mark on the world."

"Such sacrifices are often accompanied by resentment," I ventured.

Silence. The light from the fire flickered on her exquisitely chiseled face.

"How did you find Beryl?" I asked.

"She found us. She was living in Fresno at the time with her father and stepmother. She was writing, was obsessed with writing." Miss Harper continued staring into the fire as she talked. "One day Cary got a letter from her through his publisher. Accompanying it was a short story written in longhand. I still remember it well. She showed promise, a germinal imagination that simply needed shepherding. Thus the correspondence began, and months later Cary invited her to visit us, sent her a ticket. Not long after that, he bought this house and began to restore it. He did it for her. A lovely young girl had brought magic into his world."

"And you?" I asked.

She did not reply at first.

Wood shifted in the fireplace and sparks popped.

"Life was not without its complications after she moved in with us, Dr. Scarpetta," she said. "I watched what went on between them."

"Between your brother and Beryl."

"I did not want to imprison her the way he did," she said. "In Cary's relentless attempts to hold on to Beryl and have her all to himself, he lost her."

"You loved Beryl very much," I said.

"It is impossible to explain," she said, her voice catching. "It was very difficult to manage."

I continued to probe. "Your brother didn't want you to have contact with her."

"Especially during the past few months, because of her book. Cary denounced and disowned her. Her name was not mentioned in this house. He forbade me to have any sort of contact with her."

"But you did," I answered.

"In a very limited way," she said with difficulty.

"That must have been very painful for you. To be cut off from someone so dear to you."

She looked away from me, interested in the fire again.

"Miss Harper, when did you find out about Beryl's death?"

She did not reply.

"Did someone call you?"

"I heard about it on the radio the next morning," she muttered.

Dear God, I thought. How awful.

She said nothing more. Her wounds were beyond my reach, and as much as I wanted to offer a word of comfort, there was nothing I could say. So we sat in silence for what seemed a very long time. When I finally stole a glance at my watch, I saw it was almost midnight.

The house was very quiet—too quiet, I realized with a start.

After the warmth of the library, the entrance hall was as chilly as a cathedral. I opened the back door and gasped in surprise. Beneath the milky swirl of snow the drive was a solid white blanket, with barely perceptible tire tracks left when the damn cops had driven off without me. My state car had been towed long ago, and they had forgotten I was still inside the house. Damn! Damn! Damn!

When I returned to the library, Miss Harper was placing another log on the fire.

"It appears my ride went off without me," I said, and I know I sounded upset. "I'll need to use a phone."

"I'm afraid that won't be possible," she answered unemphatically. "The phones went out not long after the policeman left. It seems to happen quite often when the weather's bad."

I watched her stab the burning logs. I watched ribbons of smoke curl out from under them as sparks swarmed up the chimney.

I had forgotten.

It hadn't occurred to me until now.

"Your friend . . ." I said.

She jabbed the log again.

"The police said a friend was on her way, would be staying with you tonight . . ."

Miss Harper slowly straightened up and turned around, her face flushed from the heat.

"Yes, Dr. Scarpetta," she said. "It was so kind of you to come."

8

MISS HARPER RETURNED with more wine as the tall case clock on the landing outside the library chimed twelve times.

"The clock," she seemed compelled to explain. "It's ten minutes slow. Always has been."

The mansion's phones really were out. I had checked. The walk to town was several miles through what was now at least four inches of snow. I wasn't going anywhere.

Her brother was dead. Beryl was dead. Miss Harper was the only one left. I hoped it was a coincidence. I lit a cigarette and took a swallow of wine.

Miss Harper didn't have the physical strength to have killed her brother and Beryl. What if the killer were after Miss Harper, too? What if he came back?

My .38 was at home.

The police would be staking out the area.

In what? Snowmobiles?

I realized Miss Harper was saying something else to me.

"I'm sorry," I said, forcing a smile.

"You look cold," she repeated.

Her face was placid as she seated herself on the baroque side chair and stared into the fire. The high flames sounded like a wind-whipped flag, and infrequent gusts of wind sent ashes blowing out on the hearth. But she appeared reassured by my company. Were I in her shoes, I wouldn't have wanted to be alone, either.

"I'm fine," I lied. I *was* cold.

"I'll be glad to get you a sweater."

"Please don't trouble yourself. I'm comfortable—really."

"It's quite impossible to heat this house," she went on. "The high ceilings. And it isn't insulated. You grow accustomed to it."

I thought of my gas-heated modern house in Richmond. I thought of my queen-size bed with its firm mattress and electric blanket. I thought of the carton of cigarettes in the cupboard near the refrigerator and of the good Scotch in my bar. I thought of the drafty, dusty dark upstairs of the Cutler Grove mansion.

"I'll be fine down here. On the sofa," I said.

"Nonsense. The fire will go out soon enough." She was fidgeting with a button on her sweater, her eyes not leaving the fire.

"Miss Harper," I tried one last time. "Do you have any idea who might have done this? To Beryl, to your brother. Or why?"

"You think it's the same man." She presented this as a statement of fact, not a question.

"I have to consider it."

"I wish I could tell you something that would help," she answered. "But perhaps it doesn't matter. Whoever it is, what's done is done."

"Don't you want him punished?"

"There has been enough punishment. It won't undo what has been done," she said.

"Wouldn't Beryl want him caught?"

She turned to me, her eyes wide. "I wish you had known her."

"I think I did. I do know her in a way," I said gently.

"I can't explain . . ."

"You don't need to, Miss Harper."

"It could have been so nice . . ."

I saw her grief for an instant, her face contorted, then controlled again. She didn't need to finish the thought. It could have been so nice now that there was no one to keep Beryl and Miss Harper apart. Companions. Friends. Life is so empty when you are alone, when there is no one to love.

"I'm sorry," I said with feeling. "I'm so terribly sorry, Miss Harper."

"It is the middle of November," she replied, looking away from me again. "Unusually early for snow. The thaw will come quickly, Dr. Scarpetta. You will be able to get out by late morning. Those who forgot you will remember by then. It really was so good of you to come."

She seemed to have known that I would be here. I had the uncanny impression she had somehow planned it. Of course, that wasn't possible.

"One thing I will ask you to do," she said.

"What is that, Miss Harper?"

"Come back in the spring. Come back when it is April," she said to the flames.

"I would like that," I answered.

"The forget-me-nots will be in bloom. The bowling green will be pale blue with them. It is so lovely, my favorite time of year. Beryl and I used to pick them. Have you ever studied them up close? Or are you like most people who take them for granted, never give them a thought because they are so small? They are so beautiful if you hold them close. *So beautiful*, as if made of porcelain and painted by the perfect hand of God. We would wear them in our hair and put them in bowls of water in the house, Beryl and I. You must promise to come back in April. You will promise me that, won't you?" She turned to me, and the emotion in her eyes pained me.

"Yes, yes. Of course I will," I replied, and I meant it.

"Is there anything special you eat for breakfast?" she asked as she got up.

"Whatever you fix for yourself will be fine."

"There's plenty in the refrigerator," she remarked oddly. "Bring your wine and I'll show you to your room."

Her hand trailed the banister as she led her guest up the magnificent carved stairway to the second floor. There were no overhead lights, just lamps to light our way, and the musty air was as cold as a cellar.

"I'm on the other side of the hallway, three doors down, if you need anything," she told me, and she showed me inside a small bedroom.

The furnishings were mahogany with satinwood inlays, and on pale-blue-papered walls were several oil paintings of loosely arranged flowers and a vista of the river. The canopied bed was turned down and piled high with comforters, and an open doorway led into the tiled bath. The air was stale and smelled of dust, as if windows were never opened and nothing but memories ever stirred in here. I was sure that no one had slept in this room in many, many years.

"In the top dresser drawer is a flannel gown. There are clean towels and other necessities in the bath," Miss Harper said. "Now then, if you're all set?"

"Yes. Thank you." I smiled at her. "Good night."

I shut the door and closed its feeble latch. The gown was the only garment inside the dresser, and tucked under it was a sachet that long ago had lost its scent. Every other drawer was empty. Inside the bath was a toothbrush still wrapped in cellophane, a tiny tube of toothpaste, a bar of lavender soap never used, and plenty of towels, as Miss Harper had promised. The sink was as dry as chalk, and when I turned the gold handles the water was liquid rust. It took forever to get clear and warm enough for me to dare to wash my face.

The gown, old but clean, was the washed-out blue of forget-me-nots, I thought. Getting in bed, I pulled the musty-smelling comforters up to my chin before switching off the lamp. The pillow was plump, and I could feel the prickly twill of feathers as I pushed and shoved it into a more comfortable shape. Wide awake, my nose cold, I sat up in the darkness of a room I was certain had once been Beryl's, and I finished my wine. The house was so still I imagined I could hear the all-absorbing quiet of the snow falling beyond the window.

I wasn't aware of dozing off, but when my eyelids flew open my heart was thudding violently, and I was afraid to move. I couldn't remember the nightmare. At first I wasn't sure where I was and if the noise I heard was real. The faucet in the bathroom was leaking, drops of water slowly clinking into the sink. Floorboards beyond my latched bedroom door creaked again, quietly.

My mind raced through an obstacle course of possibilities. The dropping temperature was causing wood to creak. Mice. Someone was slowly making his way down the hall. I strained to hear, holding my breath as slippered feet whispered past my shut door. Miss Harper, I concluded. It sounded as if she was going downstairs. I tossed and turned for what seemed like an hour. Eventually, I switched on the lamp and got out of bed. It was half past three, and there wasn't a hope I could go back to sleep. Shivering beneath my borrowed gown, I put on my overcoat, unlatched the door, and followed the pitch-black hallway until I recognized the shadowy shape of the curved banister at the top of the stairs.

The chilly entrance hall was dimly illuminated by moonlight

seeping through small windows on either side of the front door. The snow had stopped and stars were out, tree branches and shrubbery formless beneath white frosting. I crept into the library, lured by the promise of heat from its crackling fire.

Miss Harper was sitting on the sofa, an afghan pulled around her. She was staring into the flames, her cheeks wet with tears she did not bother to brush away. Clearing my throat, I tentatively called her name, not wanting to startle her.

She did not move.

"Miss Harper?" I said again, louder. "I heard you come down . . ."

She was leaning against the serpentine-curved back of the sofa, her eyes unblinking as they stared dully into the fire. Her head fell limply to one side when I quickly sat next to her and pressed my fingers against her neck. She was very warm but pulseless. Pulling her down to the rug, I went from her mouth to her sternum, desperately trying to breathe life into her lungs and force her heart to beat. I don't know how long this went on. When I finally gave up, my lips were numb, the muscles in my back and arms quivering. I was trembling all over.

The telephones were still out. I could not call anyone. There was nothing I could do. I stood before the library window, parted the curtains and looked out through tears at the incredible whiteness lit up by the moon. Beyond, the river was black and I could not see across it. Somehow I managed to get her body back on the sofa and I gently covered it with the afghan while the fire burned down and the girl in the portrait receded into the shadows. Sterling Harper's death had caught me unawares and left me stunned. I sat on the rug in front of the sofa and watched the fire die. I could not keep that alive, either. In fact, I didn't even try.

I did not cry when my father died. He had been sick so many years I became expert at cauterizing my emotions. He was in bed most of my childhood. When he finally died one evening at home, my mother's terrible grief drove me to a higher ground of detachment, and it was from this seemingly safer vantage point that I honed to perfection the art of surveying the wreckage of my family.

With what seemed unflappable reserve, I watched the anarchy that broke out between my mother and my younger sister, Dorothy, who had been consummately narcissistic and irresponsible since the day she was born. I silently removed myself from the screaming matches and arguments while inwardly I ran for my life. AWOL from the wars within my house, I spent increasing lengths of time engaging the tutelage of the Gray Nuns after class or ensconcing myself in the library, where I began to realize the precocity of my mind and the rewards it would bring to me. I excelled in science and was intrigued by human biology. I was poring over *Gray's Anatomy* by the time I was fifteen, and it became the sine qua non of my self-education, the vessel of my epiphany. I was going to leave Miami for college. In an era when women were teachers, secretaries, and housewives, I was going to be a physician.

In high school I made all A's and played tennis and read during the holidays and summers while my family struggled on like wounded Confederate veterans in a world long since won by the North. I had little interest in dating and had few friends. Graduating at the top of my class, I went off to Cornell on a full scholarship; then it was Johns Hopkins for medical school, law school at Georgetown after that, then back to Hopkins for my pathology residency. I was only vaguely aware of what I was doing. The career I had embarked upon would forever return me to the scene of the terrible crime of my father's death. I would take death apart and put it back together again a thousand times. I would master its codes and take it to court. I would understand the nuts and bolts of it. But none of it brought my father back to life, and the child inside me never stopped grieving.

Embers shifted on the hearth, and I dozed in fits and starts.

Hours later the details of my prison began to materialize in the chilled blue of dawn. Pain shot through my back and legs as I stiffly got to my feet and went to the window. The sun was a pale egg over the slate-gray river, tree trunks black against the white snow. The fire was cold, and two questions were tapping at the back of my feverish brain. Would Miss Harper have died had I not been here? How convenient for her to die while I was inside her house. Why did she come down to the library? I imagined her making her way down the stairs, stoking the fire and settling on the sofa. While she stared into the flames, her heart simply stopped. Or was it the portrait she had been looking at in the end?

I switched on every lamp. Pulling a chair close to the hearth, I climbed up and lifted the unwieldy painting free of its hooks. The portrait did not seem so unsettling of color and delicate brush strokes in heavy oil paint. Dust floated free of the canvas as I climbed down and laid the painting on the floor. There was no signature or date, nor was the portrait nearly as old as I had assumed. The colors had been deliberately muted to look old, and there wasn't the slightest bit of cracking evident in the paint.

Turning it over, I examined the brown paper backing. Centered on it was a gold seal embossed with the name of a Williamsburg picture-framing shop. I make note of it and climbed back up on the chair, returning the painting to its hooks. Then I squatted before the fireplace and delicately probed the bebris with a pencil I had gotten out of my bag. On top of the charred chunks of wood was a peculiar layer of filmy white ash that wafted like cobwebs at the slightest stirring. Beneath this was a lump of what looked like melted plastic.

"No offense, Doc," Marino said, backing his car out of the lot, "but you look like hell."

"Thanks a lot," I muttered.

"Like I said, no offense. Guess you didn't get much sleep."

When I didn't show up to take care of Cary Harper's autopsy in the morning, Marino wasted no time calling the Williamsburg police. Midmorning two sheepish officers showed up at the mansion, chains clanking and chewing tracks into the smooth, heavy snow. After the depressing rounds of questions about Sterling Harper's death, her body was loaded into an ambulance headed for Richmond, and the officers deposited me at headquarters in downtown Williamsburg, where I was plied with coffee and doughnuts until Marino picked me up.

"No way I would've stayed in that house all night," Marino went on. "I don't care if it was twenty below. I'd freeze my ass off before I'd spend the night with a stiff—"

"Do you know where Princess Street is?" I interrupted.

"What about it?" His mirrored shades turned toward me.

The snow was white fire in the sun, the streets fast turning to slush.

"I'm interested in a five-oh-seven Princess Street address," I replied in a tone indicating I expected him to take me there.

The address was at the edge of the historic district, tucked between other businesses in Merchants' Square. In the recently plowed parking lot were no more than a dozen cars, their roofs thatched with snow. I was relieved to see that The Village Frame Shoppe & Gallery was open.

Marino didn't ask questions as I got out. He probably sensed I wasn't in the mood to answer any at the moment. There was only one other customer inside the gallery, a young man in a black overcoat casually riffling through a rack of prints while a woman with long blond hair worked an adding machine behind the counter.

"May I help you?" the blond woman inquired, blandly looking up at me.

"That depends on how long you've worked here," I answered.

The cool, dubious way she looked me over made me realize I probably did look like hell. I'd slept in my coat. My hair was a godawful mess. Self-consciously reaching up to smooth down a cowlick, I realized I had somehow managed to lose an earring. I told the woman who I was and drove home the point by producing the thin black wallet containing my brass medical examiner's shield.

"I've worked here two years," she said.

"I'm interested in a painting your shop framed probably before your time," I told her. "A portrait Cary Harper may have brought in."

"Oh, God. I heard about it on the radio this morning. About what happened to him. Oh, God, how awful." She was sputtering. "You'll need to speak to Mr. Hilgeman." She disappeared in back to fetch him.

Mr. Hilgeman was a tweedy, distinguished-looking gentleman who stated in no uncertain terms, "Cary Harper hasn't been in this shop in years, and no one here knew him well, at least not to my knowledge."

"Mr. Hilgeman," I said, "over the fireplace mantel in Cary Harper's library is a portrait of a blond girl. It was framed in your shop, possibly many years ago. Do you remember it?"

There wasn't the faintest spark of recognition in the gray eyes peering at me over reading glasses.

"It appears very old," I explained. "A good imitation but a rather unusual treatment of the subject. The girl is nine, ten, at the most twelve, but she's dressed more like a young woman, in white, and sitting on a small bench holding a silver hairbrush."

I could have kicked myself for not taking a Polaroid photograph of the painting. My camera was inside my medical bag and the thought had never occurred to me. I had been too distracted.

"You know," Mr. Hilgeman said, his eyes lighting up, "I think I might remember what you're talking about. A very pretty girl, but unusual. Yes. Rather suggestive, as I recall."

I didn't prod him.

"Must have been at least fifteen years ago. . . . Let me see." He touched an index finger to his lips. "No." He shook his head. "It wasn't me."

"It wasn't you? *What* wasn't you?" I asked.

"I didn't do the framing. That would have been Clara. An assistant who worked here then. I do believe—in fact I'm certain—Clara did the framing on that one. A rather expensive job and not really worth it, if you must know. The painting wasn't terribly good. Actually," he added with a frown, "it was one of her least successful efforts—"

"Her?" I interrupted. "Do you mean Clara?"

"I'm talking about Sterling Harper." He looked speculatively at me. "She's the artist." He paused. "That would have been years ago when she did a lot of painting. They had a studio in the house, as I understand it. I've never been there, of course. But she used to bring in a number of her works, most of them still lifes, landscapes. The painting you're interested in is the only portrait I recall."

"How long ago did she paint it?"

"At least fifteen years ago, as I've said."

"Did someone pose for it?" I asked.

"I suppose it could have been done from a photograph . . ." He frowned. "Actually, I really can't answer your question. But if someone posed for it, I don't know who that might have been."

I didn't show my surprise. Beryl would have been sixteen or seventeen and living at Cutler Grove then. Was it possible Mr. Hilgeman, the people in town, didn't know this?

"It's rather sad," he mused. "Such talented, intelligent people. No family, no children."

"What about friends?" I asked.

"I really don't know either of them personally," he said.

And you never will, I thought morbidly.

Marino was wiping off his windshield with a chamois cloth when I went back out into the parking lot. The melted snow and salt left by road crews had splotched and dulled his beautiful black car. He didn't look happy about it. On the pavement beneath the driver's door was an untidy collection of cigarette butts he had unceremoniously dumped from his ashtray.

"Two things," I began very seriously as we buckled up. "In the mansion's library is a portrait of a young blond girl that Miss Harper apparently had framed in this shop approximately fifteen years ago."

"Beryl Madison?" He got out his lighter.

"It may very well be a portrait of her," I replied. "But if so, it depicts her at an age much younger than she would have been when the Harpers met her. And the treatment of the subject is a little peculiar. Lolita-like . . ."

"Huh?"

"Sexy," I said bluntly. "A little girl painted to look sensual."

"Yo. So now you're going to tell me Cary Harper was a closet pedophile."

"In the first place, his sister painted the portrait," I said.

"Shit," he complained.

"Secondly," I went on, "I got the distinct impression the owner of the framing shop has no idea Beryl ever lived with the Harpers. It makes me wonder if other people know. And if not, I wonder how that's possible. She lived in the mansion for *years*, Marino. It's just a couple of miles from town. This is a *small* town."

He stared straight ahead as he drove and didn't say a word.

"Well," I decided, "it may all be idle speculation. They were reclusive. Perhaps Cary Harper did his best to hide Beryl from the world. Whatever the case, the situation doesn't sound exactly healthy. But it may have nothing to do with their deaths."

"Hell," he said shortly, "*healthy* ain't the word for it. Reclusive or not, it don't make sense for no one to know she was there. Not unless they had her locked up or chained to a bedpost. Damn perverts. I hate perverts. I hate people picking on kids. You know?" He glanced over at me again. "I really do hate that. I'm getting that feeling again."

"What feeling?"

"That Mr. Pulitzer Prize took Beryl out," Marino said. "She's going to spill the beans in her book, and he freaks, comes to see her and brings a knife."

"Then who killed him?" I asked.

"So maybe his batty sister did."

Whoever murdered Cary Harper was strong enough to inflict

blows so forceful he was rendered unconscious almost immediately, and cutting someone's throat didn't fit with a female assailant. In fact, I had never had a case in which a woman did such a thing.

After a long silence, Marino asked, "Did Old Lady Harper strike you as senile?"

"Rather eccentric. But not senile," I said.

"Crazy?"

"No."

"Based on how you've described things, it don't sound to me like her response to her brother getting whacked was exactly appropriate," he answered.

"She was in shock, Marino. People who are in shock do not react appropriately to anything."

"You thinking she committed suicide?"

"Certainly that's possible," I replied.

"You find any drugs at the scene?"

"Some over-the-counter meds, none of them lethal," I said.

"No injuries?"

"None I could see."

"So, you know what the hell killed her?" he asked, looking over at me, his face hard.

"No," I answered. "At the moment I have absolutely no idea."

"I assume you're heading back to Cutler Grove," I said to Marino as he parked behind the OCME.

"Real thrilled about it, too," he grumbled. "Go home and get some decent sleep."

"Don't forget Cary Harper's typewriter."

Marino dug in a pocket for his lighter.

"The make and model, and any used ribbons," I reminded him.

He lit a cigarette.

"And any stationery or typing paper in the house. I suggest you collect the ashes in the fireplace yourself. It's going to be extremely difficult to preserve them—"

"No offense, Doc, but you're beginning to sound like my mother or something."

"Marino," I snapped, "I'm serious."

"Yeah, you're serious, all right—seriously in need of a good night's sleep," he said.

Marino was as frustrated as I and probably needed sleep, too.

The bay was locked and empty, the cement floor mottled with oil stains. Inside the morgue I was aware of the tedious humming of electricity and generators I hardly noticed during business hours. The rush of foul-smelling air seemed unusually loud as I entered the refrigerator.

Their bodies were on gurneys parked together against the left wall. Maybe it was because I was so tired. But when I pulled the sheet back from Sterling Harper, I went weak in the knees and dropped my medical bag to the floor. I recalled the keen beauty of her face, the terror in her eyes when the mansion's back door opened and she looked out as I attended to her dead brother, my gloved hands bright red with his blood. Brother and sister were present and accounted for. That was all I needed to know. I covered her gently, shrouding a face now as empty as a rubber mask. All around were tagged and protruding naked feet.

I had vaguely noticed the yellow film box beneath Sterling Harper's gurney when I had first walked into the refrigerator. But it wasn't until I reached down to pick up my medical bag that I took a good look and realized the significance. Kodak thirty-five millimeter, twenty-four exposure. The film on state contract for my office was Fuji, and we always ordered the thirty-six exposure. The paramedics who had transported Miss Harper's body would have been in and out many hours ago, and they wouldn't have taken any photographs.

I went back out into the hallway. The light over the elevator caught my attention, and I realized it was stopped on the second floor. Someone else was in the building! It was probably just the security guard making his rounds. Then, as my scalp began to prickle, I thought of the empty film box again. Gripping the strap of my medical bag tightly, I decided to take the stairs. On the second-floor landing I slowly opened the door and listedned before stepping inside. The offices in the east wing were empty, the lights out. I turned right into the main hallway, passing the empty classroom, the library, and Fielding's office. I didn't hear or see anyone. Just to be sure, I decided as I turned into my office to call security.

When I saw him, I stopped breathing. For a terrible moment my mind wouldn't work. He was deftly and silently riffling through an open filing cabinet. The collar of a navy jacket was up around his ears, eyes masked by dark aviator glasses, hands sheathed in surgical gloves. Over a powerful shoulder was a leather strap attached to a camera. He looked as solid and hard as marble, and it wasn't possible for me to step out of sight fast enough. The gloved hands suddenly stilled.

When he lunged, it was a reflex, my medical bag looping back like an Olympic hammer. Momentum propelled it with such force between his legs the impact jarred the sunglasses from his face. He fell forward, doubling over in agony and knocked sufficiently off balance for me to send him sprawling with a kick to the ankles. He must not have felt any better when the hard metal lens of his camera was the only cushion between his ribs and the floor.

Medical impedimenta scattered as I frantically dug out of my bag the small canister of Mace I always carried, and he bellowed when the heavy stream hit him in the face. He clawed at his eyes, rolling around, screaming, while I grabbed the phone and called for help. I squirted him one more time for good measure just before the security guard hustled in. Then the cops arrived. My hysterical hostage begged to be taken to the hospital as an unsympathetic officer wrenched his arms behind his back, snapped on cuffs, and frisked him.

According to his driver's license, the intruder's name was Jeb Price, age thirty-four, address Washington, D.C. Wedged in the back of his corduroy trousers was a Smith & Wesson 9-millimeter automatic with fourteen rounds in the clip and one in the chamber.

I don't remember going into the morgue office and getting the keys off the pegboard for the other state car leased by the OCME. But I must have, because I was parking the dark blue station wagon in my driveway as night began to fall. Used to transport bodies, the car was oversize, the tailgate window discreetly covered with a screen, and in back was a removable plyboard floor that required hosing down several times a week. The car was a cross between a family wagon and a hearse, and the only thing harder to parallel park, in my opinion, was the *QE2*.

Like a zombie, I went straight upstairs without bothering to play back my telephone messages or turn off the answering machine. My right elbow and shoulder ached. The small bones in my hand hurt. Laying my clothes on a chair, I took a hot bath and numbly fell into bed. Deep, deep sleep. Sleep so deep it was like dying. Darkness was heavy and I was trying to swim through it, my body like lead, as the ringing telephone by my bed was abruptly cut off by my answering machine.

". . . don't know when I'll be able to call back, so listen. Please listen, Kay. I heard about Cary Harper . . ."

My heart was pounding as my eyes opened, Mark's urgent voice pulling me out of my torpor.

". . . Please stay out of it. Don't get involved. *Please*. I'll talk to you again as soon as I'm able . . ."

By the time I found the receiver I was listening to a dial tone. Replaying his message, I slumped against pillows and began to cry.

9

THE NEXT MORNING Marino arrived at the morgue as I was making a Y incision on Cary Harper's body.

I removed the breastplate of ribs and lifted the block of organs out of the chest cavity while Marino looked on mutely. Water drummed in sinks, surgical instruments clattered and clicked, and across the suite a long blade rasped against a whetstone as one of the morgue assistants sharpened a knife. We had four cases this morning, all of the stainless-steel autopsy tables occupied.

Since Marino didn't seem inclined to volunteer anything, I introduced the subject.

"What have you found out about Jeb Price?" I asked.

"His record check didn't come up with squat," he replied, staring off and restless. "No priors, no outstanding warrants, nothing. He ain't singing, either. If he was, it'd probably be soprano after the number you done on him. I stopped by ID right before I came down here. They're developing the film in his camera. I'll bring by a set of prints as soon as they're ready."

"Have you taken a look?"

"At the negatives," he answered.

"And?" I asked.

"Pictures he took inside the fridge. Of the Harpers' bodies," he said.

I had expected as much. "I don't suppose he's a journalist for some tabloid," I said in jest.

"Yo. Dream on."

I glanced up from what I was doing. Marino was not in a jovial mood. More disheveled than usual, he had nicked his jaw twice while shaving and his eyes were bloodshot.

"Most reporters I know don't pack nine mils loaded with Glasers," he said. "And they tend to whine when they get leaned on, ask for a quarter to call the paper's lawyer. This guy's not making a peep, a real pro. Must've picked a lock to get in. Makes his move on a Monday afternoon, a state holiday, when it's not likely anybody's going to be around. We found his ride parked about three blocks away in the Farm Fresh lot, a rental car with a cellular phone. Got enough ammo clips and magazines in the trunk to stop a small army, plus a Mac Ten machine pistol and a Kevlar vest. He ain't no reporter."

"I'm not so sure he's a *pro*, either," I commented, fitting a new blade in my scalpel. "It was sloppy to leave an empty film box inside the refrigerator. And if he really wanted to play it safe, he should have broken in at two or three in the morning, not in broad daylight."

"You're right. The film box was sloppy," Marino agreed. "But I can see why he broke in when he did. A funeral home or squad comes in to deliver a body while Price's inside the fridge, right? In the middle of the day, maybe he's smooth enough to make it appear he works here, has a legit reason for being inside. But let's say he's surprised at two A.M. No way in hell he's going to be able to explain himself at that hour."

Whatever the case, I thought, Jeb Price meant business. Glaser Safety Slugs were one of the worst things out, the cartridges packed with small shot that disperse on impact and tear through flesh and organs like a lead hailstorm. Mac Tens are a favorite occupational tool of terrorists and drug lords, the machine pistols a dime a dozen in Central America, the Middle East, and my hometown of Miami.

"You might consider putting a lock on the fridge," Marino added.

"I've already alerted Buildings and Grounds," I said.

It was a precaution I had put off for years. Funeral homes and squads had to be able to get inside the refrigerator after hours. The security guards would have to be given keys. My local medical examiners on call would have to be given keys. There would be protests. There would be problems. Damn it, I was getting so tired of problems!

Marino had turned his attention to Harper's body. It didn't require an autopsy or a genius to determine the cause of death.

"He has multiple fractures of the skull and lacerations of the brain," I explained.

"His throat was cut last, like in Beryl's case?"

"The jugular veins and carotid arteries are transected, yet his organs aren't particularly pale," I answered. "He would have hem-orrhaged to death in a matter of minutes if he'd had a blood pres-sure. In other words, he didn't bleed out enough to account for his death. He was dead or dying from his head injuries by the time his throat was cut."

"What about defense injuries?" Marino asked.

"None." I set down the scalpel to show him, one by one forcing open Harper's unwilling fingers. "No broken nails, cuts or contusions. He didn't attempt to ward off the blows of the weapon."

"Never knew what hit him," Marino commented. "He drives in after dark. The drone's waiting for him, probably hiding in the bushes. Harper parks, gets out of his Rolls. He's locking his door when the guy comes up behind him and hits him in the back of the head—"

"He has twenty percent stenosis of his LAD," I thought out loud, looking for my pencil.

"Harper goes down like a shot and the squirrel keeps swing-ing," Marino went on.

"Thirty percent of his right coronary." I scribbled notes on an empty glove packet. "No scarring from old infarcts. Heart's healthy but mildly enlarged, and he's got calcification of his aorta, moderate atherosclerosis."

"Then the guy slashes Harper's throat. Probably to make damn sure he's dead."

I looked up.

"Whoever did it wanted to make sure Harper was dead," Marino repeated.

"I don't know that I'd attribute such rational thinking to the assailant," I replied. "Look at him, Marino." I had deflected the scalp back from the skull, which was shattered like a hardboiled egg. Pointing out the fracture lines, I explained, "He was struck at least seven times with such force that none of the injuries was survivable. Then his throat was cut. It's overkill. Just as it was in Beryl's case."

"Okay. Overkill. I'm not arguing," he replied. "I'm just saying the killer wanted to make sure Beryl and Harper was dead. You nearly cut someone's damn head off, and you can walk away with the certainty your victim ain't going to be revived to tell the story."

Marino made a face as I began emptying the stomach contents into a cardboard container.

"Don't bother. I can tell you what he ate, was sitting right there. Beer nuts. And two martinis," he said.

The peanuts had barely begun clearing Harper's stomach when he died. There was nothing else but brownish fluid, and I could smell the alcohol.

I asked Marino, "What did you find out from him?"

"Not a damn thing."

I glanced at him as I labeled the container.

"I'm in the tavern drinking tonic and lime," he said. "I guess this was about quarter of. Harper walks in at five on the nose."

"How did you know it was him?" The kidneys were finely granular. I set them in the scale and jotted down the weights.

"Couldn't miss him with that mane of white hair," Marino replied. "He fit Poteat's description. I knew the second he walked in. He takes a table to himself and don't say nothing to nobody, just orders his 'usual' and eats beer nuts while he waits. I watch him for a while, then go over, pull up a chair and introduce myself. He says he's got nothing he can help me out with and he don't want to talk about it. I press him, tell him Beryl was being threatened for months, ask if he was aware of that. He looks annoyed, says he didn't know."

"Do you think he was telling the truth?" I was also wondering what the truth was about Harper's drinking. He had a fatty liver.

"No way for me to know," Marino said, flicking a cigarette ash on the floor. "Next I ask him where he was the night she was murdered, and he tells me he was in the tavern at his usual time, went home afterwards. When I ask if his sister can verify that, he tells me she wasn't home."

I looked up in surprise, the scalpel poised midair. "Where was she?"

"Out of town," he said.

"He didn't tell you where?"

"No. He said, and I quote, 'That's her business. Don't ask me.' " Marino's eyes fixed disdainfully on the sections of liver I was cutting. He added, "My favorite food used to be liver an' onions. You believe that? I don't know a single cop who's seen an autopsy and still eats liver . . ."

The Stryker saw drowned him out as I began work on the head. Marino gave up and backed away as bony dust drifted on the pungent air. Even when bodies are in good shape they smell bad when opened up. The visual experience isn't exactly Mary Poppins, either. I had to give Marino credit. No matter how awful the case, he always came to the morgue.

Harper's brain was soft, with numerous ragged lacerations. There was very little hemorrhage, verifying that he hadn't lived long after sustaining the injuries. At least his death was mercifully quick. Unlike Beryl, Harper had no time to register terror or pain or to beg for his life. His murder was different from hers in several other ways, as well. He had received no threats—at least none that we knew about. There were no sexual overtones. He had been beaten versus stabbed to death, and no articles of his clothing were missing.

"I counted one hundred and sixty-eight dollars in his wallet," I told Marino. "And his wristwatch and signet ring are present and accounted for."

"What about his necklace?" he asked.

I had no idea what he was talking about.

"He had on this thick gold chain with a medal on it, a shield, sort of like a coat of arms," he explained. "I noticed it at the tavern."

"It didn't come in with him, and I don't recall seeing it on him at the scene . . ." I started to say "last night." It wasn't last night. Harper had died early Sunday night. It was Tuesday now. I had lost all sense of time. The last two days seemed unreal, and had I not replayed Marks's message again this morning I would wonder if his call were real, too.

"So maybe the squirrel took it. Anoter souvenir," Marino said.

"That doesn't make sense," I answered. "I can understand the taking of a souvenir in Beryl's case, if her murder is the handiwork of a deranged individual who had an obsession with her. But why take something from Harper?"

"Trophies, maybe," Marino suggested. "Pelts from the hunt. Could be some hired hun who likes to keep little reminders of his jobs."

I would think a hired gun would be too careful for that," I countered.

"Yeah, you'd think so. Just like you'd think Jeb Price would be too careful to leave a film box in the fridge," he said ironically.

Peeling off my gloves, I finished labeling test tubes and other specimens I had collected. I gathered my paperwork and Marino followed me upstairs to my office.

Rose had left the afternoon newspaper on my blotter. Harper's murder and his sister's sudden death were the front-page headline. The accompanying sidebar was what ruined my day:

CHIEF MEDICAL EXAMINER ACCUSED OF "LOSING" CONTROVERSIAL MANUSCRIPT

The dateline was New York, an Associated Press release, and the lead was followed by an account of my "incapacitating" a man named Jeb Price after catching him "ransacking" my office yesterday afternoon. The allegations about the manuscript had to have come from Sparacino, I thought angrily. The bit about Jeb Price must have come from the police report, and as I shuffled through message slips, I noted that the majority of them were from reporters.

"Did you ever check out her computer disks?" I asked, tossing the paper to Marino.

"Oh, yeah," he said. "I've been through 'em."

"And did you find this book everybody's in such a tizzy about?"

Perusing the front page, he muttered, "Nope."

"It's not there?" I broke out in frustration. "It's not on her disks? How can that be if she was writing it on her computer?"

"Don't ask me," he said. "I'm just telling you I looked at maybe a dozen disks. Nothing recent on 'em. Looks like old stuff, you know, her novels. Nothing about herself, about Harper. Found a couple of old letters, including two business letters to Sparacino. They didn't excite me."

"Maybe she put the disks in a safe place before she left for Key West," I said.

"Maybe she did. But we ain't found 'em."

Just then Fielding walked in, his orangutan arms hanging out of the short sleeves of his surgical greens, his muscular hands

lightly coated with the talc lining the latex gloves he had been wearing downstairs. Fielding was his own work of art. God knows how
many hours each week he spent sculpting himself in some Nau-
tilus room somewhere. It was my theory that his obsession with
body building was inversely proportional to his obsession with his
job. A competent deputy chief, he had been on board little more
than a year and was already showing signs of burnout. The more
disenchanted he got, the bigger he got. I gave him another two years
before he retreated to the tidier, more lucrative world of hospital
pathology, or became the heir apparent to the Incredible Hulk.

"I'm going to have to pend Sterling Harper," he said, hovering
restlessly at the edge of my desk. "Her STAT alcohol's only point
oh-three, nothing in her gastric that tells me much. No bleeding,
no unusual odors. The heart's good, no evidence of old infarcts,
her coronaries clear. Brain's normal. But something was going on
with her. The liver's enlarged, around twenty-five hundred grams,
and the spleen's about a thousand with thickening of the capsule.
Some involvement of the lymph nodes, as well."

"Any metastases?" I asked.

"None on gross."

"Put a rush on the micros," I told him.

Fielding nodded and briskly left.

Marino looked questioningly at me.

"Could be a lot of things," I said. "Leukemia, lymphoma, or any
one of a number of collagen diseases—some of which are benign,
and some of which aren't. The spleen and lymph nodes react as a
component of the immune system—in other words, the spleen is
almost always involved in any blood disease. As for the big liver, that
doesn't help us much diagnostically. I won't know anything until I
can look at the histologic changes under the scope."

"You want to speak English for a change?" He lit a cigarette. "Tell me in simple terms what Doc-tor Schwarzenegger
found."

"Her immune system was reacting to something," I said. "She
was sick."

"Sick enough to account for her flaking out on her sofa?"

"That suddenly?" I said. "I doubt it."

"What about some sort of prescription drug?" he suggested.
"You know, she takes all the pills and tosses the bottle in the fire,
maybe explaining the melted plastic you found in the fireplace and

the fact we didn't find no pill bottles or nothing in the house. Just over-the-counter crap."

A drug overdose was certainly high on my list, and there wasn't any point in my worrying about it at the moment. Despite my pleading, despite promises that her case would be a top priority, the toxicology results would take days, possibly weeks.

As for her brother, I had a theory.

"I think Cary Harper was struck with a homemade slapjack, Marino," I said. "Possibly a segment of metal pipe filled with bird shot for weight, the ends packed with something like Play-Doh to hold in the shot. After several blows, a wad of the Play-Doh flew out and the shot scattered."

He thoughtfully tapped an ash. "Don't exactly fit with the 'soldier of fortune' shit we found in Price's car. Not with anything Old Lady Harper might have thought up, either."

"I assume you didn't find anything like Play-Doh, modeling clay, or birdshot inside her house."

He shook his head and said, "Hell, no."

My phone did not stop ringing the rest of the day.

Accounts of my alleged role in the disappearance of a "mysterious and valuable manuscript," and exaggerated descriptions of my "disabling an attacker" who broke into my office, had made the wire services. Other reporters were trying to cash in on the scoop, some of them prowling the OCME's parking lot or appearing in the lobby, their microphones and cameras ready like rifles. One particularly irreverent local DJ was sending out over the airwaves that I was the only woman chief in the country who wore "golden gloves instead of rubber ones." The situation was quickly getting out of control, and I was beginning to take Mark's warnings a little more seriously. Sparacino was perfectly capable of making my life miserable.

Whenever Thomas Ethridge IV had something on his mind, he dialed my direct line instead of going through Rose. I wasn't surprised when he called. I suppose I was relieved. It was late afternoon and we were sitting inside his office. He was old enough to be my father, one of those men whose homeliness in youth is gradually transformed by age into a monument of character. Ethridge had a Winston Churchill face that belonged in Parliament or a cigar smoke–filled drawing room. We had always gotten along extremely well.

"A publicity stunt? You think it likely anybody's going to believe that, Kay?" the attorney general asked as he absently fingered the rose-gold watch chain looped over his vest.

"I get the feeling *you* don't believe me," I said.

His response was to reach for a fat black Mont Blanc fountain pen and slowly unscrew the cap.

"I don't suppose anyone will get the chance to believe or dis-believe me," I added lamely. "My suspicions aren't founded on anything concrete, Tom. I make an accusation of this nature to counter what Sparacino's doing and he's going to have all the more fun."

"You're feeling very isolated, aren't you, Kay?"

"Yes. Because I am, Tom."

"Situations like this have a way of taking on a life of their own," he mused. "Problem's going to be nipping this one in the bud without generating more attention."

Rubbing his tired eyes behind horn-rimmed glasses, he turned to a fresh page in a legal pad and began making out one of his Nixonian lists, a line drawn down the center of the yellow page, advantages on one side, disadvantages on the other—advantages or disadvantages to what I had no idea. After filling half a page, one column dramatically longer than the other, he leaned back in his chair, looked up, and frowned.

"Kay," he said, "does it ever strike you that you seem to get more involved in your cases than your predecessors did?"

"I didn't know any of my predecessors," I replied.

He smiled a little. "That's not an answer to my question, Counselor."

"I honestly have never given the matter any thought," I said.

"Wouldn't expect you to," he surprised me by saying. "Wouldn't expect that at all because you're focused as hell, Kay. Which is just one of several reasons I solidly backed your appointment. The good side is you don't miss anything, are a damn good forensic patholo-gist in addition to being a fine administrator. The bad side is you tend to place yourself in jeopardy on occasion. Those strangling cases a year or so ago, for example. They might never have been solved and more women might have died were it not for you. But they almost cost you your life.

"Now this incident yesterday." He paused, then shook his head and laughed. "Though I have to admit I'm rather impressed. 'Decked him,' I believe I heard on the radio this morning. Did you *really*?"

"Not exactly," I replied uncomfortably.

"Do you know who he is, what he was looking for?"

"We're not sure," I said. "But he went inside the morgue refrigerator and took photographs. Photographs of Cary and Sterling Harper's bodies. The files he was looking through when I walked in on him didn't tell me anything."

"Alphabetized?"

"He was in the M through N drawer," I said.

"M as in Madison?"

"Possibly," I replied. "But her case is locked up in the front office. Nothing about her is in my filing cabinets."

After a long silence, he tapped the legal pad with his index finger and said, "I've been writing out what I know about these recent deaths. Beryl Madison, Cary Harper, Sterling Harper. Has all the trappings of a mystery novel, doesn't it? And now this intrigue over a missing manuscript that allegedly involves the medical examiner's office. What I have to say to you are a couple of things, Kay. First, if anybody else calls about the manuscript, I think it will make life easier if you refer the interested parties to my office. I fully expect some trumped-up lawsuit to follow. I'll get my staff involved now, see if we can head off the posse at the pass. Second, and I've been giving this a lot of careful consideration, I want you to be like an iceberg."

"What, exactly, is that supposed to mean?" I asked uneasily.

"What protrudes from the surface is but a fraction of what's really below," he answered. "This is not to be confused with keeping a low profile, even though you *will* be keeping a low profile for all practical purposes. Minimal statements to the press, making yourself as much a nonissue as possible." He began fingering his watch chain again. "Inversely proportional to your invisibility will be your level of activity, or involvement, if you will."

"My involvement?" I protested. "Is this your way of telling me to do my job, nothing but my job, and to keep the office out of the limelight?"

"Yes and no. Yes to doing your job. As for keeping the medical examiner's office out of the limelight, I'm afraid that may be out of your control." He paused, folding his hands on top of his desk. "I'm quite familiar with Robert Sparacino."

"You've met him?" I asked.

"I had the distinct misfortune of making his acquaintance in law school," he said.

I looked at him in disbelief.

"Columbia, class of 'fifty-one," Ethridge went on. "An obese, arrogant young man with a serious character defect. He was also very bright and might have graduated top of the class and gone on to clerk for the chief justice had I not gotten compulsive." He paused. "I went to Washington and enjoyed the privilege of working for Hugo Black. Robert stayed in New York."

"Has he ever forgiven you?" I asked, a cloud of suspicion gathering. "I'm assuming there must have been a lot of rivalry. Has he ever forgiven you for beating him out, graduating at the top?"

"He never fails to send me a Christmas card," Ethridge said dryly. "Generated from a computer list, his signature stamped, my name misspelled. Just impersonal enough to be insulting."

It was beginning to make more sense why Ethridge wanted all battles with Sparacino routed through the AG's office. "You don't think it's possible he's causing this trouble with me to get to you," I offered hesitantly.

"What? That the missing manuscript is all a ruse and he knows it? That he's causing a stink in the Commonwealth to in-directly give me a black eye and a lot of headaches?" He smiled grimly. "I think it's unlikely this would be the whole of his motiva-tion."

"But it might be added incentive," I commented. "He would know that any legal snafus, any potential litigation involving my office would be handled by the state's attorney. What I hear you telling me is he's a vindictive man."

Ethridge began slowly tapping his fingertips together as he stared off and said, "Let me tell you something I heard about Robert Sparacino when we were at Columbia. He's from a bro-ken home and lived with his mother while his estranged father made a lot of money on Wall Street. Apparently, the kid visited his father in New York several times a year, was precocious, a prolific reader quite taken with the literary world. On one such visit he managed to persuade his father to take him to lunch at the Algonquin on a day that Dorothy Parker and her Round Table were supposed to be there. Robert, no more than nine or ten at the time, had it all planned, according to the story, which he apparently told to several drinking buddies at Columbia. He would approach Dorothy Parker's table, offer his hand, and introduce himself by saying, 'Miss Parker, it's such a pleasure to meet you,' and so on. When he got to her table, what emerged instead was 'Miss Parker, it's such a meet to pleasure you.' Whereupon she quipped, as only she could, 'So many men have said, though none quite as young as you.' The laughter that followed mortified Sparacino, humiliated him. He never forgot it."

The image of the little fatso offering his sweaty hand and saying such a thing was so pathetic I didn't laugh. Had I been that embarrassed by a childhood hero, I never would have forgotten it, either.

"I tell you this," Ethridge said, "to demonstrate a point that has been corroborated by now, Kay. When Sparacino told this story at Columbia, he was drunk and bitter and loudly promising he would get his revenge, show Dorothy Parker and the rest of the elitist world he's not to be laughed at. And what's happened?" He looked appraisingly at me. "He's one of the most powerful book lawyers in the country, mingles freely with editors, agents, writers, all of whom may privately hate him but find it unwise not to fear him. Supposedly he regularly lunches at the Algonquin, and insists on signing all movie and book contracts there while he no doubt inwardly smirks at Dorothy Parker's ghost." He paused. "Sound farfetched?"

"No. One doesn't need to be a psychologist to figure it out," I said.

"Here's what I'm going to suggest," Ethridge said, his eyes fixed on mine. "Let me handle Sparacino. I want you to have no contact with him at all, if possible. You mustn't underestimate him, Kay. Even when you think you've told him very little, he's reading between the lines, is a master at making inferences that can be uncannily on the mark. I'm not sure what his involvement with Beryl Madison, the Harpers, really was or what his real agenda is. Perhaps a mixture of unsavory things. But I don't want him knowing any more details about these deaths than he already knows."

"He's already gotten a lot," I said. "Beryl Madison's police report, for example. Don't ask me how—"

"He's very resourceful," Ethridge interrupted. "I advise you to keep all reports out of circulation, send them only where you must. Tighten the lid on your office, beef up security, every file under lock and key. Make sure your staff releases no information about these cases to anyone unless you're absolutely certain the person calling in the request is who he says he is. Every crumb Sparacino will use to his advantage. It's a game to him. Many people could be hurt—including you. Not to mention what could happen to the cases come court time. After one of his typical publicity blitzes we'd have to change the damn venue to Antarctica."

"He may have anticipated that you'll do this," I said quietly.

"That I'd relegate myself to being the lightning rod? Step into the ring instead of letting an assistant handle it?"

I nodded.

"Well, perhaps so," he answered.

I was sure of it. I wasn't Sparacino's intended quarry. His old nemesis was. Sparacino couldn't pick on the attorney general directly. He would never get past the watchdogs, the aides, the secretaries. So Sparacino picked on me instead and was being rewarded with the desired result. The idea of being used this way only made me angrier, and Mark suddenly came to mind. What was his role in this?

"You're annoyed and I don't blame you," Ethridge said. "And you're just going to have to swallow your pride, your emotions, Kay. I need your help."

I just listened.

"The ticket that will get us out of Sparacino's amusement park, I strongly suspect, is this manuscript everyone's so interested in. Any possibility you might be able to track it down?"

I felt my face getting hot. "It never came through my office, Tom—"

"Kay," he said firmly, "that's not my question. A lot of things never come through your office and the medical examiner manages to track them down. Prescription drugs, a complaint of chest pain overheard at some point before the decedent suddenly dropped dead, suicidal ideations you somehow manage to get a family member to divulge. You have no power of enforcement, but you can investigate. And sometimes you're going to find out details no one is ever going to tell the police."

"I don't want to be an ordinary witness, Tom."

"You're an expert witness. Of course you don't want to be ordinary. It's a waste," he said.

"And the cops are usually better interrogators," I added. "They don't expect people to tell the truth."

"Do you expect it?" he asked.

"Your local friendly doctor usually expects it, expects people to tell the truth as they perceive it. They do the best they can. Most docs don't expect the patient to lie."

"Kay, you're speaking in generalities," he said.

"I don't want to be in the position—"

"Kay, the Code reads that the medical examiner shall make an investigation into the cause and manner of death and reduce his findings to writing. This is very broad. It gives you full investigative powers. The only thing you can't do is actually arrest somebody. You know that. The police are never going to find that manuscript. You're the only person who can find it." He looked levelly at me. "It's *more important* to you, to your good name, than it is to them."

There was nothing I could do. Ethridge had declared war on Sparacino, and I had been drafted.

"Find that manuscript, Kay." The attorney general glanced at his watch. "I know you. You put your mind to it, you'll find it or at least discover what's become of it. Three people are dead. One of them a Pulitzer Prize-winner whose book happens to be a favorite of mine. We need to get to the bottom of this. In addition, everything you turn up that relates to Sparacino you report back to me. You'll try, won't you?"

"Yes, sir," I replied. "Of course I'll try."

I began by badgering the scientists.

Documents examination is one of very few scientific procedures that can supply answers right before your eyes. It is as concrete as paper and as tangible as ink. By late Wednesday afternoon the section chief, whose name was Will, and Marino and I had been at it for hours. What we were discovering was a vivid reminder that not one of us is above being driven to drink.

I wasn't sure what I was hoping. Maybe it would have been a simple solution had we determined right off that what Miss Harper had burned in her fireplace was Beryl's missing manuscript. Then we might conclude that Beryl had relegated it to the safekeeping of her friend. We might assume that the work contained indiscretions that Miss Harper chose not to share with the world. Most important, we could conclude that the manuscript really had not, after all, disappeared from the crime scene.

But the amount and type of paper we were examining were not consistent with these possibilities. There were very few unburned fragments, none bigger than a dime or worth placing under the infrared-filter-covered lens of the video comparator. No technical aids or chemical tests were going to assist us in examining the remaining tissuey white curls of ash. They were so fragile we didn't dare remove them from the shallow cardboard box Marino had collected them in, and we had shut the door and vents of the documents lab to keep the room as airless as possible.

What we were doing amounted to a frustrating, painstaking task of nudging weightless ashes aside with tweezers, picking here, picking there, for a word. So far we knew that Miss Harper had burned sheets of twenty-pound rag paper imprinted with characters typed with a carbon ribbon. We could be sure of this for several reasons. Paper produced from wood pulp turns black when incinerated, while paper made from cotton is incredibly clean, its ashes wispy white like the ones in Miss Harper's fireplace. The few unburned fragments we looked at were consistent with twenty-pound stock. Finally, carbon does not burn. The heat had shrunk the typed characters to what was comparable to fine print, or approximately twenty pitch. Some words were present in their entirety, standing out blackly against the filmy white ash. The rest were hopelessly fragmented and sullied like sooty bits of tiny paper fortunes from Chinese cookies.

"*A R R I V*," Will spelled out, eyes bloodshot behind unstylish black-framed glasses, his young face weary. He was having to work at being patient.

I added the partial word to the half-filled page of my notepad.

"Arrived, arriving, arrive," he added with a sigh. "Can't think of what else it could be."

"Arrival, arriviste," I thought out loud.

"*Arriviste?*" Marino asked sourly. "What the hell is that?"

"As in social climber," I replied.

"A little too esoteric for me," Will said humorlessly.

"Probably a little too esoteric for most people," I conceded, wishing for the bottle of Advil downstairs in my pocketbook and blaming my persistent headache on eyestrain.

"Jesus," Marino complained. "Words, words, words. Never seen so many words in my damn life. Never heard of half of 'em and not sorry about the fact, either."

He was leaning back in a swivel chair, his feet propped on a desk, as he continued reading the transcription of writings Will had deciphered from the ribbon removed from Cary Harper's type-writer. The ribbon wasn't carbon, meaning the pages Miss Harper burned could not have come from her brother's typewriter. It appeared that the novelist had been working in fits and starts on yet another book attempt. Most of what Marino was looking at didn't make much sense, and when I had perused it earlier I had wondered if Harper's inspiration had been of the bottled variety.

"Wonder if you could sell this shit," Marino said.

Will had fished another sentence fragment out of the god-awful sooty mess, and I was leaning close to inspect it.

"You know," Marino went on. "They're always coming out with stuff after a famous writer dies. Most of it crap the poor guy never wanted published to begin with."

"Yes. They could call it *Table Scraps from a Literary Banquet*," I muttered.

"Huh?"

"Never mind. There's not even ten pages there, Marino," I said abstractedly. "Rather hard to get a book out of that."

"Yeah. So it gets published in *Esquire*, maybe *Playboy*, instead of a book. Probably still worth some bucks," Marino said.

"This word is definitely indicating a proper name of a place or company or something," Will mused, oblivious to the conversation around him. "*Co* is capitalized."

I said, "Interesting. Very interesting."

Marino got up to take a look.

"Be careful not to breathe," Will warned, the tweezers in his hand steady as a scalpel as he gingerly manipulated the wisp of white ash on which tiny black letters spelled out *bor Co*.

"County, company, country, college," I suggested. My blood was beginning to flow again, waking me up.

"Yeah, but what would have *bor* in it?" Marino puzzled.

"Ann Arbor?" Will suggested.

"What about a county in Virginia?" Marino asked.

We couldn't come up with any county in Virginia that ended with the letters *bor*.

"Harbor," I said.

"Okay. But followed by *Co*?" Will replied dubiously.

"Maybe something-Harbor Company," Marino said.

I looked in the telephone directory. There were five businesses with names beginning with Harbor: Harbor East, Harbor South, Harbor Village, Harbor Imports, and Harbor Square.

"Don't sound like we're in the right ball park," Marino said.

We didn't fare any better when I dialed directory assistance and asked for the names of any businesses in the Williamsburg area called Harbor-this or Harbor-that. Other than one apartment complex, there was nothing. Next I called Detective Poteat of the Williamsburg Police, and other than that same apartment complex, he couldn't think of anything, either.

"Maybe we shouldn't get too hung up on this," Marino said testily.

Will was engrossed in the box of ashes again.

Marino looked over my shoulder at the list of words we had found so far.

You, your, I, my, we, and *well* were common. Other complete words included the mortar of everyday sentence constructions—*and, is, was, that, this, which, a,* and *an*. Some words were a bit more specific, such as *town, home, know, please, fear, work, think,* and *miss*. As for incomplete words, we could only guess at what they had been in their former life. A derivation of *terrible* apparently was used numerous times for lack of any other common word we could think of that began with *terri* or *terrib*. Nuance, of course, was forever lost on us. Did the person mean terrible, as in "It is so terrible"? Did the person mean terribly, as in "I am terribly upset" or "I miss you terribly"? Or was it as benign as "It is terribly nice of you"?

Significantly, we found several remnants of the name Sterling and just as many remnants of the name Cary.

"I'm fairly certain what she burned was personal letters," I decided. "The type of paper, the words used, make me think that."

Will agreed.

"Do you remember finding any stationery in Beryl Madison's house?" I asked Marino.

"Computer paper, typing paper. That's about it. None of this high-dollar rag you're talking about," he said.

"Her printer uses ink ribbons," Will reminded us as he anchored an ash with tweezers and added, "I think we may have another one."

I took a look.

This time all that was left was *or C.*

"Beryl had a Lanier computer and printer," I said to Marino. "I think it might be a good idea to find out if that's what she always had."

"I went through her receipts," he said.

"For how many years?" I asked.

"As many as she had. Five, six," he answered.

"Same computer?"

"No," he said. "But same damn printer, Doc. Something called a sixteen-hundred, with a daisy wheel. Always used the same kind of ribbons. Got no idea what she wrote with before that."

"I see."

"Yo, glad you do," Marino complained, kneading the small of his back. "Me, I'm not seeing a goddamn thing."

10

THE FBI NATIONAL ACADEMY in Quantico, Virginia, is a brick and glass oasis in the midst of an artificial war. I would never forget my first stay there years ago. I went to bed and got up to the sound of semiautomatics going off, and when I took a wrong turn on the wooded fitness course one afternoon, I was almost flattened by a tank.

It was Friday morning. Benton Wesley had scheduled a meeting, and Marino perked up visibly as the Academy's fountain and flags came into view. I had to take two steps for his every one as I followed him inside the spacious sunny lobby of a new building that looked enough like a fine hotel to have earned the nickname Quantico Hilton. Checking his handgun at the front desk, Marino signed us in, and we clipped on visitor's passes while a receptionist buzzed Wesley to affirm our privileged clearance.

A maze of glass hyphens connect sections of offices, classrooms, and laboratories, and one can go from building to building without ever stepping outside. No matter how often I came here, I always got lost. Marino seemed to know where he was going, so I dutifully stayed on his heels and watched the parade of color-coded students pass. Red shirts and khaki trousers were police officers. Gray shirts with black fatigues tucked into spit-polished boots were new DEA agents, with the veterans dressed ominously in solid black. New FBI agents wore blue and khaki, while members of the elitist Hostage Teams wore solid white. Men and women were impeccably groomed and remarkably fit. They carried with them a mien of militaristic reserve as tangible as the odor of the gun-cleaning solvent they left in their wake.

We boarded a service elevator and Marino punched the button designated *LL* (for Low Low, so the joke goes). Hoover's secret bomb shelter is sixty feet under ground, two stories below the indoor firing range. It has always seemed appropriate to me that the Academy decided to locate its Behavioral Science Unit closer to hell than heaven. Titles change. The last I heard, the Bureau was calling profilers Criminal Investigative Agents, or CIAs (an acronym destined for confusion). The work doesn't change. There will always be pyschopaths, sociopaths, lust murderers—whatever one chooses to call evil people who find pleasure in causing unthinkable pain.

We got off the elevator and followed a drab hallway to a drab outer office. Wesley emerged and showed us into a small conference room, where Roy Hanowell was sitting at a long polished table. The fibers expert never seemed to remember me on sight from one meeting to the next. I always made a point of introducing myself when he offered his hand.

"Of course, of course, Dr. Scarpetta. How are you?" he inquired, just as he always did.

Wesley shut the door and Marino looked around, scowling when he couldn't find an ashtray. An empty Diet Coke can in a trash basket would have to do. I resisted the impulse to dig out my own pack. The Academy was about as smokeless as an intensive care unit.

Wesley's white shirt was wrinkled in back, his eyes tired and preoccupied as he began perusing paperwork inside a folder. He immediately got down to business.

"Anything new on Sterling Harper?" he asked.

I had reviewed her histology slides yesterday and wasn't unduly surprised by what I had found. Nor was I any closer to understanding her cause of sudden death.

"She had chronic myelocytic leukemia," I replied.

Wesley glanced up. "Cause of death?"

"No. In fact, I can't even be sure she knew she had it," I said.

"That's interesting," Hanowell commented. "You can have leukemia and not know it?"

"The onset of chronic leukemia is insidious," I explained. "Her symptoms could have been as mild as night sweats, fatigue, weight loss. On the other hand, it could have been diagnosed some time ago and was in remission. She wasn't in a blast crisis. There were no progressive leukemic infiltrations, and she wasn't suffering from any significant infections."

Hanowell looked perplexed. "Then what killed her?"

"I don't know," I admitted.

"Drugs?" Wesley asked, making notes.

"The tox lab is beginning its second round of testing," I answered. "Her preliminary report shows a blood alcohol of point zero-three. In addition, she had dextromethorphan on board, which is an antitussive found in numerous over-the-counter cough suppressants. At the scene we found a bottle of Robitussin on top of the sink inside her upstairs bathroom. It was more than half full."

"So that didn't do it," Wesley muttered to himself.

"The entire bottle wouldn't do it," I told him, adding, "It's puzzling, I agree."

"You'll keep me posted? Let me know what turns up on her," Wesley said. More pages turned, and he went to the next item on his agenda. "Roy's examined the fibers from Beryl Madison's case. We want to talk to you about that. And then, Pete, Kay"—he glanced up at us—"I have another matter to take up with both of you."

Wesley looked anything but happy, and I had the feeling that his reason for summoning us here wasn't going to make me happy, either. Hanowell, in contrast, was his usual unperturbed self. His hair, eyebrows, and eyes were gray. Even his suit was gray. Whenever I saw him, he always looked half asleep and gray, so colorless and calm I was tempted to wonder if he had a blood pressure.

"With one exception," Hanowell laconically began, "the fibers I was asked to look at, Dr. Scarpetta, reveal few surprises—no unusual dyes or shapes at cross sections to speak of. I have concluded that the six nylon fibers most likely came from six different origins, just as your examiner in Richmond and I discussed. Four of them are consistent with the fabrics used in automobile carpeting."

"How do you figure that?" Marino asked.

"Nylon upholstery and carpeting degrade very quickly in sunlight and heat, as you might imagine," Hanowell said. "If the fibers aren't treated with a premetalized dye, thereby adding UV and thermal stabilizers, car carpet will bleach out or rot in short order. By using X-ray fluorescence I was able to detect trace amounts of metals in four of the nylon fibers. Though I can't say with certainty the origin of these fibers is car carpeting, they are consistent with that."

"Any chance of tracing them back to a make and model?" Marino wanted to know.

"I'm afraid not," Hanowell replied. "Unless we're talking about a very unusual fiber with a patented modification ratio, tracing the darn thing back to a manufacturer is pretty futile, especially if the vehicles in question were manufactured in Japan. Let me give you an example. The precursor to the carpeting in a Toyota is plastic pellets, which are shipped from this country to Japan. There they are spun into fibers, the yarn shipped back here to be made into carpet. The carpet is then sent back to Japan to be placed inside the cars coming off the line."

He droned on. It only got more hopeless.

"We also have headaches with cars manufactured in the United States. Chrysler Corporation, for example, may procure a certain color for its carpeting from three different suppliers. Then halfway through the model year Chrysler may decide to change suppliers. Let's say you and I are both driving 'eighty-seven black LeBarons with burgundy interior, Lieutenant. Well, the suppliers for the burgundy carpet in mine may be different from the suppliers in yours. Point is, the only significance of the nylon fibers I've examined is the variety. Two may be from household carpeting. Four may be from automobile carpeting. The colors and cross sections vary. You add to this the finding of olefin, Dynel, acrylic fibers, and what you've got is a hodgepodge I find most peculiar."

"Obviously," Wesley interjected, "the killer has a profession or some other preoccupation that puts him in contact with many different types of carpeting. And when he murdered Beryl Madison, he was wearing something that caused numerous fibers to adhere to him."

Wool, corduroy or flannel could account for that, I thought. But no wool or dyed cotton fibers had been found that were thought to have come from the killer.

"What about Dynel?" I asked.

"Usually associated with women's dresses. With wigs, fake furs," Hanowell answered.

"Yes, but not exclusively," I said. "A shirt or pair of slacks made of Dynel would build up static electricity like polyester, causing everything to stick to it. This might explain why he was carrying so much trace."

"Possibly," Hanowell said.

"So maybe the squirrel was wearing a wig," Marino proposed. "We know Beryl let him in her house, translated into she didn't feel threatened. Most ladies ain't going to feel threatened by a woman at the door."

"A transvestite?" Wesley suggested.

"Could be," Marino replied. "Some of the best-looking babes you'll ever see. It's friggin' sickening. Even I can't tell with a few of 'em unless I get right up in their faces."

"If the assailant were in drag," I pointed out, "how do we account for the fibers adhering to him? If the origin of the fibers is his workplace, certainly he wouldn't have been dressed in drag at work."

"Unless he works the streets in drag," Marino said. "He's in and out of johns' rides all night long, maybe in and out of motel rooms with carpeted floors."

"Then his victim selection doesn't make any sense," I said.

"No, but the absence of seminal fluid might make sense," Marino argued. "Male transvestites, faggots, usually don't go around raping women."

"They usually don't go around murdering them, either," I answered.

"I mentioned an exception," Hanowell resumed, glancing at his watch. "This is the orange acrylic fiber you were so curious about." His gray eyes fixed impassively on me.

"The three-leaf clover shape," I recalled.

"Yes," Hanowell said, nodding. "The shape is very unusual, the purpose, as is true with other trilobals, to hide dirt and scatter light. Only place I know you'll find fibers with this shape is in Plymouths manufactured in the late seventies—the fibers are in the nylon carpeting. They're the same three-leaf clover shape at cross section as the orange fiber in Beryl Madison's case."

"But the orange fiber is acrylic," I reminded him. "Not nylon."

"That's correct, Dr. Scarpetta," he said. "I'm giving you background in order to demonstrate the unique properties of the fiber in question. The fact that it is acrylic versus nylon, the fact that bright colors such as orange are almost never used in automobile carpeting, assists us in excluding the fiber from a number of origins—including Plymouths manufactured in the late seventies. Or any other automobile you might think of."

"So you're never seen anything like this orange fiber before?" Marino asked.

"That's what I'm leading up to." Hanowell hesitated.

Wesley took over. "Last year we got in a fiber identical to this orange one in every respect when Roy was asked to examine trace recovered from a Boeing seven forty-seven hijacked in Athens, Greece. I'm sure you recall the incident," he said.

Silence.

Even Marino was momentarily speechless.

Wesley went on, his eyes dark with trouble. "The hijackers murdered two American soldiers on board and dumped their bodies on the tarmac. Chet Ramsey was a twenty-four-year-old Marine, the first to be thrown out of the plane. The orange fiber was adhering to blood on his left ear."

"Could the fiber have come from the interior of the plane?" I asked.

"It doesn't appear so," Hanowell replied. "I compared it with exemplars of carpet, seat upholstery, the blankets stored in the overhead bins, and didn't come up with a match or even a near match. Either Ramsey picked up the fiber someplace else—and this doesn't seem likely since it was adhering to wet blood—or possibly it was the result of a passive transfer from one of the terrorists to him. The only other alternative I can think of is that the fiber came from one of the other passengers, but if so, this individual would have to have touched him at some point after he was injured. According to eyewitness accounts, none of the other passengers went near him. Ramsey was taken to the front of the plane, away from the other passengers, and beaten, shot, his body wrapped in one of the plane's blankets and thrown out onto the tarmac. The blanket, by the way, was tan."

Marino said it first, and he wasn't good humored about it, "You mind explaining how the hell a hijacking in Greece is connected with two writers getting whacked in Virginia?"

"The fiber connects at least two of the incidences," Hanowell replied. "The hijacking and Beryl Madison's death. This isn't to say that the actual crimes are connected, Lieutenant. But this orange fiber is so unusual we have to consider the possibility there may be some common denominator in what happened in Athens and what is happening here now."

It was more than a possibility, it was a certainty. There was a common denominator. Person, place, or thing, I thought. It had to be one of the three, and the details were slowly materializing in my mind.

I said, "They were never able to question the terrorists. Two of them ended up dead. Another two managed to escape and have never been caught."

Wesley nodded.

"Are we even certain they *were* terrorists, Benton?" I asked.

After a pause, he answered, "We've never succeeded in tying them in with any terrorist group. But the assumption is they were making an anti-American statement. The plane was American, as were a third of its passengers."

"What were the hijackers wearing?" I asked.

"Civilian clothes. Slacks, open-neck shirts, nothing unusual," he said.

"And no orange fibers were found on the bodies of the two hijackers killed?" I asked.

"We don't know," Hanowell answered. "They were gunned down on the tarmac, and we weren't able to move fast enough to claim the bodies and fly them over here for examination along with the slain American soldiers. Unfortunately, I got only the fiber report from the Greek authorities. I never actually examined the hijackers' clothing or trace myself. Obviously, quite a lot could have been missed. But even if there had been an orange fiber or two recovered from one of the hijacker's bodies, this still wouldn't necessarily tell us the origin."

"Hey, what are you telling me?" Marino demanded. "What? I'm supposed to think we're looking for an escaped hijacker who's now killing people in Virginia?"

"We can't completely rule it out, Pete," Wesley said. "Bizarre as it may seem."

"The four men who hijacked that plane have never been associated with any group," I recalled. "We really don't know the whole of their purpose or who they were, except that two of them were Lebanese—if my memory serves me well—the other two who escaped possibly Greek. It seems to me there was some speculation at the time that the real target was an American ambassador on vacation who was scheduled to be on that flight with his family."

"This is true," Wesley said tensely. "After the American embassy in Paris was bombed several days earlier, the ambassador's travel plans were secretly changed even though the reservations weren't."

His eyes glanced past me, and he was tapping an ink pen against the knuckle of his left thumb.

He added, "We haven't ruled out the possibility the hijackers were a hit squad, professional guns hired by somebody."

"Okay, okay," Marino said impatiently. "And no one's ruled out that Beryl Madison and Cary Harper might have been murdered by a professional gun. You know, their crimes staged to look like a squirrel did 'em in."

"I suppose one place to start would be to see what else we can find out about this orange fiber, its possible origin." Then I came right out and said it. "And maybe someone ought to look a little harder at Sparacino, make sure he wasn't somehow connected with that ambassador who may have been the real target in the hijacking."

Wesley didn't respond.

Marino suddenly got interested in trimming a thumbnail with his pocketknife.

Hanowell looked around the table, and when it seemed apparent we had no more questions for him, he excused himself and left.

Marino fired up another cigarette.

"You ask me," he said, blowing out a stream of smoke, "this is turning into a damn wild goose chase. I mean, it don't add up. Why hire some international hit man to snuff a lady romance writer and a has-been novelist who ain't produced nothing in years?"

"I don't know," Wesley said. "It all depends on who had what connections. Hell, it depends on a lot of things, Pete. Everything does. All we can do is follow the evidence as best we're able. This brings me to the next item on the agenda. Jeb Price."

"He's back on the street," Marino said automatically.

I looked at him in disbelief.

"Since when?" Wesley inquired.

"Yesterday," Marino replied. "He posted bail. Fifty grand, to be exact."

"You mind telling me how he managed that?" I said, furious that Marino hadn't told me this before now.

"Don't mind at all, Doc," he said.

There were three ways to post bail, I knew. The first was on personal recognizance, the second with cash or property, the third through a bail bondsman who charged a ten percent fee and demanded a cosigner or some other sort of security to assure he wasn't left holding an empty bag if the accused decided to skip town. Jeb Price, Marino said, had opted for the latter.

"I want to know how he managed that," I said again, getting out my cigarettes and scooting the Coke can closer so we could share.

"Only one way I know of. He called his lawyer, who opened a bank escrow account and sent a passbook to Lucky's," Marino said.

"Lucky's?" I asked.

"Yo. Lucky Bonding Company on Seventeenth Street, conveniently located a block from the city jail," Marino answered. "Charlie Luck's pawnshop for prisoners. Also know as Hock & Walk. Charlie and me go back a long time, shoot the breeze, tell a few jokes. Sometimes he snitches a little, other times he zips his lip. This is one of those other times, unfortunately. Nothing I could pull on him succeeded in getting me the name of Price's lawyer, but I've got a suspicion he ain't local."

"Price obviously has connections in high places," I said.

"Obviously," Wesley agreed grimly.

"And he never talked?" I asked.

"Had the right to remain silent, and he sure as hell did," Marino answered.

"What did you find out about his arsenal?" Wesley was making notes to himself again. "You run it through ATF?"

"Marino replied, "Comes back as registered to him, and he's got a license to carry a concealed weapon, issued six years ago by some senile judge up here in northern Virginia who's since retired and moved down south somewhere. According to the background check included in the record I got from the circuit court, Price was unmarried, was working in a D.C. gold and silver exchange called Finklestein's at the time he was issued the license. And guess what? Finklestein's ain't there no more."

"What about his DMV record?" Wesley continued to write.

"No tickets. An 'eighty-nine BMW is registered to him, his address in D.C., an apartment near Dupont Circle he apparently moved out of last winter. The rental office pulled his old lease, lists him as being self-employed. I'm still running it down, will get the IRS to pull records of his tax returns for the past five years."

"Possible he's a private eye?" I asked.

"Not in the District of Columbia,"Marino answered.

Wesley looked up at me and said, "Someone hired him. For what purpose, we still don't know. Clearly, he failed in his mission. Whoever's behind it may try again. I don't want you walking in on the next one, Kay."

"Would it be stating the obvious to say I don't want that either?"

"I guess what I'm telling you," he went on like a nonsense father, "is I want you to avoid placing yourself in any situation where you might be vulnerable. For example, I don't think it's a good idea for you to be in your office when no one else is inside the building. I don't mean just on the weekends. If you work until six, seven at night, and everybody else has gone home, it's not a good idea for you to be walking out into a dark parking lot to get in your car. Possible you can leave at five when there are eyes and ears around?"

"I'll keep it in mind," I said.

"Or if you have to leave later, Kay, then call the security guard and ask him to escort you to your car," Wesley went on.

"Hell, call me, for that matter," Marino was quick to volunteer. "You got my pager number. If I'm not available, ask the dispatcher to send a car by."

Fine, I thought. Maybe if I'm lucky I'll make it home by midnight.

"Just be extremely careful." Wesley looked hard at me. "All theories aside, two people have been murdered. The killer's still out there. The victimology, the motivation are sufficiently strange for me to believe anything's possible."

His words resurfaced more than once during the drive home. When anything is possible, nothing is impossible. One plus one does not equal three. Or does it? Sterling Harper's death did not seem to belong in the same equation as the deaths of her brother and Beryl. But what if it did?

"You told me Miss Harper was out of town the night Beryl was murdered," I said to Marino. "Have you learned anything more about that?"

"Nope."

"Wherever it was she went, do you suppose she drove?" I asked.

"Nope. Only car the Harpers had was the white Rolls, and her brother had it the night of Beryl's death."

"You know that?"

"Checked it out with Culpeper's Tavern," he said. "Harper came in his usual time that night. Drove up just like he always did and left around six-thirty."

In light of recent events, I doubted anybody thought it the least bit strange when I announced at staff conference the following Monday morning that I was taking annual leave.

The assumption was that my encounter with Jeb Price had stressed me to the point I needed to get away, regroup, bury my head in the sand for a while. I didn't tell anybody where I was going because I didn't know. I just walked out, leaving behind a secretly relieved secretary and an overwhelmed desk.

Returning home, I spent the entire morning on the phone, calling every airline that serviced Richmond's Byrd Airport, the airport most convenient for Sterling Harper.

"Yes, I know there's a twenty percent penalty," I said to the USAir ticket agent. "You misunderstand. I'm not trying to change the ticket. This was weeks ago. I'm trying to find out if she ever got on the flight at all."

"The ticket wasn't for you?"

"No," I said for the third time. "It was issued in *her* name."

"Then she really needs to contact us herself."

"Sterling Harper is dead," I said. "She can't contact you herself."

A startled pause.

"She died suddenly right around the time of a trip she was supposed to go on," I explained. "If you could just check your computer . . ."

This went on. It got to where I could recite the same lines without thinking. USAir had nothing, nor did the computers for Delta, United, American, or Eastern. As far as the agents could tell from their records, Miss Harper had not flown out of Richmond during the last week of October, when Beryl Madison was murdered. Miss Harper hadn't driven, either. I seriously doubted she had taken the bus. That left the train.

An Amtrak agent named John said his computer was down

and asked if he could call me back. I hung up as someone rang my doorbell.

It was not quite noon. The day was as tart and crisp as a fall apple. Sunlight painted white rectangles in my living room and winked off the windshield of the unfamiliar silver Mazda sedan parked in my drive. The pasty, blond young man I observed through the peephole was standing back from my front door, head down, the collar of a leather jacket up around his ears. My Ruger was hard and heavy in my hand, and I stuffed it in the pocket of my warmup jacket as I unfastened the dead bolt. I didn't recognize him until we were face-to-face.

"Dr. Scarpetta?" he asked nervously.

I made no move to let him inside, my right hand in my pocket and firm around the butt of the revolver.

"Please forgive me for appearing on your doorstep like this," he said. "I called your office and was told you're on vacation. I found your name in the book and the line was busy. So I concluded you were home. I, well, I really need to talk to you. May I come in?"

He looked even more innocuous in person than he had looked on the videotape Marino had shown me.

"What is this about?" I asked firmly.

"Beryl Madison, it's about her," he said. "Uh, my name's Al Hunt. I won't take much of your time. I promise."

I backed away from the door and he stepped inside. His face got as white as alabaster when he seated himself on my living room couch and his eyes fixed briefly on the butt of the revolver protruding from my pocket as I settled in a wing chair a safe distance away.

"Uh, you've got a gun?" he said.

"Yes, I do," I answered.

"I don't like them, like guns."

"They're not very likable," I agreed.

"No, ma'am," he said. "My father took me deer hunting once. When I was a boy. He hit a doe. She was crying. The doe, she was crying, lying on her side and crying. I never could shoot anything."

"Did you know Beryl Madison?" I asked.

"The police—The police have talked to me about her," he stammered. "A lieutenant. Marino, Lieutenant Marino. He came by the car wash where I work and talked to me, then asked me down to headquarters. We talked for a long time. She used to bring her car in. That's how I met her."

As he rambled on I couldn't help but wonder what "colors" were radiating from me. Steely blue? Maybe a hint of bright red because I was alarmed and doing my best not to show it? I contemplated ordering him to leave. I considered calling the police. I couldn't believe he was sitting inside my house, and perhaps the sheer audacity on his part and mystification on mine explains why I did nothing at all.

I interrupted him. "Mr. Hunt—"

"Please call me Al."

"Al, then," I said. "Why did you want to see me? If you have information, why aren't you talking to Lieutenant Marino?"

The color rose to his cheeks and he looked uncomfortably down at his hands.

"What I have to say doesn't really belong in the category of police information," he said. "I thought you might understand."

"Why would you think that? You don't know me," I answered.

"You took care of Beryl. As a rule, women are more intuitive, more compassionate than men," he said.

Perhaps it was that simple. Perhaps Hunt was here because he believed I would not humiliate him. He was staring at me now, a wounded, woebegone look in his eyes that was on the verge of becoming panic.

He asked, "Have you ever known something with certainty, Dr. Scarpetta, even though there is absolutely no evidence to support your belief?"

"I'm not clairvoyant, if that's what you're asking," I replied.

"You're being the scientist."

"I *am* a scientist."

"But you've had the feeling," he insisted, his eyes desperate now. "You know very well what I mean, don't you?"

"Yes," I said. "I think I know what you mean, Al."

He seemed relieved and took a deep breath. "I *know* things, Dr. Scarpetta. I know who murdered Beryl."

I didn't react at all.

"I *know* him, know what he thinks, feels, why he did it," he said with emotion. "If I tell you, will you promise to treat what I say with great care, consider it seriously and not— Well, I don't want you running to the police. They wouldn't understand. You see that, don't you?"

"I will very carefully consider what you have to say," I replied.

He leaned forward on the couch, his eyes luminous in his wan El Greco face. I instinctively moved my right hand closer to my pocket. I could feel the rubber grip of the revolver against the side of my palm.

"The police already don't understand," he said. "They aren't capable of understanding me. Why I left psychology, for example. The police wouldn't understand that. I have a master's degree. And what? I worked as a nurse and now I'm working in a car wash? You don't really think the police are going to understand that, do you?"

I didn't respond.

"When I was a kid I dreamed of being a psychologist, a social worker, maybe even a psychiatrist," he went on. "It all came so naturally to me. It was what I should be, what my talents directed that I should be."

"But you're not," I reminded him. "Why?"

"Because it would have destroyed me," he said, averting his eyes. "It isn't something I have control over, what happens to me. I relate so completely to other people's problems and idiosyncrasies that the person who is me gets lost, suffocates. I didn't realize how dramatic this was until I spent time on a forensic unit. For the criminally insane. Uh, it was part of my research, my research for my thesis." He was getting increasingly distracted. "I'll never forget. Frankie. Frankie was a paranoid schizophrenic. He beat his mother to death with a stick of firewood. I got to know Frankie. I very gently walked him through his life until we reached that winter's afternoon.

"I said to him, 'Frankie, Frankie, what little thing was it? What pushed that button? Do you remember what was going through your mind, through your nerves?'

"He said he was sitting in the chair he always sat in before the fire, watching the flames burn down, when *they* began whispering to him. Whispering terrible, mocking things. When his mother walked in she looked at him the way she always did, but this time he saw it in her eyes. The voices got so loud he couldn't think and next thing he was wet and sticky and she didn't have a face anymore. He came to when the voices were still. I couldn't sleep for many nights after that. Every time I'd close my eyes I'd see Frankie crying, covered with his mother's blood. I understood him. I understood what he'd done. Whoever I talked to, whatever story I heard, it affected me the same way."

I was sitting calmly, my powers of imagination switched off, the scientist, the clinician deliberately donned like a suit of clothes.

I asked him, "Have you ever felt like killing anyone, Al?"

"Everybody's felt that way at some point," he said as our eyes met.

"Everybody? Do you really think so?"

"Yes. Every person has the capacity. Absolutely."

"Who have you felt like killing?" I asked.

"I don't own a gun or anything else, uh, dangerous," he answered. "Because I don't ever want to be vulnerable to an impulse. Once you can envision yourself doing something, once you can relate to the mechanism behind the deed, the door is cracked. It can happen. Virtually every heinous event that occurs in this world was first conceived in thought. We aren't good or bad, one or the other." His voice was trembling. "Even those classified as insane have their own reasons for why they do what they do."

"What was the reason behind what happened to Beryl?" I asked.

My thoughts were precise and clearly stated. And yet I was sick inside as I tried to block the images: the black stains on the walls, the stab wounds clustered over her breast, her books standing primly on the library shelf quietly waiting to be read.

"The person who did this loved her," he said.

"A rather brutal way to show it, don't you think?"

"Love can be brutal," he said.

"Did you love her?"

"We were very much alike."

"In what way?"

"Out of sync." He was studying his hands again. "Alone and sensitive and misunderstood. And this served to make her distant, very guarded and unapproachable. I know nothing about her—I'm saying, no one's ever told me anything about her. But I sensed the being inside her. I intuited that she was very aware of who she was, of her worth. But she was deeply angered by the price she paid for being different. She was wounded. I don't know by what. Something had hurt her. This made me care for her. I wanted to reach out because I knew I would have understood her."

"Why didn't you reach out to her?" I asked.

"The circumstances weren't right. Maybe if I'd met her some-where else," he replied.

"Tell me about the person who did this to her, Al," I said. "Would he have reached out to her had the circumstances ever been right?"

"No."

"No?"

"The circumstances would never have been right because he is inadequate and knows it," Hunt said.

His sudden transformation was disconcerting. Now he was the psychologist. His voice was calmer. He was concentrating very hard, tightly clasping his hands in his lap.

He was saying, "He has a very low opinion of himself and is unable to express feelings in a constructive manner. Attraction turns to obsession, love becomes pathological. When he loves, he has to possess because he feels so insecure and unworthy, is so easily threatened. When his secret love is not returned, he becomes increasingly obsessed. He becomes so fixated his ability to react and function becomes limited. It's like Frankie hearing the voices. Something else drives him. He no longer has control."

"Is he intelligent?" I asked.

"Reasonably so."

"What about education?"

"His problems are such that he isn't able to function in the capacity he is intellectually capable of."

"Why her?" I asked him. "Why did he select Beryl Madison?"

"She has freedom, fame, he doesn't have," Hunt replied, his eyes glazed. "He thinks he's attracted to her, but it's more than that. He wants to possess those qualities he lacks. He wants to possess her. In a sense, he wants to *be* her."

"Then you're saying he knew Beryl was a writer?" I asked.

"There is very little you can keep from him. One way or an-other, he would have found out she's a writer. He would know so much about her that when she began to pick up on it, she would have felt terribly violated and profoundly afraid."

"Tell me about that night," I said. "What happened the night she died, Al?"

"I know only what I've read in the papers."

"What have you pieced together from reading what has been in the papers?" I asked.

"She was home," he said, staring off. "And it was getting late in the evening when he appeared at her door. Most likely she let him in. At some point before midnight he left her house and the burglar alarm went off. She was stabbed to death. There was an implication of sexual assault. That's as much as I've read."

"Do you have any theories as to what might have gone on?" I asked blandly. "Speculations that go above and beyond what you've read?"

He leaned forward in the chair, his demeanor dramatically changing again. His eyes got hot with emotion. His lower lip began to quiver.

"I see scenes in my mind," he said.

"Such as?"

"Things I wouldn't want to tell the police."

"I'm not the police," I said.

"They wouldn't understand," he said. "These things I see and feel without having any reason to know them. It's like Frankie." He blinked back tears. "It's like the others. I could see what happened and understand it, even though I wasn't always given the details. But you don't always need the details. Nor are you likely to get them in most instances. You know why that is, don't you?"

"I'm not sure . . ."

"Because the Frankies in the world don't know the details, either! It's like a bad accident you can't remember. The awareness returns like waking up from a bad dream and you find yourself staring at the wreckage. The mother who no longer has a face. Or the Beryl who is bloody and dead. The Frankies *wake up* when they're running or a cop they don't remember calling pulls up in front of the house."

"Are you telling me Beryl's killer doesn't remember exactly what he did?" I asked carefully.

He nodded.

"You're quite sure of that?"

"Your most skilled psychiatrist could question him for a million years and there would never be an accurate replay," Hunt said. "The truth will never be known. It has to be re-created and, to an extent, inferred."

"Which is what you've done. Re-created and inferred." I said.

He wet his bottom lip, his breathing tremulous. "Do you want me to tell you what I see?"

"Yes," I answered.

"Much time had elapsed since his first contact with her," he began. "But she had no awareness of him as a person, though she may have seen him somewhere in the past—seen him without having any idea. His frustration, his obsessiveness had driven him to her doorstep. Something kicked that off, made it an overwhelming need to confront her."

"What?" I asked. "What kicked it off?"

"I don't know."

"What was he feeling when he decided to come after her?"

Hunt closed his eyes and said, "Anger. Anger because he couldn't make things work the way he wanted."

"Anger because he couldn't have a relationship with Beryl?" I asked.

Eyes still shut, Hunt slowly shook his head from side to side and said, "No. Maybe that's what was closest to the surface. But the root was much deeper. Anger because nothing worked the way he wanted it to in the beginning."

"When he was a child?" I asked.

"Yes."

"Was he abused?"

"He was emotionally," Hunt said.

"By whom?"

Eyes still shut, he answered, "His mother. When he killed Beryl he killed his mother."

"Do you study forensic psychiatry books, Al? Do you read about these things?" I asked.

He opened his eyes and stared at me as if he had not heard what I had said.

He went on, emotionally, "You have to appreciate how many times he had imagined the moment. It wasn't impulsive in the sense he simply rushed to her house without premeditation. The timing may have been impulsive, but his method had been planned with meticulous detail. He absolutely couldn't afford for her to be alarmed and refuse him entrance into her house. She'd call the police, give them a description. And even if he wasn't apprehended, his mask had been ripped off and he'd never be able to come near her again. He had created a scheme that was guaranteed not to fail, something that would not excite her suspicions. When he appeared at her door that night, he inspired trust. And she let him in."

In my mind I saw the man in Beryl's foyer, but I could not see his face or the color of his hair, just an indistinct figure and the glinting of the long steel blade as he introduced himself with the weapon he used to murder her.

"This is when it deteriorated for him," Hunt continued. "He won't remember what happened next. Her panic, her terror, are not pleasant for him. He had not completely thought out this part of his ritual. When she ran, tried to get away from him, when he saw the panic in her eyes, he fully realized her rejection of him. He realized the horrible thing he was doing, and his contempt for himself was acted out as contempt for her. Rage. He quickly lost control of her while he was reduced to the lowest form. A killer. A destroyer. A mindless savage tearing and cutting and inflicting pain. Her screams, her blood were awful for him. And the more he razed and defaced this temple where he had worshiped for so long, the more he couldn't bear the sight of it."

He looked at me and there was nobody home behind his eyes. His face was drained of all emotion when he asked, "Can you relate to this, Dr. Scarpetta?"

"I'm listening" was all I said.

"He is in all of us," he said.

"Does he feel remorse, Al?"

"He is beyond that," he said. "I don't think he feels good about what he did or even completely realizes what he did. He was left with confused emotions. In his mind he will not let her die. He wonders about her, relives his contacts with her, and fantasizes that his relationship with her was the deepest, most profound of all because she was thinking about him when she breathed her last and this is the ultimate closeness to another human being. In his fantasies he imagines she continues to think about him after death. But the rational part of him is unsatisfied and frustrated. No one can completely belong to another person, and this is what he begins to discover."

"What do you mean?" I asked.

"His deed could not possibly produce the desired effect," Hunt answered. "He is unsure of the closeness—just as he was never sure of his mother's closeness. The distrust again. And there are other people now who have a more legitimate reason to have a relationship with Beryl than he does."

"Like who?"

"The police." His eyes focused on me. "And you."

"Because we're investigating her murder?" I asked, a chill running up my spine.

"Yes."

"Because she has become a preoccupation for us, and our relationship with her is more public than his?" I said.

"Yes."

"Where does this lead?" I then asked.

"Cary Harper is dead."

"He killed Harper?"

"Yes."

"Why?" I nervously lit a cigarette.

"What he did to Beryl was a love thing," Hunt responded. "What he did to Harper was a hate thing. He is into hate things now. Anybody connected to Beryl is in danger. And this is what I wanted to tell Lieutenant Marino, the police. But I knew it wouldn't do any good. He— They would just think I have a loose screw."

"Who is he?" I asked. "Who killed Beryl?"

Al Hunt moved to the edge of the couch and rubbed his face in his hands. When he looked up, his cheeks were splotched red.

"Jim Jim," he whispered.

"Jim Jim?" I asked, mystified.

"I don't know." His voice broke. "I keep hearing that name in my head, hearing it and hearing it. . . ."

I sat very still.

"It was so long ago I was at Valhalla Hospital," he said.

"The forensic unit?" I broke out. "Was this Jim Jim a patient while you were there?"

"I'm not sure." The emotions were gathering in his eyes like a storm. "I hear his name and I see that place. My thoughts drift back to its dark memories. Like I'm being sucked down a drain. It was so long ago. So much blacked out now. Jim Jim. Jim Jim. Like a train chugging. The sound won't stop. I have headaches because of the sound."

"When was this?" I demanded.

"Ten years ago," he cried.

Hunt couldn't have been working on a master's thesis then, I realized. He would have been only in his late teens.

"Al," I said, "you weren't doing research in the forensic unit. You were a patient there, weren't you?"

He covered his face with his hands and wept. When he finally was in sufficient control, he refused to talk anymore. Obviously deeply distressed, he mumbled he was late for an appointment and practically ran out the door. My heart was racing and wouldn't slow down. I fixed myself a cup of coffee and paced the kitchen, trying to figure out what to do next. I jumped when the telephone rang.

"Kay Scarpetta, please."

"Speaking."

"This is John with Amtrak. I've finally got your information, ma'am. Let's see . . . Sterling Harper had a round-trip ticket on The Virginian for October twenty-seventh, returning on the thirty-first. According to my records, she was on the train, or at least somebody with her tickets was. You want the times?"

"Yes, please," I said, and I wrote them down. "What stations?"

He answered, "Originating in Fredericksburg, destination Baltimore."

I tried to call Marino. He was on the street. It was evening when he returned my call with news of his own.

"Do you want me to come?" I asked, stunned.

"Don't see no point in it," Marino's voice came over the line. "No question what he did. He wrote a note and pinned it to his undershorts. Said he was sorry, he couldn't take it no more. That's pretty much it. Nothing suspicious about the scene. We're about to clear on out. And Doc Coleman's here," he added, referring to one of my local medical examiners.

Shortly after Al Hunt left my house he drove to his own, a brick colonial in Ginter Park where he lived with his parents. He took a pad of paper and a pen from his father's study. He descended the stairs leading to the basement and removed his narrow black-leather belt. He left his shoes and trousers on the floor. When his mother went down later to put in a load of wash, she found her only son hanging from a pipe inside the laundry room.

11

A FREEZING RAIN began to fall past midnight, and by morning the world was glass. I stayed in my house Saturday, my conversation with Al Hunt replaying in my mind, startling the solitude of my private thoughts like the thawing ice suddenly crackling to the earth beyond my window. I felt guilty. Like every other mortal who has ever been touched by suicide, I had the fallacious belief that I could have done something to stop it.

Numbly, I added him to the list. Four people were dead. Two deaths were blatant, vicious homicides, two of them were not, and yet all of the cases were somehow connected. Perhaps connected by a bright orange thread. Saturday and Sunday I worked in my home office because my downtown office would only remind me that I no longer felt in charge—for that matter, I no longer felt needed. The work went on without me. People reached out to me and then were dead. Respected colleagues like the attorney general asked for answers, and I did not have anything to offer.

I fought back in the only feeble way I knew how. I stayed in front of my home computer typing out notes about the cases and poring over reference books. And I made a lot of phone calls.

I did not see Marino again until we met at the Amtrak station on Staples Mill Road Monday morning. We passed between two waiting trains, the dark, wintry air warmed by engines and smelling of oil. We found seats in the back of our train and resumed a conversation we had started inside the station.

"Dr. Masterson wasn't exactly chatty," I said about Hunt's psychiatrist as I carefully set down the shopping bag I was carrying. "But I'm suspicious he remembers Hunt a lot more clearly than he's letting on." Why was it I always got a seat with a footrest that didn't work?

Marino yawned voraciously as he pulled down his, which worked just fine. He didn't offer to exchange seats with me. If he had, I would have accepted.

He answered, "So Hunt would've been eighteen, nineteen when he was in the bin."

"Yes. He was treated for severe depression," I said.

"Yeah, well, I guess so."

"And what's that supposed to mean?" I asked.

"His type's always depressed."

"What is his *type*, Marino?"

"Let's just say the word *fag* went through my mind more'n once when I talked to him," he said.

The word *fag* went through Marino's mind more than once when he talked to anybody who was different.

The train glided forward, silently, like a boat from a pier.

"I wish you'd taped that conversation," Marino went on, yawning again.

"With Dr. Masterson?"

"No, the one with Hunt. When he dropped by your crib," he said.

"It's moot and it doesn't matter," I replied uncomfortably.

"I don't know. Seems to me like the squirrel knew an awful lot. Wish like hell he'd hung around a little longer, so to speak."

What Hunt had said in my living room would have been significant were he still alive and not armored in alibis. The police had taken apart his parents' house. Nothing was found that might have linked Hunt to the murders of Beryl Madison and Cary Harper. More to the point, Hunt was eating dinner with his parents at their country club the night of Beryl's death, and he was with his parents at the opera when Harper was murdered. The stories had been checked out. Hunt's parents were telling the truth.

We bumped, swayed, and rumbled northbound, the train whistle hooting balefully.

"The stuff with Beryl pushed him over the edge," Marino was

saying. "You want my opinion, he related to her killer to the point he freaked, took himself out of circulation, kissed off before he cracked."

"I think it's more likely Beryl reopened the old wound," I answered. "It reminded him of his inability to have relationships."

"Sounds like he and the killer are cut from the same cloth. Both of them unable to relate to women. Both of them losers."

"Hunt wasn't violent."

"Maybe he was leaning that way and couldn't live with it," Marino said.

"We don't know who killed Beryl and Harper," I reminded him. "We don't know if it was someone like Hunt. We don't know that at all, and we still have no idea about the motive. The killer could just as easily be someone like Jeb Price. Or someone called Jim Jim."

"Jim Jim my ass," he said snidely.

"I don't think we should dismiss anything at this point, Marino."

"Be my guest. You run across a Jim Jim who graduated from Valhalla Hospital and now's a part-time terrorist carrying around orange acrylic fibers on his person, give me a buzz." Settling down in his seat and shutting his eyes, he mumbled, "I need a vacation."

"So do I," I said. "I need a vacation from you."

Last night Benton Wesley had called to talk about Hunt, and I mentioned where I was going and why. He was adamant that it was unwise for me to go alone, visions of terrorists, Uzis, and Glasers dancing in his head. He wanted Marino with me, and I might not have minded had it not turned out to be such an ordeal. There were no other seats available on the six-thirty-five morning train, so Marino had booked both of us on the one leaving at four-forty-eight A.M. I ventured into my downtown office at three A.M. to pick up the Styrofoam box now inside my shopping bag. I was feeling physically punished, my sleep deficit climbing out of sight. The Jeb Prices of the world wouldn't need to do me in. My guardian angel Marino would spare them the trouble.

Other passengers were dozing, their overhead lamps switched off. Soon we were creaking slowly through the middle of Ashland and I wondered about the people living in the prim white frame homes facing the tracks. Windows were dark, bare flagpoles greeting us with stark salutes from porches. We passed sleepy storefronts—a barbershop, a stationery store, a bank—then picked up speed as we curved around the campus of Randolph-Macon College with its Georgian buildings and its frosted athletic field peopled at this early moonlit hour by a row of varicolored football sleds. Beyond the town were woods and raw red clay banks. I was leaning back in the seat, entranced by the rhythm of the train. The farther we got from Richmond the more I relaxed, and quite without intending to I drifted off to sleep.

I did not dream but was unconscious for an hour, and when I opened my eyes the dawn was blue beyond the glass and we were passing over Quantico Creek. The water was polished pewter catching light in laps and ruffles, and there were boats out. I thought of Mark. I thought of our night in New York and of times long past. I had not heard a word from him since the last cryptic message on my answering machine. I wondered what he was doing, and yet I was afraid to know.

Marino sat up, squinting groggily at me. It was time for breakfast and cigarettes, not necessarily in that order.

The dining car was half filled with semicomatose clientele who could have been sitting in any bus station in America and looked very much at home. A young man dozed to the beat of whatever was playing inside the headphones he wore. A tired woman held a squirming baby. An older couple was playing cards. We found an empty table in a corner, and I lit up while Marino went to see about food. The only positive thing I could say about the prepackaged ham and egg sandwich he came back with was that it was hot. The coffee wasn't bad.

He tore open cellophane with his teeth and eyed the shopping bag I had placed next to me on the seat. Inside it was the Styrofoam box containing samples of Sterling Harper's liver, tubes of her blood, and her gastric contents, packed in dry ice.

"How long before it thaws?" he asked.

"We'll get there in plenty of time, providing we don't make any detours," I replied.

"Speaking of plenty of time, that's exactly what we got on our hands. You mind going over it again, the bit about this cough syrup shit? I was half asleep when you were rattling on about it last night."

"Yes, half asleep just like you are this morning."

"Don't you ever get tired?"

"I'm so tired, Marino, I'm not sure I'm going to live."

"Well, you better live. I sure as hell ain't delivering those pieces an' parts by myself," he said, reaching for his coffee.

I explained with the deliberation of a taped lecture. "The active ingredient in the cough suppressant we found in Miss Harper's bathroom is dextromethorphan, an analogue of codeine. Dextromethorphan is benign unless you ingest a tremendous dose. It's the d-isomer of a compound, the name of which won't mean anything to you—"

"Oh, yeah? How do you know it won't mean nothing to me?"

"Three-methoxy-N-methylmorphinan."

"You're right. Don't mean a damn thing to me."

I went on, "There's another drug which is the l-isomer of this same compound that dextromethorphan is the d-isomer of. The l-isomer compound is levomethorphan, a potent narcotic about five times stronger than morphine. And the only difference between the two drugs as far as detection goes is that, when viewed through an optical rotatory device called a polarimeter, dextromethorphan rotates light to the right, and levomethorphan rotates light to the left."

"In other words, without this contraption you can't tell the difference between the two drugs," Marino concluded.

"Not in tox tests routinely done," I answered. "Levomethorphan comes up as dextromethorphan because the compounds are the same. The only discernible difference is they bend light in opposite directions, just as d-sucrose and l-sucrose bend light in opposite directions even though they're both structurally the same disaccharide. D-sucrose is table sugar. L-sucrose has no nutritional value to humans."

"I'm not sure I get it," Marino said, rubbing his eyes. "How can compounds be the same but different?"

"Think of dextromethorphan and levomethorphan as identical twins," I said. "They're not the same people, so to speak, but they *look* the same—except one is right-handed, the other left-handed. One is benign, the other strong enough to kill. Does that help?"

"Yeah, I guess. So how much of this levomethorphan stuff would it take for Miss Harper to snuff herself?"

"Thirty milligrams would probably do it. Fifteen two-milligram tablets, in other words," I answered.

"What then, saying she did?"

"She would very quickly slip into a deep narcosis and die."

"You think she would've known about this isomer stuff?"

"She might have," I replied. "We know she had cancer, and we also suspect she wanted to disguise her suicide, perhaps explaining the melted plastic in the fireplace and the ashes of whatever else it was she burned right before she died. It's possible she deliberately left the bottle of cough syrup out to throw us off track. After seeing that, I wasn't surprised when dextromethorphan came up in her tox."

Miss Harper had no living relatives, very few friends—if any—and she didn't strike me as someone who traveled very often. After discovering she had recently made a trip to Baltimore, the first thing that came to mind was Johns Hopkins, which has one of the finest oncology clinics in the world. A couple of quick calls confirmed that Miss Harper had made periodic visits to Hopkins for blood and bone marrow workups, a routine relating to a disease she obviously had been quite secretive about. When I was informed of her medication, the pieces suddenly snapped together in my mind. The labs in my building did not have a polarimeter or any way to test for levomethorphan. Dr. Ismail at Hopkins had promised to assist if I could supply him with the necessary samples.

It was not quite seven now, and we were on the outer fringes of D.C. Woods and swamps streamed past until the city was suddenly there, the Jefferson Memorial flashing white through a break in the trees. Tall office buildings were so close I could see plants and lampshades through spotless windows before the train plunged underground like a mole and burrowed blindly beneath the Mall.

We found Dr. Ismail inside the pharmacology lab of the oncology clinic. Opening the shopping bag, I set the small Styrofoam box on his desk.

"Are these the samples we talked about?" he asked with a smile.

"Yes," I replied. "They should still be frozen. We came here straight from the train station."

"If the concentrations are good, I can have an answer for you in a day or so," he said.

"What exactly will you do with the stuff?" Marino inquired as he looked around the lab, which looked like every lab I have ever seen.

"It's very simple, really," Dr. Ismail replied patiently. "First I will make an extract of the gastric sample. That will be the longest, most painstaking part of the test. When that is done I place the extract into the polarimeter, which looks very much like a telescope. But it has rotatory lenses. I look through the eyepiece and rotate the lenses to the left and right. If the drug in question is dextromethorphan, then it will bend light to the right, meaning the light in my field will get brighter as I rotate the lenses to the right. For levomethorphan the opposite is true."

He went on to explain that levomethorphan is a very effective pain reliever prescribed almost exclusively for people terminally ill with cancer. Because the drug had been developed here, he kept a list of all Hopkins patients who were on it. The purpose was to establish the therapeutic range. The bonus for us was he had a record of Miss Harper's treatments.

"She would come in every two months for her blood and bone marrow workups and on each visit was given a supply, about two hundred fifty two-milligram tablets," Dr. Ismail was saying as he smoothed open the pages of a thick monitoring book. "Let's see . . . Her last visit was October twenty-eighth. She should have had at least seventy-five, if not a hundred tablets left."

"We didn't find them," I said.

"A shame." He lifted dark, saddened eyes. "She was doing so well. A very lovely woman. I was always pleased to see her and her daughter."

After a moment of startled silence, I asked, "Her daughter?"

"I assume so. A young woman. Blond . . ."

Marino cut in, "She with Miss Harper last time, the last weekend in October?"

Dr. Ismail frowned and said, "No. I don't recall seeing her then. Miss Harper was alone."

"How many years had Miss Harper been coming here?" I asked.

"I'll have to pull her chart. But I know it has been several. At least two years."

"Was her daughter, the young blond woman, always with her?" I asked.

"Not so often in the early days," he answered. "But during the past year she was with Miss Harper on every visit, except for this last one in October, and possibly the one before that. I was impressed. Being so ill, well, it is nice when one has the support of family."

"Where did Miss Harper stay when she was here?" Marino's jaw muscles were flexing again.

"Most of the patients stay in hotels located nearby. But Miss Harper was fond of the harbor," Dr. Ismail said.

My reactions were slowed by tension and lack of sleep.

"You don't know what hotel?" Marino persisted.

"No. I have no idea . . ."

Suddenly I began seeing images of the fragmented typed words on filmy white ash.

I interrupted both of them. "May I see your telephone directory, please?"

Fifteen minutes later Marino and I were standing out on the street looking for a cab. The sun was bright, but it was quite cold.

"Damn," he said again. "I hope you're right."

"We'll find out soon enough," I said tensely.

In the business listings of the telephone directory was a hotel called Harbor Court. *bor Co, bor C.* I kept seeing the miniature black letters on the wisps of burned paper. The hotel was one of the most luxurious in the city, and it was directly across the street from Harbor Place.

"I tell you what I can't figure," Marino went on as another taxi passed us by. "Why all the bother? So Miss Harper kills herself, right? Why go to all the trouble to do it in such a mysterious way? Make any sense to you?"

"She was a proud woman. Suicide was probably a shameful act to her. She may not have wanted anyone to figure it out, and she may have chosen to take her life while I was inside her house."

"Why?"

"Perhaps because she didn't want her body found a week later." Traffic was terrible, and I was beginning to wonder if we were going to have to walk to the harbor.

"And you really think she knew about this isomer business?"

"I think she did," I said.

"How come?"

"Because she would wish for death with dignity, Marino. It's possible she'd premeditated suicide for quite a long time, in the event her leukemia became acute and she didn't want to suffer or make others suffer any longer. Levomethorphan was a perfect choice. In most instances, it never would have been detected—providing a cough suppressant containing dextromethorphan was found inside her house."

"No shit?" he marveled as a taxi, thank God, pulled out of traffic and headed our way. "I'm impressed. You know, I really am."

"It's tragic."

"I don't know." He peeled open a stick of gum and began to chew with vigor. "Me, I wouldn't want to be tied down to no hospital bed with tubes in my nose. Maybe I would've thought like she did."

"She didn't kill herself because of her cancer."

"I know," he said as we ventured off the curb. "But it's related. Gotta be. She's not long for this world anyway. Then Beryl gets whacked. Next, her brother gets whacked." He shrugged. "Why hang around?"

We got into the taxi and I gave the driver the address. For ten minutes we rode in silence. Then the taxi crept almost to a stop and threaded through a narrow arch leading into a brick courtyard bright with beds of ornamental cabbages and small trees. A doorman dressed in tails and a top hat was immediately at my elbow, and I found myself escorted inside a splendid light-filled lobby of rose and cream. Everything was new and clean and highly polished, with fresh flowers arranged on fine furniture, and crisp members of the hotel staff alighting where needed but not obtrusive.

We were shown to a well-appointed office, where the well-dressed manager was talking on the telephone. T. M. Bland, according to the brass nameplate on his desk, glanced up at us and quickly completed his call. Marino wasted no time telling him what we wanted.

"The list of our guests is confidential," Mr. Bland replied, smiling benignly.

Marino helped himself to a leather chair and lit a cigarette, despite the THANK YOU FOR NOT SMOKING sign in plain view on the wall, then reached for his wallet and flashed his badge.

"Name's Pete Marino," he said laconically. "Richmond P.D., Homicide. This here's Dr. Kay Scarpetta, Chief Medical Examiner of Virginia. We sure as hell understand your insistence on confidentiality, and respect your hotel for that, Mr. Bland. But you see, Sterling Harper's dead. Her brother Cary Harper's dead. And Beryl Madison's dead, too. Cary Harper and Beryl was murdered. We're not too sure yet what happened to Miss Harper. That's what we're here for."

"I read the newspapers, Detective Marino," Mr. Bland said, his composure beginning to waver. "Certainly the hotel will cooperate with the authorities in any way possible."

"Then you're telling me they was guests here," Marino said.

"Cary Harper was never a guest here."

"But his sister and Beryl Madison was."

"That is correct," Mr. Bland said.

"How often, and when was the last time?"

"I'll have to pull Miss Harper's account," Mr. Bland answered. "Will you please excuse me for a moment?"

He left us for no more than fifteen minutes, and when he returned he handed us a computer printout.

"As you can see," he said, reseating himself, "Miss Harper and Beryl Madison stayed with us six times during the past year and a half."

"Approximately every two months," I thought out loud, scanning the dates on the printout, "except for the last week in August and the last few days of October. Then it appears Miss Harper stayed here alone."

He nodded.

"What was the purpose of their visits?" Marino asked.

"Business, possibly. Shopping. Simply relaxation. I really don't know. It isn't the practice of the hotel to monitor our guests."

"And it ain't my practice to care about what your guests is up to unless they turn up dead," Marino said. "Tell me what you observed when the two ladies was here."

Mr. Bland's smile disappeared, and he nervously plucked a gold ballpoint pen off a notepad and then seemed at a loss as to what purpose the action served. Tucking the pen in the breast pocket of his starched pink shirt, he cleared his throat.

"I can only tell you what I noted," he said.

"Please do," Marino said.

"The two women made separate travel arrangements. Usually Miss Harper checked in the night before Beryl Madison did, and they often didn't leave at the same time, or, uh, together."

"What do you mean, they didn't *leave* at the same time?"

"I mean that they may have checked out on the same day, but not necessarily at the same time, and they didn't necessarily choose the same means of transportation. Not in the same cab, for example."

"Were they both headed for the train station?" I inquired.

"It seems to me Miss Madison frequently took the limo to the airport," Mr. Bland replied. "But yes. I think Miss Harper's habit was to take the train."

"What about their accommodations?" I asked, studying the printout.

"Yeah," Marino butted in. "It don't say nothing about their room on this thing." He tapped the printout with his index finger. "They stay in a double or a single? You know, one bed or two?"

His cheeks coloring at the implication, Mr. Bland replied, "They always stayed in a double room facing the water. They were guests of the hotel, Detective Marino, if you really need to know that detail, and certainly it isn't for publication."

"Hey, what do I look like, a damn reporter?"

"You're saying they stayed in your hotel free of charge?" I asked, confused.

"Yes, ma'am."

"You mind explaining that?" Marino said.

"It was the desire of Joseph McTigue," Mr. Bland answered.

"I beg your pardon?" I leaned forward and stared hard at him. "The contractor from Richmond? You're referring to *that* Joseph McTigue?"

"The late Mr. McTigue was one of the developers of much of the waterfront. His holdings include substantial interests in this hotel," Mr. Bland replied. "It was his request that we accommodate Miss Harper in any way possible, and we continued to honor this after his death."

Minutes later I was slipping a dollar bill to the doorman and Marino and I were getting into a cab.

"You mind telling me who the hell Joseph McTigue is?" Marino asked as we took off into traffic. "I got a feeling you know."

"I visited his wife in Richmond. At Chamberlayne Gardens. I told you about it."

"Ho-ly shit."

"Yes, it's rather thrown me for a loop, too," I agreed.

"You want to tell me what the hell you make of that?"

I didn't know, but I was beginning to formulate a suspicion about it.

"Sounds pretty weird to me," he went on. "For starters, the bit about Miss Harper's taking the train while Beryl usually flew, when both of them was heading in the same direction."

"It's not so strange," I said. "Certainly they couldn't travel together, Marino. Miss Harper, Beryl, couldn't risk that. They weren't supposed to have anything to do with each other, remember? If Cary Harper routinely picked up his sister at the train station, there wouldn't be a way for Beryl to suddenly disappear if she and Miss Harper were traveling together." I paused as it came to mind. "It may also be that Miss Harper was assisting with Beryl's book, giving her background information about the Harper family."

Marino was staring out his side window.

He said, "You want my opinion, I think the two ladies was closet lesbians."

I saw the driver's curious eyes in the rearview mirror.

"I think they loved each other," I said simply.

"So maybe the two of them was having a little affair, getting together every two months here in Baltimore where nobody knew 'em or paid 'em any mind.

"You know," Marino persisted, "maybe that's why Beryl decided to run to Key West. She was a fag-ette, would've felt at home there."

"Your homophobia really is rabid, not to mention tiresome, Marino. You should be careful. People might wonder about *you*."

"Yeah, right," he said, not the least bit amused.

I was silent.

He went on, "Point is, maybe Beryl found herself a little girlfriend while she was down there."

"Maybe you ought to check into that."

"No way, José. No way I'm getting bit by no goddamn mosquito in the AIDS capital of America. And talking to a bunch of queers ain't my idea of a good time."

"Have you gotten the Florida police to check out her contacts down there?" I asked seriously.

"A couple of them said they poked around. Talk about a sorry assignment. They was afraid to eat anything, drink the water. One of the queerbaits from the restaurant she wrote about in her letters is dying of AIDS even as we speak. The cops had to wear gloves the entire time."

"During the interviews?"

"Oh, yeah. Surgical masks, too—at least when they was talking to the guy dying. Didn't come up with nothing helpful, none of the information worth a damn."

"I guess not," I commented. "You treat people like lepers and they're not likely to open up to you."

"You ask me, they ought to saw off that part of Florida and send it drifting out to sea."

"Well, fortunately," I said, "nobody asked you."

There were numerous messages waiting on my answering machine when I returned home midevening.

I hoped one would be from Mark. I sat on the edge of my bed drinking a glass of wine and half-heartedly listening to the voices drifting out of the machine.

Bertha, my housekeeper, had the flu and announced she would not be able to come the next day. The attorney general wanted to meet me for breakfast tomorrow morning and went on to report that Beryl Madison's estate was suing over the missing manuscript. Three reporters had called demanding comment, and my mother wanted to know if I would prefer turkey or ham for Christmas—her not-so-subtle way of finding out if she could count on me for at least one holiday this year.

I did not recognize the breathy voice that followed.

". . . You have such pretty blond hair. Is it real or do you bleach it, Kay?"

I rewound the tape. I frantically opened the drawer of my bedside table.

". . . Is it real or do you bleach it, Kay? I left a little gift for you on your back porch."

Stunned and with Ruger in hand, I rewound the tape one more time. The voice was almost a whisper, very quiet and deliberate. A white male. I could determine no accent, sense no emotion in the tone. The sound of my feet on the stairs unnerved me, and I turned on the lights in each room I passed through. The back porch was off the kitchen, and my heart was pounding as I stepped to one side of the picture window overlooking the bird feeder and barely parted the curtains, the revolver held high, barrel pointed at the ceiling.

Light seeped from the porch, pushing back the darkness from the lawn and etching the shapes of trees in the wooded blackness at the edge of my property. The brick stoop was bare. I saw nothing on it or the steps. I curled my fingers around the doorknob and stood very still, my heart hammering as I unfastened the dead bolt.

A scraping against the wooden exterior of the door was barely perceptible as it opened, and when I saw what was looped over the outer knob I slammed the door so hard the windows shook.

Marino sounded as if I had gotten him out of bed.

"Get here now!" I exclaimed into the phone, my voice an octave higher than usual.

"Stay put," he said firmly. "Don't open the door for nobody until I get there. You got that? I'm on my way."

Four cruisers lined the street in front of my house, and in the darkness officers probed the woods and shrubbery with long fingers of light.

"The K-nine unit's on the way," Marino said, setting his portable radio upright on my kitchen table. "Seriously doubt the drone hung around, but we'll make damn sure he didn't before we book on out of here."

It was the first time I had ever seen Marino in jeans, and he might have looked casually stylish were it not for the pair of white athletic socks and penny loafers, and the gray sweatshirt one size too small. The smell of fresh coffee filled the kitchen. I was percolating a pot big enough to accommodate half the neighborhood. My eyes were darting around, looking for things to do.

"Tell it to me again real slow," Marino said as he lit a cigarette.

"I was playing back the messages on my answering machine," I repeated. "When I got to the last one it was this voice, a white male, young. You'll have to hear it for yourself. He said something about my hair, wanting to know whether I bleach it." Marino's eyes annoyingly shifted to my roots. "Then he said he'd left a present on my back porch. I came down here, looked out the window and didn't see anything. I don't know what I was expecting. I don't know. Something awful in a box, gift wrapped. When I opened the door, I heard something scraping against the wood. It was looped over the outer knob."

Inside a plastic evidence envelope in the center of the table was an unusual gold medallion attached to a thick gold chain.

"You're sure it's what Harper was wearing at the tavern?" I asked again.

"Oh, yeah," Marino replied, his face tight. "No question about it. No question where the thing's been all this time either. The squirrel took it from Harper's body and now you're getting an early Christmas present. Looks like our friend's gotten sweet on you."

"Please," I said impatiently.

"Hey. I'm taking it serious, okay?" He wasn't smiling as he slid the envelope closer and examined the necklace through the plastic. "You notice the clasp's bent, so's the little ring at the end. Looks to me like maybe it got broke when he yanked it off Harper's neck. Then he maybe fixes it with pliers. He's probably been wearin' it. Shit." He tapped an ash. "Find any injury on Harper's neck from the chain?"

"There wasn't much of his neck left," I said dully.

"Ever seen a medallion like this before?"

"No."

It looked like a coat of arms in eighteen-karat gold, but there was nothing engraved on it except the date 1906 on the back.

"Based on the four jeweler's marks stamped on the back, I think its origin is English," I said. "The marks are a universal code indicating when the medallion was made, where, and by whom. A jeweler could interpret them. I know it's not Italian—"

"Doc—"

"It would have a seven-fifty stamped on the back for eighteen-karat gold, five hundred for the equivalent of fourteen-karat—"

"Doc . . ."

"I have a jeweler consultant at Schwarzschild's—"

"Hey," Marino said loudly. "It don't matter, all right?"

I was prattling on like a hysterical old woman.

"A friggin' family tree of everybody who ever owned this necklace ain't going to tell us the most important thing—the name of the squirrel who hung it on your door." His eyes softened a little and he lowered his voice. "What you got to drink in this crib? Brandy. You got any brandy?"

"You're on the job."

"Not for me," he said, laughing. "For you. Go pour yourself this much." Touching his thumb to the middle knuckle of his index finger, he marked off two inches. "Then we'll talk."

I went to the bar and returned with a small snifter. The brandy burned going down and instantly began to spread warmth through my blood. I stopped shivering inside. I stopped shaking. Marino eyed me curiously. His attentiveness began to make me conscious of many things. I was wearing the same rumpled suit I had worn on the train back from Baltimore. My pantyhose were biting into my waist and bagging around my knees. I was aware of a maddening compulsion to wash my face and brush my teeth. My scalp itched. I was certain I looked awful.

"This guy ain't into empty threats," Marino said quietly as I sipped.

"He's probably just jerking me around because I'm involved in the case. Taunting. It's not unusual for psychopaths to taunt investigators or even send them souvenirs." I didn't really believe it. Certainly Marino didn't.

"I'm going to keep a unit or two staked out. We'll watch your house," he said. "And I got a couple rules for you. Follow them to the letter. No fooling around." He met my eyes. "For starters, whatever your normal routines are, I want you to scramble them up as much as possible. If you usually go to the grocery store on Friday afternoon, go on Wednesday next time and pick a different store. Don't ever set foot outside your house or car without looking around. You see anything that catches your eye, like a strange car parked on the street or evidence anybody's been on your property, you haul ass out of there or keep yourself locked up tight in here and call the police. When you walk inside your house, if you sense anything—I mean if you so much as get a creepy feeling—get out of here, find a phone and call the police, ask an officer to accompany you inside to make sure everything's okay."

"I've got a burglar alarm," I said.

"So did Beryl."

"She let the bastard in."

"You don't let nobody in you're not sure about."

"What's he going to do, bypass my alarm system?" I persisted.

"Anything's possible."

I remembered Wesley saying that.

"No leaving your office after dark or when nobody else is around. The same applies to your coming in. If you usually come in when it's still pretty dark, the parking lot empty, start coming in a little later. Keep your answering machine on. Tape everything. You get another call, get hold of me immediately. A couple more and we'll put a trap on your line—"

"Like you did with Beryl?" I was beginning to get angry.

He didn't respond.

"What, Marino? Will my rights be honored in the breach, too? When it's too damn late to do me any damn good?"

"You want me to sleep on your couch tonight?" he asked calmly.

Facing the morning was hard enough. I envisioned Marino in boxer shorts, a T-shirt stretched taut over his big belly as he padded barefooted in the general direction of the bathroom. He probably still left the seat up.

"I'll be fine," I said.

"You've got a license for carrying a gun, don't you?"

"Carrying a concealed weapon?" I asked. "No."

He pushed back his chair, deciding. "I'll have a little chat with Judge Reinhard in the morning. We'll get you one."

That was all. It was almost midnight.

Moments later I was alone and unable to sleep. I downed another shot of brandy, then one more, and lay in bed staring up at the dark ceiling. If you have enough bad things happen to you in life, others begin to privately question if you invite them, are a magnet that attracts misfortune or danger or dysfunction. I was beginning to wonder. Maybe Ethridge was right, I got too involved in my cases and placed myself at risk. I'd had close calls before that could have sent me spinning off into eternity.

When I finally faded into sleep, I dreamed nonsensical things. Ethridge burned a hole in his vest with a cigar ash. Fielding was working on a body that was beginning to look like a pin cushion because he couldn't find an artery that had any blood. Marino was riding a pogo stick up a steep hill and I knew he was going to fall.

12

IN THE EARLY MORNING I stood inside my dark living room, staring out at the shadows and shapes of my property.

My Plymouth wasn't back from the state garage. As I looked out at the oversize station wagon I was stuck with, I found myself wondering how difficult it would be for a grown man to hide under it and grab my foot as I unlocked the driver's door. He wouldn't need to kill me. I would die of a heart attack first. The street beyond was empty, street lights burning dimly. Peering through the barely parted draperies, I saw nothing. I heard nothing. Nothing seemed out of the ordinary. Probably nothing had seemed out of the ordinary when Cary Harper had driven home from the tavern, either.

My breakfast appointment with the attorney general was in less than an hour. I was going to be late if I didn't muster up the courage to step outside my own front door and negotiate the thirty feet of sidewalk that would lead me to my car. I studied the shrubbery and small dogwoods bordering my front lawn, scrutinizing their quiet silhouettes as the sky lightened by degrees. The moon was roundly iridescent like a white morning glory, grass silver with frost.

How had he gotten to their houses, to *my* house? He had to have some means of transportation. There had been little speculation about the killer's ability to move around. Type of vehicle is as much a part of criminal profiling as age and race are, and yet no one was commenting, not even Wesley. I wondered why as I stared at the vacant street. And Wesley's grim demeanor in Quantico still bothered me.

I voiced my concern as Ethridge and I were eating breakfast.

"It may be, simply, that there are things Wesley chooses not to tell you," he suggested.

"He's always been very open with me in the past."

"The Bureau tends to be very closemouthed, Kay."

"Wesley is a profiler," I replied. "He's always been generous with his theories and opinioins. But in this instance he's not talking. He's barely profiling these cases at all. His personality has changed. He's humorless, and he scarcely looks me in the eyes. It's weird and incredibly unnerving."

I took a deep breath.

Then Ethridge said, "You're still feeling isolated, aren't you, Kay?"

"Yes, Tom."

"And just a little paranoid."

"That, too," I said.

"Do you trust me, Kay? Do you belive I'm on your side and have your best interests in mind?" he asked.

I nodded and took another deep breath.

We were talking in quiet voices inside the dining room of the Capitol Hotel, a favorite watering hole for politicians and plutocrats. Three tables away sat Senator Partin, his well-known face more wrinkled than I remembered as he talked seriously to a young man I had seen somewhere before.

"Most of us feel isolated and paranoid during stressful times. We feel alone in the wilderness." Ethridge's eyes were kind on me, his face troubled.

"I am alone in the wilderness," I replied. "I feel that way because it's true."

"I can see why Wesley is worried."

"Of course."

"What worries me about you, Kay, is you're basing your theories on intuition, going on instinct. Sometimes that can be very dangerous."

"Sometimes it can be. But it can also be very dangerous when people begin to make things too complicated. Murder is usually depressingly simple."

"Not always, though."

"Almost always, Tom."

"You don't think Sparacino's machinations are related to these deaths?" the attorney general queried.

"I think it would be all too easy to be distracted by his machinations. What he's doing and what the killer is doing could be trains running on parallel tracks. Both of them dangerous, even deadly. But not the same. Not connected. Not driven by the same forces."

"You don't think the missing manuscript is connected?"

"I don't know."

"You're no closer to knowing?"

The interrogation made me feel as if I hadn't done my homework. I wished he hadn't asked.

"No, Tom," I admitted. "I have no idea where it is."

"Is it possible it could be what Sterling Harper burned in her fireplace right before she died?"

"I don't think so. The documents examiner looked at charred bits of paper, identified them as twenty-pound, high-quality rag. They're consistent with fine stationery or the paper lawyers use for legal documents. It's very unlikely someone would write a book draft on paper like that. It's more likely Miss Harper burned letters, personal papers."

"Letters from Beryl Madison?"

"We can't rule it out," I replied, even though I had pretty much ruled it out.

"Or perhaps Cary Harper's letters?"

"There was quite a collection of his private papers found inside the house," I said. "There's no evidence that any of it had been disturbed or recently gone through."

"If the letters were from Beryl Madison, why would Miss Harper burn them?"

"I don't know," I replied, and I knew Ethridge was thinking about his nemesis Sparacino again.

Sparacino had moved quickly. I had seen the lawsuit, all thirty-three pages of it. Sparacino was suing me, the police, the governor. The last time I had checked in with Rose, she had informed me that *People* magazine had called, and one of its photographers was out front taking pictures of my building the other day after being refused entrance beyond the lobby. I was becoming notorious. I was also becoming expert at refusing comment and making myself scarce.

"You think we're dealing with a psycho, don't you?" Ethridge asked me point-blank.

Orange acrylic fiber connected with hijackers or not, that was what I thought, and I told him so.

He looked down at his half-eaten food and when he lifted his eyes I was undone by what I saw in them. Sadness, disappointment. A terrible reluctance.

"Kay," he began, "there's no easy way to say this to you."

I reached for a biscuit.

"You need to know. No matter what is really going on or why, no matter your beliefs and private opinions, you need to hear this."

I decided I would rather smoke than eat, and got out my cigarettes.

"I have a contact. Suffice it to say he is privy to Justice Department activities—"

"This is about Sparacino," I interrupted.

"It's about Mark James," he said.

I couldn't have been more unnerved had the attorney general just sworn at me.

I asked, "What about Mark?"

"I'm wondering if I should ask *you* that, Kay."

"What do you mean, exactly?"

"The two of you were seen together in New York several weeks ago. At Gallagher's." An awkward pause as he coughed and added inanely, "I haven't been there in years."

I stared at the smoke drifting up from my cigarette.

"As I remember it, the steaks are pretty good. . . ."

"Stop it, Tom," I said quietly.

"A lot of good-hearted Irishmen in that place who don't hold back on the booze or the banter—"

"Stop it, goddamn it," I said a little too loudly.

Senator Partin stared straight at our table, his eyes mildly curious as they briefly alighted on Ethridge, then me. Our waiter was suddenly pouring more coffee and inquiring if we needed anything. I was uncomfortably warm.

"Don't bullshit me, Tom," I said. "Who saw me?"

He waved it off. "What matters is how you know him."

"I've known him for a very long time."

"That's not an answer."

"Since law school."

"You were close?"

"Yes."

"Lovers?"

"Jesus, Tom."

"I'm sorry, Kay. It's important." Dabbing his lips with his napkin, he reached for his coffee, his eyes drifting around the dining room. Ethridge was very ill at ease. "Let's just say that the two of you were together most of the night in New York. At the Omni."

My cheeks were burning.

"I don't give a damn about your personal life, Kay. I doubt anybody else does, either. Except in this one instance. You see, I'm very sorry." He cleared his throat, finally giving me his eyes again. "Dammit. Mark's pal, Sparacino, is being investigated by the Justice Department—"

"His *pal*?"

"It's very serious, Kay," Ethridge went on. "I don't know what Mark James was like when you knew him in law school, but I do know what's become of him since. I know his record. After you were spotted with him, I did some investigating. He got in serious trouble in Tallahassee seven years ago. Racketeering. Fraud. Crimes for which he was convicted and for which he actually spent time in prison. It was after all this that he ended up with Sparacino, who is suspected of being tied in with organized crime."

I felt as if a vise were rapidly squeezing the blood from my heart, and I must have become pale because Ethridge quickly handed me my glass of water and waited patiently until I composed myself. But when I met his eyes again, he picked up where he had interrupted his damaging testimony.

"Mark has never worked for Orndorff & Berger, Kay. The firm has never even heard of him. Which doesn't surprise me. Mark James couldn't possibly practice law. He was disbarred. It appears he is simply Sparacino's personal aide."

"Does Sparacino work for Orndorff & Berger?" I managed to ask.

"He's their entertainment lawyer. That much is true," he answered.

I said nothing, tears fighting to break out.

"Stay away from him, Kay," Ethridge said, his voice a rough caress in its attempt to be tender. "For God's sake, break it off. Whatever you've got going with him, break it off."

"I don't have anything going with him," I said shakily.

"When's the last time you had contact with him?"

"Several weeks ago. He called. We talked no more than thirty seconds."

He nodded as if he had expected as much. "The paranoid life. One of the poisonous fruits of criminal activity. I doubt Mark James is given to long telephone conversations, and I doubt he'll approach you at all unless there is something he wants. Tell me how it is you were with him in New York."

"He wanted to see me. He wanted to warn me about Sparacino." I added lamely, "Or this is what he said."

"And did he warn you about him?"

"Yes."

"What did he say?"

"The very sorts of things you've already mentioned about Sparacino."

"Why did Mark tell you this?"

"He said he wanted to protect me."

"Do you believe that?"

"I don't know what the hell I believe," I said.

"Are you in love with this man?"

I stared mutely at the attorney general, my eyes turning to stone.

He said very quietly, "I need to know how vulnerable you are. Please don't think I'm enjoying this, Kay."

"Please don't think I'm enjoying this either, Tom," I said, an edge to my voice.

Ethridge removed his napkin from his lap and folded it neatly, deliberately, before tucking it under the rim of his plate.

"I have reason to fear," he said, so softly I had to lean forward to hear him, "that Mark James could do you terrible damage, Kay. There is reason to suspect he's behind the break-in at your office—"

"*What* reason?" I cut him off, my voice rising. "What are you talking about? What proof—" The words caught in my throat, as Senator Partin and his young companion were suddenly at our table. I hadn't noticed them get up and head toward us. I could tell by the look on their faces they realized they had intruded upon a tense conversation.

"John, good to see you." Ethridge was pushing back his chair. "You know the chief medical examiner, Kay Scarpetta, don't you?"

"Of course, of course. Yes, how are you, Dr. Scarpetta?" The senator was shaking my hand, smiling, his eyes distant. "And this is my son, Scott."

I noticed that Scott had not inherited his father's rugged, rather coarse features or short, stocky build. The young man was incredibly handsome, tall, fit, his fine face framed by a crown of magnificent black hair. He was in his twenties, with a quiet burning insolence in his eyes that bothered me. The cordial conversation did not ease my disconcertedness, nor did I feel any better when father and son finally left us alone again.

"I've seen him somewhere before," I said to Ethridge after the waiter refilled our coffees.

"Who? John?"

"No, no—of course I've seen the senator before. I'm talking about his son. Scott. He looks very familiar."

"You've probably seen him on TV," he replied, stealing a distracted glance at his watch. "He's an actor, or trying to be one, at any rate. I think he's had a few minor roles in a couple of the soaps."

"Oh, my God," I muttered.

"Maybe a couple of bit parts in movies, too. He was out in California, now lives in New York."

"No," I said, stunned.

Ethridge put down his coffee cup and fixed calm eyes on me.

"How did he know we were having breakfast here this morning, Tom?" I asked, working hard to keep my voice steady as the images came back to me. Gallagher's. The lone young man drinking beer several tables away from where Mark and I had been sitting.

"I don't know how he knew," Ethridge replied, his eyes glinting with a secret satisfaction. "Suffice it to say that I'm not surprised, Kay. Young Partin's been shadowing me for days."

"He's not your Justice Department contact . . ."

"Good God, no," Ethridge said flatly.

"Sparacino?"

"I would think so. That would make the most sense, wouldn't it, Kay?"

"Why?"

He began studying the check, then said, "To make sure he knows what's going on. To spy. To intimidate." He glanced up at me. "Take your choice."

Scott Partin had struck me as one of these self-contained young men often a study in sullen splendor. I remembered he had been reading the *New York Times* and gloomily drinking a beer. I had been vaguely aware of him only because extremely beautiful people, like gorgeous arrangements of flowers, are difficult not to notice.

I felt a compulsion to tell Marino all about it as we rode the elevator down to the first floor of my building later that morning.

"I'm certain," I repeated. "He was sitting two tables over from us at Gallagher's."

"And he wasn't with nobody?"

"Correct. He was reading, drinking a beer. I don't think he was eating, but I really don't remember," I replied as we cut through a large storage room smelling of cardboard and dust.

My mind and heart were racing, trying to outrun yet another one of Mark's lies. Mark had said that Sparacino didn't know I was coming to New York, that it was coincidence when Sparacino appeared at the steak house. That couldn't be true. Young Partin had been sent to spy on me that night, and that could have happened only if Sparacino knew I was there with Mark.

"Well, there's another way to look at it," Marino said as we walked through the dusty bowels of my building. "Let's say one of the ways he stays alive in the Big Apple is he does some part-time snitching for Sparacino, okay? Could be Partin was sent to tail Mark, not you. Remember, Sparacino recommended the steak house to Mark—or at least this is what Mark told you. So Sparacino had reason to know Mark was going to eat there that night. Sparacino tells Partin to be there, check out what Mark's up to. Partin does, is sitting alone drinking a brew when the two of you walk in. Maybe at some point he slips out to call Sparacino, give him the scoop. Bingo! Next thing you know, Sparacino's walking in."

I wanted to believe it.

"Just a theory," Marino added.

I knew I could not believe it. The truth, I harshly reminded myself, was that Mark had betrayed me, that he was the criminal Ethridge had described.

"You got to consider all the possibilities," Marino concluded.

"Of course," I muttered.

Down another narrow corridor, we stopped before a heavy

metal door. Finding the right key, I let us inside the range where the firearms examiners conducted test fires on virtually every weapon known to man. It was a drab, lead-contaminated cinderblock room, one entire wall covered by a pegboard and lined with scores of handguns and machine pistols confiscated by the courts and eventually released to the lab. Propped up in racks were shotguns and rifles. The far wall was heavy steel reinforced in the center and pitted by thousands of rounds fired over the years. Marino headed for a corner where nude manikin torsos, hips, heads, and legs were commingled in a heap ghoulishly reminiscent of an Auschwitz common grave.

"You prefer light meat, don't you?" he asked, selecting a pale flesh-colored male chest.

I ignored him as I opened my carrying case and got out the stainless-steel Ruger. Plastic clacked as he rummaged, finally selecting a Caucasian head with brown-painted hair and eyes. This went on top of the chest, both of which Marino set on top of a cardboard box against the steel wall some thirty paces away.

"You get one clip to make him history," Marino said.

Loading wadcutters into my revolver, I glanced up as Marino withdrew a 9-millimeter pistol out of the back of his trousers. Cocking back the slide, he pulled out the clip, then snapped it back in place.

"Merry Christmas," he said, offering it to me, safety on, butt first.

"No, thank you," I said as politely as possible.

"Five pops with your piece and you're out of business."

"If I miss."

"Shit, Doc. Everybody misses a few. Problem is, with your Ruger there, a few's all you got."

"I'd rather have a few well-placed shots with mine. All that thing does is spray lead."

"It's a hell of a lot more firepower," he said.

"I know. About a hundred foot-pounds more at fifty feet than I've got with mine if I'm using Silvertips Plus ammo."

"Not to mention three times as many shots," Marino added.

I had fired 9-millimeters before and didn't like them. They weren't as accurate as my .38 special. They weren't as safe, and they could jam. I had never been one to substitute quantity for quality, and there was no substitution for being informed and practiced.

"You need only one shot," I said, placing a set of hearing protectors over my ears.

"Yeah. If it's between the damn eyes."

Steadying the revolver with my left hand, I repeatedly squeezed the trigger and shot the manikin in the head once, the chest three times, the fifth bullet grazing the left shoulder—all of it happening in a matter of seconds as head and torso flew off the box and clattered dully against the steel wall.

Wordlessly, Marino set the 9-millimeter on top of a table and slipped his .357 out of his shoulder holster. I could tell I had hurt his feelings. No doubt he had gone to a lot of trouble to find the automatic for me. He had thought I would be pleased.

"Thank you, Marino," I said.

Clicking the cylinder back in place, he slowly raised his revolver.

I started to add that I appreciated his thoughtfulness, but I knew either he couldn't hear me or he wasn't listening.

I backed away as he unloaded six rounds, the manikin head jumping crazily on the floor. Slapping in a speed loader, he started in on the torso. When he was finished, gun smoke was acrid on the air and I knew I would never want him murderously angry with me.

"Nothing like shooting a man while he's down," I said.

"You're right." He removed his earplugs. "Nothing like it."

We slid a wooden frame along an overhead track and attached to it a Score Keeper paper target. When the box of cartridges was empty and I was satisfied that I could still hit the broad side of a barn, I fired a couple of Silvertips to clean out the bore before I took a patch cloth of Hoppe's No. 9 to it. The solvent always reminded me of Quantico.

"You want my opinion?" Marino said, cleaning his gun as well. "What you need at home's a shotgun."

I said nothing as I returned the Ruger to its carrying case.

"You know, something like an autoloading Remington, three-inch magnum double-aught buck. Be like hitting the fool with fifteen thirty-two-caliber bullets—three times that you hit him with all three rounds. We're talking forty-five friggin' pieces of lead. He ain't gonna come back for more."

"Marino," I said quietly. "I'm fine, all right? I really don't need an arsenal."

He looked up to me, his eyes hard. "You got any idea what it's like to shoot a guy and he keeps on coming?"

"No, I don't," I said.

"Well, I do. Back in New York I emptied my gun on this animal who's freaked out on PCP. Hit the bastard four times in the upper body and it didn't even slow him down. It was like something out of Stephen King, the guy coming at me like the friggin' living dead."

I found some tissues in the pockets of my lab coat and began wiping gun oil and solvent off my hands.

"The squirrel who was chasing Beryl through her house, Doc, he was like that, like that lunatic I'm telling you about. Whatever his gig is, he ain't gonna slow down once he's in gear."

"The man in New York," I ventured, "did he die?"

"Oh, yeah. In the ER. We both rode to the hospital in the back of the same ambulance. That was a trip."

"You were badly hurt?"

Marino's face was unreadable as he replied, "Naw. Seventy-eight stitches. Flesh wounds. You've never seen me with my shirt off. The guy had a knife."

"How awful," I muttered.

"I don't like knives, Doc."

"I don't either," I agreed.

We headed out. I felt grimy with gun oil and gunshot residue. Shooting is much dirtier than most people might imagine.

Marino was reaching back for his wallet as we walked. Next he was handing me a small white card.

"I didn't fill out an application," I said, staring, rather dazed, at the license authorizing me to carry a concealed weapon.

"Yeah, well, Judge Reinhard owed me a favor."

"Thank you, Marino," I said.

He smiled as he held open the door for me.

———

Despite the directives of Wesley and Marino and my own good sense, I stayed inside my building until it was dark out, the parking lot empty. I had given up on my desk, and a glance at my calendar had about done me in.

Rose had been systematically reorganizing my life. Appointments had been pushed weeks ahead or canceled, and lectures and demonstration autopsies had been rerouted to Fielding. The health commissioner, my immediate boss, had tried to reach me three times, finally inquiring if I were ill.

Fielding was becoming quite adept at filling in for me. Rose was typing his autopsy protocols and micro-dictations. She was doing his work instead of mine. The sun continued to rise and set, and the office was running without a hitch because I had selected and trained my staff very well. I wondered how God had felt after He created a world that thought it did not need Him.

I did not go home right away, but drove to Chamberlayne Farms. The same outdated notices were still taped to the elevator walls. I rode up with an emaciated little woman who never took her lonely eyes off me as she clutched her walker like a bird clinging to its branch.

I had not told Mrs. McTigue I was coming. When the door to 378 finally opened after several loud knocks, she peered quizzically out from her lair of crowded furniture and loud television noise.

"Mrs. McTigue?" I introduced myself again, not at all sure she would remember me.

The door opened wider as her face lit up. "Yes. Why, of course! How grand of you to stop by. Won't you please come in?"

She was dressed in a pink quilted housecoat and matching slippers, and when I followed her into the living room she turned off the television set and removed a lap robe from the couch, where she evidently had been sitting as she snacked on nutbread and juice and watched the evening news.

"Please forgive me," I said. "I've interrupted your dinner."

"Oh, no. I was just nibbling. May I offer you some refreshment?" she was quick to say.

I politely declined, seating myself while she moved about, tidying up. My heart was tugged by memories of my own grandmother, whose humor was unflagging even as she watched her flesh fall to ruin around her ears. I would never forget her visit to Miami the summer before she died when I took her shopping, and her improvised "diaper" of men's briefs and Kotex pads sprung a safety pin and ended up around her knees in the middle of Woolworth's. She held herself together as we hurried off to find a ladies' room, both of us laughing so hard I nearly lost control of my bladder, too.

"They say we may get snow tonight," Mrs. McTigue commented when she seated herself.

"It's very damp out," I replied abstractedly. "And it certainly feels cold enough to snow."

"I don't believe they're predicting any accumulation, though."

"I don't like driving in the snow," I said, my mind working on weighty, unpleasant things.

"Perhaps we'll have a white Christmas this year. Wouldn't that be special?"

"It would be special." I was looking in vain for any evidence of a typewriter in the apartment.

"I can't remember the last time we had a white Christmas."

Her nervous conversation tried to overcome her uneasiness. She knew I had come to see her for a reason and sensed it wasn't good news.

"Are you quite sure I can't get you something? A glass of port?"

"No, thank you," I said.

Silence.

"Mrs. McTigue," I ventured. Her eyes were as vulnerable and uncertain as a child's. "I wonder if I might see that photograph again? The one you showed me last time I was here."

She blinked several times, her smile thin and pale like a scar.

"The one of Beryl Madison," I added.

"Why, certainly," she said, slowly getting up, an air of resignation about her as she went to the secretary to fetch it. Fear, or maybe it was merely confusion, registered on her face when she handed me the photograph and I also asked to see the envelope and sheet of creamy folded paper.

I knew instantly by the feel of it that the paper was twenty-pound weight, and when I tilted it toward the lamp I saw the Crane's watermark, translucent in the high-quality rag. I briefly glanced at the photograph, and by now Mrs. McTigue looked thoroughly bewildered.

"I'm sorry," I said. "I know you must be wondering what on earth I'm doing."

She was at a loss for words.

"I'm curious. The photograph looks much older than the stationery."

"It is," she replied, her frightened eyes not leaving me. "I found the photograph among Joe's papers and tucked it in the envelope for safekeeping."

"This is your stationery?" I asked as benignly as possible.

"Oh, no." She reached for her juice and carefully sipped. "It was my husband's, but I did pick it out for him. A very nice engraved stationery for his business, you see. After he passed on, I kept only the blank second sheets and envelopes. I have more than I'll ever use."

There was no way to ask her without being direct.

"Mrs. McTigue, did your husband have a typewriter?"

"Why, yes. I gave it to my daughter. She lives in Falls Church. I always write my letters out in longhand. Not so many anymore, because of my arthritis."

"What kind of typewriter?"

"Dear me. I don't recall except that it's electric and fairly new," she stammered. "Joe would trade it in on a new one every few years. You know, even when these computers came out, he insisted on handling his correspondence the way he always had. Burt—that was his office manager—urged Joe for years to start using the computer, but Joe always had to have his typewriter."

"At home or in his office?" I asked.

"Why, both. He often stayed up late working on things in his office at home."

"Did he correspond with the Harpers, Mrs. McTigue?"

She had slipped a tissue out of a pocket of her robe and was twisting it in her fingers.

"I'm sorry to ask you so many questions," I persisted gently.

She stared down at her gnarled, thin-skinned hands and said nothing.

"Please," I said quietly. "It's important or I wouldn't ask."

"It's about her, isn't it?" The tissue was shredding and she wouldn't look up.

"Sterling Harper."

"Yes."

"Please tell me, Mrs. McTigue."

"She was very lovely. And so gracious. A very fine lady," Mrs. McTigue said.

"Did your husband correspond with Miss Harper?" I asked.

"I'm quite sure he did."

"What makes you think that?"

"I came in on him once or twice when he was writing a letter. He always said it was business."

I said nothing.

"Yes. My Joe." She smiled, her eyes dead. "Such a ladies' man.

You know, he always kissed a lady's hand and made her feel the queen."

"Did Miss Harper write to him as well?" I asked hesitantly, for I did not enjoy irritating an old wound.

"Not that I'm aware."

"He wrote her but she never returned his letters?"

"Joe was a man of letters. He always said he would write a book someday. He was always reading something, don't you know."

"I can see why he would enjoy Cary Harper so much," I commented.

"Quite often when Mr. Harper was frustrated, he would call. I suppose writer's block is the term. He would call Joe and they would talk about the most interesting things. Literature and what-not." The tissue was little bits of twisted paper in her lap. "Joe's favorite was Faulkner, if you can imagine. He was also quite fond of Hemingway and Dostoyevski. When we were courting, I lived in Arlington and he was here. He would write me the most beautiful letters you can imagine."

Letters like the ones he began to write his love in later life, I thought. Letters like the ones he began to write the gorgeous, unmarried Sterling Harper. Letters she was kind enough to burn before she committed suicide, because she did not wish to shatter the heart and memories of his widow.

"You found them, then," she barely said.

"Found letters to her?"

"Yes. His letters."

"No." It was, perhaps, the most merciful half truth I had ever told. "No, I can't say that we found anything like that, Mrs. McTigue. The police found no correspondence from your husband among the Harpers' personal effects, no stationery with your husband's letterhead, nothing of an intimate nature addressed to Sterling Harper."

Her face relaxed as denial was blessedly reinforced.

"Did you ever spend any time with the Harpers? Socially, for example?" I asked.

"Why, yes. Twice that I remember. Once Mr. Harper came for a dinner party. And on one other occasion the Harpers and Beryl Madison were overnight guests."

This piqued my interest. "When were they your overnight guests?"

"Mere months before Joe passed on. I 'spect that would have

been the first of the year, just a month or two after Beryl spoke to our group. In fact, I'm sure it was because the Christmas tree was still up. I remember that. It was such a treat to have her."

"To have Beryl?"

"Oh, yes! I was so pleased. It seems the three of them had been in New York on business. They were seeing Beryl's agent, I believe. They flew into Richmond on their way home and were generous enough to stay the night with us. Or at least the Harpers stayed the night. Beryl lived here, you see. Late in the evening Joe gave her a ride back to her home. Then he took the Harpers back to Williamsburg the following morning."

"What do you remember about that night?" I asked.

"Let me see . . . I remember I fixed leg of lamb and they were late coming in from the airport because the airline lost Mr. Harper's bags."

Almost a year ago, I considered. This would have been before Beryl had begun receiving the threats—based on the information we had gotten.

"They were rather tired from the trip," Mrs. McTigue continued. "But Joe was so good. He was the most charming host you'd ever want to meet."

Could Mrs. McTigue tell? Did she know by the way her husband looked at Miss Harper that he was in love with her?

I remembered the distant look in Mark's eyes during those final days so long ago when we were together. When I knew. It was instinct. I knew he was not thinking about me, and yet I would not believe he was in love with someone else until he finally told me.

"Kay, I'm sorry," he said as we drank Irish coffee for the last time in our favorite bar in Georgetown while tiny flakes of snow spiraled down from gray skies and beautiful couples walked by bundled in winter coats and brightly knitted scarves. "You know I love you, Kay."

"But not the same way I love you," I said, my heart gripped by the worst pain I ever remember feeling.

He looked down at the table. "I never intended to hurt you."

"Of course you didn't."

"I'm sorry. I'm so sorry."

I knew he was. He really and truly was. And it didn't change a goddamn thing.

I never knew her name because I did not want to know it, and she was not the woman he said he had later married. Janet, who had died. But then, maybe that was a lie, too.

". . . he had quite a temper."

"Who did?" I asked, my eyes focusing on Mrs. McTigue again.

"Mr. Harper," she replied, and she was beginning to look very tired. "He was so irritable about his luggage. Fortunately, it came in on the very next flight." She paused. "Goodness. That seems so long ago, and it really wasn't that long ago a'tall."

"What about Beryl?" I asked. "What do you remember about her that night?"

"All of them gone, now." Her hands went still in her lap as she faced that dark, empty mirror. Everyone was dead but her, the guests from that cherished and frightful dinner party, ghosts.

"We are talking about them, Mrs. McTigue. They are still with us."

"I 'spect that's so," she said, her eyes bright with tears.

"We need their help and they need ours."

She nodded.

"Tell me about that night," I said again. "About Beryl."

"She was very quiet. I remember her watching the fire."

"What else?"

"Something happened."

"What? What happened, Mrs. McTigue?"

"She and Mr. Harper seemed to be unhappy with each other," she said.

"Why? Did they have an argument?"

"It was after the boy delivered the luggage. Mr. Harper opened one of the bags and pulled out an envelope that had papers in it. I don't really know. But he was drinking too much."

"Then what happened?"

"He exchanged some rather harsh words with his sister and Beryl. Then he took the papers and just flung them into the fire. He said, 'That's what I think of that! Trash, trash!' Or words to that effect."

"Do you know what it was he burned? A contract, perhaps?"

"I don't think so," she replied, staring off. "I remember getting the impression it was something Beryl had written. They looked like typed pages, and his anger seemed directed at her."

The autobiography she was writing, I thought. Or perhaps it was an outline that Miss Harper, Beryl, and Sparacino had discussed in New York with an increasingly enraged and out-of-control Cary Harper.

"Joe intervened," she said, lacing her misshapen fingers together, holding in her pain.

"What did he do?"

"He drove her home," she said. "He drove Beryl Madison home." She stopped, staring at me in abject fear. "It's why it happened. I know it."

"It's why *what* happened?" I asked.

"It's why they're dead," she said. "I know it. I had this feeling at the time. It was such a frightful feeling."

"Describe it to me. Can you describe it?"

"It's why they're dead," she repeated. "There was so much hate in the room that night."

13

VALHALLA HOSPITAL WAS SITUATED on a rise in the genteel world of Albemarle County, where my faculty ties with the University of Virginia brought me periodically throughout the year. Though I had often noticed the formidable brick edifice rising from a distant foothill visible from the Interstate, I had never visited the hospital for either personal or professional reasons.

Once a grand hotel frequented by the wealthy and well-known, it went bankrupt during the Depression and was bought by three brothers who were psychiatrists. They systematically set about to turn Valhalla into a Freudian factory, a rich man's psychiatric resort where families with means could tuck away their genetic inconveniences and embarrassments, their senile elders and poorly programmed kids.

It didn't really surprise me that Al Hunt had been farmed out here as a teenager. What did surprise me was that his psychiatrist seemed so reluctant to discuss him. Beneath Dr. Warner Masterson's professional cordiality was a bedrock of secrecy hard enough to break the drill bits of the most tenacious inquisitors. I knew he did not want to talk to me. He knew he had no choice.

Parking in the gravel lot designated for visitors, I went into a lobby of Victorian furnishings, Oriental rugs, and heavy draperies with ornate cornices well along their way to being threadbare. I was about to announce myself to the receptionist when I heard someone behind me speak.

"Dr. Scarpetta?"

474

I turned to face a tall, slender black man dressed in a European-cut navy suit. His hair was a sandy sprinkle, his cheekbones and forehead aristocratically high.

"I'm Warner Masterson," he said, and smiling broadly, he offered his hand.

I was about to wonder if I had forgotten him from some former encounter when he explained that he recognized me from pictures he had seen in the papers and on the television news, reminders I could do without.

"We'll go back to my office," he added pleasantly. "I trust your drive up wasn't too tiring? May I offer you something? Coffee? A soda?"

All this as he continued to walk, and I did my best to keep up with his long strides. A significant portion of the human race has no idea what it is like to be attached to short legs, and I am forever finding myself indignantly pumping along like a handcar in a world of express trains. Dr. Masterson was at the other end of a long, carpeted corridor when he finally had the presence of mind to look around. Pausing at a doorway, he waited until I caught up with him, then ushered me inside. I helped myself to a chair while he took his position behind his desk and automatically began tamping tobacco into an expensive briar pipe.

"Needless to say, Dr. Scarpetta," Dr. Masterson began in his slow, precise way as he opened a thick file folder, "I am dismayed by Al Hunt's death."

"Are you surprised by it?" I asked.

"Not entirely."

"I'd like to review his case as we talk," I said.

He hesitated long enough for me to consider reminding him of my statutory rights to the record. Then he smiled again and said, "Certainly," as he handed it over.

I opened the manila folder and began to peruse its contents as blue pipe smoke drifted over me like aromatic wood shavings. Al Hunt's admission history and physical examination were fairly routine. He was in good physical health when he was admitted on the morning of April tenth, eleven years ago. The details of his mental status examination told another story.

"He was catatonic when he was admitted?" I asked.

"Extremely depressed and unresponsive," Dr. Masterson replied. "He couldn't tell us why he was here. He wasn't able to tell

us anything. He didn't have the emotional energy to answer questions. You'll note from the record that we were unable to administer
the Stanford-Binet or the MMPI, and had to repeat these tests at
a later date."

The results were in the file. Al Hunt's score on the Stanford-
Binet intelligence test was in the 130 range, a lack of smarts certainly not his problem, not that I'd had any question. As for the
Minnesota Multiphasic Personality Inventory, he did not meet the
criteria for schizophrenia or organic mental disorder. According
to Dr. Masterson's evaluation, what Al Hunt suffered from was "a
schizotypal personality disorder with features of borderline personality, which presented as a brief reactive psychosis when he cut his
wrists with a steak knife after locking himself in the bathroom." It
was a suicidal gesture, the superficial wounds a cry for help versus a serious attempt to end his life. His mother rushed him to a
nearby hospital emergency room, where he was stitched up and released. The next morning he was admitted at Valhalla. An interview
with Mrs. Hunt revealed that the incident was precipitated by her
"husband losing his temper" with Al during dinner.

"Initially," Dr. Masterson went on, "Al would not participate
in any of the group or occupational therapy sessions or social functions the patients are required to attend. His response to anti-
depressant medication was poor, and during our sessions I could
barely get a word out of him."

When there was no improvement after the first week, Dr.
Masterson continued to explain, he considered electroconvulsive
treatment, or ECT, which is the equivalent of rebooting a computer
versus determining the reason for the errors. Though the end result
may be a healthy reconnecting of brain pathways, a realignment
of sorts, the formatting "bugs" causing the problem will inevitably
be forgotten and, possibly, forever lost. As a rule, ECT is not the
treatment of choice in the young.

"Was ECT administered?" I asked, for I was finding no record
of it in the file.

"No. Just at the point when I was deciding I had no other vi-
able alternative, a small miracle occurred during psychodrama one
morning."

He paused to relight his pipe.

"Explain psychodrama as it was conducted in this instance," I
said.

"Some of the routines are done by rote and are warm-ups, you might say. During this particular session, the patients were lined up and asked to imitate flowers. Tulips, daffodils, daisies, whatever came to mind, each person contorting himself into a flower of his private choosing. Obviously, there is much one can infer from the patient's choice. This was the first time Al had participated in anything at all. He made loops with his arms and bent his head." He demonstrated, looking more like an elephant than a flower. "When the therapist asked what flower he was, he replied, 'A pansy.' "

I said nothing, experiencing a mounting wave of pity for this lost boy we had conjured up before us.

"Of course, one's first reaction was to assume this was a reference to what Al's father thought of him," Dr. Masterson explained, cleaning his glasses with a handkerchief. "Harsh, mocking references to young Al's effeminate traits, his fragility. But it was more than that." Slipping his glasses back on, he looked steadily at me. "Are you aware of Al's color associations?"

"Remotely."

"Pansy is also a color."

"Yes. A very deep violet," I agreed.

"It is what you get if you blend the blue of depression with the red of rage. The color of bruises, the color of pain. Al's color. It is the color he said radiated from his soul."

"It is a passionate color," I said. "Very intense."

"Al Hunt was a very intense young man, Dr. Scarpetta. Are you aware that he believed he was clairvoyant?"

"Not exactly," I replied uneasily.

"His magical thinking included clairvoyance, telepathy, superstitiousness. Needless to say, these characteristics became much more pronounced during times of extreme stress, when he believed he had the ability to read other people's minds."

"Could he?"

"He was very intuitive." His lighter was out again. "I have to say there was often validity in his perceptions, and this was one of his problems. He sensed what others thought or felt and sometimes seemed to possess an inexplicable *a priori* knowledge of what they would do or what they had already done. The difficulty came, as I briefly mentioned during our telephone conversation, in that Al would project, run too far with his perceptions. He would lose himself in others, become agitated, paranoid, in part because his ego was so weak. Like water, he tended to take the shape of whatever he filled. To use a cliché, he personalized the universe."

"A dangerous way to be," I observed.

"To say the least. He's dead."

"You're saying he considered himself empathic?"

"Definitely."

"That strikes me as inconsistent with his diagnosis," I said. "People with borderline personality disorders generally feel nothing for others."

"Ah, but this was part of his magical thinking, Dr. Scarpetta. Al blamed his social and occupational dysfunction on what he believed was his overwhelming empathy for others. He truly believed he sensed and even experienced other people's pain, that he knew their minds, as I've already mentioned. In fact, Al Hunt was socially isolated."

"The staff at Metropolitan Hospital described him as having a very good bedside manner when he worked there as a nurse," I pointed out.

"Unsurprisingly," Dr. Masterson countered. "He was a nurse in the ER. He would never have survived in a long-term care unit. Al could be very attentive providing he didn't have to get close to anyone, providing he wasn't forced to truly relate to that person."

"Explaining why he could get his master's degree but then be unable to function in the setting of a psychotherapy practice," I conjectured.

"Exactly."

"What about his relationship with his father?"

"It was dysfunctional, abusive," he replied. "Mr. Hunt is a hard, overbearing man. His idea of raising a son was to beat him into manhood. Al simply did not have the emotional makeup to withstand the bullying, the manhandling, the mental boot camp that was supposed to prepare him for life. It sent him fleeing to his mother's camp, where his image of himself became increasingly confused. I'm sure it comes as no surprise to you, Dr. Scarpetta, that many homosexual males are the sons of big brutes who drive pickups with gun racks and Confederate flag bumper stickers."

Marino came to mind. I knew he had a grown son. It had never occurred to me before this moment that Marino never talked about this only son, who lived out west somewhere.

I asked, "Are you suggesting that Al was homosexual?"

"I'm suggesting he was too insecure, his feelings of inadequacy too great, for him to respond to anyone, for him to form intimate relationships of any nature. To my knowledge, he never had a homosexual encounter." His face was unreadable as he gazed over my head and sucked on his pipe.

"What happened in psychodrama that day, Dr. Masterson? What was the small miracle you mentioned? His imitation of a pansy? Was that it?"

"It cracked the lid," he said. "But the miracle, if you will, was an intense and volatile dialogue he got into with his father, who was imagined to be sitting in an empty chair in the center of the room. As this dialogue intensified, the therapist sensed what was happening and slipped into the chair and began playing the part of Al's father. By now Al was so involved he was almost in a trance. He could not distinguish the real from the imagined, and finally his rage broke."

"How did it manifest itself? Did he become violent?"

"He began to weep uncontrollably," Dr. Masterson replied.

"What was his 'father' saying to him?"

"He was assaulting him with the usual brickbats, being critical, telling him how worthless he was as a man, as a human being. Al was hypersensitive to criticism, Dr. Scarpetta. This was, in part, the root of his confusion. He thought he was sensitive to others, when, in truth, he was sensitive only to himself."

"Was Al assigned a social worker?" I asked, continuing to flip through pages and finding no entries made by any therapists.

"Of course."

"Who was it?" There appeared to be pages missing from the record.

"The therapist I just mentioned," he replied blandly.

"The therapist from psychodrama?"

He nodded.

"Is he still employed by this hospital?"

"No," Dr. Masterson said. "Jim is no longer with us—"

"Jim?" I interrupted.

He began knocking burnt tobacco out of his pipe.

"What is his last name and where is he now?" I asked.

"I regret to say that Jim Barnes died in a car accident many years ago."

"How many years ago?"

Dr. Masterson began cleaning his glasses again. "I suppose it was eight, nine years ago."

"How did it happen, and where?"

"I don't recall the details."

"How tragic," I said, as if the matter were no longer of any interest to me.

"Am I to assume you are considering Al Hunt a suspect in your case?" he asked.

"There are two cases. Two homicides," I said.

"Very well. Two cases."

"To answer your question, Dr. Masterson, it isn't my business to consider anyone a suspect in anything. That's up to the police. My interest is in gathering information about Al Hunt that might assist me in verifying that he had a history of suicidal ideations."

"Is there any question about that, Dr. Scarpetta? He hanged himself, didn't he? Could that be anything other than a suicide?"

"He was dressed oddly. A shirt and his boxer shorts," I responded matter-of-factly. "Such things often lead to speculations."

"Are you suggesting autoerotic asphyxiation?" He raised his eyebrows in surprise. "An accidental death that occurred while he was masturbating?"

"I'm doing my best to obviate that question, should it ever be asked."

"I see. For insurance reasons. In the event his family might contest what you put down on the death certificate."

"For any reason," I said.

"Are you really in doubt as to what happened?" He frowned.

"No," I replied. "I think he took his own life, Dr. Masterson. I think this was his intention when he went down to the basement, and that he may have taken his pants off when he removed his belt. The belt he used to hang himself."

"Very well. And perhaps I can clear up another matter for you, Dr. Scarpetta. Al never demonstrated violent tendencies. The only individual he ever inflicted harm upon, to my knowledge, was himself."

I believed him. I also believed there was much he wasn't telling me, that his memory lapses and vagueness were patently deliberate. Jim Barnes, I thought. *Jim Jim.*

"How long was Al's stay here?" I changed the subject.

"Four months, I believe."

"Did he ever spend time in your forensic unit?"

"Valhalla doesn't have a forensic unit per se. We have a ward called Backhall for patients who are psychotic, suffering the DTs, a danger to themselve. We don't warehouse the criminally insane."

"Was Al ever on this ward?" I asked again.

"It was never necessary."

"Thank you for your time," I said, getting up. "If you would simply mail a photocopy of this record to me, that will be fine."

"It will be my pleasure." He smiled his broad smile again, but he would not look at me. "Don't hesitate to call if there's anything further I can do."

It nagged at me as I followed the long, empty corridor to the lobby, but my instinct was not to ask about Frankie or even mention the name. Backhall. Patients who are psychotic or suffering the DTs. Al Hunt had mentioned interviewing patients confined to the forensic unit. Was this a figment of his imagination or confusion? There was no forensic unit at Valhalla. Yet there very well may have been someone named Frankie locked up on Backhall. Maybe Frankie had improved and was later moved to a different ward while Al was a patient at Valhalla? Maybe Frankie had imagined he had murdered his mother, or maybe he had wished he could?

Frankie beat his mother to death with a stick of firewood. The killer beat Cary Harper to death with a segment of metal pipe.

By the time I got to my office it was dark out and the custodians had come and gone.

Seating myself at my desk, I swiveled around to face the computer terminal. After several commands, the amber screen was before me, and moments later I was staring at Jim Barnes's case. Nine years ago on April twenty-first, he had been in a single-car accident in Albemarle County, the cause of death "closed head injuries." His blood alcohol was .18, almost twice the legal limit, and he had nortriptyline and amitriptyline on board. Jim Barnes was a man with a problem.

In the computer analyst's office down the hall, the archaic, boxy microfilm machine sat squarely on a back table like a Buddha. My audiovisual skills have never been extraordinary. After an impatient search through the film library, I found the roll I was looking for and somehow managed to thread it properly into the machine. With lights out, I watched an endless stream of fuzzy black-on-white print flow by. My eyes were beginning to ache by the time I found the case. Film quietly creaked as I worked a knob and centered the handwritten police report on the screen. At approximately ten forty-five on a Friday night, Barnes's 1973 BMW was traveling east on I-64 at a high rate of speed. When his right wheel left the pavement, he overcorrected, hit the median strip, and became airborne. Advancing the film, I found the medical examiner's initial report of investigation. In the comments section a Dr. Brown had written that the decedent was fired that afternoon from Valhalla Hospital, where he had been employed as a social worker. When he left Valhalla at approximately five P.M. that day, he was noted to be extremely agitated and angry. Barnes was unmarried when he died, and he was only thirty-one years old.

There were two witnesses listed on the medical examiner's report, individuals Dr. Brown must have interviewed. One was Dr. Masterson, the other an employee at the hospital named Miss Jeanie Sample.

Sometimes working a homicide case is like being lost. Whatever street seems even remotely promising, you follow it. Maybe, if you're lucky, a back road will eventually steer you toward the main drag. How could a therapist dead nine years have anything to do with the recent murders of Beryl Madison and Cary Harper? Yet I felt there was something, a link.

I was not looking forward to quizzing Dr. Masterson's staff, and was willing to bet he would already have warned those who counted that if I called, they were to be polite—and silent. The next morning, Saturday, I continued to let my subconscious work on this problem while I rang up Johns Hopkins, hoping Dr. Ismail might be in. He was, and he confirmed my theory. Samples derived from Sterling Harper's gastric contents and blood showed she had ingested levomethorphan shortly before death, her level eight milligrams per liter of blood, which was too high to be either survivable or accidental. She had taken her own life, and had done so in a manner that under ordinary circumstances would have gone undetected.

"Did she know that dextromethorphan and levomethorphan both come up as dextromethorphan in routine tox tests?" I asked Dr. Ismail.

"I don't recall ever discussing such a thing with her," he said. "But she was very interested in the details of her treatments and medications, Dr. Scarpetta. It is possible she could have researched the subject in our medical library. I do recall her asking numerous questions when I first prescribed levomethorphan. This was several years ago. Since it is experimental, she was curious, perhaps somewhat concerned . . ."

I was barely listening as he continued explaining and defending. I would never be able to prove Miss Harper had deliberately left the bottle of cough suppressant out where I would find it. But I was reasonably certain this was what she had done. She was determined to die with dignity and without reproach, but she did not want to die alone.

After I hung up, I fixed a cup of hot tea and paced the kitchen, pausing every so often to gaze out at the bright December day. Sammy, one of Richmond's few albino squirrels, was plundering my bird feeder again. For an instant we were eye to eye, his furry cheeks frantically working, seeds flying out from under his paws, his scrawny white tail a twitching question mark against the blue sky. We had become acquainted last winter as I stood before my window and watched his repeated attempts at leaping from a branch only to slide slowly off the coned top of the feeder, his paws grabbing wildly at thin air on his way down. After a remarkable number of tumbles to terra firma, Sammy finally got the hang of it. Every so often I would go out and throw him a handful of peanuts, and it had gotten to the point where if I didn't see him for a while, I experienced a tug of anxiety followed by joyous relief when he reappeared to clean me out again.

Sitting down at the kitchen table, a pad of paper and pen in hand, I dialed the number for Valhalla.

"Jeanie Sample, please." I did not identify myself.

"Is she a patient, ma'am?" the desk clerk asked without pause.

"No. She's an employee . . ." I acted addled. "I think so, at any rate. I haven't seen Jeanie in years."

"One moment, please."

The woman came back on the line. "We have no record of anybody by that name."

Damn. How could that be? I wondered. The telephone number listed with her name on the medical examiner's report was Valhalla's number. Had Dr. Brown made a mistake? Nine years ago, I thought. A lot could happen in nine years. Miss Sample could have moved. She could have gotten married.

"I'm sorry," I said. "Sample is her maiden name."

"Do you know her married name?"

"How awful. I should know—"

"Jean Wilson?"

I paused with uncertainty.

"We have a Jean Wilson," the voice went on. "One of our occupational therapists. Can you hold, please?" Then she was back very quickly. "Yes, her middle name is listed as Sample, ma'am. But she doesn't work on the weekend. She'll be back Monday morning at eight o'clock. Would you like to leave a message?"

"Any possibility you could tell me how to get in touch with her?"

"We're not allowed to give out home numbers." She was beginning to sound suspicious. "If you'll give me your name and number, I can try to get hold of her and ask her to call you."

"I'm afraid I won't be at this number long." I thought for a moment, then sounded dismally disappointed when I added, "I'll try again—next time I'm in the area. And I suppose I can write her at Valhalla, at your address."

"Yes, ma'am. You can do that."

"And that address is?"

She gave it to me.

"And her husband's name?"

A pause. "Skip, I believe."

Sometimes a nickname for Leslie, I thought. "Mrs. Skip or Leslie Wilson," I muttered, as if I were writing it down. "Thank you so much."

There was one Leslie Wilson in Charlottesville, directory assistance informed me, and one L. P. Wilson and one L. T. Wilson. I started dialing. The man who answered when I tried the number for L. T. Wilson told me "Jeanie" was running errands and would be home within the hour.

I knew that a strange voice asking questions over the phone wasn't going to work. Jeanie Wilson would insist on conferring with Dr. Masterson first, and that would end the matter. It is, however, a little more difficult to refuse someone who unexpectedly appears in the flesh at your door, expecially if this individual introduces herself as the chief medical examiner and has a badge to prove it.

Jeanie Sample Wilson didn't look a day over thirty in her jeans and red pullover sweater. She was a perky brunette with friendly eyes and a smattering of freckles over her nose, her long hair tied back in a ponytail. In the living room beyond the open door, two small boys were sitting on the carpet, watching cartoons on television.

"How long have you been working at Valhalla?" I asked.

She hesitated. "Uh, about twelve years."

I was so relieved I almost sighed out loud. Jeanie Wilson would have been employed there not only when Jim Barnes was fired nine years ago, but also when Al Hunt was a patient two years before that.

She was planted squarely in the doorway. There was one car in the drive, in addition to mine. It appeared her husband had gone out. Good.

"I'm investigating the homicides of Beryl Madison and Cary Harper," I said.

Her eyes widened. "What do you want from me? I didn't know them—"

"May I come inside?"

"Of course. I'm sorry. Please."

We sat inside her small kitchen of linoleum and white Formica and pine cabinets. It was impeccably clean, with boxes of cereal neatly lined on top of the refrigerator, and counters arranged with big glass jars filled with cookies, rice and pasta. The dishwasher was running, and I could smell a cake baking in the oven.

I intended to beat down any lingering resistance with bluntness. "Mrs. Wilson, Al Hunt was a patient at Valhalla eleven years ago, and for a while was a suspect in the cases in question. He was acquainted with Beryl Madison."

"Al Hunt?" She looked bewildered.

"Do you remember him?" I asked.

She shook her head.

"And you say you've worked at Valhalla twelve years?"

"Eleven and a half, actually."

"Al Hunt was a patient there eleven years ago, as I've already said."

"The name isn't familiar . . ."

"He committed suicide last week," I said.

Now she was very bewildered.

"I talked to him shortly before his death, Mrs. Wilson. His social worker died in a motor vehicle accident nine years ago. Jim Barnes. I need to ask you about him."

A flush was creeping up her neck. "Are you thinking his suicide was related, had something to do with Jim?"

It was a question impossible to answer. "Apparently, Jim Barnes was fired from Valhalla just hours before his death," I went on. "Your name—or at least your maiden name—is listed on the medical examiner's report, Mrs. Wilson."

"There was— Well, there was some question," she stammered. "You know, whether it was a suicide or an accident. I was questioned. A doctor, coroner, I don't remember. But some man called me."

"Dr. Brown?"

"I don't remember his name," she said.

"Why did he want to talk to you, Mrs. Wilson?"

"I suppose because I was one of the last people to see Jim alive. I guess the doctor called the front desk, and Betty referred him to me."

"Betty?"

"She was the receptionist back then."

"I need you to tell me everything you can remember about Jim Barnes's being fired," I said as she got up to check on the cake.

When she returned, she was a little more composed. She no longer looked unnerved. Instead, she looked angry.

She said, "Maybe it's not right to say bad things about the dead, Dr. Scarpetta, but Jim was not a nice person. He was a very big problem at Valhalla, and he should have been fired long before he was."

"Exactly how was he a problem?"

"Patients say a lot of things. They're often not very, well, credible. It's hard to know what's true and what isn't. Dr. Masterson, other therapists, would get complaints from time to time, but nothing could be proven until there was a witnessed event one morning, the morning of that day. The day Jim was fired and had the accident."

"This event was something you witnessed?" I asked.

"Yes." She stared off across the kitchen, her mouth firmly set.

"What happened?"

"I was walking through the lobby, on my way to see Dr. Masterson about something, when Betty called out to me. She was working the front desk, the switchboard, like I said — Tommy, Clay, now you keep it down in there!"

The shrieking in the other room only got louder, television channels switching like mad.

Mrs. Wilson got up wearily to see about her sons. I heard muffled smacks of hand against bottoms, after which the channel stayed put. Cartoon characters were shooting each other with what sounded like machine guns.

"Where was I?" she asked, returning to the kitchen table.

"You were talking about Betty," I reminded her.

"Oh, yes. She motioned me over and said Jim's mother was on the line, long distance, and it seemed important. I never did know what it was about, the call. But Betty asked if I could find Jim. He was in psychodrama, which is held in the ballroom. You know, Valhalla has a ballroom we use for various functions. The Saturday night dances, parties. There's a stage, an orchestra stage. From when Valhalla was a hotel. I slipped into the back, and when I saw what was going on, I couldn't believe it." Jeanie Wilson's eyes were bright with anger. She started fidgeting with the edge of a place mat. "I just stood there and watched. Jim's back was to me, and he was up on the stage with, I don't know, five or six patients. They were in chairs turned in such a way that they couldn't see what he was doing with this one patient. A young girl. Her name was Rita. Rita was maybe thirteen. Rita had been raped by her stepfather. She never talked, was functionally mute. Jim was forcing her to reenact it."

"The rape?" I asked calmly.

"The damn bastard. Excuse me. But it still upsets me."

"Understandably."

"He later claimed he wasn't doing anything inappropriate. Damn, he was such a liar. He denied everything. But I'd seen it. I knew exactly what he was doing. He was playing the role of the stepfather, and Rita was so terrified she didn't move. She was frozen in the chair. He was in her face, leaning over her, talking in a low voice. Sound carries inside the ballroom. I could hear everything. Rita was very mature, developed, for thirteen. Jim was asking her, 'Is this what he did, Rita?' He kept asking her that as he touched her. Fondled her, just as her stepfather had done, I suppose. I slipped out. He never knew I'd seen it until both Dr. Masterson and I confronted him minutes later."

I was beginning to understand why Dr. Masterson had refused to discuss Jim Barnes with me, and possibly why pages of Al Hunt's case file were absent. If something like this was ever made public, even though it had happened long ago, the hospital's reputation would take it on the nose.

"And you were suspicious Jim Barnes had done this before?" I asked.

"Some of the early complaints would indicate he had," Jeanie Wilson replied, her eyes flashing.

"Always females?"

"Not always."

"You received complaints from male patients?"

"From one of the young men. Yes. But no one took it seriously at the time. He had sexual problems anyway, supposedly had been molested or something. The very type someone like Jim would fix on because who would believe anything the poor kid said?"

"Do you remember this patient's name?"

"God." She frowned. "It was so long ago." She thought. "Frank . . . Frankie. That's it. I remember some of the patients called him Frankie. I don't recall his last name."

"How old was he?" I could feel my heart beating.

"I don't know. Seventeen, eighteen."

"What do you remember about Frankie?" I asked. "It's important. Very important."

A timer went off, and she pushed back her chair to take the cake out of the oven. While she was up, she checked on her boys again. When she returned, she was frowning.

She said, "I vaguely remember he was on Backhall for a while, right after he was admitted. Then he was moved downstairs to the second-floor ward where the men are. I had him in occupational therapy." She was thinking, an index finger touching her chin. "He was very industrious, I remember that. Made a lot of leather belts, brass rubbings. And he loved to knit, which was a little unusual. Most of the male patients won't knit, don't want to. They'll stick with leather work, make ashtrays and so on. He was very creative and really pretty skilled. And something else stands out. His neatness. He was obsessively neat, always cleaning off his work space, picking bits and pieces of whatever off the floor. Like it really bothered him if everything wasn't just right, clean." She paused, lifting her eyes to mine.

"When did he make the complaint about Jim Barnes?" I asked.

"Not too long after I started working at Valhalla." She hesitated, thinking hard. "I think Frankie had only been at Valhalla a month or so when he said something about Jim. I think he said it to another patient. In fact"—she paused, her prettily arched brows moving together in a frown—"it was actually this other patient who complained to Dr. Masterson."

"Do you remember who the patient was? The patient Frankie told this to?"

"No."

"Could it have been Al Hunt? You mentioned you hadn't been working at Valhalla long. Hunt would have been a patient eleven years ago during the spring and summer."

"I don't remember Al Hunt . . ."

"They would have been close to the same age," I added.

"That's interesting." Her eyes filled with innocent wonder as they fixed on mine. "Frankie had a friend, another teen-age boy. I do remember that. Blond. The boy was blond, very shy, quiet. I don't recall his name."

"Al Hunt was blond," I said.

Silence.

"Oh, my God."

I prodded her. "He was quiet, shy . . ."

"Oh, my God," she said again. "I bet it was him, then! And he committed suicide last week?"

"Yes."

"Did he mention Jim to you?"

"He mentioned someone he called Jim Jim."

"*Jim Jim*," she repeated. "Jeez. I don't know . . ."

"Whatever happened to Frankie?"

"He wasn't there long, two or three months."

"He went back home?" I asked.

"I would imagine so," she said. "There was something about his mother. I think he lived with his father. Frankie's mother deserted him when he was small—it was something like that, anyway. All I really remember is his family situation was sad. But then, I suppose you could say the same thing about most all the patients at

Valhalla." She sighed. "God. This is something. I haven't thought about all this in years. Frankie." She shook her head. "I wonder what ever became of him."

"You have no idea?"

"Absolutely none." She looked a long time at me, and it was coming to her. I could see the fear gathering behind her eyes. "The two people murdered. You don't think Frankie . . ."

I said nothing.

"He never was violent, not when I was working with him. He was very gentle, actually."

She waited. I did not respond.

"I mean, he was very sweet and polite to me, would watch me very closely, do everything I told him to do."

"He liked you, then," I said.

"He knitted a scarf for me. I just remembered. Red, white, and blue. I'd completely forgotten. I wonder what happened to it?" Her voice trailed off. "I must have given it to the Salvation Army or something. I don't know. Frankie, well, I think he sort of had a crush on me." She laughed nervously.

"Mrs. Wilson, what did Frankie look like?"

"Tall, thin, with dark hair." She briefly shut her eyes. "It was so long ago." She was looking at me again. "He doesn't stand out. But I don't remember him as being particularly nice looking. You know, I would remember him better, maybe, if he had been really nice looking or really ugly. So I think he was kind of plain."

"Would your hospital have any photographs of him on file?"

"No."

Silence again. Then she looked at me with surprise.

"He stuttered," she said slowly, then again with conviction.

"Pardon?"

"Sometimes he stuttered. I remember. When Frankie got extremely excited or nervous, he stuttered."

Jim Jim.

Al Hunt had meant exactly what he had said. When Frankie was telling Hunt what Barnes had done or tried to do, Frankie would have been upset, agitated. He would have stuttered. He would have stuttered whenever he talked to Hunt about Jim Barnes. Jim Jim!

I hit the first pay phone after leaving Jeanie Wilson's house. Marino, the dope, had gone bowling.

14

MONDAY ROLLED IN on a tide of clouds marbled an ominous gray that shrouded the Blue Ridge foothills and obscured Valhalla from view. Wind buffeted Marino's car, and by the time he parked at the hospital tiny flakes of snow were clicking against the windshield.

"Shit," he complained as we got out. "That's all we need."

"It's not supposed to amount to anything," I reassured him, flinching as icy flakes stung my cheeks. We bent our heads against the wind and hurried in frigid silence toward the front entrance.

Dr. Masterson was waiting for us in the lobby, his face as hard as stone behind his forced smile. When the two men shook hands, they eyed each other like unfriendly cats, and I did nothing to ease the tension, for I was frankly sick of the psychiatrist's games. He had information we wanted, and he would give it to us unvarnished and in its entirety by virtue of cooperation or a court order. He could take his pick. Without delay we accompanied him to his office, and this time he shut the door.

"Now, what may I help you with?" he asked right off as he took his chair.

"More information," I replied.

"Of course. But I must confess, Dr. Scarpetta," he went on as if Marino were not in the room, "I fail to see what else I can tell you about Al Hunt that might assist you in your cases. You've reviewed his record, and I've told you as much as I remember—"

Marino cut him off. "Yeah, well, we're here to massage that

memory of yours," he said, getting out his cigarettes. "And it ain't Al Hunt we're all that interested in."

"I don't understand."

"We're more interested in his pal," Marino said.

"What *pal*?" Dr. Masterson appraised him coldly.

"The name Frankie ring a bell?"

Dr. Masterson began cleaning his glasses, and I decided this was a favorite ploy of his for buying time to think.

"There was a patient here when Al Hunt was, a kid named Frankie," Marino added.

"I'm afraid I'm drawing a blank."

"Draw all the blanks you want, Doc. Just tell us who Frankie is."

"We have three hundred patients at Valhalla at any given time, Lieutenant," he answered. "It isn't possible for me to remember everybody who's been here, particularly those whose stay was of a brief duration."

"So, you're telling me this Frankie character didn't stay very long?" Marino said.

Dr. Masterson reached for his pipe. He had made a slip, and I could see the anger in his eyes. "I'm not *telling* you anything of the sort, Lieutenant." He began slowly tamping tobacco into the bowl. "But perhaps if you could give me a little more information about this patient, the young man you refer to as Frankie, I might at least have a glimmer. Can you tell me something about him other than that he was a 'kid'?"

I intervened. "Apparently, Al Hunt had a friend while he was here, someone he referred to as Frankie. Al mentioned him to me during our conversation. We believe this individual may have been restricted to Backhall after he was admitted, and then transferred to a different floor where he may have become acquainted with Al. Frankie has been described as tall, dark, slender. He also liked to knit, a hobby rather atypical among male patients, I should think."

"This is what Al Hunt told you?" Dr. Masterson asked unemphatically.

"Frankie was also obsessively neat," I said, evading the question.

"I'm afraid a patient's enjoyment of knitting isn't likely to be something brought to my attention," he commented, relighting his pipe.

"It's also possible he had a tendency to stutter when he was under stress," I added, controlling my impatience.

"Hmm. Perhaps someone with spastic dysphonia in his differential diagnosis. That might be a place to start—"

"The place to start is for you to cut the shit," Marino said rudely.

"Really, Lieutenant." Dr. Masterson gave him a condescending smile. "Your hostility is unwarranted."

"Yeah, yeah, and you're *unwarranted* at the moment, too. But I just might get the itch to change that in a minute, slap you with a warrant and haul your ass off to lockup for accessory to murder. How's that sound?" Marino glared at him.

"I think I've about had enough of your impertinence," he replied with maddening calm. "I don't respond well to threats, Lieutenant."

"And I don't respond well to someone jerking me around," Marino retorted.

"Who is Frankie?" I tried again.

"I assure you I don't know, offhand," Dr. Masterson replied. "But if you'll be so kind as to wait a few minutes, I'll go-see what we can pull up on our computer."

"Thank you," I said. "We'll be right here."

The psychiatrist had barely gotten out the door before Marino started in.

"What a dirt bag."

"Marino," I said wearily.

"It ain't like this joint's overrun with kids. I'm willing to bet seventy-five percent of the patients here's over the age of sixty. You know, young people would stand out in your memory, right? He knows damn well who Frankie is, probably could tell us what size shoes the drone wears."

"Perhaps."

"There's nothing *perhaps* about it. I'm telling you the guy's jerking us around."

"And he'll continue to do so as long as you antagonize him, Marino."

"Shit." He got up and went to the window behind Dr. Masterson's desk. Parting the curtains, he stared out into the bleak late morning. "I hate like shit when someone lies to me. Swear to God I'll pop 'im if I have to, nail his ass. That's the thing about shrinks that frosts me so bad. They can have Jack the Ripper for a patient and they don't care. They'll still lie to you, tuck the animal in bed and spoon-feed him chicken soup like he's Mr. Apple Pie America." He paused, mumbling inanely, "At least the snow's stopped."

Waiting until he sat back down, I said, "I think threatening to charge him with accessory to murder was a bit much."

"Got his attention, didn't I?"

"Give him a chance to save face, Marino."

He stared sullenly at the curtained window as he smoked.

"I think by now he's realizing it's in his best interest to help us," I said.

"Yeah, well, it's not in my best interest to sit around playing cat and mouse with him. Even as we speak, Frankie Fruitcake's on the street thinking his screwy thoughts, ticking away like a damn bomb about to go off."

I thought of my quiet house in my quiet neighborhood, of Cary Harper's necklace looped over the knob of my back door, and the whispery voice on my answering machine. *Is your hair naturally blond, or do you bleach it. . . .* How odd. I puzzled over the significance of that question. Why did it matter to him?

"If Frankie is our killer," I said quietly, taking a deep breath, "I can't imagine how there can be any connection between Sparacino and these homicides."

"We'll see," he muttered, lighting up another cigarette and staring sourly at the empty doorway.

"What do you mean, 'we'll see'?"

"Never ceases to surprise me how one thing leads to another," he replied cryptically.

"What? What things lead to other things, Marino?"

He glanced at his watch and cursed. "Where the hell is he, anyhow? He go out to lunch?"

"Hopefully he's tracking down Frankie's record."

"Yeah. Hopefully."

"What things lead to other things?" I asked him again. "What are you thinking about? You mind being a little more specific?"

"Let's just put it this way," Marino said. "I got a real strong feeling if it wasn't for that damn book Beryl was writing, all three of 'em would still be alive. In fact, Hunt would probably still be alive, too."

"I can't say that with certainty."

"Course you can't. You're always so goddamn objective. So I'm saying it, okay?" He looked over at me and rubbed his tired eyes, his face flushed. "I got this feeling, all right? It's telling me Sparacino, the book, is the connection. It's what initially linked the killer to Beryl, and then one thing led to another. Next, the squirrel whacks Harper. After that Miss Harper takes enough pills to kill a damn horse so she don't have to rattle around in that big crib of hers all alone while cancer eats her alive. Then Hunt's swinging from the rafters in his fuckin' undershorts."

The orange fiber with its peculiar three-leaf clover shape drifted through my mind, as did Beryl's manuscript, Sparacino, Jeb Price, Senator Partin's Hollywood son, Mrs. McTigue, and Mark. They were limbs and ligaments of a body I could not piece together. In some inexplicable way, they were the alchemy by which seemingly unrelated people and events had been fashioned into Frankie. Marino was right. One thing always leads to another. Murder never emerges full blown from a vacuum. Nothing evil ever does.

"Do you have any theories as to just what *exactly* this link might be?" I asked Marino.

"Nope, not a goddamn one," he replied with a yawn at the exact moment Dr. Masterson walked into the office and shut the door.

I noticed with satisfaction that he had a stack of case files in hand.

"Now then," he said coolly and without looking at either of us, "I found no one with the name Frankie, which I'm assuming may be a nickname. Therefore, I pulled cases by date of treatment, age, and race. What I have here are the records of six white males, excluding Al Hunt, who were patients at Valhalla during the interval you're interested in. All of them are between the ages of thirteen and twenty-four."

"How about you just let us go through them while you sit back and smoke your pipe." Marino was a little less combative, but not much.

"I would prefer to give you only their histories, for confidentiality reasons, Lieutenant. If one is of keen interest, we'll go through his record in detail. Fair enough?"

"Fair enough," I said before Marino could argue.

"The first case," Dr. Masterson began, opening the top file, "is a nineteen-year-old from Highland Park, Illinois, admitted in December of 1978 with a history of substance abuse—heroin, specifically." He flipped a page. "He was five-foot-eight, weighed one-seventy, brown eyes, brown hair. His treatment was three months in duration."

"Al Hunt wasn't admitted until that following April," I reminded the psychiatrist. "They wouldn't have been patients at the same time."

"Yes, I believe you're right. An oversight on my part. So we can strike him." He set the file on his ink blotter as I gave Marino a warning glance. I knew he was about to explode, his face as red as Christmas.

Opening a second file, Dr. Masterson resumed, "Next we have a fourteen-year-old male, blond, blue-eyed, five-foot-three, one-fifteen pounds. He was admitted in February 1979, discharged six months later. He had a history of withdrawal and fragmentary delusions, and was diagnosed as schizophrenic of the disorganized or hebephrenic type."

"You mind explaining what the hell that means?" Marino asked.

"It presented as incoherence, bizarre mannerisms, extreme social withdrawal, and other oddities of behavior. For example"—he paused to look over a page—"he would leave for the bus stop in the morning but fail to show up at school, and on one occasion was found sitting under a tree drawing peculiar, nonsensical designs in his notebook."

"Yeah. And now he's a famous artist living in New York," Marino mumbled sardonically. "His name Frank, Franklin, or begin with an *F*?"

"No. Nothing close."

"So, who's next?"

"Next is a twenty-two-year-old male from Delaware. Red hair, gray eyes, uhhhh, five-foot-ten, one-fifty pounds. He was admitted in March of 1979, discharged in June. He was diagnosed as suffering from organic delusional syndrome. Contributing factors were temporal lobe epilepsy and a history of cannabis abuse. Complications included dysphoric mood and his attempting to castrate himself while reacting to a delusion."

"What's dysphoric mean?" Marino asked.

"Anxious, restless, depressed."

"This before or after he tried to turn himself into a soprano?"

Dr. Masterson was beginning to register annoyance, and I really couldn't blame him.

"Next," Marino said like a drill sergeant.

"The fourth case is an eighteen-year-old male, black hair, brown eyes, five-foot-nine, one-forty-two pounds. He was admit-

ted in May of 1979, was diagnosed as schizophrenic of the paranoid type. His history"—he flipped a page, then reached for his
pipe—"includes unfocused anger and anxiety, with doubts about
gender identity and a marked fear of being thought of as homosexual. The onset of his psychosis apparently was related to his being
approached by a homosexual in a men's room—"

"Hold it right there." If Marino hadn't stopped him, I would
have. "We need to talk about this one. How long was he at Valhalla?"

Dr. Masterson was lighting his pipe. Taking his time glancing
through the record, he replied, "Ten weeks."

"Which would have been while Hunt was here," Marino said.

"That's correct."

"So he was approached in a men's room and lost his cookies?
What happened? *What* psychosis?" Marino asked.

Dr. Masterson was turning pages. Pushing up his glasses, he
replied, "An episode of delusional thinking of a grandiose nature.
He believed God was telling him to do things."

"What things?" Marino asked, leaning forward in his chair.

"There's nothing specific, nothing written here except that he
was talking in rather bizarre ways."

"And he was paranoid schizophrenic?" Marino asked.

"Yes."

"You want to define that? Like, what are the other symptoms?"

"Classically speaking," Dr. Masterson replied, "there are associated features which include grandiose delusions or hallucina-
tions with a grandiose content. There may be delusional jealousy,
extreme intensity in interpersonal interactions, argumentativeness,
and in some instances violence."

"Where was he from?" I asked.

"Maryland."

"Shit," Marino muttered. "He lived with both parents?"

"He lived with his father."

I said, "You're sure he was paranoid versus undifferentiated?"

The distinction was important. Schizophrenics of the undifferentiated type often exhibit grossly disorganized behavior. They
generally don't have the wherewithal to premeditate crimes and
successfully evade apprehension. The person we were looking for
was organized enough to successfully plan and execute his crimes
and escape detection.

"I'm quite sure," Dr. Masterson answered. After a pause, he
added blandly, "The patient's first name, interestingly enough, is

Frank." Then he handed me the file, and Marino and I briefly looked it over.

Frank Ethan Aims, or Frank E., and thus "Frankie" I could only conclude, had left Valhalla in late July of 1979 and soon after, according to a note Dr. Masterson had made at the time, Aims ran away from his home in Maryland.

"How do you know he ran away from home?" Marino asked, looking up at the psychiatrist. "How do you know what happened to him after he left this joint?"

"His father called me. He was very upset," Dr. Masterson said.

"Then what?"

"I'm afraid there was nothing I or anyone else could do. Frank was of legal age, Lieutenant."

"Do you recall anyone ever referring to him by the nickname Frankie?" I asked.

He shook his head.

"What about Jim Barnes? Was he Frank Aims's social worker?" I asked.

"Yes," Dr. Masterson said reluctantly.

"Did Frank Aims have a bad encounter with Jim Barnes?" I asked.

He hesitated. "Allegedly."

"Of what nature?"

"Allegedly of a sexual nature, Dr. Scarpetta. And for God's sake, I'm trying to help. I hope you'll be mindful of that."

"Hey," Marino said, "we're mindful of it, all right? I mean, we ain't planning on sending out press releases."

"Then Frank knew Al Hunt," I said.

Dr. Masterson hesitated again, his face tight. "Yes. It was Al who came forward with the accusations."

"Bingo," Marino mumbled.

"What do you mean by saying Al Hunt came forth with the accusations?" I asked.

"I mean that he complained to one of our therapists," Dr. Masterson replied, his tone beginning to sound defensive. "He also said something to me during one of our sessions. Frank was questioned and he refused to say anything. He was a very angry, withdrawn young man. It wasn't possible for me to act on what Al had said. Without Frank's corroboration, the accusations were hearsay."

Marino and I were silent.

"I'm sorry," Dr. Masterson said, and by now he was thoroughly unnerved. "I can't help you with Frank's whereabouts. I know nothing further. The last time I heard from his father must have been seven, eight years ago."

"What was the occasion of that conversation?" I queried.

"Mr. Aims called me."

"For what reason?"

"He wondered if I'd heard from Frank."

"Well, had you?" Marino asked.

"No," Dr. Masterson answered. "I've never heard a word from Frank, I'm sorry to say."

"Why did Mr. Aims want to know if you'd heard from Frank?" I put forth the critical question.

"He wanted to find him, hoped that perhaps I might have a clue as to his whereabouts. Because his mother had died. Frank's mother, that is."

"Where did she die and what happened?" I asked.

"Freeport, Maine. I'm really not clear on the circumstances."

"A natural death?" I asked.

"No," Dr. Masterson said, refusing to meet our eyes. "I'm fairly certain it wasn't."

It didn't take Marino long to track it down. He called the Freeport, Maine, police. According to their records, on the late afternoon of January 15, 1983, Mrs. Wilma Aims was beaten to death by a "burglar" who was apparently inside her house when she returned from grocery shopping. She was forty-two when she died, a petite woman with blue eyes and bleached blond hair. The case remained unsolved.

―――――――

I had no doubts about who the so-called burglar was. Marino didn't either.

He said, "So maybe Hunt really was clairvoyant, huh? He knew about Frankie's taking out his mother. That sure as hell happened a long time after the two fruitcakes was in the bin together."

We were idly watching Sammy Squirrel's antics around the bird feeder. After Marino had driven me back from the hospital and let me out at my house, I invited him in for coffee.

"You're certain Frankie wasn't employed at Hunt's car wash at any point during the past few years?" I asked.

"I don't remember any Frank or Frankie Aims on their books," he said.

"He very well may have changed his name," I said.

"Probably did if he whacked his old lady. Figured the cops might look for him." He reached for his coffee. "Problem is we don't have a recent description, and joints like Masterwash are a damn revolving door. Guys in and out all the time. Work a couple of days, a week, a month. You got any idea how many white guys are tall, thin, and dark? I'm running down names and running out of road."

We were so close but so far away. It was maddening. "The fibers are consistent with a car wash," I said in frustration. "Hunt worked in the car wash Beryl patronized, and he possibly knew her killer. Do you understand what I'm saying, Marino? Hunt knew about Frankie's killing his mother because Hunt and Frankie may have had contact after Valhalla. Frankie may have worked at Hunt's car wash, perhaps even recently. It's possible Frankie may have first fixed on Beryl when she brought her car in to be cleaned."

"They've got thirty-six employees. All but eleven of them are black, Doc, and out of that eleven honkies, six of them are women. That leaves, what? Five? Three of them is under twenty, meaning they were eight, nine, back when Frankie was at Valhalla. So we know that ain't right. The other three don't fit, either, for various other reasons."

"What various other reasons?" I asked.

"Like they was just hired during the last couple of months, weren't even working there when Beryl would have been bringing in her ride. Not to mention their physical descriptions aren't even close. One guy's got red hair, another one's a munchkin, almost as short as you are."

"Thanks a lot."

"I'll keep checking," he said, turning away from the bird feeder as Sammy Squirrel watched us with pink-rimmed eyes. "What about you?"

"What *about* me?"

"Your office downtown know you still work there?" Marino asked.

He was looking strangely at me.

"Everything's under control," I added.

"I'm not so sure about that, Doc."

"I'm quite sure of it."

"Me"—Marino wouldn't give it a rest—"I think you ain't doing so hot."

"I'm going to stay out of the office for a couple more days," I explained firmly. "I've got to track down Beryl's manuscript. Ethridge is on my case about it. And we need to see what's there. Maybe the link you were talking about."

"Just so long as you remember my rules." He pushed back from the table.

"I'm being quite careful," I assured him.

"And nothing more from him, right?"

"That's right," I said. "No calls. Not a sign of him. Nothing."

"Well, let me just remind you his style wasn't to call Beryl every day, either."

I didn't need the reminder. I didn't want him starting in again. "If he calls, I'll simply say, 'Hello, *Frankie*. What's going on?' "

"Hey. It ain't a joke." He stopped in the foyer and turned around. "You *were* kidding, right?"

"Of course." I smiled, patting his back.

"I mean, really, Doc. Don't do nothing like that. You hear him on your machine, don't pick up the damn phone—"

Marino froze as I opened the door, his eyes widening in horror.

"Holy shiiiiit . . ." He stepped out on my porch, idiotically reaching for his revolver, casting about like a madman.

I was too stunned to speak as I stared past him, the winter air alive with the crackle and roar of heat.

Marino's LTD was an inferno against the black night, flames dancing, licking up toward the quarter moon. Grabbing Marino's sleeve, I yanked him back inside the house just as the wailing of a siren sounded in the distance and the gas tank exploded. The living room windows lit up as a ball of fire shot into the sky and ignited the small dogwood trees at the edge of my yard.

"Oh, God," I cried as the power went out.

Marino's big shape paced the carpet in the dark like a crazed bull about to charge as he fumbled with his portable radio and swore.

"The fucking bastard! The fucking bastard!"

I sent Marino away shortly after the incinerated heap that was left of his beloved new car was hauled off in a flatbed truck. He had insisted on staying the night. I had insisted that the several patrol units staking out my house would suffice. He had insisted I check into a hotel, and I had refused to budge. He had his wreckage to deal with and I had mine. My street and yard were a sooty swamp, the downstairs hazy with vile-smelling smoke. The mailbox at the end of my drive looked like a blackened matchstick, and I had lost at least half a dozen boxwoods and just as many trees. More to the point, though I appreciated Marino's concern, I needed to be alone.

It was well past midnight and I was undressing in candlelight when the telephone rang. Frankie's voice seeped like a noxious vapor into my bedroom, poisoning the air I breathed, fouling the privileged refuge of my home.

Sitting on the edge of the bed, I stared blindly at the answering machine as bile crept up my throat and my heart thudded sickly against my ribs.

". . . I wish I could have stayed around to watch. Was it impre-pre-pressive, Kay? Wasn't it something? I don't like it when you have other me-me-men in your house. Now you know. Now you know."

The answering machine stopped and the message light began to blink. Shutting my eyes, I took slow, deep breaths as my heart raced, shadows from the candle flame wavering silently on the walls. How could this be happening to me?

I knew what I had to do. It was the same thing Beryl Madison had done. I wondered if I was experiencing the same fear she had felt when fleeing the car wash, the ragged heart scratched on her car door. My hands trembled violently as I opened the drawer in the bedside table and pulled out the Yellow Pages. After I made the reservations, I called Benton Wesley.

"I don't advise that, Kay," he said, instantly wide awake. "No. Under no circumstances. Listen to me, Kay—"

"I have no choice, Benton. I just wanted someone to know. You can inform Marino, if you wish. But don't interfere. Please. The manuscript—"

"Kay—"

"I've got to find it. I think that's where it is."

"Kay! You're not thinking right!"

"Look." My voice rose. "What am I supposed to do? Wait here until the bastard decides to kick in my door or blow up my car? I stay here, I'm dead. Haven't you figured that out yet, Benton?"

"You've got an alarm system. You've got a gun. He can't blow up your car with you in it. Uh, Marino called. He told me what happened. They're pretty sure someone doused a rag with gasoline, stuffed it into the gas tank. They found pry marks. He pried open the—"

"Jesus, Benton. You're not even listening to me."

"Listen. *You* listen. Please listen to me, Kay. I'll get cover for you, get someone to move in with you, all right? One of our female agents—"

"Good night, Benton."

"Kay!"

I hung up and didn't answer when he immediately called back. I listened numbly to his protests on the machine, blood pounding in my neck as the images rushed back at me, images of Marino's car hissing as flames snarled at arching blasts of water from tumescent fire hoses snaking over my street. When I had discovered the charred little corpse at the end of my driveway, something inside me snapped. The gas tank in Marino's car must have exploded at the very instant Sammy Squirrel was frantically hopping along the power line. Crazily, he leapt for safety. For a split second, his paws simultaneously made contact with the grounded transformer and primary line. Twenty thousand volts of electricity surged through his tiny body, burning him to a crisp and blowing the fuse.

I had scooped him into a shoe box and buried him in my rose garden, the idea of seeing his blackened shape in the light of morning more than I could bear.

The electricity was still out when I finished packing. I went downstairs and nursed brandy and smoked until I stopped shaking, my Ruger on top of the bar glinting in the light of hurricane lanterns. I did not go to bed. I did not look at the wreckage of my yard when I bolted out my door, my suitcase thumping against my leg and filthy water splashing my ankles as I ran to my car. I did not see a single patrol unit as I drove swiftly along my silent street. When I got to the airport shortly after five A.M., I headed straight for the ladies' room and took my handgun out of my pocketbock. Unloading it, I packed it inside my suitcase.

15

PASSING THROUGH THE BOARDING BRIDGE, I deplaned at noon into the sun-drenched concourse of Miami International Airport.

I stopped to buy the Miami *Herald* and a cup of coffee. Finding a small table halfway hidden by a potted palm, I took off my winter blazer and pushed up my sleeves. I was soaking wet, perspiration trickling down my sides and back. My eyes burned from lack of sleep, my head ached, and what I discovered when I spread open the paper did nothing to improve my condition. In the lower left-hand corner of the front page was a spectacular photograph of firefighters hosing down Marino's flaming car. Accompanying the dramatic tableau of arching water, billowing smoke, and trees igniting at the edge of my yard was the following caption:

POLICE CAR EXPLODES

Richmond firefighters work on a city homicide detective's car engulfed in flames on a quiet residential street. The Ford LTD was unoccupied when it exploded last night. There were no injuries. Arson is suspected.

At least there was no reference to whose house Marino's car had been parked in front of or why, thank God. All the same, my mother would see the photograph and she would try to call. "I wish you'd move back to Miami, Kay. Richmond sounds so awful. And the new medical examiner's office is so lovely down here, Kay—looks like something out of the movies," she would say. Oddly, it never seemed to occur to my mother that there were more homicides, shoot-outs, drug busts, race riots, rapes, and robberies in my Spanish-speaking hometown in any given year than in Virginia and the entire British Commonwealth combined.

I would call my mother later. Forgive me, Lord, but I don't have it in me to talk to her now.

Gathering my belongings, I crushed out a cigarette and immersed myself in the tide of tropical clothes, duty-free shopping bags and foreign tongues flowing toward the baggage area, my handbag pressed protectively against my side.

I didn't begin to relax until several hours later as I sped along the Seven Mile Bridge in my rental car. As I drove deeper south, the Gulf of Mexico on one side and the Atlantic on the other, I tried to remember the last time I had been to Key West. Of all the times Tony and I had visited my family in Miami, this was one outing we had never considered. I was fairly certain the last time I had made this drive, I had made it with Mark.

His passion for the beaches and the water and the sun was a devotion returned in kind. If it is possible for nature to favor one creature over another, nature favored Mark. I could scarely remember the year, much less where we had gone, on the occasion he had spent a week with my family. What I remembered with clarity were his baggy white swim trunks and the firm warmth of his hand in mine during our strolls across cool, wet sand. I remembered the startling whiteness of his teeth against his coppery skin, the health and unsuppressed joy in his eyes as he looked for shark's teeth and shells while I smiled in the shade of a wide-brimmed hat. Most of all, what I could not forget was loving a young man named Mark James more than I had thought it was possible to love anything on this earth.

What had changed him? It was hard for me to fathom that he had crossed over into enemy camps, as Ethridge believed and I had no choice but to accept. Mark was always spoiled. He carried about him a sense of entitlement that comes from being the beautiful son of beautiful people. The fruits of the world were his to enjoy, but he had never been dishonest. He had never been cruel. I couldn't even say that he had ever been condescending to those less fortunate than himself, or manipulative with those vulnerable to his charms. His only real sin was that he had not loved me enough. From the distant perch of my midlife perspective, I could forgive him for that. What I could not forgive him for was his dishonesty. I could not forgive him for deteriorating into a lesser man than the one I had once respected and adored. I could not forgive him for no longer being *Mark*.

Passing the U.S. Naval Hospital on U.S. 1, I followed the gentle shoreline curve of North Roosevelt Boulevard. Soon enough I was threading my way through a maze of Key West streets in search of Duval. Sunlight painted the narrow streets white as shadows of tropical foliage stirred by the breeze danced across the pavement. Beneath a blue sky that went on forever, huge palms and mahogany trees cradled houses and shops in spreading arms of vivid green as bougainvillea and hibiscus wooed sidewalks and porches with bright gifts of purple and red. Slowly, I passed people in sandals and shorts, and an endless parade of mopeds. There were very few children and a disproportionate number of men.

The La Concha was a tall, pink Holiday Inn of open spaces and gaudy tropical plants. I'd had no problem making reservations, ostensibly because the tourist season did not begin until the third week of December. But as I left my car in the half-empty parking lot and walked into the somewhat deserted lobby, I couldn't help but think about what Marino had said. Never in my life had I seen so many same-sex couples, and it was patently clear that running deep beneath the robust health of this tiny offshore island was a mother lode of disease. Wherever I looked, it seemed, I saw men dying. I had no phobia of catching hepatitis or AIDS, having learned long ago to cope with the theoretical danger of disease endemic to my work. Nor was I bothered by homosexuals. The older I got, the more I was of the opinion that love can be experienced in many different ways. There is no right or wrong way to love, only in how it is expressed.

As the desk clerk returned my credit card, I asked him to steer me in the general direction of the elevators, and I foggily headed up to my room on the fifth floor. Stripping down to my underwear, I crawled in bed, where I slept for the next fourteen hours.

The following day was just as glorious as the one before, and I was outfitted like any other tourist, except for the loaded Ruger in my pocketbook. My self-imposed mission was to search this island of some thirty thousand people and find two men known to me only as PJ and Walt. I knew from the letters Beryl had written in late August that they were her friends and lived in the rooming house where she had stayed. I had not the slightest clue as to the location or name of this rooming house, and it was my prayer that someone at Louie's could tell me.

I walked, a map that I had bought in the hotel gift shop in hand. Following Duval, I passed rows of shops and restaurants with balustraded balconies that brought to mind New Orleans's French Quarter. I passed sidewalk art displays and boutiques selling exotic plants, silks, and Perugina chocolates, then waited at a crossing to watch the bright yellow cars of the Conch Tour Train rattle by. I began to understand why Beryl Madison had not wanted to leave Key West. With each step I took, Frankie's threatening presence began to fade. By the time I turned left on South Street, he was as remote as Richmond's raw December weather.

Louie's was a white-frame restaurant that had once been a house, on the corner of Vernon and Waddell. Its hardwood floors were spotless, its pale-peach linen-covered tables impeccably set and arranged with exquisite fresh flowers. I followed my host through the air-conditioned dining room, to be seated on the porch where I was dazzled by the variegated blues of water meeting sky, and palms and hanging baskets of blooming plants stirring in air perfumed by the sea. The Atlantic Ocean was nearly under my feet, a bright spattering of sailboats anchored a short swim away. Ordering a rum and tonic, I thought of Beryl's letters and wondered if I were sitting where she had written them.

Most of the tables were occupied. I felt removed from the crowd, my table in a corner against the railing. To my left were four steps leading down to a wide deck, where a small group of young men and women were lounging in bathing suits near a chikee bar. I watched a sinewy Latin boy in a yellow bikini flick a cigarette butt into the water, then get up and languidly stretch. He padded off to buy another round of beers from the bearded bartender, who moved about with the ennui of one tired of his job and no longer young.

Long after I finished my salad and bowl of conch chowder, the group of young people finally clambered down back steps and waded noisily out into the water. Soon they were swimming in the direction of the anchored boats. I paid my bill and approached the bartender. He was leaning back in a chair beneath his thatched canopy, reading a novel.

"What will it be?" he drawled as he rose unenthusiastically to his feet and tucked the book under the bar.

"I was wondering if you sold cigarettes," I said. "I didn't see a machine inside."

"That's it," he said, gesturing toward a limited display behind him. I made a selection.

Slapping the pack on the bar, he charged me the outrageous sum of two dollars, and wasn't particularly gracious when I threw in another fifty cents for a tip. His eyes were a very unfriendly green, his face weathered by years of the sun, his thick, dark beard flecked with gray. He looked hostile and hardened, and I had a suspicion he had lived in Key West for quite a while.

"Do you mind if I ask you a question?" I said.

"Doesn't matter because you just did, ma'am," he answered.

I smiled. "You're right. I just did. And now I'm going to ask you another one. How long have you worked at Louie's?"

"Going on five years." He reached for a towel and began polishing the bar.

"Then you must have known a young woman who went by the name Straw," I asked, recalling from Beryl's letters that she had not used her proper name while here.

"Straw?" he repeated, frowning as he continued to polish.

"A nickname. She was blond, slender, very pretty, and came to Louie's almost every afternoon during this past summer. She would sit out at one of your tables and write."

He stopped polishing and fixed those hard eyes on me. "What's it to you? She a friend of yours?"

"She's a patient of mine." I said the only thing I could think of that was neither off-putting nor a bald-faced lie.

"Huh?" His thick eyebrows shot up. "A patient? What? You're her *doctor*?"

"That's correct."

"Well, there's not a whole lot of good you're going to do her now, *Doc*, I'm sorry to tell you." He plopped down in his chair and leaned back, waiting.

"I'm aware of that," I said. "I know she's dead."

"Yeah, I was pretty shocked when I heard about it. The cops stormed in a couple weeks back with their rubber hoses and thumbscrews. I'll tell you what my buddies told them, nobody here knows shit about what happened to Straw. She was real quiet, a real fine lady. Used to sit right over there." He pointed at an empty table not far from where I was standing. "Used to sit there all the time, just minding her own business."

"Did any of you get to know her?"

"Sure." He shrugged. "We all drank a few brews together. She was partial to Coronas and lime. But I wouldn't say the people here knew her *personally*. I mean, I'm not sure anybody could even tell you where she was from, except that it was from the land of snowbirds."

"Richmond, Virginia," I said.

"You know," he went on, "a lot of people come and go around here. Key West's a live-and-let-live place. A lot of starving artists here, too. Straw wasn't any different from a lot of people I meet—except most people I meet don't end up murdered. Damn." He scratched his beard and slowly shook his head from side to side. "It's really hard to imagine. Kind of blows your mind."

"There are a lot of unanswered questions," I said, lighting a cigarette.

"Yeah, like why the hell do you smoke? I thought doctors are supposed to know better."

"It's a filthy, unhealthy habit. And I do know better. And I think you may as well fix me a rum and tonic because I like to drink, too. Barbancourt with a twist, please."

"Four, eight, what's your pleasure?" He challenged my repertoire of fine booze.

"Twenty-five, if you've got it."

"Nope. Can only get the twenty-five-year-old stuff in the islands. So smooth it will make you cry."

"The best you've got, then," I said.

He shot his finger at a bottle behind him, familiar with its amber glass and five stars on the label. Barbancourt Rhum, aged in barrels for fifteen years, just like the bottle I had discovered in Beryl's kitchen cabinet.

"That would be wonderful," I said.

Grinning and suddenly energized, he got up from his chair, his hands moving with the dexterity of a juggler as he snapped up bottles, measuring a long stream of liquid Haitian gold without benefit of a jigger, which was followed by sparkling splashes of tonic. For the grand finale, he deftly sliced a perfect sliver of a Key lime that looked as if it had just been plucked from the tree, squeezed it into my drink and ran a bruised lemon peel around the rim of the glass. Wiping his hands on the towel he had tucked into the waistband of his faded Levi's, he slid a paper napkin across the bar and presented me with his art. It was, without question, the best rum and tonic I had ever raised to my lips, and I told him so.

"This one's on the house," he said, waving off the ten-dollar bill I extended to him. "Any doctor who smokes and knows her rum's all right by me." Reaching under the bar, he got out his own pack.

"I tell ya," he went on, shaking out the match, "I get so damn tired of hearing all this self-righteous shit about smoking and all the rest of it. You know what I mean? People make you feel like a damn criminal. Me, I say live and let live. That's my motto."

"Yes. I know exactly what you mean," I said as we took long, hungry drags.

"Always something they got to judge you for. You know, what you eat, what you drink, who you date."

"People certainly can be extremely judgmental and unkind," I answered.

"Amen to that."

He sat back down in the shade of his bottle-lined shelter while the sun baked the top of my head. "Okay," he said, "so you're Straw's doctor. What is it you're trying to find out, if you don't mind my asking?"

"There are various circumstances that occurred prior to her death that are very confusing," I said. "I'm hoping her friends might be able to clarify a few points for me—"

"Wait a minute," he interrupted, sitting up straighter in his chair. "When you say *doctor*, like what kind of doctor do you mean?"

"I examined her . . ."

"When?"

"After her death."

"Oh, shit. You telling me you're a *mortician*?" he asked in disbelief.

"I'm a forensic pathologist."

"A *coroner*?"

"More or less."

"Well, I'll be damned." He looked me up and down. "I sure as hell never would've guessed that one."

I didn't know if I had just been paid a compliment or not.

"Do they always send—what did you call it?—a forensic pa-thologist like you around, you know, tracking down information like you're doing?"

"Nobody sent me. I came of my own accord."

"Why?" he asked, his eyes dark with suspicion again. "You came one hell of a long way."

"I care about what happened to her. I care very much."

"You're telling me the cops didn't send you?"

"The cops don't have the authority to *send* me anywhere."

"Good." He laughed. "I like that."

I reached for my drink.

"Bunch of bullies. Think they're all junior Rambos." He stubbed out his cigarette. "Came in here with their damn rubber gloves on. Jesus Christ. Just how do you think *that* looked to our customers? Went to see Brent—he was one of our waiters. He's dying, man, and what do they do? The assholes wear surgical masks and stand back ten feet from his bed like he's Typhoid Mary while they're asking him shit. I swear to God, even if I'd known a thing about what happened to Beryl, I wouldn't have given them the time of day."

The name hit me like a two-by-four, and when our eyes met, I knew he realized the significance of what he had just said.

"Beryl?" I asked.

He leaned back silently in his chair.

I pressed him. "You knew her name was Beryl?"

"Like I said, the cops were here asking questions, talking about her." Uncomfortably, he lit another cigarette, unable to meet my eyes. My bartender friend was a very poor liar.

"Did they talk to you?"

"Nope. I made myself scarce when I saw what was going on."

"Why?"

"I told you. I don't like cops. I've got a Barracuda, a beat-up piece of shit I've had since I was a kid. For some reason, they've always got to pop me. Always giving me tickets for one thing or another, throwing their weight around with their big guns and Ray Bans, like they think they're stars in their own TV series or something."

"You knew her name when she was here," I said quietly. "You knew her name was Beryl Madison long before the police came."

"So what if I did? What's the big deal?"

"She was very secretive about it," I replied with feeling. "She didn't want people down here to know who she was. She didn't tell people who she was. She paid for everything in cash so she wouldn't have to use credit cards, checks, anything that might identify her.

She was terrified. She was running. She didn't want to die."

He was staring wide-eyed at me.

"Please tell me what you know. Please. I have a feeling you were her friend."

He got up, saying nothing, and stepped out from behind the bar. His back to me, he began collecting the empty bottles and other trash the young people had scattered over the deck.

I sipped my drink in silence and stared past him at the water. In the distance a bronzed young man was unfurling a deep blue sail as he prepared to set out to sea. Palm fronds whispered in the breeze and a black Labrador retriever danced along the shore, darting in and out of the surf.

"Zulu," I muttered, staring numbly at the dog.

The bartender stopped what he was doing and looked up at me. "What did you say?"

"Zulu," I repeated. "Beryl mentioned Zulu and your cats in one of her letters. She said Louie's stray animals eat better than any human."

"What letters?"

"She wrote several letters while she was here. We found them in her bedroom after she was murdered. She said the people here had become like family. She thought this was the most beautiful place in the world. I wish she'd never returned to Richmond. I wish she'd stayed right here."

The voice drifting out of me sounded as if it were coming from somebody else, and my vision was blurring. Poor sleep habits, accumulated stress, and the rum were ganging up on me. The sun seemed to dry up what little blood I had left flowing to my brain.

When the bartender finally returned to his chikee hut, he spoke with quiet emotion. "I don't know what to tell you. But yeah, I was Beryl's friend."

Turning to him, I replied, "Thank you. I'd like to think I was her friend, too. That I *am* her friend."

He looked down awkwardly, but not before I detected a softening of his face.

"You can never be real sure who's all right and who ain't," he commented. "It's real hard to know these days, that's for damn sure."

His meaning slowly penetrated my fatigue. "Have there been people asking about Beryl who *aren't* all right? People other than the police? People other than me?"

He poured himself a Coke.

"Have there been? Who?" I repeated, suddenly alarmed.

"Don't know his name." He took a big swallow of his drink. "Some good-looking guy. Young, maybe in his twenties. Dark. Fancy clothes, designer shades. Looked like he just stepped out of *GQ*. I guess this was a couple weeks ago. He said he was a private investigator, shit like that."

Senator Partin's son.

"He wanted to know where Beryl lived while she was here," he went on.

"Did you tell him?"

"Hell, I didn't even talk to him."

"Did *anybody* tell him?" I persisted.

"Not likely."

"Why isn't it likely, and are you ever going to tell me your name?"

"It's not likely because nobody knew except me and a buddy," he said. "And I'll tell you my name if you tell me yours."

"Kay Scarpetta."

"Pleased to meet you. My name's Peter. Peter Jones. My friends call me PJ."

PJ lived two blocks from Louie's in a tiny house completely overcome by a tropical jungle. The foliage was so dense I'm not sure I would have known the paint-eroded frame house was there had it not been for the Barracuda parked in front. One look at the car told me exactly why the police continually hassled its owner. The thing was a piece of subway graffiti on oversize wheels, with spoilers, headers, a rear end jacked up high, and a homemade paint job of hallucinatory shapes and designs in the psychedelic colors of the sixties.

"That's my baby," PJ said, affectionately thumping the hood.

"It's something else, all right," I said.

"Had her since I was sixteen."

"And you should keep her forever," I said sincerely as I ducked under branches and followed him into the cool, dark shade.

"It's not much," he apologized, unlocking the door. "Just one extra bedroom and john upstairs where Beryl stayed. One of these days, I guess I'll rent it out again. But I'm pretty picky about my tenants."

The living room was a hodgepodge of junkyard furniture: a couch and overstuffed chair in ugly shades of pink and green, several mismatched lamps fashioned from odd things like conch shells and coral, and a coffee table constructed from what appeared to have been an oak door in a former life. Scattered about were painted coconuts, starfish, newspapers, shoes, and beer cans, the damp air sour with decay.

"How did Beryl find out about the room you were renting?" I asked, sitting on the couch.

"At Louie's," he replied, switching on several lamps. "Her first few nights here she was staying at Ocean Key, a pretty nice hotel on Duval. I guess she figured out in a hurry that was going to cost her some bucks if she planned to stick around a while." He sat down in the overstuffed chair. "It was maybe the third time she'd come to Louie's for lunch. She would just get a salad and sit there and stare out at the water. She wasn't working on anything then. She would just sit. It was kind of weird the way she would hang around. I mean we're talking hours, like most of the afternoon. Finally, and like I said, I think it was the third time she'd come to Louie's, she wandered down to the bar and was leaning against the railing, looking out at the view. I guess I felt sorry for her."

"Why?" I asked.

He shrugged. "She looked so damn lost, I guess. Depressed or something. I could tell. So I started talking to her. She wasn't what I'd call easy, that's for sure."

"She wasn't easy to get to know," I agreed.

"She was hard as hell to hold a friendly conversation with. I asked her a couple of simple questions, like 'This your first visit here?' Or 'Where are you from?' That sort of thing. And sometimes she wouldn't even answer me. It's like I wasn't there. But it was funny. Something told me to hang in there with her. I asked her what she liked to drink. We started talking about different kinds. It sort of loosened her up, caught her interest. Next thing, I'm letting her try out a few favorites on the house. First a Corona with a twist of lime, which she went nuts over. Then the Barbancourt, like I fixed you. That was real special."

"No doubt that loosened her up quite a bit," I remarked.

He smiled. "Yeah, you got that straight. I mixed it pretty strong. We started shooting the breeze about other things, and next thing you know she's asking me about places to stay in the area. That's when I told her I had a room, and I invited her to come see it, told her to stop by later if she wanted. It was a Sunday, and I'm always off early on Sundays."

"And she came by that night?" I inquired.

"It really surprised me. I sort of figured she wouldn't show. But she did, found the place without a hitch. By then Walt was home. He used to stay at the Square selling his shit until dark. He'd just come in, and the three of us started talking and hitting it off. Next thing, we're walking around Old Town, and end up in Sloppy Joe's. Being a writer and all, she really flipped out, went on and on about Hemingway. She was one smart lady, I'll tell you that."

"Walt was selling silver jewelry," I said. "In Mallory Square."

"How'd you know that?" PJ asked, surprised.

"The letters Beryl wrote," I reminded him.

He stared off in sadness for a moment.

"She also mentioned Sloppy Joe's. I got the impression she was very fond of you and Walt."

"Yeah, the three of us could put away some beer." He picked a magazine off the floor and tossed it on the coffee table.

"You both may have been the only friends she had."

"Beryl was something." He looked at me. "She was something. I'd never met anybody like her before, and probably won't again. Once you got past that wall of hers, she was some fine lady. Smart as shit," he said again, resting his head on the back of the chair and staring up at the paint-peeled ceiling. "I used to love to hear her talk. She could say things just like that." He snapped his fingers. "In a way I couldn't if I had ten years to think about it. My sister's the same way. She teaches school in Denver. English. I've never been real quick with words. Before I bartended I did a lot of things with my hands. Construction, bricklaying, carpentry. Dabbled a little in pottery until I about starved to death. I came here because of Walt. Met him in Mississippi, of all places. In a bus station, if you can fucking believe that. We started talking, rode all the way to Louisiana together. A couple months later, we're both down here. It's so weird." He looked at me. "I mean, that was almost ten years ago. And all I got left is this dump."

"Your life is far from over, PJ," I said gently.

"Yeah." His face turned up to the ceiling, he shut his eyes.

"Where is Walt now?"

"Lauderdale, last I heard."

"I'm very sorry," I said.

"It happens. What can I say?"

There was a moment of silence and I decided it was time to take a chance.

"Beryl was writing a book while she was here."

"You got that straight. When she wasn't frapping around with the two of us, she was working on that damn book."

"It's disappeared," I said.

He didn't respond.

"The so-called private investigator you mentioned and various other people are keenly interested in it. You know that already. I believe you do."

He remained silent, his eyes shut.

"You have no good reason to trust me, PJ, but I hope you'll listen," I went on in a low voice. "I've got to find that manuscript, the manuscript Beryl was working on while she was here. I think she didn't take it back to Richmond with her when she left Key West. Can you help me?"

Opening his eyes, he peered over at me. "With all due respect, Dr. Scarpetta, saying I did know, why should I? Why should I break a promise?"

"Did you promise her you'd never tell where it is?" I asked.

"Doesn't matter, and I asked you first," he answered.

Taking a deep breath, I looked down at the dirty gold shag carpet beneath my feet as I leaned forward on the couch.

"I know of no good reason for you to break a promise to a friend, PJ," I said.

"Bullshit. You wouldn't ask me if you didn't know of a good reason."

"Did Beryl tell you about him?" I asked.

"You mean the asshole hassling her?"

"Yes."

"Yeah. I knew about it." He suddenly got up. "I don't know about you, but I'm ready for a beer."

"Please," I said, believing it was important I accept his hospitality despite my better judgment. I was still woozy from the rum.

Returning from the kitchen, he handed me a sweating bottle of ice-cold Corona, a wedge of lime floating in the long neck. It tasted wonderful.

PJ sat down and began talking again. "Straw, I mean Beryl, I guess I may as well call her Beryl, was scared shitless. To be honest, when I heard about what happened, I wasn't really surprised. I mean, it freaked me. But I wasn't really surprised. I told her to stay here. I told her to screw the rent, that she could stay. Walt and me, well, I guess it was funny, but it got to where she was sort of like our sister. The fuckhead screwed me, too."

"I beg your pardon?" I asked, startled by his sudden anger.

"That's when Walt left. It was after we heard about it. I don't know. He changed, Walt did. I can't say that what happened to her was the only reason. We had our problems. But it did something to him. He got distant and wouldn't talk anymore. Then, one morning, he left. He just left."

"This was when? Several weeks ago, when you found out from the police, when they came to Louie's?"

He nodded.

"It's screwed me, too, PJ," I said. "It's totally screwed me, too."

"What do you mean? How the hell's it screwed you, other than causing you a lot of trouble?"

"I'm living Beryl's nightmare." I was barely able to say it.

He took a swallow of beer, his eyes intense on me.

"Right now I suppose I'm running, too—for the same reason she was."

"Man, you're making my brain bleed," he said, shaking his head. "What are you talking about?"

"Did you see the photograph on the front page of this morning's *Herald*?" I asked. "A photograph of a police car burning in Richmond."

"Yeah," he said, puzzled. "I sort of remember it."

"That was in front of my house, PJ. The detective was inside my living room talking to me when his car was torched. It's not the first thing that's happened. You see, he's after me, too."

"Who is, for Christ's sake?" he asked, even though I could tell he knew.

"The man who murdered Beryl," I said with great difficulty. "The man who then butchered Beryl's mentor, Cary Harper, whom you may have heard her mention."

"Lots of times. Shit. I'm not believing this."

"Please help me, PJ."

"I don't know how I can." He became so upset he jumped out of the chair and started pacing. "Why would the pig come after you?"

"He suffers delusional jealousy. He's obsessive. He's a paranoid schizophrenic. He seems to hate anyone connected with Beryl. *I don't know why, PJ.* But I have to find out who he is. I have to find *him*," I said.

"I don't know who the hell he is. Or where the hell he is. If I did, I'd find him and tear his fucking head off!"

"I need that manuscript, PJ," I said.

"What the fuck does her manuscript have to do with it?" he protested.

So I told him. I told him about Cary Harper and his necklace. I told him about the phone calls and the fibers, and the autobiographical work Beryl was writing that I had been accused of stealing. I revealed everything I could think of about the cases while my soul withered in fear. I had never, not even once, discussed the details of a case with anyone other than the investigators or attorneys involved. When I was finished, PJ silently left the room. When he returned, he was carrying an army knapsack, which he placed in my lap.

"There," he said. "I swore to God I would never do this. I'm sorry, Beryl," he muttered. "I'm sorry."

Opening the canvas flap, I carefully pulled out what must have been close to a thousand typed pages scribbled with handwritten notes, and four computer diskettes, all of it bound in thick rubber bands.

"She told us never to let anybody have it should something happen to her. I promised."

"Thank you, Peter. God bless you," I said, and then I asked of him one last thing.

"Did Beryl ever mention anyone she referred to as 'M'?"

He stood very still and stared at his beer.

"Do you know who this person is?" I asked.

"Myself," he said.

"I don't understand."

" 'M' for 'Myself.' She wrote letters to herself," he said.

"The two letters we found," I said to him. "The ones we found on the floor of her bedroom after she was murdered, the ones that mentioned you and Walt, were addressed to 'M.' "

"I know," he said, shutting his eyes.

"How do you know?"

"I knew it when you mentioned Zulu and the cats. I knew you'd read those letters. That's when I decided you were all right, that you were who you said you were."

"Then you've read the letters, too?" I asked, stunned.

He nodded.

"We never found the originals," I muttered. "The two we found are photocopies."

"That's because she burned everything," he said, taking a deep breath, steadying himself.

"But she didn't burn her book."

"No. She told me she didn't know where she'd go next or what she'd do if he was still there, still after her. That she'd call me later on and tell me where to mail the book. And if I didn't hear from her, to hold on to it, never give it up to anyone. She never called, you know. She never fucking called." He wiped his eyes, averting his face from me. "The book was her hope, you know. Her hope of being alive." His voice caught when he added, "She never stopped hoping things would turn out all right."

"What exactly was it that she burned, PJ?"

"Her diary," he replied. "I guess you could call it that. Letters she'd been writing to herself. She said it was her therapy and that she didn't want anyone to see them. They were very private, her most private thoughts. The day before she left, she burned all her letters except two."

"The two I saw," I almost whispered. "Why? Why didn't she burn those two letters?"

"Because she wanted me and Walt to have them."

"As a remembrance?"

"Yeah," he said, reaching for his beer and roughly rubbing tears from his eyes. "A piece of herself, a record of thoughts she had while she was here. The day before she left, the day she burned the stuff, she went out and photocopied just those two. She kept the copies and gave us the originals, said it sort of made us *indentured* to each other—that was the word she used. The three of us would always be together in our thoughts as long as we had the letters."

When he walked me out, I turned around, throwing my arms around him in a hug of thanks.

I headed back to my hotel as the sun settled, palms etched against a spreading band of fire. Throngs of people clambered noisily toward the bars along Duval, and the enchanted air was alive with music, laughter, and lights. I walked with a spring in my step, the army knapsack slung over my shoulder. For the first time in weeks I was happy, almost euphoric. I was completely unprepared for what awaited me in my room.

16

I DID NOT RECALL leaving any lamps on and just assumed the house-keeping staff must have neglected to switch them off after changing the linen and emptying the ashtrays. I had already locked the door and was humming to myself as I passed the bath when I realized I was not alone.

Mark was sitting near the window, an open briefcase on the carpet beside his chair. In that moment's hesitation when my feet didn't know which way to move, his eyes met mine in speechless communication, thrilling my heart and seizing it with terror.

Pale and dressed in a winter gray suit, he looked as if he had just arrived from the airport, his suit bag propped against the bed. If he had a mental geiger counter, I was sure my knapsack was making it click like mad. Sparacino had sent him. I thought of the Ruger in my handbag, but I knew I could never turn a gun on Mark James and squeeze the trigger if it came to that.

"How did you get in?" I asked dully, standing very still.

"I'm your husband," he said, and reaching in his pocket, he displayed a hotel key to my room.

"You bastard," I whispered, my heart pounding harder.

His face blanched. He averted his eyes. "Kay—"

"Oh, God. You bastard!"

"Kay. I'm here because Benton Wesley sent me. Please." Then he got up from the chair.

I watched him in stunned silence as he produced a fifth of

whiskey from his suit bag. Walking past me to the bar, he began filling glasses with ice. His motions were slow and deliberate, as if he was doing his best not to further unnerve me. He also seemed very tired.

"Have you eaten?" he asked, handing me a drink.

Moving past him, I unceremoniously dropped the knapsack and my pocketbook on top of the dresser.

"I'm starved," he said, loosening his shirt collar and yanking off his tie. "Damn, I must have changed planes four times. Don't think I've had anything to eat but peanuts since breakfast."

I said nothing.

"I've already ordered for us," he went on quietly. "You'll be ready to eat by the time it gets here."

Moving to the window, I gazed out at the purple-gray clouds over the lights of Key West's Old Town streets. Mark pulled up a chair, slipped off his shoes, and propped his feet up on the edge of the bed.

"Let me know when you're ready for me to explain," he said, swirling ice in his glass.

"I wouldn't believe anything you said, Mark," I answered coldly.

"Fair enough. I'm paid to live a lie. I've gotten unbelievably good at it."

"Yes," I echoed, "you've gotten unbelievably good at it. How did you find me? I don't believe Benton told you. He doesn't know where I'm staying, and there must be fifty hotels on this island and just as many guesthouses."

"You're right. I'm sure there are, and it took me exactly one phone call to find you," he said.

Defeated, I sat down on the bed.

Reaching inside his suit jacket, he pulled out a folded brochure and handed it to me. "Look familiar?"

It was the same visitor's information guide Marino had found inside Beryl Madison's bedroom, a photocopy of which was included in her case file. It was the same guide I had studied countless times and then recalled two nights before when I had decided to flee to Key West. One side of it listed restaurants and places to sightsee and shop, the other was a street map bordered by advertisements, including one for this hotel, which was where I had gotten the idea to stay here.

"Benton finally got hold of me yesterday after repeated attempts," he went on. "He was pretty upset, said you'd taken off, headed here, and then we went about the business of trying to track you down. Apparently there's a photocopy of Beryl's brochure in the file he has. He assumed you would have seen it, too, and possibly even made a copy for your own record. We decided it might occur to you to use it as a guide."

"Where did you get this?" I returned the brochure to him.

"At the airport. It just so happens this hotel is the only one listed. It was the first place I called. They had a reservation in your name."

"All right. So I wouldn't make a very good fugitive."

"A damn poor one."

"It *is* where I got the idea, if you must know," I admitted angrily. "I've been through Beryl's paperwork so many times, I remembered the brochure, remembered seeing the ad for a Holiday Inn on Duval. I suppose it stood out to me because I wondered if she might have stayed here when she first arrived in Key West."

"Had she?" He lifted his glass.

"No."

As he got up to refresh our drinks, there was a knock on the door and my heart jumped as Mark casually reached around and withdrew a 9-millimeter pistol from under the back of his suit jacket. Holding it up, he looked through the peephole and returned the gun to the back of his trousers as he opened the door. Our dinner had arrived, and when Mark paid the young woman in cash, she smiled brightly and said, "Thank you, Mr. Scarpetta. I hope you enjoy your steaks."

"Why did you check in as my husband?" I demanded.

"I'll sleep on the floor. But you're not staying alone," he answered, setting covered dishes on the table near the window and uncorking the bottle of wine. Slipping out of his suit jacket and tossing it on the bed, he set the pistol on top of the dresser not far from my knapsack and within easy reach.

I waited until he had sat down to eat before asking him about the gun.

"An ugly little monster, but maybe my only friend," he replied, cutting into his steak. "And for that matter, I presume you have your thirty-eight with you, probably in your knapsack." He glanced at the knapsack on the dresser.

"It's in my pocketbook, for your information," I blurted out ridiculously. "And how in God's name did you know I have a thirty-eight?"

"Benton told me. He also said you'd recently gotten a license to carry it concealed, and he figured you weren't going many places without your piece these days." He sipped his wine, adding, "Not bad."

"Has Benton told you my dress size, too?" I asked, forcing myself to eat as my stomach begged me not to.

"Now, that he doesn't need to tell me. You still wear an eight, look just as good as you did when we were in Georgetown. Better, in fact."

"I'd greatly appreciate it if you'd stop acting like a cavalier son of a bitch and tell me how the hell you even know Benton Wesley's name, much less merit the privilege of enjoying so many little tête-à-têtes with him about me."

"Kay." He set down his fork as he met my angry gaze. "I've known Benton longer than you have. Haven't you figured it out yet? Do I have to spell it in neon lights?"

"Yes. Write it in big letters across the sky, Mark. Because I don't know what to believe. I have no idea who you are anymore. I don't trust you. In fact, at this moment I'm scared to death of you."

Leaning back in the chair, his face as serious as I had ever seen it, he said, "Kay, I'm sorry you're afraid of me. I'm sorry you don't trust me. And it makes perfect sense because very few people in this world have any idea who I am, and there are times when I'm not so sure myself. I couldn't tell you this before, but it's over." He paused. "Benton taught me in the Academy long before you got to know him."

"You're an *agent*?" I asked in disbelief.

"Yes."

"No," I said, my mind reeling. "No! *I'm not going to believe you this time, goddammit!*"

Getting up without a word, he went to the phone by the bed and dialed.

"Come here," he said, glancing over at me.

Then he handed me the receiver.

"Hello?" I recognized the voice immediately.

"Benton?" I said.

"Kay? Are you all right?"

"Mark's here," I replied. "He found me. Yes, Benton. I'm all right."

"Thank God. You're in good hands. I'm sure he'll explain."

"I'm sure he will. Thank you, Benton. Good-bye."

Mark took the receiver from me and hung up. When we returned to the table he looked at me for a long time before he spoke again.

"I left my law practice after Janet was killed. I'm still not sure why, Kay, but it doesn't matter. I worked in the field, in Detroit for a while, then went under deep cover. The bit about my working for Orndorff & Berger was all a ruse."

"You're not going to tell me Sparacino's working for the Feds, too," I said, and I was trembling.

"Hell, no," he replied, looking away from me.

"What's he involved in, Mark?"

"His minor infractions included his cheating Beryl Madison, tampering with her royalty statements like he's done with a number of his clients. And as I've already told you, he was manipulating her, playing her against Cary Harper and cooking up a big publicity scam—again, like he's done a number of times before."

"Then what you told me in New York is true."

"Certainly not everything. I couldn't tell you everything."

"Did Sparacino know I was coming to New York?" It was a question that had been tormenting me for weeks.

"Yes. I set it up, ostensibly so I could get more information from you and manipulate you into talking to him. He knew you would never agree to a discussion. So I volunteered to bring you to him."

"Jesus," I muttered.

"I thought everything was under control. I thought he wasn't on to me until we got to the restaurant. That's when I realized everything was going to hell," Mark went on.

"Why?"

"Because he had me tailed. I've known for a long time that the Partin brat's one of his snitches. It's how he pays the rent while he's waiting for bit parts in soaps, TV commercials, and underwear ads. Obviously, Sparacino was getting suspicious of me."

"Why would he send Partin? Wouldn't he realize you'd recognize him?"

"Sparacino isn't aware that I know about Partin," he said.

"Point is, when I saw Partin in the restaurant, I knew Sparacino had sent him to make sure I was really meeting with you, to see what I was up to, just like he sent the so-called Jeb Price to ransack your office."

"Are you going to tell me Jeb Price is a starving actor, too?"

"No. We arrested him in New Jersey last week. He won't be bothering anybody for a while."

"And I suppose your knowing Diesner in Chicago was also a lie," I said.

"He lives in legend. But I've never met the man."

"And I suppose your coming to see me in Richmond was a setup, too, wasn't it?" I fought back tears.

Refilling our wineglasses, he replied, "I wasn't really driving in from D.C. I'd just flown in from New York. Sparacino sent me to pick your brain, find out everything he could about Beryl's murder."

I sipped my wine, silent for a moment as I tried to regain my composure.

Then I asked, "Is he somehow involved in her murder, Mark?"

"At first that worried me," he answered. "If nothing else, I wondered if Sparacino's games with Harper had gone too far, if Harper had gone haywire and murdered Beryl. But then Harper was murdered, and as time went by, I failed to pick up on anything that would make me think Sparacino was connected with their deaths. I think he wanted me to find out everything I could about Beryl's murder because he was paranoid."

"Was he worried the police would have gone through her office, that maybe it would come out that her royalty statements were fraudulent?" I asked.

"Maybe. I do know he wants her manuscript. No question of its value. But beyond that, I'm not sure."

"What about his lawsuit, his vendetta against the attorney general?"

"It's generated a lot of publicity," Mark replied. "And Sparacino despises Ethridge, would be delighted if he could humiliate him or even run him out of office."

"Scott Partin has been down here," I informed him. "He was down here not long ago asking questions about Beryl."

"Interesting" was all he said, taking another bite of steak.

"How long have you been connected with Sparacino?"

"More than two years."

"Lord," I said.

"The Bureau set it up very carefully. I was sent in as a lawyer named Paul Barker looking for work, looking to get rich quick. I went through the moves necessary to make him hook into me. Of course he checked me out, and when certain details didn't add up, he finally confronted me. I admitted I was living under an assumed name, that I was part of the Federal Protected Witness Program. It's convoluted and difficult to explain, but Sparacino believed I had been involved in illegal activities in a former life in Tallahassee, had gotten nailed, and that the Feds had rewarded me for my testimony by fictionalizing my identity and my past."

"Had you been involved in illegal activities?" I asked.

"No."

"Ethridge is of the opinion that you have been," I said. "That you've also served time in prison."

"I'm not surprised, Kay. The federal marshals tend to be very cooperative with the Bureau. On paper, the Mark James you once knew looks pretty bad. A lawyer who crossed over, was disbarred, and spent two years in the pen."

"Am I to assume that Sparacino's connection with Orndorff & Berger is a front?" I asked.

"Yes."

"For what, Mark? There must be more to it than his publicity scams."

"We are convinced he has been laundering money for the mob, Kay. Money from narcotics trafficking. We also believed he is tied in with organized crime in the casinos. Politicians are involved, judges, other attorneys. The network is unbelievable. We've known it for quite a while, but it's dangerous business when one part of the criminal justice system attacks another. We had to have admissible evidence of guilt. That's why I was sent in. The more I uncovered, the more there was. Three months turned into six, and then it became years."

"I don't understand. His firm is legitimate, Mark."

"New York is Sparacino's own little country. He has power. Orndorff & Berger knows very little about what he does. I've never worked for the firm. They don't even know my name."

"But Sparacino does," I pressed him. "I heard him refer to you as Mark."

"Yes, he knows my real name. As I've said, the Bureau was very careful. They did quite a good job of rewriting my life, of creating a paper trail that makes the Mark James you once knew someone you wouldn't recognize, much less like." He paused, his face grim. "Sparacino and I agreed that he would refer to me as Mark in your presence. The rest of the time I was Paul. I worked for him. For a while I lived with his family. I was his loyal son, or at least this is what he thought."

"I know Orndorff & Berger never heard of you," I confessed. "I tried to call you in New York and Chicago, and they didn't know who I was talking about. I called Diesner. He didn't know who you were, either. I may not make a good fugitive, but you make an equally poor spy."

He was silent for a moment.

Then he said, "The Bureau had to bring me in, Kay. You came on the scene, and I took a lot of chances. I got emotionally involved because you were involved. I was stupid."

"I don't know how I'm suppose to respond to that."

"Drink your wine and watch the moon rise over Key West. That's the best way to respond."

"But, Mark," I said, and by now I was hopelessly caught up in him, "there's one very important point I don't understand."

"I'm quite sure there are any number of points you don't understand and may never understand, Kay. We have a lot of life between us that can't be spanned in an evening."

"You said Sparacino sicced you on me to pick my brain. How did he know you were acquainted with me? Did you tell him?"

"He introduced you into a conversation right after we heard about Beryl's murder. He said you were the medical examiner, the chief in Virginia. I panicked. I didn't want him messing with you. I decided it would be better if I did it instead."

"I appreciate the chivalry," I said ironically.

"And you should." His eyes were on mine. "I told him we had dated in a former life. I wanted him to turn you over to me. And he did."

"And that's the whole of it?" I said.

"I would like to think so, but I'm afraid my motives may have been mixed."

"Mixed?"

"I think I was enticed by the possibility of seeing you again."

"So you've said."

"I wasn't lying."

"Are you lying to me now?"

"I swear to God I'm not lying to you now," he said.

I suddenly realized I was still dressed in a polo shirt and shorts, my skin sticky, my hair a mess. I excused myself from the table and went into the bathroom. Half an hour later, I was swathed in my favorite terrycloth robe, and Mark was sound asleep on top of my bed.

He groaned and opened his eyes when I sat down beside him.

"Sparacino's a very dangerous man," I said, slowly running my fingers through his hair.

"No question about it," Mark said sleepily.

"He sent Partin. I'm not sure I understand how he knew that Beryl was ever down here."

"Because she called him from down here, Kay. He's known it all along."

I nodded, not really surprised. Beryl may have depended on Sparacino to the bitter end, but she must have begun to distrust him. Otherwise she would have left her manuscript with him and not in the hands of a bartender named PJ.

"What would he do if he knew you were here?" I asked quietly. "What would Sparacino do if he knew you and I were together in this room having this conversation?"

"Be jealous as hell."

"Seriously."

"Probably kill us if he thought he could get away with it."

"Could he get away with it, Mark?"

Pulling me close, he said into my neck, "Shit, no."

We were awakened the next morning by the sun, and after making love again we slept entangled in each other's arms until ten.

While Mark showered and shaved, I stared out at the day, and never had colors been so bright or the sun shone so magnificently on the tiny offshore island of Key West. I would buy a condo where Mark and I would make love for the rest of our lives. I would ride a bicycle for the first time since I was a child, take up tennis again, and quit smoking. I would work harder at getting along with my family, and Lucy would be our frequent guest. I would visit Louie's often and adopt PJ as our friend. I would watch sunlight dance over the sea and say prayers to a woman named Beryl Madison whose terrible death had given new meaning to my life and taught me to love again.

After brunch, which we ate in the room, I pulled Beryl's manuscript out of the knapsack while Mark looked on in disbelief.

"Is that what I think it is?" he asked.

"Yes. It's exactly what you think it is," I said.

"Where in God's name did you find it, Kay?" He got up from the table.

"She left it with a friend," I answered, and next we were propping pillows behind us, the manuscript between us on the bed as I told Mark all about my conversations with PJ.

Morning turned into afternoon, and we did not step outside the room except to place dirty dishes in the hall and replace them with sandwiches and snacks we ordered sent up as the spirit moved. For hours we said very little to each other as we turned through the pages of Beryl's Madison's life. The book was incredible, and more than once it brought tears to my eyes.

Beryl was a songbird born in a storm, a ragged bit of beautiful color clinging to the branches of a terrible life. Her mother had died, and her father had replaced her with a woman who treated Beryl with scorn. Unable to endure the world she lived in, she learned the art of creating one of her own. Writing was her way of coping, and it was a talent enhanced like artistry by the deaf and music by the blind. She could fashion from words a world I could taste, smell, and feel.

Her relationship with the Harpers was as intense as it was deranged. They were three volatile elements forming a thunderhead of unbelievable destruction when they finally lived together in that storybook mansion on its river of timeless dreams. Cary Harper bought and restored the great house for Beryl, and it was in the upstairs bedroom where I had slept that he robbed her one night of her virginity when she was only sixteen.

When she did not come down to breakfast the following morning, Sterling Harper went upstairs to check and found Beryl in a fetal position, crying. Unable to face that her famous brother had raped their surrogate daughter, Miss Harper battled the demons of her house with troops of denial. She never said a word to Beryl or attempted to intervene, but softly shut her door at night and slept her fitful sleep.

The molestation of Beryl continued, week after week, less

frequently as she got older and finally ending with the Pulitzer Prizewinner's impotence, brought on by long evenings of hard drinking and other excesses, including drugs. When the interest from his accumulated book earnings and family inheritance could no longer support his vices, he turned to his friend, Joseph McTigue, who focused his kindly attentions and skills on Harper's precarious finances, eventually making the author "not only solvent again, but wealthy enough to afford the finest whiskey by the case and cocaine binges whenever he pleased."

According to Beryl, after she moved out Miss Harper painted the portrait over the library mantel, a portrait of a child robbed of innocence, intended unconsciously or not to torment Harper forever. He drank more, wrote less, and began suffering from insomnia. He began frequenting Culpeper's Tavern, a ritual encouraged by his sister, who used those hours to conspire against him with Beryl on the phone. The final blow came in a dramatic act of defiance when Beryl, encouraged by Sparacino, violated her contract.

It was her way of reclaiming her life and, in her words, "preserving the beauty of my friend, Sterling, by pressing the memory of her between these pages like wildflowers." Beryl began her book very shortly after Miss Harper was diagnosed as having cancer. Their bond was inviolable, their love for each other immense.

Naturally, there were lengthy digressions about the books Beryl had written and the sources of her ideas. Excerpts from earlier works were included, and I suspected this might have explained the partial manuscript we found on her bedroom dresser after she was dead. It was hard to say. It was hard to know what had gone on in Beryl's mind. But I could see that her work was extraordinary, and sufficiently scandalous to have frightened Cary Harper and caused Sparacino to lust after it.

What I failed to see as the afternoon wore on was anything that raised the specter of Frankie. There was no mention in her manuscript of the ordeal that would eventually end her life. I supposed it was too much for her to contemplate. Perhaps, she hoped, it would pass with time.

I was nearing the end of Beryl's book when Mark suddenly put his hand on my arm.

"What?" I could barely tear my eyes away.

"Kay. Take a look at this," he said, lightly placing a page on top of the one I was reading.

It was the opening of Chapter Twenty-five, a page I had previously read. It took me a moment to see what I had missed. It was a very clean photocopy, and not an original typed page like all of the others.

"I thought you said this was the only copy," Mark quizzed me.

"I was under the impression that it was," I replied, mystified.

"I wonder if she made a copy and mixed up two of the pages."

"That's the way it looks," I considered. "But where is the copy, then? It hasn't turned up."

"Got no idea."

"You sure Sparacino doesn't have it?"

"I'm pretty sure I would know if he did. I've turned his office inside out during his absences and I've done the same to his house. Besides, I think he would have told me, at least when he thought we were buddies."

"I think we'd better go see PJ."

It was, we discovered, PJ's day off. He was not at Louie's or at home. Dusk was settling over the island before we finally caught up with him at Sloppy Joe's, by which time he was three sheets to the wind. I grabbed him at the bar and led him by the hand to a table.

I hastily made introductions. "This is Mark James, a friend of mine."

PJ nodded and lifted his longnecked bottle of beer in a drunken toast. He blinked several times, as if trying to clear his vision, while he openly admired my attractive masculine companion. Mark seemed oblivious.

Raising my voice above the din of the crowd and band, I said to PJ, "Beryl's manuscript. Did she make a copy of it while she was here?"

Taking a swig of beer and rocking to the music, he replied, "Don't know. She never said anything about it to me, if she did."

"But is it possible?" I persisted. "Might she have done this when she photocopied the letters she gave to you?"

He shrugged, beads of perspiration rolling down his temples, face flushed. PJ was more than drunk, he was stoned.

While Mark looked on impassively, I tried again. "Well, did she carry the manuscript with her when she went out to photocopy the letters?"

". . . Just like Bogie and Bacall . . ." PJ sang along in a hoarse baritone, slapping the edge of the table in rhythm with the mob.

"PJ!" I cried loudly.

"Man," he protested, his eyes riveted to the stage, "it's my favorite song."

So I sank back in my chair and let PJ sing his favorite song. During a brief break in the performance, I repeated my question. PJ drained his bottle of beer, then replied with surprising clarity, "All I remember is Beryl had the knapsack with her that day, okay? I gave it to her, you know. Something she could use down here to haul her shit around in. She headed off to Copy Cat or somewhere, and she sure as hell had the knapsack with her. So, yeah." He got out his cigarettes. "She might've had the book in the knapsack. And she might've made a copy of it when she copied the letters. All I know is she left me the one I handed over to you whenever it was."

"Yesterday," I said.

"Yeah, man. Yesterday." Shutting his eyes, he started slapping the edge of the table again.

"Thank you, PJ," I said.

He didn't pay any attention as we left, pushing our way out of the bar to escape into the fresh night air.

"That's what's known as an exercise in futility," Mark said as we began walking back to the hotel.

"I don't know," I answered. "But it makes sense to me that Beryl would have copied the manuscript when she copied the letters. I can't imagine her leaving her book with PJ unless she had a copy."

"After having met him, I can't imagine her doing so, either. PJ's not exactly what I'd call a reliable custodian."

"Actually he is, Mark. He's just a little carried away tonight."

"Fried is the word."

"Maybe that's what my appearance did to him."

"If Beryl copied her manuscript and carried it back to Richmond with her," Mark continued, "then whoever killed her must have stolen it."

"Frankie," I said.

"Which may explain why he next went after Cary Harper. Our friend Frankie got jealous, the thought of Harper in Beryl's bedroom driving him crazy—crazier. Harper's habit of going to Culpeper's every afternoon is in Beryl's book."

"I know."

"Frankie could have read about that, known how to find him, figured it was the best time to catch him by surprise."

"What better time than when you're half crocked and getting out of your car on a dark driveway in the middle of nowhere?" I said.

"Just surprises me he didn't go after Sterling Harper, too."

"Maybe he would have."

"You're right. He never had the chance," Mark said. "She spared him the trouble."

Reaching for each other's hands, we fell silent, our shoes quietly scuffing along the sidewalk as the breeze stirred the trees. I wanted the moment to go on forever. I dreaded the truths we had to face. It wasn't until Mark and I were in our room, drinking wine together, that I asked the question.

"What next, Mark?"

"Washington," he said, turning away to look out the window. "In fact, tomorrow. I'll be debriefed, reprogrammed." He took a deep breath. "Hell, I don't know what I'll do after that."

"What do you want to do after that?" I asked.

"I don't know, Kay. Who knows where they'll send me?" He continued staring out at the night. "And I know you're not going to leave Richmond."

"No, I can't leave Richmond. Not now. My work is my life, Mark."

"It's always been your life," he said. "My work is my life, too. That leaves very little room for diplomacy."

His words, his face were breaking my heart. I knew he was right. When I tried to speak again, the tears came.

We held each other tightly until he fell asleep in my arms. Gently disengaging myself, I got up and returned to the window, where I sat smoking, my mind obsessively turning over many things until dawn began to pink the sky.

I took a long shower. The hot water soothed me and reinforced my resolve. Refreshed and robed, I left the humid bathroom to find Mark up and ordering breakfast.

"I'm returning to Richmond," I announced firmly, sitting next to him on the bed.

He frowned. "Not a good idea, Kay."

"I've found the manuscript, you're leaving, and I don't want to wait here alone expecting Frankie, Scott Partin, or even Sparacino himself to show up," I explained.

"They haven't found Frankie. It's too risky. I'll arrange for your protection here," he protested. "Or in Miami. That's probably better. You could stay with your family for a while."

"No."

"Kay—"

"Mark, Frankie may already have left Richmond. They may not find him for weeks. They may never find him. What am I supposed to do, hide in Florida forever?"

Leaning back into the pillows, he didn't respond.

I reached for his hand. "I won't allow my life, my career to be disrupted like this, and I refuse to be intimidated any longer. I'll call Marino and arrange for him to meet me at the airport."

He wrapped both of his hands around mine. Looking into my eyes, he said, "Come back with me to D.C. Or you can stay at Quantico for a while."

I shook my head. "Nothing's going to happen to me, Mark."

He pulled me close. "I can't stop thinking about what happened to Beryl."

Neither could I.

We kissed good-bye at the Miami airport, and I walked quickly away from him and did not look back. I was awake only during the interval when I changed planes in Atlanta. The rest of the time I slept in my seat, physically and emotionally drained.

Marino met me at the gate. For once he seemed to sense my mood and followed me patiently and in silence through the terminal. The Christmas decorations and merchandise in the airport's shop windows only fed my depression. I wasn't looking forward to the holidays. I wasn't sure how or when Mark and I would see each other again. To make matters worse, when Marino and I got to the baggage area we spent an hour watching luggage make its lazy rounds on a carousel. It gave Marino an opportunity to debrief me while I got increasingly out of sorts. Finally, I reported my suitcase missing. After the tedium of filling out a detailed multiple-part form, I retrieved my car and, with Marino once again tailing me, drove home.

The dark, rainy night blessedly obscured the damage to the front yard as we parked in my driveway. Marino had reminded me earlier that they'd had no luck locating Frankie while I was away.

He wasn't taking any chances. After shining his flashlight over my property in search of broken windows or anything else hinting of an intruder, he took me through my house, turning on lights in each room, checking closets and even looking under the beds.

We were heading to the kitchen and thinking about coffee when we both recognized the code blaring out of his portable radio.

"Two-fifteen, ten-thirty-three—"

"Shit!" Marino exclaimed, snatching the radio out of his jacket pocket.

Ten-thirty-three was the code for "Mayday." Radio broadcasts were ricocheting like bullets through the air. Patrol cars were responding like jets taking off. An officer was down at a convenience store not far from where I lived. Apparently he had been shot.

"Seven-oh-seven, ten-thirty-three," Marino barked to the dispatcher that he was responding as he hurried to my front door.

"Goddamm it! Walters! He's just a fuckin' kid!" He ran out cursing into the rain, calling back to me, "Lock up tight, Doc. I'll have a couple uniform men over here right away!"

I paced the kitchen, finally sitting at the table nursing straight Scotch while a hard rain drummed the roof and beat against windowpanes. My suitcase was lost and my .38 was inside it. It was a detail I had neglected to mention to Marino, my mind dulled by exhaustion. Too jittery to go to bed, I flipped through Beryl's manuscript, which I had been wise enough to hand-carry on the plane, and sipped my drink waiting for the police to arrive.

Just before midnight my doorbell rang, startling me out of my chair.

Looking through my front door peephole and expecting the officers Marino had promised, I saw a pale young man wearing a dark slicker and some sort of uniform cap. He looked cold and wet as he hunched against the blowing rain, a clipboard held against his chest.

"Who is it?" I called out.

"Omega Courier Service from Byrd Airport," he answered. "I've got your suitcase, ma'am."

"Thank God," I said with feeling, deactivating the alarm and unlocking the door.

Incapacitating terror seized me as he put down my suitcase inside the foyer and I suddenly remembered. I had written my office address on the lost baggage claim I had filled out at the airport, not my home address!

17

DARK HAIR WAS a stringy fringe beneath his cap, and he did not look me in the eye as he said, "If you'll just si-sign this, ma'am." He handed me the clipboard as voices played madly in my mind.

"They were late coming in from the airport because the airline lost Mr. Harper's bag."

"Is your hair naturally blond, Kay, or do you bleach it?"

"It was after the boy delivered the luggage . . ."

"All of them gone, now."

"Last year we got in a fiber identical to this orange one in every respect when Roy was asked to examine trace recovered from a Boeing seven forty-seven . . ."

"It was after the boy delivered the luggage!"

Slowly I took the offered pen and clipboard from the outstretched brown leather–gloved hand.

In a voice I did not recognize, I instructed, "Would you please be so kind as to open my suitcase. I can't possibly sign anything until I make sure my belongings are present and accounted for."

For an instant his hard pale face registered confusion. His eyes widened a little as they dropped down to my upright bag, and I struck so fast he didn't have time to raise his hands to ward off the blow. The edge of the clipboard caught him in the throat, then I bolted like a wild animal.

I got as far as my dining room before I heard his footsteps coming after me. My heart was hammering against my ribs as I raced into the kitchen, my feet nearly going out from under me on the smooth linoleum as I wheeled around the butcher block and jerked the fire extinguisher off the wall near the refrigerator. The instant he burst into the kitchen I blasted him in the face with a choking storm of dry powder. A long-bladed knife clattered dully to the floor as he clutched his face with his hands and gasped. Snatching a cast-iron skillet off the stove, I swung it like a tennis racket, hitting him solidly in the belly. Struggling for breath, he doubled over and I swung again, this time at his head. My aim was off. I felt cartilage crunch beneath the flat iron bottom. I knew I had broken his nose and probably knocked out several teeth. It barely slowed him down. Dropping to his knees, coughing and partially blinded by the powder, he grabbed at my ankles with one hand, his other hand groping for the knife. Throwing the skillet at him, I kicked the knife out of the way and fled from the kitchen, slamming my hip into the sharp edge of the table and knocking my shoulder against the doorframe.

Disoriented and sobbing, I somehow managed to dig my Ruger out of my suitcase and jam two cartridges into the cylinder. By then he was almost on top of me. I was aware of the sound of the rain and his wheezing breath. The knife was inches from my throat when the third squeeze of the trigger finally struck firing pin against primer. In a deafening explosion of gas and flame, a Silvertip ripped through his abdomen, knocking him back several feet and down to the floor. He fought to sit up, glassy eyes staring at me, his face a gory mass of blood. He tried to say something as he feebly raised the knife. My ears were ringing. Steadying the gun in my shaking hands, I put the second bullet through his chest. I smelled acrid gunpowder tainted by the sweet odor of blood as I watched the light fade from Frankie Aims's eyes.

Then I fell apart, wailing as the wind and rain bore down hard against the house and Frankie's blood seeped over polished oak. My body shook as I wept, and I did not move until the telephone rang a fifth time.

All I could say was "Marino. *Oh God, Marino!*"

━━━━━━

I did not return to my office until Frankie Aims's body had been released from the morgue, his blood rinsed off the stainless-steel table, washed out pipes, and diffused into the fetid waters of the city's sewers. I was not sorry I had killed him. I was sorry he had ever been born.

"The way it's looking," Marino said as he regarded me over the depressing mountain of paperwork on top of my office desk, "is Frankie hit Richmond a year ago October. Least, that's how long he'd been renting his crib on Redd Street. A couple weeks later he got himself a job delivering lost bags. Omega's got a contract with the airport."

I said nothing, my letter opener slitting through another item of mail destined for my wastepaper basket.

"The guys who work for Omega drive their personal cars. And that's the problem Frankie run into long about last January. His 'eighty-one Mercury Lynx blew the transmission, and he didn't have the dough to fix it. No car, no job. That's when he asked Al Hunt for a favor, I think."

"Had the two of them been in contact before this?" I asked, feeling, and I'm sure sounding, burned out and distracted.

"Oh, yeah," Marino answered. "No doubt in my mind, or Benton's, either."

"What are you basing your assumptions on?"

"For starters," he said, "Frankie, it turns out, was living in Butler, Pennsylvania, a year and a half ago. We been going through Old Man Hunt's phone bills for the past five years—saves all the shit in case he gets audited, right? Turns out that during the time Frankie was in Pennsylvania, the Hunts received five collect calls from Butler. The year before that it was collect calls from Dover, Delaware, the year before that there was half a dozen or so from Hagerstown, Maryland."

"The calls were from Frankie?" I asked.

"We're still running it down. But me, I got a strong suspicion Frankie was calling Al Hunt from time to time, probably told him all about what he done to his mother. That's how Al knew so much when he talked to you. Hell, he wasn't no mind reader. He was reciting what he knew from conversations with his sicko pal. It's like the crazier Frankie got, the closer he moved to Richmond. Then, boom! A year ago he hits our lovely city and the rest's history."

"What about Hunt's car wash?" I asked. "Was Frankie a regular visitor?"

"According to a couple of guys working there," Marino said, "someone fitting Frankie's description was down there from time to time, apparently going back to last January. The first week in

February, based on receipts we found in his house, he had the engine in his Mercury overhauled to the tune of five hundred bucks, which he probably got from Al Hunt."

"Do you know if Frankie happened to be at the car wash on a day when Beryl might have brought her car in?"

"I'm guessing that's what happened. You know, he spots her for the first time when he delivers Harper's bags to the McTigues' house last January. Then what? He spots her again maybe a couple weeks later when he's hanging out at Al Hunt's car wash begging for a loan. Bingo. It's like a message to him. Then maybe he spots her again at the airport—he was in and out all the time picking up lost bags, doing who knows what. Maybe he sees Beryl this third time when she's at the airport catching a plane for Baltimore, where she's going to meet Miss Harper."

"Do you think Frankie talked to Hunt about Beryl, too?"

"No way to know. But I wouldn't be surprised. It would sure help explain why Hunt hung himself. He saw it coming—what his squirrelly pal finally did to Beryl. Then, next thing, Harper gets whacked. Hunt probably felt guilty as shit."

I shifted painfully in my chair as I shoved paper around in search of the date stamp I'd had in hand but a second ago. I ached all over and was seriously contemplating having my right shoulder X-rayed. As for my psyche, I wasn't sure what anyone could do about that. I didn't feel like myself. I wasn't sure what I felt except that it was very hard for me to sit still. It was impossible for me to relax.

I commented, "Part of Frankie's delusional thinking would be to personalize his encounters with Beryl and ascribe profound significance to them. He sees Beryl at the McTigues' house. He sees her at the car wash. He sees her in the airport. It would really set him off."

"Yeah. Now the schizo knows God's talking to him, telling him he has some connection with this pretty blond lady."

Just then Rose walked in. Taking the pink telephone message she offered to me, I added it to the pile.

"What color was his car?" I slit open another envelope. Frankie's car had been parked in my drive. I had seen it when the police arrived, when my property was pulsing with red strobe lights. But nothing had penetrated. I remembered very few details.

"Dark blue."

"And no one remembers seeing a blue Mercury Lynx in Beryl's neighborhood?"

Marino shook his head. "After dark, if he had his headlights off, the car wouldn't exactly be conspicuous."

"True."

"As for when he hit Harper, he probably pulled his ride off the road somewhere and went the rest of the way on foot." He paused. "The upholstery of the driver's seat was rotted out."

"I beg your pardon?" I asked, looking up from the letter I was glancing over.

"He had it covered with a blanket he must have swiped from one of the planes."

"The source of the orange fiber?" I inquired.

"They got to run some tests. But we're thinking that's the case. The blanket's got orangish-red pinstripes running through it, and Frankie would have been sitting on it when he drove to Beryl's house. Probably explains the terrorist shit. Some passenger was using a blanket like Frankie's during an overseas flight. The guy changes planes and it just so happens an orange fiber ends up on the one that gets hijacked in Greece. Bingo! Some poor Marine ends up with this same type of fiber stuck to his blood after he's whacked. Got any idea how many fibers must get transferred from plane to plane?"

"It's hard to imagine," I agreed, wondering why I merited being on every junk mailer's list in the United States. "And it probably also explains why Frankie carried so many fibers on his clothes. He was working in the baggage area. He was all over the airport and may even have gone inside the planes. Who knows what he did or what debris he picked up on his clothes?"

"Omega wears uniform shirts," Marino remarked. "Tan. They're made of Dynel."

"That's interesting."

"You should know that, Doc," he said, watching me closely. "He was wearing one when you shot him."

I didn't remember. I remembered only his dark rain slicker, and his face bloody and covered with the white powder from my fire extinguisher.

"Okay," I said. "So far I'm following you, Marino. But what I don't understand is how Frankie got Beryl's telephone number. It was unlisted. And how did he know she was flying in from Key

West the night of October twenty-ninth, the night she returned to Richmond? And how the hell did he know when I flew in, too?"

"The computers," he said. "All passenger info, including flight schedules, phone numbers, and home addresses, is in the computers. All we can figure is Frankie sometimes played around with the computers when one of the counters was unattended, maybe late at night or early in the morning. The airport was like his damn crib. No telling what all he was into without anybody paying him any mind. He wasn't much of a talker, a real low-profile kind of guy, the sort who slips around quiet as a cat."

"According to his Stanford-Binet," I mused, grinding the date stamp into its dried-out ink pad, "he was well above average in intelligence."

Marino said nothing.

I mumbled, "His IQ was in the upper one-twenty range."

"Yeah, yeah," Marino said somewhat impatiently.

"I'm just telling you."

"Shit. You really take those tests seriously, don't you?"

"They're a good indicator."

"They ain't gospel."

"No, I won't say that Intelligence Quotient tests are gospel," I agreed.

"Maybe I'm glad I don't know what mine is."

"You could have your IQ tested, Marino. It's never too late."

"Hope it's higher than my damn bowling score. That's all I got to say."

"Not likely. Not unless you're a pretty sorry bowler."

"I was last time I went."

I slipped off my glasses and gingerly rubbed my eyes. I had a headache that I was sure would never go away.

Marino went on, "All me and Benton can figure is Frankie got Beryl's phone number out of the computer, and after a while was monitoring her flights. I'm figuring he knew from the computer that she'd taken a plane to Miami back in July when she ran off after finding that heart scratched on her car door—"

"Any theories as to when he might have done this?" I interrupted, pulling the wastepaper basket closer.

"When she'd fly to Baltimore she'd leave her car at the airport, and the last time she met Miss Harper up there was in early July, less than a week before Beryl found that heart scratched on her door," he said.

"So he may have done it while her car was parked at the airport."

"What do you think?"

"I think that seems very plausible."

"Ditto."

"Then Beryl flees to Key West." I continued attacking my mail. "And Frankie keeps checking the computer for her return reservation. That's how he knew exactly when she'd be back."

"The night of October twenty-ninth," Marino said. "And Frankie had it all figured out. A piece of cake. He had legitimate access to the passengers' baggage, and I figure he probably checked out the bags from her flight as they were being loaded on the conveyor belt. When he finds a bag with Beryl's name tag on it, he snatches it. A little later, she's complaining that her brown leather tote bag is missing."

He didn't need to add that this was exactly the same maneuver Frankie used on me. He monitored my return from Florida. He snatched my suitcase. Then he appeared at my door, and I let him in.

The governor had invited me to a reception I had missed by a week. I supposed Fielding had gone in my place. The invitation went into the trash.

Marino went on to supply more details about what the police had discovered inside Frankie Aims's Northside apartment.

Inside his bedroom was Beryl's tote bag, containing her bloody blouse and underclothes. Inside a trunk that served as a table next to his bed was an assortment of violent pornographic magazines and a bag of small-gauge pellets that Frankie had used to fill the section of pipe he bashed against Cary Harper's head. Out of this same trunk came an envelope containing a second set of Beryl's computer disks, still taped between two stiff squares of cardboard, and the photocopy of Beryl's manuscript, including the opening page of Chapter Twenty-five that she had gotten mixed up with the original Mark and I had read. Benton Wesley's theory was that Frankie's habit was to sit up in bed reading Beryl's book while he fondled the clothes she was wearing when he murdered her. Perhaps so. What I did know with certainty was that Beryl never had a chance. When Frankie arrived at her door, he was carrying her

leather tote bag and identifying himself as a courier. Even if she recognized him from that night when he had delivered Cary Harper's
bags to the McTigues' house, there was no reason for her to give
it a second thought—just as I had not given it a second thought
until I had already opened my door.

"If only she hadn't invited him in," I muttered. My letter
opener had disappeared. Where the hell had it gone?

"It made sense that she would," Marino replied. "Frankie's all
official and smiling and wearing an Omega uniform shirt and cap.
He's got the bag, meaning he's also got her manuscript. She's relieved. She's grateful. She opens the door, deactivates the alarm,
and invites him in—"

"But why did she *reset* the alarm, Marino? I have a burglar
alarm system, too. And I have delivery men arrive occasionally,
too. If my alarm is on when UPS pulls up to the house, I deactivate it and open the door. If I'm trusting enough to invite the
person in, I'm certainly not going to reset the alarm only to have
to deactivate it and reset it again a minute later when the person
leaves."

"You ever locked your keys in your car?" Marino looked
thoughtfully at me.

"What's that got to do with anything?"

"Just answer my question."

"Of course I have." I found my letter opener. It was in my lap.

"How does it happen? In new cars, they got all kinds of safety
devices to prevent it, Doc."

"Right. And I learn them all so well I go through the motions
without a thought, and next thing my doors are locked, my keys
dangling from the ignition."

"I have a feeling that's exactly what Beryl did," Marino went
on. "I think she was obsessive about that damn alarm system she
had installed after she started getting the threats. I think she kept
it on all the time, that it was a reflex for her to punch those buttons
the minute she shut her front door." He hesitated, staring off at my
bookcase. "Kind of weird. She leaves her damn gun in the kitchen
and then resets her alarms after letting the drone inside her house.
Shows how screwy her mind was, how nervous the whole ordeal
made her."

I straightened up a stack of toxicology reports and moved them
and a pile of death certificates out of my way. Glancing around at

the tower of micro-dictations next to my microscope, I instantly felt depressed again.

"Jesus Christ," Marino finally complained. "You mind sitting still, at least until I leave? You're making me crazy."

"It's my first day back," I reminded him. "I can't help it. Look at this mess." I swept a hand over my desk. "You'd think I'd been gone a year. It will take me a month to catch up."

"I give you until eight o'clock tonight. By then everything will be back to normal, back exactly like it was."

"Thanks a lot," I said rather sharply.

"You got a good staff. They know how to keep things running when you're not here. So, what's wrong with that?"

"Not a thing." I lit a cigarette and shoved more papers aside in search of the ashtray.

Marino picked it up from the edge of the desk and moved it closer.

"Hey, it's not like you ain't needed around here," he said.

"No one is indispensable."

"Yeah, right. I knew that's what you were thinking."

"I'm not thinking anything. I'm simply distracted," I said, reaching up to the shelf to my left and fetching my datebook. Rose had crossed everything out through the end of next week. After that it was Christmas. I felt on the verge of tears, and I didn't know why.

Leaning forward to tap an ash, Marino asked quietly, "What was Beryl's book like, Doc?"

"It will break your heart and fill you with joy," I said, my eyes welling. "It's incredible."

"Yeah, well, I hope it ends up published. It will sort of keep her alive, if you know what I mean."

"I know exactly what you mean." I took a deep breath. "Mark's going to see what he can do. I suppose new arrangements will have to be made. Sparacino certainly won't be handling Beryl's business anymore."

"Not unless he does it behind bars. I guess Mark told you about the letter."

"Yes," I said. "He did."

One of the business letters from Sparacino to Beryl that Marino had found inside her house shortly after her death took on new meaning when Mark looked at it after having read her manuscript:

How interesting, Beryl, that Joe helped Cary out—makes me all the happier I originally got the two of them together when Cary bought that magnificent house. No, I don't find it curious, at all. Joe was one of the most generous men I've ever had the pleasure of knowing. I look forward to hearing more.

That simple paragraph hinted at quite a lot, though it was unlikely Beryl had a clue. I seriously doubted Beryl had any idea that when she mentioned Joseph McTigue, she was stepping dangerously close to the forbidden turf of Sparacino's own illicit domain, which included numerous dummy corporations the lawyer had formulated to facilitate his money laundering. Mark believed that McTigue, with his tremendous assets and real estate holdings, was no stranger to Sparacino's illegal ways, and that, finally, the assistance McTigue had offered a financially desperate Harper had been something less than legitimate. Because Sparacino had never seen Beryl's manuscript, he was paranoid about what she may have unwittingly revealed. When the manuscript disappeared, his incentive for getting his hands on it was more than just greed.

"He probably thought it was his lucky day when Beryl turned up dead," Marino was saying. "You know, she's not around to argue when he doctors her book, takes out anything that might point a finger at what he's really into. Then he turns around, sells the damn thing, and makes a killing. I mean, who wouldn't be interested after all the publicity he's generated? No telling where it was going to end, either—probably with pictures of the Harpers' dead bodies showing up in some tabloid. . . ."

"Sparacino never got the photographs Jeb Price took," I reminded him. "Thank God."

"Well, whatever. Point is, after all the noise, even I'd rush out to get the damn thing, and I bet I haven't bought a book in twenty years."

"A shame," I muttered. "Reading is wonderful. You should try it sometime."

We both looked up as Rose walked in again, this time carrying a long white box tied with a luxurious red bow. Perplexed, she looked around for a clear area on my desk to set it down, then finally gave up and placed it in my hands.

"What on earth . . . ?" I muttered, my mind going blank.

Pushing back my chair, I set the unexpected gift in my lap and began to untie the satin ribbon while Rose and Marino looked on. Inside the box were two dozen long-stemmed beauties shining like red jewels swathed in green tissue paper. Bending over, I shut my eyes and enjoyed their fragrance; then I opened the small white envelope tucked inside.

"When the going gets tough, the tough go skiing. In Aspen after Christmas. Break a leg and join me," the card read. "I love you, Mark."

All That Remains

This book is for Michael Congdon.
As always, thanks.

1

SATURDAY, THE LAST DAY of August, I started work before dawn. I did not witness mist burning off the grass or the sky turning brilliant blue. Steel tables were occupied by bodies all morning, and there are no windows in the morgue. Labor Day weekend had begun with a bang of car crashes and gunfire in the city of Richmond.

It was two o'clock in the afternoon when I finally returned to my West End home and heard Bertha mopping in the kitchen. She cleaned for me every Saturday and knew from past instruction not to bother with the phone, which had just begun to ring.

"I'm not here," I said loudly as I opened the refrigerator.

Bertha stopped mopping. "It was ringing a minute ago," she said. "Rang a few minutes before that, too. Same man."

"No one's home," I repeated.

"Whatever you say, Dr. Kay." The mop moved across the floor again.

I tried to ignore the disembodied answering machine message intruding upon the sun-washed kitchen. The Hanover tomatoes I took for granted during the summer I began to hoard with the approach of fall. There were only three left. Where was the chicken salad?

A beep was followed by the familiar male voice. "Doc? It's Marino . . ."

Oh, Lord, I thought, shoving the refrigerator door shut with a hip. Richmond homicide detective Pete Marino had been on the street since midnight, and I had just seen him in the morgue as I was picking bullets out of one of his cases. He was supposed to be on his way to Lake Gaston for what was left of a weekend of fishing. I was looking forward to working in my yard.

"I've been trying to get you, am heading out. You'll have to try my pager . . ."

Marino's voice sounded urgent as I snatched up the receiver. "I'm here."

"That you or your goddam machine?"

"Take a guess," I snapped.

"Bad news. They found another abandoned car. New Kent, the Sixty-four rest stop, westbound. Benton just got hold of me—"

"Another couple?" I interrupted, my plans for the day forgotten.

"Fred Cheney, white male, nineteen. Deborah Harvey, white female, nineteen. Last seen around eight last night when they drove off from the Harveys' Richmond house, on their way to Spindrift."

"And the car's in the *westbound* lane?" I inquired, for Spindrift, North Carolina, is three and a half hours east of Richmond.

"Yo. Appears they was heading in the opposite direction, back into the city. A trooper found the car, a Jeep Cherokee, about an hour ago. No sign of the kids."

"I'm leaving now," I told him.

Bertha had not stopped mopping, but I knew she had picked up every word.

"Be on my way soon as I finish up in here," she assured me. "I'll lock up and set the alarm. Don't you worry, Dr. Kay."

Fear was running along my nerves as I grabbed my purse and hurried out to my car.

There were four couples so far. Each had disappeared, eventually to be found murdered within a fifty-mile radius of Williamsburg.

The cases, dubbed by the press as The Couple Killings, were inexplicable, and no one seemed to have a clue or credible theory, not even the FBI and its Violent Criminal Apprehension Program, or VICAP, which featured a national data base run on an artificial intelligence computer capable of connecting missing persons with unidentified bodies and linking serial crimes. After the first couple's bodies were found more than two years ago, a VICAP regional team, comprising FBI Special Agent Benton Wesley and veteran Richmond homicide detective Pete Marino, was invited by local police to assist. Another couple would disappear, then two more. In each instance, by the time VICAP could be notified, by the time the National Crime Information Center, or NCIC, could even wire descriptions to police departments across America, the missing teenagers were already dead and decomposing in woods somewhere.

Turning off the radio, I passed through a tollbooth and picked up speed on I-64 East. Images, voices suddenly came back to me. Bones and rotted clothing scattered with leaves. Attractive, smiling faces of missing teenagers printed in the newspapers, and bewildered, distraught families interviewed on television and calling me on the phone.

"I'm so sorry about your daughter."

"Please tell me how my baby died. Oh, God, did she suffer?"

"Her cause of death is undetermined, Mrs. Bennett. There's nothing else I can tell you at this time."

"What do you mean you *don't know*?"

"All that remains is his bones, Mr. Martin. When soft tissue is gone, gone with it is any possible injury . . ."

"I don't want to hear your medical bullshit! I want to know what killed my boy! The cops are asking about drugs! My boy's never been drunk in his life, much less taken drugs! You hear me, lady? He's dead, and they're making him out to be some sort of punk . . ."

"CHIEF MEDICAL EXAMINER BAFFLED: Dr. Kay Scarpetta Unable to Tell Cause of Death."

Undetermined.

Over and over again. Eight young people.

It was awful. It was, in fact, unprecedented for me.

Every forensic pathologist has undetermined cases, but I had never had so many that appeared to be related.

I opened the sunroof and my spirits were lifted somewhat by the weather. The temperature was in the low eighties, leaves would be turning soon. It was only in the fall and spring that I did not miss Miami. Richmond summers were just as hot, without benefit of ocean breezes to sweep the air clean. The humidity was horrible, and in winter I fared no better, for I do not like the cold. But spring and fall were intoxicating. I drank in the change, and it went straight to my head.

The I-64 rest stop in New Kent County was exactly thirty-one miles from my house. It could have been any rest stop in Virginia, with picnic tables, grills and wooden trash barrels, brick-enclosed bathrooms and vending machines, and newly planted trees. But there was not a traveler or a truck driver in sight, and police cars were everywhere.

A trooper, hot and unsmiling in his blue-gray uniform, walked toward me as I parked near the ladies' room.

"I'm sorry, ma'am," he said, leaning close to my open window. "This rest area's closed today. I'm going to have to ask you to drive on."

"Dr. Kay Scarpetta," I identified myself, switching off the ignition. "The police asked me to come."

"For what purpose, ma'am?"

"I'm the chief medical examiner," I replied.

As he looked me over, I could see the skeptical glint in his eyes. I supposed I did not look particularly "chiefly." Dressed in a stone-washed denim skirt, pink oxford cloth shirt, and leather walking shoes, I was without the accouterments of authority, including my state car, which was in the state garage awaiting new tires. At a glance, I was a not-so-young yuppie running errands in her dark gray Mercedes, a distracted ash-blonde en route to the nearest shopping mall.

"I'll need some identification."

Digging inside my purse, I produced a thin black wallet and displayed my brass medical examiner's shield, then handed over my driver's license, both of which he studied for a long moment. I sensed he was embarrassed.

"Just leave your car here, Dr. Scarpetta. The folks you're looking for are in back." He pointed in the direction of the parking area for trucks and buses. "Have a nice one," he added inanely, stepping away.

I followed a brick walk. When I rounded the building and passed beneath the shade of trees, I was greeted by several more police cars, a tow truck with light bar flashing, and at least a dozen men in uniforms and plain clothes. I did not see the red Jeep Chero-kee until I was almost upon it. Midway along the exit ramp, it was well off the pavement in a dip and obscured by foliage. Two-door, it was coated with a film of dust. When I looked in the driver's win-dow I could see that the beige leather interior was very clean, the backseat neatly packed with various items of luggage, a slalom ski, a coiled yellow nylon ski rope, and a red-and-white plastic ice chest. Keys dangled from the ignition. Windows were partly rolled down.

Depressed tire tracks leading from the pavement were clearly visible in the sloping grass, the front chrome grille nudged up against a clump of pines.

Marino was talking to a thin, blond man, someone he introduced as Jay Morrell with the state police, whom I did not know. He seemed to be in charge.

"Kay Scarpetta," I volunteered, since Marino identified me only as "Doc."

Morrell fixed dark green Ray Bans on me and nodded. Out of uniform and sporting a mustache that was little more than teenage fuzz, he exuded the all-business bravado I associated with investigators brand-new on the job.

"Here's what we know so far." He was glancing around nervously. "The Jeep belongs to Deborah Harvey, and she and her boyfriend, uh, Fred Cheney, left the Harveys' residence last night at approximately eight P.M. They were heading to Spindrift, where the Harvey family owns a beach house."

"Was Deborah Harvey's family home when the couple left Richmond?" I inquired.

"No, ma'am." He briefly turned his shades my way. "They were already at Spindrift, had left earlier in the day. Deborah and Fred wanted to go in a separate car because they planned to return to Richmond on Monday. Both of them are sophomores at Carolina, and needed to come back early to get ready to return to school."

Marino explained as he got out his cigarettes, "Right before they left the Harvey house last night, they called up Spindrift, told one of Deborah's brothers they was heading out and would be arriving sometime between midnight and one A.M. When they didn't show up by four o'clock this morning, Pat Harvey called the police."

"*Pat Harvey?*" I looked at Marino in disbelief.

It was Officer Morrell who replied, "Oh, yeah. We got us a good one, all right. Pat Harvey's on her way here even as we speak. A chopper picked her up"—he glanced at his watch—"about a half hour ago. The father, uh, Bob Harvey, he's on the road. Was in Charlotte on business and was supposed to get to Spindrift sometime tomorrow. As far as we know, he hasn't been reached yet, doesn't know what's happened."

Pat Harvey was the National Drug Policy Director, a position the media had dubbed Drug Czar. A presidential appointee who not so long ago had been on the cover of *Time* magazine, Mrs. Harvey was one of the most powerful and admired women in America.

"What about Benton?" I asked Marino. "Is he aware Deborah Harvey is Pat Harvey's daughter?"

"He didn't say nothing about it to me. When he called, he'd just landed in Newport News—the Bureau flew him in. He was in a hurry to find a rental car. We didn't talk long."

That answered my question. Benton Wesley would not be rushing here in a Bureau plane unless he knew who Deborah Harvey was. I wondered why he had not said anything to Marino, his VICAP partner, and I tried to read Marino's broad, impassive face. His jaw muscles were flexing, the top of his balding head flushed and beaded with sweat.

"What's going on now," Morrell resumed, "is I got a lot of men stationed around to keep out traffic. We've looked in the bathrooms, poked around a little, to make sure the kids aren't in the immediate area. Once Peninsula Search and Rescue get here, we'll start in on the woods."

Immediately north of the Jeep's front hood the well-attended landscaping of the rest stop was overcome by brush and trees that within an acre became so dense I could see nothing but sunlight caught in leaves and a hawk making circles over a distant stand of pines. Though shopping malls and housing developments continued their encroachment upon I-64, this stretch between Richmond and Tidewater so far had remained unspoiled. The scenery, which I would have found reassuring and soothing in the past, now seemed ominous to me.

"Shit," Marino complained as we left Morrell and began walking around.

"I'm sorry about your fishing trip," I said.

"Hey. Ain't it the way it always goes? Been planning this damn trip for months. Screwed again. Nothing new."

"I noticed that when you pull off the Interstate," I observed, ignoring his irritation, "the entrance ramp immediately divides into two ramps, one leading back here, the other to the front of the rest stop. In other words, the ramps are one-way. It's not possible to pull into the front area for cars, then change your mind and drive back here without going a considerable distance the wrong way on the ramp and risk hitting someone. And I would guess there was a fair amount of travelers on the road last night, since it's Labor Day weekend."

"Right. I know that. It don't take a rocket scientist to figure out that somebody intended to ditch the Jeep exactly where it is because there were probably a lot of cars parked in front last night. So he takes the ramp for trucks and buses. Probably was pretty deserted back here. Nobody sees him, and he splits."

"He may also not have wanted the Jeep found right away, explaining why it's well off the pavement," I said.

Marino stared off toward the woods and said, "I'm getting too old for this."

A perpetual complainer, Marino had a habit of arriving at a crime scene and acting as if he did not want to be there. We had worked with each other long enough for me to be used to it, but this time his attitude struck me as more than an act. His frustration went deeper than the canceled fishing trip. I wondered if he had had a fight with his wife.

"Well, well," he mumbled, looking toward the brick building. "The Lone Ranger's arrived."

I turned around as the lean, familiar figure of Benton Wesley emerged from the men's room. He barely said "hello" when he got to us, his silver hair wet at the temples, the lapels of his blue suit speckled with water as if he had just washed his face. Eyes fixed impassively on the Jeep, he slipped a pair of sunglasses from his breast pocket and put them on.

"Has Mrs. Harvey gotten here yet?" he asked.

"Nope," Marino replied.

"What about reporters?"

"Nope," Marino said.

"Good."

Wesley's mouth was firmly set, making his sharp-featured face seem harder and more unreachable than usual. I would have found him handsome were it not for his imperviousness. His thoughts and emotions were impossible to read, and of late he had become such a master at walling off his personality that I sometimes felt I did not know him.

"We want to keep this under wraps as long as possible," he went on. "The minute the word's out all hell is going to break loose."

I asked him, "What do you know about this couple, Benton?"

"Very little. After Mrs. Harvey reported them missing early this morning, she called the Director at home and then he called me. Apparently, her daughter and Fred Cheney met at Carolina and had been dating since their freshman year. Both of them supposedly good, clean-cut kids. No history of any sort of trouble that might account for them getting tangled up with the wrong type of person out here—at least according to Mrs. Harvey. One thing I did pick up on was she had some ambivalence about the relationship, thought Cheney and her daughter spent too much time alone."

"Possibly the real reason for their wanting to drive to the beach in a separate car," I said.

"Yes," Wesley replied, glancing around. "More than likely that was the real reason. I got the impression from the Director that Mrs. Harvey wasn't keen on Deborah's bringing her boyfriend to Spindrift. It was family time. Mrs. Harvey lives in D.C. during the week and hadn't seen much of her daugher and two sons all summer. Frankly, I have the feeling that Deborah and her mother may not have been getting along very well of late, and may have had an argument right before the family headed off to North Carolina yesterday morning."

"What about the chance the kids might have run off together?" Marino said. "They was smart, right? Would read the papers, watch the news, maybe saw the stuff about these couples on that TV special the other week. Point is, they probably knew about the cases around here. Who's to say they didn't pull something? A pretty slick way to stage a disappearance and punish your parents."

"It's one of many scenarios we need to consider," Wesley replied. "And it's all the more reason I hope we can keep this from the media as long as possible."

Morrell joined us as we walked along the exit ramp back toward the Jeep. A pale blue pickup truck with a camper shell pulled up, and a man and a woman in dark jumpsuits and boots got out. Opening the tailgate, they let two panting, tail-wagging bloodhounds out of their crate. They snapped long leads to rings on the leather belts around their waists and grabbed each dog by its harness.

"Salty, Neptune, heel!"

I didn't know which dog was which. Both were big and light tan with wrinkled faces and floppy ears. Morrell grinned and put out his hand.

"Howya doin', fella?"

Salty, or maybe it was Neptune, rewarded him with a wet kiss and a nuzzle to the leg.

The dog handlers were from Yorktown, their names Jeff and Gail. Gail was as tall as her partner and looked just about as strong.

She reminded me of women I've seen who have spent their lives on farms, their faces lined by hard work and the sun, a stolid patience about them that comes from understanding nature and accepting its gifts and punishments. She was the search-and-rescue team captain, and I could tell from the way she was eyeing the Jeep that she was surveying it for any sign that the scene, and therefore the scents, had been disturbed.

"Nothing's been touched," Marino told her, bending over to knead one of the dogs behind the ears. "We haven't even opened the doors yet."

"Do you know if anybody else has been inside it? Maybe the person who found it?" Gail inquired.

Morrell began to explain, "The plate number went out over teletype, BOLOs, early this morning—"

"What the hell are BOLOs?" Wesley interrupted.

"Be On the Lookouts."

Wesley's face was granite as Morrell went on, tediously, "Troopers don't go through lineup, so they're not always going to see a teletype. They just get in their cars and mark on. The dispatchers started sending BOLOs over the air the minute the couple was reported missing, and around one P.M. a trucker spotted the Jeep, radioed it in. The trooper who responded said that other than looking through the windows to make sure nobody was inside, he didn't even get close."

I hoped this was true. Most police officers, even those who know better, can't seem to resist opening doors and at least rummaging through the glove compartment in search of the owner's identification.

Taking hold of both harnesses, Jeff took the dogs off to "use the potty" while Gail asked, "You got anything the dogs can scent off of?"

"Pat Harvey was asked to bring along anything Deborah might have been wearing recently," Wesley said.

If Gail was surprised or impressed by whose daughter she was looking for, she did not show it but continued to regard Wesley expectantly.

"She's flying in by chopper," Wesley added, glancing at his watch. "Should be here any minute."

"Well, just don't be landing the big bird right here," Gail commented, approaching the Jeep. "Don't need anything stirring up the place." Peering through the driver's window, she studied the inside of the doors, the dash, taking in every inch of the interior. Then she backed away and took a long look at the black plastic door handle on the outside of the door.

"Best thing's probably going to be the seats," she decided. "We'll let Salty scent off one, Neptune off the other. But first, we got to get in without screwing up anything. Anybody got a pencil or pen?"

Snatching a ballpoint Mont Blanc pen out of the breast pocket of his shirt, Wesley presented it to her.

"Need one more," she added.

Amazingly, nobody else seemed to have a pen on his person, including me. I could have sworn I had several inside my purse.

"How about a folding knife?" Marino was digging in a pocket of his jeans.

"Perfect."

Pen in one hand and Swiss army knife in the other, Gail simultaneously depressed the thumb button on the outside of the driver's door and pried back the handle, then caught the door's edge with the toe of her boot to gently pull it open. All the while I heard the faint, unmistakable thud-thud of helicopter blades growing louder.

Moments later, a red-and-white Bell Jet Ranger circled the rest stop, then hovered like a dragonfly, creating a small hurricane on the ground. All sound was drowned out, trees shaking and grass rippling in the roar of its terrible wind. Eyes squeezed shut, Gail and Jeff were squatting by the dogs, holding harnesses tight.

Marino, Wesley, and I had retreated close to the buildings, and from this vantage we watched the violent descent. As the helicopter slowly nosed around in a maelstrom of straining engines and beating air, I caught a glimpse of Pat Harvey staring down at her daughter's Jeep before sunlight whited out the glass.

She stepped away from the helicopter, head bent and skirt whipping around her legs as Wesley waited a safe distance from the decelerating blades, necktie fluttering over his shoulder like an aviator's scarf.

Before Pat Harvey had been appointed the National Drug Policy Director, she had been a commonwealth's attorney in Richmond, then a U.S. attorney for the Eastern District of Virginia. Her prosecution of high-profile drug cases in the federal system had occasionally involved victims I had autopsied. But I had never been called to testify; only my reports had been subpoenaed. Mrs. Harvey and I had never actually met.

On television and in newspaper photographs she came across as all business. She was, in the flesh, both feminine and strikingly attractive, slender, her features perfectly wrought, the sun finding hints of gold and red in her short auburn hair. Wesley made brief introductions, and Mrs. Harvey shook each of our hands with the politeness and self-assurance of a practiced politician. But she did not smile or meet anyone's eyes.

"There's a sweatshirt inside," she explained, handing a paper bag to Gail. "I found it in Debbie's bedroom at the beach. I don't know when she wore it last, but I don't think it's been recently washed."

"When's the last time your daughter was at the beach?" Gail inquired without opening the bag.

"Early July. She went there with several friends for a weekend."

"And you're sure she was the one wearing this? Possible one of her friends might have?" Gail asked casually, as though she were inquiring about the weather.

The question caught Mrs. Harvey by surprise, and for an instant doubt clouded her dark blue eyes. "I'm not sure." She cleared her throat. "I would assume Debbie was the one wearing it last, but obviously I can't swear to it. I wasn't there."

She stared past us through the Jeep's open door, her attention briefly fixed on the keys in the ignition, the silver "D" dangling from the keychain. For a long moment no one spoke, and I could see the struggle of mind against emotion as she warded off panic with denial.

Turning back to us, she said, "Debbie would have been carrying a purse. Nylon, bright red. One of those sports purses with a Velcro-lined flap. I'm wondering if you found it inside?"

"No, ma'am," Morrell replied. "At least we haven't seen anything like that yet, not from looking through the windows. But we haven't searched the interior, couldn't until the dogs got here."

"I would expect it to be on the front seat. Perhaps on the floor," she went on.

Morrell shook his head.

It was Wesley who spoke. "Mrs. Harvey, do you know if your daughter had much money with her?"

"I gave her fifty dollars for food and gas. I don't know what she might have had beyond that," she replied. "She also, of course, had charge cards. Plus her checkbook."

"You know what she had in her checking account?" Wesley asked.

"Her father gave her a check last week," she replied matter-of-factly. "For college—books, and so on. I'm fairly certain she's already deposited it. I suppose she should have at least a thousand dollars in her account."

"You might want to look into that," Wesley proposed. "Make certain the money wasn't recently withdrawn."

"I will do so immediately."

As I stood by and watched, I could sense hope blossoming in her mind. Her daughter had cash, charge cards, and access to money in a checking account. It did not appear that she had left her purse inside the Jeep, meaning she might still have it with her. Meaning she might still be alive and well and off somewhere with her boyfriend.

"Your daughter ever threaten to run away with Fred?" Marino asked her bluntly.

"No." Staring again at the Jeep, she added what she wanted to believe, "But that doesn't mean it isn't possible."

"What was her mood when you talked to her last?" Marino went on.

"We exchanged words yesterday morning before my sons and I left for the beach," she replied in a detached, flat tone. "She was upset with me."

"She know about the cases around here? The missing couples?" Marino asked.

"Yes, of course. We have discussed them, wondered about them. She knew."

Gail said to Morrell, "We ought to get started."

"Good idea."

"One last thing." Gail looked at Mrs. Harvey. "You got any idea who was driving?"

"Fred, I suspect," she answered. "When they went places together, he usually drove."

Nodding, Gail said, "Guess I'm going to need that pocketknife and pen again."

Collecting them from Wesley and Marino, she went around to the passenger's side and opened the door. She grasped one of the bloodhounds' harnesses. Eagerly, he got up and moved in perfect accord with his mistress's feet, snuffling along, muscles rippling beneath his loose, glossy coat, ears dragging heavily, as if lined with lead.

"Come on, Neptune, let's put that magic nose of yours to work."

We watched in silence as she directed Neptune's nose at the bucket seat where Deborah Harvey was presumed to have been sitting yesterday. Suddenly he yelped as if he had encountered a rattlesnake, jerking back from the Jeep, practically wrenching the harness from Gail's hand. He tucked his tail between his legs and the fur literally stood up on his back as a chill ran up my spine.

"Easy, boy. Easy!"

Whimpering and quivering all over, Neptune squatted and defecated in the grass.

2

I WOKE UP the next morning, exhausted and dreading the Sunday paper.

The headline was bold enough to be read from a block away:

DRUG CZAR'S DAUGHTER, FRIEND MISSING— POLICE FEAR FOUL PLAY

Not only had reporters gotten hold of a photograph of Deborah Harvey, but there was a picture of her Jeep being towed from the rest stop and a file photograph, I presumed, of Bob and Pat Harvey, hand in hand, walking a deserted beach in Spindrift. As I sipped coffee and read, I could not help but think about Fred Cheney's family. He was not from a prominent family. He was just "Deborah's boyfriend." Yet he, too, was missing; he, too, was loved.

Apparently, Fred was the son of a Southside businessman, an only child whose mother had died last year when a berry aneurysm ruptured in her brain. Fred's father, the story read, was in Sarasota visiting relatives when the police finally tracked him down late last night. If there were a remote possibility that his son had "run off" with Deborah, the story read, it would have been very much out of character for Fred, who was described as "a good student at Carolina and a member of the varsity swim team." Deborah was an honor student and a gymnast gifted enough to be an Olympic hopeful. Weighing no more than a hundred pounds, she had shoulder-length dark blond hair and her mother's handsome features. Fred was broad-shouldered and lean, with wavy black hair and hazel eyes. They were a couple described as attractive and inseparable.

"Whenever you saw one, you always saw the other," a friend was quoted as saying. "I think it had a lot to do with Fred's mother dying. Debbie met him right about that time, and I don't think he would have made it through without her."

Of course, the story went on to regurgitate the details of the other four Virginia couples missing and later found dead. My name was mentioned several times. I was described as frustrated, baffled, and avoiding comment. I wondered if it occurred to anyone that I continued to autopsy the victims of homicides, suicides, and accidents every week. I routinely talked to families, testified in court, and gave lectures to paramedics and police academies. Couples or not, life and death went on.

I had gotten up from the kitchen table, was sipping coffee and staring out at the bright morning when the telephone rang.

Expecting my mother, who often called at this hour on Sunday to inquire about my well-being and if I had been to Mass, I pulled out a nearby chair as I picked up the receiver.

"Dr. Scarpetta?"

"Speaking." The woman sounded familiar, but I could not place her.

"It's Pat Harvey. Please forgive me for bothering you at home." Behind her steady voice, I detected a note of fear.

"You certainly aren't bothering me," I replied kindly. "What can I do for you?"

"They searched all through the night and are still out there. They brought in more dogs, more police, several aircraft." She began to speak rapidly. "Nothing. No sign of them. Bob has joined the search parties. I'm home." She hesitated. "I'm wondering if you could come over? Perhaps you're free for lunch?"

After a long pause, I reluctantly agreed. As I hung up the telephone I silently berated myself, for I knew what she wanted from me. Pat Harvey would ask about the other couples. If I were her, it was exactly what I would do.

I went upstairs to my bedroom and got out of my robe. Then I took a long, hot bath and washed my hair while my answering machine began intercepting calls that I had no intention of returning unless they were emergencies. Within the hour I was dressed in a khaki skirt suit and tensely playing back messages. There were five of them, all from reporters who had learned that I had been summoned to the New Kent County rest stop, which did not bode well for the missing couple.

I reached for the phone, intending to call Pat Harvey back and cancel our lunch. But I could not forget her face when she had arrived by helicopter with her daughter's sweatshirt, I could not forget the faces of any of the parents. Hanging up the phone, I locked the house and got into my car.

People in public service can't afford the accouterments privacy demands unless they have some other means of income. Obviously, Pat Harvey's federal salary was a meager sliver of her family's worth. They lived near Windsor on the James in a palatial Jeffersonian house overlooking the river. The estate, which I guessed to be at least five acres, was surrounded by a high brick wall posted with "Private Property" signs. When I turned into a long drive shaded by trees, I was stopped by a sturdy wrought-iron gate that slid open electronically before I could roll down my window to reach for the intercom. The gate slid shut behind me as I drove through. I parked near a black Jaguar sedan before a Roman portico of unfluted columns, old red brick, and white trim.

As I was getting out of my car, the front door opened. Pat Harvey, drying her hands on a dish towel, smiled bravely at me from the top of the steps. Her face was pale, her eyes lusterless and tired.

"It's so good of you to come, Dr. Scarpetta." She motioned for me to enter. "Please come in."

The foyer was as spacious as a living room, and I followed her through a formal sitting room to the kitchen. Furniture was eighteenth century, Oriental rugs wall to wall, and there were original Impressionist paintings and a fireplace with beechwood logs artfully piled on the hearth. At least the kitchen looked functional and lived in, but I did not get the impression that anyone else was home.

"Jason and Michael are out with their father," she explained when I asked. "The boys drove in this morning."

"How old are they?" I inquired, as she opened the oven door.

"Jason is sixteen, Michael fourteen. Debbie is the oldest." Looking around for the potholders, she turned off the oven, then set a quiche on top of a burner. Her hands trembled as she got a knife and spatula from a drawer. "Would you like wine, tea, coffee? This is very light. I did throw together a fruit salad. Thought we'd sit out on the porch. I hope that will be all right."

"That would be lovely," I replied. "And coffee would be fine."

Distracted, she opened the freezer and got out a bag of Irish Creme, which she measured into the drip coffee maker. I watched her without speaking. She was desperate. Husband and sons were not home. Her daughter was missing, the house empty and silent.

She did not begin to ask questions until we were on the porch, sliding glass doors open wide, the river curving beyond us glinting in the sun.

"What the dogs did, Dr. Scarpetta," she began, picking at her salad. "Can you offer an interpretation?"

I could, but I did not want to.

"Obviously, the one dog got upset. But the other one didn't?" Her observation was posed as a question.

The other dog, Salty, had indeed reacted very differently than Neptune had. After he sniffed the driver's seat, Gail hooked the lead on his harness and commanded, "Find." The dog took off like a greyhound. He snuffled across the exit ramp and up through the picnic area. Then he tugged Gail across the parking lot toward the Interstate and would have gotten a nose full of traffic had she not yelled, "Heel!" I had watched them trot along the wooded strip separating west lanes from east, then across pavement, heading straight for the rest stop opposite the one where Deborah's Jeep had been found. The bloodhound finally lost the scent in the parking lot.

"Am I to believe," Mrs. Harvey continued, "that whoever was driving Debbie's Jeep last got out, cut through the westbound rest stop, and crossed the Interstate? Then this person most likely got into a car parked in the eastbound rest stop and drove away?"

"That is one possible interpretation," I replied, picking at my quiche.

"What other possible interpretation is there, Dr. Scarpetta?"

"The bloodhound picked up a scent. As for the scent of who or what, I don't know. It could have been Deborah's scent, Fred's scent, the scent of a third person—"

"Her Jeep was sitting out there for hours," Mrs. Harvey interrupted, staring off at the river. "I suppose anybody could have gotten in to look for money, valuables. A hitchhiker, transient, someone on foot who crossed over to the other side of the Interstate afterward."

I did not remind her of the obvious. The police had found Fred Cheney's wallet in the glove compartment, complete with credit cards and thirty-five dollars cash. It did not appear that the young couple's luggage had been gone through. As far as anyone could tell, nothing was missing from the Jeep except its occupants and Deborah's purse.

"The way the first dog acted," she went on matter-of-factly. "I assume this is unusual. Something frightened him. Upset him, at any rate. A different smell—not the same scent the other dog picked up. The seat where Debbie may have been sitting . . ." Her voice trailed off as she met my eyes.

"Yes. It appears that the two dogs picked up different scents."

"Dr. Scarpetta, I'm asking you to be direct with me." Her voice trembled. "Don't spare my feelings. Please. I know the dog wouldn't have gotten so upset unless there was a reason. Certainly, your work has exposed you to search-and-rescue efforts, to bloodhounds. Have you ever seen this before, the way the dog reacted?"

I had. Twice. Once was when a bloodhound sniffed a car trunk that, as it turned out, had been used to transport a murder victim whose body had been found inside a Dumpster. The other was when a scent led to an area along a hiking trail where a woman had been raped and shot.

What I said was "Bloodhounds tend to have strong reactions to pheromonal scents."

"I beg your pardon?" She looked bewildered.

"Secretions. Animals, insects, secrete chemicals. Sex attractants, for example," I dispassionately explained. "You're familiar with dogs marking their territory or attacking when they smell fear?"

She just stared at me.

"When someone is sexually aroused, anxious, or afraid, there are various hormonal changes that occur in the body. It is theorized that scent-discriminating animals, such as bloodhounds, can smell the pheromones, or chemicals, that special glands in our bodies secrete—"

She cut me off. "Debbie complained of cramps shortly before Michael, Jason, and I left for the beach. She had just started her period. Could that explain . . . ? Well, if she were sitting in the passenger's seat, perhaps this was the scent the dog picked up?"

I did not reply. What she was suggesting could not account for the dog's extreme distress.

"It's not enough." Pat Harvey looked away from me and twisted the linen napkin in her lap. "Not enough to explain why the dog started whining, the fur stood up on his back. Oh, dear God. It's like the other couples, isn't it?"

"I can't say that."

"But you're thinking it. The police are thinking it. If it hadn't been on everybody's mind from the start, you never would have been called yesterday. I want to know what happened to them. To those other couples."

I said nothing.

"According to what I've read," she pushed, "you were present at every scene, called there by the police."

"I was."

Reaching into a pocket of her blazer, she withdrew a folded sheet of legal paper and smoothed it open.

"Bruce Phillips and Judy Roberts," she began to brief me, as if I needed it. "High school sweethearts who disappeared two and a half years ago on June first when they drove away from a friend's house in Gloucester and never arrived at their respective homes. The next morning Bruce's Camaro was found abandoned off U.S. Seventeen, keys in the ignition, doors unlocked, and windows rolled down. Ten weeks later, you were called to a wooded area one mile east of the York River State Park, where hunters had discovered two partially skeletonized bodies facedown in the leaves, approximately four miles from where Bruce's car had been found ten weeks earlier."

I recalled that it was at this time VICAP was asked by local police to assist. What Marino, Wesley, and the detective from Gloucester did not know was that a second couple had been reported missing in July, a month after Bruce and Judy had vanished.

"Next we have Jim Freeman and Bonnie Smyth," Mrs. Harvey glanced up at me. "They disappeared the last Saturday in July after a pool party at the Freemans' Providence Forge home. Late that evening Jim gave Bonnie a ride home, and the following day a Charles City police officer found Jim's Blazer abandoned some ten miles from the Freeman home. Four months after that, on November twelfth, hunters in West Point found their bodies. . . ."

What I suspected she did not know, I thought, unpleasantly, was that despite my repeated requests, I was not given copies of the confidential sections of the police reports, scene photographs, or inventories of evidence. I attributed the apparent lack of cooperation to what had become a multijurisdictional investigation.

Mrs. Harvey continued relentlessly. In March of the following year, it happened again. Ben Anderson had driven from Arlington to meet his girlfiend, Carolyn Bennett, at her family's home in
Stingray Point on the Chesapeake Bay. They pulled away from the
Andersons' house shortly before seven o'clock to begin the drive
back to Old Dominion University in Norfolk, where they were
juniors. The next night a state trooper contacted Ben's parents
and reported that their son's Dodge pickup truck had been found
abandoned on the shoulder of I-64, approximately five miles east
of Buckroe Beach. Keys were in the ignition, the doors unlocked,
and Carolyn's pocketbook was beneath the passenger's seat. Their
partially skeletonized bodies were discovered six months later during deer season in a wooded area three miles south of Route 199
in York County. This time, I did not even get a copy of the police
report.

When Susan Wilcox and Mike Martin disappeared this past
February, I found out about it from the morning newspaper. They
were heading to Mike's house in Virginia Beach to spend spring
break together when, like the couples before them, they vanished.
Mike's blue van was found abandoned along the Colonial Parkway near Williamsburg, a white handkerchief tied to the antenna
signaling engine trouble that did not exist when the police went
over the van later. On May 15 a father and son out turkey hunting discovered the couple's decomposed bodies in a wooded area
between Route 60 and I-64 in James City County.

I remembered, once again, packing up bones to send to the
Smithsonian's forensic anthropologist for one final look. Eight
young people, and despite the countless hours I had spent on each
one of them, I could not determine how or why they had died.

"If, God forbid, there is a next time, don't wait until the bodies
turn up," I finally had instructed Marino. "Let me know the minute
the car is found."

"Yo. May as well start autopsying the cars since the bodies
ain't telling us nothing," he had said, trying unsuccessfully to be
funny.

"In all cases," Mrs. Harvey was saying, "doors were unlocked,
keys in the ignition, there was no sign of a struggle, and it did not
appear anything was stolen. The MOs were basically the same."

She folded her notes and slipped them back into a pocket.

"You're well informed" was all I said. I didn't ask, but presumed
she had gotten her staff to research the previous cases.

"My point is, you've been involved since the beginning," she said. "You examined all of the bodies. And yet, as I understand it, you don't know what killed these couples."

"That's right. I don't know," I replied.

"You *don't know*? Or is it that you aren't saying, Dr. Scarpetta?"

Pat Harvey's career as a prosecutor in the federal system had earned her national respect, if not awe. She was gutsy and aggressive, and I felt as if her porch suddenly had turned into a courtroom.

"If I knew their cause of death, I would not have signed them out as undetermined," I said calmly.

"But you believe they were murdered."

"I believe that young, healthy people don't suddenly abandon their cars and die of natural causes in the woods, Mrs. Harvey."

"What about the theories? What do you have to say about those? I assume they aren't new to you."

They weren't.

Four jurisdictions and at least that many different detectives were involved, each one with numerous hypotheses. The couples, for example, were recreational drug users and had met up with a dealer selling some new and pernicious designer drug that could not be detected through routine toxicology tests. Or the occult was involved. Or the couples were all members of some secret society, their deaths actually suicide pacts.

"I don't think much of the theories I've heard," I told her.

"Why not?"

"My findings do not support them."

"What do your findings support?" she demanded. "What *findings*? Based on everything I've heard and read, you don't have any goddam findings."

A haze had dulled the sky, and a plane was a silver needle pulling a white thread beneath the sun. In silence I watched the vapor trail expand and begin to disperse. If Deborah and Fred had met up with the same fate as the others, we would not find them anytime soon.

"My Debbie has never taken drugs," she continued, blinking back tears. "She isn't into any weird religions or cults. She has a temper and sometimes gets depressed like every other normal teenager. But she wouldn't—" She suddenly stopped, struggling for control.

"You must try to deal with the here and now," I said quietly.

"We don't know what has happened to your daughter. We don't know what has happened to Fred. It may be a long time before we know. Is there anything else you can tell me about her—about them? Anything at all that might help?"

"A police officer came by this morning," she replied with a deep, shaky breath. "He went inside her bedroom, took several articles of her clothing, her hairbrush. Said they were for the dogs, the clothes were, and he needed some of her hair to compare with any hairs they might find inside her Jeep. Would you like to see it? See her bedroom?"

Curious, I nodded.

I followed her up polished hardwood steps to the second floor. Deborah's bedroom was in the east wing, where she could see the sun rise and storms gather over the James. It was not the typical teenager's room. Furniture was Scandinavian, simple in design and built of gorgeous light teakwood. A comforter in shades of cool blue and green covered the queen-size bed, and beneath it was an Indian rug dominated by designs in rose and deep plum. Encyclopedias and novels filled a bookcase, and above the desk two shelves were lined with trophies and dozens of medals attached to bright cloth ribbons. On a top shelf was a large photograph of Deborah on a balance beam, back arched, hands poised like graceful birds, the expression on her face, like the details of her private sanctum, that of pure discipline and grace. I did not have to be Deborah Harvey's mother to know that this nineteen-year-old girl was special.

"Debbie picked out everything herself," Mrs. Harvey said as I looked around. "The furniture, rug, the colors. You'd never know she was in here days ago packing for school." She stared at suitcases and a trunk in a corner and cleared her throat. "She's so organized. I suppose she gets this from me." Smiling nervously, she added, "If I am nothing else, I am organized."

I remembered Deborah's Jeep. It was immaculate inside and out, luggage and other belongings arranged with deliberation.

"She takes wonderful care of her belongings," Mrs. Harvey went on, moving to the window. "I often worried that we indulged her too much. Her clothes, her car, money. Bob and I have had many discussions on the subject. It's difficult with my being in Washington. But when I was appointed last year, we decided, all of us did, that it was too much to uproot the family, and Bob's business is here. Easier if I took the apartment, came home on weekends when I could. Waited to see what would happen with the next election."

After a long pause, she went on. "I suppose what I'm trying to say is that I've never been very good at saying no to Debbie. It's difficult to be sensible when you want the best for your children. Especially when you remember your desires when you were their age, your insecurities about the way you dressed, your physical appearance. When you knew your parents couldn't afford a dermatologist, an orthodontist, a plastic surgeon. We have tried to exercise moderation." She crossed her arms at her waist. "Sometimes I'm not so sure we made the right choices. Her Jeep, for example. I was opposed to her having a car, but I didn't have the energy to argue. Typically, she was practical, wanting something safe that would get her around in any kind of weather."

Hesitantly, I inquired, "When you mention a plastic surgeon, are you referring to something specific concerning your daughter?"

"Large breasts are incompatible with gymnastics, Dr. Scarpetta," she said, not turning around. "By the time Debbie was sixteen she was overendowed. Not only was this rather embarrassing to her, but it interfered with her sport. The problem was taken care of last year."

"Then this photograph is recent," I said, for the Deborah I was looking at was an elegant sculpture of perfectly formed muscle, breasts and buttocks firm and small.

"It was taken last April in California."

When a person is missing and possibly dead, it is not uncommon for people like me to be interested in anatomical detail—whether it be a hysterectomy, a root canal, or scars from plastic surgery—that might assist in the identification of the body. They were the descriptions I reviewed in NCIC missing person forms. They were the mundane and very human features that I depended on, because jewelry and other personal effects, I had learned over the years, can't always be trusted.

"What I've just told you must never go outside this room," Mrs. Harvey said. "Debbie is very private. My family is very private."

"I understand."

"Her relationship with Fred," she continued. "It was private. Too private. As I'm sure you've noted, there are no photographs, no visible symbols of it. I have no doubt they have exchanged pictures, gifts, mementoes. But she has always been secretive about them. Her birthday was last February, for example. I noticed shortly after that she was wearing a gold ring on the pinky of her right hand. A narrow band with a floral design. She never said a word, nor did I ask. But I'm sure it was from him."

"Do you consider him a stable young man?"

Turning around, she faced me, eyes dark and distracted. "Fred is very intense, somewhat obsessive. But I can't say that he's unstable. I really can't complain about him. I simply have worried that the relationship is too serious, too . . ." She looked away, groping for the right word. "Addictive. That's what comes to mind. It's as if they are each other's drug." Shutting her eyes, she turned away again and leaned her head against the window. "Oh, God. I wish we'd never bought her that goddam Jeep."

I did not comment.

"Fred doesn't have a car. She would have had no choice . . ." Her voice trailed off.

"She would have had no choice," I said, "but to drive with you to the beach."

"And this wouldn't have happened!"

Suddenly she walked out the door to the hallway. She could not bear to be inside her daughter's bedroom one moment longer, I knew, and I followed her down the stairs and to the front door. When I reached for her hand, she turned away from me as her tears fell.

"I'm so sorry." How many times on this earth would I say that?

The front door shut quietly as I went down the steps. While driving home I prayed that if I ever encountered Pat Harvey again, it would not be in my official capacity of chief medical examiner.

3

A WEEK PASSED before I heard again from anyone connected to the Harvey-Cheney case, the investigation of which had gone nowhere, as far as I knew. Monday, when I was up to my elbows in blood in the morgue, Benton Wesley called. He wanted to talk to Marino and me without delay, and suggested we come for dinner.

"I think Pat Harvey's making him nervous," Marino said that evening. Tentative drops of rain bounced off his car windshield as we headed to Wesley's house. "I personally don't give a rat's ass if she talks to a palm reader, rings up Billy Graham or the friggin' Easter Bunny."

"Hilda Ozimek is not a palm reader," I replied.

"Half those Sister Rose joints with a hand painted on the sign are just fronts for prostitution."

"I'm aware of that," I said wearily.

He opened the ashtray, reminding me what a filthy habit smoking was. If he could cram one more butt in there, it would be a Guinness record.

"I take it you've heard of Hilda Ozimek, then," he went on.

"I really don't know much about her, except that I think she lives somewhere in the Carolinas."

"South Carolina."

"Is she staying with the Harveys?"

"Not anymore," Marino said, turning off the windshield wipers as the sun peeked out from behind clouds. "Wish the damn weather would make up its mind. She went back to South Carolina yesterday. Was flown in and out of Richmond in a private plane, if you can believe that."

"You mind telling me how anybody knows about it?" If I was surprised that Pat Harvey would resort to a psychic, I was even more surprised that she would tell anyone.

"Good question. I'm just telling you what Benton said when he called. Apparently, Broom Hilda found something in her crystal ball that got Mrs. Harvey mighty upset."

"What, exactly?"

"Beats the shit outta me. Benton didn't go into detail."

I did not inquire further, for discussing Benton Wesley and his tight-lipped ways made me ill at ease. Once he and I had enjoyed working together, our regard for each other respectful and warm. Now I found him distant, and I could not help but worry that the way Wesley acted toward me had to do with Mark. When Mark had walked away from me by taking an assignment in Colorado, he had also walked away from Quantico, where he had enjoyed the privileged role of running the FBI National Academy's Legal Training Unit. Wesley had lost his colleague and companion, and in his mind it was probably my fault. The bond between male friends can be stronger than marriage, and brothers of the badge are more loyal to each other than lovers.

A half hour later Marino turned off the highway, and soon after I lost track of the lefts and rights he took on rural routes that led us deeper into the country. Though I had met with Wesley many times in the past, it had always been at my office or his. I had never been invited to his house, located in the picturesque setting of Virginia farmland and forests, pastures surrounded by white fences, and barns and homes set back far from the roads. When we turned into his subdivision, we began to pass long driveways leading to large modern houses on generous lots, with European sedans parked before two- and three-car garages.

"I didn't realize there were Washington bedroom communities this close to Richmond," I commented.

"What? You've lived around here for four, five years and never heard of northern aggression?"

"If you were born in Miami, the Civil War isn't exactly foremost on your mind," I replied.

"I guess not. Hell, Miami ain't even in this country. Any place where they got to vote on whether English is the official language don't belong in the United States."

Marino's digs about my birthplace were nothing new.

Slowing down as he turned into a gravel drive, he said, "Not a bad crib, huh? Guess the feds pay a little better than the city."

The house was shingle style with a fieldstone foundation and projecting bay windows. Rosebushes lined the front, east, and west wings shaded by old magnolias and oaks. As we got out, I began to look for clues that might give me more insight into Benton Wesley's private life. A basketball hoop was above the garage door, and near a woodpile covered with plastic was a red rider mower sprayed with cut grass. Beyond, I could see a spacious backyard impeccably landscaped with flower beds, azaleas, and fruit trees. Several chairs were arranged close together near a gas grill, and I envisioned Wesley and his wife having drinks and cooking steaks on leisurely summer nights.

Marino rang the bell. It was Wesley's wife who opened the door. She introduced herself as Connie.

"Ben went upstairs for a minute," she said, smiling, as she led us into a living room with wide windows, a large fireplace, and rustic furniture. I had never heard Wesley referred to as "Ben" before. Nor had I ever met his wife. She appeared to be in her mid-forties, an attractive brunette with hazel eyes so light they were almost yellow, and sharp features very much like her husband's. There was a gentleness about her, a quiet reserve suggesting strength of character and tenderness. The guarded Benton Wesley I knew, no doubt, was a very different man at home, and I wondered how familiar Connie was with the details of his profession.

"Will you have a beer, Pete?" she asked.

He settled into a rocking chair. "Looks like I'm the designated driver. Better stick to coffee."

"Kay, what may I get for you?"

"Coffee would be fine," I replied. "If it's no trouble."

"I'm so glad to finally meet you," she added sincerely. "Ben's spoken of you for years. He regards you very highly."

"Thank you." The compliment disconcerted me, and what she said next came as a shock.

"When we saw Mark last, I made him promise to bring you to dinner next time he comes to Quantico."

"That's very kind," I said, managing a smile. Clearly, Wesley did not tell her everything, and the idea that Mark might have been in

Virginia recently without so much as calling me was almost more than I could bear.

When she left us for the kitchen, Marino asked, "You heard from him lately?"

"Denver's beautiful," I replied evasively.

"It's a bitch, you want my opinion. They bring him in from deep cover, hole him up in Quantico for a while. Next thing, they're sending his ass out west to work on something he can't tell nobody about. Just one more reason why you couldn't pay me enough to sign on with the Bureau."

I did not respond.

He went on, "The hell with your personal life. It's like they say, 'If Hoover wanted you to have a wife and kids, he would've issued them with your badge.' "

"Hoover was a long time ago," I said, staring out at trees churning in the wind. It looked like it was about to rain again, this time seriously.

"Maybe so. But you still ain't got a life of your own."

"I'm not sure any of us do, Marino."

"That's the damn truth," he muttered under his breath.

Footsteps sounded and then Wesley walked in, still in suit and tie, gray trousers and starched white shirt slightly wrinkled. He seemed tired and tense as he asked if we had been offered drinks.

"Connie's taking care of us," I said.

Lowering himself into a chair, he glanced at his watch. "We'll eat in about an hour." He clasped his hands in his lap.

"Haven't heard shit from Morrell," Marino started in.

"I'm afraid there are no new developments. Nothing hopeful," Wesley replied.

"Didn't assume there was. I'm just telling you that I ain't heard from Morrell."

Marino's face was expressionless, but I could sense his resentment. Though he had yet to voice any complaints to me, I suspected that he was feeling like a quarterback sitting out the season on the bench. He had always enjoyed a good rapport with detectives from other jurisdictions, and that, frankly, had been one of the strengths of VICAP's efforts in Virginia. Then the missing couple cases had begun. Investigators were no longer talking to each other. They weren't talking to Marino, and they weren't talking to me.

"Local efforts have been halted," Wesley informed him. "We didn't get any farther than the eastbound rest stop where the dog lost the scent. Only other thing to turn up is a receipt found inside the Jeep. It appears that Deborah and Fred stopped off at a Seven-Eleven after leaving the Harvey house in Richmond. They bought a six-pack of Pepsi and a couple other items."

"Then it's been checked out," Marino said, testily.

"The clerk on duty at the time has been located. She remembers them coming in. Apparently, this was shortly after nine P.M."

"And they was alone?" Marino inquired.

"It would seem so. No one else came in with them, and if there was someone waiting for them inside the Jeep, there was no evidence, based on their demeanor, to suggest that anything was wrong."

"Where is this Seven-Eleven located?" I asked.

"Approximately five miles west of the rest stop where the Jeep was found," Wesley replied.

"You said they bought a few other items," I said. "Can you be more specific?"

"I was getting to that," Wesley said. "Deborah Harvey bought a box of Tampax. She asked if she could use a bathroom, and was told it was against policy. The clerk said she directed them to the eastbound rest stop on Sixty-four."

"Where the dog lost the scent," Marino said, frowning as if confused. "Versus where the Jeep was found."

"That's right," Wesley replied.

"What about the Pepsi they bought?" I asked. "Did you find it?"

"Six cans of Pepsi were in the ice chest when the police went through the Jeep."

He paused as his wife appeared with our coffee and a glass of iced tea for him. She served us in gracious silence, then was gone. Connie Wesley was practiced at being unobtrusive.

"You're thinking they hit the rest stop so Deborah could take care of her problem, and that's where they met up with the squirrel who took them out," Marino interpolated.

"We don't know what happened to them," Wesley reminded us. "There are a lot of scenarios we need to consider."

"Such as?" Marino was still frowning.

"Abduction."

"As in kidnapping?" Marino was blatantly skeptical.

"You have to remember who Deborah's mother is."

"Yeah, I know. Mrs. Got-Rocks-the-Drug-Czar who got sworn

in because the President wanted to give the women's movement something to chew on."

"Pete," Wesley said calmly, "I don't think it wise to dismiss her as a plutocratic figurehead or token female appointee. Though the position sounds more powerful than it really is because it was never given Cabinet status, Pat Harvey does answer directly to the President. She does, in fact, coordinate all federal agencies in the war against drug crimes."

"Not to mention her track record when she was a U.S. attorney," I added. "She was a strong supporter of the White House's efforts to make drug-related murders and attempted murders punishable by death. And she was quite vocal about it."

"Her and a hundred other politicians," Marino said. "Maybe I'd be more concerned if she was one of these liberals wanting to legalize the shit. Then I have to wonder about some right-wing Moral Majority type who thinks God's told him to snatch Pat Harvey's kid."

"She's been very aggressive," Wesley said, "succeeded in getting convictions on some of the worst in the lot, has been instrumental in getting important bills passed, has withstood death threats, and several years ago even had her car bombed—"

"Yeah, an unoccupied Jag parked at the country club. And it made her a hero," Marino interrupted.

"My point," Wesley went on patiently, "is that she's made her share of enemies, especially when it comes to the efforts she's directed at various charities."

"I've read something about that," I said, trying to recall the details.

"What the public knows at present is just a scratch on the surface," Wesley said. "Her latest efforts have been directed at ACTMAD. The American Coalition of Tough Mothers Against Drugs."

"You gotta be kidding," Marino said. "That's like saying UNICEF's dirty."

I did not volunteer that I sent money to ACTMAD every year and considered myself an enthusiastic supporter.

Wesley went on, "Mrs. Harvey has been gathering evidence to prove that ACTMAD has been serving as a front for a drug cartel and other illegal activities in Central America."

"Geez," Marino said, shaking his head. "Good thing I don't give a dime to nobody except the FOP."

"Deborah and Fred's disappearance is perplexing because it seems connected to the other four couples," Wesley said. "But this could also be deliberate, someone's attempt to make us assume there is a link, when in fact there may not be. We may be dealing with a serial killer. We may be dealing with something else. Whatever the case, we want to work this as quietly as possible."

"So I guess what you're waiting for now is a ransom note or something, huh?" Marino said. "You know, some Central American thugs will return Deborah to her mother for a price."

"I don't think that's going to happen, Pete," Wesley replied. "It may be worse than that. Pat Harvey is due to testify in a congressional hearing early next year—and again, this all has to do with the illegitimate charities. There isn't anything much worse that could have happened right now than to have her daughter disappear."

My stomach knotted at the thought. Professionally, Pat Harvey did not seem particularly vulnerable, having enjoyed a spotless reputation throughout her career. But she was also a mother. The welfare of her children would be more precious to her than her own life. Her family was her Achilles' heel.

"We can't dismiss the possibility of political kidnapping," Wesley remarked, staring out at his yard thrashed by the wind.

Wesley had a family, too. The nightmare was that a crime family boss, a murderer, someone Wesley had been instrumental in bringing down would go after Wesley's wife or children. He had a sophisticated burglar alarm system in his house and an intercom outside the front door. He had chosen to live in the far-removed setting of the Virginia countryside, telephone number unlisted, address never given to reporters or even to most of his colleagues and acquaintances. Until today, even I had not known where he lived, but had assumed his home was closer to Quantico, perhaps in McLean or Alexandria.

Wesley said, "I'm sure Marino's mentioned to you this business about Hilda Ozimek."

I nodded. "Is she genuine?"

"The Bureau has used her on a number of occasions, though we don't like to admit it. Her gift, power, whatever you want to call it, is quite genuine. Don't ask me to explain. This sort of phenomenon goes beyond my immediate experience. I can tell you, however, that on one occasion she helped us locate a Bureau plane that had gone down in the mountains of West Virginia. She also predicted Sadat's assassination, and we might have had a little more forewarning about the attempt on Reagan had we listened to her words more carefully."

"You're not going to tell me she predicted Reagan's shooting," Marino said.

"Almost to the day. We didn't pass along what she'd said. Didn't, well, take it seriously, I suppose. That was our mistake, weird as it may seem. Ever since, whenever she says anything, the Secret Service wants to know."

"The Secret Service reading horoscopes, too?" Marino asked.

"I believe that Hilda Ozimek would consider horoscopes rather generic. And as far as I know, she doesn't read palms," Wesley said pointedly.

"How did Mrs. Harvey find out about her?" I asked.

"Possibly from someone within the Justice Department," Wesley said. "In any event, she flew the psychic to Richmond on Friday and apparently was told a number of things that have succeeded in making her . . . well, let's just say that I'm viewing Mrs. Harvey as a loose cannon. I'm concerned that her activities may prove to do a lot more harm than good."

"What exactly did this psychic tell her?" I wanted to know.

Wesley looked levelly at me and replied, "I really can't go into that. Not now."

"But she discussed it with you?" I inquired. "Pat Harvey volunteered to you that she had resorted to a psychic?"

"I'm not at liberty to discuss it, Kay," Wesley said, and the three of us were silent for a moment.

It went through my mind that Mrs. Harvey had not divulged this information to Wesley. He had found out in some other way.

"I don't know," Marino finally said. "Could be a random thing. I don't want to count that out."

"We can't count anything out," Wesley said firmly.

"It's been going on for two and a half years, Benton," I said.

"Yeah," Marino said. "A friggin' long time. Still strikes me as the work of some squirrel out there who fixes on couples, a jealousy-type thing because he's a loser, can't have relationships and hates other people who can."

"Certainly that's one strong possibility. Someone who routinely cruises around looking for young couples. He may frequent lovers' lanes, rest stops, the watering holes where kids park. He may go through a lot of dry runs before he strikes, then replay the homicides for months before the urge to kill again becomes irresistible and the perfect opportunity presents itself. It may be coincidence—Deborah Harvey and Fred Cheney may simply have been in the wrong place at the wrong time."

"I'm not aware there's evidence to suggest that any of the couples were parking, engaged in sexual activity, when they met up with an assailant," I pointed out.

Wesley did not respond.

"And other than Deborah and Fred, the other couples didn't appear to have pulled off at a rest stop or any other sort of 'watering hole,' as you put it," I went on. "It appears they were en route to some destination when something happened to make them pull off the road and either let someone in their car or get into this person's vehicle."

"The killer cop theory," Marino muttered. "Don't think I haven't heard it before."

"It could be someone posing as a cop," Wesley replied. "Certainly that would account for the couples pulling over and, perhaps, getting into someone else's car for a routine license check or whatever. Anybody can walk into a uniform store and buy a bubble light, uniform, badge, you name it. Problem with that is a flashing light draws attention. Other motorists notice it, and if there is a real cop in the area, he's likely to at least slow down, perhaps even pull over to offer assistance. So far, there hasn't been a single report of anyone noticing a traffic stop that might have occurred in the area and at the time that these kids disappeared."

"You would also have to wonder why wallets and purses would be left inside their cars—with the exception of Deborah Harvey, whose purse has not been found," I said. "If the young people were told to get inside a so-called police vehicle for a routine traffic violation, then why would they leave car registrations and driver's licenses behind? These are the first items an officer asks to see, and when you get inside his car, you have these personal effects with you."

"They may not have gotten into this person's vehicle willingly, Kay," Wesley said. "They think they're being stopped by a police officer, and when the guy walks up to their window, he pulls out a gun, orders them into his car."

"Risky as shit," Marino argued. "If it was me, I'd throw the damn car in gear and floorboard it the hell out of there. Always the chance someone driving by might see something, too. I mean, how do you force two people at gunpoint into your car on four, maybe five different occasions and not have anyone passing by notice a goddam thing?"

"A better question," Wesley said, looking unemphatically at me, "is how do you murder eight people without leaving any evidence, not so much as a nick on a bone or a bullet found somewhere near the bodies?"

"Strangulation, garroting, or throats cut," I said, and it was not the first time he had pressed me on this. "The bodies have all been badly decomposed, Benton. And I want to remind you that the cop theory implies the victims got inside the assailant's vehicle. Based on the scent the bloodhound followed last weekend, it seems plausible that if someone did something bad to Deborah Harvey and Fred Cheney, this individual may have driven off in Deborah's Jeep, abandoned it at the rest stop, and then taken off on foot across the Interstate."

Wesley's face was tired. Several times now he had rubbed his temples as if he had a headache. "My purpose in talking to both of you is that there may be some angles to this thing that require us to act very carefully. I'm asking for direct and open channels among the three of us. Absolute discretion is imperative. No loose talk to reporters, no divulging of information to anyone, not to close friends, relatives, other medical examiners, or cops. And no radio transmissions." He looked at both of us. "I want to be land lined immediately if and when Deborah Harvey's and Fred Cheney's bodies are found. And if Mrs. Harvey tries to get in touch with either of you, direct her to me."

"She's already been in contact," I said.

"I'm aware of that, Kay," Wesley replied without looking at me.

I did not ask him how he knew, but I was unnerved and it showed.

"Under the circumstances, I can understand your going to see her," he added. "But it's best if it doesn't happen again, better you don't discuss these cases with her further. It only causes more problems. It goes beyond her interfering with the investigation. The more she gets involved, the more she may be endangering herself."

"What? Because she turns up dead?" Marino asked skeptically.

"More likely because she ends up out of control, irrational." Wesley's concern over Pat Harvey's psychological wellbeing may have been valid, but it seemed flimsy to me. And I could not help but worry as Marino and I were driving back to Richmond after dinner that the reason Wesley had wanted to see us had nothing to do with the welfare of the missing couple.

"I think I'm feeling handled," I finally confessed as the Richmond skyline came into view.

"Join the club," Marino said irritably.

"Do you have any idea what's really going on here?"

"Oh, yeah," he replied, punching in the cigarette lighter. "I got a suspicion, all right. I think the Friggin' Bureau of Investigation's caught a whiff of something that's going to make someone who counts look bad. I got this funny feeling someone's covering his ass, and Benton's caught in the middle."

"If he is, then so are we."

"You got it, Doc."

It had been three years since Abby Turnbull had appeared in my office doorway, arms laden with fresh-cut irises and a bottle of exceptional wine. That had been the day when she had come to say good-bye, having given the Richmond *Times* notice. She was on her way to work in Washington as a police reporter for the *Post*. We had promised to keep in touch as people always do. I was ashamed I could not remember the last time I had called or written her a note.

"Do you want me to put her through?" Rose, my secretary, was asking. "Or should I take a message?"

"I'll talk to her," I said. "Scarpetta," I announced out of habit before I could catch myself.

"You still sound so damn *chiefly*," the familiar voice said.

"Abby! I'm sorry." I laughed. "Rose told me it was you. As usual, I'm in the middle of about fifty other things, and I think I've completely lost the art of being friendly on the phone. How are you?"

"Fine. If you don't count the fact that the homicide rate in Washington has tripled since I moved up here."

"A coincidence, I hope."

"Drugs." She sounded nervous. "Cocaine, crack, and semiautomatics. I always thought a beat in Miami would be the worst. Or maybe New York. But our lovely nation's capital is the worst."

I glanced up at the clock and jotted the time on a call sheet.

Habit again. I was so accustomed to filling out call sheets that I reached for the clipboard even when my hairdresser called.

"I was hoping you might be free for dinner tonight," she said.

"In Washington?" I asked, perplexed.

"Actually, I'm in Richmond."

I suggested dinner at my house, packed up my briefcase, and headed out to the grocery store. After much deliberation as I pushed the cart up and down aisles, I selected two tenderloins and the makings for salad. The afternoon was beautiful. The thought of seeing Abby was improving my mood. I decided that an evening spent with an old friend was a good excuse to brave cooking out again.

When I got home, I began to work quickly, crushing fresh garlic into a bowl of red wine and olive oil. Though my mother had always admonished me about "ruining a good steak," I was spoiled by my own culinary skills. Honestly, I made the best marinade in town, and no cut of meat could resist being improved by it. Rinsing Boston lettuce and draining it on paper towels, I sliced mushrooms, onions, and the last Hanover tomato as I fortified myself to tend to the grill. Unable to put off the task any longer, I stepped out onto the brick patio.

For a moment, I felt like a fugitive on my own property as I surveyed the flower gardens and trees of my backyard. I fetched a bottle of 409 and a sponge and began vigorously to scrub the outdoor furniture before taking a Brillo pad to the grill, which I had not used since the Saturday night in May when Mark and I last had been together. I attacked sooty grease until my elbows hurt. Images and voices invaded my mind. Arguing. Fighting. Then a retreat into angry silence that ended with making frantic love.

I almost did not recognize Abby when she arrived at my front door shortly before six-thirty. When she had worked the police beat in Richmond, her hair had been to her shoulders and streaked with gray, giving her a washed-out, gaunt appearance that made her seem older than her forty-odd years. Now the gray was gone. Her hair was cut short and smartly styled to emphasize the fine bones of her face and her eyes, which were two different shades of green, an irregularity I had always found intriguing. She wore a dark blue silk suit and ivory silk blouse, and carried a sleek black leather briefcase.

"You look very Washingtonian," I said, giving her a hug.

"It's *so good* to see you, Kay."

She remembered I liked Scotch and had brought a bottle of Glenfiddich, which we wasted no time in uncorking. Then we sipped drinks on the patio and talked nonstop as I lit the grill beneath a dusky late summer sky.

"Yes, I do miss Richmond in some ways," she was explaining. "Washington is exciting, but the pits. I indulged myself and bought a Saab, right? It's already been broken into once, had the hubcaps stolen, the hell beaten out of the doors. I pay a hundred and fifty bucks a month to park the damn thing, and we're talking four blocks from my apartment. Forget parking at the *Post*. I walk to work and use a staff car. Washington's definitely not Richmond." She added a little too resolutely, "But I don't regret leaving."

"You're still working evenings?" Steaks sizzled as I placed them on the grill.

"No. It's somebody else's turn. The young reporters race around after dark and I follow up during the day. I get called after hours only if something really big goes down."

"I've been keeping up with your byline," I told her. "They sell the *Post* in the cafeteria. I usually pick it up during lunch."

"I don't always know what you're working on," she confessed. "But I'm aware of some things."

"Explaining why you're in Richmond?" I ventured, as I brushed marinade over the meat.

"Yes. The Harvey case."

I did not reply.

"Marino hasn't changed."

"You've talked to him?" I asked, glancing up at her.

She replied with a wry smile, "Tried to. And several other investigators. And, of course, Benton Wesley. In other words, forget it."

"Well, if it makes you feel any better, Abby, nobody's talking much to me, either. And that's off the record."

"This entire conversation is off the record, Kay," she said seriously. "I didn't come to see you because I wanted to pick your brain for my story." She paused. "I've been aware of what's been going on here in Virginia. I was a lot more concerned about it than my editor was until Deborah Harvey and her boyfriend disappeared. Now it's gotten hot, real hot."

"I'm not surprised."

"I'm not quite sure where to begin." She looked unsettled.

"There are things I've not told anybody, Kay. But I have a sense that I'm walking on ground somebody doesn't want me on."

"I'm not sure I understand," I said, reaching for my drink.

"I'm not sure I do, either. I ask myself if I'm imagining things."

"Abby, you're being cryptic. Please explain."

Taking a deep breath as she got out a cigarette, she replied, "I've been interested in the deaths of these couples for a long time. I've been doing some investigating, and the reactions I've gotten from the beginning are odd. It's gone beyond the usual reluctance I often run into with the police. I bring up the subject and people practically hang up on me. Then this past June, the FBI came to see me."

"I beg your pardon?" I stopped basting and looked hard at her.

"You remember that triple homicide in Williamsburg? The mother, father, and son shot to death during a robbery?"

"Yes."

"I was working on a feature about it, and had to drive to Williamsburg. As you know, when you get off Sixty-four, if you turn right you head toward Colonial Williamsburg, William and Mary. But if you turn left off the exit ramp, in maybe two hundred yards you dead-end at the entrance of Camp Peary. I wasn't thinking. I took the wrong turn."

"I've done that once or twice myself," I admitted.

She went on, "I drove up to the guard booth and explained I'd taken a wrong turn. Talk about a creepy place. God. All these big warning signs saying things like 'Armed Forces Experimental Training Activity,' and 'Entering This Facility Signifies Your Consent to the Search of Your Person and Personal Property.' I was half expecting a SWAT team of Neanderthals in camouflage to bolt out of the bushes and haul me away."

"The base police are not a friendly lot," I said, somewhat amused.

"Well, I wasted no time getting the hell out of there," Abby said, "and, in truth, forgot all about it until four days later when two FBI agents appeared in the lobby of the *Post* looking for me. They wanted to know what I'd been doing in Williamsburg, why I'd driven to Camp Peary. Obviously, my plate number had been recorded on film and traced back to the newspaper. It was weird."

"Why would the FBI be interested?" I asked. "Camp Peary is CIA."

"The CIA has no enforcement powers in the United States.

Maybe that's why. Maybe the jerks were really CIA agents posing as FBI. Who can say what the hell is going on when you're dealing with those spooks? Besides, the CIA has never admitted that Camp Peary is its main training facility, and the agents never mentioned the CIA when they interrogated me. But I knew what they were getting at, and they knew I knew."

"What else did they ask?"

"Basically, they wanted to know if I was writing something about Camp Peary, maybe trying to sneak in. I told them if I had intended to sneak in, I would have been a little more *covert* about it than driving straight to the guard booth, and though I wasn't currently working on anything about, and I quote, 'the CIA,' maybe now I ought to consider it."

"I'm sure that went over well," I said dryly.

"The guys didn't bat an eye. You know the way they are."

"The CIA is paranoid, Abby, especially about Camp Peary. State police and emergency medical helicopters aren't allowed to fly over it. Nobody violates that airspace or gets beyond the guard booth without being cleared by Jesus Christ."

"Yet you've made that same wrong turn before, as have hundreds of tourists," she reminded me. "The FBI's never come looking for you, have they?"

"No. But I don't work for the *Post*."

I removed the steaks from the grill and she followed me into the kitchen. As I served the salads and poured wine, she continued to talk.

"Ever since the agents came to see me, peculiar things have been happening."

"Such as?"

"I think my phones are being tapped."

"Based on what?"

"It started with my phone at home. I'd be talking to someone and hear something. This has also happened at work, especially of late. A call will be transferred, and I have this strong sense that someone else is listening in. It's hard to explain." She nervously rearranged her silverware. "A static, a noisy silence, or however you want to describe it. But it's there."

"Any other peculiar things?"

"Well, there was something several weeks ago. I was standing out in front of a People's Drug Store off Connecticut, near Dupont Circle. A source was supposed to meet me there at eight P.M., then we were going to find some place quiet to have dinner and talk. And I saw this man. Clean-cut, dressed in a windbreaker and jeans, nice looking. He walked by twice during the fifteen minutes I was standing on the corner, and I caught a glimpse of him again later when my appointment and I were going into the restaurant. I know it sounds crazy, but I had the feeling I was being followed."

"Had you ever seen this man before?"

She shook her head.

"Have you seen him since?"

"No," she said. "But there's something else. My mail. I live in an apartment building. All the mailboxes are downstairs in the lobby. Sometimes I get things with postmarks that don't make sense."

"If the CIA were tampering with your mail, I can assure you that you wouldn't know about it."

"I'm not saying my mail *looks* tampered with. But in several instances, someone—my mother, my literary agent—will swear they mailed something on a certain day, and when I finally get it, the date on the postmark is inconsistent with what it should be. Late. By days, a week. I don't know." She paused. "I probably would just assume it had to do with the ineptitude of the postal service, but with everything else that's been going on, it's made me wonder."

"Why would anyone be tapping your phone, tailing you, or tampering with your mail?" I asked the critical question.

"If I knew that, maybe I could do something about it." She finally got around to eating. "This is wonderful." Despite the compliment, she didn't appear the least bit hungry.

"Any possibility," I suggested bluntly, "that your encounter with these FBI agents, the episode at Camp Peary, might have made you paranoid?"

"Obviously it's made me paranoid. But look, Kay. It's not like I'm writing another *Veil* or working on a Watergate. Washington is one shoot-out after another, the same old shit. The only big thing brewing is what's going on here. These murders, or possible murders, of these couples. I start poking around and run into trouble. What do you think?"

"I'm not sure." I uncomfortably recalled Benton Wesley's demeanor, his warnings from the night before.

"I know the business about the missing shoes," Abby said.

I did not respond or show my surprise. It was a detail that, so far, had been kept from reporters.

"It's not exactly normal for eight people to end up dead in the woods without shoes and socks turning up either at the scenes or inside the abandoned cars." She looked expectantly at me.

"Abby," I said quietly, refilling our wineglasses, "you know I can't go into detail about these cases. Not even with you."

"You're not aware of anything that might clue me in as to what I'm up against?"

"To tell you the truth, I probably know less than you do."

"That tells me something. The cases have been going on for two and a half years, and you may know less than I do."

I remembered what Marino said about somebody "covering his ass." I thought of Pat Harvey and the congressional hearing. My fear was kicking in.

Abby said, "Pat Harvey is a bright star in Washington."

"I'm aware of her importance."

"There's more to it than what you read in the papers, Kay. In Washington, what parties you get invited to mean as much as votes. Maybe more. When it comes to prominent people included on the elite guest lists, Pat Harvey is right up there with the First Lady. It's been rumored that come the next presidential election, Pat Harvey may successfully conclude what Geraldine Ferraro started."

"A vice-presidential hopeful?" I asked dubiously.

"That's the gossip. I'm skeptical, but if we have another Republican President, I personally think she's at least got a shot at a Cabinet appointment or maybe even becoming the next Attorney General. Providing she holds together."

"She's going to have to work very hard at holding herself together through all this."

"Personal problems can definitely ruin your career," Abby agreed.

"They can, if you let them. But if you survive them, they can make you stronger, more effective."

"I know," she muttered, staring at her wineglass. "I'm pretty sure I never would have left Richmond if it hadn't been for what happened to Henna."

Not long after I had taken office in Richmond, Abby's sister, Henna, was murdered. The tragedy had brought Abby and me together professionally. We had become friends. Months later she had accepted the job at the *Post*.

"It still isn't easy for me to come back here," Abby said. "In fact, this is my first time since I moved. I even drove past my old

house this morning and was halfway tempted to knock on the door,
see if the current owners would let me in. I don't know why. But
I wanted to walk through it again, see if I could handle going upstairs to Henna's room, replace that horrible last image of her with
something harmless. It didn't appear that anyone was home. And it
probably was just as well. I don't think I could have brought myself
to do it."

"When you're truly ready, you'll do it," I said, and I wanted
to tell her about my using the patio this evening, about how I
had not been able to before now. But it sounded like such a small
accomplishment, and Abby did not know about Mark.

"I talked to Fred Cheney's father late this morning," Abby said.
"Then I went to see the Harveys."

"When will your story run?"

"Probably not until the weekend edition. I've still got a lot of
reporting to do. The paper wants a profile of Fred and Deborah
and anything else I can come up with about the investigation—
especially any connection to the other four couples."

"How did the Harveys seem to you when you talked to them
earlier today?"

"Well, I really didn't talk to him, to Bob. As soon as I arrived, he
left with his sons. Reporters are not his favorite people, and I have
a feeling being 'Pat Harvey's husband' gets to him. He never gives
interviews." She pushed her half-eaten steak away and reached for
her cigarettes. Her smoking was a lot worse than I remembered it.
"I'm worried about Pat. She looks as if she's aged ten years in the
last week. And it was strange. I couldn't shake the sensation she
knows something, has already formulated her own theory about
what's happened to her daughter. I guess that's what made me most
curious. I'm wondering if she's gotten a threat, a note, some sort
of communication from whomever's involved. And she's refusing
to tell anyone, including the police."

"I can't imagine she would be that unwise."

"I can," Abby said. "I think if she thought there was any chance
Deborah might return home unharmed, Pat Harvey wouldn't tell
God what was going on."

I got up to clear the table.

"I think you'd better make some coffee," Abby said. "I don't
want to fall asleep at the wheel."

"When do you need to head out?" I asked, loading the dishwasher.

"Soon. I've got a couple of places to go before I drive back to Washington."

I glanced over at her as I filled the coffeepot with water.

She explained, "A Seven-Eleven where Deborah and Fred stopped after they left Richmond—"

"How did you know about that?" I interrupted her.

"I managed to pry it out of the tow truck operator who hung around the rest stop, waiting to haul away the Jeep. He overheard the police discussing a receipt they found in a wadded-up paper bag. It required one hell of a lot of trouble, but I managed to figure out which Seven-Eleven and what clerk would have been working around the time Deborah and Fred would have stopped in. Someone named Ellen Jordan works the four-to-midnight shift Monday through Friday."

I was so fond of Abby, it was easy for me to forget that she had won more than her share of investigative reporting awards for a very good reason.

"What do you expect to find out from this clerk?"

"Ventures like this, Kay, are like looking for the prize inside a box of Crackerjacks. I don't know the answers—in fact, I don't even know the questions—until I start digging."

"I really don't think you should wander around out there alone late at night, Abby."

"If you'd like to ride shotgun," she replied, amused, "I'd love the company."

"I don't think that's a very good idea."

"I suppose you're right," she said.

I decided to do it anyway.

4

THE ILLUMINATED SIGN was visible half a mile before we reached the exit, a "7-Eleven" glowing in the dark. Its cryptic red-and-green message no longer meant what it said, for every 7-Eleven I knew of was open twenty-four hours a day. I could almost hear what my father would say.

"Your grandfather left Verona for *this*?"

That was his favorite remark when he would read the morning paper, shaking his head in disapproval. It was what he said when someone with a Georgia accent treated us as if we weren't "real Americans." It was what my father would mumble when he heard tales of dishonesty, "dope," and divorce. When I was a child in Miami, he owned a small neighborhood grocery and was at the dinner table every night talking about his day and asking about ours. His presence in my life was not long. He died when I was twelve. But I was certain that were he still here, he would not appreciate convenience stores. Nights, Sundays, and holidays were not to be spent working behind a counter or eating a burrito on the road. Those hours were for family.

Abby checked her mirrors again as she turned off on the exit. In less than a hundred feet, she was pulling into the 7-Eleven's parking lot, and I could tell she was relieved. Other than a Volkswagen near the double glass front doors, it seemed we were the only customers.

"Coast is clear so far," she observed, switching off the ignition. "Haven't passed a single patrol car, unmarked or otherwise, in the last twenty miles."

"At least not that you know of," I said.

The night was hazy, not a star in sight, the air warm but damp. A young man carrying a twelve-pack of beer passed by us as we went inside the air-conditioned coolness of America's favorite fixes, where video games flashed bright lights in a corner and a young woman was restocking a cigarette rack behind the counter. She didn't look a day over eighteen, her bleached blond hair billowing out in a frizzy aura around her head, her slight figure clad in an orange-and-white-checked tunic and a pair of tight black jeans. Her fingernails were long and painted bright red, and when she turned around to see what we wanted, I was struck by the hardness of her face. It was as if she had skipped training wheels and gone straight to a Harley-Davidson.

"Ellen Jordan?" Abby inquired.

The clerk looked surprised, then wary. "Yeah? So who wants to know?"

"Abby Turnbull." Abby presented her hand in a very business-like fashion. Ellen Jordan shook it limply. "From Washington," Abby added. "The *Post*."

"What *Post*?"

"The *Washington Post*," Abby said.

"Oh." Instantly, she was bored. "We already carry it. Right over there." She pointed to a depleted stack near the door.

There was an awkward pause.

"I'm a *reporter* for the *Post*," Abby explained.

Ellen's eyes lit up. "No kidding?"

"No kidding. I'd like to ask you a few questions."

"You mean for a story?"

"Yes. I'm doing a story, Ellen. And I really need your help."

"What do you want to know?" She leaned against the counter, her serious expression reflecting her sudden importance.

"It's about the couple that came in here Friday night a week ago. A young man and woman. About your age. They came in shortly after nine P.M., bought a six-pack of Pepsi, several other items."

"Oh. The ones missing," she said, animated now. "You know, I shoulda never told 'em to go to that rest stop. But one of the first things they tell us when we're hired is nobody gets to use the bathroom. Personally, I wouldn't mind, especially not when the girl and boy came in. I felt so sorry for her. I mean, I sure understood."

"I'm sure you did," Abby said sympathetically.

"It was sort of embarrassing," Ellen went on. "When she bought the Tampax and asked if she could please use the bathroom, her boyfriend standing right there. Wow, I sure do wish I'd let her now."

"How did you know he was her boyfriend?" Abby asked.

For an instant, Ellen looked confused. "Well, I just assumed. They was looking around in here together, seemed to like each other a lot. You know how people act. You can tell if you're paying attention. And when I'm in here all hours by myself, I get pretty good at telling about people. Take married couples. Get 'em all the time, on a trip, kids in the car. Most of 'em come in here and I can tell they're tired and not getting along good. But the two you're talking about, they was real sweet with each other."

"Did they say anything else to you, other than needing to find a rest room?"

"We talked while I was ringing them up," Ellen replied. "Nothing special. I said the usual. 'Nice night for driving,' and 'Where ya headin'?' "

"And did they tell you?" Abby asked, taking notes.

"Huh?"

Abby glanced up at her. "Did they tell you where they were heading?"

"They said the beach. I remember that because I told 'em they was lucky. Seems whenever everybody else's heading off to fun places, I'm always stuck right here. Plus, me and my boyfriend had just broke up. It was getting to me, you know?"

"I understand." Abby smiled kindly. "Tell me more about how they were acting, Ellen. Anything jump out at you?"

She thought about this, then said, "Uh-uh. They was real nice, but in a hurry. I guess because she wanted to find a bathroom pretty bad. Mostly I remember how polite they was. You know, people come in here all the time wanting to use the bathroom and get nasty when I tell 'em they can't."

"You mentioned you directed them to the rest stop," Abby said. "Do you remember exactly what you told them?"

"Sure. I told 'em there's one not too far from here. Just get back on Sixty-four East"—she pointed—"and they'd see it in about five, ten minutes, couldn't miss it."

"Was anybody else in here when you told them this?"

"People were in and out. Lot of folks on the road." She thought for a minute. "I know there was a kid in back playing Pac Man. Same little creep always in here."

"Anybody else who might have been near the counter when the couple was?" Abby asked.

"There was this man. He came in right after the couple came in. Was looking through the magazines, ended up buying a cup of coffee."

"Was this while you were talking to the couple?" Abby relentlessly pursued the details.

"Yeah. I remember because he was real friendly and said something to the guy about the Jeep being a nice one. The couple drove up in a red Jeep. One of those fancy kinds. It was parked right in front of the doors."

"Then what happened?"

Ellen sat down on the stool in front of the cash register. "Well, that was pretty much it. Some other customers came in. The guy with the coffee left, and then maybe five minutes later, the couple left, too."

"But the man with the coffee—he was still near the counter when you were directing the couple to the rest stop?" Abby wanted to know.

She frowned. "It's hard to remember. But I think he was looking through the magazines when I was telling them that. Then it seems like the girl went off down one of the aisles to find what she needed, got back to the counter just as the man was paying for his coffee."

"You said the couple left maybe five minutes after the man did," Abby went on. "What were they doing?"

"Well, it took a couple minutes," she replied. "The girl set a six-pack of Coors on the counter, you know, and I had to card her, saw she was under twenty-one, so I couldn't sell her beer. She was real nice about it, sort of laughed. I mean, all of us were laughing about it. I don't take it personal. Hell, I used to try it, too. Anyway, she ended up buying a six-pack of sodas. Then they left."

"Can you describe this man, the one who bought the coffee?"

"Not real good."

"White or black?"

"White. Seems like he was dark. Black hair, maybe brown. Maybe in his late twenties, early thirties."

"Tall, short, fat, thin?"

Ellen stared off toward the back of the store. "Medium height, maybe. Sort of well built but not big, I think."

"Beard or mustache?"

"Don't think so. . . . Wait a minute." Her face lit up. "His hair was short. Yeah! In fact, I remember it passed through my mind he looked military. You know, there's a lot of military types around here, come in all the time on their way to Tidewater."

"What else made you think he might be military?" Abby asked.

"I don't know. But maybe it was just his way. It's hard to explain, but when you've seen enough military guys, it gets to where you can pick 'em out. There's just something about 'em. Like tattoos, for example. A lot of 'em have tattoos."

"Did this man have a tattoo?"

Her frown turned to disappointment. "I didn't notice."

"How about the way he was dressed?"

"Uhhhh . . ."

"A suit and tie?" Abby asked.

"Well, he wasn't in a suit and tie. Nothing fancy. Maybe jeans or dark pants. He might've been wearing a zip-up jacket. . . . Gee, I really can't be sure."

"Do you, by chance, remember what he was driving?"

"No," she said with certainty. "I never saw his car. He must've parked off to the side."

"Did you tell the police all this when they came to talk to you, Ellen?"

"Yeah." She was eyeing the parking lot out front. A van had just pulled up. "I told 'em pretty much the same things I told you. Except for some of the stuff I couldn't remember then."

When two teenage boys sauntered in and headed straight for the video games, Ellen returned her attention to us. I could tell she had nothing more to say and was beginning to entertain doubts about having said too much.

Apparently, Abby was getting the same message. "Thank you, Ellen," she said, backing away from the counter. "The story will run on Saturday or Sunday. Be sure you watch for it."

Then we were out the door.

"Time to get the hell out of here before she starts screaming that everything was *off the record*."

"I doubt she'd even know what the term meant," I replied.

"What surprises me," Abby said, "is that the cops didn't tell her to keep her mouth shut."

"Maybe they did but she couldn't resist the possibility of seeing her name in print."

The I-64 East rest stop where the clerk had directed Deborah and Fred was completely deserted when we pulled in.

Abby parked in front, near a cluster of newspaper vending machines, and for several minutes we sat in silence. A small holly tree directly in front of us was silver in the car's headlights, and lamps were smudges of white in the fog. I couldn't imagine getting out to use the rest room were I alone.

"Creepy," Abby muttered under her breath. "God. I wonder if it's always this deserted on a Tuesday night, or if the news releases have scared people away."

"Possibly both," I replied. "But you can be sure it wasn't deserted the Friday night Deborah and Fred pulled in."

"They may have been parked right about where we are," she mused. "Probably people all over the place, since it was the beginning of the Labor Day weekend. If this is where they encountered someone bad, then he must be a brash son of a bitch."

"If there were people all over the place," I said, "then there would have been cars all over the place."

"Meaning?" She lit a cigarette.

"Assuming this is where Deborah and Fred encountered someone, and assuming that for some reason they let him in the Jeep, then what about his car? Did he arrive here on foot?"

"Not likely," she replied.

"If he drove in," I went on, "and left his car parked out here, that wasn't going to work very well unless there was a lot of traffic."

"I see what you're suggesting. If his was the only car in this lot, and it remained out here for hours late at night, chances are a trooper might have spotted it and called it in."

"That's a big chance to take if you're in the process of committing a crime," I added.

She thought for a moment. "You know, what bothers me is that the entire scenario is random but not random. Deborah and Fred's stopping at the rest stop was random. If they happened to encounter someone bad here—or even inside the Seven-Eleven, such as the guy buying coffee—that seems random. But there's premeditation, too. Forethought. If someone abducted them, it seems like he knew what he was doing."

I did not respond.

I was thinking about what Wesley had said. A political connection. Or an assailant who went through a lot of dry runs. Assuming that the couple had not chosen to disappear, then I did not see how the outcome could be anything but tragic.

Abby put the car in gear.

It wasn't until we were on the Interstate and she was setting the cruise control that she spoke again. "You think they're dead, don't you?"

"Are you asking for a quote?"

"No, Kay. I'm not asking for a quote. You want to know the truth? Right now I don't give a damn about this story. I just want to know what the hell's going on."

"Because you're worried about yourself."

"Wouldn't you be?"

"Yes. If I thought my phones were tapped, that I was being tailed, I would be worried, Abby. And speaking of worried, it's late. You're exhausted. It's ridiculous for you to drive back to Washington tonight."

She glanced over at me.

"I've got plenty of room. You can head out first thing in the morning."

"Only if you've got an extra toothbrush, something I can sleep in, and don't mind if I pillage your bar."

Leaning back in the seat, I shut my eyes and muttered, "You can get drunk, if you want. In fact, I might just join you."

When we walked into my house at midnight, the telephone started ringing, and I answered it before my machine could.

"Kay?"

At first, the voice did not register because I was not expecting it. Then my heart began to pound.

"Hello, Mark," I said.

"I'm sorry to call so late—"

I could not keep the tension out of my voice as I interrupted. "I have company. I'm sure you remember my mentioning my friend Abby Turnbull, with the *Post*? She's here staying the night. We've been having a wonderful time catching up."

Mark did not respond. After a pause, he said, "Maybe it would be easier for you to call me, when it suits."

When I hung up, Abby was staring at me, startled by my obvious distress.

"Who in God's name was that, Kay?"

My first months at Georgetown I was so overwhelmed by law school and feelings of alienation that I kept my own counsel and distance from others. I was already an M.D., a middle-class Italian from Miami with very little exposure to the finer things in life. Suddenly I found myself cast among the brilliant and beautiful, and though I am not ashamed of my heritage, I felt socially common.

Mark James was one of the privileged, a tall, graceful figure, self-assured and self-contained. I was aware of him long before I knew his name. We first met in the law library between dimly lit shelves of books, and I will never forget his intense green eyes as we began to discuss some tort I cannot recall. We ended up drinking coffee in a bar and talking until early in the morning. After that, we saw each other almost every day.

For a year we did not sleep, it seemed, for even when we slept together our lovemaking did not permit many hours of rest. No matter how much we got of each other it was never enough, and foolishly, typically, I was convinced we would be together forever. I refused to accept the chill of disappointment that settled over the relationship during our second year. When I graduated wearing someone else's engagement ring, I had convinced myself that I had gotten over Mark, until he mysteriously reappeared not so long ago.

"Maybe Tony was a safe harbor," Abby considered, referring to my ex-husband as we drank Cognac in my kitchen.

"Tony was practical," I replied. "Or so it seemed at first."

"Makes sense. I've done it before in my own pathetic love life." She reached for her snifter. "I'll have some passionate fling, and God knows there have been few and they never last long. But when it ends, I'm like a wounded soldier limping home. I wind up in the arms of some guy with the charisma of a slug who promises to take care of me."

"That's the fairy tale."

"Right out of Grimm's," she agreed, bitterly. "They say they'll take care of you, but what they mean is they want you to be there fixing dinner and washing their shorts."

"You've just described Tony to a T," I said.

"What ever happened to him?"

"I haven't talked to him in too many years to count."

"People at least ought to be friends."

"He didn't want to be friends," I said.

"Do you still think about him?"

"You can't live six years with somebody and not think about

him. That doesn't mean I want to be with Tony. But a part of me will always care about him, hope he's doing well."

"Were you in love with him when you got married?"

"I thought I was."

"Maybe so," Abby said. "But it sounds to me as if you never stopped loving Mark."

I refilled our glasses. Both of us were going to feel like hell in the morning.

"I find it incredible that you got together again after so many years," she went on. "And no matter what's happened, I suspect Mark has never stopped loving you, either."

When he came back into my life, it was as if we had lived in foreign countries during our years apart, the languages of our pasts indecipherable to each other. We communicated openly only in the dark. He did tell me he had married and his wife had been killed in an automobile accident. I later found out he had forsaken his law practice and signed on with the FBI. When we were together it was euphoric, the most wonderful days I had known since our first year at Georgetown. Of course, it did not last. History has a mean habit of repeating itself.

"I don't suppose it's his fault he was transferred to Denver," Abby was saying.

"He made a choice," I said. "And so did I."

"You didn't want to go with him?"

"I'm the reason he requested the assignment, Abby. He wanted a separation."

"So he moves across the country? That's rather extreme."

"When people are angry, their behavior can be extreme. They can make big mistakes."

"And he's probably too stubborn to admit he made a mistake," she said.

"He's stubborn, I'm stubborn. Neither of us wins any prizes for our skills in compromising. I have my career and he has his. He was in Quantico and I was here—that got old fast, and I had no intention of leaving Richmond and he had no intention of moving to Richmond. Then he started contemplating going back on the street, transferring to a field office somewhere or taking a position at Headquarters in D.C. On and on it went, until it seemed that all we did was fight." I paused, groping to explain what would never be clear. "Maybe I'm just set in my ways."

"You can't be with someone and continue to live as you always did, Kay."

How many times had Mark and I said that to each other? It got to where we rarely said anything new.

"Is maintaining your autonomy worth the price you're paying, the price both of you are paying?"

There were days when I was no longer so sure, but I did not tell Abby this.

She lit a cigarette and reached for the bottle of Cognac.

"Did the two of you ever try counseling?"

"No."

What I told her was not entirely true. Mark and I had never gone to counseling, but I had gone alone and was still seeing a psychiatrist, though infrequently now.

"Does he know Benton Wesley?" Abby asked.

"Of course. Benton trained Mark in the Academy long before I came to Virginia," I replied. "They're very good friends."

"What's Mark working on in Denver?"

"I have no idea. Some special assignment."

"Is he aware of the cases here? The couples?"

"I would assume so." Pausing, I asked, "Why?"

"I don't know. But be careful what you say to Mark."

"Tonight was the first time he's called in months. Obviously, I say very little to him."

She got up and I led her to her room.

As I gave her a gown and showed her the bath, she went on, the effects of the Cognac becoming apparent, "He'll call again. Or you're going to call him. So be careful."

"I'm not planning on calling him," I said.

"You're just as bad as he is, then," she said. "Both of you hard-headed and unforgiving as hell. So there. That's my assessment of the situation, whether you like it or not."

"I have to be at the office by eight," I said. "I'll make sure you're up by seven."

She hugged me good night and kissed my cheek.

The following weekend I went out early and bought the *Post* and could not find Abby's story. It did not come out the next week or the week after that, and I thought this strange. Was Abby all right? Why had I not heard a word from her since our visit in Richmond?

In late October I called the *Post*'s newsroom.

"I'm sorry," said a man who sounded harried. "Abby's on leave. Won't be back until next August."

"Is she still in town?" I asked, stunned.

"Got no idea."

Hanging up, I flipped through my address book and tried her home number. I was answered by a machine. Abby did not return that call or any of the others I made during the next few weeks. It wasn't until shortly after Christmas that I began to realize what was going on. On Monday, January sixth, I came home to find a letter in my mailbox. There was no return address, but the handwriting was unmistakable. Opening the envelope, I discovered inside a sheet of yellow legal paper scribbled with "FYI. Mark," and a short article clipped from a recent issue of the *New York Times*. Abby Turnbull, I read with disbelief, had signed a book contract to write about the disappearance of Fred Cheney and Deborah Harvey, and the "frightening parallels" between their cases and those of four other couples in Virginia who had vanished and turned up dead.

Abby had warned me about Mark, and now he was warning me about her. Or was there some other reason for his sending me the article?

For a long interval I sat in my kitchen, tempted to leave an outraged message on Abby's machine or to call Mark. I finally decided to call Anna, my psychiatrist.

"You feel betrayed?" she asked when I got her on the phone.

"To put it mildly, Anna."

"You've known Abby is writing a newspaper story. Is writing a book so much worse?"

"She never told me she was writing a book," I said.

"Because you feel betrayed doesn't mean you truly have been," Anna said. "This is your perception at the moment, Kay. You will have to wait and see. And as for why Mark sent you the article, you may have to wait and see about that, too. Perhaps it was his way of reaching out."

"I'm wondering if I should consult a lawyer," I said. "See if there's something I should do to protect myself. I have no idea what might end up in Abby's book."

"I think it would be wiser to take her words at face value," Anna advised. "She said your conversations were off the record. Has she ever betrayed you before?"

"No."

"Then I suggest you give her a chance. Give her an opportunity to explain. Besides," she added, "I'm not sure how much of a book she can write. There have been no arrests, and there is no resolution as to what happened to the couple. They have yet to turn up."

The bitter irony of that remark would hit me exactly two weeks later, on January twentieth, when I was on the capitol grounds waiting to see what happened when a bill authorizing the Forensic Science Bureau to create a DNA data bank went before the Virginia General Assembly.

I was returning from the snack bar, cup of coffee in hand, when I spotted Pat Harvey, elegant in a navy cashmere suit, a zip-up black leather portfolio under her arm. She was talking to several delegates in the hall, and glancing my way, she immediately excused herself.

"Dr. Scarpetta," she said, offering her hand. She looked relieved to see me, but drawn and stressed.

I wondered why she wasn't in Washington, and then she answered my unspoken question. "I was asked to lend my support to Senate Bill One-thirty," she said, smiling nervously. "So I suppose both of us are here today for the same reason."

"Thank you. We need all the support we can get."

"I don't think you have a worry," she replied.

She was probably right. The testimony of the national drug policy director and the publicity it would generate would put considerable pressure on the Courts of Justice Committee.

After an awkward silence, with both of us glancing at the people milling about, I asked her quietly, "How are you?"

For an instant her eyes teared up. Then she gave me another quick, nervous smile and stared off down the hall. "If you'll please excuse me, I see someone I need to have a word with."

Pat Harvey was barely out of earshot when my pager went off.

A minute later I was on the phone.

"Marino's on his way," my secretary was explaining.

"So am I," I said. "Get my scene kit, Rose. Make sure everything's in order. Flashlight, camera, batteries, gloves."

"Will do."

Cursing my heels and the rain, I hurried down steps and along Governor Street, the wind tearing at my umbrella as I envisioned Mrs. Harvey's eyes that split second when they had revealed her pain. Thank God she had not been standing there when my pager had sounded its dreadful alert.

5

THE ODOR WAS NOTICEABLE from a distance. Heavy drops of rain smacked loudly against dead leaves, the sky as dark as dusk, winter-bare trees drifting in and out of the fog.

"Jesus," Marino muttered as he stepped over a log. "They must be ripe. No other smell like it. Always reminds me of pickled crabs."

"It gets worse," promised Jay Morrell, who was leading the way.

Black mud sucked at our feet, and every time Marino brushed against a tree I was showered with freezing water. Fortunately, I kept a hooded Gore-tex coat and heavy rubber boots in the trunk of my state car for scenes like this one. What I had been unable to find were my thick leather gloves, and it was impossible to navigate through the woods and keep branches out of my face if my hands were in my pockets.

I had been told there were two bodies, suspected to be a male and a female. They were less than four miles from the rest stop where Deborah Harvey's Jeep had been found last fall.

You don't know that it's them, I thought to myself with every step.

But when we reached the perimeter of the scene, my heart constricted. Benton Wesley was talking to an officer working a metal detector, and Wesley would not have been summoned unless the police were sure. He stood with military erectness, exuding the quiet confidence of a man in charge. He seemed bothered neither by the weather nor by the stench of decomposing human flesh. He was not looking around and taking in the details the way Marino and I were, and I knew why. Wesley had already looked around. He had been here long before I was called.

The bodies were lying next to each other, facedown in a small clearing about a quarter of a mile from the muddy logging road where we had left our cars. They were so badly decomposed they were partially skeletonized. The long bones of arms and legs protruded like dirty gray sticks from rotted clothing scattered with leaves. Skulls were detached and had been nudged or rolled, probably by small predators, a foot or two away.

"Did you find their shoes and socks?" I asked, not seeing either.

"No, ma'am. But we found a purse." Morrell pointed to the body on the right. "Forty-four dollars and twenty-six cents in it. Plus a driver's license, Deborah Harvey's driver's license." He pointed again, adding, "We're assuming the body there on the left is Cheney."

Yellow crime scene tape glistened wetly against the dark bark of trees. Twigs snapped beneath the feet of men moving about, their voices blending into an indistinguishable babble beneath the relentless, dreary rain. Opening my medical bag, I got out a pair of surgical gloves and my camera.

For a while I did not move as I surveyed the shrunken, almost fleshless bodies before me. Determining the sex and race of skeletal remains cannot always be done at a glance. I would not swear to anything until I could look at the pelves, which were obscured by what appeared to be dark blue or black denim jeans. But based on the characteristics of the body to my right—small bones, small skull with small mastoids, nonprominent brow ridge, and strands of long blondish hair clinging to rotted fabric—I had no reason to think anything other than white female. The size of her companion, the robustness of the bones, prominent brow ridge, large skull, and flat face were good for white male.

As for what might have happened to the couple, I could not tell. There were no ligatures indicating strangulation. I saw no obvious fractures or holes that might have meant blows or bullets. Male and female were quietly together in death, the bones of her left arm slipped under his right as if she had been holding on to him in the end, empty eye sockets gaping as rain rolled over their skulls.

It wasn't until I moved in close and got down on my knees that I noticed a margin of dark soil, so narrow it was barely perceptible, on either side of the bodies. If they had died Labor Day weekend, autumn leaves would not have fallen yet. The ground beneath them would be relatively bare. I did not like what was going through my mind. It was bad enough that the police had been tramping around out here for hours. Dammit. To move or disturb a body in any way before the medical examiner arrives is a cardinal sin, and every officer out here knew that.

"Dr. Scarpetta?" Morrell was towering over me, his breath smoking. "Was just talking to Phillips over there." He glanced in the direction of several officers searching thick underbrush about twenty feet east of us. "He found a watch and an earring, some change, all right about here where the bodies are. The interesting thing is, the metal detector kept going off. He had it right over the bodies and it was beeping. Could be from a zipper or something. Maybe a metal snap or button on their jeans. Thought you should know."

I looked up into his thin, serious face. He was shivering beneath his parka.

"Tell me what you did with the bodies in addition to running the metal detector over them, Morrell. I can see they've been moved. I need to know if this is the exact position they were in when they were discovered this morning."

"I don't know about when the hunters found them, though they claim they didn't get very close," he said, eyes probing the woods. "But yes, ma'am, this is the way they looked when we got here. All we did was check for personal effects, went into their pockets and her purse."

"I assume you took photographs before you moved anything," I said evenly.

"We started taking pictures as soon as we arrived."

Getting out a small flashlight, I began the hopeless task of looking for trace evidence. After bodies have been exposed to the elements for so many months, the chance of finding significant hairs, fibers, or other debris was slim to none. Morrell watched in silence, uneasily shifting his weight from one foot to the other.

"Have you found out anything else from your investigation that might be of assistance, assuming this is Deborah Harvey and Fred Cheney?" I asked, for I had not seen Morrell or talked to him since the day Deborah's Jeep had been found.

"Nothing but a possible drug connection," he said. "We've been told Cheney's roommate at Carolina was into cocaine. Maybe Cheney fooled around with cocaine too. That's one of the things we're considering, if maybe he and the Harvey girl met up with someone who was selling drugs and came out here."

That didn't make any sense.

"Why would Cheney leave the Jeep at a rest stop and go off with a drug dealer, taking Deborah with him, and come out here?" I asked. "Why not just buy the drugs at the rest stop and be on their way?"

"They may have come out here to party."

"Who in his right mind would come out here after dark to party or do anything else? And where are their shoes, Morrell? Are you suggesting they walked through the woods barefoot?"

"We don't know what happened to their shoes," he said.

"That's very interesting. So far, five couples have been found dead and we don't know what happened to their shoes. Not one shoe or sock has turned up. Don't you find that rather odd?"

"Oh, yes, ma'am. I think it's odd, all right," he said, hugging himself to get warm. "But right now I've got to work these two cases here without thinking about the other four couples. I've got to go with what I've got. And all I've got at the moment is a possible drug connection. I can't allow myself to get sidetracked by this serial murder business or who the girl's mother is, or I might be wrong and miss the obvious."

"I certainly wouldn't want you to miss the obvious."

He was silent.

"Did you find any drug paraphernalia inside the Jeep?"

"No. Nothing out here so far to suggest drugs, either. But we've got a lot of soil and leaves to go through—"

"The weather's awful. I'm not sure it's a good idea to begin sifting through the soil." I sounded impatient and irritable. I was put out with him. I was put out with the police. Water was trickling down the front of my coat. My knees hurt. I was losing feeling in my hands and feet. The stench was overpowering, and the loud smacking of the rain was getting on my nerves.

"We haven't started digging or using the sieves. Thought we might wait on that. It's too hard to see. The metal detector's all we've used so far, that and our eyes."

"Well, the more all of us walk around out here, the more we risk destroying the scene. Small bones, teeth, other things, get stepped on and pushed down into the mud." They had already been here for hours. It was probably too damn late to preserve the scene.

"So, you want to move them today or hold off until the weather clears?" he asked.

Under ordinary circumstances, I would have waited until the rain stopped and there was more light. When bodies have been in the woods for months, leaving them covered with plastic and in place for another day or two isn't going to make any difference. But when Marino and I had parked on the logging road, there were already several television news trucks waiting. Reporters were sitting in their cars, others braving the rain and trying to coax information out of police officers standing sentry. The circumstances were anything but ordinary. Though I had no right to tell Morrell what to do, by Code I had jurisdiction over the bodies.

"There are stretchers and body bags in the back of my car," I said, digging out my keys. "If you could have somebody get them, we'll move the bodies shortly and I'll take them on in to the morgue."

"Sure thing. I'll take care of it."

"Thanks." Then Benton Wesley was crouching next to me.

"How did you find out?" I asked. The question was ambiguous, but he knew what I meant.

"Morrell reached me in Quantico. I came right away." He studied the bodies, his angular face almost haggard in the shadow of his dripping hood. "You seeing anything that might tell us what happened?"

"All I can tell you at the moment is their skulls weren't fractured and they weren't shot in the head."

He did not respond, his silence adding to my tension.

I began unfolding sheets as Marino walked up, hands jammed into his coat pockets, shoulders hunched against the cold and rain.

"You're going to catch pneumonia," Wesley remarked, getting to his feet. "Is Richmond PD too cheap to buy you guys hats?"

"Shit," Marino said, "you're lucky they put gas in your damn car and furnish you with a gun. The squirrels in Spring Street got it better than we do."

Spring Street was the state penitentiary. It was true that it cost the state more money each year to house some inmates than a lot of police officers got paid for keeping them off the street. Marino loved to complain about it.

"I see the locals drug your ass out here from Quantico. Your lucky day," Marino said.

"They told me what they'd found. I asked if they'd called you yet."

"Yeah, well, they got around to it eventually."

"I can see that. Morrell told me he's never filled out a VICAP form. Maybe you can give him a hand."

Marino stared at the bodies, his jaw muscles flexing.

"We need to get this into the computer," Wesley went on as rain drummed the earth.

Tuning out their conversation, I arranged one of the sheets next to the female's remains and turned her on her back. She held together nicely, joints and ligaments still intact. In a climate like Virginia's, it generally takes at least a year of being exposed to the elements before a body is fully skeletonized, or reduced to disarticulated bones. Muscle tissue, cartilage, and ligaments are tenacious. She was petite, and I recalled the photograph of the lovely young athlete posed on a balance beam. Her shirt, I noted, was some sort of pullover, possibly a sweatshirt, and her jeans were zipped up and snapped. Unfolding the other sheet, I went through the same procedure with her companion. Turning over decomposed bodies is like turning over rocks. You never know what you'll find underneath, except that you can usually count on insects. My flesh crawled as several spiders skittered off, vanishing beneath leaves.

Shifting positions in a fruitless attempt to get more comfortable, I realized Wesley and Marino were gone. Kneeling alone in the rain, I began feeling through leaves and mud, searching for fingernails, small bones, and teeth. I noticed at least two teeth missing from one of the mandibles. Most likely, they were somewhere near the skulls. After fifteen or twenty minutes of this, I had recovered one tooth, a small transparent button, possibly from the male's shirt, and two cigarette butts. Several cigarette butts had been found at each of the scenes, though not all of the victims were known to smoke. What was unusual was that not one of the filters bore a manufacturer's brand mark or name.

When Morrell returned, I pointed this out to him.

"Never been to a scene where there aren't cigarette butts," he replied, and I wondered just how many scenes he could swear he had been to. Not many, I guessed.

"It's as if part of the paper has been peeled away or the end of the filter nearest the tobacco pinched off," I explained, and when this evoked no response from him, I dug in the mud some more.

Night was falling when we headed back to our cars, a somber procession of police officers gripping stretchers bearing bright orange body bags. We reached the narrow unpaved logging road as a sharp wind began to kick in from the north and the rain began to freeze. My dark blue state station wagon was equipped as a hearse. Fasteners in the plyboard floor in back locked stretchers into place so they did not slide around during transport. I positioned myself behind the wheel and buckled up as Marino climbed in, Morrell slammed shut the tailgate, and photographers and television cameramen recorded us on film. A reporter who wouldn't give up rapped on my window, and I locked the doors.

"God bless it. I hope like hell I ain't called to another one of these," Marino exclaimed, turning on the heat full blast.

I drove around several potholes.

"What a bunch of vultures." Eyeing his side mirror, he watched journalists scurrying into their cars. "Some asshole must've run his mouth over the radio. Probably Morrell. The dumb-ass. If he was in my squad, I'd send his ass back to traffic, get him transferred to the uniform room or information desk."

"You remember how to get back on Sixty-four from here?" I asked.

"Hang a left at the fork straight ahead. Shit." He cracked the window and got out his cigarettes. "Nothing like driving in a closed-up car with decomposed bodies."

Thirty miles later I unlocked the back door to the OCME and pushed a red button on the wall inside. The bay door made a loud grating noise as it opened, light spilling onto the wet tarmac. Backing in the wagon, I opened the tailgate. We slid out the stretchers and wheeled them inside the morgue as several forensic scientists got off the elevator and smiled at us without giving our cargo more than a glance. Body-shaped mounds on stretchers and gurneys were as common as the cinderblock walls. Blood drips on the floor and foul odors were unpleasantnesses you learned to step around and quietly hurry past.

Producing another key, I opened the padlock on the refrigerator's stainless-steel door, then went to see about toe tags and signing in the bodies before we transferred them to a double-decker gurney and left them for the night.

"You mind if I stop by tomorrow to see what you figure out about these two?" Marino asked.

"That would be fine."

"It's them," he said. "Gotta be."

"I'm afraid that's the way it looks, Marino. What happened to Wesley?"

"On his way back to Quantico, where he can prop his Florsheim shoes on top of his big desk and get the results over the phone."

"I thought you two were friends," I said warily.

"Yeah, well, life's funny like that, Doc. It's like when I'm supposed to go fishing. All the weather reports predict clear skies, and the minute I put the boat in the water it begins to friggin' rain."

"Are you on evening shift this weekend?"

"Not last I heard."

"Sunday night—how about coming over for dinner? Six, six-thirty?"

"Yeah, I could probably manage that," he said, looking away, but not before I caught the pain in his eyes.

I had heard his wife supposedly had moved back to New Jersey before Thanksgiving to take care of her dying mother. Since then I had had dinner with Marino several times, but he had been unwilling to talk about his personal life.

Letting myself into the autopsy suite, I headed for the locker room, where I always kept personal necessities and a change of clothes for what I considered hygienic emergencies. I was filthy, the stench of death clinging to my clothing, skin, and hair. I quickly stuffed my scene clothes inside a plastic garbage bag and taped a note to it instructing the morgue supervisor to drop it by the cleaners first thing in the morning. Then I got into the shower, where I stayed for a very long time.

One of many things Anna had advised me to do after Mark moved to Denver was to make an effort to counteract the damage I routinely inflicted upon my body.

"*Exercise.*" She had said that frightful word. "The endorphins relieve depression. You will eat better, sleep better, feel so much better. I think you should take up tennis again."

Following her suggestion had proved a humbling experience.

I had scarcely touched a racket since I was a teenager, and though my backhand had never been good, over the decades it ceased to exist at all. Once a week I took a lesson late at night, when I was less likely to be subjected to the curious stares of the cocktail and happy hour crowd lounging in the observation gallery of Westwood Racquet Club's indoor facility.

After leaving the office, I had just enough time to drive to the club, dash into the ladies' locker room, and change into tennis clothes. Retrieving my racket from my locker, I was out on the court with two minutes to spare, muscles straining as I fell into leg stretches and bravely tried to touch my toes. My blood began to move sluggishly.

Ted, the pro, appeared from behind the green curtain shouldering two baskets of balls.

"After hearing the news, I didn't think I'd be seeing you tonight," he said, setting the baskets on the court and slipping out of his warm-up jacket. Ted, perennially tan and a joy to look at, usually greeted me with a smile and a wisecrack. But he was subdued tonight.

"My younger brother knew Fred Cheney. I knew him, too, though not well." Staring off at people playing several courts away, he said, "Fred was one of the nicest guys I've ever met. And I'm not just saying that because he's . . . Well. My brother's really shook up about it." He bent over and picked up a handful of balls. "And it sort of bothers me, if you want to know the truth, that the newspapers can't get past who Fred was dating. It's like the only person who disappeared was Pat Harvey's daughter. And I'm not saying that the girl wasn't terrific and what happened to her isn't just as awful as what happened to him." He paused. "Well. I think you know what I mean."

"I do," I said. "But the other side of that is Deborah Harvey's family is being subjected to intense scrutiny, and they will never be permitted to grieve privately because of who Deborah's mother is. It's unfair and tragic any way you look at it."

Ted thought about this and met my eyes. "You know, I hadn't considered it that way. But you're right. I don't think being famous would be a whole lot of fun. And I don't think you're paying me by the hour to stand out here and talk. What would you like to work on tonight?"

"Ground strokes. I want you to run me corner to corner so I can remind myself how much I hate smoking."

"No more lectures from me on that subject." He moved to the center of the net.

I backed up to the baseline. My first forehand wouldn't have been half bad had I been playing doubles.

Physical pain is a good diversion, and the harsh realities of the day were pushed aside until the phone rang at home later as I was peeling off my wet clothes.

Pat Harvey was frantic. "The bodies they found today. I have to know."

"They have not been identified, and I have not examined them yet," I said, sitting on the edge of the bed and nudging off my tennis shoes.

"A male and a female. That's what I heard."

"So it appears at this point. Yes."

"Please tell me if there's *any* possibility it isn't them," she said.

I hesitated.

"Oh, God," she whispered.

"Mrs. Harvey, I can't confirm—"

She cut me off in a voice that was getting hysterical.

"The police told me they found Debbie's purse, her driver's license."

Morrell, I thought. The half-brained bastard.

I said to her, "We can't make identifications solely from personal effects."

"She's my daughter!"

Next would follow threats and profanity. I had been through this before with the other parents who under ordinary circumstances were as civilized as Sunday school. I decided to give Pat Harvey something constructive to do.

"The bodies have not been identified," I repeated.

"I want to see her."

Not in a million years, I thought. "The bodies aren't visually identifiable," I said. "They're almost skeletonized."

Her breath caught.

"And depending on you, we might establish identity with certainty tomorrow or it might take days."

"What do you want me to do?" she asked shakily.

"I need X rays, dental charts, anything pertaining to Deborah's medical history that you can get your hands on."

Silence.

"Do you think you could track these down for me?"

"Of course," she said. "I'll see to it immediately."

I suspected she would have her daughter's medical records be-fore sunrise, even if she had to drag half of the doctors in Richmond out of bed.

The following afternoon, I was removing the plastic cover from the OCME's anatomical skeleton when I heard Marino in the hall.

"I'm in here," I said loudly.

He stepped inside the conference room, a blank expression on his face as he stared at the skeleton, whose bones were wired together, a hook in the vertex of his skull attached to the top of an L-shaped bar. He stood a little taller than I was, feet dangling over a wooden base with wheels.

Gathering paperwork from a table, I said, "How about rolling him out for me?"

"You taking Slim for a stroll?"

"He's going downstairs, and his name's Haresh," I replied.

Bones and small wheels clattered quietly as Marino and his grinning companion followed me to the elevator, attracting amused glances from several members of my staff. Haresh did not get out very often, and as a rule, when he was spirited away from his cor-ner, his abductor was not motivated by serious intent. Last June I had walked into my office on the morning of my birthday to find Haresh sitting in my chair, glasses and lab coat on, a cigarette clamped between his teeth. One of the more preoccupied foren-sic scientists from upstairs—or so I had been told—had walked past my doorway and said good morning without noticing anything odd.

"You're not going to tell me he talks to you when you're working down here," Marino said as the elevator doors shut.

"In his own way he does," I said. "I've found having him on hand is a lot more useful than referring to diagrams in *Gray's*."

"What's the story on his name?"

"Apparently, when he was purchased years ago, there was an Indian pathologist here named Haresh. The skeleton is also Indian. Male, fortyish, maybe older."

"As in Little Bighorn Indian or the other kind that paint dots on their foreheads?"

"As in the Ganges River in India," I said as we got out on the first floor. "The Hindus cast their dead upon the river, believing they will go straight to heaven."

"I sure as hell hope this joint ain't heaven."

Bones and wheels clattered again as Marino rolled Haresh into the autopsy suite.

On top of a white sheet covering the first stainless-steel table were Deborah Harvey's remains, gray dirty bones, clumps of muddy hair, and ligaments as tan and tough as shoe leather. The stench was relentless but not as overpowering, since I had removed her clothes. Her condition was made all the more pitiful by the presence of Haresh, who bore not so much as a scratch on his bleached white bones.

"I have several things to tell you," I said to Marino. "But first I want your promise that nothing leaves this room."

Lighting a cigarette, he looked curiously at me. "Okay."

"There's no question about their identities," I began, arranging clavicles on either side of the skull. "Pat Harvey brought in dental X rays and charts this morning—"

"In person?" he interrupted, surprised.

"Unfortunately," I said, for I had not expected Pat Harvey to deliver the records herself—a miscalculation on my part, and one I wasn't likely to forget.

"That must've created quite a stir," he said.

It had.

When she pulled up in her Jaguar, she had left it illegally parked by the curb and appeared full of demands and on the verge of tears. Intimidated by the presence of the famous public official, the receptionist let her in, and Mrs. Harvey promptly set off down the hall in search of me. I think she would have come down to the morgue had my administrator not intercepted her at the elevator and ushered her into my office, where I found her moments later. She was sitting rigidly in a chair, her face as white as chalk. On top of my desk were death certificates, case files, autopsy photographs, and an excised stab wound suspended in a small bottle of formalin tinted pink by blood. Hanging on the back of the door were bloodstained clothes I was intending to take upstairs when I made evidence rounds later in the day. Two facial reconstructions of unidentified dead females were perched on top of a filing cabinet like decapitated clay heads.

Pat Harvey had gotten more than she had bargained for. She had run head-on into the hard realities of this place.

"Morrell also brought me Fred Cheney's dental records," I said to Marino.

"Then it's definitely Fred Cheney and Deborah Harvey?"

"Yes," I said, and then I directed his attention to X rays clipped to a view box on the wall.

"That ain't what I think it is." A look of amazement passed over his face as he fixed on a radiopaque spot within the shadowy outline of lumbar vertebrae.

"Deborah Harvey was shot." I picked up the lumbar in question. "Caught right in the middle of the back. The bullet fractured the spinous process and the pedicles and lodged in the vertebral body. Right here." I showed him.

"I don't see it." He leaned closer.

"No, you can't see it. But you see the hole?"

"Yeah? I see a lot of holes."

"This is the bullet hole. The others are vascular foramina, holes for the vascular vessels that supply blood to bone and marrow."

"Where are the fractured pedestals you mentioned?"

"Pedicles," I said patiently. "I didn't find them. They would be in pieces and are probably still out there in the woods. An entrance and no exit. She was shot in the back versus the abdomen."

"You find a bullet hole in her clothes?"

"No."

On a nearby table was a white plastic tray in which I had placed Deborah's personal effects, including her clothing, jewelry, and red nylon purse. I carefully lifted up the sweatshirt, tattered, black, and putrid.

"As you can see," I pointed out, "the back of it, in particular, is in terrible shape. Most of the fabric's completely rotted away, torn by predators. The same goes for the waistband of her jeans in back, and that makes sense, since these areas of her clothing would have been bloody. In other words, the area of fabric where I would expect to have found a bullet hole is gone."

"What about distance? You got any idea about that?"

"As I've said, the bullet didn't exit. This would make me suspect we're not dealing with a contact gunshot wound. But it's hard to say. As for caliber, and again I'm conjecturing, I'm thinking a thirty-eight or better, based on the size of this hole. We won't know with certainty until I crack open the vertebra and take the bullet upstairs to the firearms lab."

"Weird," Marino said. "You haven't looked at Cheney yet?"

"He's been rayed. No bullets. But no, I haven't examined him yet."

"Weird," he said again. "It don't fit. Her being shot in the back don't fit with the other cases."

"No," I agreed. "It doesn't."

"So that's what killed her?"

"I don't know."

"What do you mean, you don't know?" He looked at me.

"This injury isn't immediately fatal, Marino. Since the bullet didn't go right on through, it didn't transect the aorta. Had it done so at this lumbar level, she would have hemorrhaged to death within minutes. What's significant is that the bullet had to have transected her cord, instantly paralyzing her from the waist down. And of course, blood vessels were hit. She was bleeding."

"How long could she have survived?"

"Hours."

"What about the possibility of sexual assault?"

"Her panties and brassiere were in place," I answered. "This doesn't mean that she wasn't sexually assaulted. She could have been allowed to put her clothes back on afterward, assuming she was assaulted before she was shot."

"Why bother?"

"If you're raped," I said, "and your assailant tells you to put your clothes back on, you assume you're going to live. A sense of hope serves to control you, make you do as you're told because if you struggle with him, he might change his mind."

"It don't feel right." Marino frowned. "I just don't think that's what happened, Doc."

"It's a scenario. I don't know what happened. All I can tell you with certainty is that I didn't find any articles of her clothing torn, cut, inside out, or unfastened. And as for seminal fluid, after so many months in the woods, forget it." Handing him a clipboard and a pencil, I added, "If you're going to hang around, you might as well scribe for me."

"You plan to tell Benton about this?" he asked.

"Not at the moment."

"What about Morrell?"

"Certainly, I'll tell him she was shot," I said. "If we're talking about an automatic or semiautomatic, the cartridge case may still be at the scene. If the cops want to run their mouths, that's up to them. But nothing's coming from me."

"What about Mrs. Harvey?"

"She and her husband know their daughter and Fred have been positively identified. I called the Harveys and Mr. Cheney as soon as I was sure. I will be releasing nothing further until I've concluded the examinations."

Ribs sounded like Tinker Toys quietly clacking together as I separated left from right.

"Twelve on each side," I began to dictate. "Contrary to legend, women don't have one more rib than men."

"Huh?" Marino looked up from the clipboard.

"Have you never read Genesis?"

He stared blankly at the ribs I had arranged on either side of the thoracic vertebrae.

"Never mind," I said.

Next I began looking for carpals, the small bones of the wrist that look very much like stones you might find in a creek bed or dig up in your garden. It is hard to sort left from right, and this is where the anatomical skeleton was helpful. Moving him closer, I propped his bony hands on the edge of the table and began comparing. I went through the same process with the distal and proximal phalanges, or bones of the fingers.

"Looks like she's missing eleven bones in her right hand and seventeen in her left," I reported.

Marino scribbled this down. "Out of how many?"

"There are twenty-seven bones in the hand," I replied as I worked. "Giving the hand its tremendous flexibility. It's what makes it possible for us to paint, play the violin, love each other through touch."

It is also what makes it possible for us to defend ourselves.

It was not until the following afternoon that I realized Deborah Harvey had attempted to ward off an assailant who had been armed with more than a gun. It had gotten considerably warmer out, the weather had cleared, and the police had been sifting through soil all day. At not quite four P.M., Morrell stopped by my office to deliver a number of small bones recovered from the scene. Five of them belonged to Deborah, and on the dorsal surface of her left proximal phalange—or the top of the shaft, the longest of the index finger bones—I found a half-inch cut.

The first question when I find injury to bone or tissue is whether it is pre- or postmortem. If one is not aware of the artifacts that can occur after death, he can make serious mistakes.

People who burn up in fires come in with fractured bones and epidural hemorrhages, looking for all practical purposes as if someone worked them over and then torched the house to disguise a homicide, when the injuries are actually postmortem and caused by extreme heat. Bodies washed up on the beach or recovered from rivers and lakes often look as if a deranged killer mutilated faces, genitals, hands, and feet, when fish, crabs, and turtles are to blame. Skeletal remains get gnawed, chewed on, and torn from limb to limb by rats, buzzards, dogs, and raccoons.

Predators of the four-legged, winged, or finned variety inflict a lot of damage, but blessedly, not until the poor soul is already dead. Then nature simply begins recycling. Ashes to ashes. Dust to dust.

The cut on Deborah Harvey's proximal phalange was too neat and linear to have been caused by tooth or claw, it was my opinion. But this still left much open to speculation and suspicion, including the inevitable suggestion that I might have nicked the bone myself with a scalpel at the morgue.

By Wednesday evening the police had released Deborah's and Fred's identities to the press, and within the next forty-eight hours there were so many calls that the clerks in the front office could not manage their regular duties because all they did was answer the phone. Rose was informing everyone, including Benton Wesley and Pat Harvey, that the cases were pending while I stayed in the morgue.

By Sunday night, there was nothing more I could do. Deborah's and Fred's remains had been defleshed, degreased, photographed from every angle, the inventory of their bones completed. I was packing them in a cardboard box when the buzzer went off in back. I heard the night watchman's footsteps down the hall and the bay door open. Then Marino was walking in.

"You sleeping down here or what?" he asked.

Glancing up at him, I was surprised to note that his overcoat and hair were wet.

"It's snowing." He pulled off his gloves and set his portable radio on the edge of the autopsy table where I was working.

"That's all I need," I said, sighing.

"Coming down like a bitch, Doc. Was driving by and saw your ride in the lot. Figured you'd been in this cave since the crack of dawn and had no idea."

It occurred to me as I tore off a long strip of tape and sealed the box. "I thought you weren't on evening shift this weekend."

"Yeah, and I thought you was having me in for dinner."

Pausing, I stared curiously at him. Then I remembered. "Oh, no," I muttered, glancing up at the clock. It was past eight P.M. "Marino, I'm so sorry."

"Don't matter. Had a couple of things to follow up on, anyway."

I always knew when Marino was lying. He wouldn't look me in the eye and his face got red. It wasn't coincidence that he had seen my car in the lot. He had been looking for me, and not simply because he wanted dinner. Something was on his mind.

Leaning against the table, I gave him my full attention.

"Thought you might want to know that Pat Harvey was in Washington over the weekend, went to see the Director," he said.

"Did Benton inform you of this?"

"Yo. He also said he'd been trying to get hold of you but you ain't returning his calls. The Drug Czar's complaining that you ain't returning her calls either."

"I'm not returning anybody's calls," I replied wearily. "I've been rather preoccupied, to say the least, and I don't have anything to release at this point."

Looking at the box on the table, he said, "You know Deborah was shot, a homicide. What are you waiting for?"

"I don't know what killed Fred Cheney or if there's any possibility drugs might have been involved. I'm waiting for tox reports, and I don't intend to release a thing until those are in and I've had a chance to talk to Vessey."

"The guy at the Smithsonian?"

"I'm seeing him in the morning."

"Hope you got four-wheel drive."

"You haven't explained the purpose of Pat Harvey's going to see the Director."

"She's accusing your office of stonewalling, says the FBI is stonewalling her, too. She's pissed. Wants her daughter's autopsy report, police reports, the whole nine yards, and is threatening to get a court order and raise hell if her demands aren't met right away."

"That's crazy."

"Bingo. But if you don't mind a little advice, Doc, I think you might consider calling Benton before the night's out."

"Why?"

"I don't want you getting burned, that's why."

"What are you talking about, Marino?" I untied my surgical gown.

"The more you avoid everybody right now, the more you're adding fuel to the fire. According to Benton, Mrs. Harvey's convinced there's some sort of cover-up and all of us are involved."

When I did not reply he said, "Are you listening?"

"Yes. I've listened to every word you said."

He picked up the box.

"Incredible to think there's two people inside this thing," he marveled.

It was incredible. The box wasn't much bigger than a microwave oven and weighed ten or twelve pounds. As he placed it in the trunk of my state car, I said under my breath, "Thank you for everything."

"Huh?"

I knew he'd heard me, but he wanted me to say it again.

"I appreciate your concern, Marino. I really do. And I'm so sorry about dinner. Sometimes I really screw up."

The snow was falling fast, and as usual, he wasn't wearing a hat. Cranking the engine and turning on the heat full blast, I looked up at him and thought how odd it was that I should find him such a comfort. Marino got on my nerves more than anyone I knew, and yet I could not imagine him not being around.

Locking my door, he said, "Yeah, well you owe me."

Semifreddo di cioccolato.

"I love it when you talk dirty."

"A dessert. My specialty, you big jerk. Chocolate mousse with ladyfingers."

"Ladyfingers?" He stared pointedly in the direction of the morgue, feigning horror.

It seemed to take forever to get home. I crept along snow-covered roads, concentrating so fiercely my head was splitting by the time I was in my kitchen pouring myself a drink. Sitting at the table, I lit a cigarette and gave Benton Wesley a call.

"What have you found?" he asked immediately.

"Deborah Harvey was shot in the back."

"Morrell told me. Said the bullet was unusual. Hydra-Shok, nine millimeter."

"That's correct."

"What about her boyfriend?"

"I don't know what killed him. I'm waiting on tox results, and I need to confer with Vessey at the Smithsonian. I'm pending both cases for now."

"The longer you pend them, the better."

"I beg your pardon?"

"I'm saying that I'd like you to pend the cases for as long as possible, Kay. I don't want reports going out to anyone, not even to the parents, and especially not to Pat Harvey. I don't want anyone knowing that Deborah was shot—"

"Are you telling me that the Harveys don't know?"

"When Morrell informed me, I made him promise to keep the information under wraps. So, no, the Harveys haven't been told. Uh, the police haven't told them. They know only that their daughter and Cheney are dead." He paused, adding, "Unless you've released something that I don't know about."

"Mrs. Harvey has tried to get hold of me a number of times, but I haven't talked to her or hardly anybody else during the past few days."

"Keep it that way," Wesley said firmly. "I'm asking you to release information only to me."

"There will come a point, Benton," I said just as firmly, "when I will have to release cause and manner of death. Fred's family, Deborah's family, are entitled to that by Code."

"Hold off as long as possible."

"Would you be so kind as to tell me why?"

Silence.

"Benton?" I was about to wonder if he was still on the line.

"Just don't do anything without conferring with me first." He hesitated again. Then, "I presume you're aware of this book Abby Turnbull is under contract to write."

"I saw something about it in the paper," I answered, getting angry.

"Has she contacted you again? Uh, recently?"

Again? How did Wesley know Abby had come to see me last fall? Damn you, Mark, I thought. When he had telephoned me, I had mentioned that Abby was with me that night.

"I haven't heard from her," I replied curtly.

6

MONDAY MORNING THE ROAD in front of my house was blanketed in deep snow, the sky gray and threatening more bad weather to come. I fixed a cup of coffee and debated the wisdom of my driving to Washington. On the verge of scrapping my plans, I called the state police and learned that I-95 North was clear, the snow tapering off to less than an inch by Fredericksburg. Deciding that my state car wasn't likely to make it out of my driveway, I loaded the cardboard box in my Mercedes.

As I turned off on the Interstate, I realized that if I had a wreck or were pulled over by the police, it wasn't going to be easy explaining why I was heading north in an unofficial car with human skeletons in the trunk. Sometimes flashing my medical examiner shield wasn't enough. I never would forget flying to California carrying a large briefcase packed with sadomasochistic sexual paraphernalia. The briefcase got as far as the X-ray scanner, and the next thing I knew airport security was squiring me away for what was nothing less than an interrogation. No matter what I said, they couldn't seem to get it through their heads that I was a forensic pathologist en route to the National Association of Medical Examiners' annual meeting, where I was to give a presentation on autoerotic asphyxiation. The handcuffs, studded collars, leather bindings, and other unseemly odds and ends were evidence from old cases and did not *belong* to me.

By ten-thirty I was in D.C. and had managed to find a parking place within a block of Constitution Avenue and Twelfth. I had not been to the Smithsonian's National Museum of Natural History since attending a forensic anthropology course there several years before. When I carried the cardboard box inside a lobby fragrant with potted orchids and noisy with the voices of tourists, I wished I could leisurely peruse dinosaurs and diamonds, mummy cases and mastodons, and never know the bleaker treasures housed within these walls.

Rising from ceiling to floor in every available inch of space not visible to guests were green wooden drawers containing, among other dead things, more than thirty thousand human skeletons. Bones of every description arrived by registered mail every week for Dr. Alex Vessey to examine. Some remains were archaeological, others turned out to be bear or beaver paws or the hydrocephalic skulls of calves, human-looking artifacts found along the wayside or turned up by plows, and feared, at first, to be what was left of a person who had met a violent end. Other parcels truly did contain bad news, the bones of someone murdered. In addition to being a natural scientist and curator, Dr. Vessey worked for the FBI and assisted people like me.

Gaining clearance from the unsmiling security guard, I clipped on my visitor's pass and headed for the brass elevator that took me up to the third floor. As I passed walls of drawers inside a dimly lit, crowded corridor, the sounds of people levels below looking at the great stuffed elephant faded. I began to feel claustrophobic. I remembered being so desperate for sensory input after eight hours of class inside this place that when I finally escaped at the end of the day, crowded sidewalks were welcome, the noise of traffic a relief.

I found Dr. Vessey where I had seen him last, inside a laboratory cluttered with steel carts bearing skeletons of birds and animals, teeth, femurs, mandibles. Shelves were covered with more bones and other unhappy human relics such as skulls and shrunken heads. Dr. Vessey, white haired and wearing thick glasses, was sitting behind his desk talking on the phone. While he concluded his call, I opened the box and got out the plastic envelope containing the bone from Deborah Harvey's left hand.

"The Drug Czar's daughter?" he asked right off, taking the envelope from me.

It seemed a strange question. But, in a way, it was correctly posed, for Deborah had been reduced to a scientific curiosity, a piece of physical evidence.

"Yes," I said as he took the phalange out of the envelope and began gently turning it under the light.

"I can tell you without hesitation, Kay, that this is not a post-mortem cut. Though some old cuts can look fresh, fresh cuts can't look old," he said. "The inside of the cut is discolored from the environment in a manner consistent with the rest of the bone's surface. In addition, the way the lip of the cut is bent back tells me this wasn't inflicted on dead bone. Green bone bends. Dead bone doesn't."

"My conclusion exactly," I replied, pulling up a chair. "But you know the question will be asked, Alex."

"And it should be," he said, peering at me over the rim of his glasses. "You wouldn't believe the things that come through here."

"I suspect I would," I said, unpleasantly reminded that the degree of forensic competence dramatically varied from state to state.

"A coroner sent me a case a couple months ago, a chunk of soft tissue and bone he told me was a newborn child found in the sewer. The question was sex and race. The answer was male beagle, two weeks old. Not long before that, another coroner who didn't know pathology from plants sent in a skeleton found in a shallow grave. He had no idea how the person had died. I counted forty-some cuts, lips bent back, textbook examples of green bone plasticity. Definitely not a natural death." He cleaned his glasses with the hem of his lab coat. "Of course, I get the other, too. Bones cut during autopsy."

"Any chance this was caused by a predator?" I said, even though I didn't see how it could have been.

"Well, cuts aren't always easy to distinguish from marks made by carnivores. But I'm fairly certain we're talking about some sort of blade." Getting up, he added cheerfully, "Let's take a look."

The anthropological minutiae that drove me to distraction gave Dr. Vessey joy, and he was energized and animated as he moved to the dissecting microscope on a countertop and centered the bone on the stage. After a long, silent moment of peering through the lenses and turning the bone in the field of light, he commented, "Now, that's interesting."

I waited.

"And this was the only cut you found?"

"Yes," I said. "Perhaps you'll find something else when you

conduct your own examination. But I found nothing else except the bullet hole I mentioned. In her lumbar spine."

"Yes. You said the bullet hit the spinal cord."

"Right. She was shot in the back. I recovered the slug from her vertebra."

"Any idea of the location of the shooting?"

"We don't know where she was in the woods—or if she was even *in* the woods—when she was shot."

"And she has this cut to her hand," Dr. Vessey mused, peering into the scope again. "No way to know which came first. She would have been paralyzed from the waist down after being shot, but she still could have moved her hands."

"A defense injury?" I asked what I suspected.

"A very unusual one, Kay. The cut is dorsal versus palmar." He leaned back in the chair and looked up at me. "Most defense injuries to the hands are palmar." He held up his hands palm out. "But she took this cut to the *top* of her hand." He turned his hands palm in. "I usually associate cuts on the top of the hand with someone who is aggressive in defending himself."

"Punching," I said.

"Right. If I'm coming at you with a knife and you're punching away, you're likely to get cut on the top of your hand. Certainly, you're not going to receive a cut to your palmar surfaces, unless you unclench your fists at some point. But what's more significant is that most defense injuries are slices. The perpetrator is swinging or stabbing, and the victim raises his hands or forearms to ward off the blade. If the cut goes deep enough to strike bone, I'm usually not going to be able to tell you much about the cutting surface."

"If the cutting surface is serrated," I interpolated, "with a slice, the blade covers its own tracks."

"That's one reason this cut is so interesting," he said. "There's no question it was inflicted by a serrated blade."

"Then she wasn't sliced but *hacked*?" I asked, puzzled.

"Yes." He returned the bone to its envelope. "The pattern of serrations means that at least a half an inch of the blade must have struck the top of her hand." Returning to his desk, he added, "I'm afraid that's as much information as I can give you about the weapon and what might have occurred. As you know, there's so much variability. I can't tell you the size of the blade, for example, whether the injury occurred before or after she was shot, and what position she was in when she received the cut."

Deborah could have been on her back. She could have been kneeling or on her feet, and as I returned to my car, I began to analyze. The cut to her hand was deep and would have bled profusely. This most likely placed her on the logging road or in the woods when she received the injury, because there was no blood inside her Jeep. Did this hundred-pound gymnast struggle with her assailant? Did she try to punch him, was she terrified and fighting for her life because Fred already had been murdered? And where did the gun fit in? Why did the killer use two weapons when it did not seem he had needed a gun to kill Fred?

I was willing to bet that Fred's throat was cut. Quite likely, after Deborah was shot, her throat was cut or else she was strangled. She was not shot and left to die. She did not drag herself, half paralyzed, to Fred's side and slip her arm under his. Their bodies had been positioned this way deliberately.

Turning off Constitution, I finally found Connecticut, which eventually led me to a northwest section of the city that I suspected would have been little better than a slum were it not for the Washington Hilton. Rising from a grassy slope that covered a city block, the hotel was a magnificent white luxury liner surrounded by a troubled sea of dusty liquor stores, laundromats, a nightclub featuring "live dancers," and dilapidated row houses with broken windows boarded up and cement front stoops almost on the street. Leaving my car in the hotel's underground parking deck, I crossed Florida Avenue and climbed the front steps of a dingy tan brick apartment building with a faded blue awning in front. I pressed the button for Apartment 28, where Abby Turnbull lived.

"Who is it?"

I barely recognized the disembodied voice blaring out of the intercom. When I announced myself, I wasn't sure what Abby muttered, or maybe she simply gasped. The electronic lock clicked open.

I stepped inside a dimly lit landing with soiled tan carpet on the floor and a bank of tarnished brass mailboxes on a wall paneled in Masonite. I remembered Abby's fear about someone tampering with her mail. It certainly did not appear that one could easily get past the apartment building's front door without a key. The mailboxes required keys as well. Everything she had said to me in Richmond last fall rang false. By the time

I climbed the five flights to her floor, I was out of breath and angry.

Abby was standing in her doorway.

"What are you doing here?" she whispered, her face ashen.

"You're the only person I know in this building. So what do you think I'm doing here?"

"You didn't come to Washington just to see me." Her eyes were frightened.

"I was here on business."

Through her open doorway I could see arctic white furniture, pastel throw pillows, and abstract monotype Gregg Carbo prints, furnishings I recognized from her former house in Richmond. For an instant I was unsettled by images from that terrible day. I envisioned her sister's decomposing body on the bed upstairs, police and paramedics moving about as Abby sat on a couch, her hands trembling so violently she could barely hold a cigarette. I did not know her then except by reputation, and I had not liked her at all. When her sister was murdered, Abby at least had gotten my sympathy. It wasn't until later that she had earned my trust.

"I know you won't believe me," Abby said in the same hushed tone, "but I was going to come see you next week."

"I have a phone."

"I couldn't," she pleaded, and we were having this conversation in the hall.

"Are you going to ask me in, Abby?"

She shook her head.

Fear tingled up my spine.

Glancing past her, I asked quietly, "Is someone in there?"

"Let's walk," she whispered.

"Abby, for God's sake . . ."

She stared hard at me and raised a finger to her lips.

I was convinced she was losing her mind. Not knowing what else to do, I waited in the hall as she went inside to get her coat. Then I followed her out of the building, and for the better part of half an hour we walked briskly along Connecticut Avenue, neither of us speaking. She led me into the Mayflower Hotel and found a table in the darkest corner of the bar. Ordering espresso, I leaned back in the leather chair and regarded her tensely across the polished table.

"I know you don't understand what's going on," she began,

glancing around. At this early hour in the afternoon, the bar was almost empty.

"*Abby? Are you all right?*"

Her lower lip trembled. "I couldn't call you. I can't even talk to you inside my own fucking apartment! It's like I told you in Richmond, only a thousand times worse."

"You need to see someone," I said very calmly.

"I'm not crazy."

"You're an inch away from being completely unglued."

Taking a deep breath, she met my eyes fiercely. "Kay, I'm being followed. I'm positive my phone is being tapped, and I can't even be sure there aren't listening devices planted inside my place—which is why I couldn't ask you in. There, go ahead. Conclude that I'm paranoid, psychotic, whatever you want to think. But I live in my world and you don't. I know what I've been going through. I know what I know about these cases and what's been happening ever since I got involved in them."

"What, exactly, has been happening?"

The waitress returned with our order. After she left, Abby said, "Less than a week after I'd been in Richmond talking to you, my apartment was broken into."

"You were burglarized?"

"Oh, no." Her laugh was hollow. "Not hardly. The person—or persons—were much too clever for that. Nothing was stolen."

I looked quizzically at her.

"I have a computer at home for my writing, and on the hard disk is a file about these couples, their strange deaths. I've been keeping notes for a long time, writing them into this file. The word processing package I use has an option that automatically backs up what you're working on, and I have it set to do this every ten minutes. You know, to make sure I don't lose anything should the power go out or something. Especially in my building—"

"Abby," I interrupted. "What in God's name are you talking about?"

"What I'm saying is that if you go into a file on my computer, if you're in there for ten minutes or more, not only is a backup created, but when you save the file, the date and time are recorded. Are you following me?"

"I'm not sure." I reached for my espresso.

"You remember when I came to see you?"

I nodded.

"I took notes when I talked to the clerk at the Seven-Eleven."

"Yes. I remember."

"And I talked to a number of other people, including Pat Harvey. I intended to put the notes from these interviews into the computer after I got home. But things went haywire. As you recall, I saw you on a Tuesday night and drove back here the next morning. Well, that day, Wednesday, I talked to my editor around noon, and he was suddenly uninterested, said he wanted to hold off on the Harvey-Cheney story because the paper was going to run a series over the weekend about AIDS.

"It was strange," she went on. "The Harvey-Cheney story was hot, the *Post* was in one big hurry for it. Then I return from Richmond and suddenly have a new assignment?" She paused to light a cigarette. "As it turned out, I didn't have a free moment until Saturday, which was when I finally sat down in front of my computer to pull up this file, and there was a date and time listed after it that I didn't understand. Friday, September twentieth, two-thirteen in the afternoon *when I wasn't even home*. The file had been opened, Kay. Someone went into it, and I know it wasn't me because I didn't touch my computer—not even once—until that Saturday, the twenty-first, when I had some free time."

"Perhaps the clock in your computer was off. . . ."

She was already shaking her head. "It wasn't. I checked."

"How could anybody do that?" I asked. "How could someone break into your apartment without anyone seeing them, without your knowing?"

"The FBI could."

"Abby," I said, exasperated.

"There's a lot you don't know."

"Then fill me in, please," I said.

"Why do you think I took a leave of absence from the *Post*?"

"According to the *New York Times*, you're writing a book."

"And you're assuming I already knew I was going to write this book when I was with you in Richmond."

"It's more than an assumption," I said, feeling angry again.

"I wasn't. I swear." Leaning forward, she added in a voice trembling with emotion, "My beat was changed. Do you understand what that means?"

I was speechless.

"The only thing worse would have been to be fired, but they

couldn't do that. There was no cause. Jesus Christ, I won an investigative reporting award last year, and all of a sudden they want to switch me over to features. Do you hear me? *Features.* Now, you tell me what you make of that."

"I don't know, Abby."

"I don't know, either." She blinked back tears. "But I have my self-respect. I know there's something big going on, a story. And I sold it. There. Think what you want, but I'm trying to survive. I have to live and I had to get away from the paper for a while. Features. Oh, God. Kay, I'm so scared."

"Tell me about the FBI," I said firmly.

"I've already told you a lot. About the wrong turn I took, about ending up at Camp Peary, and the FBI agents coming to see me."

"That's not enough."

"The jack of hearts, Kay," she said as if she were telling me something I already knew.

When it dawned on her that I had no idea what she was talking about, her expression changed to astonishment.

"You don't know?" she asked.

"What jack of hearts?"

"In each of these cases, a playing card has been found." Her incredulous eyes were fixed on mine.

I vaguely remembered something from one of the few transcripts of police interviews I had seen. The detective from Gloucester had talked to a friend of Bruce Phillips and Judy Roberts, the first couple. What was it the detective had asked? I recalled it had struck me as rather peculiar. Cards. Did Judy and Bruce ever play cards? Had the friend ever seen any cards inside Bruce's Camaro?

"Tell me about the cards, Abby," I said.

"Are you familiar with the ace of spades, with how it was used in Vietnam?"

I told her I wasn't.

"When a particular outfit of American soldiers wanted to make a point after making a kill, they would leave an ace of spades on the body. In fact, a company that manufactures playing cards supplied this unit with boxes of the cards just for this purpose."

"What does this have to do with Virginia?" I asked, baffled.

"There's a parallel. Only we're not talking about an ace of spades, but a jack of hearts. In each of the first four cases, a jack of hearts was found in the abandoned car."

"Where did you get this information?"

"You know I can't tell you that, Kay. But we're talking about more than one source. That's why I'm so sure of it."

"And did one of your *sources* also tell you that a jack of hearts was found in Deborah Harvey's Jeep?"

"Was one found?" She idly stirred her drink.

"Don't toy with me," I warned.

"I'm not." She met my eyes. "If a jack of hearts was found inside her Jeep or anywhere else, I don't know about it. Obviously, it's an important detail because it would definitely link Deborah Harvey's and Fred Cheney's deaths with those of the first four couples. Believe me, I'm looking hard for that link. I'm not sure it's there. Or if it is, what it means."

"What does this have to do with the FBI?" I asked reluctantly, for I was not sure I wanted to hear her reply.

"They've been preoccupied with these cases almost from the start, Kay. And it goes way beyond VICAP's usual participation. The FBI's known about the cards for a long time. When a jack of hearts was found inside the first couple's Camaro—on the dash—no one paid much attention. Then the second couple disappeared, and there was another card, this one on the passenger seat. When Benton Wesley found out, he immediately started controlling things. He went back to the detective in Gloucester County and told him not to say a word about the jack of hearts found inside the Camaro. He told the investigator in the second case the same thing. Each time another abandoned car turned up, Wesley was on the phone with that investigator."

She paused, studying me as if trying to read my thoughts. "I guess I shouldn't be surprised you didn't know," she added. "I don't suppose it would be that hard for the police to withhold from you what was discovered inside the cars."

"It wouldn't be hard for them to do that," I replied. "Were the cards found with the bodies, that would be another matter. I don't know how that could be kept from me."

Even as I heard myself say the words, doubt whispered in the back of my mind. The police had waited hours before calling me to the scene. By the time I got there, Wesley had arrived, and Deborah Harvey's and Fred Cheney's bodies had been tampered with, searched for personal effects.

"I would expect the FBI to keep quiet about this," I continued to reason. "The detail could be critical to the investigation."

"I'm so sick of hearing shit like that," Abby said angrily. "The detail about the killer leaving a calling card, so to speak, is critical to the investigation only if the guy comes forward and confesses, says he left a card in each couple's car when there's no way for him to know about that unless he really did it. I don't think that's going to happen. And I don't think the FBI is sitting on this thing just because they want to make sure nothing screws up the investigation."

"Then why?" I asked uneasily.

"Because we're not just talking about serial murders. We're not just talking about some fruitcake out there who's got a thing about couples. This thing's political. It's got to be."

Falling silent, she caught the waitress's eye. Abby did not say another word until a second round of drinks was placed on our table and she had taken several sips.

"Kay," she continued, and she was calmer, "does it surprise you that Pat Harvey talked to me when I was in Richmond?"

"Yes, frankly."

"Have you given any thought as to why she agreed to it?"

"I suppose she would have done anything to bring her daughter back," I said. "And sometimes publicity can help."

Abby shook her head. "When I talked to Pat Harvey, she told me a lot of things that I would never have put in the paper. And it's not the first encounter I'd had with her, not by a long shot."

"I don't understand." I was feeling shaky, and it was due to more than the espresso.

"You know about her crusade against illegal charities."

"Vaguely," I replied.

"The tip that alerted her about all that originally came from me."

"From you?"

"Last year I began work on a big investigative piece about drug trafficking. As I was going along, I began to uncover a lot of things I couldn't verify, and this is where the fraudulent charities come in. Pat Harvey has an apartment here, at the Watergate, and one evening I went there to interview her, to get a couple quotes for my story. We got to talking. I ended up telling her about the allegations I'd heard to see if she could corroborate any of them. That's how it began."

"What allegations, exactly?"

"About ACTMAD, for example," Abby said. "Allegations that

some of these antidrug charities are really fronts for drug cartels and other illegal activities in Central America. I told her I'd been informed by what I considered to be reliable sources that millions of dollars donated each year were ending up in the pockets of people like Manuel Noriega. Of course, this was before Noriega was arrested. But it's believed that funds from ACTMAD and other so-called charities are being used to buy intelligence from U.S. agents and facilitate the heroin trade through Panamanian airports, customs offices, in the Far East and the Americas."

"And Pat Harvey, prior to your coming to her apartment, had heard nothing about this?"

"No, Kay. I don't think she had a clue, but she was outraged. She started investigating, and then finally went before Congress with a report. A special subcommittee was formed to investigate, and she was invited to serve as a consultant, as you probably know. Apparently, she's uncovered a great deal and a hearing has been set for this April. Some people aren't happy about it, including the Justice Department."

I was beginning to see where this was going.

"There are informants involved," Abby went on, "that the DEA, FBI, and CIA have been after for years. And you know how it works. When Congress gets involved, they have the power to offer special immunity in exchange for information. Once these informants testify in this congressional hearing, the game's over. No way the Justice Department will be able to prosecute."

"Meaning that Pat Harvey's efforts are not exactly appreciated by the Justice Department."

"Meaning that the Justice Department would be secretly thrilled if her entire investigation fell apart."

"The National Drug Policy Director, or Drug Czar," I said, "is subservient to the Attorney General, who commands the FBI and DEA. If Mrs. Harvey is having a conflict of interests with the Justice Department, why doesn't the AG rein her in?"

"Because it's not the AG she's having a problem with, Kay. What she's doing is going to make him look good, make the White House look good. Their Drug Czar is making a dent in drug crimes. What your average citizen won't understand is that as far as the FBI and DEA are concerned, the consequences of this congressional hearing aren't great enough. All that will occur is a full disclosure, the names of these charities and the truth about what they've been doing. The publicity will put groups like ACTMAD out of business, but the scumbags involved will suffer nothing more than a slap on the wrist. The agents working the cases end up with an empty bag because nobody gets put away. Bad people don't stop doing bad things. It's like closing down a nip joint. Two weeks later, it's reopened on another corner."

"I fail to see how this is connected to what's happened to Mrs. Harvey's daughter," I said again.

"Start with this. If you were at cross-purposes with the FBI," Abby said, "and maybe even doing battle with them, how would you feel if your daughter disappeared and the FBI was working the case?"

It was not a pleasant thought. "Justified or not, I would feel very vulnerable and paranoid. I suppose it would be hard for me to trust."

"You've just skimmed the surface of Pat Harvey's feelings. I think she really believes that someone used her daughter to get to her, that Deborah's not the victim of a random crime, but a hit. And she's not sure that the FBI isn't involved—"

"Let me get this straight," I said, stopping her. "Are you implying that Pat Harvey is suspicious the *FBI* is behind the deaths of her daughter and Fred?"

"It's entered her mind that the feds are involved."

"Are you going to tell me that you're entertaining this notion yourself?"

"I'm to the point of believing anything."

"Good God," I muttered under my breath.

"I know how off-the-wall it sounds. But if nothing else, I believe the FBI knows what's going on and maybe even knows who's doing it, and that's why I'm a problem. The feds don't want me snooping around. They're worried I might turn over a rock and find out what's really crawling underneath it."

"If that's the case," I reminded her, "then it would seem to me the *Post* would be offering you a raise, not sending you over to features. It's never been my impression that the *Post* is easily intimidated."

"I'm not Bob Woodward," she replied bitterly. "I haven't been there very long, and the police beat is chicken shit, usually where rookies get their feet wet. If the Director of the FBI or someone in the White House wants to talk lawsuits or diplomacy with the powers to be at the *Post*, I'm not going to be invited in on the meeting or necessarily told what's going on."

She was probably right about that, I thought. If Abby's demeanor in the newsroom was anything like it was now, it was unlikely anyone was eager to deal with her. In fact, I wasn't sure I was surprised she had been relieved of her beat.

"I'm sorry, Abby," I said. "Maybe I could understand politics being a factor in Deborah Harvey's case, but the others? How do the other couples fit? The first couple disappeared two and a half years before Deborah and Fred did."

"Kay," she said fiercely, "I don't know the answers. But I swear to God something is being covered up. Something the FBI, the government, doesn't want the public ever to find out. You mark my words, even if these killings stop, the cases will never be solved if the FBI has its way about it. That's what I'm up against. And that's what you're up against." Finishing her drink, she added, "And maybe that would be all right—as long as the killings stopped. But the problem is, *when* will they stop? And could they have been stopped before now?"

"Why are you telling me all this?" I asked bluntly.

"We're talking about innocent teenage kids who are turning up dead. Not to mention the obvious—I trust you. And maybe I need a friend."

"You're going to continue with the book?"

"Yes. I just hope there will be a final chapter to write."

"Please be careful, Abby."

"Believe me," she said, "I know."

When we left the bar it was dark out and very cold. My mind was in turmoil as we were jostled along crowded sidewalks, and I felt no better as I made the drive back to Richmond. I wanted to talk to Pat Harvey, but I did not dare. I wanted to talk to Wesley, but I knew he would not divulge his secrets to me, were there any, and more than ever I was unsure of our friendship.

The minute I was home, I called Marino.

"Where in South Carolina does Hilda Ozimek live?" I asked.

"Why? What did you find out at the Smithsonian?"

"Just answer my question, please."

"Some little armpit of a town called Six Mile."

"Thank you."

"Hey! Before you hang up, you mind telling me what went down in D.C.?"

"Not tonight, Marino. If I can't find you tomorrow, you get hold of me."

7

At 5:45 A.M., Richmond International Airport was deserted. Restaurants were closed, newspapers were stacked in front of locked-up gift shops, and a janitor was slowly wheeling a trash can around, a somnambulist picking up gum wrappers and cigarette butts.

I found Marino inside the USAir terminal, eyes shut and rain-coat wadded behind his head as he napped in an airless, artificially lit room of empty chairs and dotted blue carpet. For a fleeting moment I saw him as if I did not know him, my heart touched in a sad, sweet way. Marino had aged.

I don't think I had been in my new job more than several days when I met him for the first time. I was in the morgue performing an autopsy when a big man with an impassive face walked in and positioned himself on the other side of the table. I remembered feeling his cool scrutiny. I had the uncomfortable sensation he was dissecting me as thoroughly as I was dissecting my patient.

"So you're the new chief." He had posed the comment as a challenge, as if daring me to acknowledge that I believed I could fill a position never before held by a woman.

"I'm Dr. Scarpetta," I had replied. "You're with Richmond City, I assume?"

He had mumbled his name, then waited in silence while I removed several bullets from his homicide case and receipted them to him. He strolled off without so much as a "good-bye" or "nice to meet you," by which point our professional rapport had been established. I perceived he resented me for no cause other than my gender, and in turn I dismissed him as a dolt with a brain pickled by testosterone. In truth, he had secretly intimidated the hell out of me.

It was hard for me to look at Marino now and imagine I had ever ·found him threatening. He looked old and defeated, shirt straining across his big belly, wisps of graying hair unruly, brow drawn in what was neither a scowl nor a frown but a series of deep creases caused by the erosion of chronic tension and displeasure.

"Good morning." I gently touched his shoulder.

"What's in the bag?" he muttered without opening his eyes.

"I thought you were asleep," I said, surprised.

He sat up and yawned.

Settling next to him, I opened the paper sack and got out Styrofoam cups of coffee and cream cheese bagels I had fixed at home and heated in the microwave oven just before heading out in the dark.

"I assume you haven't eaten?" I handed him a napkin.

"Those look like real bagels."

"They are," I said, unwrapping mine.

"I thought you said the plane left at six."

"Six-thirty. I'm quite sure that's what I told you. I hope you haven't been waiting long."

"Yeah, well I have been."

"I'm sorry."

"You got the tickets, right?"

"In my purse," I replied. There were times when Marino and I sounded like an old married couple.

"You ask me, I'm not sure this idea of yours is worth the price. It wouldn't come out of my pocket, even if I had it. But it don't thrill me that you're getting soaked, Doc. It would make me feel better if you at least tried to get reimbursed."

"It wouldn't make me feel better." We had been through this before. "I'm not turning in a reimbursement voucher, and you aren't, either. You turn in a voucher and you leave a paper trail. Besides," I added, sipping my coffee, "I can afford it."

"If it would save me six hundred bucks, I'd leave a paper trail from here to the moon."

"Nonsense. I know you better than that."

"Yeah. Nonsense is right. This whole thing's goofy as shit." He dumped several packs of sugar into his coffee. "I think Abby *Turncoat* scrambled your brains."

"Thank you," I replied shortly.

Other passengers were filing in, and it was amazing the power Marino had to make the world tilt slightly on its axis. He had chosen to sit in an area designated as nonsmoking, then had carried an upright ashtray from rows away and placed it by his chair. This served as a subliminal invitation for other semiawake smokers to settle near us, several of whom carried over additional ashtrays. By the time we were ready to board there was hardly an ashtray to be found in the smoking area and nobody seemed quite sure where to sit. Embarrassed and determined to have no part in this unfriendly takeover, I left my pack in my purse.

Marino, who disliked flying more than I did, slept to Charlotte, where we boarded a commuter prop plane that reminded me unpleasantly of how little there is between fragile human flesh and empty air. I had worked my share of disasters and knew what it was like to see an aircraft and passengers scattered over miles of earth. I noted there was no rest room or beverage service, and when the engines started, the plane shook as if it were having a seizure. For the first part of the trip, I had the rare distinction of watching the pilots chat with each other, stretching and yawning until a stewardess made her way up the aisle and yanked the curtain shut. The air was getting more turbulent, mountains drifting in and out of fog. The second time the plane suddenly lost altitude, sending my stomach into my throat, Marino gripped both armrests so hard his knuckles went white.

"Jesus Christ," he muttered, and I began to regret bringing him breakfast. He looked as if he were about to get sick. "If this bucket ever makes it on the ground in one piece, I'm having a drink. I don't friggin' care what time it is."

"Hey, I'll buy," a man in front of us turned around and said.

Marino was staring at a strange phenomenon occurring in a section of the aisle directly ahead of us. Rolling up from a metal strip at the edge of the carpet was a ghostly condensation that I had never seen on any previous flight. It looked as if clouds were seeping inside the plane, and when Marino pointed this out with a loud "What the hell?" to the stewardess, she completely ignored him.

"Next time I'm going to slip phenobarbital in your coffee," I warned him between clenched teeth.

"Next time you decide to talk to some wild-ass gypsy who lives in the sticks, I ain't coming along for the ride."

For half an hour we circled Spartanburg, bumped and tossed,

fits of freezing rain pelting the glass. We could not land because of the fog, and it honestly occurred to me that we might die. I thought about my mother. I thought about Lucy, my niece. I should have gone home for Christmas, but I was so weighted down by my own concerns, and I had not wanted to be asked about Mark. *I'm busy, Mother. I simply can't get away right now.* "But it's Christmas, Kay." I could not remember the last time my mother had cried, but I always knew when she felt like it. Her voice got funny. Words were spaced far apart. "Lucy will be so disappointed," she had said. I had mailed Lucy a generous check and called her Christmas morning. She missed me terribly, but I think I missed her more.

Suddenly, clouds parted and the sun lit up windows. Spontaneously, all of the passengers, including me, gave God and pilots a round of applause. We celebrated our survival by chatting up and down the aisle as if all of us had been friends for years.

"So maybe Broom Hilda's looking out for us," Marino said sarcastically, his face covered with sweat.

"Maybe she is," I said, taking a deep breath as we landed.

"Yeah, well, be sure to thank her for me."

"You can thank her yourself, Marino."

"Yo," he said, yawning and fully recovered.

"She seems very nice. Maybe for once, you might consider having an open mind."

"Yo," he said again.

When I had gotten Hilda Ozimek's number from directory assistance and given her a call, I was expecting a woman shrewd and suspicious who bracketed every comment in dollar signs. Instead, she was unassuming and gentle, and surprisingly trusting. She did not ask questions or want proof of who I was. Her voice sounded worried only once, and this was when she mentioned that she could not meet us at the airport.

Since I was paying and in a mood to be chauffeured, I told Marino to pick out what he wanted. Like a sixteen-year-old on his first test drive to manhood, he selected a brand-new Thunderbird, black, with a sunroof, a tape deck, electric windows, leather bucket seats. He drove west with the sunroof open and the heat turned on as I went into more detail about what Abby had said to me in Washington.

"I know Deborah Harvey's and Fred Cheney's bodies were moved," I was explaining. "And now I suspect I understand why."

"I'm not sure I do," he said. "So why don't you lay it out for me one point at a time."

"You and I got to the rest stop before anyone went through the Jeep," I began. "And we didn't see a jack of hearts on the dash, on a seat, or anywhere else."

"Don't mean the card wasn't in the glove compartment or something, and the cops didn't find it until after the dogs was finished sniffing." Setting the cruise control, he added, "*If* this card business is true. Like I said, it's the first I've heard of it."

"Let's for the sake of argument assume it is true."

"I'm listening."

"Wesley arrived at the rest stop after we did, so he didn't see a card, either. Later, the Jeep was searched by the police, and you can be sure that Wesley was either on hand or he called Morrell and wanted to know what was found. If there was no sign of a jack of hearts, and I'm willing to bet that's the case, this had to have thrown Wesley a curve. His next thought may have been that either Deborah's and Fred's disappearance was unrelated to the other couples' disappearances and deaths, or else if Deborah and Fred were already dead, then it was possible that this time a card may have been left at the scene, left with the bodies."

"And you're thinking this was why their bodies was moved before you got there. Because the cops was looking for the card."

"Or Benton was. Yes, that's what I'm considering. Otherwise it doesn't make much sense to me. Benton and the police *know* not to touch a body before the medical examiner arrives. But Benton also wouldn't want to take the chance that a jack of hearts might come into the morgue with the bodies. He wouldn't want me or anyone else to find it or know about it."

"Then it would make more sense for him to just tell us to keep our mouths shut instead of him screwing around with the scene," Marino argued. "It's not like he was out there in the woods alone. There was other cops around. They would have noticed if Benton found a card."

"Obviously," I said. "But he would also realize that the fewer people who know, the better. And if I found a playing card among Deborah's or Fred's personal effects, that would go into my written report. Commonwealth's attorneys, members of my staff, families, insurance companies—other people are going to see the autopsy reports eventually."

"Okay, okay." Marino was getting impatient. "But so what? I mean, what's the big deal?"

"I don't know. But if what Abby's implying is true, these cards turning up must be a very big deal to someone."

"No offense, Doc, but I never liked Abby Turnbull worth a damn. Not when she was working in Richmond, and I sure as hell don't think better of her now that she's at the *Post*."

"I've never known her to lie," I said.

"Yeah. You've never *known* it."

"The detective in Gloucester mentioned playing cards in a transcript I read."

"And maybe that's where Abby picked up the ball. Now she's running around the block with it. Making assumptions. Hoping. All she gives a shit about is writing her book."

"She's not herself right now. She's frightened, angry, but I don't agree with you about her character."

"Right," he said. "She comes to Richmond, acts like your long-lost friend. Says she don't want nothing from you. Next thing, you have to read the *New York Times* to find out she's writing a friggin' book about these cases. Oh, yeah. She's a real friend, Doc."

I shut my eyes and listened to a country-music song playing softly on the radio. Sunlight breaking through the windshield was warm on my lap, and the early hour I had gotten out of bed hit me like a stiff drink. I dozed off. When I came to, we were bumping slowly along an unpaved road out in the middle of nowhere.

"Welcome to the big town of Six Mile," Marino announced.

"What town?"

There was no skyline, not so much as a single convenience store or gas station in sight. Roadsides were dense with trees, the Blue Ridge a haze in the distance, and houses were poor and spread so far apart a cannon could go off without your neighbor hearing it.

Hilda Ozimek, psychic to the FBI and oracle to the Secret Service, lived in a tiny white frame house with white-painted tires in the front yard where pansies and tulips probably grew in the spring. Dead cornstalks leaned against the porch, and in the drive was a rusting Chevrolet Impala with flat tires. A mangy dog began to bark, ugly as sin and big enough to give me pause as I considered getting out of the car. Then he trotted off on three legs, favoring his right front paw, as the front screen door screeched open and a woman squinted at us in the bright, cold morning.

"Be still, Tootie." She patted the dog's neck. "Now go on

around back." The dog hung his head, tail wagging, and limped off to the backyard.

"Good morning," Marino said, his feet heavy on the front wooden steps.

At least he intended to be polite, and there had been no guarantee of that.

"It is a fine morning," Hilda Ozimek said.

She was at least sixty and looked as country as corn bread. Black polyester pants were stretched over wide hips, a beige sweater buttoned up to her neck, and she wore thick socks and loafers. Her eyes were light blue, hair covered by a red head rag. She was missing several teeth. I doubted Hilda Ozimek ever looked in a mirror or gave a thought to her physical self unless she was forced to by discomfort or pain.

We were invited into a small living room cluttered with musty furniture and bookcases filled with a variety of unexpected volumes not arranged in any sort of sensible order. There were books on religion and psychology, biographies and histories, and a surprising assortment of novels by some of my favorite authors: Alice Walker, Pat Conroy, and Keri Hulme. The only hint of our hostess's otherworldly inclinations was several works by Edgar Cayce and half a dozen or so crystals placed about on tables and shelves. Marino and I were seated on a couch near a kerosene heater, Hilda across from us in an overstuffed chair, sunlight from the window behind her shining through the open blinds and painting white bars across her face.

"I hope you had no trouble, and I am so sorry I couldn't come get you. But I don't drive anymore."

"Your directions were excellent," I reassured her. "We had no problem finding your house."

"If you don't mind my asking," Marino said, "how do you get around? I didn't see a store or nothing within walking distance."

"Many people come here for readings or just to talk. Somehow, I always have what I need or can get a ride."

A telephone rang in another room, and was instantly silenced by an answering machine.

"How may I help you?" Hilda asked.

"I brought photographs," Marino replied. "The Doc said you wanted to see them. But there's a couple things I want to clear up first. No offense or nothing, Miss Ozimek, but this mind-reading stuff is something I've never put much stock in. Maybe you can help me understand it better."

For Marino to be so forthright without a trace of combativeness in his tone was uncommon, and I glanced over at him, rather startled. He was studying Hilda with the openness of a child, his expression an odd mix of curiosity and melancholy.

"First, let me say that I'm not a mind reader," Hilda replied matter-of-factly. "And I don't even feel comfortable with being called a psychic, but for lack of a better term, I suppose, that is how I am referred to and how I refer to myself. All of us have the capability. Sixth sense, some part of our brain most people choose not to use. I explain it as an enhanced intuition. I feel energy coming from people and just relay the impressions that come into my mind."

"Which is what you did when Pat Harvey was with you," he said.

She nodded. "She took me into Debbie's bedroom, showed me photographs of her, and then she took me to the rest stop where the Jeep was found."

"What impressions did you get?" I inquired.

Staring off, she thought hard for a moment. "I can't remember all of them. That's the thing. It's the same when I give readings. People come back to me later and tell me about something I said and what's happened since. I don't always remember what I've said until I'm reminded."

"Do you remember anything you said to Mrs. Harvey?" Marino wanted to know, and he sounded disappointed.

"When she showed me Debbie's picture, I knew right away the girl was dead."

"What about the boyfriend?" Marino asked.

"I saw his picture in the newspaper and knew he was dead. I knew both of them were dead."

"So you been reading about these cases in the newspaper," Marino then said.

"No," Hilda answered. "I don't take the newspaper. But I saw the boy's picture because Mrs. Harvey had clipped it out to show me. She didn't have a photograph of him, only of her daughter, you see."

"You mind explaining how you knew they was dead?"

"It was something I felt. An impression I got when I touched their pictures."

Reaching into his back pocket and pulling out his wallet, Marino said, "If I give you a picture of someone, can you do the same thing? Give me your impressions?"

"I'll try," she said as he handed her a snapshot.

Closing her eyes, she rubbed her fingertips over the photograph in slow circles. This went on for at least a minute before she spoke again. "I'm getting guilt. Now, I don't know if it's because this woman was feeling guilty when the picture was taken, or if it's because she's feeling that way now. But that's coming in real strong. Conflict, guilt. Back and forth. She's made up her mind one minute, then doubting herself the next. Back and forth."

"Is she alive?" Marino asked, clearing his throat.

"I feel that she is alive," Hilda replied, still rubbing. "I'm also getting the impression of a hospital. Something medical. Now I don't know if this means that she's sick or if someone close to her is. But something medical is involved, a concern. Or maybe it will be involved at some future point."

"Anything else?" Marino asked.

She shut her eyes again and rubbed the photograph a little longer. "A lot of conflict," she repeated. "It's as if something's past but it's hard for her to let it go. Pain. And yet she feels she has no choice. That's all that's coming to me." She looked up at Marino.

When he retrieved the photograph, his face was red. Returning the wallet to his pocket without saying a word, he unzipped his briefcase and got out a microcassette tape recorder and a manila envelope containing a series of retrospective photographs that began at the logging road in New Kent County and ended in the woods where Deborah Harvey's and Fred Cheney's bodies had been found. Hilda spread them out on the coffee table and began rubbing her fingers over each one. For a very long time she said nothing, eyes closed as the telephone continued to ring in the other room. Each time the machine intervened, and she did not seem to notice. I was deciding that her skills were in more demand than those of any physician.

"I'm picking up fear," she began talking rapidly. "Now, I don't know if it's because someone was feeling fear when these pictures were taken, or if it's because someone was feeling fear in these places at some earlier time. But fear." She nodded, eyes still shut. "I'm definitely picking it up with each picture. All of them. Very strong fear."

Like the blind, Hilda moved her fingers from photograph to

photograph, reading something that seemed as tangible to her as the features of a person's face.

"I feel death here," she went on, touching three different photographs. "I feel that strong." They were photographs of the clearing where the bodies were found. "But I don't feel it here." Her fingers moved back to photographs of the logging road and a section of woods where I had walked when being led to the clearing in the rain.

I glanced over at Marino. He was leaning forward on the couch, elbows on his knees, his eyes fixed on Hilda. So far, she wasn't telling us anything dramatic. Neither Marino nor I had ever assumed that Deborah and Fred had been murdered on the logging road, but in the clearing where their bodies were found.

"I see a man," Hilda went on. "Light-complected. He's not real tall. Not short. Medium height and slender. But not skinny. Now, I don't know who it is, but since nothing is coming to me strongly, I'll have to assume it was someone who had an encounter with the couple. I'm picking up friendliness. I'm hearing laughter. It's like he was, you know, friendly with the couple. Maybe they met him somewhere, and I can't tell you why I'm thinking this, but I'm feeling as if they were laughing with him at some point. Trusted him."

Marino spoke. "Can you see anything else about him? About the way he looked?"

She continued rubbing the photographs. "I'm seeing darkness. It's possible he has a dark beard or something dark over part of his face. Maybe he's dressed in dark clothing. But I'm definitely picking him up in connection with the couple and with the place where the pictures were taken."

Opening her eyes, she stared up at the ceiling. "I'm feeling that the first meeting was a friendly encounter. Nothing to make them worry. But then there's fear. It's so strong in this place, the woods."

"What else?" Marino was so intense, the veins were standing out in his neck. If he leaned forward another inch, he was going to fall off the couch.

"Two things," she said. "They may not mean anything but they're coming to me. I have a sense of another place that's not in these pictures, and I'm feeling this in connection with the girl. She might have been taken somewhere or gone somewhere. Now this place could be close by. Maybe it's not. I don't know, but I'm getting a sense of crowdedness, of things grabbing. Of panic, a lot of noise and motion. Nothing about these impressions is good. And then there is something lost. I'm seeing this as something metal that has to do with war. I'm not getting anything more about that except I don't feel anything bad—I'm not picking up that the object itself is harmful."

"Who lost whatever this metal thing is?" Marino inquired.

"I have a sense that this is a person who is still alive. I'm not getting an image, but I feel this is a man. He perceives the item as lost versus discarded and is not real worried about it, but there is some concern. As if whatever he has lost enters his mind now and then."

She fell silent as the telephone rang again.

I asked, "Did you mention any of this to Pat Harvey last fall?"

"When she wanted to see me," Hilda replied, "the bodies had not been found. I didn't have these pictures."

"Then you did not get any of these same impressions."

She thought hard. "We went to the rest stop and she led me right over to where the Jeep was found. I stood there for a while. I remember there was a knife."

"What knife?" Marino asked.

"I saw a knife."

"What kind of knife?" he asked, and I recalled that Gail, the dog handler, had borrowed Marino's Swiss army knife when opening the Jeep's doors.

"A long knife," Hilda said. "Like a hunting knife or maybe some kind of military knife. It seems there was something about the handle. Black and rubbery, maybe, with one of those blades I associate with cutting through hard things like wood."

"I'm not sure I understand," I said, even though I had a good idea what she meant. I did not want to lead her.

"With teeth. Like a saw. I guess serrated is what I'm trying to say," she replied.

"This is what came into your mind when you was standing out there at the rest stop?" Marino asked, staring at her in disbelief.

"I did not feel anything that was frightening," she said. "But I saw the knife, and I knew it was not the couple who had been in the Jeep when it was left where it was. I did not feel their presence at that rest stop. They were never there." She paused, closing her eyes again, brow furrowed. "I remember feeling anxiety. I had the impression of someone anxious and in a hurry. I saw darkness. Like it was night. Then someone was walking quickly. I couldn't see who it was."

"Can you see this individual now?" I asked.

"No. I can't see him."

"*Him?*" I said.

She paused again. "I believe my feeling was that it was a man."

It was Marino who spoke. "You told Pat Harvey all this when you was with her at the rest stop?"

"Some of it, yes," Hilda replied. "I don't remember everything I said."

"I need to walk around," Marino muttered, getting up from the couch. Hilda did not seem surprised or concerned as he went out, the screen door slamming shut behind him.

"Hilda," I said, "when you met with Pat Harvey, did you pick up anything about her? Did you get any sense that she knew something, for example, about what might have happened to her daughter?"

"I picked up guilt real strong, like she was feeling responsible. But this would be expected. When I deal with the relatives of someone who has disappeared or been killed, I always pick up guilt. What was a little more unusual was her aura."

"Her *aura?*"

I knew what an aura was in medicine, a sensation that can precede the onset of a seizure. But I did not think this was what Hilda meant.

"Auras are invisible to most people," she explained. "I see them as colors. An aura surrounding a person. A color. Pat Harvey's aura was gray."

"Does that mean something?"

"Gray is neither death nor life," she said. "I associate it with illness. Someone sick of body, mind, or soul. As if something is draining the color from her life."

"I suppose that makes sense when you consider her emotional state at the time," I pointed out.

"It might. But I remember that it gave me a bad feeling. I picked up that she might be in some sort of danger. Her energy wasn't good, wasn't positive or healthy. I felt she was at risk for opening herself up to harm, or maybe bringing harm upon herself through her own doings."

"Have you ever seen a gray aura before?"

"Not often."

I could not resist asking, "Are you picking up a color from me?"

"Yellow with a little brown mixed in."

"That's interesting," I said, surprised. "I never wear either color. In fact, I don't believe I have anything yellow or brown inside my house. But I love sunlight and chocolate."

"Your aura has nothing to do with colors or foods you like." She smiled. "Yellow can mean spiritual. And brown I associate with good sense, practical. Someone grounded in reality. I see your aura as being very spiritual but also very practical. Now mind you, that is my interpretation. For each person, colors mean a different thing."

"And Marino?"

"A thin margin of red. That's what I see around him," she said. "Red often means anger. But he needs more red, I think."

"You're not serious," I said, for the last thing I would have thought that Marino needed was more anger.

"When someone is low on energy, I tell them they need more red in their life. It gives energy. Makes you get things done, fight against your troubles. Red can be real good if channeled properly. But I get the sense he is afraid of what he is feeling, and this is what is weakening him."

"Hilda, have you seen pictures of the other couples who disappeared?"

She nodded. "Mrs. Harvey had their pictures. From the news-paper."

"And did you touch them, read them?"

"I did."

"What did you perceive?"

"Death," she said. "All of the young people were dead."

"What about the light-complected man who may have a beard or something dark over part of his face?"

She paused. "I don't know. But I do remember picking up this friendliness I mentioned. Their initial encounter was not one of fear. I had the impression that none of the young people were afraid at first."

"I want to ask you about a card now," I said. "You mentioned that you read people's cards. Are you talking about playing cards?"

"You can use most anything. Tarot cards, a crystal ball. It doesn't matter. These things are tools. It's whatever makes it easy for you to concentrate. But yes, I use a deck of playing cards."

"How does that work?"

"I ask the person to cut the cards, then I begin to pick one at a time and tell what impressions come to mind."

"Were you to pick the jack of hearts, would there be any special significance?" I asked.

"It all depends on the person I'm dealing with, what energy I'm picking up from this individual. But the jack of hearts is equal to the knight of cups in tarot cards."

"A good card or a bad card?"

"It depends on who the card represents in relation to the individual whose reading I'm doing," she said. "In tarot cards, cups are love and emotion cards, just as swords and pentacles are business and money cards. The jack of hearts would be a love and emotion card. And this could be very good. It could also be very bad if the love has gone sour or turned vengeful, hateful."

"How would a jack of hearts be different from a ten of hearts or queen of hearts, for example?"

"The jack of hearts is a face card," she said. "I would say this is a card that represents a man. Now a king of hearts is also a face card, but I would associate a king with power, someone who is perceived or perceives himself as in control, in charge, possibly a father or boss, something like that. A jack, like a knight, might represent someone who is perceived or perceives himself as a soldier, a defender, a champion. He might be someone who is out in the world doing battle on the business front. Maybe he's into sports, a competitor. He could be a lot of things, but since hearts are emotion, love cards, that would make me say that whoever this card represents, there is an emotional element versus a money or work element."

Her telephone rang again.

She said to me, "Don't always trust what you hear, Dr. Scarpetta."

"About what?" I asked, startled.

"Something that matters a great deal to you is causing unhappiness, grief. It has to do with a person. A friend, a romantic interest. It could be a member of your family. I don't know. Definitely someone of great importance in your life. But you are hearing and maybe even imagining many things. Be careful what you believe."

Mark, I thought, or maybe Benton Wesley. I couldn't resist asking, "Is this someone currently in my life? Someone I'm having encounters with?"

She paused. "Since I'm sensing confusion, much that is unknown, I'll have to say that it isn't someone you are currently close to. I'm feeling a distance, you know, not necessarily geographical, but emotional. Space that is making it hard for you to trust. My advice is to let it go, don't do anything about this now. A resolution will come, and I can't tell you when this will be, but it will be all right if you relax, don't listen to the confusion, or act impulsively.

"And there's something else," she went on. "Look beyond what is before you, and I don't know what this is about. But there is something you aren't seeing and it has to do with the past, something of importance that happened in the past. It will come to you and lead you to the truth, but you will not recognize its significance unless you open yourself first. Let your faith guide you."

Wondering what had happened to Marino, I got up and looked out the window.

Marino drank two bourbon and waters in the Charlotte airport, then had one more when we were in the air. He had very little to say during the trip back to Richmond. It wasn't until we were walking to our cars in the parking lot that I decided to take the initiative.

"We need to talk," I said, getting out my keys.

"I'm beat."

"It's almost five o'clock," I said. "Why don't you come to my house for dinner?"

He stared off across the parking lot, squinting in the sun. I could not tell if he was in a rage or on the verge of tears, and I wasn't sure I'd ever seen him this out of sorts.

"Are you angry with me, Marino?"

"No, Doc. Right now I just want to be alone."

"Right now, I don't think you should be."

Fastening the top button of his coat, he muttered, "See ya later," and walked off.

I drove home, absolutely drained, and was mindlessly puttering in the kitchen when my doorbell rang. Looking through the peephole, I was amazed to see Marino.

"I had this in my pocket," he explained the instant I opened the door. He handed me his canceled plane ticket and inconsequential paperwork from the rental car. "Thought you might need it for your tax records or whatever."

"Thank you," I said, and I knew this was not why he had come. I had charge card receipts. Nothing he had given to me was necessary. "I was just fixing dinner. You might as well stay since you're already here."

"Maybe for a little while." He would not meet my eyes. "Then I got things to do."

Following me into the kitchen, he sat at the table while I resumed slicing sweet red peppers and adding them to chopped onions sautéing in olive oil.

"You know where the bourbon is," I said, stirring.

He got up, heading to the bar.

"While you're at it," I called after him, "would you please fix me a Scotch and soda?"

He did not reply, but when he came back he set my drink on the counter nearby and leaned against the butcher's block. I added the onions and peppers to tomatoes sautéing in another pan, then began browning sausage.

"I don't have a second course," I apologized as I worked.

"Don't look to me like you need one."

"Spring lamb with white wine, breast of veal, or roast pork would be perfect." I filled a pot with water and set it on the stove. "I'm pretty amazing with lamb, but I'll have to give you a rain check."

"Maybe you ought to forget cutting up dead bodies and open a restaurant."

"I'll assume you mean that as a compliment."

"Oh, yeah." His face was expressionless, and he was lighting a cigarette. "So what do you call this?" He nodded at the stove.

"I call it yellow and green broad noodles with sweet peppers and sausage," I replied, adding the sausage to the sauce. "But if I really wanted to impress you, I would call it *le papardelle del Cantunzein.*"

"Don't worry. I'm impressed."

"Marino." I glanced over at him. "What happened this morning?"

He replied with a question, "You mention to anyone what Vessey told you about the hack mark's being made with a serrated blade?"

"So far, you're the only person I've told."

"Hard to figure how Hilda Ozimek came up with that, with the hunting knife with a serrated edge she claims popped into her mind when Pat Harvey took her to the rest stop."

"It is hard to understand," I agreed, placing pasta in the boiling water. "There are some things in life that can't be reasoned away or explained, Marino."

Fresh pasta takes only seconds to cook, and I drained it and transferred it to a bowl kept warm in the oven. Adding the sauce, I tossed in butter and grated fresh Parmesan, then told Marino we were ready to eat.

"I've got artichoke hearts in the refrigerator." I served our plates. "But no salad. I do have bread in the freezer."

"This is all I need," he said, his mouth full. "It's good. Real good."

I had barely touched my meal when he was ready for a second helping. It was as though Marino had not eaten in a week. He was not taking care of himself, and it was showing. His tie was in serious need of a dry cleaner, the hem on one leg of his trousers had unraveled, and his shirt was stained yellow under the arms. Everything about him cried out that he was needy and neglected, and I was as repelled by this as I was disturbed. There was no reason why an intelligent grown man should allow himself to fall into poor repair like an abandoned house. Yet I knew his life was out of control, that in a way he could not help himself. Something was terribly wrong.

I got up and retrieved a bottle of Mondavi red wine from the wine rack.

"Marino," I said, pouring each of us a glass, "whose photograph did you show to Hilda? Was it your wife?"

He leaned back in his chair and would not look at me.

"You don't have to talk about it if you don't want to. But you haven't been yourself for quite a while. It's very apparent."

"What she said freaked me out," he replied.

"What Hilda said?"

"Yeah."

"Would you like to tell me about it?"

"I haven't told no one about it." He paused, reaching for his wine. His face was hard, eyes humiliated. "She went back to Jersey last November."

"I'm not sure you've ever told me your wife's name."

"Wow," he muttered bitterly. "Ain't that a comment."

"Yes, it is. You keep an awful lot to yourself."

"I've always been that way. But I guess being a cop has made it worse. I'm so used to hearing the guys bitch and moan about their wives, girlfriends, kids. They cry on your shoulder, you think they're your brothers. Then when it's your turn to have a problem, you make the mistake of spilling your guts and next thing it's all the hell over the police department. I learned a long time ago to keep my mouth shut."

He paused, getting out his wallet. "Her name's Doris." He handed me the snapshot he had shown Hilda Ozimek this morning.

Doris had a good face and a round, comfortable body. She was standing stiffly, dressed for church, her expression self-conscious and reluctant. I had seen her a hundred times, for the world was full of Dorises. They were the sweet young women who sat on porch swings dreaming of love as they stared into nights magic with stars and the smells of summer. They were mirrors, their images of themselves reflections of the significant people in their lives. They derived their importance from the services they rendered, survived by killing off their expectations in inches, and then one day woke up mad as hell.

"We would've been married thirty years this June," Marino said as I returned the photograph. "Then suddenly she ain't happy. Says I work too much, never around. She don't know me. Things like that. But I wasn't born yesterday. That's not the real story."

"Then what is?"

"It got started last summer when her mother had a stroke. Doris went to look after her. Was up north for almost a month, getting her mother out of the hospital and into a nursing home, taking care of everything. When Doris came home, she was different. It's like she was somebody else."

"What do you think happened?"

"I know she met this guy up there whose wife died a couple years back. He's into real estate, was helping sell her mother's house. Doris mentioned him once or twice like it was no big deal. But something was going on. The phone would ring late, and when I answered it, the person would hang up. Doris would rush out to get the mail before I did. Then in November, she suddenly packs up and leaves, says her mother needs her."

"Has she been home since?" I asked.

He shook his head. "Oh, she calls now and then. She wants a divorce."

"Marino, I'm sorry."

"Her mother's in this home, you see. And Doris is looking after her, seeing this real estate guy, I guess. Upset one minute, happy the next. Like she wants to come back, but don't want to. Guilty, then don't give a damn. It's just like Hilda said when she was looking at her picture. Back and forth."

"Very painful for you."

"Hey." He tossed his napkin on the table. "She can do what she wants. Screw her."

I knew he did not mean that. He was devastated, and my heart ached for him. At the same time, I could not help but feel sympathy for his wife. Marino would not be easy to love.

"Do you want her to come home?"

"I've been with her longer than I was alive before we met. But let's face it, Doc." He glanced at me, his eyes frightened. "My life sucks. Always counting nickels and dimes, called out on the street in the middle of the night. Plan vacations and then something goes down and Doris unpacks and waits at home—like Labor Day weekend when the Harvey girl and her boyfriend disappeared. That was the last straw."

"Do you love Doris?"

"She don't believe I do."

"Maybe you should make sure she understands how you feel," I said. "Maybe you should show that you want her a lot and don't need her so much."

"I don't get it." He looked bewildered.

He would never get it, I thought, depressed.

"Just take care of yourself," I told him. "Don't expect her to do that for you. Maybe it will make a difference."

"I don't earn enough bucks, and that's it, chapter and verse."

"I'll bet your wife doesn't care so much about money. She'd rather feel important and loved."

"He's got a big house and a Chrysler New Yorker. Brand-new, with leather seats, the whole nine yards."

I did not reply.

"Last year he went to Hawaii for his vacation." Marino was getting angry.

"Doris spent most of her life with you. That was her choice, Hawaii or not—"

"Hawaii's nothing but a tourist trap," he cut in, lighting a cigarette. "Me, I'd rather go to Buggs Island and fish."

"Has it occurred to you that Doris might have grown weary of being your mother?"

"She ain't my mother," he snapped.

"Then why is it that since she left, you've begun looking like you desperately need a mother, Marino?"

"Because I don't got time to sew buttons on, cook, and clean, do shit like that."

"I'm busy, too. I find time for shit like that."

"Yeah, you also got a maid. You also probably earn a hundred G's a year."

"I would take care of myself if I earned only ten G's a year," I said. "I would do it because I have self-respect and because I *don't want* anyone to take care of me. I simply want to be cared for, and there's a very big difference between the two."

"If you got all the answers, Doc, then how come you're divorced? And how come your friend Mark's in Colorado and you're here? Don't sound to me like you wrote the book on relationships."

I felt a flush creeping up my neck. "Tony did not truly care for me, and when I finally figured that out, I left. As for Mark, he has a problem with commitments."

"And you were committed to him?" Marino almost glared at me.

I did not respond.

"How come you didn't go out west with him? Maybe you're only committed to being a chief."

"We were having problems, and certainly part of it was my fault. Mark was angry, went out west . . . maybe to make a point, maybe just to get away from me," I said, dismayed that I could not keep the emotion out of my voice. "Professionally, my going with him wouldn't have been possible, but it was never an option."

Marino suddenly looked ashamed. "I'm sorry. I didn't know that."

I was silent.

"Sounds like you and me are in the same boat," he offered.

"In some ways," I said, and I did not want to admit to myself what those ways were. "But I'm taking care of myself. If Mark ever reappears, he won't find me looking like hell, my life down the drain. I want him, but I don't *need* him. Maybe you ought to try that with Doris?"

"Yeah." He seemed encouraged. "Maybe I will. I think I'm ready for coffee."

"Do you know how to fix it?"

"You gotta be kidding," he said, surprised.

"Lesson number one, Marino. Fixing coffee. Step this way."

While I showed him the technical wonders of a drip coffee maker that required nothing more than a fifty IQ, he resumed contemplating this day's adventures.

"A part of me don't want to take what Hilda said seriously," he explained. "But another part of me has to. I mean, it sure gave me second thoughts."

"In what way?"

"Deborah Harvey was shot with a nine-millimeter. They never found the shell. Kind of hard to believe the squirrel could collect the shell out there in the dark. Makes me think Morrell and the rest of them wasn't looking in the right place. Remember, Hilda wondered if there wasn't another place, and she mentioned something lost. Something metal that had to do with war. That could be a spent shell."

"She also said this object wasn't harmful," I reminded him.

"A spent shell couldn't hurt a fly. It's the bullet that's harmful, and only when it's being fired."

"And the photographs she looked at were taken last fall," I went on. "Whatever this lost item is may have been out there then but isn't there now."

"You thinking the killer came back during daylight to look for it?"

"Hilda said the person who lost this metal object was concerned about it."

"I don't think he went back," Marino said. "He's too careful for that. Be a big damn risk. The area was crawling with cops and bloodhounds right after the kids disappeared. You can bet the killer laid low. He's got to be pretty cool to have gotten away with what he's doing for so long, whether we're talking about a psychopath or a paid hit man."

"Maybe," I said as the coffee began to drip.

"I think we should go back out there and poke around a little. You up for it?"

"Frankly, the idea has crossed my mind."

8

IN THE LIGHT of a clear afternoon, the woods did not seem so ominous until Marino and I drew closer to the small clearing. Then the faint, foul odor of decomposing human flesh was an insidious reminder. Pine tags and leaves had been displaced and piled in small mounds by the scraping of shovels and emptying of sieves. It would take time and hard rains before the tangible remnants of murder were no longer to be found in this place.

Marino had brought a metal detector and I carried a rake. He got out his cigarettes and looked around.

"Don't see any point in scanning right here," he said. "It's been gone over half a dozen times."

"I assume the path's been gone over thoroughly as well," I said, staring back at the trail we had followed from the logging road.

"Not necessarily, because the path didn't exist when the couple was taken out here last fall."

I realized what he was saying. The trail of displaced leaves and hard-packed dirt had been made by police officers and other interested parties going back and forth from the logging road to the scene.

Surveying the woods, he added, "The fact is, we don't even know where they was parked, Doc. It's easy to assume it's close to where we parked, and that they got here pretty much the same way we did. But it depends on whether the killer was actually *heading* here."

"I have a feeling the killer knew where he was going," I replied.

"It doesn't make sense to think he randomly turned down the logging road and then ended up out here after haphazardly wandering around in the dark."

Shrugging, Marino switched on the metal detector. "Can't hurt to give it a try."

We began at the perimeter of the scene, scanning the path, sweeping yards of undergrowth and leaves on either side as we slowly made our way back toward the logging road. For almost two hours we probed any opening in trees and brush that looked remotely promising for human passage, the detector's first high-frequency tone rewarding our efforts with an Old Milwaukee beer can, the second with a rusty bottle opener. The third alert did not sound until we were at the edge of the woods, within sight of our car, where we uncovered a shotgun shell, the red plastic faded by the years.

Leaning against the rake, I stared dismally back down the path, thinking. I pondered what Hilda had said about another place being involved, perhaps somewhere that the killer had taken Deborah, and I envisioned the clearing and the bodies. My first thought had been that if Deborah had broken free of the killer at some point, it may have been when she and Fred were being led in the dark from the logging road to the clearing. But as I looked through the woods, this theory didn't really make sense.

"Let's accept as a given that we're dealing with one killer," I said to Marino.

"Okay, I'm listening." He wiped his damp forehead on his coat sleeve.

"If you were the killer and had abducted two people and then forced them, perhaps at gunpoint, to come out here, who would you kill first?"

"The guy's going to be a bigger problem," he said without pause. "Me, I'm going to take him out first and save the little girl for last."

It was still difficult to imagine. When I tried to envision one person forcing two hostages to walk through these woods after dark, I continued to draw a blank. Did the killer have a flashlight? Did he know this area so well he could find the clearing blindfolded? I voiced these questions aloud to Marino.

"I've been trying to see the same thing," he said. "A couple ideas come to mind. First, he probably restrained them, tied their hands behind their back. Second, if it was me, I'd hold on to the girl, have the gun to her ribs while we're walking through the woods. This would make the boyfriend as gentle as a lamb. One false move, and his girl gets blown away. As for a flashlight? He had to have had some way of seeing out here."

"How are you going to hold a gun, a flashlight, and the girl at the same time?" I asked.

"Easy. Want me to show you?"

"Not particularly." I backed away as he reached toward me.

"The rake. Geez, Doc. Don't be so damn jumpy."

He handed me the metal detector and I gave him the rake.

"Pretend the rake's Deborah, okay? I'm yoking her around the neck with my left arm, the flashlight in my left hand, like this." He demonstrated. "In my right hand I've got the gun, which is stuck against her ribs. No problem. Fred's gonna be a couple feet in front of us, following the beam of the flashlight while I watch him like a hawk." Pausing, Marino stared down the path. "They're not going to be moving very fast."

"Especially if they're barefoot," I pointed out.

"Yeah, and I'm thinking they were. He can't tie up their feet if he's going to walk them out here. But if he makes them take off their shoes, then that's going to slow them down, make it harder for them to run. Maybe after he whacks them, he keeps the shoes as souvenirs."

"Maybe." I was thinking about Deborah's purse again.

I said, "If Deborah's hands were bound behind her back, then how did her purse get out here? It didn't have a strap, no way to loop it over her arm or shoulder. It wasn't attached to a belt, in fact it doesn't appear she was wearing a belt. And if someone were forcing you out into the woods at gunpoint, why would you take your purse with you?"

"Got no idea. That's been bothering me from the start."

"Let's give it one last try," I said.

"Oh, shit."

By the time we got back to the clearing, clouds had passed over the sun and it was getting windy, making it seem that the temperature had dropped ten degrees. Damp beneath my coat from exertion, I was cold, the muscles in my arms trembling from raking. Moving to the perimeter farthest from the path, I studied an area beyond which stretched a terrain so uninviting that I doubted even hunters ventured there. The police had dug and sifted maybe ten feet in this direction before running into an infestation of kudzu that had metastasized over the better part of an acre. Trees covered in the vine's green mail looked like prehistoric dinosaurs rearing up over a solid green sea. Every living bush, pine, and plant was slowly being strangled to death.

"Good God," Marino said as I waded out with my rake. "You're not serious."

"We won't go very far," I promised.

We did not have to.

The metal detector responded almost immediately. The tone got louder and higher pitched as Marino positioned the scanner over an area of kudzu less than fifteen feet from where the bodies had been found. I discovered that raking kudzu was worse than combing snarled hair and finally resorted to dropping to my knees and ripping off leaves and feeling around roots with fingers sheathed in surgical gloves until I felt something cold and hard that I knew wasn't what I was hoping for.

"Save it for the tollbooth," I said dejectedly, tossing Marino a dirty quarter.

Several feet away the metal detector signaled us again, and this time my rooting around on hands and knees paid off. When I felt the unmistakable hard, cylindrical shape, I gently parted kudzu until I saw the gleam of stainless steel, a cartridge case still as shiny as polished silver. I gingerly plucked it out, touching as little of its surface as possible, while Marino bent over and held open a plastic evidence bag.

"Nine-millimeter, Federal," he said, reading the head stamp through plastic. "I'll be damned."

"He was standing right around here when he shot her," I muttered, a strange sensation running along my nerves as I recalled what Hilda had said about Deborah's being in a place "crowded" with things "grabbing" at her. *Kudzu.*

"If she was shot at close range," Marino said, "then she went down not too far from here."

Wading out a little farther as he followed me with the metal detector, I said, "How the hell did he *see* to shoot her, Marino? Lord. Can you imagine this place at night?"

"The moon was out."

"But it wasn't full," I said.

"Full enough so it wouldn't have been pitch-dark."

The weather had been checked months ago. The Friday night of August thirty-first when the couple had disappeared, the temperature had been in the upper sixties, the moon three-quarters full, the sky clear. Even if the killer had been armed with a powerful flashlight, I still could not understand how he could force two hostages out here at night without being as disoriented and vulnerable as they were. All I could imagine was confusion, a lot of stumbling about.

Why didn't he just kill them on the logging road, drag their bodies several yards into the woods, and then drive away? Why did he want to bring them out here?

And yet the pattern was the same with the other couples. Their bodies also had been found in remote, wooded areas like this.

Looking around at the kudzu, an unpleasant expression on his face, Marino said, "Glad as hell this ain't snake weather."

"That's a lovely thought," I said, unnerved.

"You want to keep going?" he asked in a tone that told me he had no interest in venturing an inch farther into this gothic wasteland.

"I think we've had enough for one day." I waded out of the kudzu as quickly as possible, my flesh crawling. The mention of snakes had done me in. I was on the verge of a full-blown anxiety attack.

It was almost five, the woods gloomy with shadows as we headed back to the car. Every time a twig snapped beneath Marino's feet, my heart jumped. Squirrels scampering up trees and birds flying off branches were startling intrusions upon the eerie silence.

"I'll drop this off at the lab first thing in the morning," he said. "Then I gotta be in court. Great way to spend your day off."

"Which case?"

"The case of Bubba shot by his friend named Bubba, the only witness was another drone named Bubba."

"You're not serious."

"Hey," he said, unlocking the car doors, "I'm as serious as a sawed-off shotgun." Starting the engine, he muttered, "I'm starting to hate this job, Doc. I swear, I really am."

"At the moment you hate the whole world, Marino."

"No, I don't," he said, and he actually laughed. "I like you all right."

The last day of January began when the morning's mail brought an official communication from Pat Harvey. Brief and to the point, it stated that if copies of her daughter's autopsy and toxicology reports were not received by the end of the following week, she would get a court order. A copy of the letter had been sent to my immediate boss, the Commissioner of Health and Human Services, whose secretary was on the phone within the hour summoning me to his office.

While autopsies awaited me downstairs, I left the building and made the short walk along Franklin to Main Street Station, which had been vacant for years, then converted into a short-lived shopping mall before the state had purchased it. In a sense, the historic red building with its clock tower and red tile roof had become a train station again, a temporary stop for state employees forced to relocate while the Madison Building was stripped of asbestos and renovated. The Governor had appointed Dr. Paul Sessions commissioner two years before, and though face-to-face meetings with my new boss were infrequent, they were pleasant enough. I had a feeling today might prove a different story. His secretary had sounded apologetic on the phone, as if she knew I were being called in to be gaffed.

The commissioner resided in a suite of offices on the second level, accessible by a marble stairway worn smooth by travelers scuffing up and down steps in an era long past. The spaces the commissioner had appropriated had once been a sporting goods store and a boutique selling colorful kites and wind socks. Walls had been knocked out, plate glass windows filled in with brick, his offices carpeted, paneled, and arranged with handsome furnishings. Dr. Sessions was familiar enough with the sluggish workings of government to have settled into his temporary headquarters as if the relocation were permanent.

His secretary greeted me with a sympathetic smile that made me feel only worse as she swiveled around from her keyboard and reached for the phone.

She announced that I was here, and immediately the solid oak door across from her desk opened and Dr. Sessions invited me in.

An energetic man with thinning brown hair and large-framed glasses that swallowed his narrow face, he was living proof that marathon running was never intended for human beings. His chest was tubercular, body fat so low he rarely took his suit jacket off and frequently wore long sleeves in the summer because he was chronically cold. He still wore a splint on the left arm he had broken several months ago while running a race on the West Coast and getting tangled up in a coathanger that had eluded the feet of runners ahead of him and sent him crashing to the street. He was, perhaps, the only contender not to finish the race and end up in the newspapers anyway.

He seated himself behind his desk, the letter from Pat Harvey centered on the blotter, his face unusually stern.

"I assume you've already seen this?" He tapped the letter with an index finger.

"Yes," I said. "Understandably, Pat Harvey is very interested in the results of her daughter's examination."

"Deborah Harvey's body was found eleven days ago. Am I to conclude you don't yet know what killed her or Fred Cheney?"

"I know what killed her. His cause of death is still undetermined."

He looked puzzled. "Dr. Scarpetta, would you care to explain to me why this information has not been released to the Harveys or to Fred Cheney's father?"

"My explanation is simple," I said. "Their cases are still pending as further special studies are conducted. And the FBI has asked me to withhold releasing anything to anyone."

"I see." He gazed at the wall as if it contained a window to look out of, which it did not.

"If you direct me to release my reports, I will do so, Dr. Sessions. In fact, I would be relieved if you would order me to meet Pat Harvey's request."

"Why?" He knew the answer, but he wanted to hear what I had to say.

"Because Mrs. Harvey and her husband have a right to know what happened to their daughter," I said. "Bruce Cheney has a right to hear what we do or don't know about his son. The wait is anguish for them."

"Have you talked to Mrs. Harvey?"

"Not recently."

"Have you talked to her since the bodies were found, Dr. Scarpetta?" He was fidgeting with his sling.

"I called her when the identifications were confirmed, but I haven't talked with her since."

"Has she tried to reach you?"

"She has."

"And you have refused to talk to her?"

"I've already explained why I'm not talking to her," I said. "And

I don't believe it would be politic for me to get on the phone and tell her that the FBI doesn't want me to release information to her."

"You haven't mentioned the FBI's directive to anyone, then."

"I just mentioned it to you."

He recrossed his legs. "And I appreciate that. But it would be inappropriate to mention this business to anybody else. Especially reporters."

"I've been doing my best to avoid reporters."

"The *Washington Post* called me this morning."

"Who from the *Post*?"

He began sorting through message slips as I waited uneasily. I did not want to believe that Abby would go behind my back and over my head.

"Someone named Clifford Ring." He glanced up. "Actually, it's not the first time he's called, nor am I the only person he's attempted to milk for information. He's also been badgering my secretary and other members of my staff, including my deputy and the Secretary of Human Resources. I assume he's called you as well, which was why he finally resorted to administration, because, as he put it, 'the medical examiner won't talk to me.'"

"A lot of reporters have called. I don't remember most of their names."

"Well, Mr. Ring seems to think there's some sort of cover-up going on, something conspiratorial, and based on the direction of his questioning, he seems to have information that buttresses this."

Strange, I thought. It didn't sound to me as if the *Post* was holding off on investigating these cases, as Abby had stated so emphatically.

"He's under the impression," the commissioner continued, "that your office is stonewalling, and that it's therefore part of this so-called conspiracy."

"And I suppose we are." I worked hard to keep the annoyance out of my voice. "And that leaves me caught in the middle. Either I defy Pat Harvey or the Justice Department, and frankly, given a choice, I would prefer to accommodate Mrs. Harvey. Eventually, I will have to answer to her. She is Deborah's mother. I don't have to answer to the FBI."

"I'm not interested in antagonizing the Justice Department," Dr. Sessions said.

He did not have to outline why. A substantial portion of the commissioner's departmental budget was supplied by money from federal grants, some of which trickled down to my office to subsidize the collection of data needed by various injury prevention and traffic safety agencies. The Justice Department knew how to play hardball. If antagonizing the feds did not dry up much-needed revenues, we could at least count on our lives being made miserable. The last thing the commissioner wanted was to account for every pencil and sheet of stationery purchased with grant money. I knew how it worked. All of us would be nickel-and-dimed, papered to death.

The commissioner reached for the letter with his good arm and studied it for a moment.

He said, "Actually, the only answer may be for Mrs. Harvey to go through with her threat."

"If she gets a court order, then I will have no choice but to send her what she wants."

"I realize that. And the advantage is the FBI can't hold us accountable. The disadvantage, obviously, will be the negative publicity," he thought aloud. "Certainly, it won't shine a good light on the Department of Health and Human Services if the public knows we were forced by a judge to give Pat Harvey what she is entitled to by law. I suppose it may corroborate our friend Mr. Ring's suspicions."

The average citizen didn't even know that the Medical Examiner's Office was part of Health and Human Services. I was the one who was going to look bad. The commissioner, in good bureaucratic fashion, was setting me up to take it on the nose because he had no intention of aggravating the Justice Department.

"Of course," he considered, "Pat Harvey will come across as rather heavy-handed, as using her office to throw her weight around. She may be bluffing."

"I doubt it," I said tersely.

"We'll see." He got up from his desk and showed me to the door. "I'll write Mrs. Harvey, saying you and I talked."

I'll just bet you will, I thought.

"Let me know if I can be of any assistance." He smiled, avoiding my eyes.

I had just let him know I needed assistance. He might as well have had two broken arms. He wasn't going to lift a finger.

As soon as I got back to the office, I asked the clerks up front and Rose if a reporter from the *Post* had been calling. After searching memories and digging through old message slips, no one could come up with a Clifford Ring. He couldn't exactly accuse me of stonewalling if he'd never tried to reach me, I reasoned. All the same, I was perplexed.

"By the way," Rose added as I headed down the hall, "Linda's been looking for you, says she needs to see you right away."

Linda was a firearms examiner. Marino must have been by with the cartridge case, I thought. Good.

The toolmarks and firearms laboratory was on the third floor and could have passed for a used-gun shop. Revolvers, rifles, shotguns, and pistols covered virtually every inch of counter space, and evidence wrapped in brown paper was stacked chest high on the floor. I was about to decide that everyone was at lunch when I heard the muffled explosions of a gun discharging behind closed doors. Adjoining the lab was a small room used to test-fire weapons into a galvanized steel tank filled with water.

Two rounds later Linda emerged, .38 Special in one hand, spent bullets and cartridge cases in the other. She was slender and feminine, with long brown hair, good bones, and wide-spaced hazel eyes. A lab coat protected a flowing black skirt and pale yellow silk blouse with a gold circle pin at the throat. Were I sitting next to her on a plane and trying to guess her profession, teaching poetry or running an art gallery would have come to mind.

"Bad news, Kay," she said, setting the revolver and spent ammunition on her desk.

"I hope it doesn't pertain to the cartridge case Marino brought in," I said.

"Afraid it does. I was about to etch my initials and a lab number on it when I got a little surprise." She moved over to the comparison microscope. "Here." She offered me the chair. "A picture's worth a thousand words."

Seating myself, I peered into the lenses. In the field of light to my left was the stainless-steel cartridge case.

"I don't understand," I muttered, adjusting the focus.

Etched inside the cartridge case's mouth were the initials "J.M."

"I thought Marino receipted this to you." I looked up at her.

"He did. He came by about an hour ago," Linda said. "I asked him if he etched these initials, and he said he didn't. Not that I really thought he had. Marino's initials are P.M., not J.M., and he's been around long enough to know better."

Though some detectives initialed cartridge cases just as some medical examiners initialed bullets recovered from bodies, the fire-arms examiners discouraged the practice. Taking a stylus to metal is risky because there's always the threat one might scratch breech block, firing pin, ejector marks, or other features, such as lands and grooves, suitable for identification. Marino did know better. Like me, he always initialed the plastic bag and left the evidence inside untouched.

"Am I to believe these initials were *already* on this cartridge case when Marino brought it in?" I asked.

"Apparently so."

J.M. *Jay Morrell*, I thought, mystified. Why would a cartridge case left at the scene be marked with his initials?

Linda proposed, "I'm wondering if a police officer working the scene out there had this in his pocket for some reason, and inadvertently lost it. If he had a hole in his pocket, for example?"

"I'd find that hard to believe," I said.

"Well, I've got one other theory I'll toss out. But you aren't going to like it, and I don't like it much, either. The cartridge case could have been reloaded."

"Then why would it be marked with an investigator's initials? Who on earth would reload a cartridge case marked as evidence?"

"It's happened before, Kay, and you didn't hear this from me, all right?"

I just listened.

"The number of weapons and the amount of ammunition and cartridge cases collected by the police and submitted to the courts are astronomical and worth a lot of money. People get greedy, even judges. They take the stuff for themselves or sell it to gun dealers, other enthusiasts. I suppose it's remotely possible this cartridge case was collected by a police officer or submitted to the courts as evidence at some point, and ended up reloaded. It may be that whoever fired it had no idea someone's initials were etched inside it."

"We can't prove that this cartridge case belongs to the bullet I found in Deborah Harvey's lumbar spine, and won't be able to do so unless we recover the pistol," I reminded her. "We can't even say with certainty it's from a Hydra-Shok cartridge. All we know is it's nine-millimeter, Federal.

"True. But Federal holds the patent for Hydra-Shok ammunition, has since the late eighties. For whatever that's worth."

"Does Federal sell Hydra-Shok bullets for reloading?" I asked.

"That's the problem. No. Only the cartridges are available on the market. But that doesn't mean someone couldn't get hold of the bullets in some other way. Steal them from the factory, have a contact who steals them from the factory. I could get them, for example, if I claimed I were working on a special project. Who knows?" She retrieved a can of Diet Coke from her desk, adding, "Nothing much surprises me anymore."

"Is Marino aware of what you found?"

"I called him."

"Thank you, Linda," I said, getting up, and I was formulating my own theory, which was quite different from hers and, unfortunately, more probable. Just the thought of it made me furious. In my office I snatched up the phone and dialed Marino's pager number. He returned my call almost immediately.

"The little fuckhead," he said right off.

"Who? Linda?" I asked, startled.

"Morrell, that's who. The lying son of a bitch. Just got off the phone with him. Said he didn't know what I was talking about until I accused him of stealing evidence for reloads—asked him if he was stealing guns and live ammo, too. Said I'd have his ass investigated by Internal Affairs. Then he started singing."

"He etched his initials in the cartridge case and left it out there deliberately, didn't he, Marino?"

"Oh, yeah. They found the goddam cartridge case last week. The real one. Then the asshole leaves this goddam plant, starts whining that he was just doing what the FBI told him to do."

"Where is the real cartridge case?" I demanded, blood pounding in my temples.

"The FBI lab's got it. You and yours truly spent an entire afternoon in the woods, and guess what, Doc? The whole goddam time we was being watched. The place is under physical surveillance. Just a damn good thing neither one of us wandered behind a bush to take a piss, right?"

"Have you talked to Benton?"

"Hell, no. As far as I'm concerned, he can screw himself." Marino slammed down the receiver.

9

THERE WAS SOMETHING REASSURING about the Globe and Laurel that made me feel safe. Brick, with simple lines and not a hint of ostentation, the restaurant occupied a sliver of northern Virginia real estate in Triangle, near the U.S. Marine Corps base. The narrow strip of lawn in front was always tidy, boxwoods neatly pruned, the parking lot orderly, every car within the painted boundaries of its allotted space.

Semper Fidelis was over the door, and stepping inside I was welcomed by the cream of the "always faithful" crop: police chiefs, four-star generals, secretaries of defense, directors of the FBI and CIA, the photographs so familiar to me that the men sternly smiling in them seemed a host of long-lost friends. Maj. Jim Yancey, whose bronzed combat boots from Vietnam were on top of the piano across from the bar, strode across red Highland tartan carpet and intercepted me.

"Dr. Scarpetta," he said, grinning as he shook my hand. "I was afraid you didn't like the food when last you were here, and that's why you waited so long to come back."

The major's casual attire of turtleneck sweater and corduroy trousers could not camouflage his former profession. He was as military as a campaign hat, posture proudly straight, not an ounce of fat, white hair in a buzz cut. Past retirement age, he still looked fit enough for combat, and it wasn't hard for me to imagine him bumping over rugged terrain in a Jeep or eating rations from a can in the jungle while monsoon rains hammered down.

"I've never had a bad meal here, and you know it," I said warmly.

"You're looking for Benton, and he's looking for you. The old boy's around there"—he pointed—"in his usual foxhole."

"Thank you, Jim. I know the way. And it's so good to see you again."

He winked at me and returned to the bar.

It was Mark who had introduced me to Major Yancey's restaurant when I drove to Quantico two weekends every month to see him. As I walked beneath a ceiling covered with police patches and passed displays of old Corps memorabilia, recollections tugged at my heart. I could pick out the tables where Mark and I had sat, and it seemed odd to see strangers there now, engaged in their own private conversations. I had not been to the Globe in almost a year.

Leaving the main dining room, I headed for a more secluded section where Wesley was waiting for me in his "foxhole," a corner table before a window with red draperies. He was sipping a drink and did not smile as we greeted each other formally. A waiter in a black tuxedo appeared to take my drink order.

Wesley looked up at me with eyes as impenetrable as a bank vault, and I responded in kind. He had signaled the first round, and we were going to come out swinging.

"I am very concerned that we're having a problem with communication, Kay," he began.

"My sentiments exactly," I said with the iron-hard calm I had perfected on the witness stand. "I, too, am concerned by our problem with communication. Is the Bureau tapping my phone, tailing me as well? I hope whoever was hiding in the woods got good photographs of Marino and me."

Wesley said just as calmly, "You, personally, are not under surveillance. The wooded area where you and Marino were spotted yesterday afternoon is under surveillance."

"Perhaps if you had kept me informed," I said, holding in my anger, "I might have told you in advance when Marino and I had decided to go back out there."

"It never occurred to me you might."

"I routinely pay retrospective visits to scenes. You've worked with me long enough to be aware of that."

"My mistake. But now you know. And I would prefer that you not go back out there again."

"I have no plans to do so," I said testily. "But should the need arise, I will be happy to give you advance warning. Might as well, since you'll find out anyway. And I certainly don't need to waste my time picking up evidence that has been planted by your agents or the police."

"Kay," he said in a softer tone, "I'm not trying to interfere with your job."

"I'm being lied to, Benton. I'm told no cartridge case was recovered from the scene, only to discover it was receipted to the Bureau's laboratory more than a week ago."

"When we decided to set up surveillance, we didn't want word of it to leak," he said. "The fewer people told about what we were up to the better."

"Obviously, you must be assuming the killer might return to the scene."

"It's a possibility."

"Did you entertain this possibility with the first four cases?"

"It's different this time."

"Why?"

"Because he left evidence, and he knows it."

"If he were so worried about the cartridge case, he had plenty of time to go back and look for it last fall," I said.

"He may not know we would figure out Deborah Harvey was shot, that a Hydra-Shok bullet would be recovered from her body."

"I don't believe the individual we're dealing with is stupid," I said.

The waiter returned with my Scotch and soda.

Wesley went on, "The cartridge case you recovered was planted. I won't deny that. And yes, you and Marino walked into an area under physical surveillance. There were two men hiding in the woods. They saw everything the two of you did, including picking up the cartridge case. Had you not called me, I would have called you."

"I'd like to think you would have."

"I would have explained. Would have had no choice, really, because you inadvertently upset the apple cart. And you're right." He reached for his drink. "I should have let you know in advance; then none of this would have happened and we wouldn't have been forced to call things off, or better put, postpone them."

"What have you postponed, exactly?"

"Had you and Marino not stumbled upon what we were doing, tomorrow morning's news would have carried a story targeted at the killer." He paused. "Disinformation to draw him out, make him worry. The story will run, but not until Monday."

"And the point of it?" I asked.

"We want him to think that something turned up during the examination of the bodies. Something to make us believe he left important evidence at the scene. Alleged this, alleged that, with plenty of denials and no comments from the police. All of it intended to imply that whatever this evidence is, we've had no luck finding it yet. The killer knows he left a cartridge case out there. If he gets sufficiently paranoid and returns to look for it, we'll be waiting, watching him pick up the one we planted, get it on film, and then grab him."

"The cartridge case is worthless unless you have him and the gun. Why would he risk returning to the scene, especially if it appears that the police are busy looking around out there for this evidence?" I wanted to know.

"He may be worried about a lot of things, because he lost control of the situation. Had to have, or it would not have been necessary to shoot Deborah in the back. It might not have been necessary to shoot her at all. It appears he murdered Cheney without using a gun. How does he know what we're really looking for, Kay? Maybe it's a cartridge case. Maybe it's something else. He isn't going to be certain about the exact condition of the bodies when they were found. We don't know what he did to the couple, and he doesn't really know what you may have discovered while doing the autopsies. And he might not go back out there the day after the story runs, but he might try it a week or two later if everything seems quiet."

"I doubt your disinformation tactic will work," I said.

"Nothing ventured, nothing gained. The killer left evidence. We'd be foolish not to act on that."

The opening was too wide for me to resist walking through it. "And have you acted on evidence found in the first four cases, Benton? It's my understanding that a jack of hearts was recovered inside each of the vehicles. A detail you apparently have worked very hard to suppress."

"Who told you this?" he asked, the expression on his face unchanged. He did not even look surprised.

"Is it true?"

"Yes."

"And did you find a card in the Harvey-Cheney case?"

Wesley stared off across the room, nodding at the waiter. "I recommend the filet mignon." He opened his menu. "That or the lamb chops."

I placed my order as my heart pounded. I lit a cigarette, unable to relax, my mind frenetically groping for a way to break through.

"You didn't answer my question."

"I don't see how it is relevant to your role in the investigation," he said.

"The police waited hours before calling me to the scene. The bodies had been moved, tampered with, by the time I got there. I'm being stonewalled by investigators, you've asked me to indefinitely pend the cause and manner of Fred's and Deborah's deaths. Meanwhile, Pat Harvey is threatening to get a court order because I won't release my findings." I paused. He remained unflappable.

"Finally," I concluded, my words beginning to bite, "I make a retrospective visit to a scene without knowing it's under surveillance or that the evidence I collected was planted. And you don't think the details of these cases are relevant to my role in the investigation? I'm no longer sure I even have a role in the investigation. Or at least you seem determined to make sure I don't have one."

"I'm not doing anything of the sort."

"Then someone is."

He did not reply.

"If a jack of hearts was found inside Deborah's Jeep or somewhere near their bodies, it's important for me to know. It would link the deaths of all five couples. When there's a serial killer on the loose in Virginia, it is of great concern to me."

Then he caught me off guard. "How much have you been telling Abby Turnbull?"

"I haven't been telling her anything," I said, my heart pounding harder.

"You've met with her, Kay. I'm sure you won't deny that."

"Mark told you, and I'm sure you won't deny that."

"Mark would have no reason to know you saw Abby in Richmond or Washington unless you told him. And in any event, he would have no reason to pass this along to me."

I stared at him. How could Wesley have known I had seen Abby in Washington unless she really was being watched?

"When Abby came to see me in Richmond," I said, "Mark called and I mentioned she was visiting. Are you telling me he said nothing to you?"

"He didn't."

"Then how did you find out?"

"There are some things I can't tell you. And you're just going to have to trust me."

The waiter set down our salads, and we ate in silence. Wesley did not speak again until our main courses arrived.

"I'm under a lot of pressure," he said in a quiet voice.

"I can see that. You look exhausted, run-down."

"Thank you, Doctor," he said ironically.

"You've changed in other ways as well." I pushed the point.

"I'm sure that is your perception."

"You're shutting me out, Benton."

"I suppose I keep my distance because you ask questions that I can't answer; so does Marino. And then I feel even more pressure. Do you understand?"

"I'm trying to understand," I said.

"I can't tell you everything. Can you let it go at that?"

"Not quite. Because that's where we're at cross-purposes. I have information you need. And you have information I need. I'm not going to show you mine unless you show me yours."

He surprised me by laughing.

"Do you think we can strike a deal under these terms?" I persisted.

"It looks like I don't have much of a choice."

"You don't," I said.

"Yes, we did find a jack of hearts in the Harvey-Cheney case. Yes, I did have their bodies moved before you arrived at the scene, and I know that was poor form, but you have no idea why the cards are so significant or the problems that would be precipitated by word of them leaking. If it made the newspapers, for example. I'm not going to say anything further about that right now."

"Where was the card?" I asked.

"We found it inside Deborah Harvey's purse. When a couple of the cops helped me turn her over, we found the purse under her body."

"Are you suggesting that the killer carried her purse out into the woods?"

"Yes. It wouldn't make any sense to think that Deborah carried her purse out there."

"In the other cases," I pointed out, "the card was left in plain sight inside the vehicle."

"Exactly. Where the card was found is just one more inconsistency. Why *wasn't* it left inside the Jeep? Another inconsistency is that the cards left in the other cases are Bicycle playing cards. The one left with Deborah is a different brand. Then there's the matter of fibers."

"What fibers?" I asked.

Though I had collected fibers from all of the decomposed bodies, most of them were consistent with the victims' own clothing or the upholstery of their vehicles. Unknown fibers—what few I had found—had supplied no link between the cases, had proved useless so far.

"In the four cases preceding Deborah's and Fred's murders," Wesley said, "white cotton fibers were recovered from the driver's seat of each abandoned car."

"That's news to me," I said, irritation flaring again.

"The fiber analysis was done by our labs," he explained.

"And what is your interpretation?" I asked.

"The pattern of fibers recovered is interesting. Since the victims weren't wearing white cotton clothing at the time of their deaths, I have to assume that the fibers were left by the perpetrator, and this places him driving the victims' cars after the crimes. But we've been assuming that all along. One has to consider his clothing. And a possibility is that he was wearing some type of uniform when he encountered the couples. White cotton trousers. I don't know. But no white cotton fibers were recovered from the driver's seat of Deborah Harvey's Jeep."

"What did you find inside her Jeep?" I asked.

"Nothing that tells me anything right now. In fact, the interior was immaculate." He paused, cutting his steak. "The point is, the MO's different enough in this case to worry me a lot, because of the other circumstances."

"Because one of the victims is the Drug Czar's daughter, and you're still considering that what happened to Deborah may have been politically motivated, related to her mother's antidrug endeavors," I said.

He nodded. "We can't rule out that the murders of Deborah and her boyfriend were disguised to resemble the other cases."

"If their deaths aren't related to the others, and were a hit," I asked skeptically, "then how do you explain their killer knowing about the cards, Benton? Even I didn't find out about the jack of hearts until recently. Certainly it hasn't been in the newspapers."

"Pat Harvey knows," he startled me by saying.

Abby, I thought. And I was willing to bet that Abby had divulged the detail to Mrs. Harvey, and that Wesley knew this.

"How long has Mrs. Harvey known about the cards?" I asked.

"When her daughter's Jeep was found, she asked me if we'd recovered a card. And she called me about it again after the bodies turned up."

"I don't understand," I said. "Why would she have known last fall? It sounds to me as if she knew the details of the other cases *before* Deborah and Fred disappeared."

"She knew some of the details. Pat Harvey was interested in these cases long before she had personal motivation."

"Why?"

"You've heard some of the theories," he said. "Drug overdoses. Some new weird designer drug on the street, the kids going out in the woods to party and ending up dead. Or some drug dealer who gets his thrills by selling bad stuff in some remote place, then watching the couples die."

"I've heard the theories, and there is nothing to support them. Toxicology results were negative for drugs in the first eight deaths."

"I remember that from the reports," he said thoughtfully. "But I also assumed this didn't necessarily mean the kids hadn't been involved in drugs. Their bodies were almost skeletonized. Doesn't seem there was much left to test."

"There was some red tissue left, muscle. That's enough for testing. Cocaine or heroin, for example. We, at least, would have expected to find their metabolites of benzoylecogonine or morphine. As for designer drugs, we tested for analogues of PCP, amphetamines."

"What about China White?" he proposed, referring to a very potent synthetic analgesic popular in California. "From what I understand, it doesn't take much for an overdose and is difficult to detect."

"True. Less than one milligram can be fatal, meaning the concentration is too low to detect without using special analytical procedures such as RIA." Noting the blank expression on his face, I explained, "Radioimmunoassay, a procedure based on specific drug antibody reactions. Unlike conventional screening procedures, RIA can detect small levels of drugs, so it's what we resort to when looking for China White, LSD, THC."

"None of which you found."

"That's correct."

"What about alcohol?"

"Alcohol's a problem when bodies are badly decomposed. Some of those tests were negative, others less than point oh-five, possibly the result of decomposition. Inconclusive, in other words."

"With Harvey and Cheney as well?"

"No trace of drugs so far," I told him. "What is Pat Harvey's interest in the early cases?"

"Don't get me wrong," he replied. "I'm not saying it was a major preoccupation. But she must have gotten tips back when she was a U.S. attorney, inside information, and she asked some questions. Politics, Kay. I suppose if it had turned out that these deaths of couples in Virginia were related to drugs—either accidental deaths or drug homicides—she would have used the information to buttress her antidrug efforts."

That would explain why Mrs. Harvey seemed well informed when I had lunch at her house last fall, I thought. No doubt she had information on file in her office because of her early interest in the cases.

"When her inquiries into this didn't go anywhere," Wesley continued, "I think she pretty much let it go until her daughter and Fred disappeared. Then it all came back to her, as you can imagine."

"Yes, I can imagine. And I can also imagine the bitter irony had it turned out that drugs killed the Drug Czar's daughter."

"Don't think that hasn't crossed Mrs. Harvey's mind," Wesley said grimly.

The reminder made me tense again. "She has a right to know, Benton. I can't pend these cases forever."

He nodded to the waiter that we were ready for coffee.

"I need you to buy me more time, Kay."

"Because of your disinformation tactics?"

"We need to give that a shot, let the stories run without interference. The minute Mrs. Harvey gets anything from you, all hell's going to break loose. Believe me, I know how she'll react better than you do at this point. She'll go to the press, and in the process screw up everything we've been setting up to lure the killer."

"What happens when she gets her court order?"

"That will take time. It won't happen tomorrow. Will you stall a little longer, Kay?"

"You haven't finished explaining about the jack of hearts," I reminded him. "How could a hit man have known about the cards?"

Wesley replied reluctantly, "Pat Harvey doesn't gather information or investigate situations alone. She has aides, a staff. She talks to other politicians, any number of people, including constituents. It all depends on who she divulged information to, and who out there might have wished to destroy her, assuming that's the case, and I'm not saying it is."

"A paid hit disguised to look like the early cases," I considered. "Only the hit man made a mistake. He didn't know to leave the jack of hearts in the car. He left it with Deborah's body, inside her purse. Someone perhaps involved with the fraudulent charities Pat Harvey is supposed to testify against?"

"We're talking about bad people who know other bad people. Drug dealers. Organized crime." He idly stirred his coffee. "Mrs. Harvey's not faring too well through all this. She's very distracted. This congressional hearing isn't exactly foremost on her mind, at the moment."

"I see. And I suspect she's not exactly on friendly terms with the Justice Department, because of this hearing."

Wesley carefully set his teaspoon on the edge of his saucer. "She's not," he said, looking up at me. "What she's trying to bring about isn't going to help us. It's fine to put ACTMAD and other scams like it out of business. But it's not enough. We want to prosecute. In the past, there's been some friction between her and the DEA, FBI, also the CIA."

"And now?" I continued to probe.

"It's worse, because she's emotionally involved, has to rely on the Bureau to assist in solving her daughter's homicide. She's uncooperative, paranoid. She's trying to work around us, take matters into her own hands." Sighing, he added, "She's a problem, Kay."

"She probably says the same thing about the Bureau."

He smiled wryly. "I'm sure she does."

I wanted to continue the mental poker game to see if Wesley was keeping anything else from me, so I gave him more. "It appears that Deborah received a defensive injury to her left index finger. Not a cut, but a hack, inflicted by a knife with a serrated blade."

"Where on her index finger?" he asked, leaning forward a little.

"Dorsal." I held up my hand to show him. "On top, near her first knuckle."

"Interesting. Atypical."

"Yes. Difficult to reconstruct how she got it."

"So we know he was armed with a knife," he thought out loud. "That makes me all the more suspicious that something went wrong out there. Something happened he wasn't expecting. He may have resorted to a gun to subdue the couple, but intended to kill them with the knife. Possibly by cutting their throats. But then something went haywire. Deborah somehow got away and he shot her in the back, then maybe cut her throat to finish her off."

"And then positioned their bodies to look like the others?" I asked. "Arm in arm, facedown, and fully clothed?"

He stared at the wall above my head.

I thought of the cigarette butts left at each scene. I thought of the parallels. The fact that the playing card was a different brand and left in a different place this time proved nothing. Killers are not machines. Their rituals and habits are not an exact science or set in stone. Nothing that Wesley had divulged to me, including the absence of white cotton fibers in Deborah's Jeep, was enough to validate the theory that Fred's and Deborah's homicides were unrelated to the other cases. I was experiencing the same confusion that I felt whenever I visited Quantico, where I was never sure if guns were firing bullets or blanks, if helicopters carried marines on real business or FBI agents simulating maneuvers, or if buildings in the Academy's fictitious town of Hogan's Alley were functional or Hollywood facades.

I could push Wesley no further. He wasn't going to tell me more.

"It's getting late," he commented. "You have a long drive back."

I had one last point to make.

"I don't want friendship to interfere with all this, Benton."

"That goes without saying."

"What happened between Mark and me—"

"That's not a factor," he interrupted, and his voice was firm but not unkind.

"He was your best friend."

"I'd like to think he still is."

"Do you blame me for why he went to Colorado, left Quantico?"

"I know why he left," he said. "I'm sorry he left. He was very good for the Academy."

The FBI's strategy of drawing out the killer by way of disinformation did not materialize the following Monday. Either the Bureau had changed its mind, or it was preempted by Pat Harvey, who held a press conference the same day.

At noon, she faced cameras in her Washington office, adding to the pathos by having Bruce Cheney, Fred's father, by her side. She looked awful. Weight added by the camera and makeup could not hide how thin she had gotten or the dark circles under her eyes.

"When did these threats begin, Mrs. Harvey, and what was the nature of them?" a reporter asked.

"The first one came shortly after I began investigating the charities. And I suppose this was a little over a year ago," she said without emotion. "This was a letter mailed to my home in Richmond. I won't divulge the specific nature of what it said, but the threat was directed at my family."

"And you believe this was connected to your probe into fraudulent charities like ACTMAD?"

"There's no question about that. There were other threats, the last one as recent as two months before my daughter and Fred Cheney disappeared."

Bruce Cheney's face flashed on the screen. He was pale, blinking in the blinding haze of TV lights.

"Ms. Harvey . . ."

"Mrs. Harvey . . ."

Reporters were interrupting each other, and Pat Harvey interrupted them, the camera swinging back her way.

"The FBI was aware of the situation, and it was their opinion that the threats, the letters, were originating from one source," she said.

"Mrs. Harvey . . ."

"Ms. Harvey"—a reporter raised her voice above the commotion—"it's no secret that you and the Justice Department have different agendas, a conflict of interests arising from the investigation of the charities. Are you suggesting the FBI knew that the safety of your family was in jeopardy and *didn't do anything?*"

"It's more than a suggestion," she stated.

"Are you accusing the Justice Department of incompetence?"

"What I'm accusing the Justice Department of is conspiracy," Pat Harvey said.

Groaning, I reached for a cigarette as the din, the interruptions reached a crescendo. You've lost it, I thought, staring in disbelief at the TV inside the small medical library in my downtown office.

It got only worse. And my heart was filled with dread as Mrs. Harvey turned her cool stare to the camera and one by one ran her sword through everyone involved in the investigation, including me. She spared no one, and there was nothing sacred, including the detail of the jack of hearts.

It had been a gross understatement when Wesley had said she was uncooperative and a problem. Beneath her armor of reason was a woman crazed by rage and grief. Numbly I listened as she plainly and without reservation indicted the police, the FBI, and the Medical Examiner's Office for complicity in a "cover-up."

"They are deliberately burying the truth about these cases," she concluded, "when the act of doing so serves only their self-interest at the unconscionable expense of human lives."

"What a lot of shit," muttered Fielding, my deputy chief, sitting nearby.

"*Which* cases?" a reporter demanded loudly. "The deaths of your daughter and her boyfriend or are you referring to the four other couples?"

"All of them," Mrs. Harvey replied. "I'm referring to all of the young men and women hunted down like animals and murdered."

"What is being covered up?"

"The identity or identities of those responsible," she said as if she knew. "There has been no intervention on the part of the Justice Department to stop these killings. The reasons are political. A certain federal agency is protecting its own."

"Could you please be more specific?" a voice shot back.

"When my investigation is concluded, I will make a full disclosure."

"At the hearing?" she was asked. "Are you suggesting that the murder of Deborah and her boyfriend . . ."

"*His name is Fred.*"

It was Bruce Cheney who had spoken, and suddenly his livid face filled the television screen.

The room went silent.

"Fred. His name is *Frederick Wilson Cheney*." The father's voice trembled with emotion. "He's not just Debbie's *boyfriend*. He's dead, murdered, too. My *son!*" Words caught in his throat, and he hung his head to hide his tears.

I turned off the television, upset and unable to sit still.

Rose had been standing in the doorway, watching. She looked at me and slowly shook her head.

Fielding got up, stretched, tightened the drawstring of his surgical greens.

"She just screwed herself in front of the whole damn world," he announced, walking out of the library.

I realized as I was pouring myself a cup of coffee what Pat Harvey had said. I began to really hear it as it replayed inside my head.

"*Hunted down like animals and murdered . . .*"

Her words had the sound of something scripted. They did not strike me as glib, off the cuff or a figure of speech. *A federal agency protecting its own?*

Hunt.

A jack of hearts like a knight of cups. Someone who is perceived or perceives himself as a competitor, a defender. One who does battle, Hilda Ozimek had said to me.

A knight. A soldier.

Hunt.

━━━━━

Their murders were meticulously calculated, methodically planned. Bruce Phillips and Judy Roberts disappeared in June. Their bodies were found in mid-August, when hunting season opened.

Jim Freeman and Bonnie Smyth disappeared in July, their bodies found the opening day of quail and pheasant season.

Ben Anderson and Carolyn Bennett disappeared in March, their bodies found in November during deer season.

Susan Wilcox and Mark Martin disappeared in late February, their bodies discovered in mid-May, during spring gobbler season.

Deborah Harvey and Fred Cheney vanished Labor Day week-end and were not found until months later when the woods were crowded with hunters after rabbit, squirrel, fox, pheasant, and raccoon.

I had not assumed the pattern meant anything because most of the badly decomposed and skeletonized bodies that end up in my office are found by hunters. When someone drops dead or is dumped in the woods, a hunter is the most likely person to stumble upon the remains. But when and where the couples' bodies were discovered could have been planned.

The killer wanted his victims found, but not right away, so he killed them off season, knowing that it was probable his victims would not be discovered until hunters were out in the woods again. By then the bodies were decomposed. Gone with the tissue were the injuries he had inflicted. If rape was involved, there would be no seminal fluid. Most trace evidence would be dislodged by wind and washed away by rain. It may even be that it was important to him that the bodies be found by hunters because in his fantasies he, too, was a hunter. The greatest hunter of all.

Hunters hunted animals, I thought as I sat at my downtown desk the following afternoon. Guerrillas, military special agents, and soldiers of fortune hunted human beings.

Within the fifty-mile radius where the couples had vanished and turned up dead were Fort Eustis, Langley Field, and a number of other military installations, including the CIA's West Point, operated under the cover of a military base called Camp Peary. "The Farm," as Camp Peary is referred to in spy novels and investigative nonfiction books about intelligence, was where officers were trained in the paramilitary activities of infiltration, exfiltration, demolitions, nighttime parachute jumps, and other clandestine operations.

Abby Turnbull took a wrong turn and ended up at the entrance of Camp Peary, and days later FBI agents came looking for her.

The feds were paranoid, and I had a suspicion I might know why. After reading the newspaper accounts of Pat Harvey's press conference, I had become only more convinced.

A number of papers, including the *Post*, were on my desk, and I had studied the write-ups several times. The byline on the *Post*'s story was Clifford Ring, the reporter who had been pestering the commissioner and other personnel of the Department of Health and Human Services. Mr. Ring mentioned me only in passing when he implied that Pat Harvey was inappropriately using her public office to intimidate and threaten all involved into releasing details about her daughter's death. It was enough to make me wonder if Mr. Ring was Benton Wesley's media source, the FBI's conduit for planted releases, and that would not have been so bad, really. It was the point of the stories that I found disturbing.

What I had assumed would be dished out as the sensational exposé of the month was, instead, being bruited about as the co-lossal degradation of a woman who, just weeks before, had been talked of by some as a possible Vice President of the United States. I would be the first to say that Pat Harvey's diatribe at the press conference was reckless in the least, premature at best. But I found it odd that there was no evidence of a serious attempt at corrobo-rating her accusations. Reporters in this case did not seem inclined to get the usual incriminating "no comments" and other double-talk evasions from the governmental bureaucrats that journalists typically pursue with enthusiasm.

The media's only quarry, it seemed, was Mrs. Harvey, and she was shown no pity. The headline for one editorial was SLAUGHTERGATE? She was being ridiculed, not only in print but in political cartoons. One of the nation's most respected officials was being dismissed as a hysterical female whose "sources" included a South Carolina psychic. Even her staunchest allies were back-ing away, shaking their heads, her enemies subtly finishing her off with attacks softly wrapped in sympathy. "Her reaction is cer-tainly understandable in light of her terrible personal loss," said one Democratic detractor, adding, "I think it wise to overlook her imprudence. Consider her accusations the slings and arrows of a deeply troubled mind." Said another, "What's happened to Pat Har-vey is a tragic example of self-destruction brought on by personal problems too overwhelming to endure."

Rolling Deborah Harvey's autopsy report into my typewriter, I whited out "pending" in the manner and cause of death spaces. I typed in "homicide" and "exsanguination due to gunshot wound to lower back and cutting injuries." Amending her death certificate and CME-1 report, I went up front and made photocopies. These I enclosed with a cover letter explaining my findings and apologizing for the delay, which I attributed to the long wait for toxicology re-sults, which were still provisional. I would give Benton Wesley that much. Pat Harvey would not hear from me that I had been strong-armed by him to indefinitely pend the results of her daughter's medicolegal examination.

The Harveys were going to get it all—my findings on gross and microscopically, the fact that the first rounds of toxicology tests were negative, the bullet in Deborah's lower lumbar, the defense injury to her hand, and, pathetically, the detailed description of her clothing, or what had been left of it. The police had recovered her earrings, watch, and the friendship ring given to her by Fred for her birthday.

I also mailed copies of Fred Cheney's reports to his father, though I could go no further than saying that his son's manner of death was homicide, the cause "undetermined violence."

I reached for the phone and dialed Benton Wesley's office, only to be told he wasn't in. Next, I tried his home.

"I'm releasing the information," I said when he got on the line. "I wanted you to know."

Silence.

Then he said very calmly, "Kay, you heard her press conference?"

"Yes."

"And you've read today's paper?"

"I watched her press conference, and I've read the papers. I'm well aware that she shot herself in the foot."

"I'm afraid she shot herself in the head," he said.

"Not without some help."

A pause, then Wesley asked, "What are you talking about?"

"I'll be happy to spell it out in detail. Tonight. Face-to-face."

"Here?" He sounded alarmed.

"Yes."

"Uh, it's not a good idea, not tonight."

"I'm sorry. But it can't wait."

"Kay, you don't understand. Trust me—"

I cut him off. "No, Benton. Not this time."

10

A FRIGID WIND wreaked havoc with the dark shapes of trees, and in the scant light of the moon the terrain looked foreign and foreboding as I drove to Benton Wesley's house. There were few streetlights, and the rural routes were poorly marked. I finally stopped at a country store with a single island of gas pumps in front. Switching on the overhead lamp, I studied my scribbled directions. I was lost.

I could see the store was closed but spotted a pay phone near the front door. Pulling close, I got out, leaving headlights burning and the engine on. I dialed Wesley's number and his wife, Connie, answered.

"You've really gotten tangled up," she said after I did my best to describe where I was.

"Oh, God," I said, groaning.

"Well, it's really not that far. The problem is it's complicated getting from where you are to here." She paused, then decided, "I think the wise thing would be for you to stay put, Kay. Lock your doors and sit tight. Better if we come and you follow us. Fifteen minutes, all right?"

Backing out, I parked closer to the road, turned on the radio, and waited. Minutes passed like hours. Not a single car went by. My headlights illuminated a white fence girdling a frosty pasture across the road. The moon was a pale sliver floating in the hazy darkness. I smoked several cigarettes, my eyes darting around.

I wondered if it had been like this for the murdered couples, what it would be like to be forced barefoot and bound into the woods. They had to have known they were going to die. They had to have been terrified by what he would do to them first. I thought of my niece, Lucy. I thought of my mother, my sister, my friends. Fearing for the pain and death of one you loved would be worse than fearing for your own life. I watched as headlights grew brighter far down the dark, narrow road. A car I did not recognize turned in and stopped not far from mine. When I caught a glimpse of the driver's profile, adrenaline rushed through my blood like electricity.

Mark James climbed out of what I assumed was a rental car. I rolled down the window and stared at him, too shocked to speak.

"Hello, Kay."

Wesley had said this was not a good night, had tried to talk me out of it, and now I understood why. Mark was visiting. Perhaps Connie had asked Mark to meet me, or he had volunteered. I could not imagine my reaction had I walked through Wesley's front door and found Mark sitting in the living room.

"It's a maze to Benton's house from here," Mark said. "I suggest you leave your car. It will be safe. I'll drive you back later so you won't have a problem finding your way."

Wordlessly, I parked closer to the store, then got in his car.

"How are you?" he asked quietly.

"Fine."

"And your family? How's Lucy?"

Lucy still asked about him. I never knew what to say.

"Fine," I said again.

As I looked at his face, his strong hands on the wheel, every contour, line, and vein familiar and wonderful to me, my heart ached with emotion. I hated and loved him at the same time.

"Work's all right?"

"Please stop being so goddam polite, Mark."

"Would you rather I be rude like you?"

"I'm not being rude."

"What the hell do you want me to say?"

I replied with silence.

He turned on the radio and we drove deeper into the night.

"I know this is awkward, Kay." He stared straight ahead. "I'm sorry. Benton suggested I meet you."

"That was very thoughtful of him," I said sarcastically.

"I didn't mean it like that. I would have insisted had he not asked. You had no reason to think I might be here."

We rounded a sharp bend and turned into Wesley's subdivision.

As we pulled into Wesley's driveway, Mark said, "I guess I'd better warn you that Benton's not in a very good mood."

"I'm not either," I replied coldly.

A fire burned in the living room, and Wesley was sitting near the hearth, a briefcase open and resting against the leg of his chair, a drink on the table nearby. He did not get up when I walked in, but nodded slightly as Connie invited me to the couch. I sat on one end, Mark the other.

Connie left to get coffee, and I started in. "Mark, I know nothing of your involvement in all this."

"There isn't much to know. I was in Quantico for several days and am spending the night with Benton and Connie before returning to Denver tomorrow. I'm not involved in the investigation, not assigned to the cases."

"All right. But you're aware of the cases." I wondered what Wesley and Mark had discussed in my absence. I wondered what Wesley had said to Mark about me.

"He's aware of them," Wesley answered.

"Then I'll ask both of you," I said. "Did the Bureau set up Pat Harvey? Or was it the CIA?"

Wesley did not move or change the expression on his face. "What leads you to suppose she's been set up?"

"Obviously, the Bureau's disinformation tactics went beyond luring the killer. It was someone's intention to destroy Pat Harvey's credibility, and the press has done this quite successfully."

"Even the President doesn't have that much influence over the media. Not in this country."

"Don't insult my intelligence, Benton," I said.

"What she did was anticipated. Let's put it that way." Wesley recrossed his legs and reached for his drink.

"And you laid the trap," I said.

"No one spoke for her at her press conference."

"It doesn't matter because no one needed to. Someone made sure her accusations would come across in print as the ravings of a lunatic. Who primed the reporters, the politicians, her former allies, Benton? Who leaked that she consulted a psychic? Was it you?"

"No."

"Pat Harvey saw Hilda Ozimek last September," I went on.

"It never made the news until now, meaning the press didn't know about it until now. That's pretty low, Benton. You told me yourself that the FBI and Secret Service have resorted to Hilda Ozimek on a number of occasions. That's probably how Mrs. Harvey found out about her, for God's sake."

Connie returned with my coffee, then left again as quickly as she had appeared.

I could feel Mark's eyes on me, the tension. Wesley continued staring into the fire.

"I think I know the truth." I made no effort to disguise my outrage. "I intend to have it out in the open now. And if you can't accommodate me this way, then I don't think it will be possible for me to continue accommodating you."

"What are you implying, Kay?" Wesley looked over at me.

"If it happens again, if another couple dies, I can't guarantee that reporters won't find out what's really going on—"

"Kay." It was Mark who interrupted, and I refused to look at him. I was doing my best to block him out. "You don't want to trip up like Mrs. Harvey."

"She didn't exactly trip up on her own," I said. "I think she's right. Something *is* being covered up."

"You sent her your reports, I presume," Wesley said.

"I did. I will no longer play a part in this manipulation."

"That was a mistake."

"My mistake was not sending them to her earlier."

"Do the reports include information about the bullet you recovered from Deborah's body? Specifically, that it was nine-millimeter Hydra-Shok?"

"The caliber and brand would be in the firearms report," I said. "I don't send out copies of firearms reports any more than I send out copies of police reports, neither of which are generated by my office. But I'm interested in why you're so concerned over that detail."

When Wesley did not reply, Mark intervened. "Benton, we need to smooth this out."

Wesley remained silent.

"I think she needs to know," Mark added.

"I think I already know," I said. "I think the FBI has reason to fear the killer is a federal agent gone bad. Quite possibly, someone from Camp Peary."

Wind moaned around the eaves, and Wesley got up to tend to

the fire. He put on another log, rearranged it with the poker, and swept ashes off the hearth, taking his time. When he was seated again, he reached for his drink and said, "How did you come to this conclusion?"

"It doesn't matter," I said.

"Did someone say this to you directly?"

"No. Not directly." I got out my cigarettes. "How long has this been your suspicion, Benton?"

Hesitating, he replied, "I believe you are better off not knowing the details. I really do. It's only going to be a burden. A very heavy one."

"I'm already carrying a very heavy burden. And I'm tired of stumbling over disinformation."

"I need your assurance nothing discussed leaves here."

"You know me too well to worry about that."

"Camp Peary entered into it not long after the cases began."

"Because of the close proximity?"

He looked at Mark. "I'll let you elaborate," Wesley said to him.

I turned and confronted this man who once had shared my bed and dominated my dreams. He was dressed in navy blue corduroy trousers and a red-and-white-striped oxford shirt that I had seen him wear in the past. He was long legged and trim. His dark hair was gray at the temples, eyes green, chin strong, features refined, and he still gestured slightly with his hands and leaned forward when he talked.

"In part, the CIA got interested," Mark explained, "because the cases were occurring close to Camp Peary. And I'm sure it comes as no surprise to you that the CIA is privy to most of what goes on around their training facility. They know a lot more than anyone might imagine, and in fact, local settings and citizens are routinely incorporated into maneuvers."

"What sorts of maneuvers?" I asked.

"Surveillance, for example. Officers in training at Camp Peary often practice surveillance, using local citizens as guinea pigs, for lack of a better term. Officers set up surveillance operations in public places, restaurants, bars, shopping centers. They tail people in cars, on foot, take photographs, and so on. No one is ever aware this is going on, of course. And there's no harm done, I suppose, except that local citizens wouldn't be keen on knowing they were being tailed, watched, or captured on film."

"I shouldn't think so," I said uncomfortably.

"These maneuvers," he continued, "also include going through dry runs. An officer might feign car trouble and stop a motorist for assistance, see how far he can go in getting this individual to trust him. He might pose as a law enforcement officer, tow truck operator, any number of things. It's all practice for overseas operations, to train people how to spy and avoid being spied upon."

"And it's an MO that may parallel what's been going on with these couples," I interpolated.

"That's the point," Wesley interjected. "Someone at Camp Peary got worried. We were asked to help monitor the situation. Then when the second couple turned up dead, and the MO was the same as the first case, the pattern had been established. The CIA began to panic. They're a paranoid lot anyway, Kay, and the last thing they needed was to discover that one of their officers at Camp Peary was practicing *killing* people."

"The CIA has never admitted that Camp Peary is its main training facility," I pointed out.

"It's common knowledge," Mark said, meeting my eyes. "But you're right, the CIA has never admitted it publicly. Nor do they wish to."

"Which is all the more reason they wouldn't want these murders connected to Camp Peary," I said, wondering what he was feeling. Maybe he wasn't feeling anything.

"That and a long list of other reasons," Wesley took over. "The publicity would be devastating, and when was the last time you read anything positive about the CIA? Imelda Marcos was accused of theft and fraud, and the defense claimed that every transaction the Marcoses made was with the full knowledge and encouragement of the CIA. . . ."

He wouldn't be so tense, so afraid to look at me, if he felt nothing.

". . . Then it came out that Noriega was on the CIA's payroll," Wesley continued making his case. "Not long ago it was publicized that CIA protection of a Syrian drug smuggler made it possible for a bomb to be placed on a Pan Am seven-forty-seven that exploded over Scotland, killing two hundred and seventy people. Not to mention the more recent allegation that the CIA is financing certain drug wars in Asia to destabilize governments over there."

"If it turned out," Mark said, shifting his eyes away from me, "that teenage couples were being murdered by a CIA officer at Camp Peary, you can imagine the public's reaction."

"It's unthinkable," I said, willing myself to concentrate on the discussion. "But why would the CIA be so sure these murders are being committed by one of their own? What hard evidence do they have?"

"Most of it's circumstantial," Mark explained. "The militaristic touch of leaving a playing card. The similarities between the patterns in these cases and the maneuvers that go on both inside the Farm and on streets of nearby cities and towns. For example, the wooded areas where the bodies have been turning up are reminiscent of the 'kill zones' inside Camp Peary, where officers practice with grenades, automatic weapons, utilizing all the trade craft, such as night vision equipment, allowing them to see in the woods after dark. They also receive training in defense, how to disarm someone, maim and kill with their bare hands."

"When there was no apparent cause of death with these couples," Wesley said, "one had to wonder if they were being murdered without the use of weapons. Strangulation, for example. Or even if their throats were cut, this is associated with guerrilla warfare, taking out an enemy swiftly and in silence. You cut through his airway and he's not going to be making any noise."

"But Deborah Harvey was shot," I said.

"With an automatic or semiautomatic weapon," Wesley replied. "Either a pistol or something like an Uzi. The ammunition uncommon, associated with law enforcement, mercenary soldiers, people whose targets are human beings. You don't associate exploding bullets or Hydra-Shok ammo with deer hunting." Pausing, he added, "I would think this gives you a better idea why we don't want Pat Harvey cognizant of the type of weapon and ammunition that was used on her daughter."

"What about the threats Mrs. Harvey mentioned in her press conference?" I asked.

"That is true," Wesley said. "Not long after she was appointed National Drug Policy Director, someone did send communications threatening her and her family. It isn't true that the Bureau didn't take them seriously. She's been threatened before and we've always taken it seriously. We have an idea who's behind the more recent threats and don't believe they're related to Deborah's homicide."

"Mrs. Harvey also implicated a 'federal agency,' " I said. "Was she referring to the CIA? Is she aware of what you've just told me?"

"That concerns me," Wesley admitted. "She's made comments

to suggest she has an idea, and what she said in the press conference only increases my anxiety. She might have been referring to the CIA. Then again, maybe she wasn't. But she has a formidable network. For one thing, she has access to CIA information, providing it's relevant to the drug trade. More worrisome is that she's close friends with an ex-United Nations ambassador who is a member of the President's Foreign Intelligence Advisory Board. Members of the board are entitled to top secret intelligence briefings on any subject at any time. The board knows what's going on, Kay. It's possible Mrs. Harvey knows everything."

"So she's set up Martha Mitchell-style?" I asked. "To make sure she comes off as irrational, unreliable, so that no one takes her seriously, so that if she does blow the lid, no one will believe her?"

Wesley was running his thumb around the rim of his glass. "It's unfortunate. She's been uncontrollable, uncooperative. And the irony is, we want to know who murdered her daughter more than she does, for obvious reasons. We're doing everything within our power, have mobilized everything we can think of to find this individual—or individuals."

"What you're telling me seems patently inconsistent with your earlier suggestion that Deborah Harvey and Fred Cheney may have been a paid hit, Benton," I said angrily. "Or was that just a lot of smoke you were blowing out to hide the Bureau's real fears?"

"I don't know if they were a paid hit," he said grimly. "Frankly, there's so little we really know. Their murders could be political, as I've already explained. But if we're dealing with a CIA officer gone haywire, someone like that, the cases of the five couples may, in fact, be connected, may be serial killings."

"It could be an example of escalation," Mark offered. "Pat Harvey's been in the news a lot, especially over the past year. If we're looking for a CIA officer who's practicing homicidal maneuvers, he may have decided to target a presidential appointee's daughter."

"Thus adding to the excitement, the risk," Wesley explained. "And making the kill similar to the sorts of operations you associate with Central America, the Middle East, political neutralizations. Assassinations, in other words."

"It's my understanding that the CIA is not supposed to be in the business of assassinations, not since the Ford administration," I said. "In fact, the CIA's not even supposed to engage in coup attempts in which a foreign leader is in danger of being killed."

"That's correct," Mark replied. "The CIA's not supposed to be in that business. American soldiers in Vietnam weren't supposed to kill civilians. And cops aren't supposed to use excessive force on suspects and prisoners. When it's all reduced to individuals, sometimes things get out of control. Rules get broken."

I could not help but wonder about Abby Turnbull. How much of this did she know? Had Mrs. Harvey leaked something to her? Was this the true nature of the book Abby was writing? No wonder she suspected her phones were being bugged, that she was being followed. The CIA, the FBI, and even the President's Foreign Intelligence Advisory Board, which had a back-door entrée straight into the Oval Office, had very good reason to be nervous about what Abby was writing, and she had very good reason to be paranoid. She may have placed herself in real danger.

The wind had died down, a light fog settling over treetops as Wesley closed the door behind us. Following Mark to his car, I felt a sense of resolution and validation because of what had been said, and yet I was more unsettled than before.

I waited to speak until we left the subdivision. "What's happening to Pat Harvey is outrageous. She loses her daughter, now her career and reputation are being destroyed."

"Benton's had nothing to do with leaks to the press, any sort of 'setup,' as you put it." Mark kept his eyes on the dark, narrow road.

"It's not a matter of how I *put it*, Mark."

"I'm just referring to what you said," he replied.

"You know what's going on. Don't act naive with me."

"Benton's done everything he can for her, but she's got a vendetta against the Justice Department. To her, Benton's just another federal agent out to get her."

"If I were her, I might feel the same way."

"Knowing you, you probably would."

"And what's that supposed to mean?" I asked, as my anger, which went far deeper than Pat Harvey, surfaced.

"It doesn't mean a thing."

Minutes passed in silence as the tension grew. I did not recognize the road we were on, but I knew our time together was nearing an end. Then he turned into the store's parking lot and pulled up next to my car.

"I'm sorry we had to see each other under these circumstances," he said quietly.

I did not reply, and he added, "But I'm not sorry to see you, not sorry it happened."

"Good night, Mark." I started to get out of the car.

"Don't, Kay." He put his hand on my arm.

I sat still. "What do you want?"

"To talk to you. Please."

"If you're so interested in talking to me, then why haven't you gotten around to it before now?" I replied with emotion, pulling my arm away. "You've made no effort to say a goddam thing to me for months."

"That works both ways. I called you last fall and you never called me back."

"I knew what you were going to say, and I didn't want to hear it," I replied, and I could feel his anger building, too.

"Excuse me. I forgot that you have always had the uncanny ability of reading my mind." He placed both hands on the wheel and stared straight ahead.

"You were going to announce that there was no chance of reconciliation, that it was over. And I wasn't interested in having you put into words what I already assumed."

"Think what you want."

"It has nothing to do with what I *want* to think!" I hated the power he had to make me lose my temper.

"Look." He took a deep breath. "Do you think there's any chance we can declare a truce? Forget the past?"

"Not a chance."

"Great. Thanks for being so reasonable. At least I tried."

"Tried? It's been what? Eight, nine months since you left? What the hell have you tried, Mark? I don't know what it is you're asking, but it's impossible to forget the past. It's impossible for the two of us to run into each other and pretend there was never anything between us. I refuse to act that way."

"I'm not asking that, Kay. I'm asking if we can forget the fights, the anger, what we said back then."

I really could not remember exactly what had been said or explain what had gone wrong. We fought when we weren't sure what we were fighting about until the focus became our injuries and not the differences that had caused them.

"When I called you last September," he went on with feeling, "I wasn't going to tell you there was no hope of reconciliation. In fact, when I dialed your number I knew I was running the risk of hearing *you* say that. And when you never called me back, I was the one who made assumptions."

"You're not serious."

"The hell I'm not."

"Well, maybe you were wise to make assumptions. After what you did."

"After what *I* did?" he asked, incredulous. "What about what *you* did?"

"The only thing I did was to get sick and tired of making concessions. You never really tried to relocate to Richmond. You didn't know what you wanted and expected me to comply, concede, uproot myself whenever you figured everything out. No matter how much I love you, I can't give up what I am and I never asked you to give up what you are."

"Yes, you did. Even if I could have transferred to the field office in Richmond, that's not what I wanted."

"Good. I'm glad you pursued what you wanted."

"Kay, it's fifty-fifty. You're to blame, too."

"I'm not the one who left." My eyes filled with tears, and I whispered, "Oh, shit."

Getting out a handkerchief, he gently placed it on my lap.

Dabbing my eyes, I moved closer to the door, leaning my head against the glass. I did not want to cry.

"I'm sorry," he said.

"Your being sorry doesn't change anything."

"Please don't cry."

"I will if I want," I said, ridiculously.

"I'm sorry," he said again, this time in a whisper, and I thought he was going to touch me. But he didn't. He leaned back in the seat and stared up at the roof.

"Look," he said, "if you want to know the truth, I wish *you* had been the one who left. Then you could have been the one who screwed up instead of me."

I did not say anything. I did not dare.

"Did you hear me?"

"I'm not sure," I said to the window.

He shifted his position. I could feel his eyes on me.

"Kay, look at me."

Reluctantly, I did.

"Why do you think I've been coming back here?" he asked in a low voice. "I'm trying to get back to Quantico, but it's tough.

The timing's bad with the federal budget cuts, the economy, the Bureau's being hit hard. There are a lot of reasons."

"You're telling me you're professionally unhappy?"

"I'm telling you I made a mistake."

"I regret any professional mistakes you've made," I said.

"I'm not referring just to that, and you know it."

"Then what are you referring to?" I was determined to make him say it.

"You know what I'm referring to. Us. Nothing's been the same."

His eyes were shining in the dark. He looked almost fierce.

"Has it been for you?" he pushed.

"I think both of us have made a lot of mistakes."

"I'd like to start undoing some of them, Kay. I don't want it to end this way with us. I've felt that for a long time but . . . well, I just didn't know how to tell you. I didn't know if you wanted to hear from me, if you were seeing someone else."

I did not admit that I had been wondering the same about him and was terrified of the answers.

He reached for me, taking my hand. This time I could not pull away.

"I've been trying to sort through what went wrong with us," he said. "All I know is I'm stubborn, you're stubborn. I wanted my way and you wanted yours. So here we are. I can't say what your life has been like since I left, but I'm willing to bet it hasn't been good."

"How arrogant of you to bet on such a thing."

He smiled. "I'm just trying to live up to your image of me. One of the last things you called me before I left was an arrogant bastard."

"Was that before or after I called you a son of a bitch?"

"Before, I believe."

"As I remember it, you called me a few rather choice names as well. And I thought you just suggested that we forget what was said back then."

"And you just said *no matter how much I love you.*"

"I beg your pardon?"

" 'Love,' as in present tense. Don't try to take it back. I heard it."

He pressed my hand to his face, his lips moving over my fingers.

"I've tried to stop thinking about you. I can't." He paused, his face close to mine. "I'm not asking you to say the same thing."

But he was asking that, and I answered him.

I touched his cheek and he touched mine, then we kissed the places our fingers had been until we found each other's lips. And we said nothing more. We stopped thinking entirely until the windshield suddenly lit up and the night beyond was throbbing red. We frantically rearranged ourselves as a patrol car pulled up and a deputy climbed out, flashlight and portable radio in hand.

Mark was already opening his door.

"Everything all right?" the deputy asked, bending over to peer inside. His eyes wandered disconcertingly over the scene of our passion, his face stern, an unseemly bulge in his right cheek.

"Everything's fine," I said, horrified as I not so subtly probed the floor with my stocking foot. Somehow I had lost a shoe.

He stepped back and spat out a stream of tobacco juice.

"We were having a conversation," Mark offered, and he had the presence of mind not to display his badge. The deputy knew damn well we had been doing a lot of things when he pulled up. Conversing was not one of them.

"Well, now, if y'all intend to continue your *conversation*," he said, "I'd 'preciate it if you'd go someplace else. You know, it ain't safe to be sitting out here late at night in a car, been some problems. And if you're not from around here, maybe you hadn't heard about the couples disappearing."

He went on with his lecture, my blood running cold.

"You're right, and thank you," Mark finally said. "We're leaving now."

Nodding, the deputy spat again, and we watched him climb into his car. He pulled out onto the road and slowly drove away.

"Jesus," Mark muttered under his breath.

"Don't say it," I replied. "Let's not even get into how stupid we are. Lord."

"Do you see how damn easy it is?" He said it anyway. "Two people out at night and someone pulls up. Hell, my damn gun's in the glove compartment. I never even thought about it until he was right in my face, and then it would have been too late—"

"Stop it, Mark. Please."

He startled me by laughing.

"It's not funny!"

"Your blouse is buttoned crooked," he gasped.

Shit!

"You better hope like hell he didn't recognize you, Chief Scarpetta."

"Thank you for the reassuring thought, Mr. FBI. And now I'm going home." I opened the door. "You've gotten me into enough trouble for one night."

"Hey. You started it."

"I most certainly did not."

"Kay?" He got serious. "What do we do now? I mean, I'm going back to Denver tomorrow. I don't know what's going to happen, what I can make happen or if I should try to make anything happen."

There were no easy answers. There never had been with us.

"If you don't try to make anything happen, nothing will."

"What about you?" he asked.

"There's a lot of talking we need to do, Mark."

He turned on the headlights and fastened his seat belt. "What about you?" he asked again. "It takes two to try."

"Funny you should say that."

"Kay, don't. Please don't start in."

"I need to think." I got out my keys. I was suddenly exhausted.

"Don't jerk me around."

"I'm not jerking you around, Mark," I said, touching his cheek.

We kissed one last time. I wanted the kiss to go on for hours, and yet I wanted to get away. Our passion had always been reckless. We had always lived for moments that never seemed to add up to any sort of future.

"I'll call you," he said.

I opened my car door.

"Listen to Benton," he added. "You can trust him. What you're involved in is very bad stuff."

I started the engine.

"I wish you'd stay out of it."

"You always wish that," I said.

━━━━━

Mark did call late the following night and again two nights after that. When he called a third time, on February tenth, what he said sent me out in search of the most recent issue of *Newsweek*.

Pat Harvey's lusterless eyes stared out at America from the magazine's cover. A headline in bold, black letters read THE MURDER

OF THE DRUG CZAR'S DAUGHTER, the "exclusive" inside a rehashing of her press conference, her charges of conspiracy, and the cases of the other teenagers who had vanished and been found decomposed in Virginia woods. Though I had declined to be interviewed for the story, the magazine had found a file photograph of me climbing the steps of Richmond's John Marshall Court House. The caption read, "Chief Medical Examiner releases findings under threat of court order."

"It just goes with the turf. I'm fine," I reassured Mark when I called him back.

Even when my mother rang me up later that same night, I remained calm until she said, "There's someone here who's dying to talk to you, Kay."

My niece, Lucy, had always had a special talent for doing me in.

"How come you got in trouble?" she asked.

"I didn't get in trouble."

"The story says you did, that someone threatened you."

"It's too complicated to explain, Lucy."

"It's really awesome," she said, unfazed. "I'm going to take the magazine to school tomorrow and show it to everybody."

Great, I thought.

"Mrs. Barrows," she went on, referring to her homeroom teacher, "has already asked if you can come for career day in April . . . ?"

I had not seen Lucy in a year. It did not seem possible she was already a sophomore in high school, and though I knew she had contact lenses and a driver's license, I still envisioned her as a pudgy, needy child wanting to be tucked into bed, an *enfant terrible* who, for some strange reason, had bonded to me before she could crawl. I would never forget flying to Miami the Christmas after she was born and staying with my sister for a week. Lucy's every conscious minute, it seemed, was spent watching me, eyes following my every move like two luminous moons. She would smile when I changed her diapers and howl the instant I walked out of the room.

"Would you like to spend a week with me this summer?" I asked.

Lucy hesitated, then said disappointedly, "I guess that means you can't come for career day."

"We'll see, all right?"

"I don't know if I can come this summer." Her tone had

turned petulant. "I've got a job and might not be able to get away."

"It's wonderful you have a job."

"Yeah. In a computer store. I'm going to save enough to get a car. I want a sports car, a convertible, and you can find some of the old ones pretty cheap."

"Those are death traps," I said before I could stop myself. "Please don't get something like that, Lucy. Why don't you come see me in Richmond? We'll go around and shop for cars, something nice and safe."

She had dug a hole, and as usual, I had fallen in it. She was an expert at manipulation, and it didn't require a psychiatrist to figure out why. Lucy was the victim of chronic neglect by her mother, my sister.

"You are a bright young lady with a mind of your own," I said, changing tactics. "I know you'll make a good decision about what to do with your time and money, Lucy. But if you can fit me in this summer, maybe we can go somewhere. The beach or mountains, wherever you'd like. You've never been to England, have you?"

"No."

"Well, then, that's a thought."

"Really?" she asked suspiciously.

"Really. I haven't been in years," I said, warming up to the idea. "I think it's time for you to see Oxford and Cambridge, the museums in London. I'll arrange a tour of Scotland Yard, if you'd like, and if we could manage to get away as early as June, we might be able to get tickets for Wimbledon."

Silence.

Then she said cheerfully, "I was just teasing. I don't really want a sports car, Aunt Kay."

The next morning there were no autopsies, and I sat at my desk trying to diminish piles of paperwork. I had other deaths to investigate, classes to teach, and trials demanding my testimony, yet I could not concentrate. Every time I turned to something else, my attention was drawn back to the couples. There was something important I was overlooking, something right under my nose.

I felt it had to do with Deborah Harvey's murder.

She was a gymnast, an athlete with superb control of her body. She may not have been as strong as Fred, but she would have been quicker and more agile. I believed the killer had underestimated her athletic potential, and this was why he momentarily lost control of her in the woods. As I stared blankly at a report I was supposed to be reviewing, Mark's words came back to me. He had mentioned "kill zones," officers at Camp Peary utilizing automatic weapons, grenades, and night vision equipment to hunt each other down in fields and woods. I tried to imagine this. I began toying with a gruesome scenario.

Perhaps when the killer abducted Deborah and Fred and took them to the logging road, he had a terrifying game in store for them. He told them to take off their shoes and socks, and bound their hands behind their backs. He may have been wearing night vision goggles, which enhanced moonlight, making it possible for him to see quite well as he forced them into the woods, where he intended to track them down, one at a time.

I believed Marino was right. The killer would have gotten Fred out of the way first. Perhaps he told him to run, gave him a chance to get away, and all the while Fred was stumbling through trees and brush, panicking, the killer was watching, able to see and move about with ease, knife in hand. At the opportune moment, it would not have been very difficult for him to ambush his victim from behind, yoke arm under chin and jerk the head back, then slash through the windpipe and carotid arteries. This commando style of attack was silent and swift. If the bodies were not discovered for a while, the medical examiner would have difficulty finding a cause of death because tissue and cartilage would have decomposed.

I took the scenario further. Part of the killer's sadism might have been to force Deborah to witness her boyfriend being tracked and murdered in the dark. I was considering that once they were in the woods, the killer held her captive audience by binding her feet at the ankles, but what he did not anticipate was her flexibility. It was possible that while he was occupied with Fred, she managed to bring her bound hands under her buttocks and work her legs through her arms, thus getting her hands in front of her. This would have allowed her to untie her feet and defend herself.

I held my hands in front of me, as if they were bound at the wrists. Had Deborah locked her fingers together in a double fist and swung, and had the killer's reflex been to defensively raise his hands, in one of which he was holding the knife he had just used to murder Fred, then the hack to Deborah's left index finger made sense. Deborah ran like hell, and the killer, knocked off guard, shot her in the back.

Was I right? I could not know. But the scenario continued to play in my mind without a hitch. What didn't fit were several presuppositions. If Deborah's death was a paid hit carried out by a professional or the work of a psychopathic federal agent who had selected her in advance because she was Pat Harvey's daughter, then did this individual not know that Deborah was an Olympic-caliber gymnast? Would he not have considered that she would be unusually quick and agile and have incorporated this into his premeditations?

Would he have shot her *in the back*?

Was the manner in which she was killed consistent with the cold, calculating profile of a professional killer?

In the back.

When Hilda Ozimek had studied the photographs of the dead teenagers, she continued to pick up fear. Obviously, the victims had felt fear. But it had never occurred to me before this moment that the killer may have felt fear, too. Shooting someone in the back is cowardly. When Deborah resisted her assailant, he was unnerved. He lost control. The more I thought about it, the more I was convinced that Wesley and perhaps everybody else was wrong about this character. To hunt bound, barefoot teenagers in the woods after dark, when you have weapons, are familiar with the terrain, and are perhaps equipped with a night vision scope or goggles would be like shooting fish in a barrel. It's cheating. It's too damn easy. It did not strike me as the modus operandi I would expect were the killer an expert who thrived on taking risks.

And then there was the matter of his weapons.

If I were a CIA officer hunting human prey, what would I use? An Uzi? *Maybe.* More likely I would pick a nine-millimeter pistol, something that would do the job, nothing more, nothing less. I would use commonplace cartridges, something unremarkable. Everyday hollowpoints, for example. What I would not use was anything unusual like Exploder bullets or Hydra-Shoks.

The ammunition. Think hard, Kay! I could not remember the last time I had recovered Hydra-Shok bullets from a body.

The ammunition was originally designed with law enforcement officers in mind, the bullets having greater expansion upon impact than any other round fired from a two-inch barrel. When the lead projectile with its hollowpoint construction and distinctive raised central post enters the body, hydrostatic pressure forces the peripheral rim to flare like the petals of a flower. There's very little recoil, making it easier for one to fire repeat shots. The bullets rarely exit the body; the disruption to soft tissue and organs is devastating.

This killer was into specialized ammunition. He, no doubt, had sighted his gun by his cartridges of choice. To select one of the most lethal types of ammunition probably gave him confidence, made him feel powerful and important. He might even be superstitious about it.

I picked up the phone and told Linda what I needed.

"Come on up," she said.

When I walked into the firearms lab, she was seated before a computer terminal.

"No cases so far this year, except for Deborah Harvey, of course," she said, moving the cursor down the screen. "One for last year. One the year before that. Nothing else for Federal. But I did find two cases involving Scorpions."

"Scorpions?" I puzzled, leaning over her shoulder.

She explained, "An earlier version. Ten years before Federal bought the patent, Hydra-Shok Corporation was manufacturing basically the same cartridges. Specifically, Scorpion thirty-eights and Copperhead three-fifty-sevens." She hit several keys, printing out what she had found. "Eight years ago, we got in one case involving Scorpion thirty-eights. But it wasn't human."

"I beg your pardon?" I asked, baffled.

"Appears this victim was of the canine variety. A dog. Shot, let's see . . . three times."

"Was the shooting of the dog connected with some other case? A suicide, homicide, burglary?"

"Can't tell from what I've got here," Linda replied apologetically. "All I've got is that three Scorpion bullets were recovered from the dead dog. Never matched up with anything. I guess the case was never solved."

She tore off the printout and handed it to me.

The OCME, on rare occasion, did perform autopsies on animals. Deer shot out of season were sometimes sent in by game wardens, and if someone's pet was shot during the commission of a crime or if the pet was found dead along with its owners, we took a look, recovered bullets or tested for drugs. But we did not issue death certificates or autopsy reports for animals. It wasn't likely I was going to find anything on file for this dog shot eight years ago.

I rang up Marino and filled him in.

"You gotta be kidding," he said.

"Can you track it down without making a commotion? I don't want this raising any antennas. It may be nothing, but the jurisdiction is West Point, and that's rather interesting. The bodies of the second couple were found in West Point."

"Yeah, maybe. I'll see what I can do," he said, and he didn't sound thrilled about it.

The next morning Marino appeared while I was finishing work on a fourteen-year-old boy thrown out of the back of a pickup truck the afternoon before.

"That ain't something you got on, I hope." Marino moved closer to the table and sniffing.

"He had a bottle of aftershave in a pocket of his pants. It broke when he hit the pavement, and that's what you're smelling." I nodded at clothing on a nearby gurney.

"Brut?" He sniffed again.

"I believe so," I replied absently.

"Doris used to buy me Brut. One year she got me Obsession, if you can believe that."

"What did you find out?" I continued to work.

"The dog's name was Dammit, and I swear that's the truth," Marino said. "Belonged to some old geezer in West Point, a Mr. Joyce."

"Did you find out why the dog came into this office?"

"No connection to any other cases. A favor, I think."

"The state veterinarian must have been on vacation," I replied, for this had happened before.

On the other side of my building was the Department of Animal Health, complete with a morgue where examinations were conducted on animals. Normally, the carcasses went to the state veterinarian. But there were exceptions. When asked, the forensic pathologists indulged the cops and pitched in when the veterinarian was unavailable. During my career I had autopsied tortured dogs, mutilated cats, a sexually assaulted mare, and a poisoned chicken left in a judge's mailbox. People were just as cruel to animals as they were to each other.

"Mr. Joyce don't got a phone, but a contact of mine says he's still in the same crib," Marino said. "Thought I might run over there, check out his story. You want to come along?"

I snapped in a new scalpel blade as I thought about my cluttered desk, the cases awaiting my dictation, the telephone calls I had yet to return and the others I needed to initiate.

"Might as well," I said hopelessly.

He hesitated, as if waiting for something.

When I looked up at him, I noticed. Marino had gotten his hair cut. He was wearing khaki trousers held up by suspenders and a tweed jacket that looked brand new. His tie was clean, so was his pale yellow shirt. Even his shoes were shined.

"You look downright handsome," I said like a proud mother.

"Yeah." He grinned, his face turning red. "Rose whistled at me when I was getting on the elevator. It was kinda funny. Hadn't had a woman whistle at me in years, except Sugar, and Sugar don't exactly count."

"Sugar?"

"Hangs out on the corner of Adam and Church. Oh yeah, found Sugar, also known as Mad Dog Mama, down in an alleyway, passed out drunk as a skunk, practically ran over her sorry ass. Made the mistake of bringing her to. Fought me like a damn cat and cussed me all the way to lockup. Every time I pass within a block of her, she yells, whistles, hitches up her skirt."

"And you were worrying that you were no longer attractive to women," I said.

11

DAMMIT'S ORIGIN WAS UNDETERMINED, though it was patently clear that every genetic marker he had picked up from every dog in his lineage was the worst of the lot.

"Raised him from a pup," said Mr. Joyce as I returned to him a Polaroid photograph of the dog in question. "He was a stray, you know. Just appeared at the back door one morning and I felt sorry for him, threw him some scraps. Couldn't get rid of him to save my life after that."

We were sitting around Mr. Joyce's kitchen table. Sunlight seeped wanly through a dusty window above a rust-stained porcelain sink, the faucet dripping. Ever since we had arrived fifteen minutes ago, Mr. Joyce had not had a kind word to offer about his slain dog, and yet I detected warmth in his old eyes, and the rough hands thoughtfully stroking the rim of his coffee mug looked capable of tender affection.

"How did he get his name?" Marino wanted to know.

"Never did give him a name, you see. But I was always hollering at him. 'Dammit, shut up! Come here, dammit! Dammit, if you don't stop yapping, I'm gonna wire your mouth shut.' " He smiled sheepishly. "Got to where he thought his name was Dammit. So that's what I took to calling him."

Mr. Joyce was a retired dispatcher for a cement company, his tiny house a monument to rural poverty out in the middle of farmland. I suspected the house's original owner had been a tenant farmer, for on either side of the property were vast expanses of fallow fields that Mr. Joyce said were thick with corn in the summer.

And it had been summer, a hot, sultry July night, when Bonnie Smyth and Jim Freeman had been forced to drive along the sparsely populated dirt road out front. Then November had come, and I passed over the same road, passed right by Mr. Joyce's house, the back of my station wagon packed with folded sheets, stretchers, and body pouches. Less than two miles east of where Mr. Joyce lived was the dense wooded area where the couple's bodies had been found some two years before. An eerie coincidence? What if it wasn't?

"So tell me what happened to Dammit," Marino was saying as he lit a cigarette.

"It was a weekend," Mr. Joyce began. "Middle of August, it seems. Had all the windows open and was sitting in the living room watching TV. 'Dallas.' Funny I can remember that. Guess it means it was a Friday. Nine o'clock's when it came on."

"Then it was between nine and ten when your dog was shot," Marino said.

"That's my guess. Couldn't have been shot much before that or he'd never made it home. I'm watching TV, and next thing I hear him scratching at the door, whimpering. I knew he was hurt, just figured he'd gotten tangled up with a cat or something until I opened the door and got a good look at him."

He got out a pouch of tobacco and began to roll a cigarette in expert, steady hands.

Marino prodded him. "What did you do after that?"

"Put him in my truck and drove him to Doc Whiteside's house. About five miles northwest."

"A veterinarian?" I asked.

He slowly shook his head. "No, ma'am. Didn't have a vet or even know one. Doc Whiteside took care of my wife before she passed on. A mighty nice fellow. Didn't know where else to go, to tell you the truth. Course, it was too late. Wasn't a thing the doc could do by the time I carried the dog in. He said I ought to call the police. Only thing in season in the middle of August is crow, and no good reason in the world anybody should be out late at night shooting at crow or anything else. I did what he said. Called the police."

"Do you have any idea who might have shot your dog?" I asked.

"Like I said, Dammit was bad about chasing folks, going after cars like he was going to chew the tires off. You want my personal opinion, I've always halfway suspected it might have been a cop who done it."

"Why?" Marino asked.

"After the dog was examined, I was told the bullets came from a revolver. So maybe Dammit chased after a police car and that's how it happened."

"Did you see any police cars on your road that night?" Marino asked.

"Nope. Don't mean there wasn't one, though. And I can't be sure where the shooting happened. I know it wasn't nearby. I would've heard it."

"Maybe not if you had your TV turned up loud," Marino said.

"I would've heard it, all right. Not much sound around here, specially late at night. You live here awhile, you get to where you hear the smallest thing out of the ordinary. Even if your TV's on, the windows shut tight."

"Did you hear any cars on your road that night?" Marino asked.

He thought for a moment. "I know one went by not long before Dammit started scratching on the door. The police asked me that. I got the feeling whoever was in it is the one who shot the dog. The officer who took the report sort of thought that, too. Least, that's what he suggested." He paused, staring out the window. "Probably just some kid."

A clock gonged off-key from the living room, then silence, the passing empty seconds measured by water clinking in the sink. Mr. Joyce had no phone. He had very few neighbors, none of whom were close by. I wondered if he had children. It didn't appear he had gotten another dog or found himself a cat. I saw no sign that anybody or anything lived here except him.

"Old Dammit was worthless as hell, but he sort of grew on you. Used to give the mailman a fit. I'd stand there in the living room looking out the window, laughing so hard my eyes was streaming. The sight of it. A puny little fellow, looking around, scared to death to get out of his little mail truck. Old Dammit running in circles snapping at the air. I'd give it a minute or two before I'd start hollering, then out I'd go in the yard. All I had to do was point my finger, and off Dammit would go, tail 'tween his legs." He took a deep breath, the cigarette forgotten in the ashtray. "Lot of meanness out there."

"Yes, sir," Marino agreed, leaning back in his chair. "Meanness everywhere, even in a nice, quiet area like this. Last time I was out this way must've been two years ago, a few weeks before Thanksgiving, when that couple was found in the woods. You remember that?"

"Sure do." Mr. Joyce nodded deeply. "Never seen so much commotion. I was out getting firewood when all of a sudden these police cars come thundering past, lights flashing. Must have been a dozen of them and a couple ambulances, too." He paused, eyeing Marino thoughtfully. "Don't recall seeing you out there." Turning his attention to me, he added, "Guess you were out there, too?"

"I was."

"Thought so." He seemed pleased. "Thought you looked familiar and I've been raking my brain the whole time we've been talking, trying to figure out where I might have seen you before."

"Did you go down to the woods where the bodies were?" Marino asked casually.

"With all those police cars going right past my house, wasn't a way in the world I could just sit here. I couldn't imagine what was going on. No neighbors down that way, just woods. And I was thinking, well, if it's a hunter who got shot, then that don't make sense either. Too many cops for that. So I got in my truck and headed down the road. Found an officer standing by his car and asked him what was going on. He told me some hunters had found a couple bodies back there. Then he wanted to know if I lived nearby. Said I did, and next thing there's a detective at my door asking questions."

"Do you remember the detective's name?" Marino asked.

"Can't say I do."

"What sorts of questions did he ask?"

"Mostly wanted to know if I'd seen anybody in the area, specially around the time this young couple was thought to have disappeared. Any strange cars, things like that."

"Had you?"

"Well, I got to thinking about it after he left, and it's entered my mind now and again ever since," Mr. Joyce said. "Now, the night the police think this couple was taken out here and killed, I didn't hear a thing that I remember. Sometimes I turn in early. Could be I was asleep. But there was something that I remembered a couple months back, after this other couple was found the first of the year."

"Deborah Harvey and Fred Cheney?" I asked.

"The girl whose mother's important."

Marino nodded.

Mr. Joyce went on, "Those murders got me to thinking again about the bodies found out here, and it popped into my mind. If you noticed when you drove up, I have a mailbox out front. Well, I had a bad spell maybe a couple weeks before they think that girl and boy was killed out here several years back."

"Jim Freeman and Bonnie Smyth," Marino said.

"Yes, sir. I had the flu, was throwing up, felt like I had a toothache from head to toe. Stayed in bed what must've been two days and didn't even have the strength to go out and fetch the mail. This night I'm talking about, I was finally up and around, made myself some soup and kept it down all right. So I went out to get the mail. Must have been nine, ten o'clock at night. And right as I was walking back toward the house, I heard this car. Black as tar out and the person was creeping along with his headlights off."

"Which direction was the car going?" Marino asked.

"That way." Mr. Joyce pointed west. "In other words, he was heading away from the area down there where the woods are, back toward the highway. Could be nothing, but I remember it crossed my mind that it was strange. For one thing, there's nothing down there but farmland and woods. I just figured it was kids drinking or parking or something."

"Did you get a good look at the car?" I inquired.

"Seems like it was mid-size, dark in color. Black, dark blue, or dark red, maybe."

"New or old?" Marino asked.

"Don't know if it was brand new, but it wasn't old. Wasn't one of these foreign cars, either."

"How could you tell?" Marino asked.

"By the sound," Mr. Joyce replied easily. "These foreign cars don't sound the same as American ones. The engine's louder, chugs more, don't know exactly how to describe it, but I can tell. Just like when you were pulling up earlier. I knew you were in an American car, probably a Ford or Chevy. This car that went by with its headlights off, it was real quiet, smooth sounding. The shape of it reminded me of one of these new Thunderbirds, but I can't swear to it. Might have been a Cougar."

"It was sporty, then," Marino said.

"Depends on how you look at it. To me, a Corvette's sporty. A Thunderbird or Cougar's fancy."

"Could you tell how many people were inside this car?" I asked.

He shook his head. "Now, I got no idea about that. It was mighty dark out, and I didn't stand there staring."

Marino got a notepad out of his pocket and began flipping through it.

"Mr. Joyce," he said, "Jim Freeman and Bonnie Smyth disappeared July twenty-ninth on a Saturday night. You sure when you saw this car it was before then? Sure it wasn't later on?"

"Sure as I'm sitting here. Reason I know's because I got sick, like I told you. Started coming down with whatever it was the second week of July. I remember that because my wife's birthday's July thirteenth. I always go to the cemetery on her birthday and put flowers on her grave. Had just come home from doing that when I started feeling a little funny. The next day I was too sick to get out of bed." He stared off for a moment. "Must'ave been the fifteenth or sixteenth I went out to get the mail and saw the car."

Marino got out his sunglasses, ready to leave.

Mr. Joyce, who wasn't born yesterday, asked him, "You thinking there's something about these couples dying that's got to do with my dog being shot?"

"We're looking into a lot of things. And it's best if you don't mention this conversation to anyone."

"Won't breathe a word of it, no, sir."

"I'd appreciate it."

He walked us to the door.

"Drop by again when you can," he said. "Come July the tomatoes will be in. Got a garden out back there, best tomatoes in Virginia. But you don't have to wait till then to visit. Anytime. I'm always here."

He watched us from the porch as we drove off.

Marino gave me his opinion as we followed the dirt road back to the highway.

"I'm suspicious about the car he saw two weeks before Bonnie Smyth and Jim Freeman was killed out here."

"So am I."

"As for the dog, I have my doubts. If the dog had been shot weeks, even months, before Jim and Bonnie disappeared, I'd think we were on to something. But hell, Dammit got whacked a good five years before these couples started dying."

Kill zones, I thought. Maybe we were on to something, anyway.

"Marino, have you considered that we may be dealing with

someone for whom the place of death is more important than victim selection?"

He glanced over at me, listening.

"This individual may spend quite a long time finding just the right spot," I went on. "When that is done, he hunts, brings his quarry to this place he has carefully chosen. The place is what is most important, and the time of year. Mr. Joyce's dog was killed in mid-August. The hottest time of the year, but off season as far as hunting goes, except for crow. Each of these couples has been killed off season. In every instance, the bodies have been found weeks, months later, in season. By hunters. It's a pattern."

"Are you suggesting this killer was out scouting the woods for a place to commit murders when the dog trotted up and spoiled his plan?" He glanced over at me, frowning.

"I'm just throwing out a lot of things."

"No offense, but I think you can throw that idea right out the window. Unless the squirrel was fantasizing about whacking couples for years, then finally got around to it."

"My guess is this individual's got a very active fantasy life."

"Maybe you should take up profiling," he said. "You're beginning to sound like Benton."

"And you're beginning to sound as if you've written Benton off."

"Nope. Just not in a mood to deal with him right now."

"He's still your VICAP partner, Marino. You and I are not the only ones under pressure. Don't be too hard on him."

"You sure are into handing out free advice these days," he said.

"Just be glad it's free, because you need all the advice you can get."

"You want to grab some dinner?"

It was getting close to six P.M.

"Tonight I exercise," I replied dismally.

"Geez. Guess that's what you'll be telling *me* to do next."

Just the thought of it made both of us reach for our cigarettes.

I was late for my tennis lesson, despite my doing everything short of running red lights to get to Westwood on time. One of my shoelaces broke, my grip was slippery, and there was a Mexican buffet in progress upstairs, meaning the observation gallery was full of people with nothing better to do than eat tacos, drink margaritas, and witness my humiliation. After sending five backhands in a row sailing well beyond the baseline, I started bending my knees and slowing my swing. The next three shots went into the net. Volleys were pathetic, overheads unmentionable. The harder I tried, the worse I got.

"You're opening up too soon and hitting everything late." Ted came around to my side of the net. "Too much backswing, not enough follow-through. And what happens?"

"I consider taking up bridge," I said, my frustration turning to anger.

"Your racket face is open. Take your racket back early, shoulder turned, step, hitting the ball out front. And keep it on your strings as long as you can."

Following me to the baseline, he demonstrated, stroking several balls over the net as I watched jealously. Ted had Michelangelo muscle definition, liquid coordination, and he could, without effort, put enough spin on a ball to make it bounce over your head or die at your feet. I wondered if magnificent athletes had any concept of how they made the rest of us feel.

"Most of your problem's in your head, Dr. Scarpetta," he said. "You walk out here and want to be Martina when you'd be much better off being yourself."

"Well, I sure as hell can't be Martina," I muttered.

"Don't be so determined to win points when you ought to be working at not losing them. Playing smart, setting up, keeping the ball in play until your opponent misses or gives you an easy opening to put the ball away. Out here that's the game. Club-level matches aren't won. They're lost. Someone beats you not because they win more points than you but because you lose more points than them." Looking speculatively at me, he added, "I'll bet you're not this impatient in your work. I'll bet you hit every ball back, so to speak, and can do it all day long."

I wasn't so sure about that, but Ted's coaching did the opposite of what he had intended. It took my mind off tennis. Playing smart. Later, I pondered this at length while soaking in the tub.

We weren't going to beat this killer. Planting bullets and newspaper stories were offensive tactics that had not worked. A little defensive strategy was in order. Criminals who escape apprehension are not perfect but lucky. They make mistakes. All of them do. The problem is recognizing the errors, realizing their significance, and determining what was intentional and what was not.

I thought of the cigarette butts we'd been finding near the bodies. Had the killer intentionally left them? Probably. Were they a mistake? No, because they were worthless as evidence and we could not determine their brand. The jacks of hearts left in the vehicles were intentional, but they were not a mistake either. No fingerprints had been recovered from them, and if anything, their purpose may be to make us think what the person who had left them wanted us to think.

Shooting Deborah Harvey I was sure was a mistake.

Then there was the perpetrator's past, which was what I was considering now. He didn't suddenly go from being a law-abiding citizen to becoming an experienced murderer. What sins had he committed before, what acts of evil?

For one thing, he may have shot an old man's dog eight years ago. If I was right, then he had made another mistake, because the incident suggested he was local, not new to the area. It made me wonder if he had killed before.

Immediately after staff meeting the following morning, I had my computer analyst, Margaret, give me a printout of every homicide that had occurred within a fifty-mile radius of Camp Peary over the past ten years. Though I wasn't necessarily looking for a double homicide, that was exactly what I found.

Numbers C0104233 and C0104234. I had never heard of the related cases, which had occurred several years before I moved to Virginia. Returning to my office, I shut the doors and reviewed the files with growing excitement. Jill Harrington and Elizabeth Mott had been murdered eight years ago in September, a month after Mr. Joyce's dog was shot.

Both women were in their early twenties when they disappeared eight years before on the Friday night of September fourteenth, their bodies found the next morning in a church cemetery. It wasn't until the following day that the Volkswagen belonging to Elizabeth was located in a motel parking lot off Route 60 in Lightfoot, just outside of Williamsburg.

I began studying autopsy reports and body diagrams. Elizabeth Mott had been shot once in the neck, after which, it was conjectured, she was stabbed once in the chest, her throat cut. She was fully clothed, with no evidence of sexual assault, no bullet was recovered, and there were ligature marks around her wrists. There were no defense injuries. Jill's records, however, told another story. She bore defense cuts to both forearms and hands, and contusions and lacerations to her face and scalp consistent with being "pistol whipped," and her blouse was torn. Apparently, she had put up one hell of a struggle, ending with her being stabbed eleven times.

According to newspaper clips included in their files, the James City County police said the women were last seen drinking beer in the Anchor Bar and Grill in Williamsburg, where they stayed until approximately ten P.M. It was theorized that it was here they met up with their assailant, a "Mr. Goodbar" situation, in which the two women left with him and followed him to the motel where Elizabeth's car was later found. At some point he abducted them, perhaps in the parking lot, and forced them to drive him to the cemetery where he murdered them.

There was a lot about the scenario that didn't make sense to me. The police had found blood in the backseat of the Volkswagen that could not be explained. The blood type did not match up with either woman's. If the blood was the killer's, then what happened? Did he struggle with one of the women in the backseat? If so, why wasn't her blood found as well? If both women were up front and he was in back, then how did he get injured? If he cut himself while struggling with Jill in the cemetery, then that didn't make sense, either. After the murders, he would have had to drive their car from the cemetery to the motel, and his blood should have been in the driver's area, not in the backseat. Finally, if the man intended to murder the women after engaging in sexual activity, why didn't he just kill them inside the motel room? And why were the women's physical evidence recovery kits negative for sperm? Had they engaged in intercourse with this man and then cleaned up afterward? *Two* women with one man? A ménage à trois? Well, I supposed, there wasn't much I hadn't seen in my line of work.

Buzzing the computer analyst's office, I got Margaret on the line.

"I need you to run something else for me," I said. "A list of all drug-positive homicide cases worked by James City County Detective R. P. Montana. And I need the information right away, if you can manage it."

"No problem." I could hear her fingers clicking over the keyboard.

When I got the printout there were six drug-positive homicides investigated by Detective Montana. The names of Elizabeth Mott and Jill Harrington were on the list, because their postmortem blood was positive for alcohol. The result in each instance was insignificant, less than .05. In addition, Jill was positive for chlordiazepoxide and clidinium, the active drugs found in Librax.

Reaching for the phone, I dialed the James City County Detective Division and asked to speak to Montana. I was told he was a captain now in Internal Affairs, and my call was transferred to his desk.

I intended to be very careful. If it were perceived I was considering that the murders of the two women might be related to the deaths of the other five couples, I feared Montana would back off, not talk.

"Montana," a deep voice answered.

"This is Dr. Scarpetta," I said.

"How'ya doing, Doc? Everybody in Richmond's still shooting each other, I see."

"It doesn't seem to get much better," I agreed. "I'm surveying for drug-positive homicides," I explained. "And I wonder if I could ask you a question or two about several old cases of yours I came across in our computer."

"Fire away. But it's been a while. I may be a little fuzzy on the details."

"Basically, I'm interested in the scenarios, the details surrounding the deaths. Most of your cases occurred before I came to Richmond."

"Oh, yeah, back in the days of Doc Cagney. Working with him was something." Montana laughed. "Never forget the way he used to sometimes dig around in bodies without gloves. Nothing fazed him except kids. He didn't like doing kids."

I began reviewing the information from the computer print-out, and what Montana recalled about each case didn't surprise me. Hard drinking and domestic problems had culminated in husband shooting wife or the other way around—the Smith & Wesson divorce, as it was irreverently referred to by the police. A man tanked to the gills was beaten to death by several drunk companions after a poker game went sour. A father with a .30 blood alcohol level was shot to death by his son. And so on. I saved Jill's and Elizabeth's cases for last.

"I remember them real well," Montana said. "Weird's all I got to say about what happened to those two girls. Wouldn't have thought they were the type to go off to a motel with some guy who picked them up in a bar. Both of them college graduates, had good jobs, smart, attractive. It's my opinion the guy they met up with had to be mighty slick. We're not talking about some redneck type. I've always suspected it was someone just passing through, not from around here."

"Why?"

"Because if it was someone local, I think we might have had a little luck developing a suspect. Some serial killer, it's my opinion. Picks up women in bars and murders them. Maybe some guy on the road a lot, hits in different cities and towns, then moves on."

"Was robbery involved?" I asked.

"Didn't appear to be. My first thought when I got the cases was maybe the two girls were into recreational drugs, went off with someone to make a buy, maybe agreed to meet him at the motel to party or exchange cash for coke. But no money or jewelry was missing, and I never found out anything to make me think the girls had a history of snorting or shooting up."

"I notice from the toxicology reports that Jill Harrington tested positive for Librax, in addition to alcohol," I said. "Do you know anything about that?"

He thought for a moment. "Librax. Nope. Doesn't ring a bell."

I asked him nothing else and thanked him.

Librax is a versatile therapeutic drug used as a muscle relaxant and to relieve anxiety and tension. Jill may have suffered from a bad back or soreness due to sports injuries, or she may have had psychosomatic problems such as spasms in her gastrointestinal tract. My next chore was to find her physician. I began by calling one of my medical examiners in Williamsburg and asking him to fax the section in his Yellow Pages that listed pharmacies in his area. Then I dialed Marino's pager number.

"Do you have any police friends in Washington? Anyone you trust?" I said when Marino rang me back.

"I know a couple of guys. Why?"

"It's very important I talk to Abby Turnbull. And I don't think it's a good idea for me to call her."

"Not unless you want to take the risk of someone knowing about it."

"Exactly."

"You ask me," he added, "it's not a good idea for you to talk to her anyway."

"I understand your point of view. But that doesn't change my mind, Marino. Could you contact one of your friends up there and send him to her apartment, have him see if he can locate her?"

"I think you're making a mistake. But yeah. I'll take care of it."

"Just have him tell her I need to talk to her. I want her to contact me immediately." I gave Marino her address.

By this time, the copies of the Yellow Pages I was interested in had come off the fax machine down the hall and Rose placed them on my desk. For the rest of the afternoon, I called every pharmacy that Jill Harrington might have patronized in Williamsburg. I finally located one that had her listed in their records.

"Was she a regular customer?" I asked the pharmacist.

"Sure was. Elizabeth Mott was, too. Both of them didn't live too far from here, in an apartment complex just down the road. Nice young women, never will forget how shocked I was."

"Did they live together?"

"Let me see." A pause. "Wouldn't appear so. Different addresses and phone numbers, but the same apartment complex. Old Towne, about two miles away. Nice enough place. A lot of young people, William and Mary students out there."

He went on to give me Jill's medication history. Over a period of three years, Jill had brought in prescriptions for various antibiotics, cough suppressants, and other medications associated with the mundane flu bugs and respiratory or urinary tract infections that commonly afflict the hoi polloi. As recently as a month before her murder, she had been in to fill a prescription for Septra, which she apparently was no longer on when she died, since trimethoprim and sulfamethoxazole were not detected in her blood.

"Did you ever dispense Librax to her?" I asked.

I waited while he looked.

"No, ma'am. No record of that."

Perhaps the prescription was Elizabeth's, I considered.

"What about her friend Elizabeth Mott?" I asked the pharmacist. "Did she ever come in with a prescription for Librax?"

"No."

"Was there any other pharmacy either woman patronized that you're aware of?"

"Afraid I can't help you on that one. Got no idea."

He gave me the names of other pharmacies close by. I had already called most of them, and calls to the rest confirmed neither woman had brought in a prescription for Librax or any other drug. The Librax itself wasn't necessarily important, I reasoned. But the mystery of who had prescribed it and why bothered me considerably.

12

ABBY TURNBULL HAD BEEN a crime reporter in Richmond when Elizabeth Mott and Jill Harrington were murdered. I was willing to bet that Abby not only remembered the cases, but probably knew more about them than Captain Montana did.

The next morning she called from a pay phone and left a number where she told Rose she would wait for fifteen minutes. Abby insisted that I call her back from a "safe place."

"Is everything all right?" Rose asked quietly as I peeled off my surgical gloves.

"God only knows," I said, untying my gown.

The nearest "safe place" I could think of was a pay phone outside the cafeteria in my building. Breathless and somewhat frantic to meet Abby's deadline, I dialed the number my secretary had given me.

"What's going on?" Abby asked immediately. "Some Metro cop came by my apartment, said you'd sent him."

"That's correct," I reassured her. "Based on what you've told me, I didn't think it a good idea to call you at home. Are you all right?"

"Is that why you wanted me to call?" She sounded disappointed.

"One of the reasons. We need to talk."

There was a long silence on the line.

"I'll be in Williamsburg on Saturday," she then said. "Dinner, The Trellis at seven?"

I did not ask her why she was going to be in Williamsburg. I wasn't sure I wanted to know, but when I parked my car in Merchant's Square Saturday, I found my apprehensions diminishing with each step I took. It was hard to be preoccupied with murder and other acts of incivility while sipping hot apple cider in the sharp wintry air of one of my favorite places in America.

It was a low season for tourists, and there were still plenty of people about, strolling, browsing inside the restored shops, and riding past in horse-drawn carriages driven by liverymen in knee breeches and three-cornered hats. Mark and I had talked about spending a weekend in Williamsburg. We would rent one of the eighteenth-century carriage houses inside the Historic District, follow cobblestone sidewalks beneath the glow of gaslights and dine in one of the taverns, then drink wine before the fire until falling asleep in each other's arms.

Of course, none of it had come to pass, the history of our relationship more wishes than memories. Would it ever be different from this? Recently, he had promised me on the phone that it would. But he had promised before, and so had I. He was still in Denver and I was still here.

Inside the Silversmith's Shop, I bought a handwrought sterling silver pineapple charm and a handsome chain. Lucy would get a late Valentine's Day present from her negligent aunt. A forage inside the Apothecary Shop brought forth soaps for my guest room, spicy shaving cream for Fielding and Marino, and potpourri for Bertha and Rose. At five minutes before seven, I was inside The Trellis looking for Abby. When she arrived half an hour later, I was impatiently waiting at a table nestled against a planter of wandering jew.

"I'm sorry," she said with feeling, slipping out of her coat. "I got delayed. Got here as fast as I could."

She looked keyed up and exhausted, her eyes nervously darting about. The Trellis was doing a brisk business, people talking in low voices in the wavering shadows of candlelight. I wondered if Abby felt she had been followed.

"Have you been in Williamsburg all day?" I asked.

She nodded.

"I don't suppose I dare ask what you've been doing."

"Research" was all she said.

"Nowhere near Camp Peary, I hope." I looked her in the eye.

She got my meaning very well. "You know," she said.

The waitress arrived and then went off to the bar to get Abby a Bloody Mary.

"How did you find out?" Abby asked, lighting a cigarette.

"A better question is how did *you* find out?"

"I can't tell you that, Kay."

Of course she couldn't. But I knew. Pat Harvey.

"You have a source," I said carefully. "Let me just ask you this. Why would this source want you to know? Information wasn't passed on to you without there being motive on the source's part."

"I'm well aware of that."

"Then why?"

"The truth is important." Abby stared off. "I'm also a source."

"I see. In exchange for information, you pass on what you dig up."

She did not respond.

"Does this include me?" I asked.

"I'm not going to screw you, Kay. Have I ever?" She looked hard at me.

"No," I said sincerely. "So far, you never have."

Her Bloody Mary was set before her, and she absently stirred it with the stalk of celery.

"All I can tell you," I went on, "is you're walking on dangerous ground. I don't need to elaborate. You should realize this better than anyone. Is it worth the stress? Is your book worth the price, Abby?"

When she made no comment, I added with a sigh, "I don't guess I'm going to change your mind, am I?"

"Have you ever gotten into something you can't get out of?"

"I do it all the time." I smiled wryly. "That's where I am now."

"That's where I am, too."

"I see. And what if you're wrong, Abby?"

"I'm not the one who can be wrong," she replied. "Whatever the truth is about who's committing these murders, the fact remains that the FBI and other interested agencies are acting on certain suspicions and making decisions based on them. That's reportable. If the feds, the police, are wrong, it just adds another chapter."

"That sounds awfully cold," I said uneasily.

"I'm being professional, Kay. When you talk professionally, sometimes you sound cold, too."

I had talked to Abby directly after the body of her murdered sister was discovered. If I hadn't sounded cold on that horrible occasion, at best I had come across as clinical.

"I need your help with something," I said. "Eight years ago, two women were murdered very close to here. Elizabeth Mott and Jill Harrington."

She looked curiously at me. "You don't think—"

"I'm not sure what I'm thinking," I interrupted. "But I need to know the details of the cases. There's very little in my office reports. I wasn't in Virginia then. But there are news clips in the files. Several of them have your byline."

"It's hard for me to imagine that what happened to Jill and Elizabeth is connected to the other cases."

"So you remember them," I said, relieved.

"I will never forget them. It was one of the few times working on something actually gave me nightmares."

"Why is it hard for you to imagine a connection?"

"A number of reasons. There was no jack of hearts found. The car wasn't found abandoned on a roadside, but in a motel parking lot, and the bodies didn't turn up weeks or months after the fact decomposing in the woods. They were found within twenty-four hours. Both victims were women, and they were in their twenties, not teenagers. And why would the killer strike and then not do it again until some five years later?"

"I agree," I said. "The timing doesn't fit with the profile of your typical serial killer. And the MO seems inconsistent with the others. The victim selection seems inconsistent as well."

"Then why are you so interested?" She sipped her drink.

"I'm groping, and I'm troubled by their cases, which were never solved," I admitted. "It's unusual for two people to be abducted and murdered. There was no evidence of sexual assault. The women were killed around here, in the same area where the other murders have occurred."

"And a gun and a knife were used," Abby mused.

She knew about Deborah Harvey, then.

"There are some parallels," I said evasively.

Abby looked unconvinced but interested.

"What do you want to know, Kay?"

"Anything you might remember about them. Anything at all."

She thought for a long moment, toying with her drink.

"Elizabeth was working in sales for a local computer company and doing extremely well," she said. "Jill had just finished law school at William and Mary and had gone to work with a small firm in Williamsburg. I never did buy the notion that they went off to a motel to have sex with some creep they met in a bar. Neither of the women struck me as the type. And two of them with one man? I always thought it was strange. Also, there was blood in the backseat of their car. It didn't match either Jill's or Elizabeth's blood types."

Abby's resourcefulness never ceased to amaze me. Somehow she had gotten hold of the serology results.

"I assume the blood belonged to the killer. There was a lot of it, Kay. I saw the car. It looked as if someone had been stabbed or cut in the backseat. Possibly, this would place the killer there, but it was hard to come up with a good interpretation of what might have occurred. The police were of the opinion the women met up with this animal in the Anchor Bar and Grill. But if he rode off with them in their car and was planning to kill them, then how was he going to get back to his car later on?"

"Depends on how far the motel is from the bar. He could have walked back to his car after the murders."

"The motel is a good four or five miles from the Anchor Bar, which isn't around anymore, by the way. The women were last seen inside the bar at around ten P.M. If the killer had left his car there, it probably would have been the only one in the lot by the time he got back to it, and that wouldn't have been very bright. A cop might have noticed the car, or at least the night manager would have as he was locking up to go home."

"This doesn't preclude the killer leaving his car at the motel and abducting them in Elizabeth's, then returning later, getting into his car, and driving off," I pointed out.

"No, it doesn't. But if he drove his own car to the motel, then when did he get inside hers? The scenario of the three of them being inside a motel room together, and then forcing them to drive him to the cemetery, has never set well with me. Why go to all the trouble, the risk? They could have started screaming in the parking lot, could have resisted. Why not just murder them inside the room?"

"Was it verified that the three of them were ever inside one of the rooms?"

"That's the other thing," she said. "I questioned the clerk

who was on duty that night. The Palm Leaf, a low-rent motel off Route Sixty in Lightfoot. Doesn't exactly do a thriving business. But the clerk didn't remember either woman. Nor did he remember some guy coming in and renting a room near where the Volkswagen was found. In fact, most of the rooms in that section of the motel were vacant at the time. More important, no one checked in and then left without turning in the key. Hard to believe this guy would have had opportunity or inclination to check out. Certainly not after committing the crimes. He would have been bloody."

"What was your theory when you were working on your stories?" I asked.

"The same as it is now. I don't think they met up with their killer inside the bar. I think something happened shortly after Elizabeth and Jill left."

"Such as?"

Frowning, Abby was stirring her drink again. "I don't know. They definitely weren't the type to pick up a hitchhiker, certainly not at that late hour. And I never believed there was a drug connection. Neither Jill nor Elizabeth was found to have used coke, heroin, or anything like that, and no paraphernalia was found inside their apartments. They didn't smoke, weren't heavy drinkers. Both of them jogged, were health nuts."

"Do you know where they were heading after they left the bar? Were they going straight home? Might they have stopped somewhere?"

"No evidence if they did."

"And they left the bar alone?"

"Nobody I talked to remembered seeing them with another person while they were in the bar drinking. As I remember it, they had a couple of beers, were at a corner table talking. Nobody recalled seeing them leave with anyone."

"They might have met someone in the parking lot when they left," I said. "This individual might even have been waiting in Elizabeth's car."

"I doubt they would have left the car unlocked, but I suppose it's possible."

"Did the women frequent this bar?"

"As I remember it, they didn't frequent it, but they'd gone there before."

"A rough place?"

"That was my expectation since it was a favorite watering hole for military guys," she replied. "But it reminded me of an English pub. Civilized. People talking, playing darts. It was the sort of place I could have gone with a friend and felt quite comfortable and private. The theory was that the killer was either someone passing through town or else a military person temporarily stationed in the area. It wasn't someone they knew."

Perhaps not, I thought. But it must have been someone they felt they could trust, at least initially, and I recalled what Hilda Ozimek had said about the encounters being "friendly" at first. I wondered what would come to her if I showed her photographs of Elizabeth and Jill.

"Did Jill have any medical problems you're aware of?" I asked.

She thought about this, her face perplexed. "I don't recall."

"Where was she from?"

"Kentucky comes to mind."

"Did she go home often?"

"I didn't get that impression. I think she made it home for holidays and that was about it."

Then it wasn't likely she had a prescription for Librax filled in Kentucky where her family lived, I thought.

"You mentioned she had just begun practicing law," I went on. "Did she travel much, have reason to be in and out of town?"

She waited as our chef's salads were served, then said, "She had a close friend from law school. I can't remember his name, but I talked to him, asked him about her habits, activities. He said he was suspicious Jill was having an affair."

"What made him suspect that?"

"Because during their third year of law school she drove to Richmond almost every week, supposedly because she was job hunting, liked Richmond a lot, and wanted to find an opening in a firm there. He told me she often needed to borrow his notes because her out-of-town excursions caused her to miss classes. He thought it was strange, especially since she ended up going with a firm here in Williamsburg right after graduation. He went on and on about it because he was afraid her trips might be related to her murder, if she were seeing a married man in Richmond, for example, and perhaps threatened to expose their affair to his wife. Maybe she was having an affair with someone prominent, a successful lawyer or judge, who couldn't afford the scandal, so he silenced Jill forever. Or got someone else to, and it just so happened Elizabeth had the misfortune of being around at the time."

"What do you think?"

"The lead went nowhere, like ninety percent of the tips I get."

"Was Jill romantically involved with the student who told you this?"

"I think he would have liked for her to have been," she said. "But no, they weren't involved. I got the impression this was, in part, the reason for his suspicions. He was pretty sure of himself and figured the only reason Jill never succumbed to his charms was because she had somebody else nobody knew about. A secret lover."

"Was he ever a suspect, this student?" I asked.

"Not at all. He was out of town when the murders occurred, and that was verified beyond a doubt."

"Did you talk to any of the other lawyers in the firm where Jill worked?"

"I didn't get very far with that," Abby answered. "You know how lawyers are. In any event, she'd been with the firm only a few months before she was murdered. I don't think her colleagues knew her very well."

"Doesn't sound as if Jill was an extrovert," I remarked.

"She was described as charismatic, witty, but self-contained."

"And Elizabeth?" I asked.

"More outgoing, I think," she said. "Which I suppose she had to have been to be good in sales."

The glow of gaslight lamps pushed the darkness back from cobblestone sidewalks as we walked to the Merchant's Square parking lot. A heavy layer of clouds obscured the moon, the damp, cold air penetrating.

"I wonder what these couples would be doing now, if they'd still be with each other, what difference they might have made," Abby said, chin tucked into her collar, hands in her pockets.

"What do you think Henna would be doing?" I gently asked about her sister.

"She'd probably still be in Richmond. I guess both of us would be."

"Are you sorry you moved?"

"Some days I'm sorry about everything. Ever since Henna died, it's as if I've had no options, no free will. It's as if I've been propelled along by things out of my control."

"I don't see it that way. You chose to take the job at the *Post*, move to D.C. And now you've chosen to write a book."

"Just as Pat Harvey chose to hold that press conference and do all the other things she's done that have burned her so badly," she said.

"Yes, she has made choices, too."

"When you're going through something like this, you don't know what you're doing, even if you think you do," she went on. "And no one can really understand what it's like unless they've suffered the same thing. You feel isolated. You go places and people avoid you, are afraid to meet your eyes and make conversation because they don't know what to say. So they whisper to each other. 'See her over there? Her sister was the one murdered by the strangler.' Or 'That's Pat Harvey. Her daughter was the one.' You feel as if you're living inside a cave. You're afraid to be alone, afraid to be with others, afraid to be awake, and afraid to go to sleep because of how awful it feels when morning comes. You run like hell and wear yourself out. As I look back, I can see that everything I've done since Henna died was half crazy."

"I think you've done remarkably well," I said sincerely.

"You don't know the things I've done. The mistakes I've made."

"Come on. I'll drive you to your car," I said, for we had reached Merchant's Square.

I heard a car engine start in the dark lot as I got out my keys. We were inside my Mercedes, doors locked and seat belts on when a new Lincoln pulled up beside us and the driver's window hummed down.

I opened my window just enough to hear what the man wanted. He was young, clean cut, folding a map and struggling with it.

"Excuse me." He smiled helplessly. "Can you tell me how to get back on Sixty-four East from here?"

I could feel Abby's tension as I gave him quick directions.

"Get his plate number," she said urgently as he drove away. She dug in her pocketbook for a pen and notepad.

"E-N-T-eight-nine-nine," I read quickly.

She wrote it down.

"What's going on?" I asked, unnerved.

Abby looked left and right for any sign of his car as I pulled out of the lot.

"Did you notice his car when we got to the parking lot?" she asked.

I had to think. The parking lot was nearly empty when we had gotten there. I had been vaguely aware of a car that might have been the Lincoln parked in a poorly lit corner.

I told Abby this, adding, "But I assumed no one was in it."

"Right. Because the car's interior light wasn't on."

"I guess not."

"Reading a map in the dark, Kay?"

"Good point," I said, startled.

"And if he's from out of town, then how do you explain the parking sticker on his rear bumper?"

"Parking sticker?" I repeated.

"It had the Colonial Williamsburg seal on it. The same sticker I was given years ago when the skeletal remains were discovered at that archaeology dig, Martin's Hundred. I did a series, was out here a lot, and the sticker permitted me to park inside the Historic District and at Carter's Grove."

"The guy works here and needed directions to Sixty-four?" I muttered.

"You got a good look at him?" she asked.

"Pretty good. Do you think it was the man who followed you that night in Washington?"

"I don't know. But maybe . . . Damn it, Kay! This is making me crazy!"

"Well, enough is enough," I said firmly. "Give me that license number. I intend to do something about it."

———

The next morning Marino called with the cryptic message, "If you haven't read the *Post*, better go out and get a copy."

"Since when do you read the *Post*?"

"Since never, if I can help it. Benton alerted me about an hour ago. Call me later. I'm downtown."

Putting on a warm-up suit and ski jacket, I drove through a downpour to a nearby drugstore. For the better part of half an hour I sat inside my car, heater blasting, windshield wipers a monotonous metronome in the hard, cold rain. I was appalled by what I read. Several times it entered my mind that if the Harveys didn't sue Clifford Ring, I should.

The front page carried the first in a three-part series about

Deborah Harvey, Fred Cheney, and the other couples who had died. Nothing sacred was spared, Ring's reporting so comprehensive it included details even I did not know.

Not long before Deborah Harvey was murdered, she had confided to a friend her suspicions that her father was an alcoholic and having an affair with an airline flight attendant half his age. Apparently, Deborah had eavesdropped on a number of telephone conversations between her father and his alleged mistress. The flight attendant lived in Charlotte, and according to the story, Harvey was with her the night his daughter and Fred Cheney disappeared, which was why the police and Mrs. Harvey were unable to reach him. Ironically, Deborah's suspicions did not make her bitter toward her father but her mother, who, consumed with her career, was never home, and therefore, in Deborah's eyes, to blame for her father's infidelity and alcohol abuse.

Column after column of vitriolic print added up to paint a pathetic portrait of a powerful woman bent on saving the world while her own family disintegrated from neglect. Pat Harvey had married into money, her home in Richmond was palatial, her quarters at the Watergate filled with antiques and valuable art, including a Picasso and a Remington. She wore the right clothes, went to the right parties, her decorum impeccable, her policies and knowledge of world affairs brilliant.

Yet lurking behind this plutocratic, flawless facade, Ring concluded, was "a driven woman born in a blue-collar section of Baltimore, someone described by her colleagues as tormented by insecurity that perpetually propelled her into proving herself." Pat Harvey, he said, was a megalomaniac. She was irrational—if not rabid—when threatened or put to the test.

His treatment of the homicides that had occurred in Virginia over the past three years was just as relentless. He disclosed the fears of the CIA and FBI that the killer might be someone at Camp Peary, and served up this revelation with such a wild spin that it made everyone involved look bad.

The CIA and the Justice Department were involved in a cover-up, their paranoia so extreme they had encouraged investigators in Virginia to withhold information from each other. False evidence had been planted at a scene. Disinformation had been "leaked" to reporters, and it was even suspected that some reporters were under surveillance. Pat Harvey, meanwhile, was supposedly privy to all this, and her indignation was not exactly depicted as righteous, as evidenced by her demeanor during her infamous press conference. Engaged in a turf battle with the Justice Department, Mrs. Harvey had exploited sensitive information to incriminate and harass those federal agencies with which she had become increasingly at odds due to her campaign against fraudulent charities such as ACTMAD.

The final ingredient in this poisonous stew was me. I had stonewalled and withheld case information at the request of the FBI until forced by threat of a court order to release my reports to the families. I had refused to talk to the press. Though I had no formal obligation to answer to the FBI, it was suggested by Clifford Ring that it was possible my professional behavior was influenced by my personal life. "According to a source close to Virginia's Chief Medical Examiner," the article read, "Dr. Scarpetta has been romantically involved with an FBI Special Agent for the past two years, has frequently visited Quantico and is on friendly terms with the Academy's personnel, including Benton Wesley, the profiler involved in these cases."

I wondered how many readers would conclude from this that I was having an affair with Wesley.

Impeached along with my integrity and morals was my competence as a forensic pathologist. In the ten cases in question, I had been unable to determine a cause of death in all of them but one, and when I discovered a cut on one of Deborah Harvey's bones, I was so worried that I had inflicted this myself with a scalpel, claimed Ring, that I "drove to Washington in the snow, Harvey's and Cheney's skeletons in the trunk of her Mercedes, and sought the advice of a forensic anthropologist at the Smithsonian's National Museum of Natural History."

Like Pat Harvey, I had "consulted a psychic." I had accused investigators of tampering with Fred Cheney's and Deborah Harvey's remains at the scene, and then returned to the wooded area to search for a cartridge case myself because I did not trust the police to find it. I had also taken it upon myself to question witnesses, including a clerk at a 7-Eleven, where Fred and Deborah were last seen alive. I smoked, drank, had a license to carry my .38 concealed, had "almost been killed" on several occasions, was divorced and "from Miami." The latter somehow seemed an explanation for all of the above.

The way Clifford Ring made it sound, I was an arrogant,

gunslinging wild woman who, when it came to forensic medicine, didn't know her ass from a hole in the ground.

Abby, I thought, as I sped home over rain-slick streets. Was this what she meant last night when she referred to mistakes she had made? Had she fed information to her colleague Clifford Ring?

"That wouldn't add up," Marino pointed out later as we sat in my kitchen drinking coffee. "Not that my opinion about her's changed. I think she'd sell her grandmother for a story. But she's working on this big book, right? Don't make sense that she'd share information with the competition, especially since she's pissed off at the *Post*."

"Some of the information had to have come from her." It was hard for me to admit. "The bit about the Seven-Eleven clerk, for example. Abby and I were together that night. And she knows about Mark."

"How?" Marino looked curiously at me.

"I told her."

He just shook his head.

Sipping my coffee, I stared out at the rain. Abby had tried to call twice since I'd gotten home from the drugstore. I had stood by my machine listening to her tense voice. I wasn't ready to talk to her yet. I was afraid of what I might say.

"How's Mark going to react?" Marino asked.

"Fortunately, the story didn't mention his name."

I felt another wave of anxiety. Typical of FBI agents, especially those who had spent years under deep cover, Mark was secretive about his personal life to the point of paranoia. The paper's allusion to our relationship would upset him considerably, I feared. I had to call him. Or maybe I shouldn't. I didn't know what to do.

"Some of the information, I suspect, came from Morrell," I went on, thinking aloud.

Marino was silent.

"Vessey must have talked, too. Or at least someone at the Smithsonian did," I said. "And I don't know how the hell Ring found out that we went to see Hilda Ozimek."

Setting down his cup and saucer, Marino leaned forward and met my eyes.

"My turn to give advice."

I felt like a child about to be scolded.

"It's like a cement truck with no brakes going down a hill. You ain't going to stop it, Doc. All you can do is get out of the way."

"Would you care to translate?" I said impatiently.

"Just do your work and forget it. If you get questioned, and I'm sure you will, just say you never talked to Clifford Ring, don't know nothing about it. Brush it off, in other words. You get into a pissing match with the press and you're going to end up like Pat Harvey. Looking like an idiot."

He was right.

"And if you got any sense, don't talk to Abby anytime soon."

I nodded.

He stood up. "Meanwhile, I got a few things to run down. If they pan out, I'll let you know."

That reminded me. Fetching my pocketbook, I got out the slip of paper with the plate number Abby had taken down.

"Wonder if you could check NCIC. A Lincoln Mark Seven, dark gray. See what comes back."

"Someone tailing you?" He tucked the slip of paper in his pocket.

"I don't know. The driver stopped to ask directions. I don't think he was really lost."

"Where?" he asked as I walked him to the door.

"Williamsburg. He was sitting in the car in an empty parking lot. This was around ten-thirty, eleven last night at Merchant's Square. I was getting into my car when his headlights suddenly went on and he drove over, asked me how to get to Sixty-four."

"Huh," Marino said shortly. "Probably some dumb-shit detective working under cover, bored, waiting for someone to run a red light or make a U-turn. Might have been trying to hit on you, too. A decent-looking woman out at night alone, climbing into a Mercedes."

I didn't offer that Abby had been with me. I didn't want another lecture.

"I wasn't aware that many detectives drive new Lincolns," I said.

"Would you look at the rain. Shit," he complained as he ran to his car.

———

Fielding, my deputy chief, was never too preoccupied or busy to glance at any reflective object he happened to pass. This included plate-glass windows, computer screens, and the bulletproof security partitions separating the lobby from our inner offices. When I got off the elevator on the first floor, I spotted him pausing before the morgue's stainless-steel refrigerator door, smoothing back his hair.

"It's getting a little long over your ears," I said.

"And yours is getting a little gray." He grinned.

"Ash. Blonds go ash, never gray."

"Right." He absently tightened the drawstring of his surgical greens, biceps bulging like grapefruits. Fielding couldn't blink without flexing something formidable. Whenever I saw him hunched over his microscope, I was reminded of a steroid version of Rodin's *The Thinker*.

"Jackson was released about twenty minutes ago," he said, referring to one of the morning's cases. "That's it, but we've already got one for tomorrow. The guy they had on life support from the shoot-out over the weekend."

"What's on your schedule for the rest of the afternoon?" I asked. "And that reminds me, I thought you had court in Petersburg."

"The defendant pleaded." He glanced at his watch. "About an hour ago."

"He must have heard you were coming."

"Micros are stacked up to the ceiling in the cinder-block cell the state calls my office. That's my agenda for the afternoon. Or at least it was." He looked speculatively at me.

"I've got a problem I'm hoping you can help me with. I need to track down a prescription that may have been filled in Richmond eight or so years ago."

"Which pharmacy?"

"If I knew that," I said as we took the elevator to the second floor, "then I wouldn't have a problem. What it amounts to is we need to organize a telethon, so to speak. As many people as possible on the lines calling every pharmacy in Richmond."

Fielding winced. "Jesus, Kay, there's got to be at least a hundred."

"A hundred and thirty-three. I've already counted. Six of us with a list of twenty-two, twenty-three, each. That's fairly manageable. Can you help me out?"

"Sure." He looked depressed.

In addition to Fielding, I drafted my administrator, Rose, another secretary, and the computer analyst. We assembled in the conference room with lists of the pharmacies. My instructions were quite clear. Discretion. Not a word about what we were doing to family, friends, or the police. Since the prescription had to be at least eight years old and Jill was deceased, there was a good chance the records were no longer in the active files. I told them to ask the pharmacist to check the drugstore's archives. If he was uncooperative or reluctant to release the information, roll that call over to me.

Then we disappeared into our respective offices. Two hours later, Rose appeared at my desk, tenderly massaging her right ear.

She handed me a call sheet and could not suppress a triumphant smile. "Boulevard Drug Store at Boulevard and Broad. Jill Harrington had two prescriptions for Librax filled." She gave me the dates.

"Her physician?"

"Dr. Anna Zenner," she answered.

Good God.

Hiding my surprise, I congratulated her. "You're wonderful, Rose. Take the rest of the day off."

"I leave at four-thirty anyway. I'm late."

"Then take a three-hour lunch tomorrow." I felt like hugging her. "And tell the others mission accomplished. They can put down the phones."

"Wasn't Dr. Zenner the president of the Richmond Academy of Medicine not so long ago?" Rose asked, pausing thoughtfully in my doorway. "Seems I read something about her. Oh! She's the musician."

"She was the president of the Academy year before last. And yes, she plays the violin for the Richmond Symphony."

"Then you know her." My secretary looked impressed.

All too well, I thought, reaching for the phone.

That evening, when I was home, Anna Zenner returned my call.

"I see from the papers you have been very busy lately, Kay," she said. "Are you holding up?"

I wondered if she had read the *Post*. This morning's installment had included an interview with Hilda Ozimek and a photograph of her with the caption: "Psychic Knew All of Them Were Dead." Relatives and friends of the slain couples were quoted, and half of a page was filled with a color diagram showing where the couples' cars and bodies had been found. Camp Peary was ominously positioned in the center of this cluster like a skull and crossbones on a pirate's map.

"I'm doing all right," I told her. "And I'll be doing even better if you can assist me with something." I explained what I needed, adding, "Tomorrow I will fax you the form citing the Code giving me statutory rights to Jill Harrington's records."

It was pro forma. Yet it seemed awkward reminding her of my legal authority.

"You can bring the form in person. Dinner at seven on Wednesday?"

"It's not necessary for you to go to any trouble—"

"No trouble, Kay," she interrupted warmly. "I have missed seeing you."

13

The ART DECO PASTELS of uptown reminded me of Miami Beach. Buildings were pink, yellow, and Wedgwood blue with polished brass door knockers and brilliant handmade flags fluttering over entrances, a sight that seemed even more incongruous because of the weather. Rain had turned to snow.

Traffic was rush-hour awful, and I had to drive around the block twice before spotting a parking place within a reasonable walk of my favorite wine shop. I picked out four good bottles, two red, two white.

I drove along Monument Avenue, where statues of Confederate generals on horses loomed over traffic circles, ghostly in the milky swirl of snow. Last summer I had traveled this route once a week on my way to see Anna, the visits tapering off by fall and ending completely this winter.

Her office was in her house, a lovely old white frame where the street was blacktopped cobblestone and gas carriage lamps glowed after dark. Ringing the bell to announce my arrival just as her patients did, I let myself into a foyer that led into what was Anna's waiting room. Leather furniture surrounded a coffee table stacked with magazines, and an old Oriental rug covered the hardwood floor. There were toys in a box in a corner for her younger patients, a receptionist's desk, a coffee maker, and a fireplace. Down a long hallway was the kitchen, where something was cooking that reminded me I had skipped lunch.

"Kay? Is that you?"

The unmistakable voice with its strong German accent was punctuated by brisk footsteps, and then Anna was wiping her hands on her apron and giving me a hug.

"You locked the door after you?"

"I did, and you know to lock up after your last patient leaves, Anna." I used to say this every time.

"You are my last patient."

I followed her to the kitchen. "Do all of your *patients* bring you wine?"

"I wouldn't permit it. And I don't cook for or socialize with them. For you I break all the rules."

"Yes." I sighed. "How will I ever repay you?"

"Certainly not with your services, I hope." She set the shopping bag on a countertop.

"I promise I would be very gentle."

"And I would be very naked and very dead, and I wouldn't give a damn how gentle you were. Are you hoping to get me drunk or did you run into a sale?"

"I neglected to ask what you were cooking," I explained. "I didn't know whether to bring red or white. To be on the safe side, I got two of each."

"Remind me to never tell you what I'm cooking, then. Goodness, Kay!" She set the bottles on the counter. "This looks marvelous. Do you want a glass now, or would you rather have something stronger?"

"Definitely something stronger."

"The usual?"

"Please." Looking at the large pot simmering on the stove, I added, "I hope that's what I think it is." Anna made fabulous chili.

"Should warm us up. I threw in a can of the green chilies and tomatoes you brought back last time you were in Miami. I've been hoarding them. There's sourdough bread in the oven, and coleslaw. How's your family, by the way?"

"Lucy has suddenly gotten interested in boys and cars but I won't take it seriously until she's more interested in them than in her computer," I said. "My sister has another children's book coming out next month, and she's still clueless about the child she's supposedly raising. As for my mother, other than her usual fussing and fuming about what's become of Miami, where no one speaks English anymore, she's fine."

"Did you make it down there for Christmas?"

"No."

"Has your mother forgiven you?"

"Not yet," I said.

"I can't say that I blame her. Families should be together at Christmas."

I did not reply.

"But this is good," she surprised me by saying. "You did not feel like going to Miami, so you didn't. I have told you all along that women need to learn to be selfish. So perhaps you are learning to be selfish?"

"I think selfishness has always come pretty easily to me, Anna."

"When you no longer feel guilty about it, I will know you are cured."

"I still feel guilty, so I suppose I'm not cured. You're right."

"Yes. I can tell."

I watched her uncork a bottle to let it breathe, the sleeves of a white cotton blouse rolled up to her elbows, forearms as firm and strong as those of a woman half her age. I did not know what Anna had looked like when she was young, but at almost seventy, she was an eye-catcher with strong Teutonic features, short white hair, and light blue eyes. Opening a cupboard, she reached for bottles and in no time was handing me a Scotch and soda and fixing herself a manhattan.

"What has happened since I saw you last, Kay?" We carried our drinks to the kitchen table. "That would have been before Thanksgiving? Of course, we have talked on the phone. Your worries about the book?"

"Yes, you know about Abby's book, at least know as much as I do. And you know about these cases. About Pat Harvey. All of it." I got out my cigarettes.

"I've been following it in the news. You're looking well. A little tired, though. Perhaps a little too thin?"

"One can never be too thin," I said.

"I've seen you look worse, that's my point. So you are handling the stress from your work."

"Some days better than others."

Anna sipped her manhattan and stared thoughtfully at the stove. "And Mark?"

"I've seen him," I said. "And we've been talking on the phone.

He's still confused, uncertain. I suppose I am, too. So maybe nothing's new."

"You have seen him. That is new."

"I still love him."

"That isn't new."

"It's so difficult, Anna. Always has been. I don't know why I can't seem to let it go."

"Because the feelings are intense, but both of you are afraid of commitment. Both of you want excitement and want your own way. I noticed he was alluded to in the newspaper."

"I know."

"And?"

"I haven't told him."

"I shouldn't think you would need to. If he didn't see the paper himself, certainly someone from the Bureau has called him. If he's upset, you would hear, no?"

"You're right," I said, relieved. "I would hear."

"You at least have contact, then. You are happier?"

I was.

"You are hopeful?"

"I'm willing to see what will happen," I replied. "But I'm not sure it can work."

"No one can ever be sure of anything."

"That is a very sad truth," I said. "I can't be sure of anything. I know only what I feel."

"Then you are ahead of the pack."

"Whatever the pack is, if I am ahead of it, then that's another sad truth," I admitted.

She got up to take the bread out of the oven. I watched her fill earthenware bowls with chili, toss coleslaw, and pour the wine. Remembering the form I had brought, I got it out of my pocketbook and placed it on the table.

Anna did not even glance at it as she served us and sat down.

She said, "Would you like to review her chart?"

I knew Anna well enough to be sure she would not record details of her counseling sessions. People like me have statutory rights to medical records, and these documents can also end up in court. People like Anna are too shrewd to put confidences in print.

"Why don't you summarize," I suggested.

"I diagnosed her as having an adjustment disorder," she said.

It was the equivalent of my saying that Jill's death was due to respiratory or cardiac arrest. Whether you are shot or run over by a train, you die because you stop breathing and your heart quits. The diagnosis of adjustment disorder was a catchall straight out of the *Diagnostic and Statistical Manual of Mental Disorders*. It qualified a patient for insurance coverage without divulging one scrap of useful information about his history or problems.

"The entire human race has an adjustment disorder," I said to Anna.

She smiled.

"I respect your professional ethics," I said. "And I have no intention of amending my own records by adding information that you consider confidential. But it's important for me to know anything about Jill that might give me insight into her murder. If there was something about her life-style, for example, that might have placed her at risk."

"I respect your professional ethics as well."

"Thank you. Now that we've established our mutual admiration for each other's fairness and integrity, might we push formalities aside and hold a conversation?"

"Of course, Kay," she said gently. "I remember Jill vividly. It is hard not to remember an unusual patient, especially one who is murdered."

"How was she special?"

"Special?" She smiled sadly. "A very bright, endearing young woman. So much in her favor. I used to look forward to her appointments. Had she not been my patient, I would have liked to know her as a friend."

"How long had she been seeing you?"

"Three to four times a month for more than a year."

"Why you, Anna?" I asked. "Why not someone in Williamsburg, someone closer to where she lived?"

"I have quite a number of patients from out of town. Some come from as far away as Philadelphia."

"Because they don't want anyone to know they are seeing a psychiatrist."

She nodded. "Unfortunately, many people are terrified by the prospect of others knowing. You would be surprised at the number of people who have been in this office and left by way of the back door."

I had never told a soul I was seeing a psychiatrist, and had Anna not refused to charge me, I would have paid for the sessions in cash. The last thing I needed was for someone in Employee Benefits to get hold of my insurance claims and spread gossip throughout the Department of Health and Human Services.

"Obviously, then, Jill did not want anyone to know she was seeing a psychiatrist," I said. "And this might also explain why she had her prescriptions for Librax filled in Richmond."

"Before you called, I did not know she filled the prescriptions in Richmond. But I'm not surprised." She reached for her wine.

The chili was spicy enough to bring tears to my eyes. But it was outstanding, Anna's best effort, and I told her so. Then I explained to her what she probably already suspected.

"It's possible Jill and her friend, Elizabeth Mott, were murdered by the same individual killing these couples," I said. "Or at least, there are some parallels between their homicides and the others that cause me concern."

"I'm not interested in what you know about the cases you are involved in now, unless you feel it necessary to tell me. So I'll let you ask me questions and I'll do my best to recall what I can about Jill's life."

"Why was she so worried about anyone knowing she was seeing a psychiatrist? What was she hiding?" I asked.

"Jill was from a prominent family in Kentucky, and their approval and acceptance were very important to her. She went to the right schools, did well, and was going to be a successful lawyer. Her family was very proud of her. They did not know."

"Know what? That she was seeing a psychiatrist?"

"They did not know that," Anna said. "More importantly, they did not know she was involved in a homosexual relationship."

"Elizabeth?" I knew the answer before I asked. The possibility had crossed my mind.

"Yes. Jill and Elizabeth became friends during Jill's first year in law school. Then they became lovers. The relationship was very intense, very difficult, rife with conflict. It was a first for both of them, or at least this was how it was presented to me by Jill. You must remember that I never met Elizabeth, never heard her side. Jill came to see me, initially, because she wanted to change. She did not want to be homosexual, was hoping therapy might redeem her heterosexuality."

"Did you see any hope for that?" I asked.

"I don't know what would have happened eventually," Anna said. "All I can tell you is that based on what Jill said to me, her bond with Elizabeth was quite strong. I got the impression that Elizabeth was more at peace with the relationship than Jill, who intellectually could not accept it but emotionally could not let it go."

"She must have been in agony."

"The last few times I saw Jill it had become more acute. She had just finished law school. Her future was before her. It was time to make decisions. She began suffering psychosomatic problems. Spastic colitis. I prescribed Librax."

"Did Jill ever mention anything to you that might have given you a hint as to who might have done this to them?"

"I thought about that, studied the matter closely after it happened. When I read about it in the papers, I could not believe it. I had just seen Jill three days before. I can't tell you how hard I concentrated on everything she had ever said to me. I hoped I would recall something, any detail that might help. But I never have."

"Both of them hid their relationship from the world?"

"Yes."

"What about a boyfriend, someone Jill or Elizabeth dated from time to time? For appearances?"

"Neither dated, I was told. Not a jealousy situation, therefore, unless there was something I did not know." She glanced at my empty bowl. "More chili?"

"I couldn't."

She got up to load the dishwasher. For a while we did not speak. Anna untied her apron and hung it on a hook inside the broom closet. Then we carried our glasses and the bottle of wine into her den.

It was my favorite room. Shelves of books filled two walls, a third centered by a bay window through which she could monitor from her cluttered desk flowers budding or snow falling over her small backyard. From that window I had watched magnolias bloom in a fanfare of lemony white, I had watched the last bright sparks of autumn fade. We had talked about my family, my divorce, and Mark. We had talked about suffering and we had talked about death. From the worn leather wing chair where I sat, I had awkwardly led Anna through my life, just as Jill Harrington had done.

They had been lovers. This linked them to the other murdered couples and made the "Mr. Goodbar" theory that much more implausible, and I pointed this out to Anna.

"I agree with you," she said.

"They were last seen in the Anchor Bar and Grill. Did Jill ever mention this place to you?"

"Not by name. But she mentioned a bar they occasionally went to, a place where they talked. Sometimes they went to out-of-the-way restaurants where people would not know them. Sometimes they went on drives. Generally, these excursions occurred when they were in the midst of emotionally charged discussions about their relationship."

"If they were having one of these discussions that Friday night at the Anchor, they were probably upset, one or the other possibly feeling rejected, angry," I said. "Is it possible either Jill or Elizabeth might have gone through the motions of picking up a man, flirting, to jerk the other around?"

"I can't say that's impossible," Anna said. "But it would surprise me a great deal. I never got the impression that Jill or Elizabeth played games with each other. I'm more inclined to suspect that when they were talking that night, the conversation was very intense and they were probably unaware of their surroundings, focused only on each other."

"Anyone observing them might have overheard."

"That is the risk if one has personal discussions in public, and I had mentioned this to Jill."

"If she were so paranoid about anyone suspecting, then why did she take the risk?"

"Her resolve was not strong, Kay." Anna reached for her wine. "When she and Elizabeth were alone, it was too easy to slip back into intimacy. Hugging, comforting, crying, and no decisions were made."

That sounded familiar. When Mark and I had discussions either at his place or mine, inevitably we ended up in bed. Afterward, one of us would leave, and the problems were still there.

"Anna, did you ever consider that their relationship might have been connected to what happened to them?" I asked.

"If anything, their relationship made it seem all the more unusual. I should think that a woman alone in a bar looking to be picked up is in much greater danger than two women together who are not interested in drawing attention to themselves."

"Let's return to the subject of their habits and routines," I said.

"They lived in the same apartment complex but did not live together, and again, this was for the sake of appearances. But it was convenient. They could lead their separate lives, and then get together late at night at Jill's apartment. Jill preferred to be in her own place. I remember her telling me that if her family or other people repeatedly tried to call her late at night and she was never home, there would have been questions." She paused, thinking. "Jill and Elizabeth also exercised, were very fit. Running, I think, but they didn't always do this together."

"Where did they run?"

"I believe there was a park near where they lived."

"Anything else? Theaters, shops, malls they may have frequented?"

"Nothing comes to mind."

"What does your intuition tell you? What did it tell you at the time?"

"I felt that Jill and Elizabeth were having a stressful conversation in the bar. They probably wanted to be left alone and would have resented an intrusion."

"Then what?"

"Clearly they encountered their killer at some point that evening."

"Can you imagine how that might have happened?"

"It has always been my opinion it was someone they knew, or at least were well enough acquainted with so that they had no reason not to trust him. Unless they were abducted at gunpoint by one or more persons, either in the bar's parking lot or somewhere else they might have gone."

"What if a stranger had approached them in the bar's parking lot, asked them for a lift somewhere, claimed to have car trouble . . . ?"

She was already shaking her head. "It is inconsistent with my impressions of them. Again, unless it was someone with whom they were acquainted."

"And if the killer was impersonating a police officer, perhaps pulled them over for a routine traffic stop?"

"That's another matter. I suppose even you and I might be vulnerable to that."

Anna was looking tired, so I thanked her for dinner and her time. I knew our conversation was difficult for her. I wondered how I would feel were I in her position.

Minutes after I walked through my front door, the phone rang.

"One last thing that I remember but probably does not matter," Anna said. "Jill mentioned something about the two of them working crossword puzzles when they wanted to stay in, just the two of them, on Sunday mornings, for example. Insignificant, perhaps. But a routine, something they did together."

"A book of puzzles? Or the ones in the newspapers?"

"I don't know. But Jill did read a variety of newspapers, Kay. She usually had something with her to read while waiting for her appointment. The *Wall Street Journal*, the *Washington Post*."

I thanked her again and said next time it was my turn to cook. Then I called Marino.

"Two women were murdered in James City County eight years ago," I went straight to the point. "It's possible there's a connection. Do you know Detective Montana out there?"

"Yeah. I've met him."

"We need to get with him, review the cases. Can he keep his mouth shut?"

"Hell if I know," Marino said.

───────────

Montana looked like his name, big, rawboned, with hazy blue eyes set in a rugged, honest face topped by thick gray hair. His accent was that of a native Virginian, his conversation peppered with "yes, ma'am"s. The following afternoon he, Marino, and I met at my home, where we were ensured privacy and no interruptions.

Montana must have depleted his annual film budget on Jill and Elizabeth's case, for covering my kitchen table were photographs of their bodies at the scene, the Volkswagen abandoned at the Palm Leaf Motel, the Anchor Bar and Grill, and, remarkably, of every room inside the women's apartments, including pantries and closets. He had a briefcase bulging with notes, maps, interview transcriptions, diagrams, evidence inventories, logs of telephone tips. There is something to be said for detectives who rarely have homicides in their jurisdictions. Cases like these come along once or twice in their careers, and they work them meticulously.

"The cemetery is right next to the church." He moved a photograph closer to me.

"It looks quite old," I said, admiring weathered brick and slate.

"It is and it isn't. Was built in the seventeen-hundreds, did all right until maybe twenty years ago, when bad wiring did it in. I remember seeing the smoke, was on patrol, thought one of my neighbor's farmhouses was burning. Some historical society took an interest. It's supposed to look just like it used to inside and out.

"You get to it by this secondary road right here"—he tapped another photograph—"which is less than two miles west of Route Sixty and about four miles west of the Anchor Bar, where the girls were last seen alive the night before."

"Who discovered the bodies?" Marino asked, eyes roaming the photograph spread.

"A custodian who worked for the church. He came in Saturday morning to clean up, get things ready for Sunday. Says he had just pulled in when he spotted what looked like two people sleeping in the grass about twenty feet inside the cemetery's front gate. The bodies were visible from the church parking lot. Doesn't seem whoever did it was concerned about anybody finding them."

"Am I to assume there was no activity at the church that Friday night?" I asked.

"No, ma'am. It was locked up tight, nothing going on."

"Does the church ever have activities scheduled for Friday nights?"

"They do on occasion. Sometimes the youth groups get together on Friday nights. Sometimes there's choir practice, things like that. The point is, if you selected this cemetery in advance to kill someone, it wouldn't make a whole lot of sense. There's no guarantee the church would be deserted, not on any night of the week. That's one of the reasons I figured from the start that the murders were random, the girls just met up with someone, maybe in the bar. There isn't much about these cases to make me think the homicides were carefully planned."

"The killer was armed," I reminded Montana. "He had a knife and a handgun."

"The world's full of folks carrying knives, guns in their cars or even on their person," he said matter-of-factly.

I collected the photographs of the bodies in situ and began to study them carefully.

The women were less than a yard from each other, lying in the grass between two tilting granite headstones. Elizabeth was facedown, legs slightly spread, left arm under her stomach, right arm straight and by her side. Slender, with short brown hair, she was dressed in jeans and a white pullover sweater stained dark red around the neck. In another photograph, her body had been turned over, the front of her sweater soaked with blood, eyes the dull stare of the dead. The cut to her throat was shallow, the gunshot wound to her neck not immediately incapacitating, I recalled from her autopsy report. It was the stab wound to her chest that had been lethal.

Jill's injuries had been much more mutilating. She was on her back, face so streaked by dried blood that I could not tell what she had looked like in life, except that she had short black hair and a straight, pretty nose. Like her companion, she was slender. She was dressed in jeans and a pale yellow cotton shirt, bloody, untucked, and ripped open to her waist, exposing multiple stab wounds, several of which had gone through her brassiere. There were deep cuts to her forearms and hands. The cut to her neck was shallow and probably inflicted when she was already dead or almost dead.

The photographs were invaluable for one critical reason. They revealed something that I had not been able to determine from any of the newspaper clippings or reports I had reviewed in their cases on file in my office.

I glanced at Marino and our eyes met.

I turned to Montana. "What happened to their shoes?"

14

You know, it's interesting you should mention that," Montana replied. "I never have come up with a good explanation for why the girls took their shoes off, unless they were inside the motel, got dressed when it was time to leave, and didn't bother. We found their shoes and socks inside the Volkswagen."

"Was it warm that night?" Marino asked.

"It was. All the same, I would have expected them to put their shoes back on when they got dressed."

"We don't know for a fact they ever went inside a motel room," I reminded Montana.

"You're right about that," he agreed.

I wondered if Montana had read the series in the *Post*, which had mentioned that shoes and socks were missing in the other murder cases. If he had, it did not seem he had made the connection yet.

"Did you have much contact with the reporter Abby Turnbull when she was covering Jill's and Elizabeth's murders?" I asked him.

"The woman followed me like tin cans tied to a dog's tail. Everywhere I went, there she was."

"Do you recall if you told her that Jill and Elizabeth were barefoot? Did you ever show Abby the scene photographs?" I asked, for Abby was too smart to have forgotten a detail like that, especially since it was so important now.

Montana said without pause, "I talked to her, but no, ma'am.

I never did show her these pictures. Was right careful what I said, too. You read what was in the papers, didn't you?"

"I've seen some of the articles."

"Nothing in there about the way the girls were dressed, about Jill's shirt being torn, their shoes and socks off."

So Abby didn't know, I thought, relieved.

"I notice from the autopsy photographs that both women had ligature marks around their wrists," I said. "Did you recover whatever might have been used to bind them?"

"No, ma'am."

"Then apparently he removed the ligatures after killing them," I said.

"He was right careful. We didn't find any cartridge cases, no weapon, nothing he might have used to tie them up. No seminal fluid. So it doesn't appear he got around to raping them, or if he did, no way to tell. And both were fully clothed. Now, as far as this girl's blouse being ripped"—he reached for a photograph of Jill—"that might have happened when he was struggling with her."

"Did you recover any buttons at the scene?"

"Several. In the grass near her body."

"What about cigarette butts?"

Montana began calmly looking through his paperwork. "No cigarette butts." He paused, pulling out a report. "Tell you what we did find, though. A lighter, a nice silver one."

"Where?" Marino asked.

"Maybe fifteen feet from where the bodies were. As you can see, an iron fence surrounds the cemetery. You enter through this gate." He was showing us another photograph. "The lighter was in the grass, five, six feet inside the gate. One of these expensive, slim lighters shaped like an ink pen, the kind people use to light pipes."

"Was it in working order?" Marino asked.

"Worked just fine, polished up real nice," Montana recalled. "I'm pretty sure it didn't belong to either of the girls. They didn't smoke, and no one I talked to remembered seeing either one of them with a lighter like that. Maybe it fell out of the killer's pocket, no way to know. Could have been anybody who lost it, maybe someone out there a day or two earlier sightseeing. You know how folks like to wander in old cemeteries looking at the graves."

"Was this lighter checked for prints?" Marino asked.

"The surface wasn't good for that. The silver's engraved with these crisscrosses, like you see with some of these fancy silver fountain pens." He stared off thoughtfully. "The thing probably cost a hundred bucks."

"Do you still have the lighter and the buttons you found out there?" I asked.

"I've got all the evidence from these cases. Always hoped we might solve them someday."

Montana didn't hope it half as much as I did, and it wasn't until after he left some time later that Marino and I began to discuss what was really on our minds.

"It's the same damn bastard," Marino said, his expression incredulous. "The damn squirrel made them take their shoes off just like he done with the other couples. To slow them down when he led them off to wherever it was he planned to kill them."

"Which wasn't the cemetery," I said. "I don't believe that was the spot he had selected."

"Yo. I think he took on more than he could handle with those two. They weren't cooperating or something went down that freaked him out—maybe having to do with the blood in the back of the Volkswagen. So he made them pull over at the earliest opportunity, which just happened to be a dark, deserted church with a cemetery. You got a map of Virginia handy?"

I went back to my office and found one. Marino spread it open on the kitchen table and studied it for a long moment.

"Take a look," he said, his face intense. "The turnoff for the church is right here on Route Sixty, about two miles before you get to the road leading to the wooded area where Jim Freeman and Bonnie Smyth were killed five, six years later. I'm saying we drove right past the damn road leading to the church where the two women was whacked when we went to see Mr. Joyce the other day."

"Good God," I muttered. "I wonder—"

"Yeah, I'm wondering, too," Marino interrupted. "Maybe the squirrel *was* out there casing the woods, selecting the right spot when Dammit surprised him. He shoots the dog. About a month later, he's abducted his first set of victims, Jill and Elizabeth. He intends to force them to drive him to this wooded area, but things get out of control. He ends the trip early. Or maybe he's confused, rattled, and tells Jill or Elizabeth the wrong road to turn off on. Next thing, he sees this church and now he's really freaked, realizes they didn't turn where they were supposed to. He may not have even known where the hell they were."

I tried to envision it. One of the women was driving and the other was in the front passenger's seat, the killer in the back holding a gun on them. What had happened to cause him to lose so much blood? Had he accidentally shot himself? That was highly unlikely. Had he cut himself with his knife? Maybe, but again, it was hard for me to imagine. The blood inside the car, I had noted from Montana's photographs, seemed to begin with drips on the back of the passenger's headrest. There were also drips on the back of the seat with a lot of blood on the floor mat. This placed the killer directly behind the passenger's seat, leaning forward. Was his head or face bleeding?

A *nosebleed*?

I proposed this to Marino.

"Must'ave been one hell of a one. There was a lot of blood." He thought for a moment. "So maybe one of the women threw back an elbow and hit him in the nose."

"How would you have responded if one of the women had done that to you?" I said. "Provided you were a killer."

"She wouldn't have done it again. I probably wouldn't have shot her inside the car, but I might have punched her, hit her in the head with the gun."

"There was no blood in the front seat," I reminded him. "Absolutely no evidence that either of the women was injured inside the car."

"Hmmmm."

"Perplexing, isn't it?"

"Yeah." He frowned. "He's in the backseat, leaning forward, and suddenly starts bleeding? Perplexing as shit."

I put on a fresh pot of coffee while we began to toss around more ideas. For starters, there continued to be the problem of how one individual subdues two people.

"The car belonged to Elizabeth," I said. "Let's assume she was driving. Obviously, her hands were not tied at this point."

"But Jill's might have been. He might have tied her hands during the drive, made her hold them up behind her head so he could tie them from the backseat."

"Or he could have forced her to turn around and place her

arms over the headrest," I proposed. "This might have been when she struck him in the face, if that's what happened."

"Maybe."

"In any event," I went on, "we'll assume that by the time they stopped the car, Jill was already bound and barefoot. Next he orders Elizabeth to remove her shoes and binds her. Then he forces them at gunpoint into the cemetery."

"Jill had a lot of cuts on her hands and forearms," Marino said. "Are they consistent with her warding off a knife with her hands tied?"

"As long as her hands were tied in front of her and not behind her back."

"It would have been smarter to tie their hands behind their backs."

"He probably found that out the hard way and improved his techniques," I said.

"Elizabeth didn't have any defense injuries?"

"None."

"The squirrel killed Elizabeth first," Marino decided.

"How would you have done it? Remember, you've got two hostages to handle."

"I would have made both of them lie facedown in the grass. I would have put the gun to the back of Elizabeth's head to make her behave as I get ready to use the knife on her. If she surprised me by resisting, I might have pulled the trigger, shot her when I wasn't really intending to."

"That might explain why she was shot in the neck," I said. "If he had the gun to the back of her head and she resisted, the muzzle may have slipped. The scenario is reminiscent of what happened to Deborah Harvey, except that I seriously doubt she was lying down when she was shot."

"This guy likes to use a blade," Marino replied. "He uses his gun when things don't go down the way he planned. And so far, that's only happened twice that we know of. With Elizabeth and Deborah."

"Elizabeth was shot, then what, Marino?"

"He finishes her off and takes care of Jill."

"He fought with Jill," I reminded him.

"You can bet she struggled. Her friend's just been killed. Jill knows she don't got a chance, may as well fight like hell."

"Or else she was already fighting with him," I ventured.

Marino's eyes narrowed the way they did when he was skeptical.

Jill was a lawyer. I doubted she was naive about the cruel deeds people perpetrate upon one another. When she and her friend were being forced into the cemetery late at night, I suspected Jill knew both of them were going to die. One or both women may have begun resisting as he opened the iron gate. If the silver lighter did belong to the killer, it may have fallen out of his pocket at this point. Then, and perhaps Marino was right, the killer forced both women to lie facedown, but when he started on Elizabeth, Jill panicked, tried to protect her friend. The gun discharged, shooting Elizabeth in the neck.

"The pattern of Jill's injuries sends a message of frenzy, someone who is angry, frightened, because he's lost control," I said. "He may have hit her in the head with the gun, gotten on top of her and ripped open her shirt and started stabbing. As a parting gesture, he cuts their throats. Then he leaves in the Volkswagen, ditches it at the motel, and heads out on foot, perhaps back to wherever his car was."

"He should have had blood on him," Marino considered. "Interesting there wasn't any blood found in the driver's area, only in the backseat."

"There hasn't been any blood found in the driver's areas of any of the couples' vehicles," I said. "This killer is very careful. He may bring a change of clothing, towels, who knows what, when he's planning to commit his murders."

Marino dug into his pocket and produced his Swiss army knife. He began to trim his fingernails over a napkin. Lord knows what Doris had put up with all these years, I thought. Marino probably never bothered to empty an ashtray, place a dish in the sink, or pick his dirty clothes off the floor. I hated to think what the bathroom looked like after he had been in it.

"Abby *Turncoat* still trying to get hold of you?" he asked without looking up.

"I wish you wouldn't call her that."

He didn't respond.

"She hasn't tried in the last few days, at least not that I'm aware of."

"Thought you might be interested in knowing that she and Clifford Ring have more than a professional relationship, Doc."

"What do you mean?" I asked uneasily.

"I mean that this story about the couples Abby's been working on has nothing to do with why she was taken off the police beat." He was working on his left thumb, fingernail shavings falling on the napkin. "Apparently, she was getting so squirrelly no one in the newsroom could deal with her anymore. Things reached a head last fall, right before she came to Richmond and saw you."

"What happened?" I asked, staring hard at him.

"Way I heard it, she made a little scene right in the middle of the newsroom. Dumped a cup of coffee in Ring's lap and then stormed out, didn't tell her editors where the hell she was going or when she'd be back. That's when she got reassigned to features."

"Who told you this?"

"Benton."

"How would Benton know what goes on in the *Post*'s newsroom?"

"I didn't ask." Marino folded the knife and slipped it back into his pocket. Getting up, he wadded the napkin and put it in the trash.

"One last thing," he said, standing in the middle of my kitchen. "That Lincoln you was interested in?"

"Yes?"

"A 1990 Mark Seven. Registered to a Barry Aranoff, thirty-eight-year-old white male from Roanoke. Works for a medical supply company, a salesman. On the road a lot."

"Then you talked to him," I said.

"Talked to his wife. He's out of town and has been for the past two weeks."

"Where was he supposed to have been when I saw the car in Williamsburg?"

"His wife said she wasn't sure of his schedule. Seems he sometimes hits a different city every day, buzzes all over the place, including out of state. His territory goes as far north as Boston. As best she could remember, around the time you're talking about, he was in Tidewater, then was flying out of Newport News, heading to Massachusetts."

I fell silent, and Marino interpreted this as embarrassment, which it wasn't. I was thinking.

"Hey, what you done was good detective work. Nothing wrong with writing down a plate number and checking it out. Should make you happy you wasn't being followed by some spook."

I did not respond.

He added, "Only thing you missed was the color. You said the Lincoln was dark gray. Aranoff's ride is brown."

Later that night lightning flashed high over thrashing trees as a storm worthy of summer unloaded its violent arsenal. I sat up in bed, browsing through several journals as I waited for Captain Montana's telephone line to clear.

Either his phone was out of order or someone had been on it for the past two hours. After he and Marino had left, I had recalled a detail from one of the photographs that reminded me of what Anna had said to me last. Inside Jill's apartment, on the carpet beside a La-Z-Boy chair in the living room, was a stack of legal briefs, several out-of-town newspapers, and a copy of the *New York Times Magazine*. I have never bothered with crossword puzzles. God knows I have too many other things to figure out. But I knew the *Times* crossword puzzle was as popular as manufacturer's coupons.

Reaching for the phone, I tried Montana's home number again. This time I was rewarded.

"Have you ever considered getting Call Waiting?" I asked good-naturedly.

"I've considered getting my teenage daughter her own switchboard," he said.

"I've got a question."

"Ask away."

"When you went through Jill's and Elizabeth's apartments, I'm assuming you went through their mail."

"Yes, ma'am. Checked out their mail for quite a while, seeing what all came in, seeing who wrote them letters, went through their charge card bills, that sort of thing."

"What can you tell me about Jill's subscriptions to newspapers that were delivered by mail?"

He paused.

It occurred to me. "I'm sorry. Their cases would be in your office. . . ."

"No, ma'am. I came straight home, have 'em right here. I was just trying to think, it's been a long day. Can you hold on?"

I heard pages turning.

"Well, there were a couple of bills, junk mail. But no newspapers."

Surprised, I explained Jill had several out-of-town newspapers in her apartment. "She had to have gotten them from somewhere."

"Maybe vending machines," he offered. "Lots of them around the college. That would be my guess."

The *Washington Post* or the *Wall Street Journal*, maybe, I thought. But not the Sunday *New York Times*. Most likely that had come from a drugstore or a newsstand where Jill and Elizabeth may routinely have stopped when they went out for breakfast on Sunday mornings. I thanked him and hung up.

Switching off the lamp, I got in bed, listening as rain drummed the roof in a relentless rhythm. I pulled the covers more tightly around me. Thoughts and images drifted, and I envisioned Deborah Harvey's red purse, damp and covered with dirt.

Vander, in the fingerprints lab, had finished examining it and I had looked over the report the other day.

"What are you going to do?" Rose was asking me. Oddly, the purse was in a plastic tray on Rose's desk. "You can't send it back to her family like that."

"Of course not."

"Maybe we could just take out the charge cards and things, wash them off and send those?" Rose's face twisted in anger. She shoved the tray across her desk and screamed, "Get it out of here! I can't stand it!"

Suddenly I was in my kitchen. Through the window I saw Mark drive up, only the car was unfamiliar, but I recognized it somehow. Rummaging in my pocketbook for a brush, I frantically fixed my hair. I started to run to the bathroom to brush my teeth, but there wasn't time. The doorbell rang, just once.

He took me in his arms, whispering my name, like a small cry of pain. I wondered why he was here, why he was not in Denver.

He kissed me as he pushed the door with his foot. It slammed shut with a tremendous bang.

My eyelids flew open. Thunder cracked. Lightning lit up my bedroom again and then again as my heart pounded.

The next morning I performed two autopsies, then went upstairs to see Neils Vander, section chief of the fingerprints examination lab. I found him inside the Automated Fingerprint Identification System computer room deep in thought in front of a monitor. In hand was my copy of the report detailing the examination of Deborah Harvey's purse, and I placed it on top of his keyboard.

"I need to ask you something." I raised my voice over the computer's pervasive hum.

He glanced down at the report with preoccupied eyes, unruly gray hair wisping over his ears.

"How did you find anything after the purse had been in the woods so long? I'm amazed."

He returned his gaze to the monitor. "The purse is nylon, waterproof, and the credit cards were protected inside plastic windows, which were inside a zipped-up compartment. When I put the cards in the superglue tank, a lot of smudges and partials popped up. I didn't even need the laser."

"Pretty impressive."

He smiled a little.

"But nothing identifiable," I pointed out.

"Sorry about that."

"What interests me is the driver's license. Nothing popped up on it."

"Not even a smudge," he said.

"Clean?"

"As a hound's tooth."

"Thank you, Neils."

He was off somewhere again, gone in his land of loops and whorls.

I went back downstairs and looked up the number for the 7-Eleven Abby and I had visited last fall. I was told that Ellen Jordan, the clerk we had talked to, would not be in until nine P.M. I mowed through the rest of the day without stopping for lunch, unaware of the passing hours. I wasn't the slightest bit tired when I got home.

I was loading the dishwasher when the doorbell rang at eight P.M. Drying my hands on a towel, I walked anxiously to the front door.

Abby Turnbull was standing on the porch, coat collar turned up around her ears, face wan, eyes miserable. A cold wind rocked dark trees in my yard and lifted strands of her hair.

"You didn't answer my calls. I hope you won't refuse me entrance into your house," she said.

"Of course not, Abby. Please." I opened the door wide and stepped back.

She did not take off her coat until I invited her to do so, and when I offered to hang it up, she shook her head and draped it over the back of a chair, as if to reassure me that she did not intend to stay very long. She was dressed in faded denim jeans and a heavy-knit maroon sweater flecked with lint. Brushing past her to clear paperwork and newspapers off the kitchen table, I detected the stale odor of cigarette smoke and a pungent hint of sweat.

"Something to drink?" I asked, and for some reason I could not feel angry with her.

"Whatever you're having would be fine." She got out her cigarettes while I fixed both of us a drink.

"It's hard to start," she said when I was seated. "The articles were unfair to you, to say the least. And I know what you must be thinking."

"It's irrelevant what I'm thinking. I'd rather hear what's on your mind."

"I told you I've made mistakes." Her voice trembled slightly. "Cliff Ring was one of them."

I sat quietly.

"He's an investigative reporter, one of the first people I got to know after moving to Washington. Very successful, exciting. Bright and sure of himself. I was vulnerable, having just moved to a new city, having been through . . . well, what happened to Henna." She glanced away from me.

"We started out as friends, then everything went too fast. I didn't see what he was like because I didn't want to see it." Her voice caught and I waited in silence while she steadied herself.

"I trusted him with my life, Kay."

"From which I am to conclude that the details in his story came from you," I said.

"No. They came from my reporting."

"What does that mean?"

"I don't talk to anybody about what I'm writing," Abby said. "Cliff was aware of my involvement in these cases, but I never went into detail about them. He never seemed all that interested." She was beginning to sound angry. "But he was, more than a little. That's the way he operates."

"If you didn't go into detail with him," I said, "then how did he get the information from you?"

"I used to give him keys to my building, my apartment, when I'd go out of town so he could water my plants, bring the mail in. He could have had copies made."

Our conversation at the Mayflower came back to me. When Abby had talked about someone breaking into her computer and had gone on to accuse the FBI or CIA, I had been skeptical. Would an experienced agent open a word processing file and not realize that the time and date might be changed? Not likely.

"Cliff Ring went into your computer?"

"I can't prove it, but I know he did," Abby said. "I can't prove he's been going through my mail, but I know he has. It's no big deal to steam open a letter, reseal it, and then place it back in the box. Not if you've made a copy of the mailbox key."

"Were you aware he was writing the story?"

"Of course not. I didn't know a damn thing about it until I opened the Sunday paper! He'd let himself into my apartment when he knew I wouldn't be there. He was going through my computer, anything he could find. Then he followed up by calling people, getting quotes and information, which was pretty easy, since he knew exactly where to look and what he was looking for."

"Easy because you had been relieved of your police beat. When you thought the *Post* had backed off from the story, what your editors had really backed away from was you."

Abby nodded angrily. "The story was passed into what they viewed as more reliable hands. Clifford Ring's hands," she said.

I realized why Clifford Ring had made no effort to contact me. He would know that Abby and I were friends. Had he asked me for details about the cases, I might have said something to Abby, and he had wanted to keep Abby in the dark about what he was doing for as long as possible. So Ring had avoided me, gone around me.

"I'm sure he . . ." Abby cleared her throat and reached for her drink. Her hand shook. "He can be very convincing. He'll probably win a prize. For the series."

"I'm sorry, Abby."

"It's nobody's fault but my own. I was stupid."

"We take risks when we allow ourselves to love—"

"I'll never take a risk like that again," she cut me off. "It was always a problem with him, one problem after another. I was always the one making concessions, giving him a second chance, then a third and a fourth."

"Did the people you work with know about you and Cliff?"

"We were careful." She got evasive.

"Why?"

"The newsroom is a very incestuous, gossipy place."

"Certainly your colleagues must have seen the two of you together."

"We were very careful," she repeated.

"People must have sensed something between you. Tension, if nothing else."

"Competition. Guarding my turf. That's what he would say if asked."

And jealousy, I thought. Abby never had been good at hiding her emotions. I could imagine her jealous rages. I could imagine those observing her in the newsroom misconstruing, assuming she was ambitious and jealous of Clifford Ring, when that was not the case. She was jealous of his other commitments.

"He's married, isn't he, Abby?"

She could not stop the tears this time.

I got up to refresh our drinks. She would tell me he was unhappy with his wife, contemplating divorce, and Abby had believed he would leave it all for her. The story was as threadbare and predictable as something in Ann Landers. I had heard it a hundred times before. Abby had been used.

I set her drink on the table and gently squeezed her shoulder before I moved back to my chair.

She told me what I expected to hear, and I just looked at her sadly.

"I don't deserve your sympathy," she cried.

"You've been hurt much more than I have."

"Everybody has been hurt. You. Pat Harvey. The parents, friends of these kids. If the cases hadn't happened, I'd still be working cops. At least I'd be all right professionally. No one person should have the power to cause such destruction."

I realized she was no longer thinking about Clifford Ring. She was thinking of the killer.

"You're right. No one should have the power. And no one will if we don't allow it."

"Deborah and Fred didn't allow it. Jill, Elizabeth, Jimmy, Bonnie. All of them." She looked defeated. "They didn't want to be murdered."

"What will Cliff do next?" I asked.

"Whatever it is, it won't involve me. I've changed all my locks."

"And your fears that your phones are bugged, that you're being followed?"

"Cliff's not the only one who wants to know what I'm doing. I can't trust anyone anymore!" Her eyes filled with angry tears. "You were the last person I wanted to hurt, Kay."

"Stop it, Abby. You can cry all year and it won't do me any good."

"I'm sorry. . . ."

"No more apologies." I was very firm but gentle.

She bit her bottom lip and stared at her drink.

"Are you ready to help me now?"

She looked up at me.

"First, what color was the Lincoln we saw in Williamsburg last week?"

"Dark gray, the interior leather dark, maybe black," she said, her eyes coming alive.

"Thank you. That's what I thought."

"What's going on?"

"I'm not sure. But there's more."

"More what?"

"I've got an *assignment* for you," I said, smiling. "But first, when are you returning to D.C.? Tonight?"

"I don't know, Kay." She stared off. "I can't be there now."

Abby felt like a fugitive, and in a sense she was. Clifford Ring had run her out of Washington. It probably wasn't a bad idea for her to disappear for a while.

She explained, "There's a bed and breakfast in the Northern Neck, and—"

"And I have a guest room," I interrupted. "You can stay with me for a while."

She looked uncertain, then confessed, "Kay, do you have any idea how that would look?"

"Frankly, I don't care at the moment."

"Why not?" She studied me closely.

"Your paper has already fried me in deep fat. I'm going for broke. Things will either get worse or better, but they won't stay the same."

"At least you haven't been fired."

"Neither have you, Abby. You had an affair and acted inappropriately in front of your colleagues when you dumped coffee in your lover's lap."

"He deserved it."

"I'm quite sure he did. But I wouldn't advise your doing

battle with the *Post*. Your book is your chance to redeem yourself."

"What about you?"

"My concern is these cases. You can help because you can do
things I can't do."

"Such as?"

"I can't lie, hoodwink, finagle, cheat, badger, sneak, snipe,
snoop, and pretend to be something or somebody I'm not because
I'm an officer of the Commonwealth. But you have great range of
motion. You're a reporter."

"Thanks a lot," she protested as she walked out of the kitchen.
"I'll get my things from the car."

It was not very often I had houseguests, and the bedroom downstairs was usually reserved for Lucy's visits. Covering the hardwood
floor was an Iranian Dergezine rug with a brightly colored floral
design that turned the entire room into a garden, in the midst of
which my niece had been a rosebud or a stinkweed, depending on
her behavior.

"I guess you like flowers," Abby said absently, laying the suit
bag on top of the bed.

"The rug is a little overpowering in here," I apologized. "But
when I saw it I had to buy it, and there was no place else to put it.
Not to mention, it's virtually indestructible, and since this is where
Lucy stays, that point is important."

"Or at least it used to be." Abby went to the closet and opened
the door. "Lucy's not ten years old anymore."

"There should be plenty of hangers in there." I moved closer
to inspect. "If you need more . . ."

"This is fine."

"There are towels, toothpaste, soap in the bath." I started to
show her.

She had begun unpacking and wasn't paying any attention.

I sat down on the edge of the bed.

Abby carried suits and blouses into the closet. Coat hangers
screeched along the metal bar. I watched her in silence, experiencing a prick of impatience.

This went on for several minutes, drawers sliding, more coat
hangers screeching, the medicine cabinet in the bathroom wheezing open and clicking shut. She pushed her suit bag inside the

closet and glanced around, as if trying to figure out what to do next. Opening her briefcase, she pulled out a novel and a notebook, which she placed on the table by the bed. I watched uneasily as she then tucked a .38 and boxes of cartridges into the drawer.

It was midnight when I finally went upstairs. Before settling into bed, I dialed the number for the 7-Eleven again.

"Ellen Jordan?"

"Yeah? That's me. Who's this?"

I told her, explaining, "You mentioned to me last fall that when Fred Cheney and Deborah Harvey came in, Deborah tried to buy beer, and you carded her."

"Yeah, that's right."

"Can you tell me exactly what you did when you carded her?"

"I just said I needed to see her driver's license," Ellen said, and she sounded puzzled. "You know, I asked to see it."

"Did she get it out of her purse?"

"Sure. She had to get it out so I could look at it."

"She handed it to you, then," I said.

"Uh-huh."

"Was it inside anything? Inside a plastic window?"

"It wasn't in nothing," she said. "She just handed it over and I looked at it, then I gave it back to her." A pause. "Why?"

"I'm trying to determine if you touched Deborah Harvey's driver's license."

"Sure I did. I had to touch it to look at it." She sounded frightened. "I'm not in trouble or anything, am I?"

"No, Ellen," I replied reassuringly. "You're not in any trouble at all."

15

ABBY'S ASSIGNMENT WAS to see what she could find out about Barry Aranoff, and she left for Roanoke in the morning. The following evening, she returned just minutes before Marino appeared at my front door. I had invited him to dinner.

When he discovered Abby in the kitchen, his pupils contracted. His face turned red.

"Jack Black?" I inquired.

I returned from the bar to find Abby smoking at the table while Marino stood before the window. He had cracked the blinds and was staring sullenly out at the feeder.

"You won't see any birds at this hour, unless you're interested in bats," I said.

He did not reply or turn around.

I began to serve the salad. It wasn't until I was pouring Chianti that Marino finally took his chair.

"You didn't tell me you had company," he said.

"If I had told you, you wouldn't have come," I replied just as bluntly.

"She didn't tell me either," Abby said, testily. "So now that it's been established that we're all happy to be together, let's enjoy dinner."

If I had learned nothing else from my failed marriage to Tony, it was never to engage in confrontations if it's late at night or time to eat. I did the best I could to fill the silence with light conversation. I waited until coffee was served before speaking my mind.

"Abby's going to be staying with me for a while," I said to Marino.

"It's your business." He reached for the sugar.

"It's your business, too. We're all in this together."

"Maybe you ought to explain what it is we're all into, Doc. But first"—he looked at Abby—"I'd like to know where this little dinner scene is going to show up in your book. Then I won't have to read the whole damn thing. I can just turn to the right page."

"You know, Marino, you really can be a jerk," Abby said.

"I can be an asshole, too. You ain't had that pleasure yet."

"Thank you for giving me something to look forward to."

Snatching a pen out of his breast pocket, he tossed it across the table. "Better start writing. Wouldn't want you to quote me wrong."

Abby glared at him.

"Stop it," I said angrily.

They looked at me.

"You're acting no better than the rest of them," I added.

"Who?" Marino's face was blank.

"Everybody," I said. "I'm sick to death of lies, jealousy, power plays. I expect more of my friends. I thought you were my friends."

I pushed back my chair.

"If the two of you wish to continue taking potshots at each other, go ahead. But I've had enough."

Without looking at either of them, I carried my coffee into the living room, turned on the stereo, and closed my eyes. Music was my therapy, and I had been listening to Bach last. His Sinfonia Two, Cantata No. 29 began midflight, and I began to relax. For weeks after Mark left, I would come downstairs when I couldn't sleep, put the headphones on, and surround myself with Beethoven, Mozart, Pachelbel.

Abby and Marino had the sheepish expressions of a squabbling couple that have just made up when they joined me fifteen minutes later.

"Uh, we've been talking," Abby said as I turned off the stereo. "I explained things as best I could. We've begun to reach a level of understanding."

I was delighted to hear it.

"May as well pitch in, the three of us," Marino said. "What the hell. Abby ain't really a reporter right now, anyway."

The remark stung her a little, I could tell, but they were going to cooperate, miracle of miracles.

"By the time her book comes out, this will probably be over with. That's what matters, that it's over with. It's been almost three years now, ten kids. You include Jill and Elizabeth, we're talking twelve." He shook his head, his eyes getting hard. "Whoever's whacking these kids ain't going to retire, Doc. He'll keep on until he gets nailed. And in investigations like this, that usually happens because someone gets lucky."

"We may already have gotten lucky," Abby said to him. "Aranoff's not the man who was driving the Lincoln."

"You sure?" Marino asked.

"Positive. Aranoff's got gray hair, what little hair he has left. He's maybe five-foot-eight and must weigh two hundred pounds."

"You telling me you met him?"

"No," she said. "He was still out of town. I knocked on the door and his wife let me in. I was wearing work pants, boots. I told her I was with the power company and needed to check their meter. We got to chatting. She offered me a Coke. While I was inside, I looked around, saw a family photograph, asked her about the photo to be sure. That's how I found out what Aranoff looks like. It wasn't him, the man we saw. Not the man tailing me in Washington, either."

"I don't guess there's any possibility you read the plate number wrong," Marino asked me.

"No. Even if I had," I said, "the coincidence would be incredible. Both cars 1990 Lincoln Mark Sevens? Aranoff just happens to be traveling in the Williamsburg-Tidewater area around the same time I *erroneously* record a plate number that just happens to be his?"

"Looks like Aranoff and me are going to have to have a little discussion," Marino said.

Marino called my office later that week and said right off, "You sitting down?"

"You talked with Aranoff."

"Bingo. He left Roanoke Monday, February tenth, and hit Danville, Petersburg, and Richmond. On Wednesday the twelfth, he was in the Tidewater area, and this is where it gets real interesting. He was due in Boston on Thursday the thirteenth, which is the night you and Abby was in Williamsburg. The day before that, Wednesday the twelfth, Aranoff left his car in long-term parking at the Newport News airport. From there he flew to Boston, was up in that area buzzing around in a rental car for the better part of a week. Returned to Newport News yesterday morning, got into his car, and headed home."

"Are you suggesting someone may have stolen the tags off his car while it was in long-term parking, then returned them?" I asked.

"Unless Aranoff's lying, and I don't see any reason for that, there's no other explanation, Doc."

"When he retrieved his car, did he notice anything that might have made him think it had been tampered with?"

"Nope. We went into his garage and took a look at it. Both tags were there, screwed on nice and tight. The tags were dirty like the rest of the car and they were smudged, which may or may not mean anything. I didn't lift any prints, but whoever borrowed the tags was probably wearing gloves, which could account for the smudges. No tool or pry marks that I could see."

"Was the car in a conspicuous place in the parking lot?"

"Aranoff said he left it in pretty much in the middle of the lot, which was almost full."

"You would think if his car had been sitting out there for several days without license plates, Security or someone would have noticed," I said.

"Not necessarily. People aren't all that observant. When they leave their ride at the airport or are returning from a trip, the only thing on their mind is hauling their bags, catching their plane, or getting the hell home. Even if someone noticed, it's not likely he's going to report it to Security. Security couldn't do nothing anyway until the owner returned, then it would be up to him to report the stolen plates. As for the actual theft of the plates, that wouldn't be very hard. You go to the airport after midnight and there's not going to be anybody around. If it was me, I'd just walk into the lot like I was looking for my car, then five minutes later I'd be heading out of there with a set of plates in my briefcase."

"And that's what you think happened?"

"My theory is this," he said. "The guy who asked you directions last week wasn't no detective, FBI agent, or spook out spying. He was somebody up to no good. Could be a drug dealer, could be almost anything. I think the dark gray Mark Seven he was in is his personal car, and to be on the safe side, when he goes out to do whatever he's into, he switches plates in the event his ride is spotted in the area, maybe by cops out on patrol, whatever."

"Rather risky if he gets pulled for running a red light," I pointed out. "The license number would come back to someone else."

"True. But I don't think he plans on getting pulled. I think he's more worried about his car being spotted because he's out to break the law, something's going to go down and he don't want to take the chance his own tag number's going to be on the street when it does."

"Why doesn't he just use a rental car, then?"

"That's just as bad as having his own plate number out there. Any cop knows a rental car when he sees it. All tag numbers in Virginia begin with R. And if you track it down, its going to come back to whoever rented it. Switching tags is a better idea if you're smart enough to figure out a safe routine. It's what I'd do, and I'd probably resort to a long-term parking lot. I'd use the tags, then take them off my car and put my tags back on. I'd drive to the airport, walk out into the lot after dark, make sure no one's looking, and put the tags back on the car I'd stolen them from."

"What if the owner's already returned and found his tags stolen?"

"If the ride's no longer in the lot, I'd just pitch the tags in the nearest Dumpster. Either way I can't lose."

"Good Lord. The man Abby and I saw that night might be the killer, Marino."

"The squirrel you saw wasn't no businessman who was lost or fruitcake tailing you," he said. "He was up to something illegal. That don't mean he's a killer."

"The parking sticker . . ."

"I'm gonna track that down. See if Colonial Williamsburg can supply me with a list of everybody who's been issued one."

"The car Mr. Joyce saw going down his road with the headlights off could have been a Lincoln Mark Seven," I said.

"Could have been. Mark Sevens came out in 1990. Jim and Bonnie was murdered in the summer of 1990. And in the dark, a Mark Seven wouldn't look all that different from a Thunderbird, which was what Mr. Joyce said the car he saw looked like."

"Wesley will have a field day with this," I muttered, incredulous.

"Yeah," Marino said. "I got to call him."

———

March came in with a whispered promise that winter would not last forever. The sun was warm on my back as I cleaned the windshield of my Mercedes while Abby pumped gas. The breeze was gentle, freshly scrubbed from days of rain. People were out washing cars and riding bikes, the earth stirring but not quite awake.

Like a lot of service stations these days, the one I frequented doubled as a convenience store, and I bought two cups of coffee to go when I went inside to pay. Then Abby and I drove off to Williamsburg, windows cracked, Bruce Hornsby singing "Harbor Lights" on the radio.

"I called my answering machine before we left," Abby said.

"And?"

"Five hang-ups."

"Cliff?"

"I'm willing to make a bet," she said. "Not that he wants to talk to me. I suspect he's just trying to figure out if I'm home, has probably cruised past my parking lot a number of times, too, looking for my car."

"Why would he do that if he's not interested in talking to you?"

"Maybe he doesn't know that I've changed my locks."

"Then he must be stupid. One would think he would realize you would put two and two together when his series ran."

"He's not stupid," Abby said, staring out the side window.

I opened the sunroof.

"He knows I know. But he's not stupid," she said again. "Cliff's fooled everyone. They don't know he's crazy."

"Hard to believe he could have gotten as far as he has if he's crazy," I said.

"That's the beauty of Washington," she replied cynically. "The most successful, powerful people in the world are there and half of them are crazy, the other half neurotic. Most of them are immoral. Power does it. I don't know why Watergate surprised anyone."

"What has power done to you?" I asked.

"I know how it tastes, but I wasn't there long enough to get addicted."

"Maybe you're lucky."

She was silent.

I thought of Pat Harvey. What was she doing these days? What was going through her mind?

"Have you talked to Pat Harvey?" I asked Abby.

"Yes."

"Since the articles ran in the *Post*?"

She nodded.

"How is she?"

"I once read something written by a missionary to what was then the Congo. He recalled encountering a tribesman in the jungle who looked perfectly normal until he smiled. His teeth were filed to points. He was a cannibal."

Her voice was flat with anger, her mood suddenly dark. I had no idea what she was talking about.

"That's Pat Harvey," she went on. "I dropped by to see her before heading out to Roanoke the other day. We talked briefly about the stories in the *Post*, and I thought she was taking it all in stride until she smiled. Her smile made my blood run cold."

I didn't know what to say.

"That's when I knew Cliff's stories had pushed her over the edge. Deborah's murder pushed Pat as far as I thought she could go. But the stories pushed her further. I remember when I talked to her I had this sense that something wasn't there anymore. After a while I figured out what's not there is Pat Harvey."

"Did she know her husband was having an affair?"

"She does now."

"If it's true," I added.

"Cliff wouldn't write something that he couldn't back up, attribute to a credible source."

I wondered what it would take to push me to the edge. Lucy, Mark? If I had an accident and could no longer use my hands or went blind? I did not know what it would take to make me snap. Maybe it was like dying. Once you were gone you didn't know the difference.

We were at Old Towne shortly after noon. The apartment complex where Jill and Elizabeth had lived was unremarkable, a honeycomb of buildings that all looked the same. They were brick with red awnings announcing block numbers over the main entrances;

the landscaping was a patchwork of winter-brown grass and narrow margins of flower beds covered in woodchips. There were areas for cookouts with swing sets, picnic tables, and grills.

We stopped in the parking lot and stared up at what had been Jill's balcony. Through wide spaces in the railing two blue-and-white-webbed chairs rocked gently in the breeze. A chain dangled from a hook in the ceiling, lonely for a potted plant. Elizabeth had lived on the other side of the parking lot. From their respective residences the two friends would have been able to check on each other. They could watch lights turn on and off, know when the other got up and went to bed, when one was home or not.

For a moment, Abby and I shared a depressed silence.

Then she said, "They were more than friends, weren't they, Kay?"

"To answer that would be hearsay."

She smiled a little. "To tell you the truth, I wondered about it when I was working on the stories. It crossed my mind, at any rate. But no one ever suggested it or even hinted." She paused, staring out. "I think I know what they felt like."

I looked at her.

"It must have been the way I felt with Cliff. Sneaking, hiding, spending half your energy worrying about what people think, fearing they somehow suspect."

"The irony is," I said, putting the car in gear, "that people don't really give a damn. They're too preoccupied with themselves."

"I wonder if Jill and Elizabeth would ever have figured that out."

"If their love was greater than their fear, they would have figured it out eventually."

"Where are we going, by the way?" She looked out her window at the roadside streaming past.

"Just cruising," I said. "In the general direction of downtown."

I had never given her an itinerary. All I had said was that I wanted to "look around."

"You're looking for that damn car, aren't you?"

"It can't hurt to look."

"And just what are you going to do if you find it, Kay?"

"Write the plate number down, see who it comes back to this time."

"Well"—she started to laugh—"if you find a 1990 charcoal

Lincoln Mark Seven with a Colonial Williamsburg sticker on the rear bumper, I'll pay you a hundred dollars."

"Better get your checkbook out. If it's here, I'm going to find it."

And I did, not half an hour later, by following the age-old rule of how you find something lost. I retraced my steps. When I returned to Merchant's Square the car was sitting there big as life in the parking lot, not far from where we had spotted it the first time when its driver had stopped to ask directions.

"Jesus Christ," Abby whispered. "I don't believe it."

The car was unoccupied, sunshine glinting off the glass. It looked as if it had just been washed and waxed. There was a parking sticker on the left side of the rear bumper, the plate number ITU-144. Abby wrote it down.

"This is too easy, Kay. It can't be right."

"We don't know that it's the same car." I was being scientific now. "It looks the same, but we can't be sure."

I parked some twenty spaces away, tucking my Mercedes between a station wagon and a Pontiac, and sat behind the wheel scanning the storefronts. A gift shop, a picture-framing shop, a restaurant. Between a tobacco shop and a bakery was a bookstore, small, inconspicuous, books displayed in the window. A wooden sign hung over the door, with the name "The Dealer's Room" painted on it in Colonial-style calligraphy.

"Crossword puzzles," I said under my breath, and a chill ran up my spine.

"What?" Abby was still watching the Lincoln.

"Jill and Elizabeth liked crossword puzzles. They often went out to breakfast on Sunday mornings and picked up the *New York Times*." I was opening my door.

Abby put a hand on my arm, restraining me. "No, Kay. Wait a minute. We've got to think about this."

I settled back into the seat.

"You can't just walk in there," she said, and it sounded like an order.

"I want to buy a paper."

"What if he's in there? Then what are you going to do?"

"I want to see if it's him, the man who was driving. I think I'd recognize him."

"And he might recognize you."

" 'Dealer' could refer to cards," I thought out loud as a young woman with short curly black hair walked up to the bookstore, opened the door, and disappeared inside.

"The person who deals cards, deals the jack of hearts," I added, my voice trailing off.

"You talked to him when he asked directions. Your picture's been in the news." Abby was taking charge. "You're not going in there. I will."

"We both will."

"That's crazy!"

"You're right." My mind was made up. "You're staying put. I'm going in."

I was out of the car before she could argue. She got out, too, and just stood there, looking lost, as I walked with purpose in that direction. She did not come after me. She had too much sense to make a scene.

When I put my hand on the cold brass handle of the door, my heart was hammering. When I walked inside, I felt weak in the knees.

He was standing behind the counter, smiling and filling out a charge card receipt while a middle-aged woman in an Ultrasuede suit prattled on, ". . . That's what birthdays are for. You buy your husband a book *you* want to read . . ."

"As long as you both enjoy the same books, that's all right." His voice was very soft, soothing, a voice you could trust.

Now that I was inside the shop, I was desperate to leave. I wanted to run. There were stacks of newspapers to one side of the counter, including the *New York Times*. I could pick one up, quickly pay for it, and be gone. But I did not want to look him in the eye.

It was him.

I turned around and walked out without glancing back.

Abby was sitting in the car smoking.

"He couldn't work here and not know his way to Sixty-four," I said, starting the engine.

She got my meaning precisely. "Do you want to call Marino now or wait until we get back to Richmond?"

"We're going to call him now." I found a pay phone and was told Marino was on the street. I left him the message, "ITU-144. Call me."

Abby asked me a lot of questions, and I did my best to answer them. Then there were long stretches of silence as I drove. My stomach was sour. I considered pulling off somewhere. I thought I might throw up.

She was staring at me. I could feel her concern.

"My God, Kay. You're white as a sheet."

"I'm all right."

"You want me to drive?"

"I'm fine. Really."

When we got home, I went straight up to my bedroom. My hands trembled as I dialed the number. Mark's machine answered after the second ring, and I started to hang up but found myself mesmerized by his voice.

"I'm sorry, there's no one to answer your call right now . . ."

At the beep I hesitated, then quietly returned the receiver to its cradle. When I looked up, I found Abby in my doorway. I could tell by the look on her face that she knew what I had just done.

I stared at her, my eyes filling with tears, and then she was sitting next to me on the edge of the bed.

"Why didn't you leave him a message?" she whispered.

"How could you possibly know who I was calling?" I fought to steady my voice.

"Because it's the same impulse that overwhelms me when I'm terribly upset. I want to reach for the phone. Even now, after all of it. I still want to call Cliff."

"Have you?"

She slowly shook her head.

"Don't. Don't ever, Abby."

She studied me closely. "Was it walking into the bookstore and seeing him?"

"I'm not sure."

"I think you know."

I glanced away from her. "When I get too close, I know it. I've gotten too close before. I ask myself why it happens."

"People like us can't help it. We have a compulsion, something drives us. That's why it happens," she said.

I could not admit to her my fear. Had Mark answered the phone, I didn't know if I could have admitted it to him, either.

Abby was staring off, her voice distant when she asked, "As much as you know about death, do you ever think about your own?"

I got off the bed. "Where the hell is Marino?" I picked up the phone to try him again.

16

DAYS TURNED INTO WEEKS while I waited anxiously. I had not heard from Marino since giving him the information about The Dealer's Room. I had not heard from anyone. With each hour that passed the silence grew louder and more ominous.

On the first day of spring, I emerged from the conference room after being deposed for three hours by two lawyers. Rose told me I had a call.

"Kay? It's Benton."

"Good afternoon," I said, adrenaline surging.

"Can you come up to Quantico tomorrow?"

I reached for my calendar. Rose had penciled in a conference call. It could be rescheduled.

"What time?"

"Ten, if that's convenient. I've already talked to Marino."

Before I could ask questions, he said he couldn't talk and would fill me in when we met.

It was six o'clock before I left my office. The sun had gone down and the air felt cold. When I turned into my driveway, I noticed the lights were on. Abby was home.

We had seen little of each other of late, both of us in and out, rarely speaking. She never went to the grocery store, but would leave a fifty-dollar bill taped to the refrigerator every now and then, which more than covered what little she ate. When wine or Scotch got low, I would find a twenty-dollar bill under the bottle. Several days ago, I had discovered a five-dollar bill on top of a depleted box of laundry soap. Wandering through the rooms of my house had turned into a peculiar scavenger hunt.

When I unlocked the front door, Abby suddenly stepped into the doorway, startling me.

"I'm sorry," she said. "I heard you drive in. Didn't mean to scare you."

I felt foolish. Ever since she had moved in, I had become increasingly jumpy. I supposed I wasn't adjusting well to my loss of privacy.

"Can I fix you a drink?" she asked. Abby looked tired.

"Thanks," I said, unbuttoning my coat. My eyes wandered into the living room. On the coffee table, beside an ashtray filled with cigarette butts, were a wineglass and several reporter's notepads.

Taking off my coat and gloves, I went upstairs and tossed them on my bed, pausing long enough to play back the messages on the answering machine. My mother had tried to reach me. I was eligible to win a prize if I dialed a certain number by eight P.M., and Marino had called to tell me what time he would pick me up in the morning. Mark and I continued missing each other, talking to each other's machines.

"I've got to go to Quantico tomorrow," I told Abby when I entered the living room.

She pointed to my drink on the coffee table.

"Marino and I have a meeting with Benton," I said.

She reached for her cigarettes.

"I don't know what it's about," I continued. "Maybe you do."

"Why would I know?"

"You haven't been here much. I don't know what you've been doing."

"When you're at your office, I don't know what you're doing either."

"I haven't been doing anything remarkable. What would you like to know?" I offered lightly, trying to dispel the tension.

"I don't ask because I know how private you are about your work. I don't want to pry."

I assumed she was implying that if I asked about what she was doing I would be prying.

"Abby, you seem distant these days."

"Preoccupied. Please don't take it personally."

Certainly she had plenty to think about, with the book she was writing, what she was going to do with her life. But I had never seen Abby this withdrawn.

"I'm concerned, that's all," I said.

"You don't understand what I'm like, Kay. When I get into something, I'm consumed by it. Can't get my mind off it." She paused. "You were right when you said this book was my chance to redeem myself. It is."

"I'm glad to hear it, Abby. Knowing you, it will be a best-seller."

"Maybe. I'm not the only one interested in writing a book about these cases. My agent's already hearing rumors about other deals out there. I've got a head start, will be all right if I work fast."

"It's not your book I care about, it's you."

"I care about you, too, Kay," she said. "I appreciate what you've done for me by letting me stay here. And that won't go on much longer, I promise."

"You can stay as long as you like."

She collected her notepads and drink. "I've got to start writing soon, and I can't do that until I have my own space, my computer."

"Then you're simply doing research these days."

"Yes. I'm finding a lot of things I didn't know I was looking for," she said enigmatically as she headed for her bedroom.

When the Quantico exit came into view the following morning, traffic suddenly stopped. Apparently there had been an accident somewhere north of us on I-95, and cars weren't moving. Marino flipped on his grille lights and veered off onto the shoulder, where we bumped along, rocks pelting the undercarriage of the car, for a good hundred yards.

For the past two hours he had been giving me a complete account of his latest domestic accomplishments, while I wondered what Wesley had to tell us and worried about Abby.

"Never had any idea venetian blinds was such a bitch," Marino complained as we sped past Marine Corps barracks and a firing range. "I'm spraying them with 409, right?" He glanced over at me. "And it's taking me a minute per slat, paper towels shredding the hell all over the place. Finally I get an idea, just take the damn things out of the windows and dump them in the tub. Fill it with hot water and laundry soap. Worked like a charm."

"That's great," I muttered.

"I'm also in the process of tearing down the wallpaper in the kitchen. It came with the house. Doris never liked it."

"The question is whether *you* like it. You're the one who lives there now."

He shrugged. "Never paid it much mind, you want to know the truth. But I figure if Doris says it's ugly, it probably is. We used to talk about selling the camper and putting in an above-the-ground pool. So I'm finally getting around to that, too. Ought to have it in time for summer."

"Marino, be careful," I said gently. "Make sure what you're doing is for you."

He did not answer me.

"Don't hang your future on a hope that may not be there."

"It can't hurt nothing," he finally said. "Even if she never comes back, it can't hurt nothing for things to look nice."

"Well, you're going to have to show me your place sometime," I said.

"Yeah. All the times I've been to your crib and you've never seen mine."

He parked the car and we got out. The FBI Academy had continued to metastasize over the outer fringes of the U.S. Marine Corps base. The main building with its fountain and flags had been turned into administrative offices, and the center of activity had been moved into a new tan brick building next door. What looked like another dormitory had gone up since I had visited last. Gunfire in the distance sounded like firecrackers popping.

Marino checked his .38 at the desk. We signed in and clipped on visitor passes, then he took me on another series of shortcuts, avoiding the enclosed brick-and-glass breezeways, or gerbil tubes. I followed him through a door that led outside the building, and we walked over a loading dock, through a kitchen. We finally emerged from the back of the gift shop, which Marino strolled right through without a glance in the direction of the young female clerk holding a stack of sweatshirts. Her lips parted in unspoken protest as she viewed our unorthodox passage. Out of the store and around a corner, we entered the bar and grill called The Boardroom, where Wesley was waiting for us at a corner table.

He wasted no time getting down to business.

The owner of The Dealer's Room was Steven Spurrier. Wesley described him as "thirty-four years old, white, with black hair, brown eyes. Five-eleven, one hundred and sixty pounds." Spurrier had not yet been picked up or questioned, but he had been under constant surveillance. What had been observed so far was not exactly normal.

On several occasions he had left his two-story brick home at a late hour and driven to two bars and one rest stop. He never seemed to stay in one place very long. He was always alone. The previous week he had approached a young couple emerging from a bar called Tom-Toms. It appeared he asked for directions again. Nothing happened. The couple got in their car and left. Spurrier got into his Lincoln and eventually meandered back home. His license tags remained unchanged.

"We've got a problem with the evidence," Wesley reported, looking at me through rimless glasses, his face stern. "We've got a cartridge case in our lab. You've got the bullet from Deborah Harvey in Richmond."

"I don't have the bullet," I replied. "The Forensic Science Bureau does. I presume you've started the DNA analysis on the blood recovered from Elizabeth Mott's car."

"It will be another week or two."

I nodded. The FBI DNA lab used five polymorphic probes. Each probe had to stay in the X-ray developer for about a week, which was why I had written Wesley a letter some time ago suggesting that he get the bloody swatch from Montana and begin its analysis immediately.

"DNA's not worth a damn without a suspect's blood," Marino reminded us.

"We're working on that," Wesley said stoically.

"Yeah, well, seems like we could pop Spurrier because of the license plate. Ask his sorry ass to explain why he was driving around with Aranoff's tags several weeks back."

"We can't prove he was driving around with them. It's Kay and Abby's word against his."

"All we need is a magistrate who will sign a warrant. Then we start digging. Maybe we turn up ten pairs of shoes," Marino said. "Maybe an Uzi, some Hydra-Shok ammo, who knows what we'll find?"

"We're planning to do so," Wesley continued. "But one thing at a time."

He got up for more coffee, and Marino took my cup and his and followed him. At this early hour The Boardroom was deserted. I looked around at empty tables, the television in a corner, and tried to envision what must go on here late at night. Agents in training lived like priests. Members of the opposite sex, booze, and cigarettes were not allowed inside the dormitory rooms, which also could not be locked. But The Boardroom served beer and wine. When there were blowouts, confrontations, indiscretions, this was where it happened. I remembered Mark telling me he had broken up a free-for-all in here one night when a new FBI agent went too far with his homework and decided to "arrest" a table of veteran DEA agents. Tables had crashed to the floor, beer and baskets of popcorn everywhere.

Wesley and Marino returned to the table, and setting down his coffee, Wesley slipped out of his pearl-gray suit jacket and hung it neatly on the back of his chair. His white shirt scarcely had a wrinkle, I noticed, his silk tie was peacock blue with tiny white fleur-de-lis, and he was wearing peacock blue suspenders. Marino served as the perfect foil to this Fortune 500 partner of his. With his big belly, Marino couldn't possibly do justice to even the most elegant suit, but I had to give him credit. These days he was trying.

"What do you know about Spurrier's background?" I asked. Wesley was writing notes to himself while Marino reviewed a file, both men seeming to have forgotten there was a third person at the table.

"He doesn't have a record," Wesley replied, looking up. "Never been arrested, hasn't gotten so much as a speeding ticket in the past ten years. He bought the Lincoln in February of 1990 from a dealer in Virginia Beach, traded in an '86 Town Car, paid the rest in cash."

"He must have some bucks," Marino commented. "Drives high-dollar cars, lives in a nice crib. Hard to believe he makes that much from his bookstore."

"He doesn't make that much," Wesley said. "According to what he filed last year, he cleared less than thirty thousand dollars. But he's got assets of over half a million, a money market account, waterfront real estate, stocks."

"Jeez." Marino shook his head.

"Any dependents?" I asked.

"No," Wesley said. "Never married, both parents dead. His father was very successful in real estate in the Northern Neck. He died when Steven was in his early twenties. I suspect this is where the money comes from."

"What about his mother?" I asked.

"She died about a year after the father did. Cancer. Steven came along late in life. His mother had him when she was forty-two. The only other sibling is a brother named Gordon. He lives in Texas, is fifteen years older than Steven, married, with four kids."

Skimming his notes again, Wesley brought forth more information. Spurrier was born in Gloucester, attended the University of Virginia, where he received a bachelor's degree in English. Afterward he joined the navy, where he lasted less than four months. The next eleven months were spent working at a printing press, where his primary responsibility was to maintain the machinery.

"I'd like to know more about his months in the navy," Marino said.

"There's not much to know," Wesley answered. "After enlisting, he was sent to boot camp in the Great Lakes area. He chose journalism as his speciality and was assigned to the Defense Information School at Fort Benjamin Harrison in Indianapolis. Later he was assigned his duty station, working for the Commander-in-Chief of the Atlantic Fleet in Norfolk." He looked up from his notes. "About a month later his father died, and Steven received a hardship discharge so he could return to Gloucester to take care of his mother, who was already ill with cancer."

"What about the brother?" Marino asked.

"Apparently he couldn't get away from his job and family responsibilities in Texas." He paused, glancing at us. "Maybe there are other reasons. Obviously, Steven's relationship with his family is of interest to me, but I'm not going to know a whole lot more about it for a while."

"Why not?" I asked.

"It's too risky for me to confront the brother directly at this point. I don't want him calling Steven, tipping my hand. It's unlikely Gordon would cooperate, anyway. Family members tend to stick together in matters like this, even if they don't get along."

"Well, you've been talking to someone," Marino said.

"A couple of people from the navy, UVA, his former employer at the printing press."

"What else did they have to say about this squirrel?"

"A loner," Wesley said. "Not much of a journalist. Was more interested in reading than interviewing anyone or writing stories. Apparently, the printing press suited him rather well. He stayed in the back, had his nose in a book when things were slow. His boss said Steven loved to tinker with the presses, various machines, and kept them spotless. Sometimes he would go for days without talking to anyone. His boss described Steven as peculiar."

"His boss offer any examples?"

"Several things," Wesley said. "A woman employed by the press took off her fingertip with a paper cutter one morning. Steven got angry because she bled all over a piece of equipment he had just cleaned. His response to his mother's death was abnormal as well. Steven was reading during a lunch break when the call came from the hospital. He showed no emotion, just returned to his chair and resumed reading his book."

"A real warmhearted guy," Marino said.

"No one has described him as warmhearted."

"What happened after his mother died?" I asked.

"Then, I would assume, Steven got his inheritance. He moved to Williamsburg, leased the space at Merchant's Square, and opened The Dealer's Room. This was nine years ago."

"A year before Jill Harrington and Elizabeth Mott were murdered," I said.

Wesley nodded. "He was in the area, then. He's been in the area during all of these murders. He's been working in his bookstore since it opened, except for a period of about five months back, uh, seven years ago. The store was closed during that time. We don't know why or know where Spurrier was."

"He runs his bookstore by himself?" Marino asked.

"It's a small operation. No other employees. The store is closed on Mondays. It's been noted that when there isn't much business he just sits behind the counter and reads, and if he leaves the store before closing time he either closes early or puts a sign on the door that says he'll be back at such and such an hour. He also has an answering machine. If you're looking for a certain book or want him to search for something out of print, you can leave your request on his machine."

"It's interesting that someone so antisocial would open a business that requires him to have contact with customers, even if the contact is rather limited," I said.

"It's actually very appropriate," Wesley said. "The bookstore would serve as a perfect lair for a voyeur, someone intensely interested in observing people without having to personally interact with them. It has been noted that William and Mary students frequent his store, primarily because Spurrier carries unusual, out-of-print books in addition to popular fiction and nonfiction. He also carries a wide selection of spy novels and military magazines, which attract business from the nearby military bases. If he's the killer, then watching young, attractive couples and military personnel who come into his store would fascinate him in a voyeuristic fashion and at the same time stir up feelings of inadequacy, frustration, rage. He would hate what he envies, envy what he hates."

"I wonder if he suffered ridicule during his time in the navy," I conjectured.

"Based on what I've been told, he did, at least to a degree. Spurrier's peers considered him a wimp, a loser, while his superiors found him arrogant and aloof, even though he was never a disciplinary problem. Spurrier had no success with women and kept to himself, partly by choice and because others did not find his personality particularly attractive."

"Maybe being in the navy was the closest he ever got to being a real man," Marino said, "being what he wanted to be. His father dies and Spurrier has to take care of his sick mother. In his mind, he gets screwed."

"That's quite possible," Wesley agreed. "In any event, the killer we're dealing with would believe that his troubles are the fault of others. He would take no responsibility. He would feel his life was controlled by others, and therefore, controlling others and his environment became an obsession for him."

"Sounds like he's paying back the world," Marino said.

"The killer is showing he has power," Wesley said. "If the military aspects enter into his fantasies, and I think they do, then he believes he's the ultimate soldier. He kills without being caught. He outsmarts the enemy, plays games with them, and wins. It may be possible that he has deliberately set things up in such a way as to make those investigating the murders suspect that the perpetrator is a professional soldier, even someone from Camp Peary."

"His own disinformation campaign," I considered.

"He can't destroy the military," Wesley added, "but he could try to tarnish the image, degrade and defame it."

"Yeah, and all the while he's laughing up his sleeve," Marino said.

"I think the main point is that the killer's activities are the product of violent, sexualized fantasies that existed early on in the context of his social isolation. He believes he lives in an unjust world, and fantasy provides an important escape. In his fantasies he can express his emotions and control other human beings, he can be and get anything he wants. He can control life and death. He has the power to decide whether to injure or kill."

"Too bad Spurrier don't just *fantasize* about whacking couples," Marino said. "Then the three of us wouldn't have to be sitting here having this conversation."

"I'm afraid it doesn't work that way," Wesley said. "If violent, aggressive behavior dominates your thinking, your imagination, you're going to start acting out in ways that move you closer to the actual expression of these emotions. Violence fuels more violent thoughts, and more violent thoughts fuel more violence. After a while, violence and killing are a natural part of your adult life, and you see nothing wrong with it. I've had serial murderers tell me emphatically that when they killed, they were just doing what everybody else thinks of doing."

"Evil to him who evil thinks," I said.

It was then that I offered my theory about Deborah Harvey's purse.

"I think it's possible the killer knew who Deborah was," I said. "Perhaps not when the couple was first abducted, but he may have known by the time he killed them."

"Please explain," Wesley said, studying me with interest.

"Have either of you seen the fingerprints report?"

"Yeah, I've seen it," Marino replied.

"As you know, when Vander examined Deborah's purse he found partials, smudges on her credit cards, but nothing on her driver's license."

"So?" Marino looked perplexed.

"The contents of her purse were well preserved because the nylon purse was waterproof. And the credit cards and her driver's license were inside plastic windows and zipped inside a compartment, thus protected from the elements and the body fluids of decomposition. Had Vander not picked up anything that would be one thing. But I find it interesting that he picked up something on the credit cards but not on her driver's license, when we know that Deborah got out her license when she went inside the Seven-Eleven and tried to buy beer. So she handled the license, and Ellen Jordan, the clerk, also handled it. What I'm wondering is if the killer didn't touch Deborah's driver's license, too, and then wipe it clean afterward."

"Why would he do that?" Marino asked.

"Maybe when he was inside the car with the couple, had the gun out and was abducting them, Deborah told him who she was," I answered.

"Interesting," Wesley said.

"Deborah may have been a modest young woman, but she was well aware of her family's prominence, of her mother's power," I went on. "She may have informed the killer in hopes that he would change his mind, think that in harming them there would be hell to pay. This may have startled the killer considerably, and he may have demanded proof of her identity, at which point he may have gotten hold of her purse to see the name on her driver's license."

"Then how did the purse end up out in the woods, and why did he leave the jack of hearts in it?" Marino asked.

"Maybe to buy himself a little time," I said. "He would have known that the Jeep would be found quickly, and if he realized who Deborah was, then he was also going to know that half the law enforcement world was going to be out looking for them. Maybe he decided to play it safe by not having the jack of hearts found immediately, so he left it with the bodies instead of inside the Jeep. By placing the card inside the purse and putting the purse under Deborah's body, he ensured that the card would be found, but probably not for a long time. He changes the rules a little but still wins the game."

"Not half bad. What do you think?" Marino looked at Wesley.

"I think we may never know exactly what happened," he said. "But it wouldn't surprise me if Deborah did exactly what Kay has proposed. One thing is certain—no matter what Deborah may have said or threatened, it would have been too risky for the killer to free her and Fred because they probably would have been able to identify him. So he went through with the murders, but the unforeseen turn of events could have thrown him off. Yes," he said to me. "This could have caused him to alter his ritual. It may also be that leaving the card in Deborah's purse was his way of showing contempt toward her and who she was."

"Sort of an 'up yours,'" Marino said.

"Possibly," Wesley replied.

Steven Spurrier was arrested the following Friday when two FBI agents and a local detective who had been tailing him all day followed him to the long-term parking lot of the Newport News airport.

When Marino's call woke me before dawn, my first thought was that another couple had disappeared. It took a moment for me to comprehend what he was saying over the phone.

"They popped him while he was lifting another set of tags," he was saying. "Charged him with petit larceny. The best they could do, but at least we got our probable cause to turn him inside out."

"Another Lincoln?" I asked.

"This time a 1991, silver-gray. He's in lockup waiting to see the magistrate, no way they're going to be able to hold him on a nickel-and-dime class one misdemeanor. Best they can do is stall, take their sweet time processing him. Then he's out of there."

"What about a search warrant?"

"His crib's crawling with cops and the feds even as we speak. Looking for everything from *Soldier of Fortune* magazines to Tinker Toys."

"You're heading out there, I guess," I said.

"Yeah. I'll let you know."

It was not possible for me to go back to sleep. Throwing a robe over my shoulders, I went downstairs and switched on a lamp in Abby's room.

"It's just me," I said as she sat straight up in bed. She groaned, covering her eyes.

I told her what had happened. Then we went into the kitchen and put on a pot of coffee.

"I'd pay to be present when they search his house." She was so wired I was surprised she didn't bolt out the door.

But she stayed inside all day, suddenly industrious. She cleaned up her room, helped me in the kitchen, and even swept the patio. She wanted to know what the police had found and was smart enough to realize that driving to Williamsburg would get her nowhere, because she would not be allowed entrance into Spurrier's residence or bookstore.

Marino stopped by early that evening as Abby and I were loading the dishwasher. I knew instantly by the look on his face that his news wasn't good.

"First I'll tell you what we *didn't* find," he began. "We didn't find a friggin' thing that will convince a jury Spurrier's ever killed a housefly. No knives except the ones in his kitchen. No guns or cartridges. No souvenirs such as shoes, jewelry, locks of hair, whatever, that might have belonged to the victims."

"Was his bookstore searched as well?" I asked.

"Oh, yeah."

"And his car of course."

"Nothing."

"Then tell us what you *did* find," I asked, depressed.

"Enough weirdo stuff to make me know it's him, Doc," Marino said. "I mean, this drone ain't no Eagle Scout. He's into skin magazines, violent pornography. Plus, he's got books about the military, especially the CIA, and files filled with newspaper clippings about the CIA. All of it cataloged, labeled. The guy's neater than an old lady librarian."

"Did you find any newspaper clips about these cases?" Abby asked.

"We did, including old stories about Jill Harrington and Elizabeth Mott. We also found catalogs to a number of what I call spy shops, these outfits that sell security-survival shit, everything from bulletproof cars to bomb detectors and night vision goggles. The FBI's going to check it out, see what all he's ordered over the years. Spurrier's clothes are interesting, too. He must have half a dozen nylon warm-up suits in his bedroom, all of them black or navy blue and never worn, labels cut out of them, like maybe they were intended to be disposable, worn over his clothes and pitched somewhere after the fact."

"Nylon sheds very little," I said. "Windbreakers, nylon warm-ups aren't going to leave many fibers."

"Right. Let's see. What else?" Marino paused, finishing his drink. "Oh, yeah. Two boxes of surgical gloves and a supply of those disposable shoe-covers you wear downstairs."

"Booties?"

"Right. Like you wear in the morgue so you don't get blood on your shoes. And guess what? They found cards, four decks of them, never been opened, still in the cellophane."

"I don't suppose you found an opened deck missing a jack of hearts?" I asked, hopefully.

"No. But that don't surprise me. He probably removes the jack of hearts and then throws the rest of the cards away."

"All the same brand?"

"No. A couple different brands."

Abby was sitting silently in her chair, fingers laced tightly in her lap.

"It doesn't make sense that you didn't find any weapons," I said.

"This guy's slick, Doc. He's careful."

"Not careful enough. He kept the clippings about the murders, the warm-up suits, gloves. And he was caught red-handed stealing license tags, which makes me wonder if he wasn't getting ready to strike again."

"He had stolen tags on his car when he stopped you to ask directions," Marino pointed out. "No couple disappeared that weekend that we've heard about."

"That's true," I mused. "And he wasn't wearing a warm-up suit, either."

"He may save putting that on for last. May even keep it in a gym bag in his trunk. My guess is he has a kit."

"Did you find a gym bag?" Abby asked bluntly.

"No," Marino said. "No murder kit."

"Well, if you ever find a gym bag, or murder kit," Abby added, "then maybe you'll find his knife, gun, goggles, and all the rest of it."

"We'll be looking until the cows come home."

"Where is he now?" I asked.

"Was sitting in his kitchen drinking coffee when I left," Marino replied. "Friggin' unbelievable. Here we are tearing up his house and he's not even sweating. When he was asked about the warm-up suits, the gloves, decks of cards, and so on, he said he wasn't talking to us without his attorney present. Then he took a sip of his coffee and lit a cigarette like we wasn't there. Oh, yeah, I left that out. The squirrel smokes."

"What brand?" I asked.

"Dunhills. Probably buys them in that fancy tobacco shop next to his bookstore. And he uses a fancy lighter, too. An expensive one."

"That would certainly explain his peeling the paper off the butts before depositing them at the scenes, if that's what he did," I said. "Dunhills are distinctive."

"I know," Marino said. "They've got a gold band around the filter."

"You got a suspect's kit?"

"Oh, yeah." He smiled. "That's our little trump card that will beat his jack of hearts hands down. If we can't make these other cases, at least we got the murders of Jill Harrington and Elizabeth Mott to hang him with. DNA ought to nail his ass. Wish the damn tests didn't take so long."

After Marino left, Abby stared coolly at me.

"What do you think?" I asked.

"It's all circumstantial."

"Right now it is."

"Spurrier's got money," she said. "He's going to get the best trial lawyer money can buy. I can tell you exactly how it's going to go. The lawyer's going to suggest that his client was railroaded by the cops and the feds because of the pressure to solve these homicides. It's going to come out that a lot of people are looking for a scapegoat, especially in light of the accusations Pat Harvey has made."

"Abby . . ."

"Maybe the killer *is* someone from Camp Peary."

"You don't really believe that," I protested.

She glanced at her watch. "Maybe the feds already know who it is and have already taken care of the problem. Privately, which would explain why no other couples since Fred and Deborah have disappeared. Someone's got to pay in order to remove the cloud of suspicion, end the matter to the public's satisfaction. . . ."

Leaning back in my chair, I turned my face up to the ceiling and shut my eyes while she went on and on.

"No question Spurrier's into something or he wouldn't be stealing license plates. But he could be selling drugs. Maybe he's a cat burglar or gets his jollies from driving around with borrowed tags for a day? He's weird enough to fit the profile, but the world is full of weirdos who don't ever kill anyone. Who's to say the stuff in his house wasn't planted?"

"Please stop," I said quietly.

But she wouldn't. "It's just so goddam neat. The warm-up suits, gloves, decks of cards, pornography, and newspaper clips. And it doesn't make sense that no weapons or ammunition were found. Spurrier was caught by surprise, didn't have any idea he was under surveillance. In fact, it not only doesn't make sense, it's very convenient. One thing the feds couldn't plant was the pistol that fired the bullet you recovered from Deborah Harvey."

"You're right. They couldn't plant that." I got up from the table and began wiping the counters because I couldn't sit still.

"Interesting that the one item of evidence they couldn't plant didn't show up."

There had been stories before about the police, federal agents, planting evidence in order to frame someone. The ACLU probably had a file room full of such accusations.

"You're not listening," Abby said.

"I'm going up to take a bath," I replied wearily.

She walked over to the sink where I was wringing out the dishrag.

"Kay?"

I stopped what I was doing and looked at her.

"You want it to be easy," she admonished.

"I've always wanted things to be easy. They almost never are."

"You want it to be easy," she repeated. "You don't want to think that the people you trust could send an innocent man to the electric chair in order to cover their asses."

"No question about that. I wouldn't want to think it. I refuse to think it unless there is proof. And Marino was at Spurrier's house. He would never have gone along with it."

"He was there." She walked away from me. "But he wasn't the first one there. By the time he arrived, he would have seen what they wanted him to see."

17

THE FIRST PERSON I saw when I reached the office on Monday was Fielding.

I had come in through the bay, and he was already dressed in scrubs, waiting to get on the elevator. When I noticed the plasticized blue paper booties over his running shoes, I thought of what the police had found inside Steven Spurrier's house. Our medical supplies were on state contract. But there were any number of businesses in any city that sold booties and surgical gloves. One did not need to be a physician to purchase such items any more than one needed to be a police officer to buy a uniform, badge, or gun.

"Hope you got a good night's rest," Fielding warned as the elevator doors parted.

We stepped inside.

"Give me the bad news. What have we got this morning?" I said.

"Six posts, every one of them a homicide."

"Great," I said irritably.

"Yeah, the Knife and Gun Club had a busy weekend. Four shootings, two stabbings. Spring has sprung."

We got off on the second floor and I was already taking off my suit jacket and rolling up my sleeves when I walked into my office. Marino was sitting in a chair, his briefcase on his lap, a cigarette lit. I assumed one of the morning's cases was his until he handed me two lab reports.

"Thought you'd want to see it for yourself," he said.

Typed at the top of one report was the name Steven Spurrier.

The serology lab had already completed a workup on his blood. The other report was eight years old, the results of the workup done on the blood found inside Elizabeth Mott's car.

"Of course, it's going to be a while before the DNA results are in," Marino began to explain, "but so far so good."

Settling behind my desk, I took a moment to study the reports. The blood from the Volkswagen was type O, PGM type 1, EAP type B, ADA type 1, and EsD type 1. This particular combination could be found in approximately 8 percent of the population. The results were consistent with those of the tests conducted on the blood from Spurrier's suspect kit. He also was type O, types in other blood groups the same, but since more enzymes had been tested for, the combination had been narrowed to approximately 1 percent of the population.

"It's not enough to charge him with murder," I said to Marino. "You'd have to have more than the fact that his blood type includes him in a group of thousands of people."

"A damn shame the report from the old blood isn't more complete."

"They didn't routinely test for as many enzymes back then," I replied.

"Maybe they could do it now?" he suggested. "If we could narrow it down, that would be a big help. The damn DNA for Spurrier's blood is going to take weeks."

"They're not going to be able to do it," I told him. "The blood from Elizabeth's car is too old. After this many years the enzymes would have degraded, so the results this time would be less specific than what's on this eight-year-old report. The best you could get now is the ABO grouping, and almost half of the population is type O. We have no choice but to wait for the DNA results. Besides," I added, "even if you could lock him up this minute you know he'd make bail. He's still under surveillance, I hope."

"Being watched like a hawk, and you can bet he knows it. The good news is he's not likely to try whacking anyone. The bad news is he's got time to destroy any evidence we missed. Like the murder weapons."

"The alleged missing gym bag."

"Don't add up that we couldn't find it. We did everything short of tearing up his floorboards."

"Maybe you should have torn up his floorboards."

"Yeah, maybe."

I was trying to think where else Spurrier might have hidden a gym bag when it occurred to me. I don't know why I didn't think of it earlier.

"How is Spurrier built?" I asked.

"He ain't very big, but he looks pretty strong. Not an ounce of fat."

"Then he probably works out, exercises."

"Probably. Why?"

"If he belongs to some place, the YMCA, a fitness club, he might have a locker. I do at Westwood. If I wanted to hide something, that would be a good place to do it. No one would think twice when he walked out of the club with his gym bag in hand or when he returned the bag to his locker."

"Interesting idea," Marino said thoughtfully. "I'll ask around, see what I can find out."

He lit another cigarette and unzipped his briefcase. "I got pictures of his crib, if you're interested."

I glanced up at the clock. "I've got a houseful downstairs. We'll have to make it quick."

He handed me a thick manila envelope of eight-by-tens. They were in order, and going through them was like seeing Spurrier's house through Marino's eyes, beginning with the Colonial brick front lined with boxwoods and a brick walk leading to the black front door. In back was a paved drive leading to a garage that was attached to the house.

I spread out several more photographs and found myself inside his living room. On the bare hardwood floor was a gray leather couch near a glass coffee table. Centered on the table was a jagged brass plant growing out of a chunk of coral. A recent copy of the *Smithsonian* was perfectly aligned with the table's edges. Centered on the magazine was a remote control that I suspected operated the overhead television projector suspended like a spaceship from the whitewashed ceiling. An eighty-inch television screen was retracted into an inconspicuous vertical bar above the bookcase lined with VCR tapes, neatly labeled, and scores of hardbound volumes, the titles of which I could not make out. To one side of the bookcase was a bank of sophisticated electronic equipment.

"The squirrel's got his own movie theater," Marino said. "Got surround sound, speakers in every room. The whole setup probably cost more than your Mercedes, and he wasn't sitting back at night watching *Sound of Music*, either. Those tapes there in the bookcase"—he reached across my desk to point them out. "They're all *Lethal Weapon*-type shit, flicks about Vietnam, vigilantes. Now on the shelf right above is the good stuff. The tapes look like your everyday box office hits, but you pop one of them in the VCR and get a little surprise. The one labeled *On Golden Pond*, for example, should be called *On the Cesspool*. Hardcore violent pornography. Benton and I were together all of yesterday viewing the crap. Friggin' unbelievable. About every other minute, I felt like taking a bath."

"Did you find any home movies?"

"No. Not any photography equipment, either."

I looked at more photographs. In the dining room was another glass table, this one surrounded by transparent acrylic chairs. I noticed that the hardwood floor was bare. I had yet to see a rug or carpet in any room.

The kitchen was immaculate and modern. Windows were shrouded with gray miniblinds. There were no curtains, no draperies in any room I had seen, not even upstairs where this creature slept. The brass bed was king-size, neatly made, sheets white, but no spread. Dresser drawers pulled open revealed the warm-up suits Marino had told me about, and in boxes on the closet floor were packets of surgical gloves and booties.

"There's nothing fabric," I marveled, returning the photographs to their envelope. "I've never before seen a house that didn't have at least one rug."

"No curtains, either. Not even in the shower," Marino said. "It's enclosed in glass doors. Of course, there are towels, sheets, his clothes."

"Which he probably washes constantly."

"The upholstery in his Lincoln is leather," Marino said. "And the carpet's covered with plastic mats."

"He doesn't have any pets?"

"No."

"The way he has furnished his house may have to do with more than his personality."

Marino met my eyes. "Yeah, I'm thinking that."

"Fibers, pet hairs," I said. "He doesn't have to worry about transferring them."

"You ever thought it interesting that all of the abandoned vehicles in these cases was so clean?"

I had.

"Maybe he vacuums them after the crimes," he said.

"At a car wash?"

"A filling station, apartment complex, any place that has a coin-operated car vacuum. The murders were committed late at night. By the time he stopped somewhere to vacuum the car afterward, there wouldn't be many people out to see what he was doing."

"Maybe. Who knows what he did?" I said. "But the picture we're getting is of someone who is obsessively neat and careful. Someone very paranoid and familiar with the types of evidence that are important in forensic examinations."

Leaning back in the chair, Marino said, "The Seven-Eleven where Deborah and Fred stopped the night they disappeared, I dropped by there over the weekend and talked to the clerk."

"Ellen Jordan?"

He nodded. "I showed her a photo lineup, asked her if anybody in it looked like the man who was buying coffee in the Seven-Eleven the night Fred and Deborah was in there. She picked out Spurrier."

"She was certain?"

"Yes. Said he was wearing a jacket of some sort, dark. All she really recalled was that the guy was in dark clothes, and I'm thinking Spurrier already had on a warm-up suit when he went inside the Seven-Eleven. I've been running a lot of things through my mind. We'll start with two things we do know for a fact. The interiors of the abandoned cars were very clean, and in the four cases before Deborah and Fred, white cotton fibers were recovered from the driver's seat, right?"

"Yes," I agreed.

"Okay. I think this squirrel was out cruising for victims and spotted Fred and Deborah on the road, maybe saw them sitting real close to each other, her head on Fred's shoulder, that sort of thing. It sets him off. He tails them, pulls into the Seven-Eleven right after they do. Maybe he slips into the warm-up suit at this time, changes in his car. Maybe he already has it on. But he goes inside, hangs around looking through magazines, buying coffee and listening to what they're saying to the clerk. He overhears the clerk giving Fred and Deborah directions to the nearest rest stop where there's a bathroom. Then he leaves, speeds east on Sixty-four, turns into the rest stop and parks. He gets his bag that's got his weapons, ligatures, gloves, and so on, and makes himself scarce until Deborah and Fred pull in. He probably waits until she's gone to use the ladies' room, then he approaches Fred, feeds him some story about his car breaking down or whatever. Maybe Spurrier says he was working out at the gym, on his way home, thus explaining why he's dressed the way he is."

"Fred wouldn't recognize him from the Seven-Eleven?"

"I doubt it," Marino said. "But it don't matter. Spurrier might have been bold enough to mention that, say he was just buying coffee at the Seven-Eleven, and his car conked out right after he left. He says he's just called a wrecker and wonders if Fred could give him a lift back to his car so he can wait for the wrecker, promises that his car isn't very far down the road, et cetera. Fred agrees, then Deborah reappears. Once Spurrier's inside the Cherokee, Fred and Deborah are his."

I remembered Fred described as helpful, generous. He probably would have helped a stranger in distress, especially one as smooth and clean-cut as Steven Spurrier.

"When the Cherokee's back on the Interstate, Spurrier leans over and unzips his bag, puts on gloves, booties, and slips out his gun, points it at the back of Deborah's head. . . ."

I thought of the bloodhound's reaction when he had sniffed the seat where it was believed Deborah had been sitting. What the dog had detected was her terror.

". . . He orders Fred to drive to the spot Spurrier's already picked in advance. By the time they stop on the logging road, Deborah's hands have probably already been tied behind her back. Her shoes and socks are off. Spurrier orders Fred to take off his shoes and socks, then binds his hands. Spurrier orders them out of the Cherokee and walks them into the woods. Maybe he's wearing night vision goggles so he can see. He might have had those in his bag, too.

"Then he starts his game with them," Marino went on in a detached voice. "He takes out Fred first, then goes after Deborah. She resists, gets cut, and he shoots her. He drags their bodies to the clearing, positioning them side by side, her arm under his, like they was holding hands, holding on to each other. Spurrier smokes a few cigarettes, maybe sits out there in the dark by the bodies, enjoying the afterglow. Then he heads back to the Cherokee, takes off his warm-up, gloves, booties, puts them in a plastic bag he's got inside his gym bag. Maybe puts the kids' shoes and socks in the bag, too. He drives away, finds some deserted place with a coin-operated vacuum and cleans out the inside of the Cherokee, especially the driver's area where he's been sitting. All done, and he disposes of the trash bag, maybe in a Dumpster. I'm guessing he put something over the driver's seat at this point. Maybe a folded white sheet, a white towel in the first four cases—"

"Most athletic clubs," I interrupted, "have a linen service. They keep a supply of white towels in the locker rooms. If Spurrier does keep his murder kit in a locker somewhere—"

Marino cut me off. "Yeah, I'm reading you loud and clear. Damn. Maybe I'd better start working on that one pronto."

"A white towel would explain the white cotton fibers found," I added.

"Except he must have used something different with Deborah and Fred. Hell, who knows? Maybe he sat on a plastic trash bag this time. The point is, I'm thinking he sat on something so he didn't leave fibers from his clothes on the seat. Remember, he's not wearing the warm-up suit anymore, no way he would because it would be bloody. He drives off, dumps the Cherokee where we found it, and trots across the Interstate to the eastbound rest stop where his Lincoln's parked. He's out of there. Mission accomplished."

"There were probably a lot of cars in and out of the rest stop that night," I said. "No one was going to notice his Lincoln parked out there. But even if someone had, the tags wouldn't have come back to him because they were 'borrowed.' "

"Right. That's his last task, either returning the tags to the ride he stole them from or, if that isn't possible, just pitching them somewhere." He paused, rubbing his face in his hands. "I've got a feeling Spurrier picked an MO early on and has pretty much stuck to it in all of the cases. He cruises, spots his victims, tails them, and knows he's hit pay dirt if they pull off at some place, a bar, a rest stop, where they're going to be long enough for him to get set up. Then he makes his approach, pulls something to make them trust him. Maybe he strikes only once for every fifty times he goes out cruising. But he's still getting off on it."

"The scenario seems plausible for the five recent cases," I said. "But I don't think it works quite as well for Jill and Elizabeth. If the Palm Leaf Motel was where he'd left his car, that was some five miles from the Anchor Bar and Grill."

"We don't know that Spurrier hooked up with them at the Anchor."

"I have a feeling he did."

Marino looked surprised. "Why?"

"Because the women had been in his bookstore before," I explained. "They were familiar with Spurrier, though I doubt they knew him very well. I'm guessing that he watched them when they came in to buy newspapers, books, whatever. I suspect he sensed immediately that the two women were more than friends, and this pushed his button. He's obsessed with couples. Maybe he'd been contemplating his first killings, and he thought that two women would be easier than a man and a woman. He planned the crime long in advance, his fantasies fed every time Jill and Elizabeth came into his bookstore. He might have followed them, stalked them after hours, gone through a lot of dry runs, practicing. He had already selected the wooded area out near where Mr. Joyce lives and probably was the person who shot the dog. Then one night he follows Jill and Elizabeth to the Anchor, and this is when he decides to do it. He leaves his car somewhere, heads to the bar on foot, his gym bag in hand."

"Are you thinking he went inside the bar and watched them while they drank beer?"

"No," I said. "I think he was too careful for that. I think he hung back, waited until they came out to get into the Volkswagen. Then I think Spurrier approached them and put on the same act. His car had broken down. He was the owner of the bookstore they frequented. They had no reason to fear him. He gets inside, and very soon after his plan begins to unravel. They don't end up in the wooded area, but at the cemetery. The women, Jill, in particular, aren't very cooperative."

"And he bleeds inside the Volkswagen," Marino said. "A nosebleed, maybe. Ain't no vacuum cleaner gonna get blood out of a seat or floor mat."

"I doubt he bothered to vacuum. Spurrier probably was panicking. He probably ditched the car as quickly as he could in the most convenient spot, which turned out to be the motel. As for where his car was parked, who knows? But I'm betting he was in for a little hike."

"Maybe the episode with the two women spooked him so bad he didn't try again for five years."

"I don't think that's it," I said. "Something's missing."

The telephone rang several weeks later when I was home alone working in my study. My recorded message had barely begun when the person hung up. The phone rang again half an hour later, and this time I answered before my machine. I said hello, and the line was disconnected again.

Perhaps someone was trying to reach Abby and did not want to talk to me? Perhaps Clifford Ring had discovered where she was? Distracted, I went to the refrigerator for a snack and settled on several slices of cheese.

I was back in my study paying bills when I heard a car pull in, gravel crunching beneath tires. I assumed it was Abby until the doorbell rang.

I looked through the peephole at Pat Harvey zipped up in a red windbreaker. The hang-ups, I thought. She had made certain I was home because she wanted to speak to me face-to-face.

She greeted me with "I'm sorry to impose," but I could tell she wasn't.

"Please come in," I said reluctantly.

She followed me to the kitchen, where I poured her a cup of coffee. She sat stiffly at the table, coffee mug cradled in her hands.

"I'm going to be very direct with you," she began. "It has come to my attention that this man they arrested in Williamsburg, Steven Spurrier, is believed to have murdered two women eight years ago."

"Where did you hear this?"

"That's not important. The cases were never solved and have now been linked to the murders of the five couples. The two women were Steven Spurrier's first victims."

I noticed that the lower lid of her left eye was twitching. Pat Harvey's physical deterioration since I had seen her last was shocking. Her auburn hair was lifeless; her eyes were dull; her skin was pale and drawn. She looked even thinner than she had been during her televised press conference.

"I'm not sure I'm following you," I said tensely.

"He inspired their trust and they made themselves vulnerable. Which is exactly what he did with the others, with my daughter, with Fred."

She said all this as if she knew it for a fact. Pat Harvey had convicted Spurrier in her mind.

"But he will never be punished for Debbie's murder," she said. "I know that now."

"It is too early to know anything," I replied calmly.

"They have no proof. What was found inside his house is not

enough. It will not hold up in any court, if the cases ever go to court. You can't convict someone of capital murder just because you found newspaper clippings and surgical gloves inside his house, especially if the defense claims the evidence was planted to frame his client."

She had been talking to Abby, I thought with a sick feeling.

"The only evidence," she went on coldly, "is the blood found inside the women's car. It will all depend on DNA, and there will be questions because the cases occurred so long ago. The chain of custody, for example. Even if the prints match and the courts accept the evidence, there is no certainty that a jury will, especially since the police have yet to find the murder weapons."

"They're still looking."

"He's had plenty of time to dispose of those by now," she replied, and she was right.

Marino had discovered that Spurrier worked out at a gym not far from where he lived. The police had searched his rented locker, which not only locked with a key but had had a padlock on it. The locker was empty. The blue athletic bag Spurrier had been seen carrying around the gym had never been found, and never would be, I felt sure.

"What do you need from me, Mrs. Harvey?"

"I want you to answer my questions."

"Which questions?"

"If there is evidence I don't know about, I think you'd be wise to tell me."

"The investigation is not over. The police, the FBI are working very hard on your daughter's case."

She stared across the kitchen. "Are they talking to you?"

Instantly, I understood. No one directly involved in the investigation was giving Pat Harvey the time of day. She had become a pariah, perhaps even a joke. She was not going to admit this to me, but that's why she had appeared at my door.

"Do you believe Steven Spurrier murdered my daughter?"

"Why does my opinion matter?" I asked.

"It matters a great deal."

"Why?" I asked again.

"You don't form opinions lightly. I don't think you jump to conclusions or believe something just because you wish to. You're familiar with the evidence"—her voice trembled—"and you took care of Debbie."

I could not think of what to say.

"So I'll ask you again. Do you believe Steven Spurrier murdered them, murdered her?"

I hesitated, just for an instant, but it was enough. When I told her that I could not possibly answer such a question, and indeed, did not know the answer, she did not listen.

She got up from the table.

I watched her dissolve in the night, her profile briefly illuminated by the interior light of her Jaguar as she got in and drove away.

Abby did not come in until after I had given up waiting for her and had gone to bed. I slept fitfully and opened my eyes when I heard water running downstairs. I squinted at the clock. It was almost midnight. I got up and slipped into my robe.

She must have heard me in the hall, for when I reached her bedroom she was standing in the doorway, her pajamas a sweat suit, feet bare.

"You're up late," she said.

"So are you."

"Well, I . . ." She didn't finish her sentence as I walked inside her room and sat on the edge of the bed.

"What's up?" she asked uneasily.

"Pat Harvey came to see me earlier this evening, that's what's up. You've been talking to her."

"I've been talking to a lot of people."

"I know you want to help her," I said. "I know you've been outraged by the way her daughter's death has been used to hurt her. Mrs. Harvey's a fine woman, and I think you genuinely care about her. But she needs to stay out of the investigation, Abby."

She looked at me without speaking.

"For her own good," I added empathically.

Abby sat down on the rug, crossing her legs Indian style, and leaned against the wall.

"What did she say to you?" she asked.

"She's convinced Spurrier murdered her daughter and will never be punished for it."

"I certainly had nothing to do with her reaching such a conclusion," she said. "Pat has a mind of her own."

"Spurrier's arraignment is Friday. Does she plan to be there?"

"It's just a petit larceny charge. But if you're asking if I'm worried Pat might appear and make a scene . . ." She shook her head. "No way. It would serve no purpose for her to show up. She's not an idiot, Kay."

"And you?"

"What? Am I an idiot?" She evaded me again.

"Will you be at the arraignment?"

"Sure. And I'll tell you exactly how it will go. He'll be in and out, will plead guilty to petit larceny and get slapped with a fifteen-hundred-dollar fine. And he's going to spend a little time in jail, maybe a month at most. The cops want him to sweat behind bars for a while, break him down so he'll talk."

"How do you know that?"

"He's not going to talk," she went on. "They're going to lead him out of the courthouse in front of everyone and shove him in the back of a patrol car. It's all meant to scare and humiliate him, but it won't work. He knows they don't have enough on him. He'll bide his time in jail, then be out. A month isn't forever."

"You sound as if you feel sorry for him."

"I don't feel anything for him," she said. "Spurrier was into recreational cocaine, according to his attorney, and the night the cops caught him stealing the license tags, he was planning to make a buy. Spurrier was afraid some drug dealer would turn out to be a snitch, record his plate number, maybe give it to the cops. That's the explanation for the stolen tags."

"You can't believe that," I said heatedly.

Abby straightened out her legs, wincing a little. Without saying a word, she stood up and walked out of the room. I followed her to the kitchen, my frustration mounting. As she began to fill a glass with ice, I placed my hands on her shoulders and turned her around until we were face-to-face.

"Are you listening to me?"

Her eyes softened. "Please don't be angry with me. What I'm doing has nothing to do with you, with our friendship."

"What *friendship*? I feel as if I don't even know you anymore. You leave money around my house as if I'm nothing more than the damn maid. I don't remember the last time we ate a meal together. You never talk to me. You're so obsessed with this damn book. You see what's happened to Pat Harvey. Can't you see that the same thing is happening to you?"

Abby just stared at me.

"It's as if you've made up your mind about something," I continued to plead with her. "Why won't you tell me what it is?"

"There's nothing to make up my mind about," she said quietly, pulling away from me. "Everything's already been decided."

———

Fielding called early Saturday morning to say there were no autopsies, and exhausted, I went back to bed. It was midmorning when I got up. After a long, hot shower I was ready to deal with Abby and see if we could somehow repair our damaged relationship.

But when I went downstairs and knocked on her door, there was no answer, and when I went out to get the paper I saw her car was gone. Irritated that she had managed to avoid me again, I put on a pot of coffee.

I was sipping my second cup when a small headline caught my attention:

WILLIAMSBURG MAN GIVEN SUSPENDED SENTENCE

Steven Spurrier had not been cuffed and hauled off to jail following his arraignment the day before as Abby had predicted, I read, horrified. He pleaded guilty to petit larceny, and because he had no prior record and had always been a law-abiding citizen of Williamsburg, he was fined one thousand dollars and had walked out of the courthouse a free man.

Everything's already been decided, Abby had said.

Is this what she had been referring to? If she knew Spurrier would be released, why would she deliberately mislead me?

I left the kitchen and opened the door to her room. The bed was made, curtains drawn. Inside the bath, I noticed drops of water in the sink and the faint scent of perfume. She had not been gone long. I looked for her briefcase and tape recorder, but could not find them. Her .38 was not in its drawer. I went through dressers until I found her notepads, hidden beneath clothes.

Sitting on the edge of the bed, I frantically flipped through them. I streaked through her days and weeks as the meaning became clearer.

What had begun as Abby's crusade to discover the truth

about the couples' murders had turned into her own ambitious obsession. She seemed fascinated by Spurrier. If he was guilty, she was determined to make his story the focus of her book, to explore his psychopathic mind. If he was innocent, it would be "another Gainesville," she wrote, referring to the spree murders of university students in which a suspect became a household name and later turned out to be innocent. "Only it would be worse than Gainesville," she added. "Because of what the card implies."

Initially, Spurrier had repeatedly denied Abby's requests for interviews. Then late last week, she had tried again and he had picked up the phone. He had suggested they meet after the arraignment, telling her his attorney had "made a deal."

"He said he had read my stories in the *Post* over the years," Abby had scribbled, "and had recalled my byline from when I was in Richmond. He remembered what I had written about Jill and Elizabeth, too, and remarked that they were 'nice girls' and he'd always hoped the cops would get the 'psycho.' He also knew about my sister, said he'd read about her murder. That's the reason he finally agreed to talk to me, he said. He 'felt' for me, said he realized I understood what it was like to 'be a victim,' because what happened to my sister made me a victim, too.

" 'I am a victim,' he said. 'We can talk about that. Maybe you can help me better understand what that's all about.'

"He suggested I come to his house Saturday morning at eleven, and I agreed, providing all interviews are exclusive. He said that was fine, he had no intention of talking to anybody else as long as I told his side. 'The truth,' as he put it. Thank you, Lord! Screw you and your book, Cliff. You lose."

Cliff Ring was writing a book about these cases, too. Dear Lord. No wonder Abby had been acting so odd.

She had lied when she had told me what was going to happen at Spurrier's arraignment. She did not want me to suspect that she planned to go to his house, and she knew such a thought would never occur to me if I assumed he would be in jail. I remembered her saying that she no longer trusted anyone. She didn't, not even me.

I glanced at my watch. It was eleven-fifteen.

Marino wasn't in, so I left a message on his pager. Then I called the Williamsburg police, and the phone rang forever before a secretary answered. I told her I needed to speak to one of the detectives immediately.

"They're all out on the street right now."

"Then let me speak to whoever's in."

She transferred me to a sergeant.

Identifying myself, I said, "You know who Steven Spurrier is."

"Can't work around here and not know that."

"A reporter is interviewing him at his house. I'm alerting you so you can make sure your surveillance teams know she's there, make sure everything's all right."

There was a long pause. Paper crinkled. It sounded as if the sergeant was eating something. Then, "Spurrier's not under surveillance anymore."

"I beg your pardon?"

"I said our guys have been pulled off."

"Why?" I demanded.

"Now, that I don't know, Doc, been on vacation for the past—"

"Look, all I'm asking is you send a car by his house, make sure everything's all right." It was all I could do not to scream at him.

"Don't you worry about a thing." His voice was as calm as a mill pond. "I'll pass it along."

I hung up as I heard a car pull in.

Abby, thank God.

But when I looked out the window, it was Marino.

I opened the front door before he could ring the bell.

"Was in the area when I got your message on the beeper, so I—"

"Spurrier's house!" I grabbed his arm. "Abby's there! She's got her gun!"

The sky had turned dark and it was raining as Marino and I sped east on 64. Every muscle in my body was rigid. My heart would not slow down.

"Hey, relax," Marino said as we turned off at the Colonial Williamsburg exit. "Whether the cops are watching him or not, he ain't stupid enough to touch her. Really, you know that. He ain't going to do that."

There was only one vehicle in sight when we turned onto Spurrier's quiet street.

"Shit," Marino muttered under his breath.

Parked on the street in front of Spurrier's house was a black Jaguar.

"Pat Harvey," I said. "Oh, God."

He slammed on the brakes.

"Stay here." He was out of the car as if he had been ejected, running up the driveway in the pouring rain. My heart was pounding as he pushed the front door open with his foot, revolver in hand, and disappeared inside.

The doorway was empty when suddenly he filled it again. He stared in my direction, yelling something I could not hear.

I got out of the car, rain soaking my clothes as I ran.

I smelled the burnt gunpowder the instant I entered the foyer.

"I've called for help," Marino said, eyes darting around. "Two of them are in there."

The living room was to the left.

He was hurrying up the stairs leading to the second story as photographs of Spurrier's house crazily flashed in my mind. I recognized the glass coffee table and saw the revolver on top of it. Blood was pooled on the bare wood floor beneath Spurrier's body, a second revolver several feet away. He was facedown, inches from the gray leather couch where Abby lay on her side. She stared at the cushion beneath her cheek through drowsy, dull eyes, the front of her pale blue blouse soaked bright red.

For an instant I didn't know what to do, the roaring inside my head as loud as a windstorm. I squatted beside Spurrier, blood spilling and seeping around my shoes as I rolled him over. He was dead, shot through the abdomen and chest.

I hurried to the couch and felt Abby's neck. There was no pulse. I turned her on her back and started CPR, but her heart and lungs had given up too long ago to remember what they were supposed to do. Holding her face in my hands, I felt her warmth and smelled her perfume as sobs welled up and shook me uncontrollably.

Footsteps on the hardwood floor did not register until I realized they were too light to be Marino's. I looked up as Pat Harvey lifted the revolver off the coffee table.

I stared wide-eyed at her, my lips parting.

"I'm sorry." The revolver shook as she pointed it in my direction.

"Mrs. Harvey." My voice stuck in my throat, hands frozen in front of me, stained with Abby's blood. "Please . . ."

"Just stay there." She backed up several steps, lowering the gun a little. For some bizarre reason it occurred to me she was wearing the same red windbreaker she had worn to my house.

"Abby's dead," I said.

Pat Harvey didn't react, her face ashen, eyes so dark they looked black. "I tried to find a phone. He doesn't have any phones."

"Please put the gun down."

"He did it. He killed my Debbie. He killed Abby."

Marino, I thought. *Oh, God, hurry!*

"Mrs. Harvey, it's over. They're dead. Please put the gun down. Don't make it worse."

"It can't be worse."

"That's not true. Please listen to me."

"I can't be here anymore," she said in the same flat tone.

"I can help you. Put the gun down. Please," I said, getting up from the couch as she raised the gun again.

"No," I begged, realizing what she was going to do.

She pointed the muzzle at her chest as I lunged toward her.

"Mrs. Harvey! No!"

The explosion knocked her back and she staggered, dropping the revolver. I kicked it away and it spun slowly, heavily, across the smooth wood floor as her legs buckled. She reached for something to hold on to, but nothing was there. Marino was suddenly in the room, exclaiming "Holy shit!" He held his revolver in both hands, muzzle pointed at the ceiling. Ears ringing, I was trembling all over as I knelt beside Pat Harvey. She lay on her side, knees drawn, clutching her chest.

"Get towels!" I moved her hands out of the way and fumbled with her clothing. Untucking her blouse and pushing up her brassiere, I pressed bunched cloth against the wound below her left breast. I could hear Marino cursing as he rushed out of the room.

"Hold on," I whispered, applying pressure so the small hole would not suck in air and collapse the lung.

She was squirming and began to groan.

"Hold on," I repeated as sirens wailed from the street.

Red light pulsed through blinds covering the living room windows, as if the world outside Steven Spurrier's house were on fire.

18

MARINO DROVE ME home and did not leave. I sat in my kitchen staring out at the rain, only vaguely aware of what was going on around me. The doorbell rang, and I heard footsteps and male voices.

Later, Marino came into the kitchen and pulled out a chair across from me. He perched on the edge of it as if he wasn't planning to sit long.

"Any other places in the house Abby might have put her things, beside her bedroom?" he asked.

"I don't think so," I murmured.

"Well, we've got to look. I'm sorry, Doc."

"I understand."

He followed my gaze out the window.

"I'll make coffee." He got up. "We'll see if I remember what you taught me. My first quiz, huh?"

He moved about in the kitchen, cabinet doors opening and shutting, water running as he filled the pot. He walked out while coffee dripped, and moments later was back with another detective.

"This won't take very long, Dr. Scarpetta," the detective said. "Appreciate your cooperation."

He said something in a low voice to Marino. Then he left and Marino returned to the table, setting a cup of coffee in front of me.

"What are they looking for?" I tried to concentrate.

"We're going through the notebooks you told me about. Looking for tapes, anything that might tell us what led up to Mrs. Harvey shooting Spurrier."

"You're sure she did it."

"Oh, yeah. Mrs. Harvey did it. Damn miracle she's alive. She missed her heart. She was lucky, but maybe she won't think so if she pulls through."

"I called the Williamsburg police. I told them—"

"I know you did." He cut me off gently. "You did the right thing. You did all you could."

"They couldn't be bothered." I closed my eyes, fighting the tears.

"That wasn't it." He paused. "Listen to me, Doc."

I took a deep breath.

Marino cleared his throat and lit a cigarette. "While I was back there in your office, I talked to Benton. The FBI completed the DNA analysis of Spurrier's blood and compared it with the blood found in Elizabeth Mott's car. The DNA don't match."

"What?"

"The DNA don't match," he said again. "The detectives in Williamsburg who had been tailing Spurrier were just told yesterday. Benton had been trying to get hold of me and we kept missing each other, so I didn't know. You understand what I'm saying?"

I stared numbly at him.

"Legally, Spurrier was no longer a suspect. A pervert, yeah. We're talking the land of fruits and nuts. But he didn't murder Elizabeth and Jill. He didn't leave the blood in the car, couldn't have. If he killed these other couples, we've got no proof. To keep tailing him all the hell over the place, watching his house or banging on his door because they see he's got company, was harassment. Well, I mean there comes a point when there aren't enough cops to keep that up, and Spurrier could sue. And the FBI had backed off. So that's the way it went."

"He killed Abby."

Marino looked away from me. "Yeah, it appears so. She had her tape recorder running, we got the whole thing on tape. But that don't prove he killed the couples, Doc. It's looking like Mrs. Harvey gunned down an innocent man."

"I want to hear the tape."

"You don't want to hear it. Take my word for it."

"If Spurrier was *innocent*, then why did he shoot Abby?"

"I got an idea, based on what I heard on the tape and saw at the scene," he said. "Abby and Spurrier was talking in the living room. Abby was sitting on the couch where we found her. Spurrier heard

someone at the door and got up to answer it. I don't know why he
let Pat Harvey in. You would think he would have recognized her,
but maybe he didn't. She had on a windbreaker with a hood, and
jeans. Might have been hard to tell who she was. No way to know
how she identified herself, what she said to him. We won't know
until we can talk to her, and even then we might not know."

"But he let her in."

"He opened the door," Marino said. "Then she had her revolver
out, a Charter Arms, the one she later shot herself with. Mrs. Harvey forced him back inside the house, into the living room. Abby's
still sitting there, and the tape recorder's still running. Since Abby's
Saab was out back in the drive, Mrs. Harvey wouldn't have seen
it when she parked in front. She had no idea Abby was there, and
this diverted her attention long enough for Spurrier to go for Abby,
probably to use her as a shield. Hard to know exactly what went
down, but we know Abby had her revolver with her, probably in
her purse, which was probably next to her on the couch. She tries
to get out her gun, she and Spurrier struggle and she gets shot.
Then, before he can shoot Mrs. Harvey, she shoots him. Twice. We
checked her revolver. Three spent shells, two live."

"She said something about looking for a phone," I said dully.

"Spurrier's only got two phones. One in his bedroom upstairs,
the other in the kitchen, same color as the wall and between two
cabinets, hard as shit to see. I almost didn't find it either. It looks
like we rolled up to the house maybe minutes after the shootings,
Doc. I think Mrs. Harvey set her gun on the coffee table when she
went over to Abby, saw how bad it was and tried to find a phone to
call for help. Mrs. Harvey must have been in another room when
I walked in, maybe heard me and ducked out of sight. All I know
is when I went in, I scanned the immediate area. All I saw was
the bodies in the living room, checked their carotids and thought
Abby had a faint pulse, but I wasn't sure. I had a choice, had to
make a split-second decision. I could start searching Spurrier's crib
for Mrs. Harvey, or get you and then look. I mean, I didn't see
her when I first came in. I thought she might have gone out the
back door or upstairs," he said, obviously distressed he'd put me in
jeopardy.

"I want to hear the tape," I said again.

Marino rubbed his face in his hands, his eyes bleary and bloodshot when he looked back at me. "Don't put yourself through it."

"I have to."

Reluctantly, he got up from the table and left. When he returned, he opened a plastic evidence bag that contained a microcassette recorder. He set it upright on the table, briefly rewound a portion of the tape, and depressed the Play button.

The sound of Abby's voice filled the kitchen.

". . . I'm just trying to see your side of it, but that doesn't really explain why you drive around at night, stop and ask people things that you don't really need to know. Such as directions."

"Look, I already told you about the coke. You ever snorted coke?"

"No."

"Try it some time. You do a lot of off-the-wall things when you're high. You get confused and think you know where you're going. Then suddenly you're lost and have to ask directions."

"You said you're not doing coke anymore."

"Not anymore. No way. My big mistake. Never again."

"What about the items the police found in your house . . . ? Uh . . ." There was the faint chime of a doorbell.

"Yeah. Hold on." Spurrier sounded tense.

Footsteps receded. Voices were indistinguishable in the background. I could hear Abby shifting on the couch. Then Spurrier's disbelieving voice: "Wait. You don't know what you're—"

"I know exactly what I'm doing, you bastard." It was Pat Harvey's voice, increasing in volume. "That was my daughter you took out into the woods."

"I don't know what you're—"

"Pat. Don't!"

A pause.

"Abby? Oh my God."

"Pat. Don't do it, Pat." Abby's voice was tight with fear. She gasped as something hit the couch. "Get away from me!" A commotion, rapid breathing, and Abby screaming, "Stop! Stop!" then what sounded like a cap gun going off.

Again and again.

Silence.

Footsteps clicked across the floor and got louder. They stopped.

"Abby?"

A pause.

"Please don't die. *Abby* . . ." Pat Harvey's voice was quavering so badly I could barely hear it.

Marino reached for the recorder, turned if off, and slipped it back inside the plastic bag as I stared at him in shock.

─────

On the Saturday morning of Abby's graveside service, I waited until the crowd had thinned, then walked along a footpath beneath the shade of magnolias and oaks, dogwoods blazing fuchsia and white in the gentle spring sun.

The turnout for Abby's funeral had been small. I met several of her former Richmond colleagues and tried to comfort her parents. Marino came. So did Mark, who hugged me tight, then left with the promise he would come by my house later in the day. I needed to talk with Benton Wesley, but first I wanted a few moments alone.

Hollywood Cemetery was Richmond's most formidable city for the dead, some forty acres of rolling hills, streams, and stands of hardwood trees north of the James River. Curving streets were paved and named, with speed limits posted, the sloping grass crowded with granite obelisks, headstones, and angels of grief, many of them more than a century old. Buried here were Presidents James Monroe and John Tyler, and Jefferson Davis, and tobacco magnate Lewis Ginter. There was a soldiers' section for the Gettysburg dead, and a family plot of low-lying lawn where Abby had been buried beside her sister, Henna.

I drew up on a break in the trees, the river below glimmering like tarnished copper, muddy from recent rains. It did not seem possible that Abby was now part of this population, a granite marker weathering passing time. I wondered if she had ever gone back to her former house, to Henna's room upstairs as she had told me she intended to do when she could find the courage.

When I heard footsteps behind me, I turned to find Wesley walking slowly in my direction.

"You wanted to talk to me, Kay?"

I nodded.

He slipped off his dark suit jacket and loosened his tie. Staring out at the river, he waited to hear what was on my mind.

"There are some new developments," I began. "I called Gordon Spurrier on Thursday."

"The brother?" Wesley replied, looking at me curiously.

"Steven Spurrier's brother, yes. I didn't want to tell you about it until I'd looked into several other things."

"I haven't talked to him yet," he stated. "But he's on my list.

Just a damn shame about the DNA results, that's still a major problem."

"That's my point. There isn't a problem with the DNA, Benton."

"I don't understand."

"During Spurrier's autopsy, I discovered a lot of old therapeutic scars, one of them from a small incision made above the middle of the collarbone that I associate with someone having trouble getting in a subclavian line," I said.

"Meaning?"

"You don't run a subclavian line unless the patient has a serious problem, trauma requiring the dumping of fluids very quickly, an infusion of drugs or blood. In other words, I knew Spurrier had a significant medical problem at some point in the past, and I began contemplating that this might have something to do with the five months he was absent from his bookstore not long after Elizabeth and Jill were murdered. There were other scars, too, over his hip and lateral buttock. Minute scars that made me suspect he'd had samples of bone marrow taken before. So I called his brother to find out about Steven's medical history."

"What did you learn?"

"Around the time he disappeared from his bookstore, Steven was treated for aplastic anemia at UVA," I said. "I've talked with his hematologist. Steven received total lymphoid irradiation, chemotheraphy. Gordon's marrow was infused into Steven, and Steven then spent time in a laminar flow room, or a bubble, as most people call it. You may recall Steven's house was like a bubble, in a sense. Very sterile."

"Are you saying that the bone-marrow transplant changed his DNA?" Wesley asked, his face intense.

"For blood, yes. His blood cells had been totally wiped out by his aplastic anemia. He was HLA-typed for a suitable match, which turned out to be his brother, whose ABO type and even types in other blood group systems are the same."

"But Steven's and Gordon's DNA wouldn't be the same."

"No, not unless the brothers are identical twins, which, of course, they aren't," I said. "So Steven's blood type was consistent with the blood recovered from Elizabeth Mott's car. But at the level of DNA a discernible difference would have been noticed because Steven left the blood in the Volkswagen before his marrow transplant. When Steven's blood was recently taken for the suspect kit, what we were getting, in a sense, was Gordon's blood. What was actually compared with the DNA print of the old blood from the Volkswagen was not Steven's DNA, but Gordon's."

"Incredible," he said.

"I want the test run again on tissue from his brain because Steven's DNA in other cells will be the same as it was before the transplant. Marrow produces blood cells, so if you've had a marrow transplant you take on the blood cells of the donor. But brain, spleen, sperm cells don't change."

"Explain aplastic anemia to me," he said as we started walking.

"Your marrow is no longer making anything. It's as if you've already been irradiated, all blood cells wiped out."

"What causes it?"

"It's felt to be idiopathic; nobody really knows. But possibilities are exposure to pesticides, chemicals, radiation, organic phosphates. Significantly, benzene has been associated with aplastic anemia. Steven had worked at a printing press. Benzene is a solvent used to clean printing presses and other machinery. He was exposed to it, so his hematologist said, on a daily basis for almost a year."

"And the symptoms?"

"Fatigue, shortness of breath, fever, possibly infections, and bleeding from the gums and nose. Spurrier was already suffering from aplastic anemia when Jill and Elizabeth were murdered. He may have been having nosebleeds, which would have occurred with very little provocation. Stress always makes everything worse, and he would have been under a great deal of stress while abducting Elizabeth and Jill. If his nose had started bleeding, that would explain the blood in the back of Elizabeth's car."

"When did he finally go to the doctor?" Wesley asked.

"A month after the women were murdered. During his examination, it was discovered that his white count was low, his platelets and hemoglobin low. When your platelets are low you bleed a lot."

"He committed murders while he was that sick?"

"You can have aplastic anemia for a while before it becomes severe," I said. "Some people simply find out during a routine physical."

"Poor health and losing control of his first victims were enough to make him retreat," he thought out loud. "Years went by as he recovered and fantasized, reliving the murders and improving his techniques. Eventually, he was confident enough to start killing again."

"That could explain the long interval. But who knows what went through his mind."

"We'll never really know that," Wesley said grimly.

He paused to study an ancient grave marker before speaking again. "I have some news, too. There's a company in New York, a spy shop whose catalogs were found in Spurrier's house. After some tracking we've ascertained that four years ago he ordered a pair of night vision goggles from them. In addition, we've located a gun store in Portsmouth where he purchased two boxes of Hydra-Shok cartridges less than a month before Deborah and Fred disappeared."

"Why did he do it, Benton?" I asked. "Why did he kill?"

"I can never answer that satisfactorily, Kay. But I've talked with his former roommate at UVA, who indicated that Spurrier's relationship with his mother was unhealthy. She was very critical and controlling, belittled him constantly. He was dependent on her and at the same time probably hated her."

"What about the victimology?"

"I think he spotted young women who reminded him of what he couldn't have, the girls who had never given him the time of day. When he saw an attractive couple, it set him off because he was incapable of relationships. He took possession through murder, fused himself with and overpowered what he envied." Pausing, he added, "If you and Abby hadn't encountered him when you did, I'm not sure we would have gotten him. Scary how it works. Bundy gets pulled because a taillight's out. Son of Sam gets nailed because of a parking ticket. Luck. We were lucky."

I didn't feel lucky. Abby hadn't been lucky.

"You might find it interesting to know that since all of this has been in the news we've received a lot of phone calls from people claiming someone who fits Spurrier's description approached them outside bars, at service stations, convenience stores. It's been reported that on one occasion he actually got a ride with a couple. He claimed his car had broken down. The kids dropped him off. No problem."

"Did he approach only young male-female couples during these dry runs?" I asked.

"Not always. Thus explaining how you and Abby fit that night he stopped to ask directions. Spurrier loved the risk, the fantasy,

Kay. The killing was, in a sense, incidental to the game he was playing."

"I still don't completely understand why the CIA was so worried the killer might be from Camp Peary," I told him.

He paused, draping his suit jacket over his other arm.

"It was more than the MO, the jack of hearts," he said. "The police recovered a plastic computerized gas card in the back of Jim and Bonnie's car, on the floor under the seat. It was assumed the card had inadvertently fallen out of the killer's pocket, a jacket pocket, maybe a shirt pocket, while he was abducting the couple."

"And?"

"The company name on the gas card was Syn-Tron. After some tracking, the account came back to Viking Exports. Viking Exports is a cover for Camp Peary. The gas card is issued to Camp Peary personnel for their use at the pumps on base."

"Interesting," I said. "Abby referred to a card in one of her notepads. I assumed she was referring to the jack of hearts. She knew about the gas card, didn't she, Benton?"

"I suspect Pat Harvey told her. Mrs. Harvey had known about the card for quite a while, thus explaining her accusations during the press conference that something was being covered up by the feds."

"Obviously, she no longer believed that when she decided to kill Spurrier."

"The Director briefed her after the press conference, Kay. Had no choice but to inform her that we were suspicious the gas card was left deliberately. We were suspicious from the beginning, but that didn't mean we couldn't take it seriously. Obviously, the CIA took it very seriously."

"And this silenced her."

"If nothing else it made her think twice. Certainly, after Spurrier was arrested, what the Director had said to her made a lot of sense."

"How could Spurrier have gotten hold of a Camp Peary gas card?" I puzzled.

"Camp Peary agents frequented his bookstore."

"You're saying that he somehow stole this card from a Camp Peary customer?"

"Yes. Suppose someone from Camp Peary walked out of the bookstore leaving his wallet on the counter. By the time he came back looking for it, Spurrier could have tucked it away, said he hadn't seen it. Then he left the gas card in Jim and Bonnie's car so we would link the killings to the CIA."

"No identification number on the card?"

"The ID numbers are on stickers that had been peeled off, so we couldn't trace the card back to an individual."

I was getting tired and my feet were beginning to hurt when the parking area where we had left our cars came into view. Those who had come to mourn Abby's death were gone.

Wesley waited until I was unlocking my car before touching my arm and saying, "I'm sorry for those times . . ."

"So am I." I didn't let him finish. "We go on from here, Benton. Do whatever you can to make sure Pat Harvey isn't punished further."

"I don't think a grand jury will have a problem understanding how she's suffered."

"Did she know about the DNA results, Benton?"

"She's had a way of finding out details critical to the investigation, despite our efforts to keep them from her, Kay. I suspect she knew. Certainly, it would help explain why she did what she did. She would have believed Spurrier was never going to be punished."

I got in and put the key in the ignition.

"I'm sorriest about Abby," he added.

I nodded as I shut the door, my eyes filling with tears.

I followed the narrow road to the cemetery's entrance, passing through elaborate wrought-iron gates. The sun shone on downtown office buildings and steeples in the distance, light caught in the trees. I opened the windows and drove west toward home.